GREAT DETECTIVE STORIES

GREAT DETECTIVE STORIES

THE NINE TAILORS

DOROTHY L. SAYERS

GIDEON'S DAY

JOHN CREASEY

FUZZ

ED MCBAIN

THE BIG SLEEP

RAYMOND CHANDLER

OCTOPUS BOOKS

The Nine Tailors
first published in Great Britain in 1934 by Victor Gollancz Ltd

Gideon's Day
first published in Great Britain in 1955 by Hodder & Stoughton Ltd

Fuzz
first published in Great Britain in 1968 by Hamish Hamilton

The Big Sleep
first published in Great Britain in 1939 by Hamish Hamilton

This edition first published in Great Britain in 1984 by
Octopus Books Limited, 59 Grosvenor Street, London, W1
in collaboration with
William Heinemann, 10 Upper Grosvenor Street, London, WI
and
Martin Secker & Warburg Limited, 54 Poland Street, London W1

ISBN 0 7064 0925 6

Printed in Great Britain at The Pitman Press, Bath

CONTENTS

THE NINE TAILORS

DOROTHY L. SAYERS

FOREWORD

From time to time complaints are made about the ringing of church bells. It seems strange that a generation which tolerates the uproar of the internal combustion engine and the wailing of the jazz band should be so sensitive to the one loud noise that is made to the glory of God. England, alone in the world, has perfected the art of change-ringing and the true ringing of bells by rope and wheel, and will not lightly surrender her unique heritage.

I have to ask the indulgence of all change-ringers for any errors I may have made in dealing with their ancient craft. The surnames used in this book are all such as I have myself encountered among the people of East Anglia, but every place and person described is wholly fictitious, as are also the sins and negligences of those entirely imaginary bodies, the Wale Conservancy Board, The Fen Drainage Board and the East Level Waterways Commission.

My grateful thanks are due to Mr W. J. Redhead, who so kindly designed for me the noble Parish Church of Fenchurch St Paul and set about it with cherubims.

DOROTHY L. SAYERS

PART 1

A SHORT TOUCH OF KENT TREBLE
BOB MAJOR
(Two Courses)

704

By the Course Ends

64352

23456

8th the Observation

Call her in the middle with a double, before,
wrong and home.
Repeated once.

(TROYTE)

THE FIRST COURSE

THE BELLS ARE RUNG UP

The coil of rope which it is necessary to hold in the hand, before, and whilst raising a bell, always puzzles a learner; it gets into his face, and perhaps round his neck (in which case he may be hanged!).

TROYTE *On Change-Ringing*

'That's torn it!' said Lord Peter Wimsey.

The car lay helpless and ridiculous, her nose deep in the ditch, her back wheels cocked absurdly up on the bank, as though she were doing her best to bolt to earth and were scraping herself a burrow beneath the drifting snow. Peering through a flurry of driving flakes, Wimsey saw how the accident had come about. The narrow, hump-backed bridge, blind as an eyeless beggar, spanned the dark drain at right-angles, dropping plumb down upon the narrow road that crested the dyke. Coming a trifle too fast across the bridge, blinded by the bitter easterly snowstorm, he had overshot the road and plunged down the side of the dyke into the deep ditch beyond, where the black spikes of a thorn hedge stood bleak and unwelcoming in the glare of the headlights.

Right and left, before and behind, the fen lay shrouded. It was past four o'clock and New Year's Eve; the snow that had fallen all day gave back a glimmering greyness to a sky like lead.

'I'm sorry,' said Wimsey. 'Whereabouts do you suppose we've got to, Bunter?'

The manservant consulted a map in the ray of an electric torch.

'I think, my lord, we must have run off the proper road at Leamholt. Unless I am much mistaken, we must be near Fenchurch St Paul.'

As he spoke, the sound of a church clock, muffled by the snow, came borne upon the wind; it chimed the first quarter.

'Thank God!' said Wimsey. 'Where there is a church, there is civilisation. We'll have to walk it. Never mind the suitcases; we can send somebody for them. 'Br'rh! it's cold. I bet that when Kingsley welcomed the wild north-easter he was sitting indoors by a good fire, eating muffins. I could do with a muffin myself. Next time I accept hospitality in the Fen-country, I'll take care that it's at midsummer, or else I'll go by train. The church lies to windward of us, I fancy. It would.'

They wrapped their coats about them and turned their faces to the wind and snow. To left of them, the drain ran straight as a rule could make it, black and sullen, with a steep bank shelving down to its slow, unforgiving waters. To their right was the broken line of the sunk hedge, with, here and there, a group of poplars or willows. They tramped on in silence, the snow beating on their eyelids. At the end of a solitary mile the gaunt shape of a windmill loomed up upon the farther bank of the drain, but no bridge led to it, and no light showed.

Another half-mile, and they came to a signpost and a secondary road that turned off to the right. Bunter turned his torch upon the signpost and read upon the single arm:

'Fenchurch St Paul.'

There was no other direction; ahead, road and dyke marched on side by side into an eternity of winter.

'Fenchurch St Paul for us,' said Wimsey. He led the way into the side-road, and as he did so, they heard the clock again – nearer – chiming the third quarter.

A few hundred yards of solitude, and they came upon the first sign of life in this frozen desolation: on their left, the roofs of a farm, standing some way back from the road, and, on the right, a small, square building like a box of bricks, whose sign, creaking in the blast, proclaimed it to be the Wheatsheaf public-house. In front of it stood a small, shabby car, and from windows on the ground and first floors light shone behind red blinds.

Wimsey went up to it and tried the door. It was shut, but not locked. He called out, 'Anybody about?'

A middle-aged woman emerged from an inner room.

'We're not open yet,' she began, abruptly.

'I beg your pardon,' said Wimsey. 'Our car has come to grief. Can you direct us –?'

'Oh, I'm sorry, sir. I thought you were some of the men. Your car broke down? That's bad. Come in. I'm afraid we're all in a muddle –'

'What's the trouble, Mrs Tebbutt?' The voice was gentle and scholarly, and, as Wimsey followed the woman into a small parlour, he saw that the speaker was an elderly parson.

'The gentlemen have had an accident with their car.'

'Oh, dear,' said the clergyman. 'Such a terrible day, too! Can I be of any assistance?'

Wimsey explained that the car was in the ditch, and would certainly need ropes and haulage to get it back to the road again.

'Dear, dear,' said the clergyman again. 'That would be coming over Frog's Bridge, I expect. A most dangerous place, especially in the dark. We must see what can be done about it. Let me give you a lift into the village.'

'It's very good of you, sir.'

'Not at all, not at all. I am just getting back to my tea. I am sure you must be wanting something to warm you up. I trust you are not in a hurry to reach your destination. We should be delighted to put you up for the night.'

Wimsey thanked him very much, but said he did not want to trespass upon his hospitality.

'It will be a great pleasure,' said the clergyman, courteously. 'We see so little company here that I assure you you will be doing my wife and myself a great favour.'

'In that case – ' said Wimsey.

'Excellent, excellent.'

'I'm really most grateful. Even if we could get the car out tonight, I'm afraid the axle may be bent, and that means a blacksmith's job. But couldn't we get rooms at an inn or something? I'm really ashamed – '

'My dear sir, pray don't think twice about it. Not but what I am sure Mrs Tebbutt here would be delighted to take you in and would make you very comfortable – very comfortable indeed; but her husband is laid up with this dreadful influenza – we are suffering from quite an epidemic of it I am sorry to say – and I fear it would not be altogether convenient, would it, Mrs Tebbutt?'

'Well, sir, I don't know as how we could manage very well, under the circumstances, and the Red Cow has only one room – '

'Oh, no,' said the clergyman, quickly, 'not the Red Cow; Mrs Donnington has visitors already. Indeed, I will take no denial. You must positively come along to the Rectory. We have ample accommodation – too much, indeed, too much. My name, by the way, is Venables – I should have mentioned it earlier. I am, as you will have gathered, rector of the parish.'

'It's extremely good of you, Mr Venables. If we're really not putting you out, we will accept your invitation with pleasure. My name is Wimsey – here is my card – and this is my man, Bunter.'

The Rector fumbled for his glasses, which, after disentangling the cord, he perched very much askew on his long nose, in order to peer at Wimsey's card.

'Lord Peter Wimsey – just so. Dear me! The name seems familiar. Have I not heard of it in connection with – ah! I have it! *Notes on the Collection of Incunabula,* of course. A very scholarly little monograph, if I may say so. Yes. Dear me. It will be charming to exchange impressions with another book-collector. My library is, I fear, limited, but I have an edition of the *Gospel of Nicodemus* that may interest you. Dear me! Yes. Delightful to have met you like this. Bless my heart, there's five o'clock striking. We must be off, or I shall get a scolding from my wife. Good afternoon, Mrs Tebbutt. I hope your good man will be much improved by tomorrow; I really think he is looking better already.'

'Thank you, sir; Tom's always so pleased to see you. I'm sure you do him a lot of good.'

'Tell him to keep his spirits up. Such a nasty, depressing complaint. But he's over the worst now. I will send a little bottle of port wine as soon as he is able to take it. Tuke Holdsworth '08,' added the Rector, in an aside to Wimsey; 'couldn't harm a fly you know. Yes. Dear me! Well! We really must be going. I'm afraid my car is not much to boast of, but there's more room in it than one would think. Many's the christening party we've managed to squeeze into it, eh, Mrs Tebbutt? Will you sit beside me, Lord Peter? Your man and your – dear me! have you any luggage . . . Ah! down at Frog's Bridge? I will send my gardener to fetch it. It will be quite safe where it is; we're all honest people about here, aren't we, Mrs Tebbutt? That's right. You must have this rug about your legs – yes, I insist. No, no, thank you. I can start her up quite well. I am so well accustomed to do it. There, you see! A few good pulls and she comes up as brisk as a bell. All right behind, my man? Good. Excellent. *Good* afternoon, Mrs Tebbutt!'

The ancient car, shuddering to her marrow-bones, lurched away down the straight and narrow road. They passed a cottage, and then, quite suddenly, on their right, there loomed out of the whirling snow a grey, gigantic bulk.

'Great Heavens!' exclaimed Wimsey, 'is that your church?'

'Yes, indeed,' said the Rector, with pride. 'You find it impressive?'

'Impressive!' said Wimsey. 'Why, it's like a young cathedral. I'd no idea. How big is your parish, then?'

'You'll be surprised when I tell you,' said the Rector, with a chuckle. 'Three hundred and forty souls – no more. Astonishing, is it not? But you find the same thing all over the fens. East Anglia is famous for the size and splendour of its parish churches. Still, we flatter ourselves we are almost unique, even in this part of the world. It was an abbey foundation, and in the old days Fenchurch St Paul must have been quite an important place. How high should you say our tower was?'

Wimsey gazed up at the great pile.

'It's difficult to tell in this darkness. Not less than a hundred and thirty feet, surely.'

'Not a bad guess. A hundred and twenty-eight, to be exact, to the top of the pinnacles, but it looks more, because of the comparative lowness of the clerestory roof. There aren't many to beat us. St Peter Mancroft, of course – but that's a town church. And St Michael's, Coventry, is one hundred and thirty feet without the spire. But I would venture to back Fenchurch St Paul against them all for beauty of proportion. You will see that better when we turn the corner. Here we are. I always blow my horn here; the wall and the trees make it so very dangerous. I sometimes think we ought to have the churchyard wall set back a little, in the public interest. Ah! now you get a little idea. Very fine, is it not, the piling of the aisle and clerestory? You will be able to judge better in daylight. Here is the Rectory – just opposite the church. I always blow my horn at the gate for fear anyone should be about. The bushes make is so very dark. Ah! safely negotiated. I'm sure you will be glad to get into the warm and have a cup of tea – or possibly something stronger. I always blow my horn at the door, so as to tell my wife I am back. She gets nervous when I am out after lighting-up time; the dykes and drains make these roads so very awkward, and I am not as young as I was, I fear I am already a little late. Ah! here is my wife. Agnes, my dear, I am sorry to be a little behind time, but I have brought a guest back with me. He has had an accident with his car and will stay the night with us. The rug! Allow me! I fear that seat is something of a *res angusta*. Pray be careful of your head. Ah! all is well. My dear – Lord Peter Wimsey.'

Mrs Venables, a plump and placid figure in the lamplight from the open door, received the invasion with competent tranquillity.

'How fortunate that my husband should have met you. An accident? I do hope you are not hurt. I always say these roads are perfect death-traps.'

'Thank you,' said Wimsey. 'There is no harm done. We stupidly ran off the road – at Frog's Bridge, I understand.'

'A very nasty place – quite a mercy you didn't go into the Thirty-foot

Drain. Do come in and sit down and get yourselves warm. Your man? Yes, of course. Emily! Take this gentleman's manservant into the kitchen and make him comfortable.'

'And tell Hinkins to take the car and go down to Frog's Bridge for the luggage,' added the Rector. 'He will find Lord Peter's car there. He had better go at once, before the weather gets worse. And, Emily! tell him to send over to Wilderspin and arrange to get the car out of the dyke.'

'Tomorrow morning will do for that,' said Wimsey.

'To be sure. First thing tomorrow morning. Wilderspin is the blacksmith – an excellent fellow. He will see to the matter most competently. Dear me, yes! And now, come in, come in! We want our tea. Agnes, my dear, have you explained to Emily that Lord Peter will be staying the night?'

'That will be all right,' said Mrs Venables, soothingly. 'I do hope, Theodore, you have not caught cold.'

'No, no, my dear. I have been well wrapped up. Dear me, yes! Ha! What do I see? Muffins?'

'I was just wishing for muffins,' said Wimsey.

'Sit down, sit down and make a good meal. I'm sure you must be famished. I have seldom known such bitter weather. Would you prefer a whisky-and-soda, perhaps?'

'Tea for me,' said Wimsey. 'How jolly all this looks! Really, Mrs Venables, it's tremendously good of you to take pity upon us.'

'I'm only so glad to be able to help,' said Mrs Venables, smiling cheerfully. 'Really, I don't think there's anything to equal the dreariness of these fen roads in winter. It's most fortunate your accident landed you comparatively close to the village.'

'It is indeed.' Wimsey gratefully took in the cosy sitting-room, with its little tables crowded with ornaments, its fire roaring behind a chaste canopy of velvet overmantel, and the silver tea-vessel winking upon the polished tray. 'I feel like Ulysses, come to port after much storm and peril.'

He bit gratefully into a large and buttery muffin.

'Tom Tebbutt seems a good deal better today,' observed the Rector. 'Very unfortunate that he should be laid up just now, but we must be thankful that it is no worse. I only hope there are no further casualties. Young Pratt will manage very well, I think; he went through two long touches this morning without a single mistake, and he is extremely keen. By the way, we ought, perhaps to warn our visitor – '

'I'm sure we ought,' said Mrs Venables. 'My husband has asked you to stay the night, Lord Peter, but he ought to have mentioned that you will probably get very little sleep, being so close to the church. But perhaps you do not mind the sound of bells.'

'Not at all,' said Wimsey.

'My husband is a very keen change-ringer,' pursued Mrs Venables, 'and, as this is New Year's Eve – '

The Rector, who seldom allowed anybody else to finish a sentence, broke in eagerly.

'We hope to accomplish a real feat tonight,' he said, 'or rather, I should say, tomorrow morning. We intend to ring the New Year in with – you are not, perhaps, aware that we possess here one of the finest rings in the country?'

'Indeed?' said Wimsey. 'Yes, I believe I have heard of the Fenchurch bells.'

'There are, perhaps, a few heavier rings,' said the Rector, 'but I hardly know where you would rival us for fullness and sweetness of tone. Number seven, in particular, is a most noble old bell, and so is the tenor, and the John and Jericho bells are also remarkably fine – in fact, the whole ring is most "tuneable and sound", as the old motto has it.'

'It is a full ring of eight?'

'Oh, yes. If you are interested. I should like to show you a very charming little book written by my predecessor, giving the whole history of the bells. The tenor, Tailor Paul, was actually cast in a field next to the churchyard in the year 1614. You can still see the depression in the earth where the mould was made and the field itself is called the Bell-Field to this day.'

'And have you a good set of ringers?' inquired Wimsey, politely.

'Very good indeed. Excellent fellows and most enthusiastic. That reminds me, I was about to say that we have arranged to ring the New Year in tonight with no less,' said the Rector, emphatically, 'no less than fifteen thousand, eight hundred and forty Kent Treble Bob Majors. What do you think of that? Not bad, eh?'

'Bless my heart!' said Wimsey. 'Fifteen thousand – '

'Eight hundred and forty,' said the Rector.

Wimsey made a rapid calculation.

'A good many hours' work there.'

'Nine hours,' said the Rector, with relish.

'Well done, sir,' said Wimsey. 'Why, that's equal to the great performance of the College Youths in eighteen hundred and something.'

'In 1886,' agreed the Rector. 'That is what we aim to emulate. And, what's more, but for the little help I can give, we shall be obliged to do as well as they did, and ring the whole peal with eight ringers only. We had hoped to have twelve, but unhappily, four of our best men have been laid low by this terrible influenza, and we can get no help from Fenchurch St Stephen (which has a ring of bells, though not equal to ours) because there they have no Treble Bob ringers and confine themselves to Grandsire Triples.'

Wimsey shook his head, and helped himself to his fourth muffin.

'Grandsire Triples are most venerable,' he said solemnly, 'but you can never get the same music – '

'That's what I say,' crowed the Rector. 'You never can get the same music when the tenor is rung behind – not even with Stedman's, though we are very fond here of Stedman's and ring them, I venture to say, very well. But for interest and variety and for sweetness in the peal, give me Kent Treble Bob every time.'

'Quite right, sir,' said Wimsey.

'You will never beat it,' said Mr Venables, soaring away happily to the heights of the belfry, and waving his muffin in the air, so that the butter ran down his cuff. 'Take even Grandsire Major – I cannot help feeling it as a defect that the blows come behind so monotonously at the bobs and singles – particularly at the singles, and the fact that the treble and second are confined to a plain hunting course – '

The rest of the Rector's observations on the Grandsire method of change-ringing were unhappily lost, for at that moment Emily made her appearance at the door, with the ominous words:

'If you please, sir, could James Thoday speak to you for a moment?'

'*James* Thoday?' said the Rector. 'Why, certainly, of course. Put him in the study, Emily, and I will come in a moment.'

The Rector was not long gone, and when he returned his face was as long as a fiddle. He let himself drop into his chair in an attitude of utter discouragement.

'This,' he ejaculated, dramatically, 'is an irreparable disaster!'

'Good gracious, Theodore! What in the world is the matter?'

'William Thoday! Of all nights in the year! Poor fellow, I ought not to think of myself, but it is a bitter disappointment – a bitter disappointment.'

'Why, what has happened to Thoday?'

'Struck down,' said the Rector, 'struck down by this wretched scourge of influenza. Quite helpless. Delirious. They have sent for Dr Baines.'

'T'chk, t'chk,' said Mrs Venables.

'It appears,' went on the Rector, 'that he felt unwell this morning, but insisted – most unwisely, poor man – on driving in to Walbeach on some business or other. Foolish fellow! I thought he looked seedy when he came in to see me last night. Most fortunately, George Ashton met him in the town and saw how bad he was and insisted on coming back with him. Poor Thoday must have taken a violent chill in all this bitter cold. He was quite collapsed when they got him home and they had to put him to bed instantly, and now he is in a high fever and worrying all the time because he cannot get to the church tonight. I told his brother to make every effort to calm his mind, but I fear it will be difficult. He is so enthusiastic, and the thought that he has been incapacitated at this crisis seems to be preying on his mind.'

'Dear, dear,' said Mrs Venables, 'but I expect Dr Baines will give him something to quiet him down.'

'I hope so, sincerely. It *is* a disaster, of course, but it is distressing that he should take it so to heart. Well, well. What can't be cured must be endured. This is our last hope gone. We shall be reduced to ringing minors.'

'Is this man one of your ringers, then, padre?'

'Unfortunately, he is, and there is no one now to take his place. Our grand scheme will have to be abandoned. Even if I were to take a bell myself, I could not possibly ring for nine hours. I am not getting younger, and besides, I have an Early Service at eight o'clock, in addition to the New Year service which will not release me till after midnight. Ah, well! Man proposes and God disposes – unless' – the Rector turned suddenly and looked at his guest – 'you were speaking just now with a good deal of feeling about Treble Bob – you are not, yourself, by any chance, a ringer?'

'Well,' said Wimsey, 'I used at one time to pull quite a pretty rope. But whether, at this time of day – '

'Treble Bob?' inquired the Rector, eagerly.

'Treble Bob, certainly. But it's some time since – '

'It will come back to you,' cried the Rector, feverishly. 'It will come back. Half an hour with the handbells – '

'My dear!' said Mrs Venables.

'Isn't it wonderful?' cried the Rector. 'Is it not really providential? That just at this moment we should be sent a guest who is actually a ringer and accustomed to ringing Kent Treble Bob?' He rang for the maid. 'Hinkins must go round at once and call the lads together for a practice ring on the handbells. My dear, I am afraid we shall have to monopolise the dining-room, if you don't mind. Emily, tell Hinkins that I have here a gentleman who can ring the peal with us and I want him to go round immediately – '

'One moment, Emily. Theodore, is it quite fair to ask Lord Peter Wimsey, after a motor accident, and at the end of a tiring day, to stay up ringing bells from midnight to nine o'clock? A short peal, perhaps, if he really does not mind, but even so, are we not demanding rather a lot of his good nature?'

The Rector's mouth dropped like the mouth of a hurt child, and Wimsey hastened to his support.

'Not in the least, Mrs Venables. Nothing would please me more than to ring bells all day and all night. I am not tired at all. I really don't need rest.

I would far rather ring bells. The only thing that worries me is whether I shall be able to get through the peal without making stupid mistakes.'

'Of course you will, of course you will,' said the Rector, hurriedly. 'But as my wife says – really, I am afraid I am being very thoughtless. Nine hours is too much. We ought to confine ourselves to five thousand changes or so –'

'Not a bit of it,' said Wimsey. 'Nine hours or nothing. I insist upon it. Probably, once you have heard my efforts, it will be nothing.'

'Pooh! nonsense!' cried the Rector. 'Emily, tell Hinkins to get the ringers together here by – shall we say half-past six? I think they can all be here by then, except possibly Pratt, who lives up at Tupper's End, but I can make the eighth myself. How delightful this is! Positively, I cannot get over the amazing coincidence of your arrival. It shows the wonderful way in which Heaven provides even for our pleasures, if they be innocent. I hope, Lord Peter, you will not mind if I make a little reference to it in my sermon tonight? At least, it will hardly be a sermon – only a few thoughts appropriate to the New Year and its opportunities. May I ask where you usually ring?'

'Nowhere, nowadays; but when I was a boy I used to ring at Duke's Denver, and when I go home at Christmas and so on, I occasionally lay hand to a rope even now.'

'Duke's Denver? Of course – St John ad-Portam-Latinam – a beautiful little church; I know it quite well. But I think you will admit that our bells are finer. Well, now, if you will excuse me, I will just run and put the dining-room in readiness for our practice.'

He bustled away.

'It is very good of you to indulge my husband's hobby,' said Mrs Venables; 'this occasion has meant so much to him, and he has had so many disappointments about it. But it seems dreadful to offer you hospitality and then keep you hard at work all night.'

Wimsey again assured her that the pleasure was entirely his.

'I shall insist on your getting a few hours rest at least,' was all Mrs Venables could say. 'Will you come up now and see your room? You will like a wash and brush-up at any rate. We will have supper at 7.30, if we can get my husband to release you by then, and after that, you really must go and lie down for a nap. I have put you in here – I see your man has everything ready for you.'

'Well, Bunter,' said Wimsey, when Mrs Venables had departed, leaving him to make himself presentable by the inadequate light of a small oil-lamp and a candle, 'that looks a nice bed – but I am not fated to sleep in it.'

'So I understand from the young woman, my lord.'

'It's a pity you can't relieve me at the rope, Bunter.'

'I assure your lordship that for the first time in my existence I regret that I have made no practical study of campanology.'

'I am always so delighted to find that there are things you cannot do. Did you ever try?'

'Once only, my lord, and on that occasion an accident was only narrowly averted. Owing to my unfortunate lack of manual dexterity I was very nearly hanged in the rope, my lord.'

'That's enough about hanging,' said Wimsey, peevishly. We're not detecting now, and I don't want to talk shop.'

'Certainly not, my lord. Does your lordship desire to be shaved?'

'Yes – let's start the New Year with a clean face.'

'Very good, my lord.'

Descending, clean and shaven, to the dining-room, Wimsey found the table moved aside and eight chairs set in a circle. On seven of the chairs sat seven men, varying in age from a gnarled old gnome with a long beard to an embarrassed youth with his hair plastered into a cowlick, in the centre, the Rector stood twittering like an amiable magician. 'Ah! there you are! Splendid! excellent! Now, lads, this is Lord Peter Wimsey, who has been providentially sent to assist us out of our difficulty. He tells me he is a little out of practice, so I am sure you will not mind putting in a little time to enable him to get his hand in again. Now I must introduce you all. Lord Peter, this is Hezekiah Lavender, who has pulled the tenor for sixty years and means to pull it for twenty years longer, don't you, Hezekiah?'

The little gnarled man grinned toothlessly and extended a knobbly hand.

'Proud to meet you, my lord. Yes, I've pulled old Tailor Paul a mort o' times now. Her and me's well acquainted, and I means to go on a-pulling of her till she rings the nine tailors for me, that I do.'

'I hope you will long be spared to do it, Mr Lavender.'

'Ezra Wilderspin,' went on the Rector. 'He's our biggest man, and he pulls the smallest bell. That's often the way of things, isn't it? He is our blacksmith, by the way, and has promised to get your car put right for you in the morning.'

The blacksmith laughed sheepishly, engulfed Wimsey's fingers in an enormous hand and retired to his chair in some confusion.

'Jack Godfrey,' continued the Rector. 'Number Seven. How's Batty Thomas going now, Jack?'

'Going fine, thank you, sir, since we had them new gudgeons put in.'

'Jack has the honour of ringing the oldest bell we have,' added the Rector. 'Batty Thomas was cast in 1338 by Thomas Belleyetere of Lynn; but she gets her name from Abbot Thomas who recast her in 1380 – doesn't she, Jack?'

'So she do, sir,' agreed Mr Godfrey. Bells, it may be noted, like ships and kittens, have a way of being female, whatever names they are given.

'Mr Donnington, the landlord of the Red Cow, our church-warden,' went on the Rector, bringing forward a long, thin man with a squint. 'I ought to have mentioned him first of all, by right of his office, but then you see, though he himself is very distinguished, his bell is not so ancient as Tailor Paul or Batty Thomas. He takes charge of Number Six – Dimity, we call her – a comparative newcomer in her present shape, though her metal is old.'

'And a sweeter bell we haven't got in the ring,' averred Mr Donnington, stoutly. 'Pleased to meet you, my lord.'

'Joe Hinkins, my gardener. You have already met, I think. He pulls Number Five. Harry Gotobed, Number Four; our sexton, and what better name could a sexton have? And Walter Pratt – our youngest recruit, who is going to ring Number Three and does it very well indeed. So glad you were able to get here in time, Walter. That's all of us. You, Lord Peter, will take poor William Thoday's bell, Number Two. She and Number Five were recast in the same year as Dimity – the year of the old Queen's Jubilee; her name is Sabaoth. Now, let's get to work. Here is your handbell; come and sit next to Walter Pratt. Our good old friend Hezekiah will be the conductor, and you'll find he can sing out his calls as loud and clear as the bells, for all he's seventy-five years past. Can't you, Granddad?'

'Ay, that I can,' cried the old man, cheerfully. 'Now, boys, if you be ready, we'll ring a little touch of 96, just to put this gentleman in the way of it, like. You'll remember, my lord, that you starts by making the first snapping lead with the treble and after that you goes into the slow hunt till she comes down to snap with you again.'

'Right you are,' said Wimsey. 'And after that I make the thirds and fourths.'

'That's so, my lord. And then it's three steps forward and one back till you lay the blows behind.'

'Carry on, sergeant-major.'

The old man nodded, adding: 'And you, Wally Pratt, mind what you're about, and don't go a-follerin' your course bell beyond third place. I've telled yew about that time and again. Now, are you ready, lads – go!'

The art of change ringing is peculiar to the English, and, like most English peculiarities, unintelligible to the rest of the world. To the musical Belgian, for example, it appears that the proper thing to do with a carefully tuned ring of bells is to play a tune upon it. By the English campanologist, the playing of tunes is considered to be a childish game, only fit for foreigners; the proper use of bells is to work out mathematical permutations and combinations. When he speaks of the music of his bells, he does not mean musician's music – still less what the ordinary man calls music. To the ordinary man, in fact, the pealing of bells is a monotonous jangle and a nuisance, tolerable only when mitigated by remote distance and sentimental association. The change-ringer does, indeed, distinguish musical differences between one method of producing his permutations and another; he avers, for instance, that where the hinder bells run 7, 5, 6, or 5, 6, 7, or 5, 7, 6, the music is always prettier, and can detect and approve, where they occur, the consecutive fifths of Tittums and the cascading thirds of the Queen's change. But what he really means is, that by the English method of ringing with rope and wheel, each several bell gives forth her fullest and her noblest note. His passion – and it gives a passion – finds its satisfaction in mathematical completeness and mechanical perfection, and as his bell weaves her way rhythmically up from lead to hinder place and down again, he is filled with the solemn intoxication that comes of intricate ritual faultlessly performed. To any disinterested spectator, peeping in upon the rehearsal, there might have been something a little absurd about the eight absorbed faces; the eight tense bodies poised in a spellbound circle on the edges of eight dining-room chairs; the eight upraised right hands, decorously wagging the handbells upward and downward; but to the performers, everything was serious and important as an afternoon with the Australians at Lords.

Mr Hezekiah Lavender having called three successive bobs, the bells came back into rounds without mishap.

'Excellent,' said the Rector. 'You made no mistake about that.'

'All right, so far,' said Wimsey.

'The gentleman will do well enough,' agreed Mr Lavender. 'Now, boys, once again. What 'ull we make it this time, sir?'

'Make it a 704,' said the Rector, consulting his watch. 'Call her in the middle with a double, before, wrong and home, and repeat.'

'Right you are, sir. And you, Wally Pratt, keep your ears open for the treble and your eyes on your course bell, and don't go gapin' about or you'll have us all imbrangled.'

The unfortunate Pratt wiped his forehead, curled his boots tightly round the legs of his chair, and took a firm hold of his bell. Whether out of nervousness or for some other cause, he found himself in trouble at the beginning of the seventh lead, 'imbrangled' himself and his neighbours very successfully and broke into a severe perspiration.

'Stand!' growled Mr Lavender, in a disgusted tone. 'If that's the way you mean to set about it, Wally Pratt, we may just so well give up the ringing of this here peal. Surely you know by this time what to do at a bob?'

'Come, come,' said the Rector. 'You mustn't be disheartened, Wally. Try again. You forgot to make the double dodge in 7, 8, didn't you?'

'Yes, sir.'

'Forgot!' exclaimed Mr Lavender, waggling his beard. 'Now, just yew take example by his lordship here. *He* didn't go forgettin' things, none the more for bein' out o' practice.'

'Come, come, Hezekiah,' cried the Rector again. 'You mustn't be hard on Wally. We haven't all had sixty years' experience.'

Mr Lavender grunted, and started the whole touch again from the beginning. This time Mr Pratt kept his head and his place and the ringing went on successfully through to its conclusion.

'Well rung, all,' cried the Rector. 'Our new recruit will do us credit, I think, Hezekiah?'

'I almost fell down in the second lead, though,' said Wimsey, laughing. 'I as nearly as possible forgot to lay the four blows in fourths place at the bob. However, nearly isn't quite.'

'You'll keep your place all right, my lord,' said Mr Lavender. 'As for you, Wally Pratt – '

'I think,' said the Rector hastily, 'we'd better run across to the church now and let Lord Peter get the feel of his bell. You may as well all come over and ring the bells up for service. And, Jack, see to it that Lord Peter's rope is made comfortable for him. Jack Godfrey takes charge of the bells and ropes,' he added in explanation, 'and keeps them in apple-pie order for us.'

Mr Godfrey smiled.

'We'll need to let the tuckings down a goodish bit for his lordship,' he observed, measuring Wimsey with his eye; 'he's none so tall as Will Thoday, not by a long chalk.'

'Never you mind,' said Wimsey. 'In the words of the old bell-motto: I'd have it to be understood that though I'm little, yet I'm good.'

'Of course,' said the Rector, 'Jack didn't mean anything else. But Will Thoday is a very tall man indeed. Now where did I put my hat? Agnes, my dear! Agnes! I can't find my hat. Oh, here, to be sure. And my muffler – I'm so much obliged to you. Now, let me just get the key of the belfry and we – dear me, now! When did I have that key last?'

'It's all right, sir,' said Mr Godfrey. 'I have all the keys here, sir.'

'The church-key as well?'

'Yes, sir, and the key of the bell-chamber.'

'Oh, good, good – excellent. Lord Peter will like to go up into the bell-chamber. To my mind, Lord Peter, the sight of a ring of good bells – I beg your pardon, my dear?'

'I said. Do remember dinner-time, and don't keep poor Lord Peter too long.'

'No, no, my dear, certainly not. But he will like to look at the bells. And the church itself is worth seeing. Lord Peter. We have a very interesting twelfth-century font, and the roof is considered to be one of the finest specimens – yes, yes, my dear, we're just going.'

The hall-door was opened upon a glimmering world. The snow was still falling fast; even the footprints made less than an hour earlier by the ringers were almost obliterated. They straggled down the drive and crossed the road. Ahead of them, the great bulk of the church loomed dark and gigantic. Mr Godfrey led the way with an old-fashioned lantern through the lych-gate and along a path bordered with tombstones to the south door of the church, which he opened, with a groaning of the heavy lock. A powerful ecclesiastical odour, compounded of ancient wood, varnish, dry rot, hassocks, hymn-books, paraffin lamps, flowers and candles, all gently baking in the warmth of slow-combustion stoves, billowed out from the interior. The tiny ray of the lantern picked out here the poppyhead on a pew, here the angle of a stone pillar, here the gleam of brass from a mural tablet. Their footsteps echoed queerly in the great height of the clerestory.

'All Transitional here,' whispered the Rector, 'except the Late Perpendicular window at the end of the north aisle, which of course you can't see. Nothing is left of the original Norman foundation but a couple of drums at the base of the chancel arch, but you can trace the remains of the Norman apse, if you look for it, underneath the Early English sanctuary. When we have more light, you will notice – Oh, yes, Jack, yes, by all means. Jack Godfrey is quite right, Lord Peter – we must not waste time. I am apt to be led away by my enthusiasm.'

He conducted his guest westwards under the tower arch, and thence, in the wake of Godfrey's lantern, up a steep and winding belfry stair, its stone treads worn shallow with the feet of countless long-dead ringers. After a turn or so, the procession halted; there was a jingling of keys and the lantern moved away to the right through a narrow door. Wimsey, following, found himself in the ringing-chamber of the belfry.

It was in no way remarkable, except in being perhaps a little loftier than the average, on account of the exceptional height of the tower. By daylight, it was well lit, having a fine window of three lights on each of its three exterior sides, while low down in the eastern wall, a couple of unglazed openings, defended by iron bars against accident, gave upon the interior of the church, a little above the level of the clerestory windows. As Jack Godfrey set the lantern on the floor, and proceeded to light a paraffin lamp which hung against the wall, Wimsey could see the eight bellropes, their woollen sallies looped neatly to the walls, and their upper ends vanishing mysteriously into the shadows of the chamber roof. Then the light streamed out and the walls took shape and colour. They were plainly plastered, with a painted motto in Gothic lettering running round below the windows: 'They Have Neither Speech nor Language but their Voices are Heard Among Them, their Sound is Gone Forth into All Lands.' Above this, various tablets of wood, brass and even stone, commemorated the ringing of remarkable peals in the past.

'We shall hope to put up a new tablet after tonight,' said the Rector's voice in Wimsey's ear.

'I only hope I may do nothing to prevent it,' said Wimsey. 'I see you have the old regulations for your ringers. Ah! "Keep stroak of time and goe not out. Or elles you forfeit out of doubt. For every fault a Jugg of beer." It doesn't say how big a jug, but there is something about the double g that suggests size and potency. "If a bell you over throw 'Twill cost you sixpence ere you goe." That's cheap, considering the damage it does. On the other hand, sixpence for every swear or curse is rather on the dear side, I think, don't you, padre? Where's this bell of mine?'

'Here, my Lord.' Jack Godfrey had unhitched the rope of the second bell, and let down to its full length the portion of rope below the sallie.

'When you've got her raised,' he said, 'we'll fix them tuckings proper. Unless you'd like me to raise her for you?'

'Not on your life,' said Wimsey. 'It's a poor ringer that can't raise his own bell.' He grasped the rope and pulled it gently downwards, gathering the slack in his left hand. Softly, tremulously, high overhead in the tower, Sabaoth began to speak, and her sister's after her as the ringers stood to their ropes. 'Tin-tin-tin,' cried Gaude in her silvery treble; 'tan-tan,' answered Sabaoth; 'din-din-din,' 'dan-dan-dan,' said John and Jericho, climbing to their places; 'bim, bam, bim, bam,' Jubilee and Dimity followed; 'bom,' said Batty Thomas; and Tailor Paul, majestically lifting up her great bronze mouth, bellowed 'bo, bo, bo,' as the ropes hauled upon the wheels.

Wimsey brought his bell competently up and set her at backstroke while the tuckings were finally adjusted, after which, at the Rector's suggestion, a few rounds were rung to let him 'get the feel of her.'

'You can leave your bell up, boys,' said Mr Hezekiah Lavender, graciously, when this last rehearsal was concluded, 'but don't you go a-taking that for what they calls preceedent, Wally Pratt. And listen here, all on you; don't make no mistake. You comes here, sharp at the quarter to eleven, see – and you rings same as usual for service, and after Rector has finished his sermon, you comes up here again quiet and decent and takes your places. Then, while they're a-singin' their 'ymn, I rings the nine tailors and the 'alf-minute passing-strokes for Old Year, see. Then you takes your ropes in hand and waits for the clock to strike. When she's finished striking, I say "Go!" and mind as you're ready to go. And when Rector's done down below, he's promised to come up and give a 'and from time to time to any man as needs a rest, and I'm sure it's very kind of him. And I take leave to suppose, Alf Donnington, as you won't forget the usual.'

'Not me,' said Mr Donnington. 'Well, so long, boys.'

The lantern led the way from the ringing-chamber, and a great shuffling of feet followed it.

'And now,' said the Rector, 'and now, Lord Peter, you will like to come and see – Dear me!' he ejaculated, as they groped upon the dark spiral stair, 'where in the world is Jack Godfrey? Jack! He has gone on down with the others. Ah, well, poor fellow, no doubt he wants to get home to his supper. We must not be selfish. Unfortunately he has the key of the bell-chamber, and without it we cannot conduct our researches. However, you will see much better tomorrow. Yes, Jack, yes – we are coming. Do be careful of these stairs – they are very much worn, especially on the inside. Here we are, safe and sound. Excellent! Now, before we go, Lord Peter, I should so much like to show you – '

The clock in the tower chimed the three-quarters.

'Bless my heart!' cried the Rector, conscience-striken, 'and dinner was to be at half-past! My wife – we must wait till tonight. You will get a general idea of the majesty and beauty of our church if you attend the service, though there are many most interesting details that a visitor is almost bound to miss if they are not pointed out to him. The font, for instance – Jack! bring the lantern here a moment – there is one point about our font which is most uncommon, and I should like to show it to you. Jack!'

But Jack, unaccountably deaf, was jingling the church keys in the porch, and the Rector, sighing a little, accepted defeat.

'I fear it is true,' he said as he trotted down the path, 'that I am inclined to lose count of time.'

'Perhaps,' replied Wimsey politely, 'the being continually in and about this church brings eternity too close.'

'Very true,' said the Rector, 'very true – though there are mementoes enough to mark the passage of time. Remind me tomorrow to show you the tomb of Nathaniel Perkins – one of our local worthies and a great sportsman. He refereed once for the great Tom Sayers, and was a notable figure at all the "mills" for miles around, and when he died – Here we are at home. I will tell you later about Nathaniel Perkins. Well, my dear, we're back at last! Not so *very* late after all. Come along, come along. You must make a good dinner, Lord Peter, to fit you for your exertions. What have we hear? Stewed oxtail? Excellent! Most sustaining! I trust, Lord Peter, you can eat stewed oxtail. For what we are about to receive . . .'

THE SECOND COURSE

THE BELLS IN THEIR COURSES

When mirth and pleasure is on the wing we ring;
At the departure of a soul we toll.

Ringers' Rules at Southhill, Bedfordshire

After dinner, Mrs Venables resolutely asserted her authority. She sent Lord Peter up to his room, regardless of the Rector, who was helplessly hunting through a set of untidy bookshelves in search of the Rev. Christopher Woollcott's *History of the Bells of Fenchurch St Paul*.

'I can't imagine what has become of it,' said the Rector: 'I fear I'm sadly unmethodical. But perhaps you would like to look at this – a trifling contribution of my own to campanological lore. I know, my dear, I know – I must not detain Lord Peter – it is thoughtless of me.'

'You must get some rest yourself, Theodore.'

'Yes, yes, my dear. In a moment. I was only – '

Wimsey saw that the one way to quiet the Rector was to desert him without compunction. He retired, accordingly, and was captured at the head of the stairs by Bunter, who tucked him firmly beneath the eiderdown with a hot-water bottle and shut the door upon him.

A roaring fire burned in the grate. Wimsey drew the lamp closer to him, opened the little brochure presented to him by the Rector, and studied the title-page:

An Inquiry into
the Mathematical Theory
of the
IN AND OUT OF COURSE
together with
Directions for
Calling Bells into Rounds
from any position
in all the recognised Methods
upon a
New and Scientific Principle
by
THEODORE VENABLES, M.A.
Rector of Fenchurch St Paul
sometime Scholar of Caius Coll: Camb:
author of
'Change-ringing for Country Churches,'
'Fifty Short Touches of Grandsire Triples,' etc.
'God is gone up with a merry noise.'
MCMII

The letterpress was of a soporofic tendency; so was the stewed oxtail; the room was warm; the day had been a tiring one; the lines swam before Lord Peter's eyes. He nodded; a coal tinkled from the grate; he roused himself with a jerk and read: '. . . if the 5th is in course after the 7th (says Shipway), and 7th after the 6th, they are right, when the small bells, 2, 3, 4, are brought as directed in the preceding peals; but if 6, 7, are together without the 5th, call the 5th into the hunt . . .'

Lord Peter nodded away into dreams.

He was roused by the pealing of bells.

For a moment, memory eluded him – then he flung the eiderdown aside and sat up, ruffled and reproachful, to encounter the calm gaze of Bunter.

'Good God! I've been asleep! Why didn't you call me? They've begun without me.'

'Mrs Venables gave orders, my lord, that you were not to be disturbed until half-past eleven, and the reverend gentleman instructed me to say, my lord, that they would content themselves with ringing six bells as a preliminary to the service.'

'What time is it now?'

'Nearly five minutes to eleven, my lord.'

As he spoke, the pealing ceased, and Jubilee began to ring the five-minute bell.

'Dash it all!' said Wimsey. 'This will never do. Must go and hear the old boy's sermon. Give me a hairbrush. Is it still snowing?'

'Harder than ever, my lord.'

Wimsey made a hasty toilet and ran downstairs, Bunter following him decorously. They let themselves out by the front door, and, guided by Bunter's electric torch, made their way through the shrubbery and across the road to the church, entering just as the organ boomed out its final notes. Choir and parson were in their places and Wimsey blinking in the yellow lamplight, at length discovered his seven fellow-ringers seated on a row of chairs beneath the tower. He picked his way cautiously over the coco-nut matting towards them, while Bunter, who had apparently acquired all the necessary information beforehand, made his unperturbed way to a pew in the north aisle and sat down beside Emily from the Rectory. Old Hezekiah Lavender greeted Wimsey with a welcoming chuckle and thrust a prayer-book under his nose as he knelt down to pray.

'Dearly beloved brethren – '

Wimsey scrambled to his feet and looked round.

At first glance he felt himself sobered and awe-stricken by the noble proportion of the church, in whose vast spaces the congregation – though a good one for so small a parish in the dead of a winter's night – seemed almost lost. The wide nave and shadowy aisles, the lofty span of the chancel arch – crossed, though not obscured, by the delicate fan-tracery and crenellated moulding of the screen – the intimate and cloistered loveliness of the chancel, with its pointed arcading, graceful ribbed vault and five narrow east lancets, led his attention on and focused it first upon the remote glow of the sanctuary. Then his gaze, returning to the nave, followed the strong yet slender shafting that sprang fountain-like from floor to foliated column-head, spraying into the light, wide arches that carried the clerestory. And there, mounting to the steep pitch of the roof, his eyes were held entranced with wonder and delight. Incredibly aloof, flinging back the light in a dusky shimmer of bright hair and gilded out-spread wings, soared the ranked angels, cherubim and seraphim, choir over choir, from corbel and hammer-beam floating face to face uplifted.

'My God!' muttered Wimsey, not without reverence. And he softly repeated to himself: 'He rode upon the cherubins and did fly; He came flying upon wings of the wind.'

Mr Hezekiah Lavender poked his new colleague sharply in the ribs, and Wimsey became aware that the congregation had settled down to the General Confession, leaving him alone and agape upon his feet. Hurriedly he turned the leaves of his prayer-book and applied himself to making the proper responses. Mr Lavender, who had obviously decided that he was either a half-wit or a heathen, assisted him by finding the psalms for him and by bawling every verse loudly in his ear.

'. . . Praise Him in the cymbals and dances: praise Him upon the strings and pipe.'

The shrill voices of the surpliced choir mounted to the roof, and seemed to find their echo in the golden mouths of the angels.

'Praise Him upon the well-tuned cymbals; praise Him upon the loud cymbals.

'Let everything that hath breath praise the Lord.'

The time wore on towards midnight. The Rector, advancing to the chancel steps, delivered, in his mild and scholarly voice, a simple and moving little address, in which he spoke of praising God, not only upon the strings and pipe, but upon the beautiful bells of their beloved church, and alluded, in his gently pious way, to the presence of the passing stranger – 'please do not turn round to stare at him; that would be neither courteous nor reverent' – who had been sent 'by what men call chance' to assist in this work of devotion. Lord Peter blushed, the Rector pronounced the Benediction, the organ played the opening bars of a hymn and Hezekiah Lavender exclaimed sonorously: 'Now, lads!' The ringers, with

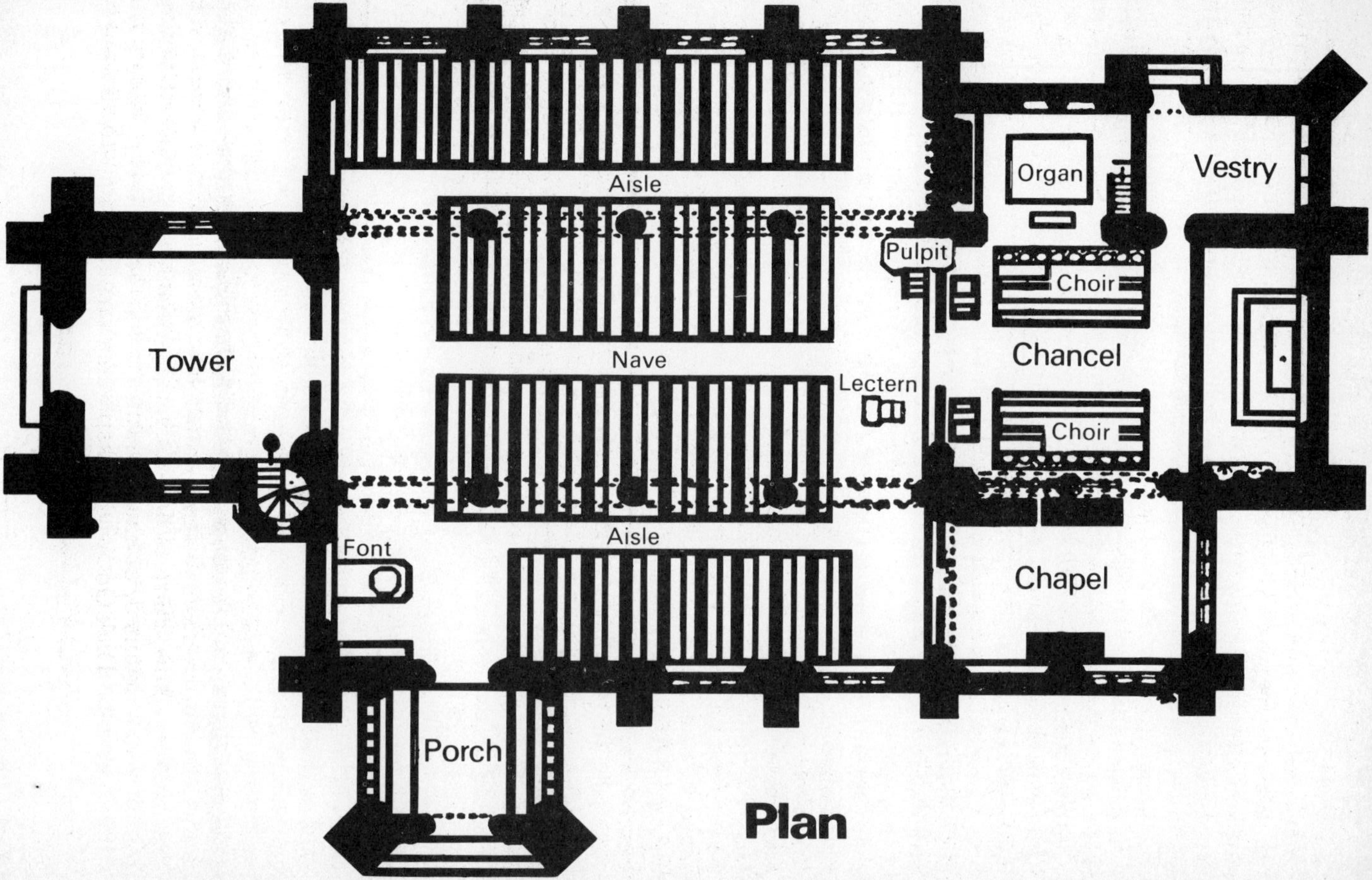
Tower
Aisle
Nave
Aisle
Font
Porch
Pulpit
Lectern
Organ
Choir
Chancel
Choir
Vestry
Chapel

Plan

much subdued shuffling, extricated themselves from their chairs and wound their way up the belfry stair. Coats were pulled off and hung on nails in the ringing-chamber, and Wimsey, observing on a bench near the door an enormous brown jug and nine pewter tankards, understood, with pleasure, that the landlord of the Red Cow had, indeed, provided 'the usual' for the refreshment of the ringers.

The eight men advanced to their stations, and Hezekiah consulted his watch.

'Time!' he said.

He spat upon his hands, grasped the Sallie of Tailor Paul, and gently swung the great bell over the balance.

Toll-toll-toll; and a pause; toll-toll-toll; and a pause; toll-toll-toll; the nine tailors, or teller-strokes, that mark the passing of a man. The year is dead; toll him out with twelve strokes more, one for every passing month. Then silence. Then, from the faint, sweet tubular chimes of the clock overhead, the four quarters and the twelve strokes of midnight. The ringers grasped their ropes.

'Go!'

The bells gave tongue: Gaude, Sabaoth, John, Jericho, Jubilee, Dimity, Batty Thomas and Tailor Paul, rioting and exulting high up in the dark tower, wide mouths rising and falling, brazen tongues clamouring, huge wheels turning to the dance of the leaping ropes. Tin tan din dan bim bam bom bo – tan tin din dan bam bim bo bom – tin tan dan din bim bam bom bo – tan tin dan din bam bim bo bom – tan dan tin bam din bo bim bom – every bell in her place striking tuneably, hunting up, hunting down, dodging, snapping, laying her blows behind, making her thirds and fourths, working down to lead the dance again. Out over the flat, white wastes of fen, over the spear-straight, steel-dark dykes and the wind-bent, groaning poplar trees, bursting from the snow-choked louvres of the belfry, whirled away southward and westward in gusty blasts of clamour to the sleeping counties went the music of the bells – little Gaude, silver Sabaoth, strong John and Jericho, glad Jubilee, sweet Dimity and old Batty Thomas, with great Tailor Paul bawling and striding like a giant in the midst of them. Up and down went the shadows of the ringers upon the walls, up and down went the scarlet sallies flickering roofwards and floorwards, and up and down, hunting in their courses, went the bells of Fenchurch St Paul.

Wimsey, his eye upon the ropes and his ear pricked for the treble's shrill tongue speaking at lead, had little attention to give to anything but his task. He was dimly conscious of old Hezekiah, moving with the smooth rhythm of a machine, bowing his ancient back very slightly at each pull to bring Tailor Paul's great weight over, and of Wally Pratt, his face anxiously contorted and his lips moving in the effort to keep his intricate course in mind. Wally's bell was moving down now towards his own, dodging Number Six and passing her, dodging Number Seven and passing her, passing Number Five, striking her two blows at lead, working up again, while the treble came down to take her place and make her last snapping lead with Sabaoth. One blow in seconds place and one at lead, and Sabaoth, released from the monotony of the slow hunt, ran out merrily into her plain hunting course. High in the air above them the cock upon the weather-vane stared out over the snow and watched the pinnacles of the tower swing to and fro with a slowly widening sweep as the tall stalk of stone gathered momentum and rocked like a windblown tree beneath his golden feet.

The congregation streamed out from the porch, their lanterns and torches flitting away into the whirling storm like sparks tossed from a bonfire. The Rector, pulling off his surplice and stole, climbed in his cassock to the ringing-chamber and sat down upon the bench, ready to give help and counsel. The clock's chimes came faintly through the voices of the bells. At the end of the first hour the Rector took the rope from the hand of the agitated Wally and released him for an interval of rest and refreshment. A soft glugging sound proclaimed that Mr Donnington's 'usual' was going where it would do most good.

Wimsey, relieved at the end of the third hour, found Mrs Venables seated among the pewter pots, with Bunter in respectful attendance beside her.

'I do hope,' said Mrs Venables, 'that you are not feeling exhausted.'

'Far from it; only rather dry.' Wimsey remedied this condition without further apology, and asked how the peal sounded.

'Beautiful!' said Mrs Venables, loyally. She did not really care for bell-music, and felt sleepy; but the Rector would have felt hurt if she had withdrawn her sympathetic presence.

'It's surprising, isn't it?' she added, 'how soft and mellow it sounds in here. But of course there's another floor between us and the bell-chamber.' She yawned desperately. The bells rang on. Wimsey, knowing that the Rector was well set for the next quarter of an hour, was seized with a fancy to listen to the peal from outside. He slipped down the winding stair and groped his way through the south porch. As he emerged into the night, the clamour of the bells smote on his ears like a blow. The snow was falling less heavily now. He turned to his right, knowing that it is unlucky to walk about a church widdershins, and followed the path close beneath the wall till he found himself standing by the west door. Sheltered by the towering bulk of the masonry, he lit a sacrilegious cigarette, and, thus fortified, turned right again. Beyond the foot of the tower, the pathway ended, and he stumbled among the grass and tombstones for the whole length of the aisle, which, on the side, was prolonged to the extreme east end of the church. Midway between the last two buttresses on the north side he came upon a path leading to a small door; this he tried, but found it locked, and so passed on, encountering the full violence of the wind as he rounded the east end. Pausing a moment to get his breath, he looked out over the Fen. All was darkness, except for a dim stationary light which might have been shining from some cottage window. Wimsey reckoned that the cottage must lie somewhere along the solitary road by which they had reached the Rectory, and wondered why anybody should be awake at three o'clock on New Year's morning. But the night was bitter and he was wanted back at his job. He completed his circuit, re-entered by the south porch and returned to the belfry. The Rector resigned the rope to him, warning him that he had now to make his two blows behind and not to forget to dodge back into eighth's place before hunting down.

At six o'clock, the ringers were all in pretty good case. Wally Pratt's cow-lick had fallen into his eyes, and he was sweating freely, but was still moving well within himself. The blacksmith was fresh and cheerful, and looked ready to go on till next Christmas. The publican was grim but determined. Most unperturbed of all was the aged Hezekiah, working grandly as though he were part and parcel of his rope, and calling his bobs without a tremor in his clear old voice.

At a quarter to eight the Rector left them to prepare for his early service. The beer in the jug had sunk to low tide and Wally Pratt, with an hour and a half to go, was beginning to look a little strained. Through the southern window a faint reflection of the morning light came, glimmering frail and blue.

At ten minutes past nine the Rector was back in the belfry, standing watch in hand with a beaming smile on his face.

At thirteen minutes past nine the treble came shrilling triumphantly into her last lead.

Tin tan din dan bim bam bom bo.

Their long courses ended, the belts came faultlessly back into rounds, and the ringers stood.

'Magnificent, lads, magnificent!' cried Mr Venables. 'You've done it, and it couldn't have been better done.'

'Eh!' admitted Mr Lavender, 'it was none so bad.' A slow toothless grin overspread his countenance. 'Yes, we done it. How did it sound from down below, sir?'

'Fine,' said the Rector. 'As firm and true as any ringing I have ever heard. Now you must all be wanting your breakfasts. It's all ready for you at the Rectory. Well now, Wally, you can call yourself a real ringer now, can't you? You came through it with very great credit – didn't he, Hezekiah?'

'Fair to middlin',' said Mr Lavender grudgingly. 'But you takes too much out o' yourself, Wally. You've no call to be gettin' all of a muck o' sweat that way. Still, you ain't made no mistakes an' that's something, but I see you a mumblin' and countin' to yourself all the time. If I've telled yew once I've telled yew a hundred times to keep your eye on the ropes and then you don't need – '

'There, there!' said the Rector. 'Never mind, Wally, you did very well indeed. Where's Lord Peter – oh! there you are. I'm sure we owe you a great deal. Not too fatigued, I hope?'

'No, no,' said Wimsey, extricating himself from the congratulatory handshakes of his companions. He felt, in fact, exhausted to dropping-point. He had not rung a long peal for years, and the effort of keeping alert for so many hours had produced an almost intolerable desire to tumble down in a corner and go to sleep. 'I – ah – oh – I'm perfectly all right.'

He swayed as he walked and would have pitched headlong down the steep stair, but for the blacksmith's sustaining arm.

'Breakfast,' said the Rector, much concerned, 'breakfast is what we all want. Hot coffee. A very comforting thing. Dear me, yes, I for one am looking forward to it very much. Ha! the snow has ceased falling. Very beautiful, this white world – if only there were not a thaw to follow. This will mean a lot of water down the Thirty foot, I expect. Are you sure you're all right? Come along, then, come along! Why, here is my wife – come to chide my tardiness, I expect. We're just coming, my dear – Why, Johnson, what is it?'

He addressed a young man in chauffeur's livery, who was standing at Mrs Venables's side. Mrs Venables broke in before he could reply.

'My dear Theodore – I have been saying, you can't go just yet. You must have something to eat – '

Mr Venables put the interruption aside with an unexpected, quiet authority.

'Agnes, my dear, permit me. Am I wanted, Johnson?'

'Sir Henry sent me to say, sir, that the mistress was very bad this morning and they're afraid she's sinking, sir, and she is very anxious to receive the Sacrament if you could see your way – '

'Good Heavens!' exclaimed the Rector. 'So ill as that? Sinking? I am terribly grieved to hear it. Of course, I will come immediately. I had no idea – '

'No more hadn't any of us, sir. It's this wicked influenza. I'm sure nobody ever thought yesterday – '

'Oh, dear, oh, dear! I hope it's not as bad as you fear! But I mustn't delay. You shall tell me about it as you go. I will be with you in one moment. Agnes, my dear, see that the men get their breakfasts and explain to them why I cannot join them. Lord Peter, you must excuse me. I shall be with you later. Bless my heart! Lady Thorpe – what a scourge this influenza is!'

He trotted hurriedly back into the church. Mrs Venables looked ready to cry, between anxiety and distress.

'Poor Theodore! After being up all night – of course he has to go, and we ought not to think about ourselves. Poor Sir Henry! An invalid himself! Such a bitter morning, and no breakfast! Johnson, please say to Miss Hilary how sorry I am and ask if there is anything I can do to help Mrs Gates. The housekeeper, you know, Lord Peter – such a nice woman, and the cook away on holiday, it does seem so hard. Troubles never come singly. Dear me, you must be famished. Do come along and be looked after. You'll be sure to send round, Johnson, if you want any help. Can Sir Henry's nurse manage, I wonder? This is such an isolated place for getting any help. Theodore! are you sure you are well wrapped up?'

The Rector, who now rejoined them, carrying the Communion vessels in a wooden case, assured her that he was well protected. He was bundled into the waiting car by Johnson, and whirled away westwards towards the village.

This untoward incident cast a certain gloom over the breakfast table, though Wimsey, who felt his sides clapping together like an empty portmanteau, was only too thankful to devour his eggs and bacon and coffee in peace. Eight pairs of jaws chumped steadily, while Mrs Venables dispensed the provisions in a somewhat distracted way, interspersing her hospitable urgings with ejaculations of sympathy for the Thorpe family and anxiety for her husband's well-being.

'Such a lot of trouble as the Thorpes have had, too, one way and another,' she remarked. 'All that dreadful business about old Sir Charles, and the loss of the necklace, and that unfortunate girl and everything, though it was a merciful thing the man died, after killing a warder and all that, though it upset the whole family very much at the time. Hezekiah, how are you getting on? A bit more bacon, Mr Donnington? Hinkins, pass Mr Godfrey the cold ham. And of course, Sir Henry never has been strong since the War, poor man. Are you getting enough to eat down there, Wally? I do hope the Rector won't be kept too long without his breakfast. Lord Peter, a little more coffee?'

Wimsey thanked her, and asked what, exactly, was the trouble about old Sir Charles and the necklace.

'Oh, of course, you don't know. So silly of me! Living in this solitary place, one imagines that one's little local excitements are of world-wide importance. It's rather a long story, and I shouldn't have mentioned it at all' – here the good lady lowered her voice – 'if Will Thoday had been here. I'll tell you after breakfast. Or ask Hinkins. He knows all about it. How is William Thoday this morning, I wonder? Has anybody heard?'

'He's mortal bad, ma'am, I'm afraid,' replied Mr Donnington, taking the question to himself. 'I saw my missus after service, and she told me she'd heard from Joe Mullins as he was dreadful delirious all night, and they couldn't hardly keep him in his bed, on account of his wanting to get up and ring.'

'Dear, dear! It's a good thing for Mary that they've got James at home.'

'So it is,' agreed Mr Donnington. 'A sailor's wonderful handy about the house. Not but what his leave's up in a day or two, but it's to be hoped as they'll be over the worst by then.'

Mrs Venables clucked gently.

'Ah!' said Hezekiah. ''Tis a mortal bad thing, this influenza. And it do take the young and strong cruel often, and leave the old uns be. Seems like old fellers like me is too tough fer it.'

'I hope so, Hezekiah, I'm sure,' said Mrs Venables. 'There! Ten o'clock striking, and the Rector not back. Well, I suppose one couldn't expect – why, there's the car coming up the drive! Wally, would you please ring that bell? I want some fresh eggs and bacon for the Rector, Emily, and you'd better take the coffee out and hot it up for him.'

Emily took out the jug, but returned almost immediately.

'Oh, if you please, ma'am, the Rector says, will you all excuse him, please, and he'll take his breakfast in the study. And oh! if you please, ma'am, poor Lady Thorpe's gone, ma'am, and if Mr Lavender's finished, he's please to go over to the church at once and ring the passing bell.'

'Gone!' cried Mrs Venables. 'Why, what a terrible thing!'

'Yes, ma'am. Mr Johnson says it was dreadful sudden. The Rector hadn't hardly left her room, ma'am, when it was all over, and they don't know how they're to tell Sir Henry.'

Mr Lavender pushed back his chair and quavered to his ancient feet.

'In the midst of life,' he said solemnly, 'we are in death. Terrible true that is, to be sure. If so be as you'll kindly excuse me, ma'am, I'll be leaving you now, and thank you kindly. Good mornin' to you all. That were a fine peal we rung, none the more for that, and now I'll be gettin' to work on old Tailor Paul again.'

He shuffled sturdily out, and within five minutes they heard the deep and melancholy voice of the bell ringing, first the six tailors for a woman and then the quick strokes which announce the age of the dead. Wimsey counted them up to thirty-seven. Then they ceased, and were followed by the slow tolling of single strokes at half-minute intervals. In the dining-room, the silence was only broken by the shy sound of hearty feeders trying to finish their meal inconspicuously.

The party broke up quietly. Mr Wilderspin drew Wimsey to one side and explained that he had sent around to Mr Ashton for a couple of farm-horses and a stout rope, and hoped to get the car out of the ditch in a very short time, and would then see what was needed in the way of repairs. If his lordship cared to step along to the smithy in an hour or so, they could go into consultation about the matter. His (Mr Wilderspin's) son George was a great hand with motors, having had considerable experience with farm engines, not to mention his own motorbike. Mrs Venables retired into the study to see that her husband had everything he wanted and to administer such consolation as she might for the calamity that had befallen the parish. Wimsey, knowing that his presence at Frog's Bridge would not help and would probably only hinder the breakdown team, begged his hostess not to trouble about him, and wandered out into the garden. At the back of the house, he discovered Joe Hinkins polishing the Rector's aged car. Joe accepted a cigarette, passed a few remarks about the ringing of the peal, and thence slid into conversation about the Thorpe family.

'They live in the big red-brick house t'other side the village. A rich family they were once. They do say as they got their land through putting money into draining of the Fen long ago under the Earl of Bedford. You'd know all about that, my lord, I dare say. Anyhow, they reckon to be an old family hereabouts. Sir Charles, he was a fine, generous gentleman; did a lot of good in his time, though he wasn't what you'd call a rich man, not by no means. They do say his father lost a lot of money up in London, but I don't know how. But he farmed his land well, and it was a rare trouble to the village when he died along of the burglary.'

'What burglary was that?'

'Why, that was the necklace the mistress was talking about. It was when young Mr Henry – that's the present Sir Henry – was married. The year of the War, it was, in the spring – April 1914 – I remember it very well. I was a youngster at the time, and their wedding-bells was the first long peal I ever rang. We gave them 5,040 Grandsire Triples, Holt's Ten-part Peal – you'll find the record of it in the church yonder, and there was a big supper at the Red House afterwards, and a lot of fine visitors came down for the wedding. The young lady was an orphan, you see, and some sort of connection with the family, and Mr Henry being the heir they was married down here. Well, there was a lady come to stay in the house, and she had a wonderful fine emerald necklace – worth thousands and thousands of pounds it was – and the very night after the wedding, when Mr Henry and his lady was just gone off for their honeymoon, the necklace was stole.'

'Good lord!' said Wimsey. He sat down on the running-board of the car and looked as encouraging as he could.

'You may say so,' said Mr Hinkins, much gratified. 'A big sensation it made at the time in the parish. And the worst part of it was, you see, that one of Sir Charles's own men was concerned in it. Poor gentleman, he never held up his head again. When they took this fellow Deacon and it came out what he'd done – '

'Deacon was – ?'

'Deacon, he was the butler. Been with them six years, he had, and married the housemaid, Mary Russell, that's married to Will Thoday, him as rings Number Two and has got the influenzy so bad.'

'Oh!' said Wimsey. 'Then Deacon is dead now, I take it.'

'That's right, my lord. That's what I was a-telling you. You see, it 'appened this way. Mrs Wilbraham woke up in the night and saw a man standing by her bedroom window. So she yelled out, and the fellow jumped out into the garden and dodged into the shrubbery, like. So she screamed again, very loud, and rang her bell and made a to-do, and everybody came running out to see what was the matter. There was Sir Charles and some gentlemen that was staying in the house, and one of them had a shotgun. And when they got downstairs, there was Deacon in his coat and trousers just running out at the back door, and the footman in pyjamas; and the chauffeur as slept over the garage, he came running out too, because the first thing as Sir Charles did, you see, was to pull the house-bell what they had for calling the gardener. The gardener, he came too, of course, and so did I, because, you see, I was the gardener's boy at the time, and wouldn't never have left Sir Charles, only for him having to cut down his establishment, what with the War and paying Mrs Wilbraham for the necklace.'

'Paying for the necklace?'

'Yes, my lord. That's just where it was, you see. It wasn't insured, and though of course nobody could have held Sir Charles responsible he had it on his conscience as he ought to pay Mrs Wilbraham the value of it, though how anybody calling herself a lady could take the money off him I don't understand. But as I was a-saying, we all came out and then one of the gentlemen see the man a-tearing across the lawn, and Mr Stanley loosed off the shot-gun at him and hit him, as we found out afterwards, but he got away over the wall, and there was a chap waiting for him on the other side with a motor-car, and he got clear away. And in the middle of it all, out comes Mrs Wilbraham and her maid, a-hollering that the emerald necklace has been took.'

'And didn't they catch the man?'

'Not for a bit, they didn't, my lord. The chauffeur, he gets the car out and goes off after them, but by the time he'd got started up, they were well away. They went up the road past the church, but nobody knew whether they'd gone through Fenchurch St Peter or up on to the Bank, and even then they might have gone either by Dykesey and Walea or Walbeach way, or over the Thirty-foot to Leamholt or Holport. So the chauffeur went after the police. You see, barring the village constable at Fenchurch St Peter there's no police nearer than Leamholt, and in those days they didn't have a car at the police-station even there, so Sir Charles said to send the car for them would be quicker than telephoning and waiting till they came.'

'Ah!' said Mrs Venables, suddenly popping her head in at the garage door. 'So you've got Joe on to the Thorpe robbery. He knows a lot more about it than I do. Are you sure you aren't frozen to death in this place?'

Wimsey said he was quite warm enough, thanks, and he hoped the Rector was none the worse for his exertions.

'He doesn't seem to be,' said Mrs Venables, 'but he's rather upset, naturally. You'll stay to lunch of course. No trouble at all. Can you eat shepherd's pie. You're sure? The butcher doesn't call today, but there's always cold ham.'

She bustled away. Joe Hinkins passed a chamois leather thoughtfully over a headlight. 'Carry on,' said Wimsey.

'Well, my lord, the police did come and of course they hunted round a good bit, and didn't we bless them, the way they morrised over the flower-beds, a-looking for footprints and breaking down the tulips. Anyhow, there 'twas, and they traced the car and got the fellow that had been shot in the leg. A well-known jewel thief he was, from London. But you see, they said it must have been an inside job, because it turned out as the fellow as jumped out o' the window wasn't the same as the London man, and the long and the short of it was, they found out as the inside man was this here Deacon. Seems the Londoner had been keeping his eye on that necklace, like, and had got hold of Deacon and got him to go and steal the stuff and drop it out of the window to him. They was pretty sure of their ground – I think they found finger-prints and such like – and they arrested Deacon. I remember it very well, because they took him one Sunday morning, just a-coming out of church, and a terrible job it was to take him; he near killed a constable. The robbery was on the Thursday night, see? and it had took them that time to get on to it.'

'Yes, I see. How did Deacon know where to find the jewels?'

'Well, that was just it, my lord. It came out as Mrs Wilbraham's maid had let out something, stupid-like, to Mary Russell – that is, her as had married Deacon, and she, not thinking no harm, had told her husband. Of course, they had them two women up too. All the village was in a dreadful way about it, because Mary was a very decent, respectable girl, and her father was one of our sidesmen. There's not an honester, better family in the Fenchurches than what the Russells are. This Deacon, he didn't come from these parts, he was a Kentish man by birth. Sir Charles brought him down from London. But there wasn't no way of getting him out of it, because the London thief – Cranton, he called himself, but he had other names – he blew the gaff and gave Deacon away.'

'Dirty dog!'

'Ah! but you see, he said as Deacon had done him down and so, if Cranton was telling the truth, he had. Cranton said as Deacon dropped out nothing but the empty jewel-case and kept the necklace for himself. He went for Deacon 'ammer-and-tongs in the dock and tried for to throttle him. But, of course, Deacon swore as it was all a pack of lies. His tale was, that he heard a noise and went to see what was the matter, and that when Mrs Wilbraham saw him in her room, he was just going to give chase to Cranton. He couldn't deny he'd been in the room, you see, because of the finger-prints and that. But it went against him that he'd told a different story at the beginning, saying as how he'd gone out by the back door, hearing somebody in the garden. Mary supported that, and it's a fact that the back door was unbolted when the footman got to it. But the lawyer on the other side said that Deacon had unbolted the door himself beforehand, just in case he had to get out by the window, so as to leave himself a way back into the house. But as for the necklace, they never could settle that part of it, for it wasn't never found. Whether Cranton had it, and was afraid to get rid of it, like or whether Deacon had it and hid it, I don't know and no more does anybody. It ain't never turned up to this day, nor yet the money Cranton said he'd given Deacon, though they turned the place upside-down looking for both on 'em. And the upshot was, they acquitted the two women, thinking as how they'd only been chattering silly-like, the way women do, and they sent Cranton and Deacon to prison for a good long stretch. Old Russell, he couldn't face the place after that, and he sold up and went off, taking Mary with him. But when Deacon died – '

'How was that?'

'Why, he broke prison and got away after killing a warder. A bad lot, was Deacon. That was in 1918. But he didn't get much good by it, because he fell into a quarry or some such place over Maidstone way, and they found his body two years later, still in his prison clothes. And as soon as he heard about it, young William Thoday, that had always been sweet on Mary went after her and married her and brought her back. You see, nobody here ever believed as there was anything against Mary. That was ten years ago, and they've got two fine kids and get along first-class. This fellow Cranton got into trouble again after his time was up and was sent back to prison, but he's out again now, so I'm told, and Jack Priest – that's the bobby at Fenchurch St Peter – he says he wouldn't wonder if we heard something about that necklace again, but I don't know. Cranton may know where it is, and again he may not, you see.'

'I see. So Sir Charles compensated Mrs Wilbraham for the loss of it.'

'Not Sir Charles, my lord. That was Sir Henry. He came back at once, poor gentleman, from his honeymoon, and found Sir Charles terrible ill. He'd had a stroke from the shock, when they took Deacon, feeling responsible-like, and being over seventy at the time. After the verdict, Mr Henry as he was then, told his father he'd see that the thing was put right, and Sir Charles seemed to understand him; and then the War came and Sir Charles never got over it. He had another stroke and passed away, but Mr Henry didn't forget, and when the police had to confess as they'd almost give up hope of the necklace, then he paid the money, but it came very hard on the family. Sir Henry got badly wounded in the Salient and was invalided home, but he's never been the same man since, and they say he's in a pretty bad way now. Lady Thorpe dying so sudden won't do him no good, neither. She was a very nice lady and very much liked.'

'Is there any family?'

'Yes, my lord; there's one daughter, Miss Hilary. She'll be fifteen this month. She's just home from school for the holidays. It's been a sad holiday for her, and no mistake.'

'You're right,' said Lord Peter. 'Well, that's an interesting tale of yours, Hinkins. I shall look out for news of the Wilbraham emeralds. Ah! here's my friend Mr Wilderspin. I expect he's come to say that the car's on deck again.'

This proved to be the case. The big Daimler stood outside the Rectory gate, forlornly hitched to the back of a farm waggon. The two stout horses who drew it seemed, judging by their sleek complacency, to have no great opinion of it. Messrs. Wilderspin senior and junior, however, took a hopeful view of the matter. A little work on the front axle, at the point where it had come into collision with a hidden milestone would, they thought, do wonders with it, and, if not, a message could be sent to Mr Brownlow at Fenchurch St Peter, who ran a garage, to come and tow it away with his lorry. Mr Brownlow was a great expert. Of course, he might be at home or he might not. There was a wedding on at Fenchurch St Stephen, and Mr Brownlow might be wanted there to take the wedding-party to church, they living a good way out along Digg's Drove, but if necessary the postmistress could be asked to telephone and find out. She would be the right party to do it, since leaving out the post-office, there was no other telephone in the village, except at the Red House, which wouldn't be convenient at a time like the present.

Wimsey, looking dubiously at his front axle, thought it might perhaps be advisable to procure the skilled assistance of Mr Brownlow and said he would approach the postmistress for that purpose, if Mr Wilderspin would give him a lift into the village. He scrambled up, therefore, behind Mr Ashton's greys, and the procession took its way past the church for the better part of a quarter of a mile, till it reached the centre of the village.

The parish church of Fenchurch St Paul, like a good many others in that part of the country, stands completely isolated from the village itself, with only the Rectory to neighbour it. The village itself is grouped about a crossroads, one arm of which runs southward to Fenchurch St Stephen and northwards to join the Fenchurch St Peter road a little south of the Thirty-foot; while the other, branching off from the same road by the church, degenerates at the western end of the village into a muddy drove by which, if you are not particular about your footing, you may, if you like, emerge once more on to the road by the Thirty-foot at Frog's Bridge. The three Fenchurches thus form a triangle, with St Paul to the north, St Peter to the south, and St Stephen to the west. The L.N.E.R. line connects St Peter with St Stephen, passing north to cross the Thirty-foot at Dykesey Viaduct on its way to Leamholt.

Of the three, Fenchurch St Peter is the largest and most important, possessing, in addition to a railway station, a river with two bridges. It has, however, but a bare and uninteresting church built in the latest and worst period of Perpendicular, with a slate spire and no bells to speak of. Fenchurch St Stephen has a railway station – through only, as it were, by accident, though lying more or less upon the direct line between Leamholt and St Peter. Still, there the station is; moreover, there is a church with a respectable fourteenth-century tower, a rather remarkable rood-screen, a Norman apse and a ring of eight bells. Fenchurch St Paul is the smallest village, and has neither river nor railway; it is, however, the oldest; its church is by far the largest and the noblest, and its bells beyond question the finest. This is due to the fact that St Paul is the original abbey foundation. The remains of the first Norman church and a few stones which mark the site of the old cloisters may still be seen to east and south of the existing chancel. The church itself, with the surrounding glebe, stands on a little mound rising some ten or twelve feet above the level of the village – an elevation which, for the Fens, is considerable and, in ancient times, was sufficient to save church and abbey from inundation during the winter months. As for the river Wale, Fenchurch St Peter had no right to boast about that, for did not the old course of the Wale run close by St Paul's church, until the cutting of Potter's Lode in King James I's time drained away its water by providing them with a shorter and more direct channel? Standing on the roof of the tower at Fenchurch St

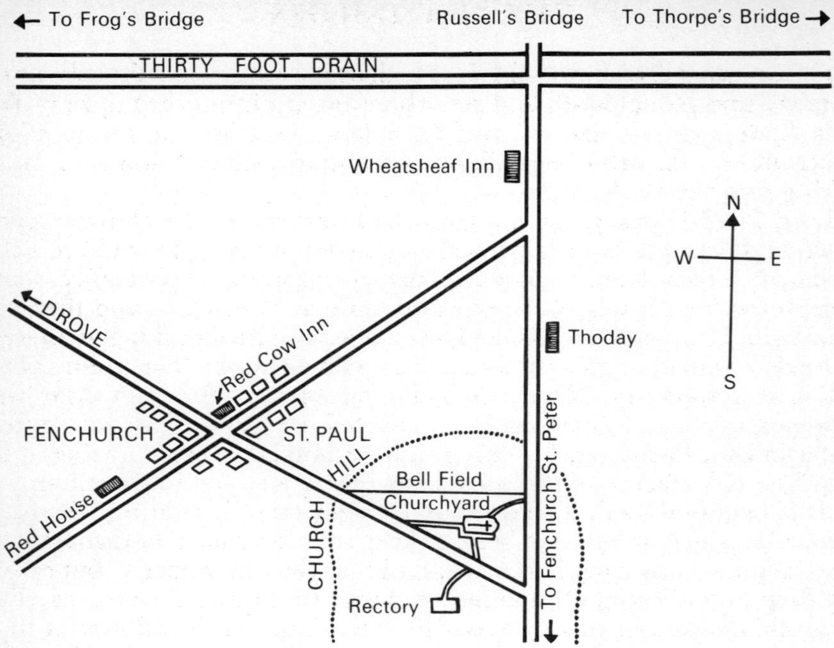
To Frog's Bridge
Russell's Bridge
To Thorpe's Bridge
THIRTY FOOT DRAIN
Wheatsheaf Inn
N
W
E
S
DROVE
Red Cow Inn
Thoday
FENCHURCH
ST. PAUL
HILL
Bell Field
Churchyard
CHURCH
Red House
Rectory
To Fenchurch St. Peter

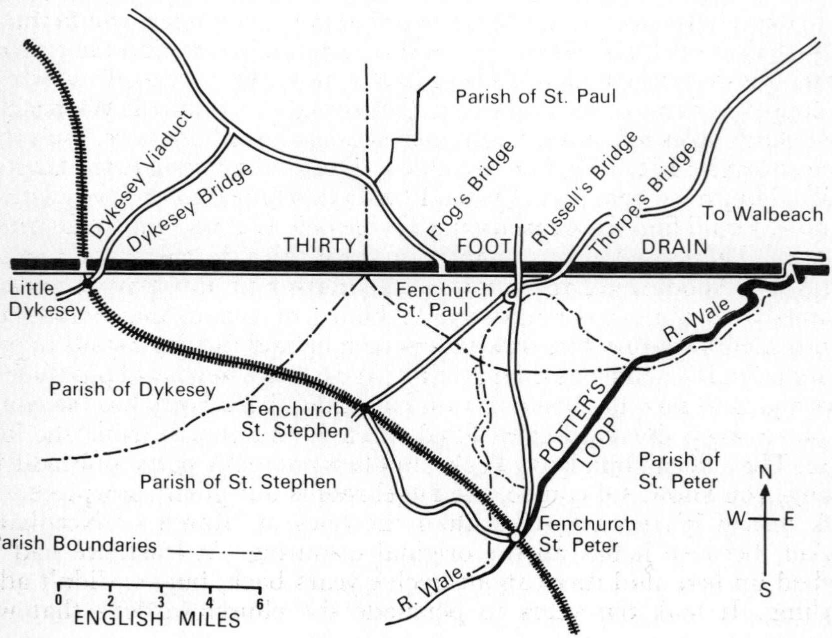
Parish of St. Paul
Dykesey Viaduct
Dykesey Bridge
Frog's Bridge
Russell's Bridge
Thorpe's Bridge
To Walbeach
THIRTY
FOOT
DRAIN
Little Dykesey
Fenchurch St. Paul
R. Wale
Parish of Dykesey
Fenchurch St. Stephen
POTTER'S LOOP
Parish of St. Peter
Parish of St. Stephen
N
W
E
S
Fenchurch St. Peter
Parish Boundaries
R. Wale
0 2 3 4 6
ENGLISH MILES

Paul, you can still trace the old river bed, as it wanders circuitously across meadow and ploughland, and see where the straight green dyke of Potter's Lode spans it like a string to a bow. Outside the group of the Fenchurches, the land rises slightly all round, being drained by cross-dyking into the Wale.

Lord Peter Wimsey, having seen the front axle of the Daimler taken down and decided that Mr Brownlow and Mr Wilderspin could possibly fix it up between them, dispatched his message from the post office, sent a wire to the friends who were expecting him at Walbeach, and then cast about him for some occupation. The village presented nothing of interest, so he determined to go and have a look at the church. The tolling of the bell had ceased and Hezekiah had gone home; the south door was, however, open, and entering, he discovered Mrs Venables putting fresh water in the altar vases. Catching sight of him as he stood gazing at the exquisite oak tracery of the screen, she came forward to greet him.

'It *is* beautiful, isn't it? Theodore is so proud of his church. And he's done a lot, since we've been here, to keep it looking nice. Fortunately the man before us was conscientious and did his repairs properly, but he was *very* Low and allowed all manner of things that quite shocked us. This beautiful chapel, for instance, would you *believe* that he allowed it to be used for furnace-coke? Of course, we had all that cleared out. Theodore would like a lady-altar here, but we're afraid the parishioners would think it popish. Yes – it's a magnificent window, isn't it? Later than the rest, of course, but so fortunate that it's kept its old glass. We were so afraid when the Zeppelins came over. You know, they dropped a bomb at Walbeach, only twenty miles off, and it might just as easily have been here. Isn't the parclose lovely? Like lace, I always think. The tombs belong to the Gaudy family. They lived here up to Queen Elizabeth's time, but they've all died out now. You'll find the name on the Treble bell: GAUDE, GAUDY, DOMINI IN LAUDE. There used to be a chantry on the north side, corresponding to this: Abbot Thomas's chantry, it was, and that's his tomb. Batty Thomas is named after him – a corruption of "Abbot", of course. Some vandal in the nineteenth century tore down the screen behind the choir stalls to put the organ in. It's a hideous thing, isn't it? We put in a new set of pipes a few years ago, and now the bellows want enlarging. Poor Potty has his work cut out to keep the wind-chest filled when Miss Snoot is using the full organ. They all call him Potty Peake, but he's not really potty, only a little lacking, you know. Of course, the angel roof is our great showpiece – I think myself it's even lovelier than the ones at March or Needham Market, because it has all the original colouring. At least, we had it touched up here and there about twelve years back, but we didn't add anything. It took ten years to persuade the churchwardens that we could put a little fresh gold-leaf on the angels without going straight over to Rome, but they're proud of it now. We hope to do the chancel roof too, one day. All these ribs ought to be painted, you can still see traces of colour, and the bosses ought to be gilt. The east window is Theodore's *bête noire.* That dreadful crude glass – about 1840, I think it is. Quite the worst period, Theodore says. The glass in the nave has all gone, of course – Cromwell's men. Thank goodness they left part of the clerestory. I suppose it was rather a job to get up there. The pews are modern; Theodore got them done ten years ago. He'd have preferred chairs, but the congregation wouldn't have liked it, being used to pews, and he had them copied from a nice old design that wasn't too offensive. The old ones were terrible – like bathrooms – and there was a frightful gallery along both sides, blocking the aisle windows completely and ruining the look of the pillars. We had that taken down at the same time. It wasn't needed, and the school-children *would* drop hymn-books and things on people's heads. Now, the choir-stalls are different. *They* are the original monks' stalls, with misereres. Isn't the carving fine? There's a piscina in the sanctuary, but not a very exciting one.'

Wimsey admitted that he was unable to feel great excitement about piscinas.

'And the altar-rails are very poor, of course – Victorian horrors. We want very much to put up something better in their place when we can find the money. I'm sorry I haven't the key to the tower. You'd like to go up. It's a wonderful view, though it's all ladders above the ringing-chamber. It makes my head swim, especially going over the bells. I think bells are rather frightening, somehow. Oh, the font, You must look at the font. That carving is supposed to be quite remarkable. I forget exactly what it is that's so special about it – stupid of me. Theodore must show you, but he's been sent for in a hurry to take a sick woman off to hospital, right away on the other side of the Thirty-foot, across Thorpe's Bridge. He rushed off almost before he'd finished his breakfast.'

('And they say,' thought Wimsey, 'that Church of England parsons do nothing for their money.')

'Would you like to stay on and look round? Do you mind locking the door and bringing the key back? It's Mr Godfrey's key – I can't *think* where Theodore has put his bunch. It does seem wrong to keep the church locked, but it's such a solitary place. We can't keep an eye on it from the Rectory because of the shrubbery and there are sometimes very unpleasant-looking tramps about. I saw a most horrible man go past only the other day, and not so long ago someone broke open the alms-box. That wouldn't have mattered so much, because there was very little in it, but they did a lot of wanton damage in the sanctuary – out of disappointment,

I suppose, and one can't really allow that, can one?'

Wimsey said, No, one couldn't, and Yes, he would like to look round the church a little longer and would remember about the key. He spent the first few minutes after the good lady had left him putting a suitable donation into the alms-box and in examining the font, whose carvings were certainly curious and, to his mind, suggestive of a symbolism neither altogether Christian nor altogether innocent. He noted a heavy old cope-chest beneath the tower, which, on being opened, proved to contain nothing more venerable than a quantity of worn bellropes, and passed on into the north aisle, noticing that the corbels supporting the principals of the angel-roof were very appropriately sculptured with cherubs' heads. He brooded for a little time over the tomb of Abbot Thomas, with its robed and mitred effigy. A stern old boy, he thought, this fourteenth-century cleric, with his strong, harsh face, a ruler rather than a shepherd of his people. Carved panels decorated the sides of the tomb, and showed various scenes in the life of the abbey; one of them depicted the casting of a bell, no doubt of 'Batty Thomas', and it was evident that the Abbot had taken particular pride in his bell, for it appeared again, supporting his feet, in place of the usual cushion. Its decorations and mottoes were realistically rendered: on the shoulder: + NOLI + ESSE + INCREDVLVS + SED + FIDELIS +; on the sound-bow: + *Abbat Thomas sett mee heare + and bad mee ringe both lovd and cleer* +1380 + ; and on the waist: O SANCTE THOMA, which inscription, being embellished with an abbot's mitre, left the spectator in a pleasing uncertainty whether the sanctity was to be attributed to the Apostle or the ecclesiastic. It was as well that Abbot Thomas had died long before the spoliation of his house by King Henry. Thomas would have made a fight for it, and his church might have suffered in the process. His successor, douce man, had meekly acquiesced in the usurpation, leaving his abbey to moulder to decay, and his church to be purified peaceably by the reformers. So, at least, the Rector informed Wimsey over the shepherd's pie at lunch.

It was only very reluctantly that the Venables consented to let their guest go; but Mr Brownlow and Mr Wilderspin between them had made such good progress on the car that it was ready for use by two o'clock, and Wimsey was anxious to press on to Walbeach before dusk set in. He started off, therefore, speeded by many handshakes and much earnest solicitation to come again soon and help to ring another peal. The Rector, at parting, thrust into his hands a copy of *Venables on the In and Out of Course*, while Mrs Venables insisted on his drinking an amazingly powerful hot whisky-and-water, to keep the cold out. As the car turned right along the Thirty-foot Bank Wimsey noticed that the wind had changed. It was hauling round to the south, and, though the snow still lay white and even over the Fen, there was a softness in the air.

'Thaw's coming, Bunter.'

'Yes, my lord.'

'Ever seen this part of the country when the floods are out?'

'No, my lord.'

'It looks pretty desolate; especially round about the Welney and Mepal Washes, when they let the waters out between the Old and New Bedford Rivers, and across the fen between Over and Earith Bridge. Acres of water, with just a bank running across it here and there or a broken line of willows. Hereabouts I think it's rather more effectively drained. Ah! look – over to the right – that must be Van Leyden's Sluice that turns the tide up the Thirty-foot Drain – Denver Sluice again on a smaller scale. Let's look at the map. Yes, that's it. See here's where the Drain joins the Wale, but it meets it at a higher level; if it wasn't for the Sluice, all the Drain water would turn back up the Wale and flood the whole place. Bad engineering – but the seventeenth-century engineers had to work piecemeal and take things as they found 'em. That's the Wale coming down through Potter's Lode from Fenchurch St Peter. I shouldn't care for the sluice-keeper's job – dashed lonely, I should think.'

They gazed at the ugly little brick house, which stood up quaintly on their right, like a pricked ear, between the two sides of the Sluice. On the one side a weir, with a small lock, spanned the Thirty-foot, where it ran into the Wale six feet above the course of the river. On the other, the upper course of the Wale itself was spanned by a sluice of five gates, which held the Upper Level waters from turning back up the river.

'Not another house within sight – oh, yes – one cottage about two miles further up the bank. Boo! Enough to make one drown one's self in one's own lock. Hullo! what happens to the road here? Oh, I see; over the Drain by the bridge and turn sharp right – then follow the river. I do wish everything wasn't so rectangular in this part of the world. Hoops-a-daisy, over she goes! There's the sluice-keeper running out to have a look at us. I expect we're his great event of the day. Let's wave our hats to him – Hullo-ullo! Cheerio! – I'm all for scattering sunshine as we pass. As Stevenson says, we shall pass this way but once – and I devoutly hope he's right. Now then, what's this fellow want?'

Along the bleak white road a solitary figure, plodding towards them, had stopped and extended both arms in appeal. Wimsey slowed the Daimler to a halt.

'Excuse me stopping you, sir,' said the man, civilly enough. 'Would you be good enough to tell me if I'm going right for Fenchurch St Paul?'

'Quite right. Cross the bridge when you come to it and follow the Drain along in the direction you are going till you come to the signpost. You can't miss it.'

'Thank you, sir. About how far would it be?'

'About five and a half miles to the signpost and then half a mile to the village.'

'Thank you very much, sir.'

'You've got a cold walk, I'm afraid.'

'Yes, sir – not a nice part of the country. However, I'll be there before dark, that's a comfort.'

He spoke rather low, and his voice had a faint London twang; his drab overcoat, though very shabby, was not ill-cut. He wore a short, dark, pointed beard and seemed to be about fifty years old, but kept his face down when talking as if evading close scrutiny.

'Like a fag?'

'Thank you very much, sir.'

Wimsey shook a few cigarettes out of his case and handed them over. The palm that opened to receive them was calloused, as though by heavy manual labour, but there was nothing of the countryman about the stranger's manner or appearance.

'You don't belong about these parts?'

'No, sir.'

'Looking for work?'

'Yes, sir.'

'Labourer?'

'No, sir. Motor mechanic.'

'Oh, I see. Well, good luck to you.'

'Thank you, sir. Good afternoon, sir.'

'Good afternoon.'

Wimsey drove on in silence for about half a mile. Then he said:

'Motor mechanic possibly, but not recently, I think. Stone-quarrying's more about the size of it. You can always tell an old lag by his eyes, Bunter. Excellent idea to live down the past, and all that, but I hope our friend doesn't put anything across the good Rector.'

PART 2

A FULL PEAL OF GRANDSIRE TRIPLES
(Holt's Ten-Part Peal)

5,040

By the Part Ends

First Half	*Second Half*
246375	257364
267453	276543
275634	264735
253746	243657
235476	234567

2nd the Observation.

Call her: 1st Half) Out of the hunt, middle, in and out at 5, right, middle, wrong, right, middle and into the hunt (4 times repeated).

2nd Half) Out of the hunt, wrong, right, middle, wrong, right, in and out at 5, wrong and into the hunt (4 times repeated).

The last call in each half is a single; Holt's Single must be used in ringing this peal.

THE FIRST PART

MR GOTOBED IS CALLED WITH A DOUBLE

Thou shalt pronounce this hideous thing
With cross, and candle, and bell-knelling.

JOHN MYRC: *Instructions for Parish Priests (15th Century)*

Spring and Easter came late together that year to Fenchurch St Paul. In its own limited, austere and almost grudging fashion the Fen acknowledged the return of the sun. The floods withdrew from the pastures; the wheat lifted its pale green spears more sturdily from the black soil; the stiff thorns bordering dyke and grass verge budded to a softer outline; on the willows, the yellow catkins danced like little bell-rope sallies, and the silvery pussies plumped themselves for the children to carry to church on Palm Sunday; wherever the grim banks were hedge-sheltered, the shivering dog-violets huddled from the wind.

In the Rectory garden, the daffodils were (in every sense of the word) in full blow, for in the everlasting sweep and torment of wind that sweeps across East Anglia, they tossed desperately and madly. 'My poor daffodils!' Mrs Venables would exclaim, as the long leaf-tufts streamed over like blown water, and the golden trumpets kissed the ground, 'this dreadful old wind! I don't know how they stand it!' She felt both pride and remorse as she cut them – sound stock varieties, Emperor, Empress, Golden Spur – and took them away to fill the altar-vases and the two long, narrow, green-painted tin troughs that on Easter Sunday stood one on either side of the chancel screen. 'The yellow looks so bright,' thought Mrs Venables, as she tried to persuade the blossoms to stand upright among the glossy green of periwinkle and St. John's Wort, 'though it really seems a shame to sacrifice them.'

She knelt before the screen on a long red cushion, borrowed from a pew-seat to protect her 'bones' from the chill of the stone floor. The four brass altar-vases stood close beside her, in company with a trug full of flowers and a watering-can. Had she tried to fill them at the Rectory and carry them over, the sou'wester would have blown them into ruin before she had so much as crossed the road. 'Tiresome things!' muttered Mrs Venables, as the daffodils flopped sideways, or slid helplessly out of sight into the bottom of the trough. She sat up on her heels and reviewed her work, and then turned, hearing a step behind her.

A red-haired girl of fifteen, dressed in black, had come in, bearing a large sheaf of pheasant-eye narcissi. She was tall and thin and rather gawky, though with promise of becoming some day a striking-looking woman.

'Are these any use to you, Mrs Venables? Johnson's trying to get the arums along, but the wind's so terrific, he's afraid they'll be broken all to bits in the barrow. I think he'll have to pack them into the car, and drive them down in state.'

'My dear Hilary, how kind of you! Yes, indeed – I can do with all the white flowers I can get. These are beautiful, and *what* a delicious scent! Dear things! I thought of having some of our plants stood along there in front of Abbot Thomas, with some tall vases among them. And the same on the other side under old Gaudy. But I am *not*' – here she became very much determined – 'I am *not* gong to tie bunches of greenery on to the font and the pulpit this year. They can have that at Christmas and Harvest Festival, if they like, but at Easter it's unsuitable and absurd, and now that old Miss Mallow's gone, poor dear, there's no need to go on with it.'

'I hate Harvest Festivals. It's a shame to hide up all this lovely carving with spiky bits of corn and vegetable marrows and things.'

'So it is, but the village people like it, you know. Harvest Festival is *their* festival, Theodore always says. I suppose it's wrong that it should mean so much more to them than the Church seasons, but it's natural. It was much worse when we came here – before you were born or thought of, you know. They actually used to drive spikes into the pillars to hold up wreaths of evergreens. Quite wicked. Just thoughtlessness, of course. And at Christmas they had horrible texts all across the screens and along the abominable old gallery – done in cottonwool on red flannel. Disgusting, dirty old things. We found a great bundle of them in the vestry when we came here, full of moths and mice. The Rector put his foot down about *that*.'

'And I suppose half the people went over to the Chapel.'

'No, dear – only two families, and one of them has come back since – the Wallaces, you know, because they had some sort of dispute with the Minister about their Good Friday beanfeast. Something to do with the tea-urns, but I forget what. Mrs Wallace is a funny woman; she takes offence rather easily, but so far – touch wood' – (Mrs Venables performed this ancient pagan rite placidly on the oak of the screen) – 'so far, I've managed to work in quite smoothly with her over the Women's Institute. I wonder if you'd just step back a little way and tell me if these two sides match.'

'You want a few more daffs on the decani side, Mrs Venables.'

'Here? Thank you, dear. Is that better? Well, I think it will have to do. Oo-oh! my poor old bones! Yes, it'll pass in a crowd with a push, as they say. Oh, here's Hinkins with the aspidistras. People may say what they like about aspidistras, but they do go on all the year round and make a background. That's right, Hinkins. Six in front of this tomb and six on the other side – and have you brought those big pickle-jars? They'll do splendidly for the narcissi, and the aspidistras will hide the jars and we can put some ivy in front of the pots. Hinkins, you might fill up my watering-can. How is your father today, Hilary? Better, I hope.'

'I'm afraid he isn't any better, Mrs Venables. Doctor Baines is very much afraid he won't get over it. Poor old Dad!'

'Oh, my dear! I'm terribly sorry. This has been a dreadful time for you. I'm afraid the shock of your dear mother's death coming so suddenly was too much for him.'

The girl nodded.

'We'll hope and pray it isn't as bad as the doctor thinks. Dr Baines always takes a pessimistic view of everything. I except that's why he's only a country practitioner, because I think he's really very clever; but patients do like a doctor to be cheerful. Why don't you get a second opinion?'

'We're going to. There's a man called Hordell coming down on Tuesday. Dr Baines tried to get him today, but he's away for Easter.'

'Doctors oughtn't to go away,' said Mrs Venables, rather uncharitably. The Rector never took holidays at the greater festivals, and scarcely ever at any other time, and she could not quite see that there was any necessity for the rest of the world to do so.

Hilary Thorpe laughed rather ruefully.

'I feel a little like that myself. But he's supposed to be the very best man there is, and we're hoping that a couple of days won't make all that difference.'

'Good gracious, no, I hope not,' said the Rector's wife. 'Is that Johnson with the arums? Oh, no, it's Jack Godfrey. I expect he's going up to grease the bells.'

'Is he? I'd like to watch him. May I go up to the belfry, Mrs Venables?'

'I'm sure you may, my dear. But do be careful. I never think those great high ladders are really safe.'

'Oh, I'm not afraid of them. I love looking at the bells.'

Hilary hastened down the church and caught Jack Godfrey up just as he emerged from the winding stairs into the ringing chamber.

'I've come to watch you do the bells, Mr Godfrey. Shall I be in your way?'

'Why, no, Miss Hilary, I'd be very pleased for you to come. You better go first up them ladders, so as I can help you if you was to slip.'

'I shan't slip,' said Hilary, scornfully. She climbed briskly up the thick and ancient rungs, to emerge into the chamber which formed the second story of the tower. It was empty, except for the case which housed the chiming mechanism of the church clock, and the eight bell-ropes rising through the sallie-holes in the floor to vanish through the ceiling in the same way. Jack Godfrey followed her up soberly, carrying his grease and cleaning-rags.

'Be a bit careful of the floor, Miss Hilary', he urged, 'it's none too good in places.'

Hilary nodded. She loved this bare, sun-drenched room, in whose four tall walls were four tall windows. It was like a palace of glass lifted high into the air. The shadows of the splendid tracery of the south window lay scrawled on the floor like a pattern of wrought iron on a gate of brass. Looking down through the dusty panes, she could see the green fen spread out mile upon mile.

'I'd like to go up to the top of the tower, Mr Godfrey.'

'All right, Miss Hilary; I'll take you up, if so be as there's time when I've done with the bells.'

The trap-door that led to the bell-chamber was shut; a chain ran down from it, vanishing into a sort of wooden case upon the wall. Godfrey produced a key from his bunch and unlocked this case, disclosing the counterpoise. He pulled it down and the trap swung open.

'Why is that kept locked, Mr Godfrey?'

'Well, Miss Hilary, now and again it has happened as the ringers has left the belfry door open, and Rector says it ain't safe. You see, that Potty Peake might come a-traipsing round, or some of they mischeevious lads might come up here and get larking about with the bells. Or they might go up the tower and fall off and hurt theirselves. So Rector said to fix a lock the way they couldn't get the trap-door open.'

'I see.' Hilary grinned a little. 'Hurt theirselves' was a moderate way of expressing the probable result of a hundred-and-twenty-foot fall. She led the way up the second ladder.

By contrast with the brilliance below, the bell-chamber was sombre and almost menacing. The main lights of its eight great windows were darkened throughout their height; only through the slender panelled tracery above the slanting louvres the sunlight dripped rare and chill, striping the heavy beams of the bell-cage with bars and splashes of pallid gold, and making a curious fantastic patterning on the spokes and rims of the wheels. The bells, with mute black mouths gaping downwards, brooded in their ancient places.

Mr Godfrey, eyeing them with the cheerful familiarity born of long use, fetched a light ladder that stood against the wall, set it up carefully against one of the cross-beams, and prepared to mount.

'Let me go up first, or I shan't see what you're doing.'

Mr Godfrey paused and scratched his head. The proposal did not seem quite safe to him. He voiced an objection.

'I shall be quite all right; I can sit on the beam. I don't mind heights one bit. I'm very good at gym.'

Sir Henry's daughter was accustomed to have her own way, and got it – with the stipulation that she should hold on very tightly by the timber of the cage and not let go or 'morris about'. The promise being given, she was assisted to her lofty perch. Mr Godfrey, whistling a lively air between his teeth, arranged his materials methodically about him and proceeded with his task, greasing the gudgeons and trunnions, administering a spot of oil to the pulley-axle, testing the movement of the slider between the blocks and examining the rope for signs of friction where it passed over wheel and pulley.

'I've never seen Tailor Paul as close as this before. She's a big bell, isn't she?'

'Pretty fair,' said Jack Godfrey, approvingly, giving the bell a friendly pat on her bronze shoulder. A shaft of sunshine touched the soundbow, lighting up a few letters of the inscription, which ran, as Hilary very well knew:

NINE + TAYLERS + MAKE + A + MANNE + IN + CHRIST +
IS + DETH + ATT + END + IN + ADAM + YET + BEGANNE +
1614

'She've done her bit in her time, have old Tailor Paul – many a good ring have we had out of her, not to say a sight of funerals and passing-bells. And we rung her with Gaude for them there Zeppelin raids, to give the alarm like. Rector was saying the other day as she did soon ought ter be quarter-turned, but I don't know. Reckon she'll go a bit longer yet. She rings out true enough to my thinking.'

'You have to ring the passing-bell for everyone that dies in the parish, don't you, whoever they are?'

'Yes, dissenter and church alike. That was laid down by old Sir Martin Thorpe, your great-great-grandfather, when he left the money for the bell-fund. "Every Christian soul" was the words in his will. Why, we even had to ring for that woman as lived up the Long Drove, as was a Roman Catholic. Old Hezekiah was rare put out.' Mr Godfrey chuckled reminiscently. '"What, ring old Tailor Paul for a Roman?" he says. "You wouldn't call the like o' them Christians, would you, Rector?" he says. "Why, Hezekiah," says Rector, "we was all Romans in this country once; this church was built by Romans," he says. But Hezekiah, he wouldn't see it. He never had much education, you see. Well, now, Miss Hilary, that'll do for Tailor Paul, I'm thinking, so if you'll give me your hand I'll be helping you down.'

Gaude, Sabaoth, John, Jericho, Jubilee, and Dimity each in her turn was visited and anointed. When, however, it came to the turn of Batty Thomas, Mr Godfrey displayed a sudden and unexpected obstinacy.

'I'm not taking you up to Batty Thomas, Miss Hilary, she's an unlucky bell. What I mean, she's a bell that has her fancies and I wouldn't like for to risk it.'

'What *do* you mean?'

Mr Godfrey found it difficult to express himself more plainly.

'She's my own bell,' he said; 'I've rung her close on fifteen years now and I've looked after her for ten, ever since Hezekiah got too old for these here ladders. Her and me knows one another and she've no quarrel with me nor I with her. But she's queer-tempered. They do say as how old Batty down below, what had her put up here, was a queer sort of man and his bell's took after him. When they turned out the monks and that – a great many years ago, that'd be – they do say as Batty Thomas tolled a whole night through on her own like, without a hand laid to the rope. And when Cromwell sent his men to break up the images an' that, there was a soldier come up here into the belfry, I don't know for what, maybe to damage the bells, but anyhow, up he come; and some of the others, not knowing he was here, began to haul on the ropes, and it seems as how the bells must have been left mouth up. Careless ringers they must have been in those days, but anyhow, that's how 'twas. And just as this soldier was leaning over to look at the bells. Batty Thomas came swinging down and killed him dead. That's history, that is, and Rector says as how Batty Thomas saved the church, because the soldiers took fright and ran away thinking it was a judgement, though to my thinking, it was just carelessness, leaving the bell that fashion. Still, there it was. And then, there was a poor lad in old Rector's time learning to ring, and he tried to raise Batty Thomas and got hisself hanged in the rope. A terrible thing that was, and there again, I say it was carelessness and the lad didn't ought to have been let practice all alone, and it's a thing Mr Venables never will allow. But you see, Miss Hilary, Batty Thomas has killed two men, and while it's quite understandable as there was carelessness both times or it wouldn't have happened – well! I wouldn't like to take any risks, like I said.'

And with this as his last word on the subject, Mr Godfrey mounted aloft to grease the gudgeons of Batty Thomas unassisted. Hilary Thorpe dissatisfied but recognising an immovable obstacle when she met one, wandered vaguely about the belfry, scuffing up the dust of ages with her square-toed, regulation-pattern school shoes and peering at the names which bygone rustics had scrawled upon the plastered walls. Suddenly in a remote corner, something gleamed white in a bar of sunlight. Idly she picked it up. It was a sheet of paper, flimsy and poor in quality and ruled in small, faint squares. It reminded her of the letters she occasionally received from a departed French governess and, when she examined it, she saw that it was covered with writing in the very same purple ink that she associated with 'Mad'm'selle,' but the hand was English – very neat, and yet somehow not the hand of a well-educated person. It had been folded in four and its under side was smeared with fine dust from the floor on which it had lain, but it was otherwise fairly clean.

'Mr Godfrey!'

Hilary's voice was so sharp and excited that Jack Godfrey was quite startled. He very nearly fell off the ladder, adding thereby one more to Batty Thomas's tale of victims.

'Yes, Miss Hilary?'

'I've found such a funny thing here. Do come and look at it.'

'In one moment, Miss Hilary.'

He finished his task and descended. Hilary was standing in a splash of sunshine that touched the brazen mouth of Tailor Paul and fell all about her like Danaë's shower. She was holding the paper where the light could catch it.

'I found this on the floor. Do listen to it. It's absolutely loony. Do you think Potty Peake could have written it?'

Mr Godfrey shook his head.

'I couldn't say, I'm sure Miss Hilary. He's queer, is Potty, and he did use to come up here one time, before Rector locked up the trap-door chain. But that don't look to me like his writing.'

'Well, I don't think anybody but a lunatic could have written it. Do read it. It's so funny.' Hilary giggled, being of an age to be embarrassed by lunacy.

Mr Godfrey set down his belongings with deliberation, scratched his head and perused the document aloud, following the lines with a somewhat grimy forefinger.

> 'I thought to see the fairies in the fields, but I saw only the evil elephants with their black backs. Woe! how that sight awed me! The elves danced all around and about while I heard voices calling clearly. Ah! how I tried to see – throw off the ugly cloud – but no blind eye of a mortal was permitted to spy them. So then came minstrels, having gold trumpets, harps and drums. These played very loudly beside me, breaking that spell. So the dream vanished, whereat I thanked Heaven. I shed many tears before the thin moon rose up, frail and faint as a sickle of straw. Now though the Enchanter gnash his teeth vainly, yet shall he return as the Spring returns. Oh, wretched man! Hell gapes, Erebus now lies open. The mouths of Death wait on thy end.'

'There, now,' said Mr Godfrey, astonished. 'That's a funny one, that is. Potty it is, but, if you follow me, it ain't Potty neither. Potty ain't no scholar. This here, now, about Ereebus – what do you take that to mean?'

'It's a kind of an old name for hell,' said Hilary.

'Oh, that's what it is, is it? Chap that wrote this seems to have got that there place on his mind, like. Fairies, too, and elephants. Well, I don't know. Looks like a bit of a joke, don't it now? Perhaps' – (his eye brightened with an idea) – 'perhaps somebody's been copying out something out of a book. Yes, I wouldn't wonder if that's what this is. One of them old-fashioned books. But it's a funny thing how it got up here. I'd show it to Rector, Miss Hilary, that's what I'd do. He knows a lot of books and maybe he'd know where it come from.'

'That's a good idea. I will. But it's awfully mysterious, isn't it? Quite creepy. Can we go up the tower now, Mr Godfrey?'

Mr Godfrey was quite willing, and together they climbed the last long ladder, stretching high over the bells and leading them out by way of a little shelter like a dog-kennel on to the leaded roof of the tower. Leaning against the wind was like leaning against a wall. Hilary pulled off her hat and let her thick bobbed hair blow out behind her, so that she looked like one of the floating singing angels in the church below. Mr Godfrey had no eyes for this resemblance; he thought Miss Hilary's angular face and straight hair rather unattractive, if the truth were known. He contended himself with advising her to hold tight by the iron stays of the weather-cock. Hilary paid no attention to him, but advanced to the parapet, leaning over between the pierced battlements to stare out southward over the Fen. Far away beneath her lay the churchyard, and, while she looked, a little figure, quaintly foreshortened, crawled beetle-like from the porch and went jogging down the path. Mrs Venables, going home to lunch. Hilary watched her struggle with the wind at the gate across the road and enter the Rectory garden. Then she turned and moved to the east side of the tower, and looked out along the ridged roofs of the nave and chancel. A brown spot in the green churchyard caught her eye and her heart seemed to turn over in her body. Here, at the north-east angle of the church, her mother lay buried, her grave not yet turfed over; and now it looked as though, before long, the earth would have to be opened up again to let the husband join his wife. 'Oh, God!' said Hilary, desperately, 'don't let Dad die – You can't – You simply can't.' Beyond the churchyard wall lay a green field, and in the middle of the field there was a slight hollow. She knew that hollow well. It had been there now for over three hundred years. Time had made it shallower, and in three hundred years more it might disappear altogether, but there it still was – the mark left by the great pit dug for the founding of Tailor Paul.

Jack Godfrey spoke close beside her.

'Time I was getting along now, Miss Hilary.'

'Oh, yes. I'm sorry. I wasn't thinking. Are you ringing a peal tomorrow?'

'Yes, Miss Hilary. We're going to have a try at Stedman's. They're difficult to ring, are Stedman's, but very fine music when you get them going proper. Mind your head, Miss Hilary. A full peal of 5,040 we're going to give them – that's three hours. It's a fortnit thing as Will Thoday's all right again, because neither Tom Tebbutt nor young George Wilderspin is what you might call reliable in Stedman's, and of course, Wally Pratt's no good at all. Excuse me one minute, Miss Hilary, while I gather up my traps. But to my mind, there's more interest, as you might say, in Stedman's than in any other method, though it takes a bit of thinking about to keep it all clear in one's head. Old Hezekiah don't so much care about it, of course, because he likes the tenor rung in. Triples ain't much fun for him, he says, and it ain't to be wondered at. Still, he's an old man now, and you couldn't hardly expect him to learn Stedman's at his age, and what's more, if he could, you'd never get him to leave Tailor Paul. Just a moment, Miss Hilary, while I lock up this here counterpoise. But give me a nice peal of Stedman's and I ask no better. We never had no Stedman's till Rector come, and it took him a powerful long time to learn us to ring them. Well I mind the trouble we had with them. Old John Thoday – that's Will's father, he's dead and gone now – he used to say, "Boy's," he said, "it's my belief the Devil himself couldn't get no sense out of this dratted method." And Rector fined him sixpence for swearing, like it says in they old rules. Mind you don't slip on the stair, Miss Hilary, it's terrible worn. But we learned Stedman to rights, none the more for that, and to my mind it's a very pretty method of ringing. Well, good morning to you, Miss Hilary.'

The peal of 5,040 Stedman's Triples was duly rung on Easter Sunday morning. Hilary Thorpe heard it from the Red House, sitting beside the great old four-poster bed, as she had sat on New Year's morning to hear the peal of Treble Bob Major. Then the noise of the bells had come full and clear; today, it reached her only in distant bursts, when the wind, rollicking away with it eastward, bated for a moment or veered round a little to the south.

'Hilary!'

'Yes, Dad.'

'I'm afraid – if I go west this time – I'll be leaving you rottenly badly off, old girl.'

'I don't care a dash about that, old thing. Not that you are going west. But if you did. I should be quite all right.'

'There'll be enough to send you to Oxford, I dare say. Girls don't seem to cost much there – your uncle will see to it.'

'Yes – and I'm going to get a scholarship, anyway. And I don't want money. I'd rather make my own living. Miss Bowler says she doesn't think anything of a woman who can't be independent.' (Miss Bowler was the English mistress and the idol of the moment.) 'I'm going to be a writer, Dad. Miss Bowler says she wouldn't wonder if I'd got it in me.'

'Oh? What are you going to write? Poetry?'

'Well, perhaps. But I don't suppose that pays very well. I'll write novels. Best sellers. The sort that everybody goes potty over. Not just bosh ones, but like *The Constant Nymph*.'

'You'll want a bit of experience before you can write novels, old girl.'

'Rot, Daddy. You don't want experience for writing novels. People write them at Oxford and they sell like billy-ho. All about how awful everything was at school.'

'I see. And when you leave Oxford, you write one about how awful everything was at college.'

'That's the idea. I can do that on my head.'

'Well, dear, I hope it'll work. But, all the same, I feel a damned failure, leaving you so little. If only that rotten necklace had turned up! I was a fool to pay that Wilbraham money for it, but she as good as accused the old Governor of being an accessory, and I – '

'Oh, Dad, please – *please* don't go on about that silly necklace. Of course you couldn't do anything else about it. And I don't want the beastly money. And, anyhow, you're not going to peg out yet.'

But the specialist, arriving on Tuesday, looked grave and, taking Dr Baines aside, said to him kindly:

'You have done all you could. Even if you had called me in earlier, it would have made no possible difference.'

And to Hilary, still kindly:

'We must never give up hope, you know, Miss Thorpe. I can't disguise from you that your father's condition is serious, but Nature has marvellous powers of recuperation . . .'

Which is the medical man's way of saying that, short of miraculous intervention, you may as well order the coffin.

On the following Monday afternoon, Mr Venables was just leaving the cottage of a cantankerous and venomous-tongued old lady on the extreme outskirts of the parish, when a deep, booming sound smote his ear from afar. He stood still with his hand upon the gate.

'That's Tailor Paul,' said the Rector to himself.

Three solemn notes and a pause.

'Man or woman?'

Three notes, and then three more.

'Man,' said the Rector. He still stood listening. 'I wonder if poor old Merryweather has gone at last? I hope it isn't that boy of Hensman's.' He counted twelve strokes, and waited. But the bell tolled on, and the Rector breathed a sigh of relief. Hensman's boy, at least, was safe. He hastily reckoned up the weaklings of his flock. Twenty strokes, thirty strokes – a man of full age. 'Heaven send,' thought the Rector, 'it isn't Sir Henry. He seemed better when I saw him yesterday.' Forty strokes, forty-one, forty-two. Surely it must be old Merryweather – a happy release for him, poor old man. Forty-three, forty-four, forty-five, forty-six. Now it must go on – it could not stop at that fatal number. Old Merryweather was eighty-four. The Rector strained his ears. He must have missed the next stroke – the wind was pretty strong, and his hearing was perhaps not as good as it had been.

But he waited full thirty seconds before Tailor Paul spoke again; and after that there was silence for another thirty seconds.

The cantankerous old lady, astonished to see the Rector stand so long bare-headed at her gate, came hobbling down the garden path to know what it was all about.

'It's the passing-bell,' said Mr Venables, 'they have rung the nine tailors and forty-six strokes, and I'm afraid it must be for Sir Henry.'

'Oh, dear,' said the cantankerous old woman. 'That's bad. Terrible bad, that is.' A peevish kind of pity came into her eyes. 'What's to become of Miss Hilary now, with her mother and father gone so quick, and her only fifteen, and nobody to keep her in check? I don't hold with girls being left to look arter themselves. They're troublesome at the best and they didn't ought to have their parents took away from them.'

'We mustn't question the ways of Providence,' said the Rector.

'Providence?' said the old woman. 'Don't yew talk to me about Providence. I've had enough o' Providence. First he took my husband, and then he took my 'taters, but there's One above as'll teach him to mend his manners, if he don't look out.'

The Rector was too much distressed to challenge this remarkable piece of theology.

'We can but trust in God, Mrs Giddings,' he said, and pulled up the starting-handle with a jerk.

Sir Henry's funeral was fixed for the Friday afternoon. This was an occasion of mournful importance to at least four persons in Fenchurch St Paul. There was Mr Russell, the undertaker, who was a cousin of that same Mary Russell who had married William Thoday. He was determined to excel himself in the matter of polished oak and brass plates, and his hammer and plane had been keeping up a dismal little harmony of their own during the early part of the week. His, also, was the delicate task of selecting the six bearers so that they might be well-matched in height and step. Mr Hezekiah Lavender and Mr Jack Godfrey went into conference about the proper ringing of a muffled peal – Mr Godfrey's business being to provide and adjust the leather buffets about the clappers of the bells, and Mr Lavender's to arrange and conduct the ringing. And Mr Gotobed, the sexton, was concerned with the grave – so much concerned that he had declined to take part in the peal, preferring to give his whole mind to the graveside ceremonies, although his son, Dick, who assisted him with the spadework, considered himself quite capable of carrying on on his own. There was not, indeed, very much to do in the way of digging. Rather to Mr Gotobed's disappointment. Sir Henry had expressed a wish to be buried in the same grave with his wife, so that there was little opportunity for any fine work in the way of shaping, measuring and smoothing the sides of the grave. They had only to cast out the earth – scarcely yet firm after three rainy months – make all neat and tidy and line the grave with fresh greenery. Nevertheless, liking to be well beforehand with his work, Mr Gotobed took measures to carry this out on the Thursday afternoon.

The Rector had just come in from a round of visits, and was about to sit down to his tea, when Emily appeared at the sitting-room door.

'If you please, sir, could Harry Gotobed speak to you for a moment?'

'Yes, certainly. Where is he?'

'At the back door, sir. He wouldn't come in on account of his boots being dirty.'

Mr Venables made his way to the back door; Mr Gotobed stood awkwardly on the step, twirling his cap in his hands.

'Well, Harry, what's the trouble?'

'Well, sir, it's about this here grave. I thought I better come and see you, being as it's a church matter. You see, when Dick and me come to open it up, we found a corpus a-lying inside of it, and Dick says to me – '

'A corpse? Well, of course there's a corpse. Lady Thorpe is buried there. You buried her yourself.'

'Yes, sir, but this here corpus ain't Lady Thorpe's corpus. It's a man's corpus, that's what it is, and it du seem as though it didn't have no right to be there. So I says to Dick – '

'A man's corpse! What do you mean? Is it in a coffin?'

'No, sir, no coffin. Just an ordinary suit o' clothes, and he du look as though he's a-been a-laying there a goodish while. So Dick says, "Dad," he says, "this looks like a police matter to me. Shall I send for Jack Priest?" he says. And I says, "No," I says, "this here is church property, this is, and Rector did ought to be told about it. That's only right and respectful," I says. "Throw a bit o' summat over it," I says, "while I goes and fetches Rector, and don't let any o' they boys come into the churchyard." So I puts on my coat and comes over, because we don't rightly know what to do about it.'

'But what an extraordinary thing, Harry!' exclaimed the Rector, helplessly. 'I really – I never – who is this man? Do you know him?'

'It's my belief, sir, his own mother wouldn't know him. Perhaps you'd like to step across and take a look at him?'

'Why, yes, of course, I'd better do that. Dear me, dear me! how very perplexing. Emily! Emily! have you seen my hat anywhere? Ah, thank you. Now, Harry. Oh, Emily, please tell Mrs Venables that I am unexpectedly detained, and not to wait tea for me. Yes, Harry, I'm quite ready now.'

Dick Gotobed had spread a tarpaulin over the half-open grave, but he lifted this as the Rector approached. The good gentleman gave one look and averted his eyes hastily. Dick replaced the tarpaulin.

'This is a very terrible thing,' said Mr Venables. He had removed his clerical felt in reverence for the horrid thing under the tarpaulin, and stood bewildered, his thin grey hair ruffled by the wind. 'We must certainly send for the constable – and – and' – here his face brightened a little – 'and for Dr Baines, of course. Yes, yes – Dr Baines will be the man. And, Harry, I think I have read that it is better in these cases to disturb things as little as possible. Er – I wonder who this poor fellow can possibly be. It's nobody belonging to the village, that's certain, because if anybody was missing we should have heard about it. I cannot imagine how he can have come here.'

'No more can't we, sir. Looks like he was a proper stranger. Excuse me, sir, but didn't we ought to inform the coroner of this here?'

'The coroner? Oh, dear! yes, naturally; I suppose there will have to be an inquest. What a dreadful business this is! Why, we haven't had an inquest in the village since Mrs Venables and I came to the Rectory, and that's close on twenty years. This will be a very shocking blow for Miss Thorpe, poor child. Her parent's grave – such a fearful desecration. Still, it can't be hushed up, of course. The inquest – well, well, we must try to keep our wits about us. I think, Dick, you had better run up to the post office and get a call put through to Dr Baines and ask him to come over at once and you had better ring through to St Peter and get someone to send a message to Jack Priest. And you, Harry, had better stay here and keep an eye on – on the grave. And I will go up to the Red House myself and break the shocking news to Miss Thorpe, for fear she should hear it in an abrupt and painful way from somebody else. Yes, I think that is what I had better do. Or perhaps it would be more suitable if Mrs Venables were to go round. I must consult her. Yes, yes, I must consult Mrs Venables. Now, Dick, off you go, and be sure you don't say a word about this to anybody till the constable comes.'

There is no doubt that Dick Gotobed did his best in the matter, but, since the post office telephone lived in the postmistress's sitting-room, it was not altogether easy to keep any message confidential. At any rate, by the time P.C. Priest arrived, rather blown, upon his push-cycle, a small knot of men and women had gathered in and about the churchyard, including Hezekiah Lavender, who had run as fast as his ancient legs could carry him from his cottage-garden and was very indignant with Harry Gotobed for not letting him lift the tarpaulin.

''Ere!' said the constable, running his machine adroitly into the midst of a bunch of children clustered round the lychgate and tipping himself bodily sideways. ''Ere! what's all this? You run along home to yer mothers, see? And don't let me catch you here again. 'Afternoon, Mr Venables, sir. What's the trouble here?'

'There's been a body found in the churchyard,' said Mr Venables.

'Body, eh?' said the constable. 'Well, it's come to the right place, ain't it? What have you done with it? Oh, you've left it where you found it. Quite right, sir. And where might that be? Oh, 'ere. *I* see. All right; let's have a look at him. Oh! ah! that's it, is it? Why, Harry, whatever have you been a-doing of? Tryin' to bury him?'

The rector began to explain, but the constable stopped him with an upraised hand.

'One moment, sir. We'll take this here matter in the proper and correct order. Just a moment while I gets out my notebook. Now, then. Date. Call received 5.15 pee hem. Proceeded to the churchyard, arriving 5.30 pee hem. Now, who found this here body?'

'Dick and me.'

'Name?' said the constable.

'Go on, Jack. You know me well enough.'

'That don't matter. I've got to do it in the proper way. Name?'

'Harry Gotobed.'

'Hoccupation?'

'Sexton.'

'Righto, Harry. Go ahead.'

'Well, Jack, we was a-openin' this here grave, which is Lady Thorpe's grave what died last New Year's Day, for to be ready for her 'usband's body, see, what's to be buried tomorrow. We begins to shovel away the earth, one at each end, like, and we hadn't got much more than a foot or so below ground level, as you might say, when Dick drives his spade down a good spit, and he says to me, "Dad," he says, "there's something in here." And I says to him, "What's that?" I says, "what do you mean? Something in here?" and then I strikes my spade down hard and I feels something sort of between hard and soft, like, and I says, "Dick," I says, "that's a funny thing, there *is* something here." So I says, "Go careful, my boy," I says "because it feels funnylike to me," I says. So we starts at one end and shovels away gentle, and arter a bit we sees something sticking up like it might be the toe of a boot. So I says, "Dick," I says, "that's a boot, that is." And he says, "You're right, Dad, so 'tis." So I says, "Looks to me like we begun at the wrong end of this here, so to say." So he says, "Well, Dad, now we've gone so far we may as well have a look at him." So we gets a-shovellin' again, still going very careful, and arter a bit more we sees something lookin' like 'air. So I says, "You put that there shovel away and use your 'ands, because we don't want to spile it." And he says, "I don't like it." And I says, "Don't you be a fool, my boy. You can wash your 'ands, can't you, when you've done?' So we clears away very careful, and at last we sees him plain. And I says, "Dick, I don't know who he is or nor yet how he got here, but he didn't ought to be here." And Dick says, "shall I go for Jack Priest?" And I says, "No. 'Tis Church ground and we better tell Rector." So that's what we done.'

'And I said,' put in the Rector, 'that we had better send at once for you and for Dr Baines – and here he is, I see.'

Dr Baines, a peremptory-looking little man, with a shrewd Scotch face, came briskly up to them.

'Good afternoon, Rector. What's happened here? I was out when your message came, so I – Good Lord!'

A few words put him in possession of the facts, and he knelt down by the graveside.

'He's terribly mutilated – looks as though somebody had regularly beaten his face in. How long has he been here?'

'That's what we'd like you to tell us, Doctor.'

'Half a minute, half a minute, sir,' interrupted the policeman. 'What day was it you said you buried Lady Thorpe, Harry?'

'January 4th, it were,' said Mr Gotobed, after a short interval for reflection.

'And was this here body in the grave when you filled it up?'

'Now don't you be a fool, Jack Priest,' retorted Mr Gotobed. ''Owever can you suppose as we'd fill up a grave with this here corpus in it? It ain't a thing as a man might drop in careless like, without noticing. If it was a pocket-knife or a pennypiece, that'd be another thing, but when it comes to the corpus of a full-grown man, that there question ain't reasonable.'

'Now, Harry, that ain't a proper answer to my question. I knows my duty.'

'Oh, all right. Well, then, there weren't no body in that there grave when I filled it up on January 4th – leavin' out, of course, Lady Thorpe's body. That was there, I don't say it wasn't, and for all I know it's there still. Unless him as put this here corpus where it is took the other away with him, coffin and all.'

'Well,' said the doctor, 'it can't have been here longer than three months, and so far as I can tell, it hasn't been there much less. But I'll tell you that better when you get it out.'

'Three months, eh?' Mr Hezekiah Lavender had pushed his way to the front. That 'ud be about the time that stranger chap disappeared – him as was stayin' at Ezra Wilderspin's and wanted a job to mend up moty-cars and sich. He had a beard, too, by my recollection.'

'Why, so he had,' cried Mr Gotobed. 'What a head you have on you, Hezekiah! That's who it is, sure-lie. To think o' that, now! I always thought that chap was after no good. But who could have gone for to do a thing like this here?'

'Well,' said the doctor. 'If Jack Priest has finished with his interrogation, you may as well get the body dug out. Where are you going to put it? It won't be a very nice thing to keep hanging about.'

'Mr Ashton have a nice airy shed, sir, If we was to ask him, I dessay he could make shift to move his ploughs out for the time being. And it's got a decent-sized window and a door with a lock to it.'

'That'll do well. Dick, run round and ask Mr Ashton and get him to lend us a cart and a hurdle. How about getting hold of the coroner, Rector? It's Mr Compline, you know, over at Leamholt. Shall I ring him up when I get back?'

'Oh, thank you, thank you. I should be very grateful.'

'All right. Can they carry on now, Jack?'

The constable signified his assent, and the digging was resumed. By this time the entire village seemed to have assembled in the churchyard and it was with the greatest difficulty that the children were prevented from crowding round the grave, since the grown-ups who should have restrained them were themselves struggling for positions of vantage. The Rector was just turning upon them with the severest rebuke he knew to utter, when Mr Lavender approached him.

'Excuse me, sir, but did I ought to ring Tailor Paul for that there?'

'Ring Tailor Paul? Well, really, Hezekiah, I hardly know.'

'We got to ring her for every Christian soul dyin' in the parish,' protested Mr Lavender. 'That's set down for us. And seemin'ly he must a-died in the parish, else why should anybody go for to bury him here?'

'True, true, Hezekiah.'

'But as for bein' a Christian soul, who's to say?'

'That, I fear, is beyond me, Hezekiah.'

'As to bein' a bit behindhand with him,' went on the old man, 'that ain't no fault of ours. We only knowed today as he'd died, so it stands to reason we couldn't ring for him earlier. But Christian – well, there! that's a bit of a puzzle, that is.'

'We'd better give him the benefit of the doubt, Hezekiah. Ring the bell by all means.'

The old man looked dubious, and at length approached the doctor.

'How old?' said the latter, looking round in some surprise. 'Why, I don't know. It's hard to say. But I should think he was between forty and fifty. Why do you want to know? The bell? Oh, I see. Well, put it at fifty.'

So Tailor Paul tolled the mysterious stranger out with nine strokes and fifty and a hundred more, while Alf Donnington at the Red Cow and Tom Tebbutt at the Wheatsheaf did a roaring trade and the Rector wrote a letter.

THE SECOND PART

LORD PETER IS CALLED INTO THE HUNT

Hunting is the first part of change ringing which it is necessary to understand.

TROYTE *On Change-Ringing.*

'My dear Lord Peter (wrote the Rector),

'Since your delightful visit to us in January, I have frequently wondered, with a sense of confusion, what you must have thought of us for not realising how distinguished an exponent of the methods of Sherlock Holmes we were entertaining beneath our roof. Living so very much out of the world, and reading only The Times *and the* Spectator, *we are apt, I fear, to become somewhat narrow in our interests. It was only when my wife wrote to her cousin Mrs Smith (whom you may know, perhaps, as she lives in Kensington) and mentioned your stay with us, that we were informed, by Mrs Smith's reply, what manner of man our guest was.*

'In the hope that you will pardon our lamentable ignorance, I venture to write and ask you to give us some advice out of your great experience. This afternoon we have been jerked rudely out of 'the noiseless tenor of our way,' by a most mysterious and shocking occurrence. On opening the grave of the late Lady Thorpe to receive the body of her husband – whose sad death you no doubt saw in the Obituary columns of the daily Press – our sexton was horrified to discover the dead body of a completely strange man, who appears to have come by his end in some violent and criminal manner. His face has been terribly mutilated, and – what seems even more shocking – the poor fellow's hands have been cut right off at the wrists! Our local police have, of course, the matter in hand, but the sad affair is of peculiar and painful interest to me (being in some sort connected with our parish church), and I am somewhat at a loss to know how I personally should proceed. My wife, with her usual great practical ability, suggested that we should seek your aid and advice, and Superintendent Blundell of Leamholt, with whom I have just had an interview, most obligingly says that he will give you every facility for investigation should you care to look into the matter personally. I hardly like to suggest to so busy a man that you should actually come and conduct your investigations on the spot, but, in case you thought of doing so, I need not say how heartily welcome you would be at the Rectory.

'Forgive me if this letter is somewhat meandering and confused; I am writing in some perturbation of mind. I may add that our Ringers retain a most pleasant and grateful recollection of the help you gave us with our

famous peal, and would, I am sure, wish me to remember them to you.
'With kindest regards from my wife and myself,

'Most sincerely yours,
'THEODORE VENABLES.'

'P.S. – My wife reminds me to tell you that the inquest is at 2 o'clock on Saturday.'

This letter, dispatched on the Friday morning, reached Lord Peter by the first post on Saturday. He wired that he would start for Fenchurch St Paul at once, joyfully cancelled a number of social engagements, and at two o'clock was seated in the Parish Room, in company with a larger proportion of the local population that had probably ever gathered beneath one roof since the spoliation of the Abbey.

The coroner, a florid-faced country lawyer, who seemed to be personally acquainted with everybody present, got to work with the air of an immensely busy person, every moment of whose time was of value.

'Come now, gentlemen . . . No talking over there *if* you please . . . all the jury this way . . . Sparkes, give out these Testaments to the jury . . . choose a foreman, please . . . Oh! you have chosen Mr Donnington . . . very good . . . Come along, Alf . . . take the Book in your right hand . . . diligently inquire . . . Sovereign Lord the King . . . man unknown . . . body . . . view . . . skill and knowledge . . . help you God . . . kiss the Book . . . sit down . . . table over there . . . now the rest of you . . . take the Book in your right hand . . . your *right* hand, Mr Pratt . . . don't you know your left from your right, Wally? . . . No laughing, please, we've no time to waste . . . same oath that your foreman . . . you and each of you severally to keep . . . help you God . . . kiss the Book . . . on that bench by Alf Donnington . . . Now then, you know what we're here for . . . inquire how this man came by his death . . . witnesses to identity . . . understand no witnesses to identity . . . Yes, Superintendent? . . . Oh, I see . . . why didn't you say so? Very well . . . this way, please . . . I beg your pardon, sir? . . . Lord Peter . . . do you mind saying that again . . . Whimsy? Oh, no H . . . just so . . . Wimsey with an E . . . quite . . . occupation? . . . what? . . . Well, we'd better say, Gentleman . . . now then, my lord, you say you can offer evidence as to identity?'

'Not exactly, but I rather think . . .'

'One moment, please . . . take the Book in your right hand . . . evidence . . . inquiry . . . truth, whole truth and nothing but the truth . . . kiss the Book . . . yes . . . name, address, occupation we've got all that . . . If you can't keep that baby quiet, Mrs Leach, you'll have to take it out . . . Yes?'

'I have been taken to see the body, and from my observation I think it possible that I saw this man on January 1st last. I do not know who he was, but if it is the same man he stopped my car about half a mile beyond the bridge by the sluice and asked the way to Fenchurch St Paul. I never saw him again, and had never seen him before to my knowledge.'

'What makes you think it may be the same man?'

'The fact that he is dark and bearded and that the man I saw also appeared to be wearing a dark suit similar to that worn by deceased. I say "appeared", because he was wearing an overcoat, and I only saw the legs of his trousers. He seemed to be about fifty years of age, spoke in a low voice with a London accent and was of fairly good address. He told me that he was a motor-mechanic and was looking for work. In my opinion, however . . .'

'One moment. You say you recognise the beard and the suit. Can you swear . . . ?'

'I cannot swear that I definitely recognise them. I say that the man I saw resembled the deceased in these respects.'

'You cannot identify his features?'

'No: they are too much mutilated.'

'Very well. Thank you. Are there any more witnesses to identity?'

The blacksmith rose up rather sheepishly.

'Come right up to the table, please. Take the Book . . . truth . . . truth . . . truth . . . Name Ezra Wilderspin well, now, Ezra, what have you got to say?'

'Well, sir, if I was to say I recognised the deceased, I should be telling a lie. But it's a fact that he ain't unlike a chap that come along same as his lordship here says, last New Year's Day a-looking for a job along of me. Said he was a motor-mechanic out o' work. Well, I told him I might do with a man as knowed somethin' about motors, so I takes him on and gives him a trial. He did his work pretty well near as I could judge, for three days, livin' in our place, and then, all of a sudden, off he goes in the middle of the night and we never seen no more of him.'

'What night was that?'

'Same day as they buried her ladyship it was . . .'

Here a chorus of voices broke in:

'January 4th, Ezra! that's when it were.'

'That's right. Saturday, January 4th, so 'twere.'

'What was the name of this man?'

'Stephen Driver, he called hisself. Didn't say much; only that he'd been trampin' about a goodish time, lookin' for work. Said he'd been in the Army, and in and out of work ever since.'

'Did he give you any references?'

'Why, yes, sir, he did, come to think on it. He give me the name of a garridge in London where he'd been, but he said it had gone bankrupt and shut up. But he said if I was to write to the boss, he'd put in a word for him.'

'Have you got the name and address he gave you?'

'Yes, sir. Leastways, I think the missus put it away in the teapot.'

'Did you take up the reference?'

'No, sir. I did think of it but being no great hand at writing I says to myself I'd wait till the Sunday, when I'd have more time, like. Well, you see, before that he was off, so I didn't think no more about it. He didn't leave nothing behind him, bar an old toothbrush. We 'ad to lend him a shirt when he came.'

'You had better see if you can find that address.'

'That's right, sir. Liz!' (in a stentorian bellow). 'You cut off home and see if you can lay your 'and on that bit o' paper what Driver give me.'

Voice from the back of the room: 'I got it here, Ezra,' followed by a general upheaval, as the blacksmith's stout wife forced her way to the front.

'Thanks, Liz,' said the coroner. 'Mr Tasker, 103 Little James St, London, W.C. Here, Superintendent, you'd better take charge of that. Now Ezra, is there anything more you can tell us about this man Driver?'

Mr Wilderspin explored his stubble with a thick forefinger.

'I dunno as there is, sir.'

'Ezra! Ezra! don't yew remember all them funny questions he asked?'

'There now,' said the blacksmith, 'the missus is quite right. That was a funny thing about them questions, that was. He said he 'adn't never been in this here village before, but he knowed a friend as had and the friend had told him to ask after Mr Thomas. "Mr Thomas!" I says. "There ain't no Mr Thomas in this village, nor never has been to my knowledge." "That's queer," he says, "but maybe he's got another name as well. Far as I can make out," he says, "this Thomas ain't quite right in his 'ead. My friend said as he was potty, like." "Why," I says, "you can't mean Potty Peake? Because Orris is his Chrissen name." "No," he says, "Thomas was the name. Batty Thomas, that's right. And another name my friend gi'n me," he says, "was a fellow called Paul – a tailor or some'in o' that, living next door to him, like." "Why," I says to him, "your friend's been havin' a game with you. Them ain't men's names, them's the names of bells," I says. "Bells?" he says. "Yes," I says, "church bells, that's what they is. Batty Thomas and Tailor Paul, they call 'em." And then he went on and asked a sight o' questions about they bells "Well," I says, "if you want to know about Batty Thomas and Tailor Paul, you better ask

Rector,' I says. 'He knows all about they old bells." I dunno if he ever went to Rector, but he come back one day – that was the Friday – and says he been in the church and see a bell carved on old Batty Thomas's tomb, like, and what did the writing on it mean. And I says to ask Rector, and he says: "Did all bells have writing on 'em," and I says, "Mostly"; and arter that he didn't say no more about it.'

Nobody being able to make very much sense out of Mr Wilderspin's revelations, the Rector was called, who said that he remembered having seen the man called Stephen Driver on one occasion when he was distributing the parish magazine at the smithy, but that Driver had said nothing then, or at any other time, about bells. The Rector then added his own evidence about finding the body and sending for the police, and was dismissed in favour of the sexton.

Mr Gotobed was very voluble, repeating, with increased circumlocutory detail and reference to what he had said to Dick and Dick to him, the account he had originally given to the police. He then explained that Lady Thorpe's grave had been dug on the 3rd of January and filled in on the 4th, immediately after the funeral.

'Where do you keep your tools, Harry?'

'In the coke-house, sir.'

'Where's that?'

'Well, sir, it's down underneath the church – where Rector says the old cryp used to be. Makes a sight o' work, that it du, a-carryin' coke up and down they stairs and through the chancel and sweepin' up arter it. You can't 'elp it a-dribbling out o' the scuttle, do as you like.'

'Is the door kept locked?'

'Oh, yes, sir, always kept locked. It's the little door under the organ, sir. You can't get to it without you have the key and the key of the west door as well. That is to say, either the key of the west door or one of the church keys, sir, if you take my meaning. I has the west door key, bein' 'andiest for me where I live, but either of the others would do as well.'

'Where do you keep these keys?'

'Hanging up in my kitchen, sir.'

'Has anybody else got a key to the coke-house door?'

'Yes, sir; Rector has all the keys.'

'Nobody else?'

'Not as I knows, sir. Mr Godfrey hasn't them all, only the key of the cryp.'

'I see. When these keys are in your kitchen, I suppose any of your family has access to them?'

'Well, sir, in a manner of speakin', yes, but I 'opes as how you ain't tryin' to put anything on me and my missus, nor yet Dick, let alone the children. I been sexton in this here village twenty year follerin' on Hezekiah, and none of us ain't never yet been suspected of 'ittin' strangers over the 'ead and buryin' of them. Come to think of it, this chap Driver came round to my place one morning on a message and 'ow do I know what he did? Not but what, if he'd a-took the keys I'd be bound to miss them; still, none the more for that . . .'

'Come, come, Harry! Don't talk nonsense. You don't suppose this unfortunate man dug his own grave and buried himself? Don't waste time.'

(Laughter, and cries of 'That's a good 'un, Harry!')

'Silence, *if* you please. Nobody's accusing you of anything. Have you in fact ever missed the keys at any time?'

'No, sir,' (sulkily).

'Or even noticed that your tools had been disturbed?'

'No, sir.'

'Did you clean them after digging Lady Thorpe's grave?'

''Course I cleaned 'em. I always leaves me tools clean.'

'When did you use them next after that?'

This puzzled Mr Gotobed for a moment. The voice of Dick supplied helpfully: 'Massey's baby.'

('Don't prompt the witness, please.')

'That's right,' agreed Mr Gotobed. 'Massey's baby it were, as you can see by the Register. And that 'ud be about a week later – ah! just about.'

'You found the tools clean and in their right place when you dug the grave for Mrs Massey's baby?'

'I ain't noticed nothing different.'

'Not at any time since?'

'No, sir.'

'Very well. That will do. Constable Priest.'

The constable, taking the oath briskly, informed the court of his having been called to the scene of action, having communicated with Superintendent Blundell, having assisted at the removal of the body and of having helped to search the clothes of the deceased. He then made way for the Superintendent, who corroborated his evidence and produced a brief list of the dead man's belongings. These were: a suit of navy-blue serge of poor quality, much deteriorated by its burial in the earth, but apparently purchased fairly recently from a well-known firm of cheap outfitters; much-worn vest and pants, bearing (unexpectedly enough) the name of a French manufacturer; a khaki shirt (British army type); a pair of working-man's boots, nearly new; a cheap spotted tie. In his pockets they had found a white cotton handkerchief; a packet of Woodbines; twenty-five shillings and eightpence in cash; a pocket-comb; a ten-centime piece; and a short length of stiff wire, bent at one end into a hook. The body had worn no overcoat.

The French money and underclothing and the piece of wire were the only objects which seemed to suggest any kind of clue. Ezra Wilderspin was recalled, but could not bring to mind that Driver had ever said anything about France, beyond mentioning that he had served in the war; and the Superintendent, asked whether he thought the wire could be anything in the nature of a pick-lock, shook his head, and said it didn't look like anything of that sort to *him*.

The next witness was Dr Baines, and his evidence produced the only real sensation of the day. He said:

'I have examined the body of deceased and made an autopsy. I should judge the subject to be a man aged between 45 and 50. He appears to have been well nourished and healthy. Taking into account the nature of the soil, which tends to retard putrefaction, the position of the body when found, that is, about two feet beneath the level of the churchyard and from three to four feet beneath the actual surface of the mound. I should judge the extent of decomposition found to indicate that deceased had been lying in the grave between three and four months. Decay does not proceed so rapidly in a buried body as in one exposed to the air, or in a clothed body as in a naked body. In this case, the internal organs and the soft tissues were all quite distinguishable and fairly well preserved. I made a careful examination and could discover no signs of external injury on any part of the body except upon the head, arms, wrist and ankles. The face had apparently been violently battered in with some blunt instrument which had practically reduced all the anterior – that is, the front – part of the skull to splinter. I was not able to form any exact estimate of the number of blows inflicted, but they must have been numerous and heavy. On opening the abdomen – '

'One moment, Doctor. I take it we may assume that the deceased died in consequence of one or some of these blows upon the skull?'

'No; I do not think that the blows were the cause of death.'

At this point an excited murmur ran around the little hall, and Lord Peter Wimsey was distinctly observed to rub his finger-tips lightly with a gratified smile.

'Why do you say that, Dr Baines?'

'Because, to the best of my judgement and belief, all the blows were inflicted after death. The hands also were removed after death, apparently with a short, heavy knife, such as a jacknife.'

Further sensation; and Lord Peter Wimsey audibly observed: 'Splendid!'

Dr Baines added a number of technical reasons for his opinion, chiefly connected with the absence of any extravasation of blood and the general appearance of the skin; adding, with proper modesty, that he was, of course, not an expert and could only proffer his opinion for what it was worth.

'But why should anybody inflict such savage injuries on a dead body?'

'That,' said the doctor dryly, 'is outside my province. I am not a specialist in lunacy or neurosis.'

'That is true. Very well, then. In your opinion, what was the cause of death?'

'I do not know. On opening the abdomen, I found the stomach, intestine, liver and spleen considerably decomposed, the kidneys, pancreas and oesophagus in a fairly good state of preservation.' (Here the doctor wandered off into medical detail.) 'I could not see,' he resumed, 'any superficial signs of disease or injury by poison. I, however, removed certain organs' (he enumerated them) 'and placed them in sealed jars' (further technical details) 'and propose dispatching them today for expert examination by Sir James Lubbock. I should expect to receive his report in about a fortnight's time – possibly earlier.'

The coroner expressed himself satisfied with this suggestion, and then went on:

'You mentioned injuries to the arms and ankles, Doctor; what was the nature of those?'

'The skin of the ankles seemed to have been very much broken and abraded – as though the ankles had been tightly bound with cord or rope which had cut through the socks. The arms also showed the pressure marks of a rope above the elbows. These injuries were undoubtedly inflicted before death.'

'You suggest that somebody tied the deceased up with ropes, and then, by some means or other, brought about his death?'

'I think that the deceased was undoubtedly tied up – either by another person or by himself. You may remember that there was a case in which a young man at one of the universities died in circumstances which suggested that he had himself bound his own wrists and arms.'

'In that case, the cause of death was suffocation, I believe?'

'I believe it was. I do not think that was the case here. I found nothing to indicate it.'

'You do not, I suppose, suggest that the deceased went so far as to bury himself?'

'No; I do not suggest that.'

'I am glad to hear it,' said the coroner, sarcastically. 'Can you suggest any reason why, if a man had accidentally or intentionally killed himself by tying himself up – ?'

'After tying himself up; the tying of the arms and ankles would not in themselves be likely to cause death.'

'After tying himself up – why somebody else should then come along, smash his face in and then bury him secretly?'

'I could suggest a variety of reasons; but I do not think that is my province.'

'You are very correct, Doctor.'

Dr Baines bowed.

'He might, I suppose, have perished of starvation, if he had tied himself up and been unable to free himself.'

'No doubt. Sir James Lubbock's report will tell us that.'

'Have *you* anything further to tell us?'

'Only that, as a possible aid to identification, I have made as careful a note as I can – in view of the extensive mutilation of the jaws – of the number and condition of deceased's teeth, and of the dental work done upon them at various times. I have handed this note over to Superintendent Blundell in order that he may issue an inquiry.'

'Thank you, Doctor; that will no doubt be very helpful.'

The coroner paused, glanced through his notes and then turned to the Superintendent.

'In the circumstances, Superintendent, it seems to be advisable to adjourn the inquest until you have completed your investigations. Shall we say, till today fortnight? Then, if you should see your way to making any charge against anybody in connection with this crime, or accident, or whatever it is, we may if you like adjourn the inquiry *sine die*.'

'I think that would be the best way, Mr Compline.'

'Very well, Gentlemen, we will adjourn until today fortnight.'

The jury, a little puzzled and disappointed at not being asked for any opinion, filed slowly out from behind the long trestle table at which they had been seated – a table dedicated, under happier circumstances, chiefly to parish teas.

'A beautiful case,' said Lord Peter, enthusiastically, to Mr Venables. 'Quite charming. I am uncommonly grateful to you for drawing my attention to it. I wouldn't have missed it for the world. I like your doctor.'

'We consider him a very able man.'

'You must introduce me to him; I feel that we should get on well together. The coroner doesn't like him. Some trifling personal antagonism, no doubt. Why, here is my old friend Hezekiah! How do you do, Mr Lavender? How's Tailor Paul?'

There was general greeting. The Rector caught the arm of a tall, thin man hurrying past their little group.

'Just a moment, Will, I want to introduce you to Lord Peter Wimsey. Lord Peter, this is Will Thoday, whose bell you rang on your last visit.'

Hands were shaken.

'Very sorry I was to miss that peal,' said Thoday. 'But I was pretty bad, wasn't I, Rector?'

'You were indeed. You don't look to have quite got over it yet.'

'I'm all right, sir, except for being troubled by a bit of a cough. But that'll pass away with the spring weather coming.'

'Well, you must take care of yourself. How's Mary?'

'Fine, sir, thank you. She was for coming to this here inquest, but I said as it wasn't no place for a woman. I'm thankful I got her to stop at home.'

'Yes; the doctor's evidence was very disagreeable. Children all right? That's splendid. Tell your wife Mrs Venables will be coming round to see her in a day or two. Yes, she's very well; thank you – distressed, naturally, by all this sad business. Ah! There's Dr Baines. Doctor! Lord Peter Wimsey wants very much to make your acquaintance. You'd better come and have a cup of tea at the Rectory. Good day, Will, good day! . . . I don't like the looks of that fellow,' added the Rector, as they turned towards the Rectory. 'What do you think of him, Doctor?'

'He's looking a bit white and strained today. Last week I thought he was a lot better, but he had a bad bout of it and he's rather a nervous subject. You don't expect farm-labourers to have nerves, do you, Lord Peter? But they're human, like the rest of us.'

'And Thoday is a very superior man,' said the Rector, as though superiority conveyed a licence to keep a nervous system. 'He used to farm his own land till these bad times set in. Now he works for Sir Henry – that is to say, he did. I'm sure I don't know what will happen now, with only the poor child left at the Red House. I suppose the trustee will let the place, or put in a steward to run it for her. It doesn't bring in very much these days, I fear.'

At this point a car overtook them and stopped a little way ahead. It proved to contain Superintendent Blundell and his assistants, and the Rector, apologising fussily for his remissness, made him and Wimsey acquainted with one another.

'Pleased to meet you, my lord. I've heard of you through my old friend Inspector Snugg. He's retired now – did you know? – and got a nice little place the other side of Leamholt. He often talks about you. Says you used to pull his leg something cruel. This is a bad job, this is. Between you and me, my lord, what was it you were going to say when the coroner interrupted you – about this chap Driver's not being a motor-mechanic?'

'I was going to say that he gave me the impression of having done most of his manual labour lately at Princetown or somewhere like that.'

'Ah!' said the Superintendent, thoughtfully. 'Struck you that way, did he? How was that?'

'Eyes, voice, attitude – all characteristic, what?'

'Ah!' said the Superintendent again. 'Ever heard of the Wilbraham emeralds, my lord?'

'Yes.'

'You know that Nobby Cranton's out again? And it seems he ain't reported himself lately, neither. Last heard of six months ago in London. They've been looking for him. Maybe we've found him. In any case, I wouldn't be surprised if we was to hear of those emeralds again before very long.'

'Loud cheers!' said Wimsey. 'I'm all for a treasure-hunt. This is all confidential, of course?'

'If you please, my lord. You see, if somebody thought it worth while to kill Cranton and smash him up and bury him, *and* cut off his hands where he keeps his fingerprints, there's somebody in this village that knows something. And the less they think we guess, the more free they'll act and speak. And that's why, my lord, I was rather glad when the reverend gentleman suggested you coming down here. They'll talk freer to you than to me – see?'

'Perfectly. I'm a terrific success at pottering round asking sloppy questions. And I can put away quite a lot of beer in a good cause.'

The Superintendent grinned, begged Wimsey to come and see him at any time, clambered into his car and drove off.

The great difficulty about any detective inquiry is knowing where to start. After some thought Lord Peter made out the following lists of queries:

A. Identity of the Corpse

1. Was it Cranton? – Wait for report on teeth and police report.
2. Consider the question of the ten-centime piece and the French underclothing. Has Cranton been in France? When? If not Cranton, is anyone known in the village also known to have been in France at any period since the war?
3. The destruction of the hands and features after death suggests that the murderer had an interest in making recognition impossible. If the body is Cranton, who knew Cranton (a) by sight? (b) personally?
(Note: Deacon knew him; but Deacon is dead. Did Mary Thoday know him?) Many people must have seen him at the trial.

B. The Wilbraham Emeralds

1. Resulting from the above: Was Mary Thoday (formerly Mary Deacon, née Russell) really after all concerned in the theft?
2. Who really had the emeralds – Deacon or Cranton?
3. Where are the emeralds now? Did Cranton (if it was Cranton) come to Fenchurch St Paul to look for them?
4. If the answer to 3 is 'Yes,' why did Cranton wait till now to make his search? Because some fresh information had lately reached him? Or merely because he was continuously in prison till just lately? (Ask the Superintendent.)
5. What is the meaning of 'Driver's' interest in Batty Thomas and Tailor Paul? Is anything to be gained from a study of the bells and/or their mottoes?

C. The Crime

1. What did deceased die of? (Wait for experts' report.)
2. Who buried (and presumably also killed) him?
3. Can any clue to the time of the burial be gained by looking up the weather reports? (Snow? rain? Footprints?)
4. Whereabouts did the murder take place? The churchyard? the church? somewhere in the village?
5. If the sexton's tools were used, who had access to them? ('Driver,' apparently, but who else?)

Quite a lot of questions, thought his lordship, and some of them unanswerable till outside reports came in. The matter of the bell-mottoes could, of course, be looked into at once. He sought the Rector and asked whether he could without too much trouble, lay his hand on Woollcott's *History of the Bells of Fenchurch St Paul,* which he had once spoken about. The Rector thought he could, and after he had hunted through all his study shelves and enlisted the aid of Mrs Venables and Emily, the book was in fact discovered in a small room devoted to the activities of the Clothing Club ('and how it could have got there I cannot imagine!'). From this work Wimsey distilled the following facts interesting to archaeologists, but not immediately suggestive of anything in the way of corpses or emeralds:

BATTY THOMAS (No. 7. Weight 30½ cwt. Note: D).

The oldest bell in the ring in her present form, and oldest still in her original metal. First cast by Thomas Belleyetere of Lynn in 1338. Recast, with additional metal, by Abbot Thomas of

Fenchurch (fl: 1356–1392) in 1380. (This abbot also built the tower and the greater part of the existing nave, though the aisle windows were enlarged in Perpendicular style by Abbot Martin, *circ.* 1423.)

INSCRIPTIONS
Shoulder
NOLI + ESSE + INCREDVLVS + SED + FIDELIS +
Waist
O SANCTE THOMA.
Soundbow
ABBAT . THOMAS . SETT . MEE . HEARE . AND . BAD .
MEE . RINGE . BOTH . LOVD . AND . CLEER . 1380 .

No record of any other bells at this time, though there was probably at least one other. We know, however, that in the reign of Elizabeth there was a ring of five bells in D of which

JOHN (No. 3. Weight 8 cwt. Note: A).
Was the original treble. She bears the name of her founder, John Cole, an itinerant founder of the period.

INSCRIPTION
Soundbow
JHON . COLE . MAD . MEE . JHON . PRESBYTER . PAYD
. MEE . JHON . EVAGELIST . AID . MEE . MDLVII .

JERICHO(No. 4. Weight 8½ cwt. Note: G).
Was the No. 2 of the old peal and her maker seems to have thought aggressively well of her.

INSCRIPTION
Shoulder
FROM . IERICHO . TO IOHN . AGROAT . YR . IS . NOE .
BELLE . CAN . BETTER . MY . NOTE . 1559 .

Of the original No. 4, nothing is known. The original No. 3 (F#) was a poor bell, flat in pitch and weak in quality. In James I's reign, this bell was further flattened by the grinding away of its inner surface so as to produce some sort of approximation to F♮, and the great tenor bell was added to make a ring of six in C.

TAILOR PAUL (No. 8. Weight 41 cwt. Note: C).
A very noble bell of superb truth and tone. She was cast in the Bellfield by the church. (See parish records.)

INSCRIPTIONS
Shoulder
PAVLE + IS + MY + HONOVR + THAT + SAME +
Soundbow
NINE + TAYLERS + MAKE + A + MANNE + IN + CHRIST + IS + DETH + ATT + END + IN + ADAM + YAT + BEGANNE + 1614

The bells survived the tumults of the Great Rebellion, and in the later part of the century, when the fashion for change-ringing set in, a new treble and second were added to bring the number up to eight.

GAUGE (Treble. Weight 7 cwt. Note: C).
The gift of the Gaudy family, she bears a 'canting' motto.

INSCRIPTION
Soundbow
GAVDE . GAUDY . DNI . IN . LAVDE . MDCLXVI .

The No. 2 of that period was known as *Carolus,* having been given in honour of the King's Restoration. This bell, however, was cracked in the 18th century, as a result of the abominable practice of 'clapping' the two smallest bells for occasional services, so that the ring was again reduced to six, of which No. 5 (F♮) had always been unsatisfactory. In the first half of the 19th century (that period of ecclesiastical apathy) the worm was allowed to get into the timbers of the bell-cage, as a result of which No. 6 (the Elizabethan No. 4) fell and was broken. Nothing was done until the eighties, when an energetic High Church rector called public attention to the bad state of the bells. Subscriptions were raised, the framework of the bell-cage was repaired and put in order, and three bells were recast:

SABAOTH (No. 2. Weight 7¼ cwt. Note: B).
Was the gift of the Rector.

INSCRIPTIONS
Shoulder
SANCTUS . SANCTUS . SANCTUS . DOMINUS . DEUS . SABAOTH

Soundbow

RECAST BY JOHN TAYLOR OF LOUGHBOROUGH 1887.

DIMITY (No. 6. Weight 14 cwt. Note: E).

Was given in memory of Sir Richard Thorpe, who died in 1883.

INSCRIPTIONS

Shoulder

RECAST BY JOHN TAYLOR OF LOUGHBOROUGH 1887.

Soundbow

IN . PIAM . MEMORIAM . RICARDI . THORPE . ARMIGERI . NUNC . DIMITTIS . DOMINE . SERVUM . TUUM . IN . PACE .

JUBILEE (No. 5. Weight 9½ cwt. Note: F♮).

The funds for this bell were raised by public subscription in commemoration of the Queen's Jubilee.

INSCRIPTIONS

Shoulder

JUBILATE . DEO . OMNIS . TERRA .

Waist

RECAST . IN . THE . YEAR . OF . THE . QUEEN'S . JUBILEE . BY . JOHN . TAYLOR . AND . CO . E. HINKINS . AND . B. DONNINGTON . CHURCHWARDENS.

Wimsey puzzled his head for some time over this information, but without very much result. The dates, the weights and the mottoes – was there anything here that could serve as a guide to buried treasure? Batty Thomas and Tailor Paul had been particularly mentioned, but try as he would, for him they had neither speech nor language. After a time he gave up his calculations. Possibly there was something about the bells themselves that did not appear in Mr Woollcott's work. Something written or carved on the timbers, possibly. He must go up and look some time.

It was Sunday morning. As he lifted his head from his calculations, he heard the bells begin to ring for matins. He hastened out in the hall, where he found his host winding the grandfather clock.

'I always wind it when the bells begin on a Sunday morning,' explained Mr Venables, 'otherwise I might forget. I fear I am none too methodical. I hope you will not feel obliged to come to church merely because you are our guest. I always make a point of telling our visitors that they are quite free to do as they wish. What time do *you* make it? Ten thirty-seven – we will put the hands at 10.45. He always loses about a quarter of an hour during the week, you see, and by putting him a little forward each time he is wound, we strike a happy mean. If you will just remember that he is always *fast* on Sundays, Mondays and Tuesday, *right* on Wednesdays, and *slow* on Thursdays, Fridays and Saturdays, you will find him a very reliable guide.

Wimsey said he was sure of it, and turned to find Bunter at his elbow, offering him with one hand his hat and with the other two leather-bound volumes on a small salver.

'You see, padre, we have every intention of going to church; we have, in fact, come prepared. Hymns A. & M. – I suppose that is the right work?'

'I took the liberty of ascertaining as much beforehand, my lord.'

'Of course you did, Bunter. You always ascertain everything. Why, padre, what's the trouble? Have you lost anything?'

'I – er – it's very odd – I could have declared that I laid them down just here. Agnes! Agnes, my dear! Have you seen those banns anywhere?'

'What is it, Theodore?'

'The banns, my dear. Young Flavel's banns. I know I had them with me. I always write them out on a slip of paper, you see, Lord Peter; it is so very inconvenient to carry the register to the lectern. Now what in the world – ?'

'Are they on the top of the clock, Theodore?'

'My dear, what a – ! Bless me, though, you are quite right. How did that come about, I wonder! I must have put them up there unconsciously when I was picking up the key. Very strange indeed, but the little mishap is now remedied, thanks to my wife. She always knows where I have put things. I believe she knows the workings of my mind better than I do myself. Well, I must go across to the church now. I go early, because of the choirboys. My wife will show you the Rectory pew.'

The pew was conveniently situated for observation, towards the rear of the nave on the north side. From it, Mrs Venables was able to survey the south porch, by which the congregation entered, and also to keep an admonitory eye on the school-children who occupied the north aisle, and to frown at those who turned round to stare or make faces. Lord Peter, presenting a placid front to the inquisitive glances of his fellow-worshippers, also watched the south porch. There was a face he was particularly anxious to see. Presently he saw it. William Thoday came in, and with him a thin, quietly dressed woman accompanied by two little girls. He guessed her to be about forty, though, as is frequently the case with country women, she had lost most of her front teeth and looked older. But he could still see in her the shadow of the smart and pretty parlourmaid that she must have been sixteen years before. It was, he thought, an honest face, but its expression was anxious and almost apprehensive – the face of a woman who had been through trouble and awaited, with nervous anticipation, the next shock which fate might hold in store for her. Probably, thought Wimsey, she was worried about her husband. He did not look well; he, too, had the air of being braced in self-defence. His uneasy eyes wandered about the church and then returned, with a curious mingling of wariness and protective affection, to his wife. They took their seats almost immediately opposite the Rectory pew, so that Wimsey from his corner seat was able to watch them without any appearance of particularity. He gained the impression, however, that Thoday felt his scrutiny and resented it. He turned his eyes away, therefore, and fixed them on the splendours of the angel roof, lovelier than ever in the soft spring sunshine that streamed through the rich reds and blues of the clerestory windows.

The pew which belonged to the Thorpe family was empty, except for an upright, middle-aged gentleman who was pointed out in a whisper by Mrs Venables as being Hilary Thorpe's uncle from London. The housekeeper, Mrs Gates, and the Red House servants sat in the south aisle. In the pew immediately in front of Wimsey was a stout little man in a neat black suit, who, Mrs Venables further informed him, was Mr Russell, the village undertaker, and a cousin of Mary Thoday. Mrs West, the postmistress, arrived with her daughter, and greeted Wimsey, whom she remembered from his last visit, with a smile and something between a nod and a bob. Presently, the bells ceased, with the exception of the five-minute bell, and the ringers came clattering up to their places. Miss Snoot, the schoolmistress, struck into a voluntary, the choir came in from the vestry with much noise of hobnailed boots, the Rector entered his stall.

The service was devoid of incident, except that Mr Venables again mislaid the banns, which had to be fetched from the vestry by the tenor on the cantoris side, and that, in his sermon, he made a solemn little allusion to the unfortunate stranger whose funeral was to take place on the morrow, whereat Mr Russell nodded, with an air of importance and approbation. The Rector's progress to the pulpit was marked by a loud and gritty crunching, which caused Mrs Venables to mutter in an exasperated tone, 'that's the coke again – Gotobed *will* be so careless with it.' At the conclusion, Wimsey found himself stranded with Mrs Venables in the porch, while handshakings and inquiries passed.

Mr Russell and Mr Gotobed came out together, busily talking, and the former was introduced to Lord Peter.

'Where are they a-putting of him, Harry?' asked Mr Russell, eagerly turning from ceremony to business.

'Over on the north side, next to old Susan Edwards,' replied the sexton. 'We got him dug last night, all very fit and proper. Maybe his lordship would like to come and see.'

Wimsey expressed suitable interest, and they made their way round to the other side of the church.

'We're giving him a nice bit of elm,' said Mr Russell, with some satisfaction, when the handsome proportions of the grave had been duly admired. 'He did ought by rights to have come on the parish, and that means deal, as you know, but the Rector says to me, "Poor fellow," he says, "let's put him away nice and seemly, and I'll pay for it," he says. And I've trued up the boards good and tight, so there won't be no unpleasantness. Of course, lead would be the right thing for him, but it ain't a thing as I'm often asked for, and I didn't think as I could get it in time, and the fact is, the sooner he's underground again, the better. Besides, lead is cruel 'ard work on the bearers. Six of them we're giving him – wouldn't want to be thought lacking in respect for the dead, however come by, so I says to Rector, "No, sir," I says, "not that old handcart," I says, "but six bearers just the same as if he was one of ourselves." And Rector, he quite agreed with me. Ah! I daresay there'll be a sight of folk come in from round about, and I wouldn't like them to see the thing done mean or careless like.'

'That's right,' said Mr Gotobed. 'I've heerd as there's a reglar party comin' from St Stephen in John Brownlow's sharrer. It'll be a rare frolic for 'em.'

'Rector's giving a wreath, too,' pursued Mr Russell, 'and Miss Thorpe's sending another. And there'll be a nice bunch o' flowers from the school-children and a wreath from the Women's Institute. My missus was round collecting the pennies just as soon as we knowed we'd have the buryin' of him.'

'Ah! she's a quick worker and no mistake,' said the sexton, admiringly.

'Ah! and Mrs Venables, she made the money up to a guinea, so it'll be a real good one. I like to see a nice lot of flowers at a funeral. Gives it tone, like.'

'Is it to be choral?'

'Well, not what you might call fully choral, but just a 'ymn at the graveside. Rector says, "Not too much about parted friends," he says. "'Twouldn't be suitable, seeing we don't know who his friends was." So I says, "What about *God moves in a myster'ous way?*" I says. "That's a good solemn-like, mournful 'ymn, as we all knows the tune on, and if anything can be said to be myster'ous, it's this here death," I says. So that's what was settled.'

'Ah!' said the voice of Mr Lavender, 'you're right there, Bob Russell. When I was a lad, there wasn't none of this myster'ousness about. Everything was straightforward an' proper. But ever since eddication come in, it's been nothing but puzzlement, and fillin' up forms and 'ospital papers and sustificates and such, before you can get even as much as your Lord George pension.'

'That may be, Hezekiah,' replied the sexton, 'but to my mind it all started with that business of Jeff Deacon at the Red House, bringin' strangers into the place. First thing as 'appened arter that was the war, and since then we been all topsy-turvy like.'

'As to the war,' said Mr Russell, 'I daresay we'd a had that anyhow, Jeff Deacon or no Jeff Deacon. But in a general way you're quite right. He was a bad 'un, was Jeff, though even now, poor Mary won't hear a word again him.'

'That's the way with women,' said Mr Lavender, sourly. 'The wusser a man is, the more they dotes on him. Too soft-spoken he were, to my liking, were that Deacon. I don't trust these London folk, if you'll excuse me, sir.'

'Don't mention it,' said Wimsey.

'Why, Hezekiah,' remonstrated Mr Russell, 'you thought a sight o' Jeff Deacon yourself at one time. Said he was the quickest chap at learning Kent Treble Bob as you ever had to do with.'

'That's a different thing,' retorted the old gentleman. 'Quick he was, there ain't no denyin', and he pulled a very good rope. But quickness in the 'ed don't mean a good 'eart. There's many evil men is as quick as monkeys. Didn't the good Lord say as much? The children o' this world is wiser in their generation than the children o' light. He commended the unjust steward, no doubt, but he give the fellow the sack just the same, none the more for that.'

'Ah, well,' said the sexton, 'Jeff Deacon 'ull be put in his proper place where he've gone, and the same with the poor chap, whoever he be. We ain't got nothing to meddle wi' that, only to do our dooties in the station whereto we are called. That's Scripture, that is, and so I says, Give him a proper funeral for we don't know when it may be our turn next.'

'That's very true, Harry; very true, that is. It may be you or me to be 'it on the 'ed one o' these days – though who can be going about to do such things beats me. Now then, Potty, what do you want here?'

'Nothing, nothing, Bob. Only to see where you was a-putting of the dead 'un. Ah! he was reglar smashed up, he were, weren't he? Beat all to a pulp, eh? Whack! whack! I a-liked to a-seen that, I would.'

'Clear off,' said the undertaker. 'I'm disgusted wi' you, Potty Fair disgusted. Don't you get talkin' that a-way, or I'll tell Rector on you, and he won't let you blow the organ no more. See? What do you mean by it?'

'Nothing, Bob, nothing.'

'That's a good thing.'

Mr Russell watched the imbecile uneasily as he shuffled away, his big head rolling and his hands swinging loosely at his sides.

'He's getting very queer, is Potty,' said he. 'I 'ope as he's safe. I reckon he did ought to be shut up.'

'No, no,' said the sexton. "Potty's safe enough. I don't 'old with these 'ere asylums.'

At this point Mrs Venables joined them to take possession of her guest.

'Poor little Hilary Thorpe wasn't in church,' she observed. 'Such a nice child. I should have liked you to see her. But she's quite prostrated, poor child, so Mrs Gates tells me. And you know, the village people do stare so at anybody who's in trouble and they will want to talk and condole. They mean well, but it's a terrible ordeal. I'll take you along to the Red House one day. Come along now – I'm sure you want your dinner.'

THE THIRD PART

LORD PETER IS TAKEN FROM LEAD AND MAKES THIRD PLACE

The bell that the treble takes from lead makes thirds place and returns to lead again; while the bells in 4, 5 and 6, 7 dodge when the place is made.

Rules for Ringing Grandsire Triples

Lord Peter watched the coffin borne up the road.

'Here comes my problem,' said he to himself, 'going to earth on the shoulders of six stout fellows. Finally, this time, I suppose, and I don't seem to have got very much out of it. What a gathering of the local worthies – and how we are all enjoying it! Except dear old Venables – he's honestly distressed . . . This everlasting tolling makes your bones move in your body . . . Tailor Paul . . . For Mr Paul . . . two mortal tons of bawling bronze . . . "I am the Resurrection and the Life . . ." that's all rather sobering. This chap's first resurrection was ghastly enough – let's hope there won't be another this side of Doomsday . . . Silence that dreadful bell! . . . Tailor Paul . . . though even that might happen, if Lubbock finds anything funny . . . "Though after my skin worms destroy this body . . ." How queer that fellow Thoday looks . . . something wrong there, I shouldn't wonder . . . Tailor Paul . . . "We brought nothing into this world and it is certain we can carry nothing out . . ." except our secrets, old Patriarch; we take those with us all right.' The deep shadows of the porch swallowed up priest, corpse and bearers, and Wimsey, following with Mrs Venables, felt how strange it was that he and she should follow that strange corpse as sole and unexpected mourners.

'And people may say what they like,' thought Wimsey again, 'about the services of the Church of England, but there was genius in the choosing of these psalms. 'That I may be certified how long I have to live' – what a terrifying prayer; Lord, let me never be certified of anything of the kind. "A stranger with Thee and a sojourner" – that's a fact, God knows . . . "Thou hast set our misdeeds before Thee" . . . very likely, and why should I, Peter Wimsey, busy myself with digging them up? I haven't got so very much to boast about myself, if it comes to that . . . Oh, well . . . "world without end, Amen." Now the lesson, I suppose we sit down for this – I'm not very well up in the book of words . . . This is the place where the friends and relations usually begin to cry – but there's nobody here to do it – not a friend, nor a – How do I know that? I don't know it. Where's the man or woman who would have recognised that face, if the murderer hadn't taken all those pains to disfigure it? . . . That red-haired kid must be Hilary Thorpe . . . decent of her to come . . . interesting type . . . I can see her making a bit of a splash in five year's time . . . "I have fought with beasts at Ephesus" . . . what on earth has that got to do with it? . . . "raised a spiritual body" – what does old Donne say?' God knows in what part of the world every grain of every man's dust lies . . . He whispers, he hisses, he beckons for the bodies of his saints" . . . do all these people believe that? Do I? Does anybody? We all take it pretty placidly, don't we? "In a flash, at a trumpet crash, this Jack, joke, poor potsherd, patch, matchwood, immortal diamond is – immortal diamond." Did the old boys who made that amazing roof believe? Or did they just make those wide wings and adoring hands for fun, because they liked the pattern? At any rate, they made them *look* as though they believed something, and that's where they have us beat. What next? Oh, yes, out again to the grave, of course. Hymn 373 . . . there must be some touch of imagination in the good Mr Russell to have suggested this, though he looks as if he thought of nothing but having tinned salmon for his tea . . . "Man that is born of woman . . ." not very much further to go now; we're coming into the straight . . . "Thou knowest, Lord, the secrets of our hearts . . ." I knew it, I knew it! Will Thoday's going to faint . . . No, he's got hold of himself again. I shall have to have a word with that gentleman before long . . . "for any pains of death, to fall from Thee." Damn it! that goes home. Why? Mere splendour of rhythm, I expect – there were plenty of worse pains . . . "Our dear brother departed" . . . *brother* . . . we're all dear when we're dead, even if beforehand somebody hated us enough to tie us up and . . . Great Scott, yes! What about that rope?'

The problem of the rope – absurdly overlooked and now absurdly insistent – took such possession of Wimsey that he forgot to join in the Lord's Prayer; nor had he even wits to spare for a sardonic commentary on the means used by Providence to deliver this our brother out of the miseries of this sinful world. He was amazed that he had not earlier seized upon the rope as a clue to the labyrinth. For the tying-up of the dead man implied so much.

Where had the rope come from? How had it happened to be handy for the tying-up, and where had that tying taken place? You might kill a man in hot blood, but you did not first tie him. The death of a bound man meant premeditation – a calf roped for the shambles. The rope had been removed before burial; there was a horrid thrift about that . . . At this point Wimsey shook himself. There was no need to fancy things; there were plenty of other reasons for the removal of the rope. It had been removed before death. It had been removed and replaced where it came from, lest its absence should arouse suspicion. It had been removed for the same reason that the face had been mutilated – lest anyone finding the body should recognise it. Finally, it had been removed because it had tied the body *to* something – and that, perhaps, was the likeliest reason. For the body must have been brought from somewhere – how? Car, lorry, cart, waggon, wheelbarrow, truck . . . ? It reminded one of 'Tinker tailor . . .'

'Everything *very* nicely done, Mr Russell,' said Mrs Venables.

'Yes'm?' said Mr Russell. 'Very glad you think so, 'm. We done what we could to the best of our ability.'

'I'm sure,' said Mrs Venables, 'that if his own people had been here, they couldn't have wished for anything *nicer*.'

'No'm,' agreed Mr Russell, much gratified, 'and it's a pity they couldn't a-been present, for there's no doubt a handsome funeral is a great comfort to them as is left. Of course, it ain' so grand as a London funeral would be – ' He glanced wistfully at Wimsey.

'But much nicer,' said Wimsey, in a ridiculous echo of Mrs Venables. 'You see, it has so much more of the personal touch.'

'That's very true,' said the undertaker, much encouraged. 'Why, I dessay these London men get as much as three or four funerals every week, and it stands to reason as they can't put the same 'eart into it – let alone not knowing the parties. Well, I'll be getting along now. There's someone wants to speak to you, my lord.'

'No,' said Wimsey, firmly, to a gentleman in well-worn tweeds, who approached briskly. 'I have no story for the *Morning Star*. Nor for the other paper. Hop it. I have other things to do.'

'Yes,' added Mrs Venables, addressing the reporter as though he were an importunate child at a school treat, 'run along now, the gentleman's busy. How tiresome these newspapers are! You must get sick to death of them. Come along, I want to introduce you to Hilary Thorpe. Hilary, my dear, how are you? Very sweet of you to come – so trying for you. How is your uncle? This is Lord Peter Wimsey.'

'I'm ever so glad to meet you, Lord Peter. Dad used to read all about your cases – he'd have loved to have a talk with you. You know, I think he'd have been frightfully amused to think of being mixed up in one himself – if only it hadn't been Mother's grave. I'm glad he didn't know about that. But it is a mystery, isn't it? And he was – well, quite a kid about mysteries and things.'

'Was he? I should have thought he'd had about enough of them.'

'You mean about the necklace? That was pretty awful for him, poor dear. Of course, it all happened before I was born, but he often used to talk about it. He always used to say he believed Deacon was the worst of the two men, and that Granddad ought never to have had him in the house. It was funny, but I believe he rather took a liking to the other man – the London thief. He only saw him at the trial, of course, but he said he was an amusing beggar and he believed he was telling the truth.'

'That's dashed interesting.' Lord Peter turned suddenly and savagely on the young man from the *Morning Star*, who still hovered at a little distance. 'See here, my lad, if you don't make a noise like a hoop and roll away, I shall have something to say to your editor. I will not have this young lady followed about and bothered by you. Go right away, and if you're good I'll see you later and tell you any lies you like. See? Now vanish! . . . Curse the Press!'

'That lad's a sticker,' said Miss Thorpe. 'He badgered poor Uncle nearly out of his senses this morning. That's Uncle, talking to the Rector. He's a Civil Servant, and he disapproves of the Press altogether. He disapproves of mysteries, too. It's rotten for Uncle.'

'I expect he'll disapprove of me.'

'Yes, he does. He thinks your hobby unsuited to your position in life. That's why he's rather carefully avoiding an introduction. Uncle's a comic old bird, but he isn't a snob and he's rather decent, really. Only he's not a bit like Dad. You and Dad would have got on splendidly. Oh, by the way – you know where Dad and Mother are buried, don't you? I expect that was the first place you looked at.'

'Well, it was; but I'd rather like to look at it again. You see, I'm wondering just exactly how the – the – '

'How they got the body there? Yes, I thought you'd be wondering that. I've been wondering, too. Uncle doesn't think it's nice of me to wonder anything of the sort. But it really makes things easier to do a little wondering, I mean, if you're once interested in a thing it makes it seem less real. That's not the right word, though.'

'Less personal?'

'Yes; that's what I mean. You begin to imagine how it all happened, and gradually it gets to feel more like something you've made up.'

'H'm!' said Wimsey. 'If that's the way your mind works, you'll be a writer one day.'

'Do you think so? How funny; That's what I want to be. But why?'

'Because you have creative imagination, which works outwards, till finally you will be able to stand outside your own experience and see it as something you have made, existing independently of yourself. You're lucky.'

'Do you really think so?' Hilary looked excited.

'Yes – but your luck will come more at the end of life than at the beginning, because the other sort of people won't understand the way your mind works. They will start by thinking you dreamy and romantic, and then they'll be surprised to discover that you are really hard and heartless. They'll be quite wrong both times – but they won't ever know it, and *you* won't know it at first, and it'll worry you.'

'But that's just what the girls say at school. How did you know? . . . Though they're all idiots – mostly, that is.'

'Most people are,' said Wimsey, gravely, 'but it isn't kind to tell them so. I expect you do tell them so. Have a heart; they can't help it . . . Yes, this is the place. Well, you know, it isn't very much overlooked, is it? That cottage is the nearest – whose is that?'

'Will Thoday's.'

'Oh, is it? . . . And after that, there's only the Wheatsheaf and a farm. Whose is the farm?'

'That's Mr Ashton's place. He's quite a well-to-do kind of man, one of the churchwardens. I liked him very much when I was a kid; he used to let me ride on the farm horses.'

'I've heard of him; he pulled my car out of the ditch one day – which reminds me. I ought to call and thank him personally.'

'That means you want to ask him questions.'

'If you *do* see through people as clearly as that, you oughtn't to make it so brutally plain to them.'

'That's what Uncle calls my unfeminine lack of tact. He says it comes of going to school and playing hockey.'

'He may be right. But why worry?'

'I'm not worrying – only, you see, Uncle Edward will have to look after me now, and he thinks it's all wrong for me to be going to Oxford . . . What are you looking at? The distance from the South gateway?'

'Uncomfortably discerning woman – yes, I was. You could bring the body in a car and carry it round without too much difficulty. What's that, there, close by the north wall of the churchyard? A well?'

'Yes; that's the well where Gotobed gets the water for washing out the porch and scrubbing the chancel and all that. I think it's rather deep. There used to be a pump there at one time, but the village people used to come and use it for drinking water, when the village well ran dry, and Mr Venables had to stop it because he said it wasn't sanitary, drinking water out of a graveyard; so he took the pump away, and paid for having the village-well dug deeper and put in order. He's frightfully good old sort. When Gotobed wants water he has to haul it up as best he can in a bucket. He grumbles a lot about it. The well's a great nuisance, anyway, because it makes the graves on that side very damp, and sometimes in the winter you can't dig them properly. It was worse before Mr Venables had the churchyard drained.'

'Mr Venables seems to do a lot for the parish.'

'He does. Dad used to subscribe to things, of course, but Mr Venables generally starts things, when it's anything to do with the Church. At least, when it's things like drains, is probably Mrs Venables. Why did you want to know about the well?'

'I wanted to know whether it was used or disused. As it's used, of course nobody would think of hiding anything large in it.'

'Oh, you mean the body? No, that wouldn't have done.'

'All the same,' said Wimsey . . . 'Look here! forgive my asking, but, supposing your father hadn't died when he did, what sort of tombstone would he have been likely to put up to your mother? Any idea?'

'None at all. He hated tombstones and wouldn't discuss them, poor darling. It's horrid to think that he's got to have one.'

'Quite. So that for all anybody knew, he might have had a flat stone put down, or one of those things with a marble kerb round and chips in the middle.'

'A thing like a fender? Oh, no! he'd never have done *that*. And certainly not chips. They always reminded him of that fearfully genteel kind of coffee-sugar you get at the sort of places where everything's served on mats and all the wine-glasses are coloured.'

'Ah! but did the murderer know you father's feelings about coffee-sugar and wine-glasses?'

'Sorry – I don't know what you're driving at.'

'My fault; I'm always so incoherent. I mean – when there are such lots of good places for putting bodies – dykes and drains and so on, why cart one at great risk and trouble to a churchyard to plant it where it might quite easily be dug up by a stonemason smoothing away the earth for a fenderful of marble chips? I know the body was a good two feet below ground-level, but I suppose they have to dig down a bit when they set up gravestones. It all seems so odd and so rash. And yet, of course, I can see the fascination of the idea. You'd think a grave was about the last place where anyone would look for a stray body. It was sheer bad luck that it should have had to be opened up again so soon. All the same – when you think of the job of getting it here, and digging away at night in secret – ! But it looks as though it must have been done that way, because of the rope-marks, which show that the man was tied up somewhere first. It must, I mean, all have been deliberate and thought-out beforehand.'

'Then the murderer couldn't have thought about it earlier than New Year's day when Mother died. I mean, he couldn't have counted on having a grave handy.'

'Of course he couldn't; but it may have happened at any time since.'

'Surely not at *any* time. Only within a week or so after Mother died.'

'Why?' asked Wimsey, quickly.

'Why, because old Gotobed would be certain to notice if anybody had been digging his grave about after the earth had been firmed up properly. Don't you think it must have happened quite soon – probably while the wreaths were still on the grave? They stayed there for a week, and then they looked dead and beastly, and I told Gotobed to chuck them away.'

'That's an idea,' said Wimsey. 'I never thought about that – not having had very much to so with the digging of graves. I must ask Gotobed about it. Can you remember how long the snow lay after your mother died?'

'Let me see. It stopped snowing on New Year's Day, and they swept the path up to the south door. But it didn't start to thaw till – wait! I know! It was during the night of the second though it had been getting sort of warmer for two days, and the snow was kind of damp. I remember quite well now. They dug the grave on the third, and everything was all sloshy. And on the day of the funeral it rained like billy-oh! It was dreadful. I don't think I shall ever forget it.'

'And that took all the snow away, of course.'

'Oh, yes.'

'So it would have been easy enough for anybody to get to the grave without leaving footprints. Yes, I suppose you never noticed yourself that the wreaths had been moved, or anything?'

'Oh, no! As a matter of fact, I didn't come here much. Dad was so ill, I had to be with him – and anyway, I didn't think of Mother as being *here*, you know. Lord Peter, I think all this business about graves is hateful, don't you? But I'll tell you who would have noticed anything, and that's Mrs Gates – our housekeeper, you know. She came down every day. She's a perfect ghoul. She kept on trying to talk to me about it, and I wouldn't listen to her. She's quite nice, really, but she ought to live in a Victorian novel, where people wear crêpe and weep into the teacups . . . Oh, dear! there's Uncle Edward looking for me. He looks quite dyspeptic with disapproval. I'm going to introduce you to him, just to embarrass the poor dear . . . Uncle Edward! This is Lord Peter Wimsey. He's been so kind. He says I have a creative imagination, and ought to be a writer.'

'Ah! how do you do?' Mr Edward Thorpe, forty-four, very correct and formal, presented a bland Civil Service front to the impact of Wimsey's personality. 'I believe I have met your brother, the Duke of Denver. I hope he is quite well . . . Quite . . . quite so . . . It is very good of you to take an interest in my niece's young ambitions. All these young women mean to do great things, don't they? But I tell her, authorship is a good stick, but a bad crutch. Very distressing business, this. I am so sorry she should be dragged into it, but of course, in her position, the village people expect her to – ah! – enter into their – ah! – their – um – '

'Amusements?' suggested Wimsey. It came upon him with a shock that Uncle Edward could not be many years older than himself. He felt for him the apprehensive reverence which one feels for a quaint and brittle piece of antiquity.

'For anything which touches them nearly,' said Mr Thorpe. Gallant fellow! Deeply disapproving, he yet sought to defend his niece against criticism. 'But I am taking her away for a little peace and quietness,' he added. 'Her aunt, unhappily, was unable to come to Fenchurch – she suffers sadly from rheumatoid arthritis – but she is looking forward to seeing Hilary at home.'

Wimsey, glanced at Hilary's sullen face, saw rebellion rising; he knew exactly the kind of woman who would have married Uncle Edward.

'In fact,' said Mr Thorpe, 'we are leaving tomorrow. I am so sorry we cannot ask you to dine, but under the circumstances – '

'Not at all,' said Wimsey.

'So I fear it must be a case of Hail and Farewell,' continued Mr Thorpe, firmly. 'Delighted to have met you. I could wish that it were under happier circumstances. Ah – good afternoon. Please remember me to your brother when you see him.'

'Warned off!' said Wimsey, when he had shaken hands with Uncle Edward and bestowed on Hilary Thorpe a grin of understanding sympathy. 'Why? Corrupting the morals of youth? Or showing too much zeal about digging up the family mystery? Is Uncle Edward a dark horse or a plain ass, I wonder? Did he go to his brother's wedding? I must ask Blundell. Where is Blundell? I wonder if he is free tonight?'

He hastened to catch the Superintendent, who had dutifully attended the funeral, and arranged to run over to Leamholt after dinner. Gradually the congregation melted away. Mr Gotobed and his son Dick removed their official 'blacks' and fetched the spades that leaned against the wall near the covered well.

As the earth thudded heavily upon the coffin lid, Wimsey joined the small group that had gathered to discuss the ceremony and read the cards upon the wreaths. He stooped idly to examine an exceptionally handsome and exotic floral tribute of pink and purple hothouse exhibits, wondering who could have gone to so much expense for the unknown victim. With a slight shock he read, on a visiting card: 'With reverent sympathy. Lord Peter Wimsey. St Luke xii. 6.'

'Very appropriate,' said his lordship, identifying the text after a little thought (for he had been carefully brought up). 'Bunter, you are a great man.'

'What I really want to know,' said Lord Peter, as he stretched comfortable legs upon the Superintendent's hearth, 'is the relation between Deacon and Cranton. How did they get into touch? Because a lot seems to turn on that.'

'So it does,' agreed Mr Blundell; 'but the trouble is, we have only got their words to go on, and which was the biggest liar, the Lord God only knows, though Mr Justice Bramhill made a guess. There's no doubt of one thing, and that is that they knew each other in London. Cranton was one of those smooth-spoken, gentlemanly sort of crooks that you meet hanging about the lounge in cheap-smart restaurants – you know the type. He'd been in trouble before, but he gave out he was a reformed character, and made quite a spot of money writing a book. At least, I suppose somebody wrote it for him, but he had his name put on the cover, and all that. There've been several of that sort since the War, but this chap was a smart lad – a bit ahead of his time, really. He was thirty-five in 1914; not educated anything to speak of, but with a kind of natural wit, sharpened by having had to look out for himself, if you take my meaning.'

'Just so. A graduate in the University of the World.'

'That's very well put,' said Mr Blundell, welcoming the cliché as an inspiration. 'Very cleverly put indeed. Yes – that's just what he was. Deacon, now, he was different. A very superior man indeed, he was, and a great reader. In fact, the chaplain down at Maidstone said he was quite a remarkable scholar in his way, with a poetic imagination, whatever that may be exactly. Sir Charles Thorpe took quite a fancy to the fellow, treated him friendly and all that, and gave him the run of the library. Well, these two met in some dance place or other, some time in 1912, when Sir Charles was staying in London. Cranton's story is that some girl that Deacon had picked up – Deacon was always after a skirt – pointed him out to Deacon as the author of this book I was telling you about, and that Deacon made out to be tremendously interested in the book and pumped him a lot about crooks and their doings and the way they worked their little games and all that. He said Deacon made a dead set at him and wouldn't leave him alone, and was always kind of hinting that he was bound to go back to the old life in the end. Deacon said different. He said that what interested him was the literary side of the business, as he called it. Says he thought, if a crook could write a book and make money, why not a butler? According to him, it was Cranton made a dead set at *him*, and started pumping him about what sort of place he'd got, and suggesting if there was anything to be pinched, they should pinch it together and go shares, Deacon working the inside part of the job and Cranton seeing to the rest – finding a fence and settling the terms and so on. I daresay it was six of one and half-a-dozen of the other, if you ask me. A pretty pair they were, and no mistake.'

The Superintendent paused to take a long draught of beer from a pewter mug and then resumed.

'You understand,' he said, 'this was the story they told after we'd got hold of 'em both for the robbery. At first, naturally, they both lied like Ananias and swore they'd never seen each other before in their lives, but when they found what the prosecution had up against them, they changed their tune. But there was this about it. As soon as Cranton realised that the game was up, he adopted this story and stuck to it. In fact, he pleaded guilty at the trial and his one idea seemed to be to get Deacon into trouble and have him gaoled good and hard. He said Deacon had double-crossed him and he was out to get his own back – though whether there was any truth in that, or whether he thought he would get off easy by making himself out to be the poor unfortunate victim of temptation, or whether it was all pure malice, I don't know. The jury had their own idea about it, and so had the judge.

'Well, now. In April 1914 this wedding of Mr Henry Thorpe's came along, and it was pretty well known that Mrs Wilbraham was going to be there with her emerald necklace. There wasn't a thief in London that didn't know all about Mrs Wilbraham. She's a sort of cousin of the Thorpe's, a lot of times removed, and long way back, and she's got a stack of money and the meanness of fifty thousand Scotch Jews rolled into one. She'll be about eighty-six or seven now and getting childish, so I'm told;

but in those days she was just eccentric. Funny old lady, stiff as a ramrod, and always dressed in black silks and satins – very old-fashioned – with jewels and bangles and brooches and God knows what stuck all over her. That was one of her crazes, you understand. And another was, that she didn't believe in insurance and she didn't believe a lot in safes, neither. She had a safe in her town house, naturally and kept her stuff locked up in it, but I don't suppose she'd have done that if the safe hadn't been put in by her husband when he was alive. She was too mean to buy as much as a strong-box for herself, and when she went away on a visit, she preferred to trust to her own wits. Mad as a March hare, she must have been,' said the Superintendent, thoughtfully, 'but there! you'd be surprised what a lot of these funny old ladies there are going about loose in the world. And, of course, nobody ever liked to say anything to her, because she was disgustingly rich and had the full disposal of her own property. The Thorpes were about the only relations she had in the world, so they invited her to Mr Henry's wedding, though it's my belief they all hated the sight of her. If they hadn't have asked her, she'd have taken offence, and – well, there! You can't offend your rich relations, can you?'

Lord Peter thoughtfully refilled his own beer-mug and said, 'Not on my account.'

'Well, then,' pursued the Superintendent, 'here's where Cranton and Deacon tell different tales again. According to Deacon, he got a letter from Cranton as soon as the wedding-day was announced, asking him to come and meet him at Leamholt and discuss some plan for getting hold of the emeralds. According to Cranton, it was Deacon wrote to him. Neither of 'em could produce a scrap of evidence about it, one way or the other, so, there again, you paid your money and you took your choice. But it was proved that they did meet in Leamholt and that Cranton came along the same day to have a look at the house.

'Very good. Now Mrs Wilbraham had a lady's maid, and if it hadn't been for her and Mary Thoday, the whole thing might have come to nothing. You'll remember that Mary Thoday was Mary Deacon then. She was housemaid at the Red House, and she'd got married to Deacon at the end of 1913. Sir Charles was very kind to the young couple. He gave them a nice bedroom to themselves away from the other servants, just off a little back stair that runs up by the butler's pantry, so that it was quite like a little private home for them. The plate was all kept in the pantry, of course, and it was supposed to be Deacon's job to look after it.

'Now, this maid of Mrs Wilbraham's – Elsie Bryant was her name – was a quick, smart sort of girl, full of fun and high spirits, and it so happened that she'd found out what Mrs Wilbraham did with her jewels when she was staying away from home. It seems the old girl wanted to be too clever by half. I think she must have been reading too many detective stories, if you ask me, but anyway, she got it into her head that the best place to keep valuables wasn't a jewel-case or a strong-box or anything of that kind, that would be the first thing a burglar would go for, but some fancy place where nobody would think of looking, and, to cut a long story short, the spot she pitched upon was – if you'll excuse me mentioning it – was underneath one of the bedroom utensils. You may well laugh – so did everybody in court, except the judge, and he happened to get a fit of coughing at the time and his handkerchief was over his face, so nobody could see how he took it. Well, this Elsie, she was a bit inquisitive, as girls are, and one day – not very long before the wedding – she managed to take a peep through a keyhole or something of that kind, and caught the old lady just in the act of putting the stuff away. Naturally, she couldn't keep a thing like that to herself, and when she and her mistress got to Fenchurch – which they did a couple of days before the wedding – the first thing she had to do was to strike up a bosom friendship with Mary Deacon (as she was then) for the express purpose, as it seems to me, of telling her all about it in confidence. And, of course, Mary, being a devoted wife and all that, had to share the joke with her husband. I dare say it's natural. Anyhow, counsel for the defence made a big point of it, and there's no doubt it was that utensil kept Elsie and Mary out of quod. "Gentlemen," he said to the jury, in his speech, "I see you smiling over Mrs Wilbraham's novel idea of a safe-deposit, and I've no doubt you're looking forward to passing the whole story on to your wives when you get home. And, that being so, you can very well enter into the feelings of my client Mary Deacon and her friend, and see how – in the most innocent manner in the world – the secret was disclosed to the one man who might have been expected to keep it quiet." He was a clever lawyer, he was, and had the jury eating out of his hand by the time he'd done with them.

'Now we've got to guess again. There was a telegram sent off to Cranton from Leamholt – no doubt about that, for we traced it. He said it came from Deacon, but Deacon said that if anybody sent it, it must have been Elsie Bryant. She and Deacon were both in Leamholt that afternoon, but we couldn't get the girl at the post office to recognise either of them, and the telegram was written in block letters. To my mind, that points to Deacon, because I doubt if the girl would have thought of such a thing, but needless to say, when the two of them were told to show a specimen of their printing, it wasn't a mite like the writing on the form. Whichever of them it was, either they were pretty clever, or they got somebody else to do it for them.

'You say you've heard already about what happened that night. What you want to know is the stories Cranton and Deacon told about it. Here's where Cranton, to my mind, shows up better than Deacon, unless he was very deep indeed. He told a perfectly consistent tale from start to finish. It was Deacon's plan first and last. Cranton was to come down in a car and be under Mrs Wilbraham's window at the time mentioned in the telegram. Deacon would then throw out the emerald necklace, and Cranton would go straight off with it to London and get it broken up and sold, dividing the loot fifty-fifty with Deacon, less £50 he'd given him on account. Only he said that what came out of the window was only the jewel-case and not the emeralds, and he accused Deacon of taking the stuff himself and rousing the house on purpose to put the blame on him – on Cranton, that is. And, of course, if that was Deacon's plan, it was a very good one. He would get the stuff and the kudos as well.

'The trouble was, of course, that none of this came out till some time after Cranton had been arrested, so that when Deacon was taken and made his first statement to the police, he didn't know what story he'd got to meet. The first account he gave was very straightforward and simple, and the only trouble about it was that it obviously wasn't true. He said he woke up in the night and heard somebody moving about in the garden, and at once he said to his wife; 'I believe there's somebody after the plate. Then, he said, he went downstairs, opened the back door and looked out, in time to see somebody on the terrace under Mrs Wilbraham's window. Then (according to him) he rushed back indoors and upstairs, just quick enough to catch a fellow making off through Mrs Wilbraham's window.'

'Hadn't Mrs Wilbraham locked her door?'

'No. She never did, on principle – afraid of fire, or something. He said he shouted loudly to alarm the house, and then the old lady woke up and saw him at the window. In the meantime the thief had climbed down by the ivy and got away. So he rushed off downstairs and found the footman just coming out of the back door. There was a bit of confusion about the back door part of the story, because Deacon didn't explain, first go-off, how he happened to be in Mrs Wilbraham's bedroom at all. His very first tale, to Sir Charles had been that he went straight out when he heard the noise in the garden, but by the time the police got him, he'd managed to fit the two accounts together, and said that he'd either been too upset at the time to explain himself clearly or else that everybody else had been too upset to understand what he said. Well, that was all right, until they started to unearth all the history of his having met Cranton before, and the telegram and so on. Then Cranton, seeing that the game was up, told his tale in full, and of course, that made it pretty awkward for Deacon. He couldn't deny it altogether, so he now admitted knowing Cranton, but said it was Cranton who had tried to tempt him into stealing the emeralds, while he had been perfectly sea-green incorruptible. As for the telegram, he denied that altogether, and put it on Elsie. And he denied the £50 altogether, and it's a fact that they never traced it to him.

'Of course, they cross-examined him pretty fiercely. They wanted to know, first, why he hadn't warned Sir Charles about Cranton, and secondly, why he'd told a different tale at first. He declared that he thought Cranton had given up all idea of the theft, and he didn't want to frighten anybody; but that when he heard noises in the garden, he guessed what was happening. He also said that afterwards he was afraid to own up to knowing Cranton for fear he should be accused of complicity. But it sounded a pretty thin story, and neither the judge nor the jury believed a word of it. Lord Bramhill spoke very severely to him after the verdict, and said that if it hadn't been his first offence, he'd have given him the heaviest sentence it was in his power to bestow. He called it aggravated larceny of the very worst type, being committed by a servant in a position of trust, in a dwelling-house and his master's dwelling-house at that, and accompanied by the opening of a window, which made it into burglary, and then he had violently resisted arrest, and so forth and so on; and in the end he gave Deacon eight years' penal servitude and told him he was lucky to get off with that. Cranton was an old offender and might have got a lot more, but the judge said he was unwilling to punish him much more heavily than Deacon, and gave him ten years. So that was that. Cranton went to Dartmoor, and served his full time as a perfectly good old lag, without giving much trouble to anybody. Deacon, being a first offender, went to Maidstone, where he set up to be one of those model prisoners – which is a kind you always want to look out for, because they are always up to some mischief or other. After nearly four years – early in 1918, it was – this nice, refined, well-conducted convict made a brutal attack on a warder and broke prison. The warder died, and of course the whole place was scoured for Deacon, without any success. I daresay, what with the War and one thing and another, they hadn't as many men to carry on the job as they ought to have had. Anyhow, they didn't find him, and for two years he enjoyed the reputation of being about the only man who had ever broken prison successfully. Then his bones turned up in one of those holes – deneholes, I think they call them, in a wood in North Kent, so they found it was one up to the prison system after all. He was still in his convict clothes and his skull was smashed in, so he must have tumbled over during the night – probably within a day or two of his escape. And that was the end of *him*.'

'I suppose there's no doubt he was guilty.'

'Not the slightest. He was a liar from beginning to end, and a clumsy liar at that. For one thing, the ivy on the Red House showed clearly enough that nobody had climbed down by it that night – and, in any case, his final story was as full of holes as a sieve. He was a bad lot, and a murderer as well, and the country was well rid of him. As for Cranton, he behaved pretty well for a bit after he came out. Then he got into trouble again for receiving stolen goods, or goods got by false pretences or something, and back he went into quod. He came out again last June, and they kept tabs on him till the beginning of September. Then he disappeared, and they're still looking for him. Last seen in London – but I shouldn't be surprised if we'd seen the last of him today. It's my belief, and always was, that Deacon had the necklace, but what he did with it, I'm damned if I know. Have another spot of beer, my lord. It won't do you any harm.'

'Where do you think Cranton was, then, between September and January?'

'Goodness knows. But if he's the corpse, I should say France, at a guess. He knew all the crooks in London, and if anybody could wangle a forged passport, he could.'

'Have you got a photograph of Cranton?'

'Yes, my lord, I have. It's just come. Like to have a look at it?'

'Rather!'

The Superintendent brought out an official photograph from a bureau which stood, stacked neatly with documents, in a corner of the room. Wimsey studied it carefully.

'When was this taken?'

'About four years ago, my lord, when he went up for his last sentence. That's the last we have.'

'He had no beard then. Had he one in September?'

'No, my lord. But he'd have plenty of time to grow one in four months.'

'Perhaps that's what he went to France for.'

'Very likely indeed, my lord.'

'Yes – well – I can't be dead positive, but I think this is the man I saw on New Year's Day.'

'That's very interesting,' said the Superintendent.

'Have you shown the photograph to any of the people in the village?'

Mr Blundell grinned ruefully.

'I tried it on the Wilderspins this afternoon, but there! Missus said it was him, Ezra said 'twas nothing like him – and a bunch of neighbours agreed heartily with both of them. The only thing is to get a beard faked on to it and try 'em again. There's not one person in a hundred can swear to a likeness between a bearded face and one that's clean-shaven.'

'H'm, too true. Defeat thy favour with an usurped beard . . . And, of course, you couldn't take the body's finger-prints, since he had no hands.'

'No, my lord, and that's a sort of an argument, in a way, for it's being Cranton.'

'If it *is* Cranton, I suppose he came here to look for the necklace, and grew a beard so that he shouldn't be recognised by the people that had seen him in court.'

'That's about it, my lord.'

'And he didn't come earlier simply because he had to let his beard grow. So much for my bright notion that he might have received some message within the last few months. What I can't understand is that stuff about Batty Thomas and Tailor Paul. I've been trying to make out something from the inscriptions on the bells, but I might as well have left it alone. Hear the tolling of the bells, iron bells – though I'd like to know when church bells were ever made of iron – what a world of solemn thought their monody compels! Was Mr Edward Thorpe at his brother's wedding, do you know?'

'Oh, yes, my lord. He was there, and a terrible row he made with Mrs Wilbraham after the theft. It upset poor old Sir Charles very much, Mr Edward as good as told the old lady that it was all her own fault, and he wouldn't hear a word against Deacon. He was certain Elsie Bryant and Cranton had fixed it all up between them. I don't believe myself that Mrs Wilbraham would ever have cut up so rough if it weren't for the things Mr Edward said to her, but she was – is – a damned obstinate old girl, and the more he swore it was Elsie, the more *she* swore it was Deacon. You see, Mr Edward had recommended Deacon to his father – '

'Oh, had he?'

'Why, yes. Mr Edward was working in London at the time – quite a lad, he was, only twenty-three – and hearing that Sir Charles was wanting a butler, he sent Deacon down to see him.

'What did he know about Deacon?'

'Well, only that he did work well and looked smart. Deacon was a waiter in some club that Mr Edward belonged to, and it seems he mentioned that he wanted to try private service, and that's how Mr Edward came to think of him. And, naturally, having recommended the fellow he had to stick up for him. I don't know if you've met Mr Edward Thorpe, but if you have, my lord, you'll know that anything that belongs to him is always perfect. He's never been known to make a mistake, Mr Edward hasn't – and so, you see, he couldn't possibly have made a mistake about Deacon.'

'Oh, yes?' said Wimsey. 'Yes, I've met him. Frightful blithering ass. Handy thing to be, sometimes. Easily cultivated. Five minutes' practice before the glass every day, and you will soon acquire that vacant look so desirable for all rogues, detectives and government officials. However, we will not dwell on Uncle Edward. Let us return to our corpse. Because, Blundell, after all, even if it is Cranton, come to look for emeralds – who killed him, and why?'

'Why,' returned the policeman, 'supposing he found the emeralds all right and somebody lammed him on the head and took them off him. What's wrong with that?'

'Only that he doesn't seem to have been lammed on the head.'

'That's what Dr Baines says; but we don't know that he's right.'

'No – but anyway, the man was killed somehow. Why kill him, when you'd already got him tied up and could take the emeralds without any killing at all?'

'To prevent him squealing. Stop! I know what you're going to say – Cranton wasn't in a position to squeal. But he was, don't you see. He'd already been punished for the theft – they couldn't do anything more to him for that, and he'd only to come and tell us where the stuff was to do himself quite a lot of good. You see his game. He could have done the sweet injured innocence stuff. He'd say: "I always told you Deacon had the stuff, so the minute I could manage it, I went down to Fenchurch to find it, and I did find it – and of course I was going to take it straight along to the police-station like a good boy, when Tom, Dick or Harry came along and took it off me. So I've come and told you all about it, and when you lay your hands on Tom, Dick or Harry and get the goods you'll remember it was me gave you the office." Oh, yes – that's what he could have done, and the only thing we'd have been able to put on him would be failing to report himself, and if he'd put us on to getting the emeralds, he'd be let off light enough, you bet. No! anybody as wanted those emeralds would have to put Cranton where he couldn't tell any tales. That's clear enough. But as to who it was, that's a different thing.'

'But how was this person to know that Cranton knew where the necklace was? And how did he know, if it comes to that? Unless it really was he who had them after all, and he hid them somewhere in Fenchurch instead of taking them to London. It looks to me as though this line of argument was going to make Cranton the black sheep after all.'

'That's true. How'd he come to know? He can't have got the tip from anybody down here, or they'd have got the stuff for themselves, and not waited for him. They've had long enough to do it, goodness knows. But why should Cranton have left the stuff behind him?'

'Hue and cry. Didn't want to be caught with it on him. He may have parked it somewhere when he drove off, meaning to come back and fetch it later. You never know. But the longer I look at these photographs, the more positive I feel that the man I met was Cranton. The official decription agrees, too – colour of eyes and all that. And if the corpse isn't Cranton, what's become of him?'

'There you are,' said Mr Blundell. 'I don't see as we can do much more till we get the reports from London. Except, of course, as regards the burying. We ought to be able to get a line on that. And what you say about Miss Thorpe's notion – I mean, as to the wreaths and that – may have something in it. Will you have a chat with this Mrs Gates, or shall I? I think you'd better tackle Mr Ashton. You've got a good excuse for seeing him, and if I went there officially, it might put somebody on his guard. It's a nuisance, the churchyard being so far from the village. Even the Rectory doesn't overlook it properly, on account of the shrubbery.'

'No doubt that circumstance was in the mind of the murderer. You mustn't quarrel with your bread and butter, Superintendent. No difficulty, no fun.'

'Fun?' said the Superintendent. 'Well, my lord, it's nice to be you. How about Gates?'

'You'd better do Gates. If Miss Thorpe's leaving tomorrow, I can't very well call without looking a nosey parker. And Mr Thorpe doesn't approve of me. I daresay he's issued an order: No information. But *you* can invoke all the terrors of the law.'

'Not much, I can't. Judges' Rules and be damned. But I'll have a try. And then there's – '

'Yes, there's Will Thoday.'

'Ah! . . . but if Miss Thorpe's right, he's out of it. He was laid up in bed from New Year's Eve till the 14th January. I know that for certain. But somebody in his house may have noticed something. It'll be a bit of a job getting anything out of them, though. They've had a taste of the dock once, and they'll get frightened, ten to one, the minute they see me.'

'You needn't worry about that. You can't very well frighten them worse than they're frightened already. Go and read the Burial Service to them and watch their reactions.'

'Oh!' said the Superintendent. 'Religion's a bit out of my line, except on Sundays. All right – I'll take on that part of it. Maybe, if I don't mention that dratted necklace . . . but there, my mind's that full of it, it'll be a mercy if it don't slip out.'

Which shows that policemen, like other people, are at the mercy of their subconscious preoccupations.

THE FOURTH PART

LORD PETER DODGES WITH MR BLUNDELL AND PASSES HIM

'Dodging' is taking a retrograde movement, or moving a place backwards out of the ordinary hunting course. . . . She will be seen to dodge with a bell, and pass a bell alternately throughout her whole work.
TROYTE

'Well now, ma'am,' said Superintendent Blundell.

'Well, officer?' retorted Mrs Gates.

It is said, I do not know with how much reason, that the plain bobby considers 'officer' a more complimentary form of address than 'my man', or even 'constable'; while some people, of the Disraelian school of thought, affirm that an unmerited 'sergeant' is not taken amiss. But when a highly refined lady with a grey glacé gown and a grey glacé eye addresses a full-blown Superintendent in plain clothes as 'officer', the effect is not soothing, and is not meant to be so. At this rate, thought Mr Blundell, he might just as well have sent a uniformed inspector, and had done with it.

'We should be greatly obliged, ma'am,' pursued Mr Blundell, 'for your kind assistance in this little matter.'

'A little matter?' said Mrs Gates. 'Since when have murder and sacrilege been considered little matters in Leamholt? Considering that you have had nothing to do for the last twenty years but run in a few drunken labourers on market day, you seem to take your new responsibilities very coolly. In my opinion, you ought to call in the assistance of Scotland Yard. But I suppose, since being patronised by the aristocracy, you consider yourself quite competent to deal with any description of crime.'

'It does not lie with me, ma'am, to refer anything to Scotland Yard. That is a matter for the Chief Constable.'

'Indeed?' said Mrs Gates, not in the least disconcerted. 'Then why does the Chief Constable not attend to the business himself? I should prefer to deal directly with him.'

The Superintendent explained patiently that the interrogation of witnesses was not, properly speaking, the duty of the Chief Constable.

'And why should I be supposed to be a witness? I know nothing about these disgraceful proceedings.'

'Certainly not, ma'am. But we require a little information about the late Lady Thorpe's grave, and we thought that a lady with your powers of observation would be in a position to assist us.'

'In what way?'

'From information received, ma'am, it appears probable that the outrage may have been committed within a very short period after Lady Thorpe's funeral. I understand that you were a frequent visitor at the graveside after the melancholy event – '

'Indeed? And who told you that?'

'We have received information to that effect, ma'am.'

'Quite so. But from whom?'

'That is the formula we usually employ, ma'am,' said Mr Blundell, with a dim instinct that the mention of Hilary would only make bad worse. 'I take it, that is a fact, is it not?'

'Why should it not be a fact? Even in these days, some respect may be paid to the dead, I trust.'

'Very proper indeed, ma'am. Now can you tell me whether, on any occasion when you visited the grave, the wreaths presented the appearance of having been disturbed, or the earth shifted about, or anything of that kind?'

'Not,' said Mrs Gates, 'unless you refer to the extremely rude and vulgar behaviour of that Mrs Coppins. Considering that she is a Noncomformist, you would think she would have more delicacy than to come into the churchyard at all. And the wreath itself in the worst possible taste. I suppose she was entitled to send one if she liked, considering the great and many favours she had always received from Sir Charles's family. But there was no necessity whatever for anything so large and ostentatious. Pink hot-house lilies in January were entirely out of place. For a person in her position, a simple bunch of chrysanthemums would have been ample to show respect, without going out of her way to draw attention to herself.'

'Just so, ma'am,' said the Superintendent.

'Merely because,' pursued Mrs Gates, 'I am here in a dependent position, that does not mean that I could not have afforded a floral tribute quite as large and expensive as Mrs Coppins. But although Sir Charles and his lady, and Sir Henry and the late Lady Thorpe after them, were always good enough to treat me rather as a friend than a servant, I know what is due to my position, and should never have dreamed of allowing my modest offering to compete in any way with those of the Family.'

'Certainly not, ma'am,' agreed the Superintendent, heartily.

'I don't know what you mean by "Certainly not,"' retorted Mrs Gates. 'The Family themselves would have raised no objection, for I may say that they have always looked on me as one of themselves, and seeing that I have been housekeeper here thirty years, it is scarcely surprising that they should.'

'Very natural indeed, ma'am. I only meant that a lady like yourself would, of course, take the lead in setting an example of good taste and propriety, and so forth. My wife,' added Mr Blundell, lying with great determination and an appearance of the utmost good faith, 'my wife is always accustomed to say to our girls, that for an example of ladylike behaviour, they cannot do better than look up to Mrs Gates of the Red House at Fenchurch. Not' – (for Mrs Gates looked a little offended) – 'that Mrs Blundell would presume to think our Betty and Ann in any way equal to *you*, ma'am, being only one of them in the post office and the other a clerk in Mr Compline's office, but it does young people no harm to look well above themselves, ma'am, and my wife always says that if they will model themselves upon Queen Mary, or – since they cannot have very much opportunity of studying her Gracious Majesty's behaviour – upon Mrs Gates of the Red House, they can't fail to grow up a credit to their parents, ma'am.'

Here Mr Blundell – a convinced Disraelian – coughed. He thought he had done that rather well on the spur of the moment, though, now he came to think of it, 'deportment' would have been a better word than 'behaviour'.

Mrs Gates unbent slightly, and the Superintendent perceived that he would have no further trouble with her. He looked forward to telling his wife and family about this interview. Lord Peter would enjoy it, too. A decent sort of bloke, his lordship, who would enjoy a bit of a joke.

'About the wreath, ma'am,' he ventured to prompt.

'I am telling you about it. I was disgusted – really *disgusted*, officer, when I found that Mrs Coppins had had the *impertinence* to remove my wreath and put her own in its place. There were of course, a great many wreaths at Lady Thorpe's funeral, some of them extremely handsome, and I should have been quite content if my little tribute had been placed on the roof of the hearse, with those of the village people. But Miss Thorpe would not hear of it. Miss Thorpe is always very thoughtful.'

'A very nice young lady,' said Mr Blundell.

'Miss Thorpe is one of the Family,' said Mrs Gates, 'and the Family are always considerate of other people's feelings. True gentlefolk always are. Upstarts are not.'

'That's very true indeed, ma'am,' said the Superintendent, with so much earnestness that a critical listener might almost have supposed the remark to have a personal application.

'My wreath was placed upon the coffin itself,' went on Mrs Gates, 'with the wreaths of the Family. There was Miss Thorpe's wreath, and Sir Henry's, of course, and Mr Edward Thorpe's and Mrs Wilbraham's and mine. There was quite a difficulty to get them all upon the coffin, and I was quite willing that mine should be placed elsewhere, but Miss Thorpe insisted. So Mrs Wilbraham's was set up against the head of the coffin, and Sir Henry's and Miss Thorpe's and Mr Edward's *on* the coffin, and mine was given a position at the foot – which was practically the same thing as being on the coffin itself. And the wreaths from the Servants' Hall and the Women's Institute were on one side of the Rector's wreath and Lord Kenilworth's wreath were on the other side. And the rest of the flowers were placed, naturally, on top of the hearse.'

'Very proper, I'm sure, ma'am.'

'And consequently,' said Mrs Gates, 'after the funeral, when the grave was filled in, Harry Gotobed took particular notice that the Family's wreaths (among which I include mine) were placed in suitable positions on the grave itself. I directed Johnson the chauffeur to attend to this – for it was a very rainy day, and it would not have been considerate to ask one of the maids to go – and he assured me that this was done. I have always found Johnson sober and conscientious in his work and I believe him to be a perfectly truthful man, as such people go. He described to me exactly where he placed the wreaths, and I have no doubt that he carried out his duty properly. And in any case, I interrogated Gotobed the next day, and he told me the same thing.'

'I daresay he did,' thought Mr Blundell, and in his place I'd have done the same. I wouldn't get a fellow into trouble with this old cat, not if I knew it.' But he merely bowed and said nothing.

'You may judge of my surprise,' went on the lady, 'when, on going down the next day after Early Service to see that everything was in order, I found Mrs Coppins's wreath – not at the side, where it should have been – but *on* the grave, as if she were somebody of importance, and *mine* pushed away into an obscure place and actually covered up, so that nobody could see the card at all. I was extremely angry, as you may suppose. Not that I minded in the least where my poor little remembrance was placed, for that can make no difference to anybody, and it is the thought that counts. But I was so much incensed by the woman's insolence – merely because I had felt it necessary to speak to her one day about the way in which her children behaved in the post office. Needless to say, I got nothing from her but impertinence.'

'That was on the 5th of January, then?'

'It was the morning after the funeral. That, as you say, would be Sunday the fifth. I did not accuse the woman without proof. I had spoken to Johnson again, and made careful inquiries of Gotobed, and they were both positive of the position in which the wreaths had been left the night before.'

'Mightn't it have been some of the school-children larking about, ma'am?'

'I could well believe anything of *them*,' said Mrs Gates, 'they are always ill-behaved, and I have frequently had to complain to Miss Snoot about them, but in this case the insult was too pointed. It was quite obviously and definitely aimed at myself, by that vulgar woman. Why a small farmer's wife should give herself such airs, I do not know. When I was a girl, village people knew their place, and kept it.'

'Certainly,' replied Mr Blundell, 'and I'm sure we were all much happier in those days. And so, ma'am you never noticed any disturbance except on that one occasion?'

'And I should think that was quite enough,' replied Mrs Gates. 'I kept a very good look-out after that, and if anything of a similar kind had occurred again, I should have complained to the police.'

'Ah, well,' said the Superintendent, as he rose to go, you see it's come round to us in the end, and I'll have a word with Mrs Coppins, ma'am, and you may be assured it won't happen again. Whew! What an old catamaran!' (this to himself, as he padded down the rather neglected avenue beneath the budding horse-chestnuts). 'I suppose I had better see Mrs Coppins.'

Mrs Coppins was easily found. She was a small, shrewish woman with light hair and eyes which boded temper.

'Oh, well,' she said, 'Mrs Gates did have the cheek to say it was me. As if I'd have touched her mean little wreath with a hayfork. Thinks she's a lady. No real lady would think twice about where her wreath was or where it wasn't. Talking that way to me, as if I was dirt! Why shouldn't we give Lady Thorpe as good a wreath as we could get? Ah! she was a sweet lady – a *real* lady, she was – and her and Sir Henry were that kind to us when we were a bit put about, like, the year we took his farm. Not that we were in any real difficulty – Mr Coppins has always been a careful man. But a question of capital at the right moment, you see, we couldn't just have laid our hands on it at the moment, if it hadn't been for Sir Henry. Naturally, it was all paid back – with the proper interest. Sir Henry said he didn't want interest, but that isn't Mr Coppins's way. Yes – January 5th, it would be – and I'm quite sure none of the children had anything to do with it, for I asked them. Not that my children would go and do such a thing, but you know what children are. And it's quite true that her wreath was where she said it was, last thing on the evening of the funeral, for I saw Harry Gotobed and the chauffeur put it there with my own eyes, and they'll tell you the same.'

They did tell the Superintendent so, at some considerable length; after which, the only remaining possibility seemed to be the school-children. Here, Mr Blundell enlisted the aid of Miss Snoot. Fortunately, Miss Snoot was not only able to reassure him that none of her scholars was in fault ('for

I asked them all very carefully at the time, Superintendent, and they assured me that they had not, and the only one I might be doubtful of is Tommy West and he had a broken arm at the time, through falling off a gate'); she was also able to give valuable and unexpected help as regards the time at which the misdemeanour was committed.

'We had a choir-practice that night, and when it was over – that would be about half-past seven – the rain had cleared up a little, and I thought I would just go and give another little look at dear Lady Thorpe's resting-place; so I went round with my torch, and I quite well remember seeing Mrs Coppins's wreath standing up against the side of the grave next to the church, and thinking what a beautiful one it was and what a pity the rain should spoil it.'

The Superintendent felt pleased. He found it difficult to believe that Mrs Coppins or anybody else had gone out to the churchyard on a dark, wet Saturday night to remove Mrs Gates's wreath. It was surely much more reasonable to suppose that the burying of the corpse had been the disturbing factor, and that brought the time of the crime down to some hour between 7.30 p.m. on the Saturday and, say, 8.30 on the Sunday morning. He thanked Miss Snoot very much and, looking at his watch, decided that he had just about time to go along to Will Thoday's. He was pretty sure to find Mary at home, and, with luck, might catch Will himself when he came home to dinner. His way led him past the churchyard. He drove slowly, and, glancing over the churchyard wall as he went, observed Lord Peter Wimsey, seated in a reflective manner and apparently meditating among the tombs.

''Morning!' cried the Superintendent cheerfully. ''Morning, my lord!'

'Oy,' responded his lordship. 'Come along here a minute. You're just the man I wanted to see.'

Mr Blundell stopped his car at the lych-gate, clambered out, grunting (for he was growing rather stout), and made his way up the path.

Wimsey was sitting on a large, flat tombstone, and in his hands was about the last thing the Superintendent might have expected to see, namely, a large reel of line, to which, in the curious, clumsy-looking but neat and methodical manner of the fisherman, his lordship was affixing a strong cast adorned with three salmon-hooks.

'Hullo!' said Mr Blundell. 'Bit of an optimist, aren't you? Nothing but coarse fishing about here.'

'Very coarse,' said Wimsey. 'Hush! While you were interviewing Mrs Gates, where do you think I was? In the garage, inciting our friend Johnson to theft. From Sir Henry's study. Hist! not a word!'

'A good many years since he went fishing, poor soul,' said Mr Blundell, sympathetically.

'Well, he kept his tackle in good order all the same,' said Wimsey, making a complicated knot and pulling it tight with his teeth. 'Are you busy, or have you got time to look at something?'

'I was going along to Thoday's, but there's no great hurry. And, by the way, I've got a bit of news.'

Wimsey listened to the story of the wreath.

'Sounds all right,' he said. He searched in his pocket, and produced a handful of lead sinkers, some of which he proceeded to affix to his cast.

'What in the world are you thinking of catching with that?' demanded Mr Blundell. 'A whale?'

'Eels,' replied his lordship. He weighed the line in his hand and gravely added another piece of lead.

Mr Blundell, suspecting some kind of mystification, watched him in discreet silence.

'That will do,' said Wimsey, 'unless eels swim deeper than ever plummet sounded. Now come along. I've borrowed the keys of the church from the Rector. He had mislaid them, of course, but they turned up eventually among the Clothing Club accounts.'

He led the way to the cope-chest beneath the tower, and threw it open

'I have been chattin' with our friend Mr Jack Godfrey. Very pleasant fellow. He tells me that a complete set of new ropes was put in last December. One or two were a little dicky, and they didn't want to take any chances over the New Year peal, so they renewed the lot while they were about it. These are the old ones, kept handy in case of sudden catastrophe. Very neatly coiled and stowed. This whopper belongs to Tailor Paul. Lift 'em out carefully – eighty feet or so of rope is apt to be a bit entanglin' if let loose on the world. Batty Thomas. Dimity. Jubilee. John. Jericho. Sabaoth. But where is little Gaude? Where and oh where is she? With her sallie cut short and her rope cut long, where and oh where can she be? No – there's nothing else in the chest but the leather buffets and a few rags and oilcans. No rope for Gaude. *Gaudeamus igitur, juvenes dum sumus.* The mystery of the missing bell-rope. *Et responsum est ab omnibus: Non est inventus – -a* or *-um.'*

The Superintendent scratched his head and gazed vaguely about the church.

'Not in the stove,' said Wimsey. 'My first thought, of course. If the burying was done on Saturday, the stoves would be alight, but they've be banked down for the night, and it would have been awkward if our Mr Gotobed had raked out anything unusual on Sunday morning with his little scraper. As a matter of fact, he tells me that one of the first things he does on Sunday morning is to open the top thingumajig on the stove and take a look inside to see that the flue-pipe is clear. Then he stirs it up a-top, rakes it out at the bottom door and sets it drawing for the day. I don't *think* that was where the rope went. I hope not, anyway, I think the murderer used the rope to carry the body by, and didn't remove it till he got to the graveside. Hence these salmon-hooks.'

'The well?' said Mr Blundell, enlightened.

'The well,' replied Wimsey. 'What shall we do, go fishing?'

'I'm on; we can but try.'

'There's a ladder in the vestry,' said Wimsey. 'Bear a hand. Along this way – out through the vestry door – and here we are. Away, my jolly boys, we're all bound away. Sorry! forget this was consecrated ground. Now then – up with the cover. Half a jiff. We'll sacrifice half a brick to the water-gods. Splosh! – it's not so very deep. If we lay the ladder over the mouth of the well, we shall get a straight pull.'

He extended himself on his stomach, took the reel in his left hand and began to play the line cautiously out over the edge of the ladder, while the Superintendent illuminated the proceedings with a torch.

The air came up cold and dank from the surface of the water. Far below a circle of light reflected the pale sky and the beam of the torch showed hooks and line working steadily downwards. Then a tiny break in the reflection marked the moment when the hook touched the water.

A pause. Then the whirr of the reel as Wimsey rewound the line.

'More water than I thought. Where are those leads? Now then, we'll try again.'

Another pause. Then:

'A bite, Super, a bite! What's the betting it's an old boot? It's not heavy enough to be the rope. Never mind. Up she comes. Ahoy! up she rises! Sorry, I forgot again. Hullo, 'ullo, 'ullo! What's this? Not a boot, but the next thing to it. A hat! Now then, super! Did you measure the head of the corpse? You did? Good! then we shan't need to dig him up again to see if his hat fits. Stand by with the gaff. Got him! Soft felt, rather the worse for wear and water. Mass production. London maker. Exhibit One. Put it aside to dry. Down she goes again . . . *And* up she comes. Another tiddler. Golly! what's this? Looks like a German sausage. No, it isn't. No, it isn't. It's a sallie. Sallie in our alley. She is the darling of my heart. Little Gaude's sallie. Take her up tenderly, lift her with care. Where the sallie is, the rest will be . . . Hoops-a-daisy! . . . I've got it . . . It's caught somewhere . . . No, don't pull too hard, or the hook may come adrift. Ease her. Hold her . . . Damn! . . . Sorry, undamn! I mean, how very provoking, it's got away . . . *now* I've got it . . . Was that the ladder cracking or my breastbone, I wonder? Suprisin'ly sharp edge a ladder has . . . There now, there now! there's your eel – all of a tangle. Catch hold. Hurray!'

'It's not all here,' said the Superintendent, as the slimy mass of rope was hauled over the edge of the well.

'Probably not,' said Wimsey, 'but this is one of the bits that were used to do the tying. He's cut it loose and left the knots in.'

'Yes. Better not touch the knots, my lord. They might tell us something about who tied 'em.'

'Take care of the knots and the noose will take care of itself. Right you are. Here we go again.'

In process of time, the whole length of the rope – as far as they could judge – lay before them in five sections, including the sallie.

'Arms and ankles tied separately. Then body tied up to something or other and the slack cut off. And he removed the sallie because it got in the way of his knots. H'm!' said Mr Blundell. 'Not very expert work, but effective, I dare say. Well, my lord, this is a very interesting discovery of yours. But – it's a bit of a facer, isn't it? Puts rather a different complexion on the crime, eh?'

'You're right, Super. Well, one must face up to things, as the lady said when she went to have her face lifted. Hullo! what the – '

A face, perched in a bodiless sort of way on the churchyard wall, bobbed suddenly out of sight as he turned, and then bobbed up again.

'What the devil do you want, Potty?' demanded the Superintendent.

'Oh, nothing,' replied Potty. 'I don't want nothing. Who're you goin' to hang with that there, mister? That's a rope, that is. They've got eight on 'em hanging up the tower there,' he added, confidentially. 'Rector don't let me go up there no more, because they don't want nobody to know. But Potty Peake knows. One, two, three, four, five, six, seven, eight – all hung up by the neck. Old Paul, he's the biggest – Tailor Paul – but there did ought to be nine tailors by rights. I can count, you see; Potty can count. I've counted 'em over time and again on my fingers. Eight. And one is nine. And one is ten – but I ain't telling you *his* name. Oh, no. He's waiting for the nine tailors – one, two, three, four – '

'Here, you hop it!' cried the Superintendent, exasperated. 'And don't let me catch you hanging round here again.'

'Who's a-hanging? Listen – you tell me, and I'll tell you. There is Number Nine a-coming, and that's a rope to hang him, ain't it, Mister? Nine of 'em, and eight's there already. Potty knows. Potty can say. But he won't. Oh, no! Somebody might be listening.' His face changed to its usual vacant look and he touched his cap.

'Good-day, sir. Good-day, mister. I got to feed the pigs, that's Potty's work. Yes, that's right. They pigs did ought to be fed. 'Morning, sir; 'morning, mister.'

He slouched away across the fields towards a group of outhouses some distance away.

'There!' said Mr Blundell, much vexed. 'He'll go telling everybody about this rope. He's got hanging on the brain, ever since he found his mother hanging in the cowhouse when he was a kid. Over at Little Dykesey, that was, a matter of thirty year back. Well, it can't be helped. I'll get these things taken along to the station, and come back later on for Will Thoday. It'll be past his lunch-time now.'

'It's past mine, too,' said Wimsey, as the clock chimed the quarter past one. 'I shall have to apologise to Mrs Venables.'

'So you see, Mrs Thoday,' said Superintendent Blundell, pleasantly, 'if anybody can help us over this awkward business it's you.'

Mary Thoday shook her head.

'I'm sure I would if I could, Mr Blundell, but there! how can I? It's right enough to say I was up all night with Will. I hardly had my clothes off for a week, but he was that bad, and the night after they laid poor Lady Thorpe to rest, he was just as bad as he could be. It turned to pneumonia, you know, and we didn't think as we should ever pull him through. I'm not likely to forget that night, nor the day neither. Sitting here, listening to old Tailor Paul and wondering if he was going to ring for Will before the night was out.'

'There, there!' said her husband, embarrassed, and sprinkling a great quantity of vinegar on his tinned salmon, 'it's all over now, and there's no call to get talking that way.'

'Of course not,' said the Superintendent. 'Not but what you had a pretty stiff time of it, didn't you, Will? Delirious and all that kind of thing. I'll lay. I know what pneumonia is, for it carried off my old mother-in-law in 1922. It's a very trying thing to nurse, is pneumonia.'

'So 'tis,' agreed Mrs Thoday. 'Very bad he was that night. Kept on trying to get out of his bed and go to church. He thought they was ringing the peal without him, though I kept on telling him that was all rung and finished with New Year's Day. A terrible job I had with him, and nobody to help me, Jim having left us that very morning. Jim was a great help while he was here, but he had to go back to his ship. He stayed as long as he could, but of course he's not his own master.'

'No,' said Mr Blundell. 'Mate on a merchantman, isn't he? How's he getting along? Have you heard from him lately?'

'We had a postcard last week from Hong Kong,' said Mary, 'but he didn't say much. Only that he was well and love to the children. He hasn't sent nothing but postcards this voyage, and he must be terrible busy, for he's such a man for writing letters as a rule.'

'They'll be a bit shorthanded, maybe,' said Will. 'And it's an anxious time for men in his line of business, freights being very scarce and hard to come by. It'll be all this depression, I suppose.'

'Yes, of course. When do you expect him back?'

'Not for I don't know when,' replied Will. The Superintendent looked sharply at him, for he seemed to detect a note almost of satisfaction in his tone. 'Not if trade's decent, that is. You see, his ship don't make regular trips. She follows cargo, as they call it, tramping round from port to port wherever there's anything to be picked up.'

'Ah, yes, of course. What's the name of the ship, again?'

'The *Hannah Brown.* She belongs to Lampson & Blake of Hull. Jim is doing very well, I'm told, and they set great store by him. If anything happened to Captain Woods, they'd give the ship to Jim. Wouldn't they, Will?'

'So he says,' replied Thoday uneasily. 'But it don't do to count on anything these days.'

The contrast between the wife's enthusiasm and the husband's lack of it was so marked, that Mr Blundell drew his own conclusions.

'So Jim's been making trouble between 'em, has he?' was his unspoken comments. 'That explains a lot. But it doesn't help me much. Better change the subject.'

'Then you didn't happen to see anything going on at the church that night?' he said. 'No lights moving about? Nothing of that kind?'

'I didn't move from Will's bedside all night,' replied Mrs Thoday, with a hesitating glance at her husband. 'You see, he was so ill, and if I left him a minute, he'd be throwing the clothes off and trying to get up. When it wasn't the peal that was in his mind, it was the old trouble – you know.'

'The old Wilbraham affair?'

'Yes. He was all muddled up in his head, thinking the – the – that dreadful trial was on and he had to stand by me.'

'That'll *do*!' cried Thoday, suddenly, pushing his plate away so violently that the knife and fork clattered from the plate upon the table. 'I won't have you fretting yourself about that old business no more. All that's dead and buried. If it come up in my mind when I wasn't rightly in my senses, I can't help that. God knows, I'd be the last to put you in mind of it if I'd been able to help myself. You did ought to know that.'

'I'm not blaming you, Will.'

'And I won't have nothing more said about it in my house. What do you want to come worrying her this way, Mr Blundell? She's told you as she don't know a thing about this chap that was buried, and that's all there is to it. What I may have said and done, when I was ill, don't matter a hill of beans.'

'Not a scrap,' admitted the Superintendent, 'and I'm very sorry such an allusion should have come up, I'm sure. Well, I won't keep you any longer. You can't assist me and that's all there is to it. I'm not saying it isn't a disappointment, but a policeman's job's all disappointments, and one must take the rough with the smooth. Now I'll be off and let the youngsters come back to their tea. By the way, what's wrong with the parrot?'

'We've put him in the other room,' said Will, with a scowl. 'He's taken to shrieking fit to split your head.'

'That's the worst of parrots,' said Mr Blundell. 'He's a good talker, though. I've never heard a better.'

He bade them a cheerful good evening and went out. The two Thoday children – who had been banished to the woodshed during the discussion of murders and buryings, unsuited to their sex and tender years – ran down to open the gate for him.

''Evening, Rosie,' said Mr Blundell, who never forgot anybody's name, ''evening, Evvie. Are you being good girls at school?'

But, the voice of Mrs Thoday calling them at that moment to their tea, the Superintendent received but a brief answer to his question.

Mr Ashton was a farmer of the old school. He might have been fifty years old, or sixty or seventy, or any age. He spoke in a series of gruff barks, and held himself so rigidly that if he had swallowed a poker it could only have produced unseemly curves and flexions in his figure. Wimsey, casting a thoughtful eye upon his hands, with their gnarled and chalky joints, concluded, however, that his unbending aspect was due less to austerity than to chronic arthritis. His wife was considerably younger than himself; plump where he was spare, bounce-about where he was stately, merry where he was grave, and talkative where he was monosyllabic. They made his lordship extremely welcome and offered him a glass of home-made cowslip wine.

'It's not many that makes it now,' said Mrs Ashton. 'But it was my mother's recipe, and I say, as long as there's peggles to be got, I'll make my peggle wine. I don't hold by all this nasty stuff you get at the shops. It's good for nothing but to blow out the stomach and give you gas.'

'Ugh!' said Mr Ashton, approvingly.

'I quite agree with you, Mrs Ashton,' said his lordship. 'This is excellent.' And so it was. 'It is another kindness I have to thank you for.' And he expressed his gratitude for the first-aid given to his car the previous January.

'Ugh!' said Mr Ashton. 'Pleased, I'm sure.'

'But I always hear of Mr Ashton engaged in some good work or other,' went on his lordship. 'I believe he was the Good Samaritan who brought poor William Thoday back from Walbeach the day he was taken ill.'

'Ugh!' repeated Mr Ashton. 'Very fortunate we happened to see him. Ugh! Very bad weather for a sick man. Ugh! Dangerous thing, influenza.'

'Dreadful,' said his wife. 'Poor man – he was quite reeling with it as he came out of the Bank. I said to Mr Ashton, "How terrible bad poor Will do look, to be sure! I'm sure he's not fit to go home." And sure enough, we hadn't got but a mile or so out of the town when we saw his car drawn up by the side of the road, and him quite helpless. It was God's mercy he didn't drive into the Drain and kill himself. And with all that money on him, too! Dear, dear! What a terrible loss it would have been. Quite helpless and out of his head he was, counting them notes over and dropping of them all over the place. "Now, Will," I said, "you just put them notes back in your pocket and keep quiet and we'll drive you home. And you've no call to worry about the car," I said, "for we'll stop at Turner's on the way and get him to bring it over next time he comes to Fenchurch. He'll do it gladly, and he can go back on the bus." So he listened to me and we got him into our car and brought him home. And a hard time he had, dear, dear! He was prayed for in church two weeks running.'

'Ugh!' said Mr Ashton.

'What he ever wanted to come out for in such weather I can't think,' went on Mrs Ashton, 'for it wasn't market day, and we wouldn't have been there ourselves, only for Mr Ashton having to see his lawyer about Giddins's lease, and I'm sure if Will had wanted any business done, we'd have been ready to do it for him. Even if it was the Bank, he could have trusted us with it. I should think. It's not as though Mr Ashton couldn't have taken care of two hundred pounds, or two thousand, for that matter. But Will Thoday was always very close about his business.'

'My dear!' said Mr Ashton, 'ugh! It may have been Sir Henry's business. You wouldn't have him anything but close about what's not, rightly speaking, his affair.'

'And since when, Mr Ashton,' demanded his lady, 'has Sir Henry's family banked at the London and East Anglia? Let alone that Sir Henry was always a deal too considerate to send a sick man out to do business for him in a snowstorm? I've told you before that I don't believe that two hundred pounds had anything to do with Sir Henry, and you'll find out one of these days I'm right, as I always am. Aren't I, now?'

'Ugh!' said Mr Ashton. 'You make a lot of talk, Maria, and some of it's bound to be right. Funny if it wasn't, now and again. Ugh! But you've no call to be interfering with Will's money. You leave that to him.'

'That's true enough,' admitted Mrs Ashton, amiably. 'I do let my tongue run on a bit, I'll allow. His lordship must excuse me.'

'Not at all,' said Wimsey. 'In a quiet place like this, if one doesn't talk about one's neighbours, what is there to talk about? And the Thodays are really your near neighbours, aren't they? They're very lucky. I'll be bound, when Will was laid up, you did a good bit of the nursing, Mrs Ashton.'

'Not as much as I'd have liked,' said Mrs Ashton. 'My daughter was took ill at the same time – half the village was down with it, if it comes to that. I managed to run in now and again, of course – 'twouldn't be friendly else – and our girl helped Mary with the cooking. But what with being up half the night – '

This gave Wimsey his opportunity. In a series of tactful inquiries he led the conversation to the matter of lights in the churchyard.

'There, now!' exclaimed Mrs Ashton. 'I always thought as there might be something in that tale as little Rosie Thoday told our Polly. But children do have so many fancies, you never know.'

'Why, what tale was that?' asked Wimsey.

'Ugh! foolish nonsense, foolish nonsense,' said Mr Ashton. 'Ghosts and what not.'

'Oh, *that's* foolish enough, I dare say,' retorted his lady, 'but you know well enough, Luke Ashton, that the child might be telling truth, ghost or no ghost. You see, your lordship, it's this way. My girl Polly – she's sixteen now and going out to service next autumn, for whatever people may say and whatever airs they may give themselves, I will maintain there's nothing like good service to train a girl up to be a good wife, and so I told Mrs Wallace only last week. It's not standing behind a counter all day selling ribbons and bathing-dresses (if they call them dresses, with no legs and no backs and next to no fronts neither) will teach you how to cook a floury potato, let alone the tendency to fallen arches and varicose veins. Which,' added Mrs Ashton triumphantly, 'she couldn't hardly deny, suffering badly from her legs as she do.'

Lord Peter expressed his warm appreciation of Mrs Ashton's point of view and hinted that she had been about to say that Polly –

'Yes, of course. My tongue do run on and no mistake, but Polly's a good girl, though I say it, and Rosie Thoday's always been a pet of Polly's like, ever since she was quite a baby and Polly only seven. Well then, it was a good time ago, now – when would it be, Luke? End of January, maybe, near enough – it was pretty near dark at six o'clock, so it couldn't be much later – well, call it end of January – Polly comes on Rosie and Evvie sitting together under the hedge just outside their place, both of them crying. "Why, Rosie," says Polly, "what's the matter?" And Rosie says, Nothing, now that Polly's come and can they walk with her to the Rectory, because their Dad has a message for Rector. Of course, Polly was willin' enough, but she couldn't understand what they was cryin' about, and then, after a bit – for you know how difficult it is to get children to tell you what they're frightened on – it comes out that they're afraid to go past the churchyard in the dark. Well, Polly being a good girl, tells 'em there's no call to be frighted, the dead being in the arms of our Saviour and not having the power to come out o' their graves not to do no harm to nobody. But that don't comfort Rosie, none the more for that, and in the end Polly makes out that Rosie's seen what she took to be the spirit of Lady Thorpe a-flittin' about her grave. And it seems the night she see her was the night of the funeral.'

'Dear me,' said Wimsey. 'What exactly did she see?'

'No more than a light, by what Polly could make out. That was one of the nights Will Thoday was very bad, and it seems Rosie was up and about helping her mother – for she's a good, handy, child is Rosie – and she looks out o' the window and sees the light just a-rising out of where the grave would be.'

'Did she tell her mother and father?'

'Not then, she didn't. She didn't like to, and I remember well, as a child I was just the same, only with me it was a funny sort of thing that used to groan in the washhouse, which I took to be bears – but as to telling anybody, I'd ha' died first. And so would Rosie, only that night her father wanted her to go a message to the Rectory and she tried everything to get off doing it, and at last he got angry and threatened to take a slipper to her. Not that he meant it, I don't suppose,' said Mrs Ashton, 'for he's a kind man as a rule, but he hadn't hardly got over his illness and he was fratchety, like, as sick people will be. So then Rosie made up her mind to tell him what she seen. Only that made him angrier still, and he said she was to go and no more nonsense, and never to speak about ghosts and such like to him again. If Mary had been there, she'd a-gone, but she was out getting his medicine from Dr Baines, and the bus don't come back till half-past seven and Will wanted the message sent particular, though I forget now what it were. So Polly told Rosie it couldn't have been Lady Thorpe's spirit, for that was at rest, and if it had been, Lady Thorpe wouldn't do harm to a living soul; and she said Rosie must a-seen Harry Gotobed's lantern. But it couldn't well a-been that, for by what the child said it was one o'clock in the morning past that Rosie see the light. Dear me an' all! I'm sure if I'd a-known then what I know now, I'd a-paid more attention to it.'

Superintendent Blundell was not pleased when this conversation was repeated to him.

'Thoday and his wife had better be careful,' he observed.

'They told you the exact truth, you know,' said Wimsey.

'Ah!' said Mr Blundell. 'I don't like witnesses to be so damned particular about exact truth. They get away with it as often as not, and then where are you? Not but what I did think of speaking to Rosie, but her mother called her away double quick – and no wonder! Besides, I don't care, somehow, for pumping kids about their parents. I can't help thinking of my own Betty and Ann.'

If that was not quite the exact truth, there was a good deal of truth in it; for Mr Blundell was a kindly man.

THE FIFTH PART

TAILOR PAUL IS CALLED BEFORE WITH A SINGLE

The canal has been dangerously ignored. Each year of the Republic, our family have reported to the Capital that there were silted channels and weakened dykes in our neighbourhood. My husband and Maida's father have just interviewed the present President. They were received politely, but their conclusion is that nothing will be done.
NORA WALN *The House of Exile*

Lord Peter Wimsey sat in the schoolroom at the Rectory, brooding over a set of underclothing. The schoolroom was, in fact, no longer the schoolroom, and had not been so for nearly twenty years. It had retained its name from the time when the Rector's daughters departed to a real boarding-school. It was now devoted to Parish Business, but a fragrance of long-vanished governesses still hung about it – governesses with straight-fronted corsets and high-necked frocks with bell sleeves, who wore their hair *à la* Pompadour. There was a shelf of battered lesson-books, ranging from *Little Arthur's England* to Hall & Knight's *Algebra,* and a bleached-looking Map of Europe still adorned one wall. Of this room, Lord Peter had been made free, 'except,' as Mrs Venables explained, 'on Clothing Club nights, when I am afraid we shall have to turn you out.'

The vest and pants were spread upon the table, as though the Clothing Club, in retiring, had left some forlorn flotsam and jetsam behind. They had been washed, but there were still faint discolorations upon them, like the shadow of corruption, and here and there the fabric had rotted away, as the garments of mortality will, when the grave has had its way with them. Wafted in through the open window came the funeral scent of jonquils.

Wimsey whistled gently as he examined the underclothes, which had been mended with scrupulous and economical care. It puzzled him that

Cranton, last seen in London in September, should possess a French vest and pants so much worn and so carefully repaired. His shirt and outer garments – now also clean and folded – lay on a chair close at hand. They, too, were well worn, but they were English. Why should Cranton be wearing second-hand French underclothes?

Wimsey knew that it would be hopeless to try tracing the garments through the makers. Underwear of this mark and quality was sold by the hundred thousand in Paris and throughout the provinces. It lay stacked up outside the great linen-drapers' shops, marked 'Occasions,' and thrifty housewives bought it there for cash. There was no laundry-mark; the washing had doubtless been done at home by the housewife herself or the *bonne à tout faire*. Holes here and there had been carefully darned; under the armpits, patches of a different material had been neatly let in; the wrists of the vest, frayed with use, had been oversewn; buttons had been renewed upon the pants. Why not? One must make economies. But they were not garments that anyone would have gone out of his way to purchase, even at a second-hand dealer's. And it would be hard for even the most active man to reduce his clothes to such a state of senility in four months' wear.

Lord Peter thrust his fingers into his hair till the sleek yellow locks stood upright. 'Bless his heart!' thought Mrs Venables, looking in upon him through the window. She had conceived a warm maternal affection for her guest. 'Would you like a glass of milk, or a whisky-and-soda, or a cup of beef-tea?' she suggested, hospitably. Wimsey laughed and thanked her, but declined.

'I hope you won't catch anything from those dreadful old clothes,' said Mrs Venables. 'I'm sure they can't be healthy.'

'Oh, I don't expect to get anything worse than brain-fever,' said Wimsey. 'I mean' – seeing Mrs Venables look concerned – 'I can't quite make out these underthings. Perhaps you can suggest something.' Mrs Venables came in, and he laid his problem before her.

'I'm sure I don't know,' said Mrs Venables, gingerly examining the objects before her. 'I'm afraid I'm not a Sherlock Holmes. I should think the man must have had a very good, hard-working wife, but I can't say more.'

'Yes, but that doesn't explain why he should get his things in France. Especially as everything else is British. Except, of course, the ten-centime piece, and they're common enough in this country.'

Mrs Venables, who had been gardening and was rather hot, sat down to consider the question.

'The only thing I can think of,' she said, 'is that he got his English clothes as a disguise – you said he came here in disguise, didn't you? But, of course, as nobody would see his underneaths, he didn't bother to change them.'

'But that would mean that he came from France.'

'Perhaps he did. Perhaps he was a Frenchman. They often wear beards, don't they?'

'Yes; but the man I met wasn't a Frenchman.'

'But you don't know he was the man you met. He may be somebody quite different.'

'Well, he *may*,' said Wimsey, dubiously.

'He didn't bring any other clothes with him, I suppose?'

'No; not a thing. He was just a tramping out-of-work. Or he said he was. All he brought was an old British trenchcoat, which he took with him, and a toothbrush. He left that behind him. Can we wangle a bit of evidence out of that? Can we say that he must have been murdered because, if he had merely wandered away, he would have taken his toothbrush with him? And if he was the corpse, where is his coat? For the corpse had no coat.'

'I can't imagine,' replied Mrs Venables, 'and that reminds me, do be careful when you go down the bottom of the garden. The rooks are building and they *are* so messy. I should wear a hat if I were you. Or there's always an old umbrella in the summer-house. Did he leave his hat behind too?'

'In a sense he did,' said Wimsey. 'We've found that, in rather a queer place. But it doesn't help us much.'

'Oh!' said Mrs Venables, 'how tiresome it all is. I'm sure you'll wear your brains right out with all these problems. You mustn't overdo yourself. And the butcher says he has some nice calf's liver today; only I don't know if you can eat it. Theodore is very fond of liver-and-bacon, though I always think it's rather rich. And I've been meaning to say, it's very good of that nice manservant of yours to clean the silver and brass so beautifully, but he really shouldn't have troubled. I'm quite used to giving Emily a hand with it. I hope it isn't very dull for him here. I understand he's a great acquisition in the kitchen and extraordinarily good at music-hall imitations. Twice as good as the talkies, Cook says.'

'Is he indeed?' said Wimsey. 'I had no idea of it. But what I don't know about Bunter would fill a book.'

Mrs Venables bustled away, but her remarks remained in Wimsey's mind. He put aside the vest and pants, filled a pipe and wandered down the garden, pursued by Mrs Venables with an ancient and rook-proof linen hat, belonging to the Rector. The hat was considerably too small for him, and the fact that he immediately put it on, with expressions of gratitude, may attest the kind heart which, despite the poet, is frequently found in close alliance with coronets; though the shock to Bunter's system was severe when his master suddenly appeared before him, wearing this grotesque headgear, and told him to get the car out and accompany him on a short journey.

'Very good, my lord,' said Bunter. 'Ahem! there is a fresh breeze, my lord.'

'All the better.'

'Certainly, my lord. If I may venture to say so, the tweed cap or the grey felt would possibly be better suited to the climatic conditions.'

'Eh? Oh! Possibly you are right, Bunter. Pray restore this excellent hat to its proper place, and if you should see Mrs Venables, give her my compliments and say that I found its protection invaluable. And, Bunter, I rely on you to keep a check upon your Don Juan fascination and not strew the threshold of friendship with the wreckage of broken hearts.'

'Very good, my lord.'

On returning with the grey felt, Bunter found the car already out and his lordship in the driving-seat.

'We are going to try a long shot, Bunter, and we will begin with Leamholt.'

'By all means, my lord.'

They sped away up the Fenchurch Road, turned left along the Drain, switchbacked over Frog's Bridge without mishap and ran the twelve or thirteen miles to the little town of Leamholt. It was market day, and the Daimler had to push her way decorously through droves of sheep and pigs and through groups of farmers, who stood carelessly in the middle of the street, disdaining to move till the mudguards brushed their thighs. In the centre of one side of the market-place stood the post office.

'Go in here, Bunter, and ask if there is any letter here for Mr Steven Driver, to be left till called for.'

Lord Peter waited for some time, as one always waits when transacting business in rural post offices, while pigs lurched against his bumpers and bullocks blew down his neck. Presently, Bunter returned, having drawn a blank despite a careful search conducted by three young ladies and the postmaster in person.

'Well, never mind,' said Wimsey. 'Leamholt is the post town, so I thought we ought to give it the first chance. The other possibilities are Holport and Walbeach, on this side of the Drain. Holport is a long way off and rather unlikely. I think we'll try Walbeach. There's a direct road from here – at least, as direct as any fen road ever is . . . I suppose God could have made a sillier animal than a sheep, but it is very certain that He never did . . . Unless it's cows. Hoop, there, hup! hup! get along with you, Jemima!'

Mile after mile the flat road reeled away behind them. Here a windmill, there a solitary farmhouse, there a row of poplars strung along the edge of a reed-grown dyke. Wheat, potatoes, beet, mustard and wheat again, grassland, potatoes, lucerne, wheat, beet and mustard. A long village street with a grey and ancient church tower, a red-brick chapel, and the vicarage set in a little oasis of elm and horse-chestnut, and then once more dyke and windmill, wheat, mustard and grassland. And as they went, the land flattened more and more, if a flatter flatness were possible, and the windmills became more numerous, and on the right hand the silver streak of the Wale River came back into view, broader now, swollen with the water of the Thirty-foot and of Harper's Cut and St Simon's Eau, and winding and spreading here and there, with a remembrance of its ancient leisure. Then, ahead of the great circle of the horizon, a little bunch of spires and roofs and a tall tree or so, and beyond them the thin masts of shipping. And so, by bridge and bridge the travellers came to Walbeach, once a great port, but stranded now far inland with the silting of the marshes and the choking of the Wale outfall; yet with her maritime tradition written unerringly upon her grey stones and timber warehouses, and the long lines of her half-deserted quays.

Here, at the post office in the little square (Lord Peter waited in the pleasant hush that falls on country towns where all days but market days are endless Sabbaths) Bunter was absent for some time, and, when he emerged, did so with a trifle less than his usual sedateness, while his usually colourless face was very slightly flushed about the cheekbones.

'What luck?' inquired Wimsey, genially.

To his surprise, Bunter replied by a hasty gesture enjoining silence and caution. Wimsey waited till he had taken his place in the car and altered his question to:

'What's up?'

'Better move on quickly, my lord,' said Bunter, 'because, while the manoeuvre has been attended with a measure of success, it is possible that I robbed His Majesty's mails by obtaining a postal packet under false pretences.'

Long before this handsome period had thundered to its close, the Daimler was running down a quiet street behind the church.

'What *have* you been doing, Bunter?'

'Well, my lord, I inquired, as instructed, for a letter addressed to Mr Stephen Driver, poste restante, which might have been lying here some time. When the young person inquired how long a time, I replied, according to our previous arrangement, that I had intended to visit Walbeach a few weeks ago, but had been prevented from doing so, and that I understand that an important letter had been forwarded to me at this address under a misapprehension.'

'Very good,' said Wimsey. 'All according to Cocker.'

'The young person, my lord, then opened a species of safe or locker, and searched in it, and after the expiration of a considerable period, turned round with a letter in her hand and inquired what name I had said.'

'Yes? These girls are very bird-witted. It would have been more surprising if she hadn't asked you to repeat the name.'

'Quite so, my lord. I said, as before, that the name was Stephen or Steve Driver, but at the same time I observed from where I was standing that the letter in her hand bore a blue stamp. There was only the counter between us, and, as you are aware, my lord, I am favoured with excellent sight.'

'Let us always be thankful for blessings.'

'I hope I may say that I always am, my lord. On seeing the blue stamp, I added quickly (calling to mind the circumstances of the case) that the letter had been posted in France.'

'Very good, indeed,' said Wimsey, nodding approval.

'The young person, my lord, appeared to be puzzled by this remark. She said, in a doubtful tone, that there was a letter from France, which had been lying in the post office for three weeks, but that it was addressed to another person.'

'Oh, hell!' said Wimsey.

'Yes, my lord; that thought passed through my own mind. I said, "Are you quite sure, that you have not mistaken the handwriting?" I am happy to say, my lord, that the young person – being young, and, no doubt, inexperienced – succumbed to this somewhat elementary strategy. She answered immediately, "Oh, no – it's as plain as print: M. Paul Taylor." At that point – '

'Paul Taylor!' cried Wimsey, in sudden excitement. 'Why, that was the name – '

'Precisely, my lord. As I was about to say, at that point it was necessary to act promptly. I said at once: "Paul Taylor? Why, that is the name of my chauffeur." You will excuse me, my lord, if the remark should appear to carry any disrespectful implication, seeing that you were at that moment in the car and might conceivably be supposed to be the person alluded to, but in the momentary agitation of my spirits, my lord, I was not in a position to think as quickly or as clearly as I should have wished.'

'Bunter,' said his lordship, 'I warn you that I am growing dangerous. Will you say at once, yes or no, did you get that letter?'

'Yes, my lord, I did. I said, of course, that since the letter for my chauffeur was there, I would take it to him, adding some facetious observations to the effect that he must have made a conquest while we were travelling abroad and that he was a great man for the ladies. We were quite merry on the subject, my lord.'

'Oh, were you?'

'Yes, my lord. At the same time, I said it was exceedingly vexatious that my own letter should have gone astray, and I requested the young person to institute another search. She did so, with some reluctance, and in the end I went away, after remarking that the postal system in this country was very undependable and that I should certainly write to *The Times* about it.'

'Excellent. Well, it's all very illegal, either way, but we'll get Blundell to put it right for us – I'd have suggested his doing it himself, but it was such a shot at a venture that I didn't think he'd cotton to it, and I hadn't a devil of a lot of faith in it myself. And anyway' – here Wimsey was seized with an uprush of candour to the lips – 'anyway, it was *my* jolly old idea and I wanted us to have the fun of it ourselves. Now, don't start apologising any more. You were perfectly brilliant in two places and I'm as bucked as hell. What's that. It mayn't be the right letter? Rot! It *is* the right letter. It's damn well got to be the right letter, and we're going to go straight along to the Cat and Fiddle, where the port is remarkable and the claret not to be despised, to celebrate our deed of darkness and derring do.'

Accordingly, within a very short time, Wimsey and his follower found themselves established in a dark old upper room, facing away from the square looking out upon the squat, square church tower, with the rooks wheeling over it and the seagulls swooping and dipping among the gravestones. Wimsey ordered roast lamb and a bottle of the far from despicable claret and was soon in conversation with the waiter, who agreed with him that things were very quiet.

'But not so quiet as they used to be, sir. The men working on the Wash Cut make a difference to the town. Oh, yes, sir – the Cut's nearly finished now, and they say it will be opened in June. It will be a good thing, so they say, and improve the draining very much. It's hoped as it will scour the river out ten feet or more and take the tide up again to the head of the Thirty-foot Drain, like it was in the old days, by what they tell us. Of course, I don't know about that, sir, for it seems that was in Oliver Cromwell's time, and I've only been here twenty year, but that's what the Chief Engineer says. They've brought the Cut to within a mile of the town now, sir, and there's to be a great opening in June, with a gala and a cricket match and sports for the young people, sir. And they say as they're asking the Duke of Denver to come down and open the Cut, but we haven't heard yet if he'll come.'

'He'll come all right,' said Wimsey. 'Dash it, he shall come. He does no work and it will do him good.'

'Indeed, sir?' said the waiter, a little dubiously, not knowing the cause of this certainty, but unwilling to offend. 'Yes, sir, it would be much appreciated in the town if he were to come. Will you take another potato, sir?'

'Yes, please,' said Wimsey. 'I'll make a point of jogging old Denver up to do his duty. We'll all come. Great fun. Denver shall present gold cups to all the winners and I will present silver rabbits to all the losers, and with luck somebody will fall into the river.'

'That,' said the waiter, seriously, 'will be very gratifying.'

Not till the port (Tuke Holdsworth '08) was set upon the table did Wimsey draw the letter from his pocket and gloat upon it. It was addressed in a foreign hand to 'M. Paul Taylor, Poste Restante, Walbeach, Lincolnshire, Angleterre.'

'My family,' observed Lord Peter, 'have frequently accused me of being unrestrained and wanting in self-control. They little know me. Instead of opening this letter at once, I reserve it for Superintendent Blundell. Instead of rushing off at once to Superintendent Blundell, I remain quietly at Walbeach and eat roast mutton. It is true that the good Blundell is not at Leamholt today, so that nothing would be gained if I did rush back, but still – it just shows you. The envelope bears a postmark which is only half-decipherable, but which I make out to be something ending in y in the department of either Marne or Seine-et-Marne – a district endeared to many by the recollection of mud, blood, shell-holes and trench-feet. The envelope is of slightly worse quality than even the majority of French envelopes, and the writing suggests that it was carried out with what may be called a post office pen and ink to match, by a hand unaccustomed to the exercise. The ink and pen mean little, for I have never yet encountered in any part of France a pen and ink with which any normal person could write comfortably. But the handwriting is suggestive, because, owing to the system of State education in that country, though all the French write vilely, it is rare to find one who writes very much more vilely than the rest. The date is obscure, but, since we know the time of arrival, we may guess the time of dispatch. Can we deduce anything further from this envelope?'

'If I may be allowed to say so, my lord, it is possibly a little remarkable that the name and address of the sender does not appear on the back.'

'That is well observed. Yes, Bunter, you may have full marks for that. The French, as you have no doubt often noticed, seldom head their letters with an address as we do in England, though they occasionally write at the foot some such useless indication as "Paris" or "Lyon", without adding the number of the house and the name of the street. They do, however, frequently place these necessary indications on the flap of the envelope, in the hope that they may be thrown into the fire and irrecoverably lost before the letter is answered or even read.'

'It has sometimes occurred to me, my lord, to be surprised at that habit.'

'Not at all, Bunter. It is quite logical. To begin with, it is a fixed idea with the French that the majority of letters tend to be lost in the post. They put no faith in Government departments, and I think they are perfectly right. They hope, however, that if the post office fails to deliver the letter to the addressee, it may, in time, return it to the sender. It seems a forlorn hope, but they are again perfectly right. One must explore every stone and leave no avenue unturned. The Englishman, in his bluff, hearty way, is content that under such circumstances the post office should violate his seals, peruse his correspondence, extract his signature and address from the surrounding verbiage, supply a fresh envelope and return the whole to him under the blushing pseudonym of "Hubbykins" or Dogsbody" for the entertainment of his local postman. But the Frenchman, being decorous, not to say secretive, by nature, thinks it better to preserve his privacy by providing, on the exterior of the missive, all the necessary details for the proper functioning of this transaction. I do not say he is wrong, though I do think it would be better if he wrote the address in both places. But the fact that this particular letter provides no address for the return does perhaps suggest that the sender was not precisely out for publicity. And the devil of it is, Bunter, that ten to one there will be no address on the inside, either. No matter. This is very excellent port. Be good enough to finish the bottle, Bunter, because it would be a pity to waste it and if I have any more I shall be too sleepy to drive.'

They took the direct road back from Walbeach to Fenchurch following the bank of the river.

'If this country had been drained intelligently and all of a piece,' remarked Wimsey, 'by running all the canals into the rivers instead of the rivers into the canals, so as to get a good scour of water, Walbeach might still be a port and the landscape would look rather less like a crazy quilt. But what with seven hundred years of greed and graft and laziness, and perpetual quarrelling between one parish and the next, and the mistaken impression that what suits Holland must suit the Fens, the thing's a mess. It answers the purpose, but it might have been a lot better. Here's the place where we met Cranton – if it was Cranton. By the way, I wonder if that fellow at the sluice saw anything of him. Let's stop and find out. I love dawdling round locks.'

He twisted the car across the bridge and brought it to a standstill close beside the sluice-keeper's cottage. The man came out to see what was wanted and was lured, without difficulty, into a desultory conversation, beginning with the weather and the crops and going on to the Wash Cut, the tides and the river. Before very long, Wimsey was standing on the narrow wooden footbridge that ran across the sluice, gazing down thoughtfully into the green water. The tide was on the ebb and the gates partly open, so that a slow trickle ran through them as the Wale water discharged itself sluggishly towards the sea.

'Very picturesque and pretty,' said Wimsey. 'Do you ever get artists and people along here to paint it?'

The sluice-keeper didn't know as he did.

'Some of those piers would be none the worse for a bit of stone and mortar,' went on Wimsey; 'and the gates look pretty ancient.'

'Ah!' said the sluice-keeper. 'I believe you.' He spat into the river. 'This here sluice has been needing repairs – oh! a matter of twenty year, now. And more.'

Then why don't they do it?'

'Ah!' said the sluice-keeper.

He remained lost in melancholy thought for some minutes, and Wimsey did not interrupt him. Then he spoke, weightily, and with long years of endurance in his voice.

'Nobody knows whose job this here sluice is, seemin'ly. The Fen Drainage Board, now – they say as it did oughter be done by the Wale Conservancy Board. And *they* say the Fen Drainage Board did oughter see to it. And now they've agreed to refer it, like, to the East Level Waterways Commission. But they ain't made their report yet.' He spat again and was silent.

'But,' said Wimsey, 'suppose you got a lot of water up this way, would the gates stand it?'

'Well, they might and they mightn't,' replied the sluicekeeper. 'But we don't get much water up here these days. I have heard tell as it was different in Oliver Cromwell's time, but we don't get a great lot now.'

Wimsey was well used to the continual intrusion of the Lord Protector upon the affairs of the Fen, but he felt it to be a little unjustified in the present case.

'It was the Dutchmen built this sluice, wasn't it?' he said.

'Ah!' agreed the sluice-keeper. 'Yes, that's who built this sluice. To keep the water out. In Oliver Cromwell's time this country was all drowned every winter, so they say. So they built this sluice. But we don't get much water up nowadays.'

'You will, though, when they've finished the New Wash Cut.'

'Ah! So they say. But I don't know. Some says it won't be no different. And some says as it'll drown the land round about Walbeach. All I know, they've spent a sight of money, and where's it coming from? To my mind, things was all very well as they was.'

'Who's responsible for the Wash Cut? The Fen Drainage Board?'

'No, that's the Wale Conservancy, that is.'

'But it must have occurred to them that it might make a difference to this sluice. Why couldn't they do it all at the same time?'

The fenman gazed at Wimsey with a slow pity for his bird-witted feebleness of mind.

'Ain't I telling yew? They don't rightly know if it did oughter be paid for by the Fen Drainage or the Wale Conservancy. Why,' and a note of pride crept into his tone, 'they've had five law actions about this here sluice. Ah! they took one on 'em up to Parliament, they did. Cost a heap of money, so they say.'

'Well, it seems ridiculous,' said Wimsey. 'And with all this unemployment about, too. Do you get many of the unemployed tramping round this way?'

'Times we do, times we don't.'

'I remember meeting a chap along the Bank last time I was down here – on New Year's Day. I thought he looked a bit of a tough nut.'

'Oh, him? Yes. He got took on at Ezra Wilderspin's place, but he soon had enough o' that. Didn't want to do no work. Half on 'em don't. He came along askin' for a cup o' tea, but I told him to get out. It wasn't tea he was lookin' for. Not him. I know his sort.'

'I suppose he'd come from Walbeach.'

'I suppose he had. He said so, anyhow. Said he'd been trying to get work on the Wash Cut.'

'Oh? He told me he was a motor mechanic.'

'Ah!' The sluice-keeper spat once more into the tumbling water. 'They'd say anything.'

'He looked to me as though he'd worked a good bit with his hands. Why shouldn't there be work for men on the Cut? That's what I was saying.'

'Yes, sir, it's easy to say them things. But with plenty o' skilled men out of a job, they don't need to go taking on the like of him. That's where it is, you see.'

'Well,' said Wimsey, 'I still think that the Drainage Board and the Conservancy Board and the Commission between them ought to be able to absorb some of these men and give you a fresh set of gates. However, it's not business, and I'll have to be pushing along.'

'Ah!' said the sluice-keeper. 'New Gates? Ah!'

He remained hanging on the rail and spitting thoughtfully into the water till Wimsey and Bunter had regained the car. Then he came hobbling after them.

'What I says is,' he observed, leaning so earnestly over the door of the Daimler that Wimsey hurriedly drew back his feet, thinking that the usual expectoration was about to follow, 'what I says is, Why don't they refer it to Geneva? Why don't they refer it to Geneva? Then we might get it, same time as they gets disarmament, see?'

'Ha, ha!' said Wimsey, rightly supposing this to be irony. 'Very good! I must tell my friends about that. Good work, what? Why don't they refer it to Geneva? Ha, ha!'

'That's right,' said the sluice-keeper, anxious that the point of the jest should not be lost. 'Why don't they refer it to Geneva? see?'

'Splendid!' said Wimsey. 'I won't forget that. Ha, ha, ha!'

He gently released the clutch. As they moved away, he glanced back and saw the sluice-keeper convulsed by the remembrance of his own wit.

Lord Peter's misgiving's about the letter were duly confirmed. He honourably submitted it, unopened, to Superintendent Blundell, as soon as the latter returned from attendance at the Quarter Sessions where he had been engaged all day. The Superintendent was alarmed by Wimsey's unorthodox raid on the post office, but pleased by his subsequent discretion, and readily allowed him full credit for zeal and intelligence. Together they opened the envelope. The letter, which bore no address, was written on thin paper of the same poor quality as the envelope, and began:

'*Mon cher mari* – '

'Hey!' said Mr Blundell. 'What's that mean? I'm not much of a French scholar, but doesn't *mari* mean "husband"?'

'Yes. "My dear husband", it begins.'

'I never knew that Cranton – dash it!' exclaimed Mr Blundell. 'Where does Cranton come into this? I never heard of his having any wife at all, let alone a French one.'

'We don't know that Cranton comes into it at all. He came to St Paul and asked for a Mr Paul Taylor. This, presumably, is addressed to the Paul Taylor he asked for.'

'But they said Paul Taylor was a bell.'

'Tailor Paul is a bell, but Paul Taylor may be a person.'

'Who is he, then?'

'God knows. Somebody with a wife in France.'

'And the other chap, Batty Something – is he a person?'

'No, he's a bell. But he may be a person, too.'

'They can't both be persons,' said Mr Blundell, 'it's not reasonable. And where is this Paul Taylor, anyhow?'

'Perhaps he was the corpse.'

'Then where's Cranton? They can't,' added the Superintendent, both be the corpse. That's not reasonable, either.'

'Possibly Cranton gave one name to Wilderspin and another to his correspondent.'

'Then what did he mean by asking for Paul Taylor at Fenchurch St Paul?'

'Perhaps that was the bell, after all.'

'See here,' said Mr Blundell, 'it doesn't seem reasonable to me. This Paul Taylor or Tailor Paul can't be both a bell and a person. At least, not both at once. It sounds kind of, well, batty to me.'

'Why bring Batty into it? Batty is a bell. Tailor is a bell. Paul Taylor is a person, because he gets a letter. You can't send letters to a bell. If you did you'd be batty. Oh, bother!'

'Well, I don't understand it,' said Mr Blundell. 'Stephen Driver, he's a person, too. You don't say he's a bell, do you? What I want to know is, which of 'em all is Cranton. If he's been and fixed himself up with a wife in France between this and last September – I mean, between this and January – no, I mean between September and January – I mean – here, dash it all, my lord, let's read the blooming letter. You might read it out in English, would you? My French is a bit off, these days.'

> *'My dear husband'* (Wimsey translated).
> *' – You told me not to write to you, without great urgency, but three months are past and I have no news of you. I am very anxious, asking myself if you have not been taken by the military authorities. You have assured me that they could not now have you shot, the War being over so long ago, but it is known that the English are very strict. Write, I beseech you, a little word to say that you are safe. It begins to be very difficult to do the work of the farm alone, and we have had great trouble with the Spring sowing. Also the red cow is dead. I am obliged to carry the fowls to market myself, because Jean is too exigent, and prices are very low. Little Pierre helps me as much as he can, but he is only nine. Little Marie has had the whooping-cough and the Baby also. I beg your pardon if I am indiscreet to write to you, but I am very much troubled. Pierre and Marie send kisses to their papa.*
>
> *'Your loving wife,*
> *'SUZANNE.'*

Superintendent Blundell listened aghast; then snatched the paper from Wimsey, as though he mistrusted his translation and thought to tear out some better meaning from the words by mere force of staring at them.

'Little Pierre – nine years old – kisses to their papa – and the red cow's dead – t'cha!' He did a little arithmetic on his fingers. 'Nine years ago, Cranton was in gaol.'

'Step-father, perhaps?' suggested Wimsey.

Mr Blundell paid no heed. 'Spring sowing – since when has Cranton turned farmer? And what's all that about military authorities? And the War. Cranton never was in the War. There's something here I can't make head or tail of. See here, my lord – this can't be Cranton. It's silly, that's what it is. It can't be Cranton.'

'It begins to look as if it wasn't,' said Wimsey. 'But I still think it was Cranton I met on New Year's Day.'

'I'd better get on the telephone to London,' said Mr Blundell. 'And then I'll have to be seeing the Chief Constable about this. Whatever it is, it's got to be followed up. Driver's disappeared and we've found a body that looks like his and we've got to do something about it. But France – well, there! How we're to find this Suzanne I don't know, and it'll cost a mint of money.'

THE SIXTH PART

MONSIEUR ROZIER HUNTS THE TREBLE DOWN

The remaining bell . . . does nothing but plain hunting, and is therefore said to be 'in the hunt with the Treble.'
TROYTE *On Change-Ringing*

There are harder jobs in detective work than searching a couple of French departments for a village ending in 'y' containing a farmer's wife whose first name is Suzanne whose children are Pierre, aged nine, Marie and a baby of unknown age and sex, and whose husband is an Englishman. All the villages in Marne district end, indeed, in 'y', and Suzanne, Pierre and Marie are all common names enough, but a foreign husband is rarer. A husband named Paul Taylor would, of course, be easily traced, but both Superintendent Blundell and Lord Peter were pretty sure that 'Paul Taylor' would prove to be an alias.

It was about the middle of May when a report came in from the French police which looked more hopeful than anything previously received. It came through the Sûreté, and originated with M. le commissaire Rozier of Chateau-Thierry in the Department of Marne.

It was so exceedingly promising that even the Chief Constable, who was a worried gentleman with an itch for economy, agreed that it ought to be investigated on the spot.

'But I don't know whom to send,' he grumbled. 'Dashed expensive business, anyhow. And then there's the language. Do you speak French, Blundell?'

The Superintendent grinned sheepishly. 'Well, sir, not to say speak it. I could ask for a spot of grub in an *estaminet*, and maybe swear at the garsong a bit. But examining witnesses – that's a different question.'

'I can't go myself,' said the Chief Constable, sharply and hastily, as though anticipating a suggestion that nobody had had the courage to make. 'Out of the question.' He tapped his fingers on his study table and stared vaguely over the Superintendent's head at the rooks wheeling high over the elms at the end of the garden. 'You've done your best, Blundell, but I think we had better hand the thing over, lock, stock and barrel, to Scotland Yard. Perhaps we ought to have done so earlier.'

Mr Blundell looked chagrined. Lord Peter Wimsey, who had come with him, ostensibly in case help should be needed to translate the commissaire's letter, but actually because he was determined not to be left out of anything, coughed gently.

'If you would entrust the inquiry to me, sir,' he murmured, 'I could pop over in two ticks – at my own expense, of course,' he added, insinuatingly.

'I'm afraid it would be rather irregular,' said the Chief Constable, with the air of one who only needs to be persuaded.

'I'm more reliable than I look, really I am,' said his lordship. 'And my French is my one strong point. Couldn't you swear me in as a special constable or something? with a natty little armlet and a truncheon? Or isn't interrogation part of a special constable's duties?'

'It is not,' said the Chief Constable. 'Still,' he went on, 'still – I suppose I might stretch a point. And I suppose' – he looked hard at Wimsey – 'I suppose you'll go in any case.'

'Nothing to prevent me from making a private tour of the battlefields,' said Wimsey, 'and, of course, if I met one of my old Scotland Yard pals knocking round there, I might join up with him. But I really think that, in these hard times, we ought to consider the public purse, don't you, sir?'

The Chief Constable was thoughtful. He had no real wish to call in Scotland Yard. He had an idea that a Yard man might make himself an officious nuisance. He gave way. Within two days, Wimsey was being cordially received by M. le commissaire Rozier. A gentleman who has *'des relations intimes'* with the Paris Sûreté, and who speaks perfect French, is likely to be well received by country *commissaires de police*. M. Rozier produced a bottle of very excellent wine, entreated his visitor to make himself at home, and embarked upon his story.

'It does not in any way astonish me, milord, to receive an inquiry concerning the husband of Suzanne Legros. It is evident that there is there a formidable mystery. For ten years I have said to myself, 'Aristide Rozier, the day will come when your premonition concerning the so-called Jean Legros will be justified.' I perceive that the day is at hand, and

I congratulate myself upon my foresight.'

'Evidently,' said Wimsey, 'M. le commissaire possesses a penetrating intelligence.'

'To lay the matter clearly before you, I am obliged to go back to the summer of 1918. Milord served in the British Army? Ah! then milord will remember the retreat over the Marne in July. *Quelle histoire sanglante!* On that occasion the retreating armies were swept back across the Marne pell-mell and passed in disorder through the little village of C——y, situated upon the left bank of the river. The village itself, you understand, milord, escaped any violent bombardment, for it was behind the frontline trenches. In that village lived the aged Pierre Legros and his grandaughter Suzanne. The old man was eighty years of age and refused to leave his home. His grandchild, then aged twenty-seven, was a vigorous and industrious girl who, single-handed, kept the farm in a sort of order throughout the years of conflict. Her father, her brother, her affianced husband had all been killed.

'About ten days after the retreat, it was reported that Suzanne Legros and her grandfather had a visitor at the farm. The neighbours had begun to talk, you understand, and the curé, the reverend Abbé Latouche, now in paradise, thought it his duty to inform the authorities here. I myself, you comprehend, was not here at that time; I was in the Army; but my predecessor, M. Dubois, took steps to investigate the matter. He found that there was a sick and wounded man being kept at the farm. He had suffered a severe blow upon the head and various other injuries. Suzanne Legros, and her grandfather, being interrogated, told a singular story.

'She said that, on the second night after the retreat had passed through the village, she went to a distant outhouse and there found this man lying sick and burning with fever, stripped to his underclothing, with his head roughly bandaged. He was dirty and bloodstained and his clothes were bedaubed with mud and weeds as though he had been in the river. She contrived to carry him home with the old man's help, washed his wounds and nursed him as best she might. The farm is a couple of kilometres distant from the village itself, and she had no one whom she could send for assistance. At first, she said, the man had raved in French about the incidents of the battle, but afterwards he had fallen into a heavy stupor, from which she could not rouse him. When seen by the curé and by the commissaire he lay inert, breathing heavily and unconscious.

'She showed the clothing in which she had found him – a vest, underpants, socks, and shirt of regulation army pattern, very much stained and torn. No uniform; no boots, no identity disc; no papers. It seemed evident that he had been in the retreat and had been obliged to swim across the river in making his way back from the front line – this would account for the abandoning of his boots, uniform and kit. He seemed to be a man of some thirty-five or forty years of age, and when first seen by the authorities, he had a dark beard of about a week's growth.'

'Then he had been clean-shaven?'

'It would seem so, milord. A doctor from the town was found to go out and see him, but he could only say that it appeared to be a severe case of injury to the brain from the wound in the head. He advised ameliorative measures. He was only a young student of small experience, incapacitated from the Army by reason of frail health. He has since died.

'It was first supposed that they had only to wait till the man came to himself to learn who he was. But when, after three more weeks of coma, he slowly regained consciousness, it was found that his memory, and, for some time, his speech also, was gone. Gradually, the speech was regained, though for some time he could express himself only in a thick mumbling manner, with many hesitations. It seemed that there were injuries to the locutory centres in the brain. When he was well enough to understand and make himself understood he was, naturally, interrogated. His replies were simply that his mind was a blank. He remembered nothing of his past – but nothing. He did not know his name, or his place of origin; he had no recollection of the war. For him, his life began in the farmhouse at C——y.'

M. Rozier paused impressively, while Wimsey registered amazement.

'Well, milord, you will understand that it was necessary to report the case at once to the Army authorities. He was seen by a number of officers, none of whom could recognise him, and his portrait and measurements were circulated without result. It was thought at first that he might be an Englishman – or even a Boche – and that, you understand, was not agreeable. It was stated, however, that when Suzanne first found him, he had deliriously muttered in French, and the clothes found upon him were undoubtedly French also. Nevertheless, his description was issued to the British Army, again without result, and, when the Armistice was signed, inquiries were extended to Germany. But they knew nothing of him there. Naturally, these inquiries took some time, for the Germans had a revolution, as you know, and everything was much disordered. In the meanwhile, the man had to live somewhere. He was taken to hospital – to several hospitals – and examined by psychologists, but they could make nothing of him. They tried – you understand, milord – to set traps for him. They suddenly shouted words of command at him in English, French and German, thinking that he might display an automatic reaction. But it was to no purpose. He seemed to have forgotten the war.'

'Lucky devil!' said Wimsey, with feeling.

'*Je suis de votre avis.* Nevertheless, a reaction of some kind would have been satisfying. Time passed, and he became no better. They sent him back to us. Now you know, milord, that it is impossible to repatriate a man who has no nationality. No country will receive him. Nobody wanted this unfortunate man except Suzanne Legros and her *bon-papa*. They needed a man to work on the farm and this fellow, though he had lost his memory, had recovered his physical strength and was well suited for manual labour. Moreover, the girl had taken a fancy to him. You know how it is with women. When they have nursed a man, he is to them in a manner their child. Old Pierre Legros asked leave to adopt this man as his son. There were difficulties – *que coulez-vous?* But, *enfin,* since something had to be done with the man, and he was quiet and well behaved and gave no trouble, the consent was obtained. He was adopted under the name of Jean Legros and papers of identity were made out for him. The neighbours began to be accustomed to him. There was a man – a fellow who had thought of marrying Suzanne – who was his enemy and called him *sale Boche* – but Jean knocked him down one evening in the *estaminet* and after that there was no more heard of the word Boche. Then, after a few years it became known that Suzanne had the wish to marry him. The old curé opposed the match – he said it was not known but that the man was married already. But the old curé died. The new one knew little of the circumstances. Besides, Suzanne had already thrown her bonnet over the windmill. Human nature, milord, is human nature. The civil authorities washed their hands of the matter; it was better to regularise the position. So Suzanne Legros wedded this Jean, and their eldest son is now nine years of age. Since that time there has been no trouble – only Jean still remembers nothing of his origin.'

'You said in your letter,' said Wimsey, 'that Jean had now disappeared.'

'Since five months, milord. It is said he is in Belgium, buying pigs, cattle, or I know not what. But he has not written, and his wife is concerned about him. You think you have some information about him?'

'Well,' said Wimsey, 'we have a corpse. And we have a name. But if this Jean Legros has conducted himself in the manner you describe, then the name is not his, though the corpse may be. For the man whose name we have was in prison in 1918 and for some years afterwards.'

'Ah! then you have no further interest in Jean Legros?'

'On the contrary. An interest of the most profound. We still have the corpse.'

'*A la bonne heure,*' said M. Rozier cheerfully. 'A corpse is always something. Have you any photograph? any measurements? any marks of identification?'

'The photograph will assuredly be of little use, since the corpse when found was four months old and the face had been much battered. Moreover, his hands had been removed at the wrists. But we have measurements and two medical reports. From the latest of these, recently received from a London expert, it appears that the scalp bears the mark of an old scar, in addition to those recently inflicted.'

'Aha! that is perhaps some confirmation. He was, then, killed by being beaten on the head, your unknown?'

'No,' said Wimsey. 'All the head injuries were inflicted after death. The expert opinion confirms that of the police-surgeon on this point.'

'He died, then, of what?'

'There is the mystery. There is no sign of fatal wound, or of poison, or of strangling, nor yet of disease. The heart was sound; the intestines show that he had not died of starvation – indeed, he was well nourished, and had eaten a few hours before his death.'

'*Tiens!* an apoplexy, then?'

'It is possible. The brain, you understand, was in a somewhat putrefied condition. It is difficult to say with certainty, though there are certain signs that there had been effusion of blood into the cortex. But you comprehend that. If a thundering apoplexy killed this man, it was not so obliging as to bury him also.'

'Perfectly. You are quite right. Forward, then, to the farm of Jean Legros.'

The farm was a small one, and did not seem to be in too flourishing a state. Broken fences, dilapidated outhouses and ill-weeded fields spoke of straightened means and a lack of the necessary labour. The mistress of the house received them. She was a sturdy, well-muscled woman of some forty-years of age, and carried in her arms a nine-month-old child. At the sight of the commissaire and his attendant gendarme a look of alarm came unmistakably into her eyes. Another moment, and it had given place to that expression of mulish obstinacy which no one can better assume at will than the French peasant.

'M. le commissaire Rozier?'

'Himself, madame. This gentleman is milord Vainsé, who has voyaged from England to make certain inquiries. It is permitted to enter?'

It was permitted, but at the word 'England' the look of alarm had come again; and it was not lost on either of the men.

'Your husband, Mme Legros,' said the commissaire, coming brusquely to the point, 'he is absent from home. Since how long?'

'Since December, M. le commissaire.'

'Where is he?'

'In Belgium.'

'Where, in Belgium?'

'Monsieur, in Dixmude, as I suppose.'

'You suppose? You do not know? You have had no letter from him?'

'No, monsieur.'

'That is strange. What took him to Dixmude?'

'Monsieur, he had taken the notion that his family lived perhaps at Dixmude. You know, without doubt, that he had lost his memory. *Eh, bein!* In December, one day, he said to me "Suzanne, put a record on the gramaphone." I put on the record of a great *diseuse,* reciting *Le Carillon,* a poem of Verhaeren, to music. *C'est un morceau très impressionnant.* At that moment, filled with emotion where the carillons are named turn and turn, my husband cried out: "Dixmude! There is then a town of Dixmude in Belgium?" "But certainly," I replied. He said, "But that name says something to me! I am convinced, Suzanne, that I have a beloved mother residing in Dixmude. I shall not rest till I have gone to Belgium to make inquiries about this dear mother." M. le commissaire, he would listen to nothing. He went away, taking with him our small savings, and since that time I have heard nothing from him.'

'Histoire très touchante,' said the commissaire, drily. 'You have my sympathy, madame. But I cannot understand that your husband should be a Belgian. There were no Belgian troops engaged at the third battle of the Marne.'

'Nevertheless, monsieur, his father may have married a Belgian. He may have Belgian relations.'

'C'est vrai. He left you no address?'

'None, monsieur. He said he would write on his arrival.'

'Ah! And he departed how? By the train?'

'Oh, yes, monsieur.'

'And you have made no inquiries? From the mayor of Dixmude, for example?'

'Monsieur, you understand that I was sufficiently embarrassed. I did not know where to begin with such an inquiry.'

'Nor of us, the police, who exist for that? You did not address yourself to us?'

'M. le commissaire, I did not know – I could not imagine – I told myself every day, "Tomorrow he will write," and I waited, *en enfin –'*

'Et enfin – it did not occur to you to inform yourself. *C'est bien remarquable.* What gave you the idea that your husband was in England?'

'In England, monsieur?'

'In England, madame. You wrote to him under the name of Paul Taylor, did you not?' At the town of Valbesch in the county of Laincollone?' The commissaire excelled himself in the rendering of those barbarian place-names. 'At Valbesch in Laincollone you address yourself to him in the name of Paul Taylor – *voyons, madame, voyons,* and you tell me now that you suppose him to be all the time in Belgium. You will not deny your own handwriting, I suppose? Or the names of your two children? Or the death of the red cow? You do not imagine that you can resurrect the cow?'

'Monsieur – '

'Come, madame. During all these years you have been lying to the police, have you not? You knew very well that your husband was not a Belgian but an Englishman? That his name was actually Paul Taylor? That he had not lost his memory at all? Ah! you think that you can trifle with the police in that way? I assure you, madame, that you will find it a serious matter. You have falsified papers, that is a crime!'

'Monsieur, monsieur – '

'That is your letter?'

'Monsieur, since you have found it, I cannot deny it. But – '

'Good, you admit the letter. Now, what is this about falling into the hands of the military authorities?'

'I do not know, monsieur. My husband – monsieur, I implore you to tell me, where is my husband?'

The commissaire Rozier paused, and glanced at Wimsey, who said:

'Madame, we are greatly afraid that your husband is dead.'

'*Ah, mon dieu! je le savais bien.* If he had been alive he would have written to me.'

'If you will help us by telling the truth about your husband, we may be able to identify him.'

The woman stood looking from one to the other. At last she turned to Wimsey:

'You, milord, you are not laying a trap for me? You are sure that my husband is dead?'

'Come, come,' said the commissaire, 'that makes no difference. You must tell the truth, or it will be the worse for you.'

Wimsey took out the attaché case in which he had brought the underclothing which had been found upon the corpse.

'Madame,' he said, 'we do not know whether the man who wore these is your husband, but on my honour, the man who wore these is dead and they were taken from his body.'

Suzanne Legros turned the garments over, her work-hardened fingers slowly tracing each patch and darn. Then, as though the sight of them had broken down something in her, she dropped into a chair and laid her head on the mended vest and burst out into loud weeping.

'You recognise the garments?' asked the commissaire presently, in a milder tone.

'Yes, they are his, I mended these garments myself. I understand that he is dead?'

'In that case,' said Wimsey, 'you can do him no harm by speaking.'

When Suzanne Legros had recovered herself a little, she made her statement, the commissaire calling in his attendant gendarme to take a shorthand note of it.

'It is true that my husband was not a Frenchman or a Belgian. He was an Englishman. But it is true also that he was wounded in the retreat of 1918. He came to the farm one night. He had lost much blood and was exhausted. Also his nerves were shattered, but it is not true that he had lost his memory. He implored me to help him and to hide him, because he did not want to fight any more. I nursed him till he was well and then we arranged what we should say.'

'It was shameful, madame, to harbour a deserter.'

'I acknowledge it, monsieur, but consider my position. My father was dead, my two brothers killed, and I had no one to help me with the farm. Jean-Marie Picard, that was to have married me, was dead also. There were so few men left in France, and the war had gone on so long. And also, monsieur, I grew to love Jean. And his nerves were greatly deranged. He could not face any more fighting.'

'He should have reported to his unit and applied for sick leave,' said Wimsey.

'But then,' said Suzanne, simply, 'they would have sent him back to England and separated us. And besides, the English are very strict. They might have thought him a coward and shot him.'

'It appears at least, that he made you think so,' said Monsieur Rozier.

'Yes, monsieur. I thought so and he thought so too. So we arranged that he should pretend to have lost his memory, and since his French accent was not good, we decided to make out that his speech was affected by his injury. And I burnt his uniform and papers in the copper.'

'Who invented the story – you or he?'

'He did, monsieur. He was very clever. He thought of everything.'

'And the name also?'

'The name also.'

'And what was his real name?'

She hesitated. 'His papers were burnt, and he never told me anything about himself.'

'You do not know his name. Was it then not Taylor?'

'No, monsieur. He adopted that name when he went back to England.'

'Ah! and what did he go to England for?'

'Monsieur, we were very poor, and Jean said that he had property in England which could be disposed of for a good sum, if only he could get hold of it without making himself known. For, you see, if he were to reveal himself he would be shot as a deserter.'

'But there was a general amnesty for deserters after the war.'

'Not in England, monsieur.'

'He told you that?' said Wimsey.

'Yes, milord. So it was important that nobody should know him when he went to fetch the property. Also there were difficulties which he did not explain to me, about selling the goods – I do not know what they were – and for that he had to have the help of a friend. So he wrote to this friend and presently he received a reply.'

'Have you that letter?'

'No, monsieur. He burnt it without showing it to me. This friend asked him for something – I did not quite understand that, but it was some sort of guarantee, I think. Jean shut himself up in his room for several hours the next day to compose his answer to the letter, but he did not show that to me, either. Then the friend wrote back and said he could help him, but it would not do for Jean's name to appear – neither his own name nor the name of Legros, you understand. So he chose the name of Paul Taylor, and he laughed very much when the idea came to him to call himself so. Then the friend sent him papers made out in the name of Paul Taylor, British subject. I saw those. There was a passport with photograph; it was not very much like my husband, but he said they would not pay great attention to it. The beard was like his.'

'Had your husband a beard when you first knew him?'

'No, he was clean-shaven, like all the English. But of course, he grew his beard when he was ill. It altered him very much, because he had a small chin, and with the beard it looked bigger. Jean took with him no luggage: he said he would buy clothes in England, because then he would again look like an Englishman.'

'And you know nothing of the nature of this property in England?'

'Nothing whatever, monsieur.'

'Was it land, securities, valuables?'

'I know nothing about it, monsieur. I asked Jean often, but he would never tell me.'

'And you expect us to believe you do not know your husband's real name?'

Again the hesitation. Then: 'No, monsieur, I do not know. It is true that I saw it upon his papers, but I burnt those and I do not now remember it. But I think it began with a C, and I should know it if I saw it again.'

'Was it Cranton?' asked Wimsey.'

'No, I do not think it was that, but I cannot say what it was. As soon as he was able to speak at all, he told me to give him his papers, and I asked him then what his name was, because I could not pronounce it – it was English and difficult – and he said that he would not tell me his name then, but I could call him what I liked. So I called him Jean, which was the name of my *fiancé*, who was killed.'

'I see,' said Wimsey. He hunted through his pocket-book and laid the official photograph of Cranton before her. 'Is that your husband as you first knew him?'

'No, milord. That is not my husband. It is not in the least like him.' Her face darkened. 'You have deceived me. He is not dead and I have betrayed him.'

'He is dead,' said Wimsey. 'It is this man who is alive.'

'And now,' said Wimsey, 'we are no nearer than before to a solution.'

'*Attendez*, milord. She has not yet told all she knows. She does not trust us, and she is concealing the name. Only wait, and we shall find the means to make her speak. She still thinks that her husband may be alive. But we shall convince her. We shall have this man traced. It is some months old, the trail, but it will not be too difficult. That he started from here by train to go to Belgium I already know, by my inquiries. When he sailed for England, it was doubtless from Ostend – unless, *voyons,* milord, what resources could this man command?'

'How can I tell? But we believe that this mysterious property had to do with an emerald necklace of many thousands of pounds value.'

'*Ah, voilà!* It would be worth while to spend money, then. But this man, you say he is not the man you thought. If that other man was the thief how does this one come into it?'

'There is the difficulty. But look! There were two men concerned in the theft; one, a London *cambrioleur,* the other, a domestic servant. We do not know which of them had the jewels; it is a long story. But you heard that this Jean Legros wrote to a friend in England, and that friend may have been Cranton, the burglar. Now Legros cannot have been the servant who stole the jewels in the first place, for that man is dead. But before dying, the thief may have communicated to Legros the secret of where the emeralds are hidden, and also the name of Cranton. Legros then writes to Cranton and proposes a partnership to find the jewels. Cranton does not believe, and asks for proof that Legros really knows something. Legros sends a letter which satisfies Cranton, and Cranton in turn procures the necessary papers for Legros. Then Legros goes to England and meets Cranton. Together they go and discover the jewels. Then Cranton kills his confederate, so as to have all for himself. How is that, monsieur? For Cranton also has disappeared.'

'It is very possible, milord. In that case, both the jewels and the murderer are in England – or wherever this Cranton may be. You think, then, that the other dead man the servant, communicated the hiding-place of the necklace – to whom?'

'Perhaps to some fellow-prisoner who was only in gaol for a short term.'

'And why should he do that?'

'In order that this fellow-prisoner should provide him with a means of escape. And the proof is that the servant did break prison and escape, and afterwards his dead body was found in a pit many miles from the prison.'

'Aha! the affair begins to outline itself. And the servant – how did he come to be found dead? Eh?'

'He is supposed to have fallen over the edge of the pit in the dark. But I begin to think that he was killed by Legros.'

'Milord, our thoughts chime together. Because, *voyez-vous,* this story of desertion and military authorities will not hold water. There is more than a desertion behind this change of name and this fear of the British police. But if the man was an old gaol-bird, and had committed a murder into the bargain, the thing understands itself. Twice he changes his name, so that he shall not be traced even to France, because he, Legros, under his English name, had enlisted after his release from prison and the records of your Army might reveal him. Only, if he was in the Army, it is strange that he should have found the leisure to plan a prison-breaking for his comrade and commit murder. No, there are still difficulties, but the outline of the plot is clear and will develop itself more clearly still as we proceed. In the meanwhile, I will undertake inquiries here and in Belgium. I think, milord, we must confine ourselves to the ordinary passenger-routes, or even to the ports. A motor-boat might well make the journey to the coast of Laincollone. Your police, also, will make inquiries on their part. And when we have shown the progress of Legros from the front door of his house to his grave in England, then, I think, Mme Suzanne will speak a little more. And how, milord, I beg you will honour us by sharing our dinner tonight. My wife is an excellent cook, if you will condescend to a *cuisine bourgeoise* garnished with a tolerable *vin de Bourgogne*. Monsieur Delavigne of the Sûreté informs me that you have the reputation of a *gourmet,* and it is only with a certain diffidence that I make the suggestion, but it would give Mme Rozier unheard-of delight if you would give her the pleasure of making your acquaintance.'

'Monsieur,' said Lord Peter, 'I am infinitely obliged to you both.'

THE SEVENTH PART

PLAIN HUNTING

First, Lucas Mortis; then Terra Tenebrosa; next, Tartarus, after that, Terra Oblivionis; then Herebus; then Barathrum; then Gehenna; and then Stagnum Ignis.

SHERIDAN LEFANU: *Wylder's Hand*

'Well,' said Superintendent Blundell, 'if that's how it is, we've got to find Cranton. But it's a funny thing to me. From what they tell me, I wouldn't have thought Cranton was the man for that sort of job. He's never been suspected of killing anyone, and he never looked to me like a killer. And you know, my lord, that it's very rare for one of them sort of smart burglars to go all off the rails and take to violence. What I mean, it isn't in them, as a rule, if you get my meaning. It's true he went for Deacon in the dock but that was more of a scrimmage, as you might say, and I don't think he meant much harm. Supposing as it was the other chap that killed Cranton? He might have changed clothes with him to prevent identification.'

'So he might. But what becomes of that old scar on the head? That seems to fit in with the body being this fellow they call Jean Legros. Unless Cranton had a scar too.'

'He'd no scar up to last September,' said the Superintendent, thoughtfully. 'No, I reckon you're right, and that won't work. Some of the measurements seem a bit different, too – though, of course, it's not easy to be as accurate as all that when you're comparing a live man with a four-months-old corpse. And there were so many teeth gone and busted from the corpse that we've not got much out of that, either. No, we've got to find Cranton. If he's alive, he's lying uncommon low. Looks as though he'd done something pretty bad – I give you that.'

The conversation took place in the churchyard, where Mr Blundell had been undertaking an exhaustive search for unspecified clues. The Superintendent thoughtfully decapitated a nettle, and resumed:

'Then there's that chap Will Thoday. I can't make him out at all. I'll swear he knows something – but what *can* he know? It's as certain as anything can be that he was sick in bed when it all happened. He sticks to that, and says he knows nothing. What can you do with a man who says he knows nothing? Why, nothing. And as for his wife, *she* couldn't have tied a man up and buried him. She's not a powerful sort of woman by any means. And I've got hold of the children. It went against me to do it, but I did it all the same. And they say their Mother and Dad were both in the house all night. There's one other person might know something, and that's James Thoday. Look here, my lord, here's a queer thing. James Thoday left Fenchurch St Paul on January 4th, early in the morning, to join his ship. He was seen to go, all right – the station-master saw him. But he never got to Hull that day. I've been on to Lampson & Blake, and they say they had a wire from him to say he couldn't get back in time, but would arrive on the Sunday night – which he did. Had some story of being taken suddenly ill – and they say he looked ill enough when he did arrive. I've told them to get in touch with him as quick as they can.'

'Where was the wire sent from?'

'London. From a post office near Liverpool Street. About the time when the train Jim Thoday took at Dykesey would get up there. Looks as though he'd been taken queer on the way up.'

'He might have picked up influenza from his brother.'

'So he might. Still, he was fit to sail the next day, and it looks funny, don't you think? He'd have had plenty of time to go up to London and come down here again. He wouldn't come to Dykesey, of course, but he might have come part of the way by train and done the rest by car or motor-bike or what-not.'

Wimsey whistled. 'You think he was in with Will over the thing. Yes, I see. Will is in a conspiracy with Legros to get the emeralds – is that it? And he gets flu and can't do the job himself, so he arranges with Brother Jim to do it for him. Then Jim meets Legros and kills him and buries him and vamooses with the emeralds to Hong Kong. Well, that would explain one thing, and that is, why those infernal stones haven't been put on the European market. He could easily get rid of them over in the East. But look here, Super – how did Will Thoday get into touch with Legros in the first place? It was easy when we put it all on Cranton, because he could have got the papers and things made out for Legros by one of his pals in Town. But you can't imagine that Thoday produced forged papers and provided Legros with his passage facilities and all that. How would a fellow like that know how to set about it?'

Mr Blundell shook his head.

'But there's that two hundred pounds,' he said.

'So there is, but that was after Legros had started.'

'And when Legros was killed, the money was returned to the bank.'

'Was it?'

'Oh, yes. I had a word with Thoday. He made no difficulties. He said he had an idea of purchasing a bit of land and starting to farm again on his own, but that, after his illness, he gave up the idea, thinking that for some time he wouldn't be strong enough. He gave me permission to go over his bank account. It was all in order – no suspicious withdrawals of money up to that £200 on December 31st, and that was paid in again in January, as soon as he was able to get about. And it's true about the land, too. He did think of buying it. All the same, £200 all in one-pound notes – '

The Superintendent broke off, and made a sudden dive behind a tall tombstone. There was a squeak and a scuffle. Mr Blundell emerged, rather flustered. His large hand held Potty Peake's coat-collar in a firm grip.

'Now, you clear off,' said the Superintendent, giving his captive a rough, but not unkindly, shake. 'You'll get yourself in trouble, my lad, hanging round the churchyard and listening to private conversations. See?'

'Ar!' said Potty, 'you needn't choke a fellow. You needn't choke poor Potty. If you knew what Potty knows – '

'What do you know?'

Potty's eyes gleamed cunningly.

'I seen him – Number Nine – I seen him a-talking to Will in the church. But the tailors was too much for him. Him with the rope – he got him, and he'll get you too. Potty knows. Potty ain't lived all these years, in and out of the church, for nothing.'

'Who was talking to Will in the church?'

'Why, him!' Potty jerked his head towards the Thorpe grave. 'Him they found over there. The black-bearded man. There's eight in the belfry and one in the grave. That makes nine. You think Potty can't count, but he can. But him as calls the peal – you won't get him, oh, no!'

'See here,' said Wimsey, 'you're a clever fellow, Potty. When did you see Will Thoday talking to the black-bearded man? See if you can count that far.'

Potty Peake grinned at him. 'Potty can count all right,' he said, with great satisfaction. 'Oh, yes.' He began an elaborate calculation on his fingers. 'Ah! it was Monday night, that's when it was. There was cold pork and beans for dinner – that's good, cold pork and beans. Ah! Parson he preached about thankfulness. Be thankful for Christmas, he says. There was roast fowl, Christmas Day, and boiled pork and greens Sunday and be thankful, that's what Parson says. So Potty slips out at night, for to be thankful again. You got to go to church to be thankful proper, ain't you, sir? And there was the church door standing open. So Potty creeps in, careful-like, see? And there's a light in the vestry. Potty was frightened. There's things hanging in the vestry. Ah! So Potty hides behind ole Batty Thomas, and then Will Thoday comes in, and Potty hears them talking in the vestry. "Money", Will says. 'Tis a great wickedness, is money. And then Will Thoday he cries out – he fetched a rope from the chest and – ah! Potty's afraid. He thinks about hanging. Potty don't want to see no one hanged. Potty runs away. He looks in at the vestry window, and there's the black-bearded man a-laying on the floor, and Will a-standing over him with the rope. Ah, dear! oh, dear! Potty don't like ropes. Potty's allus a-dreamin' of ropes. One, two, three, four, five, six, seven, eight – and this one's nine. Potty seen him a-hangin' there. Ooh!'

'I think you was a-dreaming all the time,' said the Superintendent. 'There's nobody hanged that I know of.'

'I see him a-hanging,' persisted Potty. 'Terrible it were. But don't you pay no attention. 'Tis only one o' poor Potty's dreams.' His face changed. 'You lemme go, mister, I gotter feed my pigs.'

'Bless my heart,' said Superintendent Blundell.' 'And what do you suppose we're to make of that?'

Wimsey shook his head.

'I think he saw something – or how did he know that the rope was gone from the cope-chest? But as for hanging, no! He's crazed about hanging. Got a hanging complex, or whatever they call it. The man wasn't hanged. Which Monday night do you suppose Potty meant?'

'Can't be January 6th, can it?' said the Superintendent. 'The body was buried on the 4th, as far as we can make out. And it can't very well be December 30th, because Legros only got here on January 1st – if that was Legros you saw. And besides, I can't make out whether he means Sunday or Monday, with his boiled pork!'

'I can,' said Wimsey. 'He had boiled pork and greens on Sunday, and Parson told him to be thankful and so he was. And on Monday, he had the pork cold with beans – probably the tinned variety if I know the modern countrywoman – and he felt thankful again. So he went down to the church to be thankful in the proper place. It would be some time in the evening, as there was a light in the vestry.'

'That's right. Potty lives with an aunt of his – a decent old soul, but not very sharp. He's always slipping out at night. They're cunning as the devil, these naturals. But which evening was it?'

'The day after Parson had preached on thankfulness,' said Wimsey. 'Thankfulness for Christmas. That looks like December 30th. Why not? You don't know that Legros didn't get here before January 1st. That's when Cranton got here.'

'But I thought we'd washed Cranton out of it,' objected Mr Blundell, 'and put Will Thoday in his place.'

'Then who was it I met on the road over the bridge?'

'That must have been Legros.'

'Well, it may be – thought I still think it was Cranton, or his twin brother. But if I met Legros on January 1st, he can't have been hanged by Will Thoday on December 30th. And in any case, he wasn't hanged.

And,' said Wimsey, triumphantly, 'we still don't know how he did die!'

The Superintendent groaned.

'What I say is, we've got to find Cranton, somehow. And as for December 30th, how are you going to be sure of that, anyway?'

'I shall ask the Rector which day he preached about thankfulness. Or Mrs Venables. She's more likely to know.'

'And I'd better see Thoday again. Not that I believe a single word Potty says. And how about Jim Thoday? How does he come into it now?'

'I don't know. But one thing I'm sure of, Super. It was no sailor put those knots into Gaude's rope. I'll take my oath on that.'

'Oh, well!' said the Superintendent.

Wimsey went back to the house and found the Rector in his study, busily writing out a touch of Treble Bob Major.

'One moment, my dear boy,' he said, pushing the tobacco-jar towards his guest, 'one moment. I am just pricking this little touch to show Wally Pratt how to do it. He has got himself "imbrangled" as they call it – fine old English word, that. Now what has the foolish lad done here? The ninth lead should bring Queen's change – let me see, let me see – 51732468, 15734286 – that's the first thirds and fourths all right – 51372468, 15374286 – and that's the first fourths and thirds – 13547826 – ah! here is the trouble! The eighth should be at home. What has happened? – To be sure! What a beetleheaded cuckoo I am! He has forgotten to make the bob. She can't come home till she's called.' He ran a red-ink line down the page and started to write figures furiously. 'There! 51372468, 15374286 – and *now* she comes home like a bird! – 13572468. That's better. Now it should come round at the second repeat. I will just check it. Second to fifth, third to second – yes, yes – that brings 15263748, with Tittums at the end of the second course, and repeated once again brings it round. I will just jot down the lead-ends for him to check it by. Second to third, third to fifth, fourth to second, fifth to seventh, sixth to fourth, seventh to eighth, eighth to sixth for the plain lead. Then the bob. Plain, bob, bob, three plain and a bob. I cannot understand why red ink should distribute itself so lavishly over one's person. There! I have a large smear on my cuff! Call her in the middle, in and out and home. Repeat twice. A lovely little touch.' He pushed aside several sheets of paper covered with figures, and transferred a quantity of red ink from his fingers to his trouser-leg. 'And now, how are you getting along? Is there anything I can do to help you?'

'Yes, padre. You can tell me on which Sunday this winter you preached about thankfulness.'

'Thankfulness? Well, now, that's rather a favourite subject of mine. Do you know, I find people very much disposed to grumble – I do indeed –

and when you come to think of it, they might all be very much worse off. Even the farmers. As I said to them last Harvest Festival – oh! you were asking about my Thankfulness sermon – well, I nearly always preach about it at Harvest Festival . . . Not so long ago as that? . . . Let me think. My memory is getting very unreliable, I fear . . .' He made a dive for the door. 'Agnes, my dear! Can you spare us a moment? . . . My wife is sure to remember . . . My dear, I am so sorry to interrupt you, but can you recollect when I last preached about Thankfulness? I touched on the subject in my Tithe sermon, I remember – would you be thinking of that? Not that we have had any trouble about tithe in this parish. Our farmers are very sensible. A man from St Peter came to talk to me about it, but I pointed out to him that the 1918 adjustment was made in the farmer's interests and that if they thought they had reason to complain of the 1925 Act, then they should see about getting a fresh adjustment made. But the law, I said, is the law. Oh, on the matter of tithe I assure you I am adamant. Adamant.'

'Yes, Theodore,' said Mrs Venables, with rather a wry smile, 'but if you didn't so often advance people money to pay the tithe with, they mightn't be as reasonable as they are.'

'That's different,' said the Rector, hurriedly, 'quite different. It's a matter of principle, and any small personal loan has nothing to do with it. Even the best of women don't always grasp the importance of a legal principle, do they, Lord Peter? My sermon dealt with the principle. The text was: "Render unto Caesar". Though whether Queen Anne's Bounty is to be regarded as Caesar or as God – and sometimes, I admit, I feel that it is a little unfortunate that the Church should appear to be on Caesar's side, and that disestablishment and disendowment – '

'A Caesarian operation is indicated, so to speak?' suggested Wimsey.

'A – ? Oh, yes! Very good,' said the Rector. 'My dear, that is very good, don't you think? I must tell the Bishop – no, perhaps not. He is just a leetle bit strait-laced. But it is true – if only one could separate the two things, the temporal and the spiritual – but the question I ask myself is always, the churches themselves – the buildings – our own beautiful church – what would become of it in such a case?'

'My dear,' said Mrs Venables, 'Lord Peter was asking about your sermons on Thankfulness. Didn't you preach one on the Sunday after Christmas? About Thankfulness for the Christmas message? Surely you remember. The text was taken from the Epistle for the day; "Thou art no more a servant, but a son." It was about how happy we ought to be as God's children and about making a habit of saying "Thank-you, Father" for all the pleasant things of life, and being as pleasant-tempered as we should wish our own children to be. I remember it so well, because Jackie and Fred Holliday got quarrelling in church over those prayer-books we gave them and had to be sent out.'

'Quite right, my dear. You always remember everything. That was it, Lord Peter. The Sunday after Christmas. It comes back to me very clearly now. Old Mrs Giddings stopped me in the porch afterwards to complain that there weren't enough plums in her Christmas pudding.'

'Mrs Giddings is an ungrateful old wretch,' said his wife.

'Then the next day *was* the 30th December,' said Wimsey. 'Thanks, padre, that's very helpful. Do you recollect Will Thoday coming round to see you on the Monday evening, by any chance?'

The Rector looked helplessly at his wife, who replied readily enough:

'Of course he did, Theodore. He came to ask you something about the New Year's peal. Don't you remember saying how queer and ill he looked? Of course, he must have been working up for that attack of flu, poor man. He came late – about 9 o'clock – and you said you couldn't understand why he shouldn't have waited till the morning.'

'True, true,' said the Rector. 'Yes, Thoday came round to me on the Monday night. I hope you are not – well! I mustn't ask indiscreet questions, must I?'

'Not when I don't know the answers,' said Wimsey, with a smile and a shake of the head. 'About Potty Peake, now. Just how potty is he? Can one place any sort of reliance on his account of anything?'

'Well,' said Mrs Venables, 'sometimes one can and sometimes one can't. He get mixed up, you know. He's quite truthful, as far as his understanding goes, but he gets fancies and then tells them as if they were facts. You can't trust anything he says about ropes or hanging – that's his little peculiarity. Otherwise – if it was a question of pigs, for instance, or the church organ – he's quite good and reliable.'

'I see,' said Wimsey. 'Well, he has been talking a good bit about ropes and hanging.'

'Then don't believe a word of it,' replied Mrs Venables, robustly. 'Dear me! here's that Superintendent coming up the drive. I suppose he wants you.'

Wimsey caught Mr Blundell in the garden and headed him away from the house.

'I've seen Thoday,' said the Superintendent. 'Of course he denies the whole story. Says Potty was dreaming.'

'But how about the rope?'

'There you are! But that Potty was hiding behind the churchyard wall when you and I found the rope in the well, and how much he may have heard, I don't know. Anyway, Thoday denies it, and short of charging him with the murder, I've got to take his word for it. You know these dratted regulations. No bullying of witnesses. That's what they say. And whatever Thoday did or didn't do, he couldn't have buried the body, so where are you? Do you think any jury is going to convict on the word of a village idiot like Potty Peake? No. Our job's clear. We've got to find Cranton.'

That afternoon, Lord Peter received a letter.

Dear Lord Peter,
I have just thought of something funny you ought to know about, though I don't see how it can have anything to do with the murder. But in detective stories the detective always wants to know about anything funny, so I am sending you the paper. Uncle Edward wouldn't like me writing to you, because he says you encourage me about wanting to be a writer and mixing myself up in police work – he is *a silly old stick-in-the-mud! So I don't suppose Miss Garstairs – that's our H.M. – would let me send you a letter, but I'm putting this into one to Penelope Dwight and I do hope she sends it on all right.*

'I found the paper lying in the belfry on the Saturday before Easter Day and I meant to show it to Mrs Venables because it was so funny, but Dad dying made me forget all about it. I thought it must be some rubbish of Potty Peake's, but Jack Godfrey says it isn't Potty's writing, but it's quite mad enough to be him, isn't it? Anyway, I thought you might like to have it. I don't see how Potty could have got hold of that foreign paper, do you?

'I hope you are still getting on well with the investigations. Are you still at Fenchurch St Paul? I am writing a poem about the founding of Tailor Paul. Miss Bowler says it is quite good and I expect they will put it in the School Magazine. That will be one in the eye for Uncle Edward, anyhow. He can't stop me being printed in the School Mag. Please write if you have time and tell me if you find out anything about the paper.

Yours sincerely,
HILARY THORPE.

'A colleague, as Sherlock Holmes would say, after my own heart,' said Wimsey, as he unfolded the thin enclosure. 'Oh, lord! "I thought to see the fairies in the fields" – a lost work by Sir James Barrie, no doubt! Literary sensation of the year. "But I saw only the evil elephants with their black backs." This is neither rhyme nor reason. Hum! there is a certain dismal flavour about it suggestive of Potty, but no reference to hanging, so I conclude that it is not his – he surely couldn't keep King

Charles's Head out of it so long. Foreign paper – wait a minute! I seem to know the look of that paper. By God, yes! Suzanne Legros's letter! If the paper isn't the dead spit of this I'm a Dutchman. Let me think. Suppose this was the paper Jean Legros sent to Cranton, or Will Thoday, or whoever it was? Blundell had better have a look at it. Bunter, get the car out. And what do you make of this?'

'Of this, my lord? I should say that it was written by a person of no inconsiderable literary ability, who had studied the works of Sheridan Lefanu and was, if I may be permitted the expression, bats in the belfry, my lord.'

'It strikes you that way? It does not look to you like a cipher message, or anything of that kind?'

'It had not occurred to me to regard it in that light, my lord. The style is cramped, certainly, but it is cramped in what I should call a consistent manner, suggestive of – ah! – literary rather than mechanical effort.'

'True, Bunter, true. It certainly isn't anything simple and bucolic of the every-third-word type. And it doesn't look as if it was meant to be read with a grid, because, with the possible exception of "gold", there isn't a single word in it that's significant – or could be significant of anything but moonshine. That bit about the moon is rather good, of its kind. Mannered, but imaginative. "Frail and faint as a sickle of straw." Alliteration's artful aid, what? "So then came minstrels, having gold trumpets, harps and drums. These played very loudly beside me, breaking that spell." Whoever wrote that had an ear for a cadence. Lefanu, did you say? That's not a bad shot, Bunter. It reminds me a little of that amazing passage in *Wylder's Hand* about Uncle Lorne's dream.'

'That was the passage I had in mind, my lord.'

'Yes. Well – in that case the victim was due to "be sent up again, at last, a thousand, a hundred, ten and one, black marble steps, and then it will be the other one's turn." He *was* sent up again, Bunter, wasn't he?'

'From the grave, my lord? I believe that was so. Like the present unknown individual.'

'As you say – very like him. "Hell gapes, Erebus now lies open," as our correspondent has it. "The mouths of Death wait on thy end." Does he mean anything by that, Bunter?'

'I could not say, my lord.'

'The word "Erebus" occurs in the Lefanu passage too, but there, if I remember rightly, it is spelt with an H. If the man who wrote this got his inspiration there, he knew enough, at any rate, about Erebus to be familiar with both spellings. All very curious, Bunter mine. We'll go along to Leamholt and get the two sheets of paper put side by side.'

There was a great wind blowing over the fen, and immense white clouds sailing fast in the wide blue dome of sky. As they drew up before the police-station at Leamholt, they met the Superintendent just about to step into his own car.

'Coming to see me, my lord?'

'I was. Were you coming to see me?'

'Yes.'

Wimsey laughed.

'Things are moving. What have you got?'

'We've got Cranton.'

'No!'

'Yes, my lord. They've run him to earth in a place in London. I heard from them this morning. Seems he's been ill, or something. Anyway, they've found him. I'm going up to interrogate him. Would you like to come?'

'Rather! Shall I run you up there? Save the Force a bit of money, you know, on train fares. And be quicker and more comfortable.'

'Thank you very much, my lord.'

'Bunter, wire to the Rector that we have gone to Town. Hop in, Super. You will see how safe and swift modern methods of transport are when there is no speed limit. Oh, wait a moment. While Bunter is wiring, have a look at this. It reached me this morning.'

He handed over Hilary Thorpe's letter and the enclosure.

'Evil elephants?' said Mr Blundell. 'What in the name of goodness is all this about?'

'I don't know. I'm hoping your friend Cranton can tell us.'

'But it's potty.'

'I don't think Potty could rise to such heights. No, I know what you mean – don't trouble to explain. But the paper, Superintendent, the paper!'

'What about it? Oh, I get you. You think this came from the same place as Suzanne Legros's letter. I shouldn't wonder if you're right. Step in and we'll have a look. By Jove, my lord, and you *are* right. Might have come out of the same packet. Well, I'll be – Found in the belfry, you say. What do you think it all means, then?'

'I think this is the paper that Legros sent to his friend in England – the "guarantee" that he composed, shut up in his room for so many hours. And I think it's the clue to where the emeralds were hidden. A cipher, or something of that sort.'

'Cipher, eh? It's a queer one, then. Can you read it?'

'No, but I jolly well will. Or find somebody who can. I'm hoping that Cranton will read it for us. I bet he won't though,' added his lordship, thoughtfully. 'And even if we do read it, it isn't going to do us much good, I'm afraid.'

'Why not?'

'Why, because you can bet your sweet life that the emeralds were taken away by whoever it was killed Legros – whether it was Cranton or Thoday or somebody else we don't know about yet.'

'I suppose that's a fact. Anyhow, my lord, if we read the cipher and find the hiding-place, and the stuff's gone, that'll be pretty good proof that we're working along the right lines.'

'So it will. But,' added Wimsey, as the Superintendent and Bunter piled into the car and were whisked away out of Leamholt at a speed which made the policeman gasp, 'if the emeralds are gone, and Cranton says he didn't take them, and we can't prove he did, and we can't find out who Legros really was, or who killed him, why then – where are we?'

'Just where we were before,' said Mr Blundell.

'Yes,' said Wimsey. 'It's like Looking-Glass Country. Takes all the running we can do to stay in the same place.'

The Superintendent glanced about him. Flat as a chess-board, and squared like a chess-board with intersecting dyke and hedge, the fen went flashing past them.

'Very like Looking-Glass Country,' he agreed, 'same as the picture in the book. But as for staying in the same place – all I can say is, it don't look like it, my lord – not where you're concerned.'

THE EIGHTH PART

LORD PETER FOLLOWS HIS COURSE BELL TO LEAD

I will again urge on the young conductor the great advantage that it will be to him to write out touches or even whole peals . . . whereby be will gain a great insight into the working of the bells.
TROYTE *On Change-Ringing*

'Well, of course,' admitted Mr Cranton, grinning up ruefully from his pillow into Lord Peter's face, 'if your lordship recognises me, that's done it. I'll have to come clean, as the sheet said to the patent washer. It's a fact I was in Fenchurch St Paul on New Year's Day, and a lovely place it is to start a happy New Year in, I don't think. And it's true I failed to report myself as from last September. And if you ask me, I think it's damned slack of you flatties not to have dug me out earlier. What we pay rates and taxes for I don't know.'

He stopped and shifted restlessly.

'Don't waste your breath in giving us lip,' said Chief Inspector Parker of the C.I.D., kindly enough. 'When did you start growing that face-fungus? In September? I thought so. What was the idea? You didn't think it was becoming, did you?'

'I didn't,' said Mr Cranton. 'Went to my heart, I may say, to disfigure myself. But I thought. "They'll never know Nobby Cranton with his handsome features all hidden in black hair," so I made the sacrifice. It's not so bad now, and I've got used to it, but it looked horrible while it was growing. Made me think of those happy times when I lived on His Majesty's bounty. Ah! and look at my hands. They've never got over it. I ask you, how can a gentleman carry on with his profession after all those years of unrefined manual labour? Taking the bread out of a man's mouth, I call it.'

'So you had some game on, which started last September,' said Parker, patiently. 'What was it, now? Anything to do with the Wilbraham emeralds, eh?'

'Well, to be frank, it was,' replied Nobby Cranton. 'See here, I'll tell you the truth about that. I didn't mind – I never *have* minded – being put inside for what I did do. But it's offensive to a gentleman's feelings when his word isn't believed. And when I said I never had those emeralds, I meant what I said. I never did have them, and you know it. If I had had them, I wouldn't be living in a hole like this, you can bet your regulation boots. I'd have been living like a gentleman on the fat of the land. Lord!' added Mr Cranton, 'I'd have had 'em cut up and salted away before you could have said "knife". Talk about tracing them – you'd never have traced them the way I'd have worked it.'

'So you went to Fenchurch St Paul to try and find them, I suppose?' suggested Wimsey.

'That's right, I did. And why? Because I knew they must be there. That swine – you know who I mean – '

'Deacon?'

'Yes, Deacon.' Something that might have been fear and might have been mere anger twisted the sick man's face. 'He never left the place. He couldn't have got them away before you pinched him. You watched his correspondence, didn't you? If he'd have packed them up and posted them, you'd have known it, eh? No. He had them there – somewhere – I don't know – but he had them. And I meant to get them, see? I meant to get them, and I meant to bring them along and show 'em to you and make you take back what you said about my having had them. Pretty silly, you'd have looked, wouldn't you, when you had to own up that I was right?'

'Indeed?' said Parker. 'That was the idea, was it? You were going to find the stuff and bring it along like a good little boy?'

'That's right.'

'No idea of making anything out of them, of course?'

'Oh, dear, no,' replied Cranton.

'You didn't come to us in September and suggest that we should help you to find them?'

'Well, I didn't,' agreed Mr Cranton. 'I didn't want to be bothered with a lot of clumsy cops. It was my own little game, see? All my own work, as the pavement-artists say.'

'Delightful,' said Parker.' And what made you think you knew where to look for them?'

'Ah!' said Mr Cranton, cautiously. 'Something Deacon once said gave me an idea. But he was a liar about that, too. I never met such a liar as that fellow was. He was so crooked, you could have used his spine for a safety-pin. It serves me right for having to do with menials. A mean, sneaking spirit, that's what you find in that sort. No sense of honour at all.'

'Very likely,' said the Chief Inspector. 'Who is Paul Taylor?'

'There you are!' said Mr Cranton, triumphantly. 'Deacon said to me – '

'When?'

'In the – oh, well! – in the dock, if you will excuse my mentioning such a vulgar place. "Want to know where those shiners are?" he said. "Ask Paul

Taylor or Batty Thomas" – and grinned all over his face. "Who're they?" said I. "You'll find 'em in Fenchurch," he said, grinning still more. "But you aren't likely to see Fenchurch again in a hurry," he said. So then I biffed him one – excuse the expression – and the blinking warder interfered.'

'Really?' said Parker, incredulously.

'Cross my heart and wish to die,' said Mr Cranton. 'But when I got down to Fenchurch, you see, I found there were no such people – only some rubbish about bells. So I dismissed the matter from my mind.'

'And sneaked off on the Saturday night. Why?'

'Well, to be frank with you,' replied Mr Cranton, 'there was an individual in that place I didn't like the looks of, I got the idea that my face struck a chord in her mind, in spite of the exterior decoration. So, not wishing for argument – which is always ungentlemanly – I went quietly away.'

'And who was the penetrating individual?'

'Why, that woman – Deacon's wife. We had stood shoulder to shoulder, as you might say, under unfortunate circumstances, and I had no wish to renew the acquaintance. I never expected to see *her* in that village, and candidly, I thought she showed a lack of taste.'

'She came back when she married a man named Thoday,' said Wimsey.

Married again, did she?' Cranton's eyes narrowed. 'Oh, I see. I didn't know that. Well, I'm damned!'

'Why the surprise?'

'Why? – Oh, well – somebody wasn't too particular, that's all.'

'See here,' said Parker, 'you may as well tell the truth now. Did that woman have anything to do with the theft of the emeralds?'

'How should I know? But to be frank, I don't believe she did. I think she was just a plain fool. Deacon's cat's-paw. I'm sure the fellow put her on to find out about the stuff, but I don't think she was wise to what she was doing. Honestly, I don't think so, because I can't see that man Deacon giving his game away. But hell! What do I know about it?'

'You don't think she knows where the stuff is?'

Cranton thought for a moment. Then he laughed.

'I'd pretty well take my oath she doesn't.'

'Why?'

He hesitated.

'If she knew and was straight, she'd have told the police, wouldn't she? If she knew and was crooked, she'd have told me or my pals. No. You won't get it out of her.'

'H'm! You say you think she recognised you?'

'I got a sort of idea that she was beginning to find my face familiar. Mind you, it was only a kind of hunch I got. I might have been wrong. But I anticipated argument, and I have always considered argument ill-bred. So I went away. In the night. I was working for the blacksmith – an excellent fellow, but crude. I didn't want any argument with him, either. I just went quietly home to think things out, and then I got laid up with rheumatic fever, and it's left my heart dickey, as you see.'

'Quite so. How did you get rheumatic fever?'

'Well, wouldn't anybody get rheumatic fever, if he'd fallen into one of those cursed dykes? I never saw such a country, never. Country life never did suit me – particularly in the blasted middle of winter, with a thaw going on. I was damn nearly found dead in a ditch, which is no end for a gentleman.'

'You didn't investigate the matter of Batty Thomas and Tailor Paul any further, then?' said Parker, placidly putting aside the eloquence which Mr Cranton seemed ready to lavish on any side-issue. 'I am referring to the bells. You did not, for instance, visit the belfry, to see if the emeralds were hidden up there?'

'No, of course I didn't. Besides,' went on Mr Cranton, much too hastily, 'the confounded place was always locked.'

'You tried it, then?'

'Well, to be frank, I may just have laid my hand on the door, so to speak.'

'You never went up into the bell-chamber?'

'Not me.'

'Then how do you account for that?' demanded Parker, suddenly producing the mysterious cipher and thrusting it under the sick man's eyes.

Mr Cranton turned extremely white.

'That?' he gasped. 'That? – I never – ' He fought for breath. 'My heart – here, give me some of the stuff in that glass – '

'Give it him,' said Wimsey, 'he's really bad.'

Parker gave him the medicine with a grim face. After a time the blue pallor gave place to a healthier colour, and the breathing became more natural.

'That's better,' said Cranton. 'You startled me. What did you say? That? I never saw that before.'

'You're lying,' said the Chief Inspector, curtly. 'You have seen it. Jean Legros sent it to you, didn't he?'

'Who's he? Never heard of him.'

'That's another lie. How much money did you send him to get him to England?'

'I tell you I never heard of him,' repeated Cranton, sullenly. 'For God's sake, can't you leave me alone? I tell you I'm ill.'

He looked ill enough. Parker swore under his breath.

'Look here, Nobby, why not come across with the truth? It'll save us bothering you. I know you're ill. Cough it up and get it over.'

'I know nothing about it. I've told you – I went down to Fenchurch and I came away again. I never saw that paper and I never heard of Jean What's-his-name. Does that satisfy you?'

'No, it doesn't.'

'Are you charging me with anything?'

Parker hesitated. 'Not as yet,' he said.

'Then you've got to take my answer,' said Mr Cranton, faintly, but as one who is sure of his position.

'I know that,' said Parker, 'but, hang it, man! do you *want* to be charged? If you'd rather come down with us to the Yard – '

'What's the idea? What have you got to charge me with? You can't try me for stealing those bloody emeralds all over again. I haven't got them. Never seen them – '

'No; but we might charge you with the murder of Jean Legros.'

'No – no – no!' cried Cranton. 'It's a lie! I never killed him. I never killed anybody. I never – '

'He's fainted,' said Wimsey.

'He's dead,' said Superintendent Blundell, speaking for the first time.

'I hope to goodness not,' said Parker. 'No – it's all right, but he looks pretty queer. Better get hold of that girl. Here, Polly!'

A woman came in. She gave one resentful glance at the three men and hurried across to Cranton.

'If you've killed him,' she muttered, 'it's murder. Coming and threatening one that's as sick as him. You get out, you great bullies. He's done nobody any harm.'

'I'll send the doctor along,' said Parker. 'And I'll be coming to see him again. And when I do come, see that I find him here all right. Understand? We shall want him elsewhere, you know, as soon as he's fit to be moved. He hasn't reported himself since last September.'

The girl shrugged a disdainful shoulder, and they left her bending over the sick man.

'Well, Superintendent,' said Parker. 'I'm afraid that's the best we can do for you at the moment. The man's not shamming – he's really ill. But he's holding something out on us. All the same, I don't think it's murder, somehow. That wouldn't be like Cranton. He knew that paper all right.'

'Yes,' said Wimsey. 'Produced quite a reaction, didn't it? He's frightened about something, Charles. What is it?'

'He's frightened about the murder.'

'Well,' said Blundell, 'it looks to me as though he did it. He admits he was there, and that he ran away on the night the body was buried. If he didn't do it, who did? He could have got the key of the crypt from the sexton all right, we know that.'

'So he could,' said Wimsey, 'but he was a stranger to the place. How did he know where the sexton kept his tools? Or where to find the bell-rope? He might have noticed the well, of course, in the daytime, but it's funny that he should have had the whole scheme so pat. And where does Legros come into it? If Deacon told Cranton in the dock where to find the emeralds, where was the sense of bringing Legros to England? He didn't want him. And, if he did for some reason need Legros, and killed him to get the emeralds, where are the emeralds? If he sold them, you ought to have found it out by now. If he's still got them, you'd better have a hunt for them.'

'We'll search the house,' said Parker, dubiously, 'but I don't somehow think he's got them. He wasn't alarmed about the emeralds. It's a puzzle. But we'll turn the place upside-down, and if they're here, we'll get them.'

'And if you do,' said Blundell, 'then you can arrest that chap for the murder. Whoever's got the emeralds did the murder. I'm sure of that.'

'Where thy treasure is, there shall thy heart be also,' said Wimsey. 'The heart of this crime is down at St Paul. That's my prophecy, Charles. Will you have a bet on it?'

'No, I won't,' said the Chief Inspector. 'You're right too often, Peter, and I've no money to waste.'

Wimsey went back to Fenchurch St Paul and shut himself up with the cipher. He had untwisted cryptograms before, and he felt certain that this would prove to be a simple one. Whether the inventor was Cranton or Jean Legros or Will Thoday or any other person connected with the affair of the Wilbraham emeralds, he was hardly likely to be an expert in the art of secret writing. Yet the thing had the signs of a cunning hand about it. He had never seen a secret message that looked so innocent. Sherlock Holmes's Little Dancing Men were, by comparison, obviously secretive.

He tried various simple methods, such as taking every second, third or fourth letter, or skipping letters in accordance with a set combination of figures, but without result. He tried assigning a number to each letter and adding the results, word by word and sentence by sentence. This certainly produced enough mathematical problems to satisfy a Senior Wrangler, but none of them seemed to make sense. He took all the bell-inscriptions and added them up also, with and without the dates, but could find nothing significant. He wondered whether the book contained the whole of what was on the bells. Leaving his papers strewn over the table, he went to the Rector to borrow the keys to the belfry. After a slight delay, caused by the keys having been taken downstairs by mistake for the keys of the wine-cellar, he secured them and made his way to the church.

He was still puzzled about the finding of the cryptogram. The keys jingled together in his hand – the two great keys of the west and south doors, all by themselves on a steel chain, and then, in a bunch on a ring together, the keys of the crypt and vestry, the key of the belfry, the key of the ringing-chamber and the key that unlocked the counterpoise of the belfry. How had Cranton known where to find them? He could, of course, have taken them from the sexton's house – if he had known already. But if 'Stephen Driver' had been asking questions about the church keys, somebody would have taken notice of it. The sexton had the keys of the west door and of the crypt. Had he the other keys as well? Wimsey suddenly turned back and shot the question through the study window at the Rector, who was struggling with the finances of the Parish Magazine.

Mr Venables rubbed his forehead.

'No,' he said at last. 'Gotobed has the west-door key and the key of the crypt, as you say, and he also has the key of the belfry stair and of the ringing-chamber, because he rings the single bell for Early Service and sometimes deputises for Hezekiah when he's ill. And Hezekiah has the keys of the south porch and the belfry stair and the ringing-chamber, too. You see, Hezekiah was sexton before Gotobed, and he likes to keep his privilege of ringing the passing-bell, though he's too old for the other work, and he has the necessary keys. But neither of them has the key to the counterpoise. They don't need it. The only people who have that are Jack Godfrey and myself. I have a complete set of everything, of course, so that if one of the others is lost or mislaid, I can supply it.'

'Jack Godfrey – has he the key of the crypt as well?'

'Oh, no – he doesn't need that.'

Curiouser and curiouser, thought Wimsey. If the man who left the paper in the bell-chamber was the same man who buried the body, then either he took *all* the Rector's keys, or he had access to *two* sets, and those two sets had to be Jack Godfrey's (for the key of the counterpoise) and Gotobed's (for the key of the crypt). And if the man had been Cranton, then how did he *know*? Of course, the criminal might have brought his own spade (though that added to the complication). If so he must have had either the Rector's keys or Jack Godfrey's. Wimsey went round to the back and got hold of Emily and Hinkins. They were both quite sure that they had never seen the man who called himself Stephen Driver inside the Rectory gates, much less inside the Rector's study, which was the proper place for the keys when they were in their proper place.

'But they weren't there at all, my lord,' said Emily, 'because, if you remember, they keys was missing on New Year's night, and it wasn't till near a week after we found them in the vestry – bar the key of the church porch and that was in the lock where Rector left it after choir-practice.'

'After choir-practice? On the Saturday?'

'That's right,' said Hinkins. 'Only, don't you remember, Emily, Rector said it couldn't have been him as left it, because it was gone a-missing, and he didn't have it on Saturday and had to wait for Harry Gotobed?'

'Well, I don't know,' said Emily, 'but that's where it was. Harry Gotobed said he found it there when he went to ring for Early Service.'

More confused than ever, Wimsey trotted back to the study window. Mr Venables, arrested with a carrying-figure at the tip of his pen, was at first not very clear in his recollection, but said presently that he believed Emily was right.

'I must have left the keys in the vestry the week before,' he suggested, 'and whoever left the church last after choir-practice must have found the church key and used it – but who that would be, I don't know, unless it was Gotobed. Yes, it would be Gotobed, because he would wait behind to make up the stoves. But it was funny that he should leave the key in the lock. Dear me! You don't think it could have been the murderer, do you?'

'I do, indeed,' said Wimsey.

'There now!' exclaimed the Rector. 'But if I left the keys in the vestry, how did he get in to find them? He couldn't get in without the church key. Unless he came to choir-practice. Surely, nobody belonging to the choir – '

The Rector looked horribly distressed. Wimsey hastened to comfort him.

'The door would be unlocked during choir-practice. He might have slipped in then.'

'Oh, yes – of course! How stupid I am! No doubt that is what occurred. You have relieved my mind very much.'

Wimsey had not, however, relieved his own mind. As he resumed his way to the church, he turned the matter over. If the keys had been taken on New Year's Eve, then Cranton had not taken them. Cranton had not arrived till New Year's Day. Will Thoday had come, unnecessarily, to the Rectory on December 30th, and might have taken the keys then, but he had certainly not been in the church on the night of January 4th to restore them. It remained possible that Will Thoday had taken the keys and the mysterious James Thoday had returned them – but in that case, what was Cranton doing in the business? And Wimsey felt sure that Cranton knew something about the paper found in the bell-chamber.

Meditating thus, Wimsey let himself into the church, and, unlocking the door in the tower, made his way up the spiral stair. As he passed through the ringing-chamber, he noticed with a smile that a new board had made its appearance on the wall, announcing that: 'On New Year's morning, 19—, a peal of 15,840 Kent Treble Bob Major was Rung in 7 Hours and 15 Minutes, the Ringers being: Treble, Ezra Wilderspin; 2, Peter D. B. Wimsey; 3, Walter Pratt; 4, Henry Gotobed; 5, Joseph Hinkins; 6, Alfred Donnington; 7, John P. Godfrey; Tenor, Hezekiah Lavender; Theodore Venables, Rector, assisting. Our Mouths shall shew forth Thy Praise.' He passed up through the great, bare clock-chamber, released the counterpoise and climbed again till he came out beneath the bells. There he stood for a moment, gazing up into their black mouths while his eyes grew accustomed to the semi-darkness. Presently their hooded silence oppressed him. A vague vertigo seized him. He felt as though they were slowly collapsing together and coming down upon him. Spellbound, he spoke their names: Gaude, Sabaoth, John, Jericho, Dimity, Batty Thomas and Tailor Paul. A soft and whispered echo seemed to start from the walls and die stealthily among the beams. Suddenly he shouted in a great voice: 'Tailor Paul!' and he must somehow have hit upon a harmonic of the scale, for a faint brazen note answered him, remote and menacing, from overhead.

'Come!' said Wimsey, pulling himself together, 'this won't do. I'm getting as bad as Potty Peake, coming here and talking to the bells. Let's find the ladder and get to work.'

He switched on his torch and turned it on the dim corners of the belfry. It showed him the ladder, and it showed him something else also. In the gloomiest and dustiest corner of the floor, there was a patch that was not so dusty. He stepped forward eagerly, the menace of the bells forgotten. Yes, there was no mistake. A portion of the floor had at some fairly recent time been scrubbed, for the dust which in other places lay centuries thick was here only a thin film.

H knelt to examine it, and new thoughts went swooping and turning through his brain like bats. Why should anybody trouble to swab the floor of a belfry, unless to remove some very sinister stain. He saw Cranton and Legros climbing to the belfry, with the cipher in their hands for guidance. He saw the green glint of the jewels, dragged from their old hiding-place in the light of the lantern. He saw the sudden leap, the brutal blow, and the blood gushing to the floor, the cipher fluttering, unheeded, into a corner. And then the murderer, trembling and glancing over his shoulder, as he snatched the emeralds from dead fingers, took up the body and stumbled panting down the creaking ladders. The sexton's spade from the crypt, the bucket and scrubbing-brush from the vestry, or wherever they were kept, the water from the well –

There he stopped. The well? The well meant the rope, and what had the rope to do with this? Had it been used merely as a convenient means to carry the corpse? But the experts had been so sure that the victim had been bound before he was dead. And besides, there were the blow and the blood. It was all very well making horrible pictures for one's self, but there had been no blow till the man had been dead too long to leave any pool of blood. And if there was no blood, why scrub the floor?

He sat back on his heels and looked up again to the bells. If their tongues could speak, they could tell him what they had seen, but they had neither speech nor language. Disappointed, he again took up the torch and searched further. Then he broke out into a harsh and disgusted laughter. The whole cause of the mystery revealed itself absurdly. An empty quart beer-bottle lay there, rolled into an obscure place behind a quantity of worm-eaten beams that were stacked against the wall. Here was a pretty ending to his dreams! Some unlicensed trespasser on consecrated ground – or possibly some workman legitimately engaged in repairs to the bell-cage – had spilt his beer and had tidily removed the stains, while the bottle, rolling out of sight, had been forgotten. No doubt that was all. Yet a lingering suspicion caused Wimsey to take up the bottle very carefully, by means of a finger inserted into the neck. It was not very dusty. It could not, he thought, have lain there long. It would bear somebody's finger-prints – perhaps.

He examined the rest of the floor very carefully, but could find only a few jumbled footprints in the dust – large, male prints, he thought. They might be Jack Godfrey's or Hezekiah Lavender's, or anybody's. Then he took the ladder and made an exhaustive search of the bells and timbers. He found nothing. No secret mark. No hiding-place. And nothing whatever suggestive of fairies or elephants, enchanters or Erebus. After several dirty and fatiguing hours, he descended again, carrying the bottle as his sole reward.

Curiously enough, it was the Rector who solved the cipher. He came into the schoolroom that night as the hall-clock struck eleven, thoughtfully bearing a glass of hot toddy in one hand and an old-fashioned foot-muff in the other.

'I do hope you are not working yourself to death,' he said, apologetically. 'I have ventured to bring a little comfort for the inner man. These nights of early summer are so chilly. And my wife thinks you might like to put your feet in this. There is always a draught under that door. Allow me – it is slightly moth-eaten, I fear, but still affords protection. Now, you must not let me disturb you. Dear me! What is that? Are you pricking out a peal? Oh, no, – I see they are letters, not figures. My eyesight is not as good as it was. But I am rudely prying into your affairs.'

'Not a bit, padre. It does look rather like a peal. It's still this wretched cipher. Finding that the number of letters formed a multiple of eight. I had written it out in eight columns, hoping forlornly that something might come of it. Now you mention it, I suppose one might make a simple sort of cipher out of a set of changes.'

'How could you do that?'

'Well, by taking the movements of one bell and writing the letters of your message in the appropriate places and then filling up the places of the other bells with arbitraries. For instance. Take a Plain Course of Grandsire Doubles,[1] and suppose you want to convey the simple and pious message "Come and worship". You would select one bell to carry the significants – let us say, No. 5. Then you would write out the beginning of your plain course, and wherever No. 5 came you would put one letter of your message. Look.'

He rapidly scribbled down the two columns:

'Then you could fill up the other places with any sort of nonsense letters – say XLOCMP, JQIWON, NAEMMB, TSHEZP, and so on. Then you would write the whole thing out in one paragraph, dividing it so as to look like words.'

'Why?' inquired the Rector.

'Oh, just to make it more difficult. You could write, for example, "XLOC MPJQI. WON NAE M MBTS! HEZP?" and so on to the end. It wouldn't matter what you did. The man who received the message and had the key would simply divide the letters into six columns again, run his pencil along the course of No. 5 and read the message.'

1 2 3 4 5 6	
2 1 3 5 4 6	– – – C – –
2 3 1 4 5 6	– – – – O –
3 2 4 1 5 6	– – – – M –
3 4 2 5 1 6	– – – E – –
4 3 5 2 1 6	– – A – – –
4 5 3 1 2 6	– N – – – –
5 4 1 3 2 6	D – – – – –
5 1 4 2 3 6	W – – – – –
1 5 2 4 3 6	– O – – – –
1 2 5 3 4 6	– – R – – –
2 1 5 4 3 6	– – S – – –
2 5 1 3 4 6	– H – – – –
5 2 3 1 4 6	I – – – – –
5 3 2 4 1 6	P – – – – –
etc.	

[1] 'Doubles' is the name given to a set of changes rung on 5 bells, the tenor (No. 6) being rung last or 'behind' in each change.

'Dear me!' said Mr Venables, 'so he would! How very ingenious. And I suppose that with a little further ingenuity, the cipher might be made to convey some superficial and misleading information. I see, for instance, that you already have the word WON and the Scotch expression NAE. Could not the idea be extended further, so that the entire message might appear completely innocuous?'

'Of course it could. It might look like this.' Wimsey flicked Jean Legros's communication with his finger.

'Have you – ? But pardon me. I am unwarrantably interfering. Still – have you tried this method on the cryptogram?'

'Well, I haven't,' admitted Wimsey. 'I've only just thought of it. Besides, what would be the good of sending a message like that to Cranton, who probably knows nothing about bell-ringing? And it would take a bell-ringer to write it, and we have no reason to suppose that Jean Legros was a ringer. It is true,' he added thoughtfully, 'that we have no reason to suppose he was not.'

'Well, then,' said the Rector. 'Why not try? You told me, I think, that this paper was picked up in the belfry. Might not the person to whom it was sent, though not himself a ringer and not knowing how to interpret it, have connected it in his mind with the bells and supposed that the key was to be found in the belfry? No doubt I am very foolish, but it appears to me to be possible.'

Wimsey struck his hand on the table.

'Padre, that's an idea! When Cranton came to Fenchurch St Paul, he asked for Paul Taylor, because Deacon had told him that Tailor Paul or Batty Thomas knew where the emeralds were. Come on. Have at it. We'll ask Tailor Paul ourselves.'

He picked up the paper on which he had already written the cryptogram in eight columns.

'We don't know what method the fellow used, or which bell to follow. But we'll take it that the bell is either Batty Thomas or Tailor Paul. If the method is Grandsire Triples, it can't be Tailor Paul, for the Tenor would be rung behind the whole way and we should find the message running down the last column. And it's not likely to be Grandsire Major, because you never ring that method here. Let us try Batty Thomas. What does the 7th bell give us? GHILSTETHCWA. That's not very encouraging. For form's sake we'll try the other bells. No. No. No. Could the man possibly have started off with a bob or single?'

'Surely not.'

'Well, you never know. He's not pricking a peal, he's only making a cipher and he might do something unusual on purpose.'

His pencil traced the letter again.

'No. I can't make anything of it. Wash out Grandsires. And I think we can probably wash out Stedman's, too – that would keep the significants too close together. Try Kent Treble Bob, and we'll take Tailor Paul first, since the Tenor is the usual observation bell for that method. She starts in the 7th place, H. Then 8th place, E. Back to 7th, S; to 6th, I; to 5th, T. "HESIT." Well, it's pronounceable, at any rate. Dodge up into 6ths place, T again. Down to 5th, E; to 4th, T; to 3rds, H. "HESITTETH." Hullo, padre! we've got two words, anyhow. "He sitteth." Perhaps "He" is the necklace. We'll carry on with this.'

The Rector, his glasses sliding down his long nose with excitement, pored over the paper as the pencil made its rapid way down the letters.

'"He sitteth between" – it's part of a verse from Psalm xcix – there, what did I tell you? "He sitteth between the cherubims." Now, what can that mean? Oh, dear! there is some mistake – the next letter should be a B – "be the earth never so unquiet."'

'Well, it isn't a B; it's another T. There isn't a B anywhere. Wait a moment. THE is coming – no, THEI – no, as you were. It's THE ISLES. I can't help it, padre. It couldn't come like that by accident. Just a second, and we'll have it all sorted out and then you can say what you like . . . Oy! what's happened here at the end? Oh, dash it! I was forgetting. This must be the end of the lead. Yes' – he calculated rapidly – 'it is, and we've got to make the 3rds and 4ths. There you are. Message complete; and what it means is more than I can tell you.'

The Rector polished his glasses and stared.

'It's verses from three psalms,' he said. 'Most singular. "He sitteth between the cherubims"; that's Ps. xcix. 1. Then "The isles may be glad thereof"; that's Ps. xcvii. 1. Both those psalms begin alike: "Dominus regnavit", "The Lord is King". And then we get, "as the rivers in the south". That's Ps. cxxvi. 5, "In convertendo", "When the Lord turned the captivity of Sion". This is a case of *obscurum per obscuriora* – the interpretation is even more perplexing than the cipher.'

'Yes,' said Wimsey. 'Perhaps the figures have something to do with it. We have 99. 1. 97. 1. 126. 5. Are they to be taken as one figure 9919711265? or to be left as they are? or re-divided? The permutations are almost endless. Or perhaps they ought to be added. Or converted into letters on some system we haven't discovered yet. It can't be a simple a = 1 substitution. I refuse to believe in a message that runs IIAIGIABFE. I shall have to wrestle with this quite a lot more. But you have been simply marvellous, padre. You ought to take to deciphering codes as a profession.'

'It was pure accident,' said Mr Venables, simply, 'and due entirely to my failing vision. That is a curious thing. It has given me the idea for a sermon about evil being overruled for good. But I should never have thought of the possibility that one might make a cipher out of change-ringing. Most ingenious.'

'It could have been done still more ingeniously,' said Wimsey. 'I can think of lots of ways to improve it. Suppose – but I won't waste time with supposing. The point is, what the dickens is one to do with 99. 1. 97. 1. 126. 5?'

He clutched his head between his hands, and the Rector, after watching him for a few minutes, tiptoed away to bed.

I T H O U G H T	L Y C L O U D B	N Y T E A R S B
T O S E E T H E	U T N O B L I N	E F O R E T H E
F A I R I E S I	D E Y E O F A M	T H I N M O O N
N T H E F I E L	O R T A L W A S	R O S E U P F R
D S B U T I S A	P E R M I T T E	A I L A N D F A
W O N L Y T H E	D T O S P Y T H	I N T A S A S I
E V I L E L E P	E M S O T H E N	C K L E O F S T
H A N T S W I T	C A M E M I N S	R A W N O W T H
H T H E I R B L	T R E L S H A V	O U G H T H E E
A C K B A C K S	I N G G O L D T	N C H A N T E R
W O E H O W T H	R U M P E T S H	G N A S H H I S
A T S I G H T A	A R P S A N D D	T E E T H V A I
W E D M E T H E	R U M S T H E S	N L Y Y E T S H
E L V E S D A N	E P L A Y E D V	A L L H E R E T
C E D A L L A R	E R Y L O U D L	U R N A S T H E
O U N D A N D A	Y B E S I D E M	S P R I N G R E
B O U T W H I L	E B R E A K I N	T U R N S O H W
E I H E A R D V	G T H A T S P E	R E T C H E D M
O I C E S C A L	L L S O T H E D	A N H E L L G A
L I N G C L E A	R E A M V A N I	P E S E R E B U
R L Y A H H O W	S H E D W H E R	S N O W L I E S
I T R I E D T O	E A T I T H A N	O P E N T H E M
S E E T H R O W	K E D H E A V E	O U T H S O F D
O F F T H E U G	N I S H E D M A	E A T H W A I T
		O N T H Y E N D

THE NINTH PART

EMILY TURNS BUNTER FROM BEHIND

Let the bell that the Treble turns from behind make thirds place, and return behind again.

Rules for Change-Making on Four Bells

'I should like,' panted Emily between her sobs, 'to give my week's warning.'

'Good gracious, Emily,' cried Mrs Venables, pausing as she passed through the kitchen with a pail of chicken-feed, 'what on earth is the matter with you?'

'I'm sure,' said Emily, 'I ain't got no fault to find with you and Rector as has always been that kind, but if I'm to be spoken to so by Mr Bunter, which I'm not his servant and never want to be and ain't no part of my duties, and anyway how was I to know? I'm sure I'd have cut my right hand off rather than disoblige his lordship, but I did ought to have been told and it ain't my fault and so I told Mr Bunter.'

Mrs Venables turned a little pale. Lord Peter presented no difficulties, but Bunter she found rather alarming. But she was of the bulldog breed, and had been brought up in the knowledge that a servant was a servant and that to be afraid of a servant (one's own or anybody else's) was the first step to an Avernus of domestic inefficiency. She turned to Bunter, standing white and awful in the background.

'Well now, Bunter,' she said firmly. 'What is all this trouble about?'

'I beg your pardon, madam,' said Bunter in a stifled manner. 'I fear that I forgot myself. But I have been in his lordship's service now for going on fifteen years (counting my service under him in the war), and such a thing has never yet befallen me. In the sudden shock and the bitter mortification of my mind, I spoke with considerable heat. I beg, madam, that you will overlook it. I should have controlled myself better. I assure you that it will not occur again.'

Mrs Venables put down the chicken-pail.

'But what was it all about?'

Emily gulped, and Bunter pointed a tragic finger at a beer-bottle which stood on the kitchen table.

'That bottle, madam, was entrusted to me yesterday by his lordship. I placed it in a cupboard in my bedroom, with the intention of photographing it this morning, before despatching it to Scotland Yard. Yesterday evening, it seems that this young woman entered the room during my absence, investigated the cupboard and removed the bottle. Not content with removing it, she dusted it.'

'If you please, 'm,' said Emily, 'how was I to know it was wanted? A nasty, dirty old thing. I was only a-dusting the room, 'm and I see this old bottle on the cupboard shelf, and I says to myself, "Look at that dusty old bottle, why however did that get there? It must have got left accidental." So I takes it down and when Cook sees it she says, "Why, whatever have you got there, Emily? That'll just do," she says, "to put the methylated." So I gives it a dust – '

'And now the finger-prints have all gone,' concluded Bunter in a hollow tone, 'and what to say to his lordship I do not know.'

'Oh, dear! oh dear!' said Mrs Venables, helplessly. Then she seized on the one point of domestic economy which seemed to call for inquiry. 'How did you come to leave your dusting so late?'

'If you please, 'm, I don't know how it was. I got all behind yesterday, somehow, and I said to myself, 'Better late than never,' and I'm sure I'd only have known – '

She wept loudly, and Bunter was touched.

'I am sorry I expressed myself with so much acerbity,' he said, 'and I take blame to myself for not removing the key from the cupboard door. But you will understand my feelings, madam, when I think of his lordship innocently waking to a new day, if I may say so, and not knowing of the blow which is in store for him. It goes to my heart, if you will pardon my mentioning the organ in such a connection. There, madam, is his morning tea, only waiting for my hand to put the boiling water to it, and I feel, madam, as though it were the hand of a murderer with no perfumes of Arabia – supposing such to be a suitable to my situation – could sweeten. He has rung twice,' added Bunter, in desperate tones, 'and he will know by the delay that something of a calamitous nature has occurred – '

'Bunter!'

'My lord!' cried Bunter, in a voice like prayer.

'What the devil has happened to my tea? What the – ? Oh, I beg your pardon, Mrs Venables. Excuse my language and my bath-robe, won't you? I didn't know you were here?'

'Oh, Lord Peter!' exclaimed Mrs Venables, 'such a dreadful thing's happened. Your man is so terribly upset, and this silly girl – she meant well, of course, and it's all a mistake – but we've dusted all the finger-prints off your bottle!'

'Wah-ha-ha!' sobbed Emily. 'O-oh! Wah-ha-ha! I did it. I dusted it. I didn't know – ho-ho.'

'Bunter,' said his lordship, 'what is the verse about the struck eagle stretched upon the plain. Never through something clouds to soar again?

It expresses my feelings exactly. Take up my tea and throw the bottle in the dustbin. What's done cannot be undone. In any case the finger-prints were probably of no importance. William Morris once wrote a poem called *The Man Who Never Laughed Again.* If the shout of them that triumph, the song of them that feast, should never again be heard upon my lips, you will know why. My friends will probably be devoutly thankful. Let it be a warning to you never to seek for happiness out of a bottle. Emily, if you cry any more, your young man won't know you from Sunday. Don't worry about the bottle Mrs Venables – it was a beastly bottle, anyhow, and I always loathed the sight of it. It is a beautiful morning for early rising. Allow me to carry the chicken-pail. I beg you will not give another thought to the bottle, or Emily either. She's a particularly nice girl, isn't she? What's her surname, by the way?'

'Holliday,' said Mrs Venables. 'She's a niece of Russell's, the undertaker, you know, and some sort of relation to Mary Thoday, though of course, everybody is, in this village, related to somebody or the other, I mean. It comes of being such a small place, though now that they all have motor-bicycles and the buses running twice a week it isn't so bad, and there won't be so many unfortunate creatures like Potty Peake. All the Russells are very nice, superior people.'

'Just so,' said Lord Peter Wimsey. He did a certain amount of thinking as he spooned out mash into the chicken-trough.

He spent the early part of the morning in fresh unavailing study of the cryptogram, and as soon as he thought the pubs would be open, went round to the Red Cow for a pint of beer.

'Bitter, my lord?' inquired Mr Donnington with his hand upon the tap.

Wimsey said No, not today. He would have a bottle of Bass for a change.

Mr Donnington produced the Bass, observing that his lordship would find it in very nice condition.

'Condition is nine-tenths of the bottle,' said Wimsey, 'and a lot of it depends upon the bottling. Who are your bottlers?'

'Griggs of Walbeach,' said Mr Donnington. 'Very sound people they are, too; I've got no complaints to make. Just you try for yourself – though you can tell by the look of it, if you see what I mean. Clear as a bell – though, of course, you have to be able to trust your cellarman. I had a chap once that never could be taught not to pack his Bass 'ead down in the basket, same as if it was stout. Now stout will stand being stood on its 'ead, though it's not a thing I ever would do myself and I don't recommend it, but Bass *must* be stood right ways up and not shook about if you're to do justice to the beer.'

'Very true indeed,' said Wimsey. 'There's certainly nothing wrong with this. Your health. Won't you take something yourself?'

'Thank you, my lord, I don't mind if I do. Here's luck. Now, that,' said Mr Donnington, raising the glass to the light, 'is as nice a glass of Bass as you could wish to see.'

Wimsey asked whether he did much with Quart bottles.

'Quarts?' said Mr Donnington. 'No. Not with quarts, I don't. But I believe Tom Tebbutt down at the Wheatsheaf does a bit. Griggs bottles for him, too.'

'Ah!' said Wimsey.

'Yes. There's one or two prefers quarts. Though, mind you, most of the business about here is draught. But there's a farmer here and there as likes the quarts delivered at their homes. Ah! in the old days they all did their own brewing – there's plenty farms now with the big brewing coppers still standing, and there's a few as still cures their own sides of bacon – Mr Ashton's one on 'em, he won't have nothing new-fangled. But what with these chain stores and their grocery vans, and the girls all wanting to be off to the pictures in their silk stockings and so many things coming in tins, it's not many places where you can see a bit of real home-cured. And look at the price of pig-feed. What I say is, the farmers did ought to have some protection. I was brought up a Free Trader myself, but times has changed. I don't know if you've ever thought of these things, my lord. They may not come your way. Or – there – I'm forgetting. Maybe you sit in the 'Ouse of Lords, now. Harry Gotobed will have it that that's so, but I said he was mistook – but there! you'll know better than me about that.'

Wimsey explained that he was not qualified to sit in the House of Lords. Mr Donnington observed with pleasure that in that case the sexton owed him half-a-crown, and while he made a note of the fact on the back of an envelope, Wimsey escaped and made his way to the Wheatsheaf.

Here, by exercising a certain amount of tact, he obtained a list of those households to which Bass was regularly supplied in quarts. Most of those names were those farmers in outlying places, but as an afterthought, Mrs Tebbutt mentioned one which made Wimsey prick up his ears.

'Will Thoday, he had a few while Jim was at home – a dozen or so, it might be. He's a nice chap, is Jim Thoday – makes you laugh by the hour telling his tales of foreign parts. He brought back that there parrot for Mary, though as I says to her, that bird ain't no proper example for the children. How it do go on, to be sure. I'm sure, if you'd heard what it said to Rector the other day! I didn't know where to look. But it's my belief, Rector didn't understand half of it. He's a real gentleman, is Mr Venables, not like old parson. He was a kind man, too, but different from Rector, and they say he used to swear something surprising in a clergyman. But there, poor man! He had a bit of a weakness, as they say. "Do as I say, don't do as I do" – that's what he used to say in his sermons. Terrible red in the face he were, and died sudden, of a stroke.'

Wimsey tried in vain to steer the conversation back to Jim Thoday. Mrs Tebbutt was fairly launched into reminiscences of Old Rector, and it was half an hour before he was able to make his way out of the Wheatsheaf. Turning back towards the Rectory, he found himself at Will Thoday's gate. Glancing up the path, he saw Mary, engaged in hanging out washing. He suddenly determined on a frontal attack.

'I hope you'll forgive me, Mrs Thoday,' he said, when he had announced himself and been invited to enter, 'if I take your mind back to a rather painful episode. I mean to say, bygones are bygones and all that and one hates digging anything up, what? But when it comes to dead bodies in other people's graves and so on, well, sometimes one gets pondering about them and all that sort of thing, don't you know.'

'Yes, indeed, my lord. I'm sure if there's anything I can do to help, I will. But as I told Mr Blundell, I never knew a thing about it, and I can't imagine how it came there. That was the Saturday night he was asking me about, and I'm sure I've thought and thought, but I couldn't call to mind as I'd seen anything.'

'Do you remember a man who called himself Stephen Driver?'

'Yes, my lord. Him that was at Ezra Wilderspin's. I remember seeing him once or twice. They said at the inquest that the body might have been him.'

'But it wasn't,' said Wimsey.

'Wasn't it, my lord?'

'No. Because we've found this chap Driver and he's still alive and kicking. Had you ever seen Driver before he came here?'

'I don't think so, my lord; no, I can't say as I ever did.'

'He didn't remind you of anybody?'

'No, my lord.'

She appeared to be answering quite frankly, and he could not see any signs of alarm in voice or expression.

'That's odd,' said Wimsey, 'because he says that he ran away from St Paul because he thought you had recognised him.'

'Did he? Well, that's a strange thing, my lord.'

'Did you ever hear him speak?'

'I don't think I ever did, my lord.'

'Suppose he hadn't been wearing a beard, now – would he remind you of anybody?'

Mary shook her head. Like most people, she found the effort of imagination beyond her.

'Well, do you recognise this?'

He took out a photograph of Cranton, taken at the time of the Wilbraham emeralds affair.

'That?' Mrs Thoday turned pale. 'Oh, yes, my lord. I remember him. That was Cranton, that took the necklace and was sent to prison same time as – as my first husband, my lord. I expect you know all about that. That's his wicked face. Oh, dear! it's given me quite a turn, seeing that again.'

She sat down on a bench and stared at the photograph.

'This isn't – it couldn't be Driver?'

'That's Driver,' said Wimsey. 'You had no idea of it?'

'That I never had, my lord. If I'd ever had such a thought, I'd have spoken to him, don't you fear! I'd have got out of him where he put those emeralds to. You see, my lord, that was what went so hard against my poor husband, this man saying as my husband had kept the necklace himself. Poor Jeff, there's no doubt he was tempted – all through my fault, my lord, talking so free – and he did take the jewels, I'm sorry to say. But he didn't have them afterwards. It was this Cranton had them all the time. Don't you think it hasn't been a bitter hard cross to me, my lord, all these years, knowing as I was suspected? The jury believed what I said, and so did the judge, but you'll find some as thinks now that I had a hand in it and knew where the necklace was. But I never did, my lord, never. If I'd been able to find it, I'd have crawled to London on my hands and knees to give it back to Mrs Wilbraham. I know what poor Sir Henry suffered with the loss of it. The police searched our place, and I searched it myself, over and over – '

'Couldn't you take Deacon's word for it?' asked Wimsey, softly.

She hesitated, and her eyes clouded with pain.

'My lord, I did believe him. And yet, all the same – well! it was such a terrible shock to me that he could have done such a thing as to rob a lady in the master's house, I didn't know but what he mightn't perhaps have done the other too. I didn't rightly know what to believe, if you understand me, my lord. But *now* I feel quite sure that my husband was telling the truth. He was led away by this wicked Cranton, there's no doubt of that, but that he was deceiving us all, afterwards, I don't believe. Indeed, my lord, I don't think he was – I'm quite sure of it in my own mind.'

'And what do you suppose Cranton came down here for?'

'Doesn't that show, my lord, that it was him as hid them after all? He must have got frightened and hid them away in some place that night, before he got away.'

'He says himself that Deacon told him in the dock that the emeralds were here, and he was to ask Tailor Paul and Batty Thomas to find them for him.'

Mary shook her head. 'I don't understand that, my lord. But if my husband had said such a thing to him then, Cranton wouldn't have kept quiet about it. He'd have told the jury, he was that mad with Jeff.'

'Would he? I'm not so sure. Suppose Deacon told Cranton where to find the emeralds, don't you think Cranton would have waited in the hope of getting hold of them when he came out of prison? And mightn't he have come down here last January to look for them? And then, thinking you'd spotted him, mightn't he have run away in a fright?'

'Well, my lord, I suppose he might. But then, who would that poor dead man be?'

'The police think he may have been an accomplice of Cranton's, who helped him to find the emeralds and was killed for his pains. Do you know whether Deacon made any friends among the other convicts or the warders at Maidstone?'

'I couldn't say, I'm sure, my lord. He was allowed to write now and again, of course, but naturally he wouldn't tell anybody a thing like that, because his letters would be read.'

'Naturally. I wondered whether perhaps you'd had a message from him at some time – through a released prisoner, or anything like that?'

'No, my lord, never.'

'Have you ever seen this writing?'

He handed her the cryptogram.

'That writing? Why, of course – '

'Shut up, you fool! Shut up, you bloody fool! Come on, Joey! Show a leg there!'

'Good lord!' exclaimed Wimsey, startled. Peering round the door into the inner room, he encountered the bright eye of a grey African parrot fixed knowingly upon his. At sight of a stranger, the bird stopped talking, cocked its head aslant, and began to sidle along its perch.

'Damn your eyes!' said his lordship, pleasantly. 'You made me jump.'

'Aw!' said the bird, with a long, self-satisfied chuckle.

'Is that the bird your brother-in-law gave you? I've heard about him from Mrs Tebbutt.'

'Yes, my lord, that's him. He's a wonderful talker, but he does swear and that's the truth.'

'I've no use for a parrot that doesn't,' said Wimsey. 'Seems unnatural. Let me see – what were we – ? Oh, yes, that bit of writing You were just saying – '

'I said, of course I'd never seen it before, my lord.'

Wimsey could have sworn that she had been going to say just the opposite. She was looking at – no, not at, but through and past him, with the face of someone who sees an incredible catastrophe approaching.

'It's queer-looking stuff, isn't it?' she went on, in a flat voice, 'don't seem to mean anything. What made you think I should know anything about the like of that?'

'We had an idea that it might have been written by some man your late husband knew at Maidstone. Did you ever hear of anyone called Jean Legros?'

'No, my lord. That's a French name, isn't it? I've never seen a Frenchman, except a few of those Beljums that came over here in the war.'

'And you never knew anyone called Paul Taylor?'

'No, never.'

The parrot laughed heartily.

'Shut up, Joey!'

'Shut up, you fool! Joey, Joey, Joey! Scratch a poll, then. Aw!'

'Oh, well,' said Wimsey. 'I just wondered.'

'Where did that come from?'

'What? Oh, this? It was picked up in the church, and we had an idea it might be Cranton's. But he says it isn't, you know.'

'In the *church*?'

As though the words were a cue, the parrot picked it up, and began muttering excitedly:

'Must go to church. Must go to church. The bells. Don't tell Mary. Must go to church. Aw! Joey! Joey! Come on, Joey! Must go to church.'

Mrs Thoday stepped hurriedly into the other room and flung a cloth over the cage, while Joey squawked protestingly.

'He goes on like that,' she said. 'Gets on my nerves. He picked it up the night Will was so bad. They were ringing the peal, and it worried him, like, that he couldn't be there. Will gets that angry with Joey when he starts mocking him. Shut up, now, Joey, do.'

Wimsey held out his hand for the cryptogram, which Mary surrendered – reluctantly, he thought, and as though her thoughts were elsewhere.

'Well, I mustn't bother you any more, Mrs Thoday. I just wanted to clear up that little point about Cranton. I expect you are right after all, and he just came down here to snoop about on his own. Well, you aren't likely to be bothered with him again. He's ill, and in any case, he'll have to go back to prison to work out his time. Forgive my bargin' along and botherin' you about what's best forgotten.'

But all the way back to the Rectory, he was haunted by Mary Thoday's eyes and by the hoarse muttering voice of the parrot:

'The bells! the bells! Must go to the church! Don't tell Mary!'

Superintendent Blundell clicked his tongue a good deal over all this.

'It's a pity about the bottle,'.he said. 'Don't suppose it would have told us anything, but you never know. Emily Holliday, eh? Of course, she's a cousin of Mary Thoday's. I'd forgotten that. That woman beats me – Mary, I mean. Damned if I know what to make of her, or her husband either. We're in touch with those people at Hull, and they're arranging to get James Thoday shipped back to England as soon as possible. We told them he might be wanted as a witness. Best way to work it – he can't skip his orders; or if he does, we'll know there's something wrong and go after him. It's a queer business altogether. As regards that cipher, what do you say to sending it along to the Governor of Maidstone? If this fellow Legros or Taylor or whatever he is was ever in there, they may be able to spot the handwriting.'

'So they may,' said Wimsey, thoughtfully. 'Yes, we'll do that. And I'm hoping we'll hear from M. Rozier again soon. The French haven't any of our inhibitions about dealing with witnesses.'

'Lucky them, my lord,' replied Mr Blundell, with fervour.

THE TENTH PART

LORD PETER IS CALLED WRONG

And he set the cherubims within the inner house: and they stretched forth the wings of the cherubims.

1 *Kings vi.* 27

And above were costly stones. 1 *Kings vii.* 11

'I hope,' said the Rector on the following Sunday morning, 'there is nothing wrong with the Thodays. Neither Will nor Mary was at Early Service. I've never known them both miss before, except when he was ill.'

'No more they were,' said Mrs Venables. 'Perhaps Will has taken a chill again. These winds are very treacherous. Lord Peter, do have another sausage. How are you getting along with your cipher?'

'Don't rub it in, I'm hopelessly stuck.'

'I shouldn't worry,' said Mr Venables. 'Even if you have to lie still a whole pull now and again, you'll soon find yourself back in the hunt.'

'I wouldn't mind that,' said Wimsey. 'It's lying behind the whole way that gets on my nerves.'

'There's always something that lies behind a mystery,' said the Rector, mildly enjoying his little witticism. 'A solution of some kind.'

'What I say is,' observed Mrs Venables darkly, 'there are always wheels within wheels.'

'And where there's a wheel there's usually a rope,' added his lordship.

'Unhappily,' said the Rector, and there was a melancholy pause.

Anxiety about the Thodays was somewhat allayed by their appearance together at Matins, but Wimsey thought he had never seen two people look so ill and unhappy. In wondering about them, he lost all consciousness of what was going on about him, sat down for the Venite, lost the Psalms for the day, embarked on a loud and solitary 'For thine is the Kingdom' at the end of the second 'Our Father,' and only pulled himself together when Mr Venables came down to preach his sermon. As usual, Mr Gotobed had failed to sweep the chancel properly, and a hideous crunching of coke proclaimed the Rector's passage to the pulpit. The Invocation was pronounced, and Wimsey sank back with a sigh of relief into the corner of the pew, folded his arms and fixed his gaze firmly on the roof.

'Who hast exalted thine only son with great triumph into the Heavens. Those words are from the collect for the day. What do they mean to us? What picture do we make of the glory and triumph of Heaven? Last Thursday we prayed that we also might in heart and mind thither ascend and continually dwell, and we hope that after death we shall be admitted – not only in heart and mind but in soul and body – to that blessed state where cherubium and seraphim continually sing their songs of praise. It is a beautiful description that the Bible gives us – the crystal sea and the Lord sitting between the cherubims, and the angels with their harps and crowns of gold, as the old craftsmen imagined them when they built this beautiful roof that we are so proud of – but do we, do you and I really believe – ?'

It was hopeless. Wimsey's thoughts were far away again. 'He rode upon the cherubim and did fly. He sitteth between the cherubims.' He was suddenly reminded of the little architect who was come down to advise about the church roof at Duke's Denver. 'You see, your Grace, the rot has got into the timbers; there are holes behind those cherrybims you could put your hand in.' *He sitteth between the cherubims*. Why, of course! Fool that he was – climbing up among the bells to look for cherubims when they were here over his head, gazing down at him, their blank golden eyes blind with excess of light. The cherubim? Nave and aisle were thick with cherubim, as autumn leaves in Vallombrosa. Nave and aisle – 'the *isles* may be glad thereof' – and then the third text – 'as the rivers in the *south*.' Between the cherubims in the south aisle – what could be clearer than that? In his excitement he nearly shot out of his seat. It only remained to discover which particular pair of cherubims was concerned, and that ought not to be very difficult. The emeralds themselves would be gone, of course, but if one could find even the empty hiding place, that would prove that the cryptogram was connected with the necklace and that all the queer tragedy brooding over Fenchurch St Paul was in some way connected with the emeralds too. Then, if the handwriting of the cryptogram could be traced back to Maidstone Gaol and to Jean Legros they would know who Legros was, and with luck they would also link him up with Cranton. After that, if Cranton could escape from the murder charge, he would be a lucky man.

Over the Sunday beef and Yorkshire pudding, Wimsey tackled the Rector.

'How long ago was it, sir, that you took away the galleries from the aisles?'

'Let me see,' said Mr Venables, 'about ten years ago, I think. Yes, that is right. Ten years. Hideous, cumbersome things they were. They ran right across the aisle windows, obscuring all the upper tracery and blocking the light, and were attached to the arcading. As a matter of fact, what with those horrible great pews, like bathing machines, sprouting up from the floor, and the heavy galleries, you could scarcely see the shafts of the pillars at all.'

'Or anything else,' said his wife. 'I always used to say it was regular blind man's holiday underneath those galleries.'

'If you want to see what it was like,' added the Rector, 'go and look at Upwell Church near Wisbech. You'll find the same sort of gallery in the north aisle there (though ours was larger and uglier), and they have an angel roof, too, though not as fine as ours, because their angels are only attached to the roof itself, instead of being on the hammer-beams. In fact, you can't see the angels in their north aisle, at all, unless you climb up into the gallery.'

'I suppose there was the usual amount of opposition when you took the galleries down?'

'A certain amount, of course. There are always some people who oppose any change. But it did seem absurd, when the church was far too large for the parish in any case, to have all that unnecessary seating. There was plenty of room for the school-children in the aisle.'

'Did anybody sit in the gallery besides the school-children?'

'Oh, yes. The Red House servants and a few of the oldest inhabitants, who had been there from time immemorial. Indeed, we really had to wait for one poor old soul to die before we embarked on the improvements. Poor old Mrs Wilderspin, Ezra's grandmother. She was ninety-seven and came regularly to church every Sunday, and it would have broken her heart to have turned her out.'

'Which side did the Red House servants sit?'

'At the west end of the south aisle. I never liked that, because one couldn't see what they were doing, and sometimes their behaviour wasn't as reverent as it might have been. I do not think the House of God is a proper place for flirtation, and there was so much nudging and giggling that it really was very unseemly.'

'If that woman Gates had done her duty and sat with the servants it would have been all right,' said Mrs Venables, 'but she was far too much of a lady. She always had to have her own seat, just inside the south door, for fear she should feel faint and have to go out.'

'Mrs Gates is not a robust woman, my dear.'

'Rubbish!' said Mrs Venables. 'She eats too much and gets indigestion, that's all.'

'Perhaps you are right, my dear.'

'I can't stand the woman,' said Mrs Venables. 'The Thorpes ought to sell that place, but apparently they can't under Sir Henry's will. I don't see how it can be kept up, and the money would be more use to Hilary Thorpe than the great tumbledown house. Poor little Hilary! If it hadn't been for that horrible old Wilbraham creature and her necklace – I suppose there's no hope of recovering the necklace, Lord Peter, after all this time?'

'I'm afraid we're a day after the fair. Though I'm pretty sure it was in this parish up to last January.'

'In the parish? Where?'

'I think it was in the church,' said Wimsey. 'That was a very powerful sermon of yours this morning, padre. Very inspiring. It inspired me to guess the riddle of the cryptogram.'

'No!' exclaimed the Rector. 'How did it do that, I wonder?'

Wimsey explained.

'Good gracious! How very remarkable! We must investigate the place at once.'

'Not at once, Theodore.'

'Well, no, my dear, I didn't mean today. I'm afraid it wouldn't do to take ladders into the church on Sunday. We are still rather touchy here about the Fourth Commandment. Besides, I have the Children's Service this afternoon and three baptisms, and Mrs Edwards is coming to be churched. But, Lord Peter, how do you suppose the emeralds got up in the roof?'

'Why, I was just thinking about that. Isn't it true that this fellow Deacon was arrested after church on Sunday morning? I expect he got some idea of what was going to happen to him, and concealed his loot somehow during the service.'

'Of course, he was sitting up there that morning. Now I understand why you asked so many questions about the gallery. What a sad villain the man must have been! He really did – what is that word they use when one malefactor deceives another?'

'Double-cross?' suggested Wimsey.

'Ah! that is the very expression I was looking for. He did double-cross his accomplice. Poor man! I mean the accomplice. Ten years in prison for a theft of which he never enjoyed the fruits. One cannot help feeling some sympathy for him. But in that case, Lord Peter, who constructed the cryptogram?'

'I think it must have been Deacon, because of the bell-ringing.'

'Ah, yes. And then he gave it to this other man, Legros. Why did he do that?'

'Probably as an inducement to Legros to help him to escape from Maidstone.'

'And Legros waited all these years before making use of it?

'Legros obviously had very good reasons for keeping out of England. Eventually he must have passed the cryptogram on to somebody here – Cranton, perhaps. Possibly he couldn't decipher it himself, and in any case he wanted Cranton's help to get back from France.'

'I see. Then they found the emeralds and Cranton killed Legros. How sad it makes me to think of all this violence for the sake of a few stones!'

'It makes me still sadder to think of poor Hilary Thorpe and her father,' said Mrs Venables. 'You mean to say that while they needed that money so badly, the emeralds were hidden in the church all the time within a few feet of them?'

'I'm afraid so.'

'And where are they now? Has this man Cranton got them? Why hasn't somebody found tnem by now? I can't think what the police are doing.'

Sunday seemed an unusually long day. On the Monday morning, a great many things happened at once.

The first thing was the arrival of Superintendent Blundell, in great excitement.

'We've got that letter from Maidstone,' he announced, 'and whose do you suppose the writing is?'

'I've been thinking it over,' said Wimsey. 'I think it must have been Deacon's.'

'There!' said Mr Blundell, disappointed. 'Well, you're quite right, my lord; it is.'

'It must be the original cipher,' said Wimsey. 'When we found out that it had to do with bell-ringing, I realised that Deacon must be the author. To have two bell-ringing convicts in Maidstone Gaol at once seemed rather too much of a coincidence. And then, when I showed the paper to Mrs Thoday, I felt sure that she recognised the writing. It might have meant that Legros had written to her, but it was still more likely that she knew it to be her husband's.'

'Well, then, how did it come to be written on that foreign paper?'

'Foreign paper is much of a muchness,' said Wimsey. 'Did Lady Thorpe ever have a foreign maid? Old Lady Thorpe, I mean.'

'Sir Charles had a French cook,' said the Superintendent.

'At the time of the theft?'

'Yes. She left them when the war broke out, I remember. She wanted to get back to her family, and they scraped her across on one of the last boats.'

'Then that's clear enough. Deacon invented his cryptogram before he actually hid the emeralds. He couldn't have taken it into prison with him. He must have handed it to somebody – '

'Mary,' said the Superintendent, with a grim smile.

'Perhaps. And she must have sent it to Legros. It's all rather obscure.'

'Not so obscure as that, my lord.' Mr Blundell's face grew still grimmer. 'I thought it was a bit reckless, if you'll excuse me, showing that paper to Mary Thoday. She's skipped.'

'Skipped?'

'First train to town this morning. And Will Thoday with her. A precious pair.'

'Good God!'

'You may say so, my lord. Oh, we'll have them, don't you fear. Gone off, that's what they've done, and the emeralds with them.'

'I admit,' said Wimsey, 'I didn't expect that.'

'Didn't you?' said Mr Blundell. 'Well, I didn't either, or I'd have kept a sharper eye on them. And by the way, we know now who that Legros fellow was.'

'You're a perfect budget of news today, Super.'

'Ah! well – we've had a letter from your friend M. Rozier. He had that woman's house searched, and what do you think they found? Legros's identification disc – no less. Any more guesses coming, my lord?'

'I might make a guess, but I won't. I'll buy it. What was the name?'

'Name of Arthur Cobbleigh.'

'And who's Arthur Cobbleigh when he's at home?'

'You hadn't guessed that, then?'

'No – my guess was quite different. Go on, Super. Spill the beans.'

'Well, now. Arthur Cobbleigh – seems he was just a bloke. But can you guess where he came from?'

'I've given up guessing.'

'He came from a little place near Dartford – only about half a mile from the wood where Deacon's body was found.'

'Oho! now we're coming to it.'

'I got on the phone straight away as soon as this letter came. Cobbleigh was a chap aged somewhere about twenty-five in 1914. Not a good record. Labourer. Been in trouble once or twice with the police for petty thieving and assault. Joined up in the first year of the war and considered rather a good riddance. Last seen on the last day of his leave in 1918, and that day was just two days after Deacon's escape from prison. Left his home to rejoin his unit. Never seen again. Last news of him. "Missing believed killed" in the retreat over the Marne. Officially, that is. Last actual news of him – over there!'

The Superintendent jerked his thumb in the general direction of the churchyard.

Wimsey groaned.

'It makes no sense, Super, it makes no sense! If this man Cobbleigh joins up in the first year of the war, how on earth could he have been elaborately in league with Deacon, who went to Maidstone in 1914? There was no time. Damn it! You don't get a man out of quod in a few spare hours spent on leave. If Cobbleigh had been a warder – if he'd been a fellow-convict – if he'd been anything to do with the prison, I could understand it. Had he a relation in the gaol or anything of that sort. There must have been something more to it than that.'

'Must there? Look here, my lord, how's this? I've been working this thing out coming over, and this is what I make out of it. Deacon bust away from a working-party, didn't he? He was found still wearing his prison dress, wasn't he? Doesn't that show his escape wasn't planned out elaborately beforehand? They'd have found him fast enough, if he hadn't gone and pitched down that denehole, wouldn't they? Now, you listen to this and see if it don't hold water. I can see it plain as a pikestaff. Here's this Cobbleigh – a hard nut, by all accounts. He's walking through the wood on the way from his mother's cottage, to take the train to Dartford for wherever he might be going to join up with the troops going back to France. Somewhere on that moor he finds a chap lurking about. He collars him, and finds he's pinched the escaped convict that everybody's looking for. The convict says, "Let me go, and I'll make you a rich man," see? Cobbleigh's got no objection to that. He says, "Lead me to it. What is it?" The convict says, "The Wilbraham emeralds, that's what it is." Cobbleigh says, "Coo! tell us some more about that. How'm I to know you ain't kidding me? You tell us where they are and we'll see about it." Deacon says, "No fear – catch me telling you, without you helps me first." Cobbleigh says, "You can't help yourself," he says, "I only got to give you up and then where'll you be?" Deacon says, "You won't get much out o' that. You stick by me and I'll put hundreds of thousands of pounds in your hands." They go on talking, and Deacon, like a fool, let's out that he's made a note of the hiding-place and had it on him. "Oh, have you?" says Cobbleigh, "then you damn well take that." And lams him over the head. Then he goes over him and finds the paper, which he's upset to find he can't make head or tail of. Then he has another look at Deacon and sees he's done him good and proper. "Oh, hell!" he says, "that's torn it. I better shove him out of the way and clear off." So he pops him down the hole and makes tracks for France. How's that, so far?'

'Fine, full-blooded stuff,' said Wimsey. 'But why should Deacon be carrying a note of the hiding-place about with him? And how did it come to be written on foreign paper?'

'I don't know. Well, say it was like you said before. Say he'd given the paper to his wife. He spills his wife's address like a fool, and then it all happens the way I said. Cobbleigh goes back to France, deserts, and gets taken care of by Suzanne. He keeps quiet about who he is, because he don't know whether Deacon's body's been found or not and he's afraid of being had up for murder if he goes home. Meanwhile, he's stuck to the paper – no, that's wrong. He writes to Mrs Deacon and gets the paper out of her.'

'Why should she give it up?'

'That's a puzzler. Oh, I know! I've got it this time. He tells her he's got the key to it. That's right. Deacon told him, "My wife's got the cipher, but she's a babbling fool and I ain't trusted her with the key. I'll give you the key and that'll show you I know what I'm talking about." Then Cobbleigh kills him, and when he thinks it's safe he writes to Mary and she sends him the paper.'

'The original paper?'

'Why, yes.'

'You'd think she'd keep that and send him a copy.'

'No. She sends the original, so that he can see it's in Deacon's writing.'

'But he wouldn't necessarily know Deacon's writing.'

'How's she to know that? Cobbleigh works out the cipher and they help him to get across.'

'But we've been into all that and decided the Thodays couldn't do it.'

'All right, then. The Thodays bring Cranton into it. Cobbleigh comes over, anyhow, under the name of Paul Taylor, and he comes along to Fenchurch and they get the emeralds. Then Thoday kills him, and *he* takes the emeralds. Meanwhile, along comes Cranton to see what's happening and finds they've been ahead of him. He clears off and the Thodays go about looking innocent till they see we're getting a bit close on their trail. Then *they* clear.'

'Who did the killing, then?'

'Any one of them, I should say.'

'And who did the burying?'

'Not Will, anyhow.'

'And how was it done? And why did they want to tie Cobbleigh up? Why not kill him straight off with a bang on the head? Why did Thoday take £200 out of the bank and put it back again? When did it all happen? Who was the man Potty Peake saw in the church on the night of the 30th? And, above all, why was the cipher found in the belfry of all places?'

'I can't answer everything at once, can I? That's the way it was done between 'em, you can take it from me. And now I'm going to have Cranton charged, and get hold of those precious Thodays, and if I don't put my hand on the emeralds among them, I'll eat my hat.'

'Oh!' said Wimsey, 'that reminds me. Before you came, we were just going to look at the place where Deacon hid those jolly old emeralds. The Rector solved the cipher – '

'Him?'

'He. So, just for fun, and by way of shutting the stable door after the steed was stolen, we're going to climb up aloft and have a hunt among the cherubims. In fact, the Rector is down at the church, champing his bit at this very moment. Shall we go?'

'Sure – though I haven't a lot of time to waste.'

'I don't suppose it will take long.'

The Rector had procured the sexton's ladder and was already up in the south aisle roof, covering himself with cobwebs as he poked about vaguely among the ancient oak.

'The servants sat just about here,' he said, as Wimsey came in with the Superintendent. 'But now I come to think of it, we had the painters up here last year, and they ought to have found anything there was to be found.'

'Perhaps they did,' said Wimsey; and Mr Blundell uttered a low moam.

'Oh, I hope not, I really think not. They are most honest men.' Mr Venables came down from the ladder. 'Perhaps you had better try. I am not clever about these things.'

'Beautiful old work this is,' said his lordship. 'All pegged together. There's a lot of this old rafter work down at Duke's Denver, and when I was a kid I made rather a pretty cache for myself in a corner of the attic. Used to keep tiddly-winks counters in it and pretend it was a pirate's hoard. Only it was a dickens of a job getting them out again. I say! Blundell! do you remember that wire hook you found in the corpse's pocket?'

'Yes, my lord. We never made out what that was for.'

'I ought to have known,' said Wimsey. 'I made a thing very like it for the pirate's hoard.' His long fingers were working over the beams, gently pulling at the thick wooden pegs which held them together. 'He must have been able to reach it from where he sat. Aha! what did I tell you? This is the one. Wriggle her gently and out she comes. Look!'

He wrenched at one of the pegs, and it came out in his hand. Originally, it had passed right through the beam and must have been over a foot in length, tapering from the size of a penny-piece at one end to something over half-an-inch at the other. But at some time it had been sawn off about three inches from the thick end.

'There you are,' said Wimsey. 'An old schoolboy cache originally, I expect. Some kid got pushing it from the other end and found it was loose. Probably shoved it clean out. At least, that's what I did, up in the attic. Then he took it home and sawed six inches or so out of the middle of it. Next time he comes to church he brings a short rod with him. He pushes the thin end back into place again with the rod, so that the hole doesn't show from the other side. Then he drops in his marbles or whatever he wanted to hide, and plugs up the big end again with this. And there he is, with a nice little six-inch hidey-hole where nobody would ever dream of looking for it. Or so he thinks. Then – perhaps years afterwards – along comes friend Deacon. He's sitting up here one day, possibly a little bored with the sermon (sorry, padre!). He starts fidgeting with the peg, and out it comes – only three inches of it. Hullo! says he, here's a game! Handy place if you wanted to pop any little thing away in a hurry. Later on, when he does want to pop his little shiners away in a hurry, he thinks of it again. Easy enough. Sits here all quiet and pious, listening to the First Lesson. Puts his hand down at his side, slips out the plug, slides the emeralds out of his pocket, slips them into the hole, pops back the plug. All over before his reverence says "Here endeth". Out into the sunshine and slap into the arms of our friend the Super here and his merry men. "Where are the emeralds?" they say. "You can search me," says he. And they do, and they've been searching ever since.'

'Amazing!' said the Rector. Mr Blundell uttered a regrettable expression, remembered his surroundings and coughed loudly.

'So now we see what the hook was for,' said Wimsey. 'When Legros, or Cobbleigh, whichever you like to call him, came for the loot – '

'Stop a minute,' objected the Superintendent. 'That cipher didn't mention anything about a hole, did it? It only mentioned cherubims. How did he know he needed a hook to get necklaces out of cherubims?'

'Perhaps he'd had a look at the place first. But of course, we know he did. That must have been what he was doing when Potty Peake saw him and Thoday in the church. He spotted the place then, and came back later. Though why he should have waited five days I couldn't tell you. Possibly something went wrong. Anyway, back he came, armed with his hook, and hitched the necklace out. Then, just as he was coming down the ladder, the accomplice took him from behind, tied him up and – and then – and then did away with him by some means we can't account for.'

The Superintendent scratched his head.

'You'd think he might have waited for a better place to do it in, wouldn't you, my lord? Putting him out here in the church, and all that bother of burying him and what not. Why didn't he go while the going was good, and shove Cobbleigh into the dyke or something on the way home?'

'Heaven knows,' said Wimsey. 'Anyhow, there's your hiding-place and there's the explanation of your hook.' He thrust the end of his fountain pen into the hole. 'It's quite deep – no, by Jove, it's not! it's not! it's only a shallow hole after all, not much longer than the peg. We can't, surely, have made a mistake. Where's my torch? Dash it! (Sorry, padre.) Is that wood? or is it – ? Here, Blundell, find me a mallet and a short, stout rod or stick of some kind – not too thick. We'll have this hole clear.'

'Run across to the Rectory and ask Hinkins,' suggested Mr Venables, helpfully.

In a few minutes' time, Mr Blundell returned, panting, with a short iron bar and a heavy wheel-spanner. Wimsey had shifted the ladder and was examining the narrow end of the oaken peg on the east side of the beam. He set one end of the bar firmly against the peg and smote lustily with the spanner. An ecclesiastical bat, startled from its resting-place by the jar, swooped out with a shriek, the tapered end of the peg shot smartly through the hole and out at the other side, and something else shot out with it – something that detached itself in falling from its wrapping of brown paper and cascaded in a flash of green and gold to the Rector's feet.

'Bless my heart!' cried Mr Venables.

'The emeralds!' yelled Mr Blundell. 'The emeralds, by God! And Deacon's fifty pounds with them.'

'And we're wrong, Blundell,' said Lord Peter. 'We've been wrong from start to finish. Nobody found them. Nobody killed anybody for them. Nobody deciphered the cryptogram. We're wrong, wrong, out of the hunt and wrong!'

'But we've got the emeralds,' said the Superintendent.

PART 3

A SHORT TOUCH OF STEDMAN'S TRIPLES
(Five Parts)

840

By the Part Ends
5 6 1 2 3 4
3 4 1 5 6 2
6 2 1 3 4 5
4 5 1 6 2 3
2 3 1 4 5 6
Treble the observation.

Call her the last whole turn, out quick, in slow, the second half turn and out slow. Four times repeated.
(TROYTE)

THE FIRST PART

THE QUICK WORK

The work of each bell is divided in three parts, viz. the quick work, dodging, and slow work.
TROYTE *On Change-Ringing*

Lord Peter Wimsey passed a restless day and night and was very silent the next day at breakfast.

At the earliest possible moment he got his car and went over to Leamholt.

'Superintendent,' he said, 'I think I have been the most unmitigated and unconscionable ass that ever brayed in a sleuth-hound's skin. Now, however, I have solved the entire problem, with one trivial exception. Probably you have done so too.'

'I'll buy it,' said Mr Blundell. 'I'm like you, my lord, I'm doing no more guessing. What's the bit you haven't solved, by the way?'

'Well, the murder,' said his lordship, with an embarrassed cough. 'I can't quite make out who did that, or how. But that, as I say, is a trifle. I know who the dead man was, why he was tied up, where he died, who sent the cryptogram to whom, why Will Thoday drew £200 out of the bank and put it back again, where the Thodays have gone and why and when they will return, why Jim Thoday missed his train, why Cranton came here, what he did and why he is lying about it, and how the beer-bottle got into the belfry.'

'Anything else?' asked Mr Blundell.

'Oh, yes. Why Jean Legros was silent about his past, what Arthur Cobbleigh did in the wood at Dartford, what the parrot was talking about and why the Thodays were not at Early Service on Sunday, what Tailor Paul had to do with it and why the face of the corpse was beaten in.'

'Excellent,' said Mr Blundell. 'Quite a walking library, aren't you, my lord? Couldn't you go just a step further and tell us who we're to put the handcuffs on?'

'I'm sorry. I can't do that. Dash it all, can't I leave one little titbit for a friend?'

'Well,' said Mr Blundell, 'I don't know that I ought to complain. Let's have the rest of it and perhaps we'll be able to do the last bit on our own.'

Lord Peter was silent for a moment.

'Look here, Super,' he said at last. 'This is going to be a dashed painful sort of story. I think I'd like to test it a bit before I come out with it. Will you do something yourself, first? You've got to do it in any case, but I'd rather not say anything till it is done. After that, I'll say anything you like.'

'Well?'

'Will you get hold of a photograph of Arthur Cobbleigh and send it over to France for Suzanne Legros to identify?'

'That's got to be done, naturally. Matter of routine.'

'If she identifies it, well and good. But if she's stubborn and refuses, will you give her this note, just as it is, and watch her when she opens it?'

'Well, I don't know about doing that personally, my lord, but I'll see that this Monsieur Rozier does it.'

'That will do. And will you also show her the cryptogram?'

'Yes, why not? Anything else?'

'Yes,' said Wimsey, more slowly. 'The Thodays. I'm a little uncomfortable about the Thodays. You're trailing them, I suppose?'

'What do you think?'

'Exactly. Well, when you've put your hands on them, will you let me know before you do anything drastic? I'd rather like to be there when you question them.'

'I've no objection to that, my lord. And this time they'll have to come across with some sort of story, Judge's Rules or no Judge's Rules, even if it breaks me.'

'You won't have any difficulty about that,' said Wimsey. 'Provided, that is, you catch them within a fortnight. After that, it will be more difficult.'

'Why within a fortnight?'

'Oh, come!' expostulated his lordship. 'Isn't it obvious? I show Mrs Thoday the cipher. On Sunday morning neither she nor her husband attends Holy Communion. On Monday they depart to London by the first train. My dear Watson, it's staring you in the face. The only real danger is – '

'Well?'

'The Archbishop of Canterbury. A haughty prelate, Blundell. An arbitrary prince. But I don't suppose they'll think about him, somehow. I think you may risk him.'

'Oh, indeed! And how about Mr Mussolini and the Emperor of Japan?'

'Negligible. Negligible,' replied his lordship, with a wave of the hand. 'Likewise the Bishop of Rome. But get on to it Blundell, get on to it.'

'I mean to,' said Mr Blundell, with emphasis. 'They'll not get out of the country, that's a certainty.'

'So it is, so it is. Of course, they'll be back here by tomorrow fortnight, but that will be too late. How soon do you expect Jim Thoday back? End of the month? Be sure he doesn't give you the slip. I've an idea he may try to.'

'You think he's our man?'

'I don't know, I tell you. I don't want him to be. I rather hope it's Cranton.'

'Poor old Cranton,' said the Superintendent, perversely, 'I rather hope it isn't. I don't like to see a perfectly good jewel-thief stepping out of his regular line, so to speak. It's disconcerting that's what it is. Besides, the man's ill. However, we shall see about that. I'll get on to this Cobbleigh business and settle it.'

'Right!' said Wimsey. 'And I think, after all, I'll ring up the Archbishop. You never know.'

'Dotty!' said Mr Blundell to himself. 'Or pulling my leg. One or the other.'

Lord Peter Wimsey communicated with the Archbishop, and appeared to be satisfied with the result. He also wrote to Hilary Thorpe, giving her an account of the finding of the emeralds. 'So you see,' he said, 'your Sherlocking was very successful. How pleased Uncle Edward will be.' Hilary's reply informed him that old Mrs Wilbraham had taken the necklace and restored the money paid in compensation – all without comment or apology. Lord Peter haunted the Rectory like an unhappy ghost. The Superintendent had gone to town in pursuit of the Thodays. On Thursday things began to happen again.

Telegram from Commissaire Rozier to Superintendent Blundell:

Suzanne Legros no knowledge Cobbleigh identifies photograph in sealed envelope as her husband identification supported by mayor here do you desire further action.

Telegram from Superintendent Blundell to Lord Peter Wimsey:

Suzanne Legros rejects Cobbleigh identifies sealed photograph who is it unable trace Thodays in London.

Telegram from Superintendent Blundell to Commissaire Rozier:

Please return papers immediately detain Legros pending further information.

Telegram from Lord Peter Wimsey to Superintendent Blundell:

Surely you know by this time try all churches registrars.

Telegram from Superintendent Blundell to Lord Peter Wimsey:

Vicar St Andrews Bloomsbury says asked perform marriage by licence William Thoday Mary Deacon both of that parish was it Deacon.

Telegram from Lord Peter Wimsey to Superintendent Blundell:

Yes of course you juggins charge Cranton at once.

Telegram from Superintendent Blundell to Lord Peter Wimsey:

Agreed juggins but why charge Cranton Thodays found and detained for inquiry.

Telegram from Lord Peter Wimsey to Superintendent Blundell:

Charge Cranton first joining you in town.

After dispatching this wire, Lord Peter summoned Bunter to pack up his belongings and asked for a private interview with Mr Venables, from which both men emerged looking distressed and uneasy.

'So I think I'd better go,' said Wimsey. 'I rather wish I hadn't come buttin' into this. Some things may be better left alone, don't you think? My sympathies are all in the wrong place and I don't like it. I know all about not doing evil that good may come. It's doin' good that evil may come that is so embarrassin'.'

'My dear boy,' said the Rector, 'it does not do for us to take too much thought for the morrow. It is better to follow the truth and leave the result in the hand of God. He can foresee where we cannot, because He knows all the facts.'

'And never has to argue ahead of His data, as Sherlock Holmes would say? Well, padre, I dare say you're right. Probably I'm tryin' to be too clever. That's me every time. I'm sorry to have made so much unpleasantness, anyhow. And I really would rather go away now. I've got that silly modern squeamishness that doesn't like watchin' people suffer. Thanks awfully for everything. Good-bye.'

Before leaving Fenchurch St Paul, he went and stood in the churchyard. The grave of the unknown victim still stood raw and black amid the grass, but the grave of Sir Henry and Lady Thorpe had been roofed in with green turves. Not far away there was an ancient box tomb; Hezekiah Lavender was seated on the slab, carefully cleaning the letters of the inscription. Wimsey went over and shook hands with the old man.

'Makin' old Samuel fine and clean for the summer,' said Hezekiah. 'Ah! Beaten old Samuel by ten good year, I have. I says to Rector, "Lay me aside old Samuel," I says, "for everybody to see as I beaten him." An' I got Rector's promise. Ah! so I have. But they don't write no sech beautiful poetry these here times.'

He laid a gouty finger on the inscription, which ran:

Here lies the Body of SAMUEL SNELL
That for fifty Years pulled the Tenor Bell.
Through Changes of this Mortal Race
He Laid his Blows and Kept his Place
Till Death that Changes all did Come
To Hunt him Down and Call him Home.
His Wheel is broke his Rope is Slackt
His Clapper Mute his Metal Crackt,
Yet when the great Call summons him from Ground
He shall be Raised up Tuneable and Sound.
MDCXCVIII
Aged 76 years

'Ringing Tailor Paul seems to be a healthy occupation,' said Wimsey. 'His servants live to a ripe old age, what?'

'Ah!' said Hezekiah. 'So they du, young man, so they du, if so be they're faithful tu 'un an' don't go a-angerin' on 'un. They bells du know well who's a-haulin' of 'un. Wunnerful understandin' they is. They can't abide a wicked man. They lays in wait to overthrow 'un. But old Tailor Paul can't say I ain't done well by her an' she allus done well by me. Make righteousness your course bell, my lord, an' keep a-follerin' on her an' she'll see you through your changes till Death calls you to stand. Yew ain't no call to be afeared o' the bells if so be as yew follows righteousness.'

'Oh, quite,' said Wimsey, a little embarrassed.

He left Hezekiah and went into the church, stepping softly as though he feared to rouse up something from its sleep. Abbot Thomas was quiet in his tomb; the cherubims, open-eyed and open-mouthed, were absorbed in their everlasting contemplation; far over him he felt the patient watchfulness of the bells.

THE SECOND PART

NOBBY GOES IN SLOW AND COMES OUT QUICK

It is a frightful plight. Two angels buried him . . . in Vollombrosa by night; I saw it, standing among the lotus and hemlock.

J. SHERIDAN LEFANU: *Wylder's Hand*

Mr Cranton was in an infirmary as the guest of His Majesty the King, and looked better than when they had last seen him. He showed no surprise at being charged with the murder of Geoffrey Deacon, twelve years or so after that gentleman's reputed decease.

'Right!' said Mr Cranton. 'I rather expected you'd get on to it, but I kept on hoping you mightn't. I didn't do it, and I want to make a statement. Do sit down. These quarters aren't what I could wish for a gentleman, but they seem to be the best the Old Country can offer. I'm told they do it much prettier in Sing Sing. England, with all thy faults, I love thee still. Where do you want me to begin?'

'Begin at the beginning,' suggested Wimsey, 'go on till you get to the end and then stop. May he have a fag, Charles?'

'Well, my lord and – no,' said Mr Cranton, 'I won't say gentlemen. Seems to go against the grain, somehow. Officers, if you like, but not gentlemen. Well, my lord and officers. I don't need to tell you that I'm a deeply injured man. I said I never had those shiners, didn't I? And you see I was right. What you want to know is, how did I first hear that Deacon was still on deck? Well, he wrote me a letter, that's how. Somewhere about last July, that would be. Sent it to the old crib, and it was forwarded on – never you mind who by.'

'Gammy Pluck,' observed Mr Parker, distantly.

'I name no names,' said Mr Cranton. 'Honour among – gentlemen. I burnt that letter, *being* an honourable gentleman, but it was some story, and I don't know that I can do justice to it. Seems that when Deacon made his getaway, after an unfortunate encounter with a warder, he had to sneak about Kent in a damned uncomfortable sort of way for a day or two. He said the stupidity of the police was almost incredible. Walked right over him twice, he said. One time they trod on him. Said he'd never realised so vividly before why a policeman was called a flattie. Nearly broke his fingers standing on them. Now I,' added Mr Cranton, 'have rather small feet. Small and well-shod. You can always tell a gentleman by his feet.'

'Go on, Nobby,' said Mr Parker.

'Anyhow, the third night he was out there lying doggo in a wood somewhere, he heard a chap coming along that wasn't a flattie. Rolling drunk, Deacon said he was. So Deacon pops out from behind a tree and pastes the fellow one. He said he didn't mean to do him in, only put him out, but he must have struck a bit harder than what he meant. Mind you, that's only what he said, but Deacon always was a low kind of fellow and he'd laid out one man already and you can't hang a chap twice. Anyway, he found he'd been and gone and done it, and that was that.

'What he wanted, of course, was duds, and when he came to examine the takings, he found he'd bagged a Tommy in uniform with all his kit. Well, that wasn't very surprising, come to think of it. There were a lot of those about in 1918, but it sort of took Deacon aback. Of course, he knew there was a war on – they'd been told all about that – but it hadn't, as you might say, come home to him. This Tommy had some papers and stuff on him and a torch, and from what Deacon could make out, looking into the thing rather hurriedly in a retired spot, he was just coming off his leaf and due to get back to the Front. Well, Deacon thought, any hole's better than Maidstone Gaol, so here goes. So he changes clothes with the Tommy down to his skin, collars his papers and what not, and tips the body down the hole. Deacon was a Kentish man himself, you see, and knew the place. Of course, he didn't know the first thing about soldiering – however, needs must and all that. He thought his best way was to get up to Town and maybe he'd find some old pal up there to look after him. So he tramped off – and eventually he got a lift on a lorry or something to a railway station. He did mention the name, but I've forgotten it. He picked some town he'd never been in – a small place. Anyway, he found a train going to London and he piled into it. That was all right; but somewhere on the way, in got a whole bunch of soldiers, pretty lit-up and cheery, and from the way they talked, Deacon began to find out what he was up against. It came over him, you see, that here he was, all dressed up as a perfectly good Tommy, and not knowing the first thing about the War, or drill or anything, and he knew if he opened his mouth he'd put his foot in it.'

'Of course,' said Wimsey. 'It'd be like dressing up as a Freemason. You couldn't hope to get away with it.'

'That's it. Deacon said it was like being among people talking a foreign language. Worse; because Deacon did know a bit about foreign languages. He was an educated sort of bloke. But this Army stuff was beyond him. So all he could do was to pretend to be asleep. He said he just rolled up in his corner and snored, and if anybody spoke to him he swore at them. It worked quite well, he said. There was one very pesistent bloke, though, with a bottle of Scotch. He kept on shoving drinks at Deacon and he took a few, and then some more, and by the time he got to London he was pretty genuinely sozzled. You see, he'd had nothing to eat, to speak of, for a coupla days, except some bread he'd managed to scrounge from a cottage.'

The policeman who was taking all this down in shorthand scratched stolidly on over the paper. Mr Cranton took a drink of water and resumed.

'Deacon said he wasn't very clear what happened to him after that. He wanted to get out of the station and go off somewhere, but he found it wasn't so easy. The darkened streets confused him, and the persistent fellow with the bottle of Scotch seemed to have taken a fancy to him. This bloke talked all the time, which was lucky for Deacon. He said he remembered having some more drinks and something about a canteen, and tripping over something and a lot of chaps laughing at him. And after that he must really have fallen asleep. The next thing he knew, he was in a train again, with Tommies all around him, and from what he could make out, they were bound for the Front.'

'That's a very remarkable story,' said Mr Parker.

'It's clear enough,' said Wimsey. 'Some kindly soul must have examined his papers, found he was due back and shoved him on to the nearest transport, bound for Dover, I suppose.'

'That's right,' said Mr Cranton. 'Caught in the machine' as you might say. Well, all he could do was to lie doggo again. There were plenty of others who seemed to be dog-tired and fairly well canned and he wasn't in any way remarkable. He watched what the others did, and produced his papers at the right time and all that. Fortunately, nobody else seemed to belong to his particular unit. So he got across. Mind you,' added Mr Cranton, 'I can't tell you all the details. I wasn't in the War myself, being otherwise engaged. You must fill up the blanks for yourself. He said he was damned seasick on the way over, and after that he slept in a sort of cattle-waggon and finally they bundled him out at last in the dark at some ghastly place or other. After a bit he heard somebody asking if there was anyone belonging to his unit. He knew enough to say "Yes, sir," and stand forward – and then he found himself foot-slogging over filthy road full of holes with a small party of men and an officer. God! he said it went on for hours and he thought they must have done about a hundred miles, but I daresay that was an exaggeration. And he said there was a noise like merry hell going on ahead, and the ground began to shake, and he suddenly grasped what he was in for.'

'This is an epic,' said Wimsey.

'I can't do justice to it,' said Mr Cranton, 'because Deacon never knew what he was doing and I don't know enough to make a guess. But I gather he walked straight into a big strafe. Hell let loose, he said, and I shouldn't wonder if he began to think kindly of Maidstone Gaol and even of the condemned cell. Apparently he never got to the trenches, because they were being shelled out of them and he got mixed up in the retreat. He lost his party and something hit him on the head and laid him out. Next thing he knew he was lying in a shell-hole along with somebody who'd been dead some time. I don't know. I couldn't follow it all. But after a bit he crawled out. Everything was quiet and it was coming on dark, so he must have lost a whole day somehow. He'd lost his sense of direction, too, he said. He wondered about, and fell in and out of mud and holes and wire, and in the end he stumbled into a shed where there was some hay and stuff. But he couldn't remember much about that, either, because he'd had a devil of a knock on the head and he was getting feverish. And then a girl found him.'

'We know all about that,' said the Superintendent.

'Yes, I daresay you do. You seem to know a lot. Well, Deacon was pretty smart about that. He got round the soft side of the girl and they made up a story for him. He said it was fairly easy pretending to have lost his memory. Where the doctor blokes made a mistake was trying to catch him out with bits of Army drill. He'd never done any, so of course he didn't have to pretend not to recognise it. The hardest part was making out that he didn't know any English. They nearly got him on that, once or twice. But he did know French, so he did his best to seem intelligent about that. His French accent was pretty good, but he pretended to have lost his speech, so that any mumbling or stammering might be put down to that, and in the intervals he practised talking to the girl till he was word-perfect. I must say, Deacon had brains.'

'We can imagine all that part,' said Parker. 'Now tell us about the emeralds.'

'Oh, yes. The thing that started him on that was getting hold of an old English newspaper which had a mention of the finding of a body in the dene-hole – his own body, as everone thought. It was a 1918 paper, of course, but he only came across it in 1924 – I forget where. It turned up, the way things do. Somebody's used it to wrap something sometime, and I think he came across it in an estaminet. He didn't bother about it, because the farm was doing pretty well – he'd married the girl by then, you see – and he was quite happy. But later on, things began to go badly, and it worried him to think about those sparklers all tucked away doing no good to anybody. But he didn't know how to start getting hold of them, and he got a vertical breeze up every time he thought of that dead warder and the chap he'd thrown down the hole. However, in the end, he called to mind yours truly, and figured it out that I'd be out on my own again. So he wrote me a letter. Well, as you know, I wasn't out. I was inside again, owing to a regrettable misunderstanding, so I didn't get the letter for some time, my pals thinking it wasn't quite the sort of thing to send to the place where I was. See? But when I came out again, there was the letter waiting for me.'

'I wonder he made *you* his confidant,' observed Parker. 'There had been – shall we say, ungentlemanly words passed on the subject.'

'Ah!' said Mr Cranton. 'There had, and I had something to say about that when I wrote back. But you see, he'd nobody else to go to, had he? When all's said and done, there's nobody like Nobby Cranton to handle a job like that in a refined and competent manner. I give you my word I nearly told him to go and boil himself, but in the end I said, No! Let bygones be bygones. So I promised to help the blighter. I told him I could fix him up with money and papers and get him across all right. Only I told him he'd have to give me a bit more dope on the thing first. Otherwise, how was I to know he wouldn't double-cross me again, the dirty skunk?'

'Nothing more likely,' said Parker.

'Ah! and he did, too,' blast his worm-eaten little soul! I said he'd have to tell me where the stuff was. And, would you believe it, the hound wouldn't trust me! Said, if he told me that, I might get in and pinch the bleeding lot before he got there!'

'Incredible!' said Parker. 'Of course you wouldn't do such a thing as that.'

'Not me,' replied Nobby. 'What do *you* think?' He winked. 'Well, we went on writing backwards and forwards till we reached what they call an impasse. At last he wrote and said he'd send me a what d'you call – a cipher, and if I could make out from that where the shiners were, I was welcome. Well, he sent the thing, and I couldn't make head or tail of it, and I told him so. Then he said, All right; if I didn't trust him I could go down to Fenchurch and ask for a tailor called Paul as lived next door to Batty Thomas, and they'd give me the key, but, he says, you'd do better to leave it to me, because I know how to handle them. Well, I didn't know, only I thought to myself if these two chaps come in on it they'll want their share, and they might turn sour on me, and it seemed to me I was safer with Deacon, because he stood to lose more than I did. Call me a mug if you like, but I sent him over the money and some perfectly good papers. Of course, he couldn't come as Deacon and he didn't want to come as Legros, because there might be a spot of trouble over that, and he suggested his papers should be made out as Paul Taylor. I thought it a bit silly myself, but he seemed to think it would be a good joke. Now, of course, I know why. So the papers were made out, with a lovely photograph – a real nice job, that was. Might have been anybody. As a matter of fact, it was a composite. It looked very convincing, and had quite a look of all sorts of people. Oh, yes! and I sent him some clothes to meet him at Ostend, because he said his own things were too Frenchy. He came across on the 29th December. I suppose you got on to that?'

'Yes,' said Blundell, 'we did, but it didn't help us a lot.'

'That bit went all right. He sent me a message from Dover. Telephoned from a public call-box – but I'll forgive you for not tracing that. He said he was going straight through and would come along up to London with the stuff next day or the day after, or as soon as he could. Anyway, he would get a message through somehow. I wondered whether I oughtn't to go down to Fenchurch myself – mind you, I never trusted him – but I wasn't altogether keen, in spite of my face-fungus. I'd grown that on spec, you understand. I didn't want you people following me about too much. And besides, I had one or two other irons in the fire. I'm coming clean, you see.'

'You'd better,' said Parker, ominously.

'I didn't get any message on the 30th, nor yet on the 31st, and I thought I'd been had proper. Only I couldn't see what he had to gain by double-crossing me. He needed me to handle the goods – or so I thought. Only then it struck me he might have picked up some other pal over at Maidstone or abroad.'

'In that case, why bring you into it at all?'

'That's what I thought. But I got so windy, I thought I'd better go down to the place and see what was happening. I didn't want to leave a trail, so I went over to Walbeach – never mind how, that's off the point –'

'Probably Sparky Bones or the Fly-catcher,' put in Parker, thoughtfully.

'Ask no questions and you'll hear no lies. My pal decanted me a few miles out and I footslogged it. I made out I was a tramp labourer, looking for work on the New Cut. Thank God, they weren't taking on any hands, so they didn't detain me.'

'So we gathered.'

'Ah! I suppose you would go nosey-parkering round there. I got a lift part of the way to Fenchurch and walked the rest. Beastly country it is, too, as I said before. I'm not doing my hiking thereabouts, I can tell you.'

'That was when we ran across one another, I think,' said Wimsey.

'Ah! and if I'd known who I had the pleasure of stopping I'd have walked off home,' said Mr Cranton, handsomely. 'But I didn't know, so I trotted along and – but there! I expect you know that part of it.'

'You got a job with Ezra Wilderspin and made inquiries for Paul Taylor.'

'Yes – and a nice business that was!' exclaimed Nobby with indignation. 'Mr Paul Bleeding Taylor and Mr Batty Thomas! Bells, if you please! And not a hide nor hair of *my* Paul Taylor to be seen or heard of. I tell you, that made me think a bit. I didn't know if he'd been and gone, or if he'd been pinched on the way, or if he was lurking about round the corner or what. And that chap Wilderspin – he was a good hand at keeping a hardworking man's nose to the grindstone, curse him! "Driver, come here!" "Steve, do this!" I didn't have a minute to call my own. All the same, I started to think quite a lot about that cipher. I took the idea that maybe it had to do with those bells. But could I get into the confounded belfry? No, I couldn't. Not openly, I mean. So I made out to do it one night and see if I could make sense of the thing up there. So I made a couple or so of pick-locks, the forge being handy for the job, and on Saturday night I just let myself quietly out of Ezra's back-door.

'Now, look here. What I'm going to tell you is gospel truth. I went down to that church a bit after midnight, and the minute I put my hand on the door, I found it was open. What did I think? Why, I thought Deacon must be in there on the job. Who else was it likely to be, that time of night? I'd been in the place before and made out where the belfry door was, so I went along nice and quiet, and that was open, too. "That's all right," I thought. "Deacon's here, and I'll give him Tailor Paul and Batty Thomas for not keeping me posted. I got up into a sort of place with ropes in it – damn nasty, I thought they looked. And then there was a ladder and more ropes a-top of that. And then another ladder and a trap-door.'

'Was the trap-door open?'

'Yes, and I went up. And I didn't half like it, either. Do you know, when I got up into the next place – Gee! there was a queer feel about it. Not a sound, but like as if there might be people standing round. And dark! It was a pitch-black beast of a night and raining like hell, but I never met anything like the blackness of that place. And I felt as if there was hundreds of eyes watching me. Talk about the heebie-jeebies! Well there!

'After a bit, with still not a sound, I sort of pulled myself together and put my torch on. Say, have you ever been up in that place? Ever seen those bells? I'm not what you'd call fanciful in a general way, but there was something about the bells that gave me the fantods.'

'I know,' said Wimsey, 'they look as if they were going to come down on you.'

'Yes, *you* know,' said Nobby, eagerly. 'Well, I'd got to where I wanted, but I didn't know where to begin. I didn't know the first thing about bells, or how to get to them or anything. And I couldn't make out what had happened to Deacon. So I looked round on the floor with the torch and – Boo! – there he was!'

'Dead?'

'Dead as a door-nail. Tied up to a big kind of post, and a look on his face

– there! I don't want to see a face like that again. Just as though he'd been struck dead and mad all at one go, if you see what I mean.'

'I suppose there's no doubt he was dead?'

'Dead?' Mr Cranton laughed. 'I never saw anyone deader.'

'Stiff?'

'No, not stiff. But cold, my God! I just touched him. He swung on the ropes and his head had fallen over – well, it looked as if he'd got what was coming to him, anyhow, but worse. Because, to do them justice, they're pretty quick on the drop, but he looked as if it had lasted for a good long time.'

'Do you mean the rope was round his neck?' demanded Parker, a little impatiently.

'No. He wasn't hanged. I don't know what killed him. I was just looking to see, when I heard somebody starting to come up the tower. I didn't stop, you bet. There was another ladder, and I legged it up that as high as I could go, till I got to a sort of hatch leading out on to the roof, I suppose, I squatted inside that and hoped the other fellow wouldn't take it into his head to come up after me, I wasn't keen on being found up there at all, and the body of my old pal Deacon might want some explaining. Of course, I could have told the truth, and pointed out that the poor bloke was cold before I got there, but me having pick-locks in my pocket rather jiggered up that bit of the alibi. So I sat tight. The chap came up into the place where the body was and started moving round and shuffling about, and once or twice he said "Oh, God!" in a groaning sort of voice. Then there was a nasty sort of thump, and I reckoned he'd got the body down on the floor. Then after a bit I heard him pulling and hauling, and presently his steps went across the floor very low and heavy, and a bumping noise, like he was dragging old Deacon after him. I couldn't see him at all from where I was, because from my corner I could only see the ladder and the wall opposite, and he was right away on the other side of the room. After that there was more scuffling, and a sort of bumping and sliding, and I took it he was getting the body down the other ladder. And I didn't envy him the job, neither.

'I waited up there and waited, till I couldn't hear him any more, and then I began to wonder what I should do next. So I tried the door on to the roof. There was a bolt inside, so I undid that and stepped out. It was raining like blazes and pitch-black, but out I crawled and got to the edge of the tower and looked over. How high is that cursed tower? Hundred and thirty feet, eh? Well, it felt like a thousand and thirty. I'm no cat-burglar, nor yet a steeplejack. I looked down, and I saw a light moving about right away up the other end of the church, miles away beneath me in the graveyard. I tell you I hung on to that blinking parapet with both hands and I got a feeling in my stomach as though me and the tower and everything was crumbling away and going over. I was glad I couldn't see more than I did.

'Well, I thought, you'd better make tracks, Nobby, while the dirty work's going on down there. So I came in again carefully and bolted the door after me and started to come down the ladder. It was awkward going in the dark and after a bit I switched my torch on, and I wished I hadn't. There I was, and those bells just beneath me – and, God! how I hated the look of them. I went all cold and sweaty and the torch slipped out of my hand and went down, and hit one of the bells. I'll never forget the noise it made. It wasn't loud, but kind of terribly sweet and threatening, and it went humming on and on, and a whole lot of other notes seemed to come out of it, high up and clear and close – right in my ears. You'll think I'm loony, but I tell you that bell was alive. I shut my eyes and hung on to the ladder and wished I'd chosen a different kind of profession – and that'll show you what a state I was in.'

'You've got too much imagination, Nobby,' said Parker.

'You wait, Charles,' said Lord Peter. 'You wait till you get stuck on a ladder in a belfry in the dark. Bells are like cats and mirrors – they're always queer, and it doesn't do to think too much about them. Go on, Cranton.'

'That's just what I couldn't do,' said Nobby, frankly. 'Not for a bit. It felt like hours, but I daresay it wasn't more than five minutes. I crawled down at last – in the dark, of course, having lost the torch. I groped round after it and found it, but the bulb had gone, naturally, and I hadn't any matches. So I had to feel for the trap-door, and I was terrified of pitching right down. But I found it at last, and after that it was easier, though I had a nasty time on the spiral staircase. The steps are all worn away, and I slipped about, and the walls were so close I couldn't breathe. My man had left all the doors open, so I knew he'd be coming back, and that didn't cheer me up much, either. When I was out in the church I hared it for all I was worth to the door. I tripped over something on the way, too, that made an awful clatter. Something like a big metal pot.'

'The brass ewer at the foot of the font,' said Wimsey.

'They didn't ought to keep it there,' said Mr Cranton, indignantly. 'And when I got out through the porch, I had to pussyfoot pretty gently over the beastly creaking gravel. In the end I got away and then I ran – golly, how I ran! I hadn't left anything behind at Wilderspin's, bar a shirt they'd lent me and a toothbrush I'd bought in the village, and I wasn't going back there. I ran and ran like hell, and the rain was something cruel. And it's a hell of a country. Ditches and bridges all over the place. There was a car came past one time, and trying to get out of the light, I missed my footing and rolled down the bank into a ditch full of water. Cold? It was like an ice-bath. I fetched up at last in a barn near a railway station and shivered there till morning, and presently a train came along, so I got on that. I forget the name of the place, but it must have been ten or fifteen miles away from Fenchurch. By the time I got up to London I was in a fever, I can tell you; rheumatic fever, or so they said. And you see what it's done to me. I pretty nearly faded out, and I rather wish I had. I'll never be fit for anything again. But that's the truth and the whole truth, my lord, and officers. Except that when I came to look myself over. I couldn't find Deacon's cipher. I thought I'd lost it on the road, but if you picked it up in the belfry, it must have come out of my pocket when I pulled the torch out. I never killed Deacon, but I knew I'd have a job to prove I didn't and that's why I spun you a different tale the first time you came.'

'Well,' said Chief Inspector Parker, 'let's hope it'll be a lesson to you to keep out of belfries.'

'It will,' replied Nobby fervently. 'Every time I see a church tower now it gives me the jim-jams. I'm done with religion, I am, and if I ever go inside a church-door again, you can take and put me in Broadmoor.'

THE THIRD PART

WILL THODAY GOES IN QUICK AND COMES OUT SLOW

For while I held my tongue, my bones consumed away through my daily complaining.

Psalm xxxii. 3

Wimsey thought he had never seen such utter despondency on any face as on William Thoday's. It was the face of a man pushed to the last extremity, haggard and grey, and pinched about the nostrils like a dead man's. On Mary's face there was anxiety and distress, but something combative and alert as well. She was still fighting, but Will was obviously beaten.

'Now then, you two,' said Superintendent Blundell, 'lets hear what you have to say for yourselves.'

'We've done nothing we need be ashamed of,' said Mary.

'Leave it to me, Mary,' said Will. He turned wearily to the Superintendent. 'Well,' he said, 'you've found out about Deacon, I suppose. You know that he done us and ours a wrong that can't be put right. We been trying, Mary and me, to put right as much as we can, but you've stepped in. Reckon we might have known we couldn't keep it quiet, but what else could we do? There's been talk enough about poor Mary down in the village, and we thought the best thing was to slip away, hoping to make an honest woman of her without asking the leaves of all they folk with long tongues as 'ud only be too glad to know something against us. And why shouldn't we? It weren't no fault of ours. What call have you got to stop us?'

'See here, Will,' said Mr Blundell, 'it's rough luck on you, and I'm not saying as 'tisn't, but the law's the law. Deacon was a bad lot, as we all know, but the fact remains somebody put him away, and it's our job to find out who did it.'

'I ain't got nothing to say about that,' said Will Thoday, slowly. 'But it's cruel hard if Mary and me – '

'Just a moment,' said Wimsey. 'I don't thing you quite realise the position, Thoday. Mr Blundell doesn't want to stand in the way of your marriage, but, as he says, somebody did murder Deacon, and the ugly fact remains that you were the man with the best cause to do it. And that means, supposing a charge were laid against you, and brought into court – well, they might want this lady to give evidence.'

'And if they did?' said Will.

'Just this,' said Wimsey. 'The law does not allow a wife to give evidence against her husband.' He waited while this sank in. 'Have a cigarette, Thoday. Think it out.'

'I see,' said Thoday, bitterly. 'I see. It comes to this – there ain't no end to the wrong that devil done us. He ruined my poor Mary and brought her into the dock once, and he robbed her of her good name and made bastards of our little girls, and now he can come between us again at the altar rails and drive her into the witness-box to put my neck in the rope. If ever a man deserved killing, he's the one, and I hope he's burning in hell for it now.'

'Very likely he is,' said Wimsey, 'but you see the point. If you don't tell us the truth now – '

'I've nothing to tell you but this,' broke in Thoday in a kind of desperation. 'My wife – and she *is* my wife in God's sight and mine – she never knew nothing about it. Not one word. And she knows nothing now, nothing but the name of the man rotting in that grave. And that's the truth as God sees us.'

'Well,' said Mr Blundell, 'you'll have to prove that.'

'That's not quite true, Blundell,' said Wimsey, 'but I dare day it could be proved. Mrs Thoday – '

The woman looked quickly and gratefully at him.

'When did you first realise that your first husband had been alive till the beginning of this year, and that you were, therefore, not legally married to Will Thoday here?'

'Only when you came to see me, my lord, last week.'

'When I showed you that piece of writing in Deacon's hand?'

'Yes, my lord.'

'But how did that – ?' began the Superintendent. Wimsey went on, drowning his voice.

'You realised then that the man buried in Lady Thorpe's grave must be Deacon.'

'It came over me, my lord, that that must be the way of it. I seemed to see a lot of things clear that I hadn't understood before.'

'Yes, You'd never doubted till that moment that Deacon had died in 1918?'

'Not for a moment, my lord. I'd never have married Will else.'

'You have always been a regular communicant?'

'Yes, my lord.'

'But last Sunday you stayed away.'

'Yes, I did, my lord. I couldn't come here, knowing as me and Will wasn't properly married. It didn't seem right, like.'

'Of course not,' said Wimsey. 'I beg your pardon Superintendent. I'm afraid I interrupted you,' he added, blandly.

'That's all very well,' said Mr Blundell. 'You said you didn't recognise that writing when his lordship showed it to you.'

'I'm afraid I did. It wasn't true – but I had to make up my mind quick – and I was afraid – '

'I'll bet you were. Afraid of getting Will into trouble, hey? Now, see here, Mary, how did you know that paper wasn't written donkey's years ago? What made you jump so quick to the idea Deacon was the corpse in the Thorpe grave? Just you answer me that, my girl, will you?'

'I don't know,' she said, faintly. 'It came over me all of a sudden.'

'Yes, it did,' thundered the Superintendent. 'And why? Because Will had told you about it already, and you knew the game was up. Because you'd seen that there paper before – '

'No, no!'

'I say, Yes. If you hadn't have known something, you'd have had no cause to deny the writing. You knew *when* it was written – now, didn't you?'

'That's a lie!' said Thoday.

'I really don't think you're right about that, Blundell,' said Wimsey, mildly, 'because, if Mrs Thoday had known about it all along, why shouldn't she have gone to Church last Sunday morning? I mean, don't you see, if she'd brazened it out all those months, why shouldn't she do it again?'

'Well,' retorted the Superintendent, 'and how about Will? He's been going to church all right, ain't he? You aren't going to tell me *he* knew nothing about it either.'

'Did he, Mrs Thoday?' inquired Wimsey, gently.

Mary Thoday hesitated.

'I can't tell you about that,' she said at last.

'Can't you, by God?' snapped Mr Blundell. 'Well, now, will you tell me – ?'

'It's no good, Mary,' said Will. 'Don't answer him. Don't say nothing. They'll only twist your words round into what you don't mean. We've got nothing to say and if I got to go through it, I got to go through it and that's all about it.'

'Not quite,' said Wimsey. 'Don't you see that if you tell us what you know, and we're satisfied that your wife knows nothing – then there's nothing to prevent your marriage from going through straight away? That's right, isn't it, Super?'

'Can't hold out any inducement, my lord,' said the Superintendent, stolidly.

'Of course not, but one can point out an obvious fact. You see,' went on Wimsey, 'somebody *must* have known something, for your wife to have jumped so quickly to the conclusion that the dead man was Deacon. If she hadn't already been suspicious about you – if *you* were perfectly ignorant and innocent the whole time – then *she* had the guilty knowledge. It would work all right that way, of course. Yes, I see now that it would. If she knew, and told you about it – then *you* would be the one with the sensitive conscience. *You* would have told *her* that you couldn't kneel at the altar with a guilty woman –'

'Stop that!' said Thoday. 'You say another word and I'll – Oh, my God! it wasn't that, my lord. She never knew. I did know. I'll say that much, I won't say no more, only that. As I hope to be saved, she never knew a word about it.'

'As you hope to be saved?' said Wimsey. 'Well, well. And you did know, and that's all you've got to tell us?'

'Now, look here,' said the Superintendent, 'you'll have to go a bit further than that, my lad. When did you know?'

'When the body was found,' replied Thoday, 'I knew then.' He spoke slowly, as though every word were being wrenched out of him. He went on more briskly: 'That's when I knew who it was.'

'Then why didn't you say so?' demanded Blundell.

'What, and have everybody know me and Mary wasn't married. Likely, ain't it?'

'Ah!' said Wimsey. 'But why didn't you get married then?'

Thoday shifted uncomfortably in his chair.

'Well, you see, my lord – I hope as Mary needn't ever know. It was a bitter hard thing for her, wasn't it? And the children. We couldn't ever put that right, you see. So I made up my mind to say nothing about it and take the sin – if it was a sin – on my shoulders. I didn't want to make no more trouble for her. Can't you understand that? Well, then – when she found it out, through seeing that there paper – ' He broke off and started again. 'You see, ever since the body was found I'd been worried and upset in my mind, like, and I daresay I was a bit queer in my ways and she'd noticed it – when she asked me if the dead man was Deacon after all, why, then I told her as it was, and that's how it all came about.'

'And how did you know who the dead man was?'

There was a long silence.

'He was terribly disfigured, you know,' went on Wimsey.

'You said you thought he was – that he'd been in prison,' stammered Thoday, 'and I said to myself – '

'Half a mo',' broke in the Superintendent, 'when did you ever hear his lordship say that? It wasn't brought out at the inquest, nor yet at the adjournment, because we were most particularly careful to say nothing about it. Now then!'

'I heard something about it from Rector's Emily,' said Thoday, slowly. 'She happened to hear something his lordship said to Mr Bunter.'

'Oh, *did* she?' snapped Mr Blundell. 'And how much more did Rector's Emily overhear, I'd like to know. That beer-bottle, now! Who told her to dust the fingerprints off it – come, now!'

'She didn't mean no harm about that,' said Will. 'It was nothing but the girl's curiosity. You know how they are. She came over next day and told Mary all about it. In a rare taking, she was.'

'Indeed!' said the Superintendent, unbelievingly. 'So *you* say. Never mind. Let's go back to Deacon. You heard that Emily heard something his lordship said to Mr Bunter about the dead man having been in prison. Was that it? And what did you think of that?'

'I said to myself, it must be Deacon. I said, here's that devil come out of his grave to trouble us again, that's what I said. Mind you, I didn't exactly know, but that's what I said to myself.'

'And what did you imagine he had come for?'

'How was I to know? I thought he'd come, that's all.'

'You thought he'd come after the emeralds, didn't you?' said the Superintendent.

For the first time a look of genuine surprise and eagerness came into the haunted eyes. 'The emeralds? Was *that* what he was after? Do you mean he had them after all? Why, we always thought the other fellow – Cranton – had got them.'

'You didn't know that they had been hidden in the church?'

'In the church?'

'We found them there on Monday,' explained his lordship, placidly, 'tucked away in the roof.'

'In the roof of the church? Why, then, *that* was what he – The emeralds found? Thank God for that! They'll not be able to say now as Mary had any hand in it.'

'True,' said Wimsey. 'But you were about to say something else, I rather fancy. "That was what he – ?' What? "That was what he was after when I found him in the church." Was that it?'

'No, my lord. I was going to say – I was just going to say, that was what he did with them.' A fresh wave of anger seemed to sweep over him. "The dirty villain! He did double-cross that other fellow after all.'

'Yes,' agreed his lordship. 'I'm afraid there's not much to be said in favour of the late Mr Deacon. I'm sorry, Mrs Thoday, but he was really rather an unsatisfactory person. And you're not the only one to suffer. He married another woman over in France, and she's left with three small children too.'

'Poor soul!' said Mary.

'The damned scoundrel!' exclaimed Will, 'if I'd have known that, I'd – '

'Yes?'

'Never mind,' growled the farmer. 'How did he come to be in France? How did he – ?'

'That's a long story,' said Wimsey, 'and rather far from the point at issue. Now, let's get your story clear. You heard that the body of a man who might have been a convict had been found in the churchyard, and though the face was quite unrecognisable, you were – shall we say inspired? to identify him with Geoffrey Deacon, whom you had supposed to have died in 1918. You said nothing about it till your wife, the other day, saw a bit of Deacon's handwriting, which might have been written at any time, and was – shall we again say inspired? – with the same idea. Without waiting for any further verification, you both rushed away to town to get remarried, and that's the only explanation you can give. Is that it?'

'That's all I can say, my lord.'

'And a damned thin story too,' observed Mr Blundell, truculently. 'Now, get this, Will Thoday. You know where you stand as well as I do. You know you're not bound to answer any questions now unless you like. But there's the inquest on the body; we can have that reopened, and you can tell your story to the coroner. Or you can be charged with the murder and tell it to a judge and jury. Or you can come clean now. Whichever you like. See?'

'I've nothing more to say, Mr Blundell.'

'I tell thee all, I can no more,' observed Wimsey thoughtfully. 'That's a pity, because the public prosecutor may get quite a different sort of story fixed in his mind. He may think, for instance, that you knew Deacon was alive because you had met him in the church on the night of December 30th.'

He waited to see the effect of this, and resumed:

'There's Potty Peake, you know. I don't suppose he's too potty to give evidence about what he saw and heard that night from behind Abbot Thomas's tomb. The black-bearded man and the voices in the vestry and Will Thoday fetching the rope from the cope-chest. What took you into the church, by the way? You saw a light, perhaps. And went along and found the door open, was that it? And in the vestry, you found a man doing something that looked suspicious. So you challenged him and when he spoke you knew who it was. It was lucky that the fellow didn't shoot you, but probably you took him unawares. Anyway, you threatened to give him up to justice and then he pointed out that would put your wife and children in an unpleasant position. So you indulged in a little friendly chat – did you speak? In the end, you compromised. You said you would keep quiet about it and get him out of the country with £200 in pocket, but you hadn't got it at the moment and in the meantime you would put him in a place of safety. Then you fetched a rope and tied him up. I don't know how you kept him quiet while you went to fetch it. Did you give him a straight left to the jaw, or what? . . . You won't help me? . . . Well, never mind. You tied him up and left him in the vestry while you went round to steal Mr Venables's keys. It's a miracle you found them in the right place, by the way. They seldom are. Then you took him up into the belfry, because the bell-chamber was nice and handy and had several locks to it, and was easier than escorting him out through the village. After that you brought him some food – perhaps Mrs Thoday could throw some light on that. Did you miss a quart bottle of beer or so about that time, Mrs Thoday? Some of those you got in for Jim? By the way, Jim is coming home and we'll have to have a word with him.'

Watching Mary's face, the Superintendent saw it contract suddenly with alarm, but she said nothing. Wimsey went on remorselessly.

'The next day you went over to Walbeach to get the money. But you weren't feeling well, and on the way home you broke down completely and couldn't get back to let Deacon out. That was damned awkward for you, wasn't it? You didn't want to confide in your wife. Of course, there was Jim.'

Thoday raised his head.

'I'm not saying anything one way or other, my lord, except this. I've never said one word to Jim about Deacon – not one word. Nor he to me. And that's the truth.'

'Very well,' said Wimsey. 'Whatever else happened, in between December 30th and January 4th, somebody killed Deacon. And on the night of the 4th, somebody buried the body. Somebody who knew him and took care to mutilate his face and hands beyond recognition. And what everybody will want to know is, at what moment did Deacon cease to be Deacon and become the body? Because that's rather the point, isn't it? We know that you couldn't very well have buried him yourself, because you were ill, but the killing is a different matter. You see, Thoday, he didn't starve to death. He died with a full tummy. *You* couldn't have fed him after the morning of December 31st. If you didn't kill him then, who took him his rations in the interval? And who, having fed him and killed him rolled him down the belfry ladder on the night of the 4th, with a witness sitting in the roof of the tower – a witness who had seen him and recognised him? A witness who – '

'Hold on, my lord,' said the Superintendent. 'The woman's fainted.'

THE FOURTH PART

THE SLOW WORK

Who shut up the sea with doors . . . and brake up for it my decreed place?
Job xxxviii. 8, 10

'He won't say anything,' said Superintendent Blundell.

'I know he won't,' said Wimsey. 'Have you arrested him?'

'No, my lord, I haven't. I've sent him home and told him to think it over. Of course, we could easily get him on being an accessory after the fact in both cases. I mean, he was shielding a known murderer – that's pretty clear, I fancy; and he's also shielding whoever killed Deacon, if he didn't do it himself. But I'm taking the view that we'll be able to handle him better after we've interrogated James. And we know James will be back in England at the end of the month. His owners have been very sensible. They've given him orders to come home, without saying what he's wanted for. They've arranged for another man to take his place and he's to report himself by the next boat.'

'Good! It's a damnable business, the whole thing. If ever a fellow deserved a sticky death, it's this Deacon brute. If the law had found him the law would have hanged him, with loud applause from all good citizens. Why should we hang a perfectly decent chap for anticipating the law and doing our dirty work for us?'

'Well, it *is* the law, my lord,' replied Mr Blundell, 'and it's not my place to argue about it. In any case, we're going to have a bit of a job to hang Will Thoday, unless it's as an accessory before the fact. Deacon was killed on a full stomach. If Will did away with him on the 30th, or the 31st, why did he go to collect the £200. If Deacon was dead, he wouldn't want it. On the other hand, if Deacon wasn't killed till the 4th, who fed him in the interval? If James killed him, why did he trouble to feed him first? The thing makes no sense.'

'Suppose Deacon was being fed by somebody,' said Wimsey, 'and suppose he said something infuriatin' and the somebody killed him all of a sudden in a frenzy, not meanin' to?'

'Yes, but how did he kill him? He wasn't stabbed or shot or clouted over the head.'

'Oh, I don't *know*,' said Wimsey. 'Curse the man! He's a perfect nuisance, dead or alive, and whoever killed him was a public benefactor. I wish I'd killed him myself. Perhaps I did. Perhaps the Rector did. Perhaps Hezekiah Lavender did.'

'I don't suppose it was any of those,' said Mr Blundell, stolidly. 'But it might have been somebody else, of course. There's that Potty, for instance. He's always wandering round the church at night. Only he'd have to get into the bell-chamber, and I don't see how he could. But I'm waiting for James. I've got a hunch that James may have quite a lot to tell us.'

'Have you? Oysters have beards, but they don't wag them.'

'If it comes to oysters,' said the Superintendent, 'there's ways and means of opening 'em – *and* you needn't swallow 'em whole, neither. You're not going back to Fenchurch?'

'Not just at present. I don't think there's very much I can do down there for a bit. But my brother Denver and I are going to Walbeach to open the New Cut. I expect we shall see you there.'

The only other thing of interest that happened during the next week or so was the sudden death of Mrs Wilbraham. She died at night and alone – apparently from mere old age – with the emeralds clasped in her hand. She left a will drawn up fifteen years earlier, in which she left the whole of her very considerable estate to her Cousin Henry Thorpe 'because he is the only honest man I know.' That she should cheerfully have left her only honest relative to suffer the wearing torments of straitened means and anxiety throughout the intervening period seemed to be only what anybody might have expected from her enigmatic and secretive disposition. A codicil, dated on the day after Henry's death, transferred the legacy to Hilary, while a further codicil, executed a few days before her own death, not only directed that the emeralds which had caused all the disturbance should be given to 'Lord Peter Wimsey who seems to be a sensible man and to have acted without interested motives,' but also made him Hilary's trustee. Lord Peter made a wry face over this bequest. He offered the necklace to Hilary, but she refused to touch it; it had painful associations for her. It was, indeed, only with difficulty that she was persuaded to accept the Wilbraham estate. She hated the thought of the testatrix; and besides, she had set her heart on earning her own living. 'Uncle Edward will be worse than ever,' she said. 'He will want me to marry some horrible rich man, and if I want to marry a poor one, he'll say he's after the money. And anyway, I don't want to marry anybody.'

'Then don't,' said Wimsey. 'Be a wealthy spinster.'

'And get like Aunt Wilbraham? Not me!'

'Of course not. Be a nice wealthy spinster.'

'Are there any?'

'Well, there's me. I mean, I'm a nice wealthy bachelor. Fairly nice, anyway. And it's fun to be rich. I find it so. You needn't spend it all on yachts and cocktails, you know. You could build something or endow something or run something or the other. If you don't take it, it will go to some ghastly person – Uncle Edward or somebody – whoever is Mrs Wilbraham's next-of-kin, and they'd be sure to do something silly with it.'

'Uncle Edward would,' said Hilary, thoughtfully.

'Well, you've got a few years to think it over,' said Wimsey. 'When you're of age, you can see about throwing it into the Thames. But what I'm to do with the emeralds I really don't know.'

'Beastly things,' said Hilary. 'They've killed grandfather, and practically killed Dad, and they've killed Deacon and they'll kill somebody else before long. I wouldn't touch them with a barge-pole.'

'I'll tell you what. I'll keep them till you're twenty-one, and then we'll form ourselves into a Wilbraham Estate Disposals Committee and do something exciting with the whole lot.'

Hilary agreed; but Wimsey felt depressed. So far as he could see, his interference had done no good to anybody and only made extra trouble. It was a thousand pities that the body of Deacon had ever come to light at all. Nobody wanted it.

The New Wash Cut was opened with great rejoicing at the end of the month. The weather was perfect, the Duke of Denver made a speech which was a model of the obvious, and the Regatta was immensely successful. Three people fell into the river, four men and an old woman were had up for being drunk and disorderly, a motor-car became entangled with a tradesman's cart and young Gotobed won First Prize in the Decorated Motor-cycle section of the Sports.

And the River Wale, placidly doing its job in the midst of all the disturbance, set to work to scour its channel to the sea. Wimsey, leaning over the wall at the entry to the Cut, watched the salt water moving upward with the incoming tide, muddied and chafing along its new-made bed. On his left, the crooked channel of the old river lay empty of its waters, a smooth expanse of shining mud.

'Doing all right,' said a voice beside him. He turned and found that it was one of the engineers.

'What extra depth have you given her?'

'Only a few feet, but she'll do the rest herself. There's been nothing the matter with this river except that silting of the outfall and the big bend below here. We've shortened her course now by getting on for three miles and driven a channel right out into the Wash beyond the mudbanks. She'll make her own outfall now, if she's left to herself. We're expecting her to grind her channel lower by eight to ten feet – possibly more. It'll make all the difference to the town. It's a scandal, the way the thing's been let go. Why, as it is, the tide scarcely gets up higher than Van Leyden's Sluice. After this, it'll probably run up as far as the Great Leam. The whole secret with these Fen rivers is to bring back all the water you can into its natural course. Where the old Dutchmen went wrong was in dispersing it into canals and letting it lie about all over the place. The smaller the fall of the land, the bigger weight of water you need to keep the outfall scoured. You'd think it was obvious, wouldn't you? But it's taken people hundreds of years to learn it.'

'Yes,' said Wimsey. 'I suppose all this extra water will go up the Thirty-Foot?'

'That's right. It's practically a straight run now from the Old Bank Sluice to the New Cut Outfall – thirty-five miles – and this will carry off a lot of the High Level water from Leamholt and Lympsey. At present the Great Leam has to do more work than it should – they've always been afraid to let the Thirty-Foot take its fair proportion of the flood-water in winter, because, you see, when it got down to this point it would have overflowed the old river-bed and drowned the town. But now the New Cut will carry it clean off, and that will relieve the Great Leam and obviate the floods round Frogglesham, Mere Wash and Lympsey Fen.'

'Oh!' said Wimsey. 'I suppose the Thirty-Foot Dyke will stand the strain?'

'Oh, dear, yes,' said the engineer, cheerfully. 'It was meant to from the beginning. In fact, at one time, it had to. It's only within the last hundred years that the Wale has got so badly silted up. There's been a good deal of shifting in the Wash – chiefly owing to tidal action, of course, and the Nene Outfall Cut, and that helped to cause the obstruction, don't you see. But the Thirty-Foot worked all right in the old days.'

'In the Lord Protector's time, I suppose,' said Wimsey. 'And now you've cleared the Wale Outfall, no doubt the obstruction will go somewhere else.'

'Very likely,' replied the engineer, with unimpaired cheerfulness. 'These mudbanks are always shifting about. But in time I daresay they'll clear the whole thing – unless, of course, they really take it into their heads to drain the Wash and make a job of it.'

'Just so,' said Wimsey.

'But as far as it goes,' continued the engineer, 'this looks pretty good. It's to be hoped our dam over there will stand up to the strain. You'd be surprised at the scour you get with these quiet-looking rivers. Anyhow, this embankment is all right – I'll take my oath of that. You watch the tide-mark. We've marked the old low level and the old high level – if you don't see the one lowered and the other raised by three or four feet within the next few months, you can call me – a Dutchman. Excuse me a minute – I just want to see that they're making that dam good over there.'

He hurried off to superintend the workmen who were completing the dam across the old course of the river.

'And how about my old sluice-gates?'

'Oh!' said Wimsey, looking round, 'it's you, is it?'

'Ah!' The sluice-keeper spat copiously into the rising water. 'It's me. That's who it is. Look at all this money they been spending. Thousands. But as for them gates of mine, I reckon I can go and whistle for 'em.'

'No answer yet from Geneva?'

'Eh?' said the sluice-keeper. 'Oh! Ah! Meaning what I said? Ah! that were a good 'un, weren't it? Why don't they refer it to the League of Nations? Ah and why don't they? Look at thisher great scour o' water a-coming' up. Where's that a-going to? It's got to go somewhere, ain't it?'

'No doubt,' said Wimsey. 'I understand it's to go up the Thirty-Foot.'

'Ah!' said the sluice-keeper. 'Always interfering with things, they are.'

'They're not interfering with your gates, anyway.'

'No, they ain't, and that's just where it is. Once you starts interferin' with things you got to go on. One thing leads to another. Let 'm bide, that's what I say. Don't go digging of 'em up and altering of 'em. Dig up one thing and you got to dig up another.'

'At the rate,' objected Wimsey, 'the Fens would still be all under water.'

'Well, in a manner of speaking, so they would,' admitted the sluice-keeper. 'That's very true. So they would. But none the more for that, they didn't ought to come a-drowning of us now. It's all right for him to talk about letting the floods out at the Old Bank Sluice. Where's it all a-going to? It comes up, and it's got to go somewhere, and it comes down and it's got to go somewhere, ain't it?'

'At the moment I gather it drowns the Mere Wash and Frogglesham and all those places.'

'Well, it's their water, ain't it?' said the sluice-keeper. 'They ain't got no call to send it down here.'

'Quite,' said Wimsey, recognising the spirit that had hampered the Fen drainage for the last few hundred years, 'but as you say yourself, it's got to go somewhere.'

'It's their water,' retorted the man obstinately. 'Let 'em keep it. It won't do us no good.'

'Walbeach seems to want it.'

'Ah! them!' The sluice-keeper spat vehemently. 'They don't know what they want. They're always a-wantin' some nonsense or other. And there's always some fool to give it 'em, what's more. All I wants is a new set of gates, but I don't look like getting of 'em. I've asked for 'em time and again. I asked that young feller there. "Mister," I says to him, "How about a new set o' gates for my sluice?" "That ain't in our contract," he says. "No," I says, "and drowning half the parish ain't in your contract neither, I suppose." But he couldn't see it.'

'Well, cheer up,' said Wimsey. 'Have a drink.'

He did, however, feel sufficient interest in the matter to speak to the engineer about it when he saw him again.

'Oh, I think it's all right,' said that gentleman. 'We did, as a matter of fact, recommend that the gates should be repaired and strengthened, but you see, the damned thing's all tied up in some kind of legal bother. The fact is, once you start on a job like this, you never know where it's going to end. It's all piecemeal work. Stop it up in one place and it breaks out in another. But I don't think you need worry about this part of it. What *does* want seeing to is the Old Bank Dyke – but that's under a different authority altogether. Still, they've undertaken to make up their embankment and put in some fresh stonework. If they don't there'll be trouble, but they can't say we haven't warned them.'

'Dig up one thing,' thought Wimsey, 'and you have to dig up another. I wish we'd never dug up Deacon. Once you let the tide in, it's got to go somewhere.'

James Thoday, returning to England as instructed by his employers, was informed that the police wanted him as a witness. He was a sturdy man, rather older than William, with bleak blue eyes and a reserved manner. He repeated his original story, without emphasis and without details. He had been taken ill in the train after leaving Fenchurch. He had attributed the trouble to some sort of gastric influenza. When he got to London, he had felt quite unable to proceed, and had telegraphed to that effect. He had spent part of that day huddled over the fire in a public house near Liverpool Street; he thought they might remember him there. They could not give him a bed for the night and, in the evening, feeling a little better he had gone out and found a room in a back street. He could not recall the address, but it had been a clean, pleasant place. In the morning he found himself fit to continue his journey, though still very weak and tottery. He had, of course, seen English papers mentioning the discovery of the corpse in the churchyard, but knew nothing further about it, except, of course, what he had heard from his brother and sister-in-law, which was very little. He had never had any idea who the dead man was. Would he be surprised to hear that it was Geoffrey Deacon? He would be very much surprised indeed. The news came as a terrible shock to him. That would be a bad job for his people.

Indeed, he looked startled enough. But there had been a tenseness of the muscles about his mouth which persuaded Superintendent Blundell that the shock had been caused, not so much by hearing the dead man's name as by hearing that the police knew it.

Mr Blundell, aware of the solicitude with which the Law broods over the interest of witnesses, thanked him and proceeded with his inquiries. The public house was found, and substantiated the story of the sick sailor who had sat over the fire all day drinking hot toddies; but the clean and pleasant woman who had let her room to Mr Thoday was not so easy of identification.

Meanwhile, the slow machinery of the London police revolved and, from many hundreds of reports, ground out the name of a garage proprietor who had hired out a motor-bicycle on the evening of the 4th January to a man answering to the description of James Thoday. The bicycle had been returned on the Sunday by a messenger, who had claimed and taken away the deposit, minus the charge for hire and insurance. No, not a district messenger: a youth, who looked like an ordinary out-of-work.

On hearing this, Chief Inspector Parker, who was dealing with the London end of the inquiry, groaned dismally. It was too much to expect this nameless casual to turn up. Ten to one, he had pocketed the surplus deposit and would be particularly unwilling to inform the world of the fact.

Parker was wrong. The man who had hired the bicycle had apparently made the fatal mistake of picking an honest messenger. After prolonging inquiry and advertisement a young Cockney made his appearance at New Scotland Yard. He gave his name as Frank Jenkins, and explained that he had only just seen the advertisement. He had been seeking work in various places, and had drifted back to Town in time to be confronted with the police inquiry on a notice board at the Labour Exchange.

He very well remembered the episode of the motor-bike It had struck him as funny at the time. He had been hanging round a garage in Bloomsbury in the early morning of January 5th, hoping to pick up a job when he sees a bloke coming along on this here bike. The bloke was short and stocky, with blue eyes, and sounded like he might be the boss of some outfit or other – he spoke sharp and quick, like he might be accustomed to giving orders. Yes, he might have been an officer in the mercantile marine, very likely. Come to think of it, he did look a bit like a sailor. He was dressed in a very wet and dirty motoring coat and wore a cap, pulled down over his face, like. This man had said: 'Here, sonny, d'you want a job?' On being told 'Yes,' he had asked: 'Can you ride a motor-bike?' Frank Jenkins had replied, 'Lead me to it guvnor'; whereupon he had been told to take the machine back to a certain garage, to collect the deposit and to bring it to the stranger outside the Rugby Tavern at the corner of Great James Street and Chapel Street, when he would receive something for his pains. He had done his part of the business, and hadn't took more than an hour, all told (returning by bus), but when he arrived at the Rugby Tavern, the stranger was not there, and apparently never had been there. A woman said she had seen him walking away in the direction of Guildford Street. Jenkins had hung about till the middle of the morning, but had seen no sign of the man in the motor-coat. He had therefore deposited the money with the landlord of the Tavern, with a message to say that he could wait no longer and had kept back half-a-crown – that being the amount he thought fair to award himself for the transaction. The landlord would be able to tell them if the sum had ever been claimed.

The landlord being interrogated, brought the matter to mind. Nobody answering the description of the stranger had ever called for the money, which, after a little search and delay, was produced intact in a dirty envelope. Enclosed with it was the garage-proprietor's receipt made out in the name of Joseph Smith, at a fictitious address.

The next thing was, obviously to confront James Thoday with Frank Jenkins. The messenger identified his employer immediately; James Thoday persisted, politely, that there was some mistake. What next, thought Mr Parker.

He put the question to Lord Peter, who said:

'I think it's time for a spot of dirty work, Charles. Try putting William and James alone with a microphone or whatever you call the beastly gadget. It may not be pretty, but you'll probably find that it works.'

In these circumstances, therefore, the brothers met for the first time since James had left William on the morning of January 4th. The scene was a waiting-room at Scotland Yard.

'Well, William,' said James.

'Well, James,' said William.

There was a silence. Then James said:

'How much do they know?'

'Pretty well everything, by what I can make out.'

There was another pause. Then James spoke again in a constrained voice:

'Very well. Then you had better let me take the blame. I'm not married, and there's Mary and the kids to be thought of. But in God's name, man, couldn't you have got rid of the fellow without killing him?'

'That,' said William, 'is just what I was going to ask *you*.'

'You mean to say that it wasn't you who did away with him?'

'Of course not. I'd be a fool to do it. I'd offered the brute two hundred pounds to go back where he came from. If I hadn't a-been ill, I'd a-got him away all right, and that's what I thought you'd a-done. My God! when he come up out o' that grave, like judgement Day, I wished you'd killed me along of him.'

'But I never laid hand on him, Will, till after he was dead. I saw him there, the devil, with that ghastly look on his face, and I never blamed you for what you'd done. I swear I never blamed you, Will – only for being such a fool as to do it. So I broke his ugly face in, so that no one should ever guess who he was. But they've found out, seemingly. It was cursed bad luck, that grave being opened so soon. Maybe it'd have been better if I'd carried him out and thrown him in the Drain, but it's a long way to go, and I thought we'd be safe enough.'

'But, see here, James – if you didn't kill him, who did?'

It was at this point that Superintendent Blundell, Chief Inspector Parker and Lord Peter Wimsey walked in on the pair of them.

THE FIFTH PART

THE DODGING

Then whispered they of a violated grave – of a disfigured body.
EDGAR ALLAN POE: *Berenice*

The only difficulty was that the two witnesses who had formerly refused to speak could now hardly speak fast enough and spoke both together. Chief Inspector Parker was obliged to call for silence.

'All right,' he said. 'You've both been suspecting each other and shielding each other. We've grasped that. Now that we've got that clear, let's have the story. William first.' He added the usual caution.

'Well, sir,' replied William, briskly, 'I don't know as I've much to tell you, because his lordship here seems to have worked it all out surprising neat. What my feelings were when he told me just what I did that night I won't say – but what I do want to make as clear as I can is that my poor wife never knew one thing about it, first to last. Why, that was my whole trouble all the time – how to keep it from her.

'I'll begin right at the beginning, with the night of December 30th. I was just coming home, pretty late for me, from seeing to one of the cows that had gone sick up at Sir Henry's place, and as I was passing the church, I thought I saw somebody a-creeping up to the porch and going in. It was a dark night, of course, but, if you remember, sir, it had begun to snow, and I could see something moving, like, against the white. So I thinks, that's Potty up to his games again – I better send him off home. So I goes up to the church door, and I sees footmarks going all along the path as far as the porch, and there they seems to stop. So I say, "Hallo!" and looks about a bit. That's queer, I says to myself, where's the beggar got to? So I goes round the church, and I sees a light a-moving about and going towards the vestry. Well, I thinks, maybe it's Rector. And then I thinks, well, maybe it ain't. So I comes back to the door, and there's no key in it, like there would be in the ordinary way if Rector had been inside. So I pushes the door and it opens. And in I goes. And then I hears somebody a-moving about and bumping, like, up in the chancel. I goes along quiet, having rubber boots on, that I was wearing for the fields, and when I gets round behind the chancel screen I sees a light and hears the bloke in the vestry, so in I goes and there's a fellow a-tugging away at the ladder Harry Gotobed uses for seeing to the lamps and that, what's always kept a-lying along the wall. He had his back to me, and on the table I see a kind of a dark lantern and something else as had no right to be there, and that's a revolver. So I catches hold of the revolver and said, loud and sharp, "What are you doing there?" And he jumped round pretty damn quick and made a dive for the table. "No, you don't," I said, "I've got your gun and I know how to use it. What are you after?" Well, he started some sort of tale about being out of work and tramping about and wanting a place to sleep in, and I said, "That won't wash. How about this gun? Hands up," I said, "let's see what else you've got on you." So I went through his pockets and brought out what looked to me like a set of pick-locks. "Well, my lad," I said, "that's quite enough for me. You're for it." And he looked at me, and laughed like hell, and said, "Think again. Will Thoday." And I said, "How do you know my name?" and then I looked again and said, "My God, it's Geoff Deacon!" And he said, "Yes; and you're the man that's married my wife." And he laughed again. And then it come over me just what it all meant.'

'How did he know that?' asked Wimsey. 'He didn't get it from Cranton.'

'That was the other scoundrel? No, he told me he'd meant to come after Mary, but hearing from some fellow at Leamholt that she was married, he thought he'd better have a scout round first. I couldn't make out why he'd come back to the place at all, and he wouldn't tell me. I see it now, it was the emeralds. He did say something about me keeping quiet and he'd make it worth my while, but I told him I'd have no truck with him. I asked him where he'd been, but he just laughed and said, "Never you mind." And I asked what he wanted in Fenchurch, and he said he wanted money. So I made out that he'd meant to come blackmailing Mary. Well, that made me see red, and I was in half a mind to give him up to the police and take what was coming to us, but when I thought about Mary and the kids – well, I couldn't face it. I was wrong, of course, but when I remembered all the talk there'd been – well, I wanted to spare her that. He knew just how I stood, the devil, and he stood there grinning at me.

'So in the end, I made a devil's bargain with him. I said I'd hide him and give him the money to get out of the country, and then I thought what was I to do with him? I'd got his pick-locks all right, but I didn't trust him none the more for that, and I was afraid to go out of the church with him, where we might run up against somebody. And then I got the idea of putting him up in the bell-chamber. So I told him what I meant to do and he agreed. I thought I could get the keys from the Rector all right, so, just for the time being, I pushed him into the cupboard where the surplices hang and locked him in. Then I thought that he might easily break his way out while I was over at the Rectory, so I went down and fetched a rope from the chest and came back and tied him up. You see, I didn't believe that tale of his about sleeping in the vestry. Robbing the church was what

I thought he was after. And besides, if I went away and left him, what was to stop him getting out and hiding somewhere and slugging me over the head when I got back? I'd no key to the church door, neither, and he might have made off.'

'Good thing for you if he had,' suggested Mr Blundell.

'Yes – so long as nobody else caught him. Anyhow, I got the keys. I put up some story to the Rector – it must have been a pretty lame one – the old gentleman was a bit puzzled, I think. He kept on saying how queer I looked, and insisted on getting me a drop of his port. While he was fetching it, I just nipped the keys off the nail by the door. I know what you're going to say – suppose he'd mislaid them as usual? Well, I'd have had to try some dodge on Jack Godfrey or else change my plans – but there they were and I didn't bother with any "ifs". I went back to the church and untied Deacon's legs and made him walk up the belfry stairs in front of me, like taking a pig to market. It wasn't difficult: I had the revolver, you see.'

'And you tied him up to a beam in the bell-chamber?'

'Yes, sir, I did. And wouldn't you a-done? Just think of yourself carrying victuals and stuff up one o' they ladders in the dark, with a murderer roaming loose at the top all ready to bash your head in the moment you popped it up above floor level. I tied him up good and proper, though it were a bit of a job with the rope being so thick. "Stay you there," I said, "and I'll bring you something to eat in the morning and see you out of the country before you're twenty-four hours older." He cursed like a devil, but I paid no attention to him. It was all I could do to keep my hand offen him, and I'm often minded to think it's a wonder I didn't kill him then and there.'

'But had you made any plans for shipping him off?'

'Yes, I had. I'd been over to Walbeach the day before with Jim here, and we'd had a bit of a talk with a pal of his – a queer old skipper on a Dutch cargo boat that was lying there, taking in some sort of freight – I never rightly gathered what it was – but I got the notion the old boy wouldn't find much come amiss to him.'

'You're right there, Will,' put in Jim grinning.

'So I found. It wasn't the best plan, maybe, but it was all I could do in the time. I couldn't think very clear, to tell you the truth. I was terrible put about in my mind and my head was buzzing like a thresher. I suppose 'twas the flu coming on. I don't know how I got through that evening at home, looking at Mary and the kids and knowing what I knew. Fortunately, she knew I was worried over the cow and put it all down to that – at least, I thought so. I tossed and turned all night, and the only thing to comfort me was the blessed snow coming down and hiding all they footprints we'd left round the church.

'Next morning I was damned ill, but I couldn't stop to think of that. I slipped out well before daybreak, with some bread and cheese and beer in an old tool-bag. Jim heard me and called out to know what was up. So I said I was going over to see the cow – and so I did, only I took the church on the way.

'Deacon was all right, only very bad-tampered and perished wi' cold, so I left him my old coat – not wanting him to be frozen to death. And I tied him up by his elbows and ankles, leaving his hands free, as he could help himself to his victuals but not untie himself. Then I went on to see to the cow and found her better. After breakfast I got the old car out and ran her over to Walbeach, feeling worse and worse all the time. I found my skipper, just getting ready to sail. I had a word with him, and he agreed to wait until ten o'clock that night and carry my passenger, no questions asked. Two hundred and fifty pounds was the price he wanted and I agreed to pay it. I got the money and gave him the fifty then and there, promising him the rest when I got Deacon aboard. I got into the car and started back – and you know what happened afterwards.'

'That's very clear,' said Parker. 'I needn't tell you that you were compounding a serious felony by helping a convicted murderer to escape from justice. Speaking as a policeman, I am shocked; speaking as a human being, I have every sympathy for you. Now, you.' He turned to Jim. 'I imagine your part of it comes in here.'

'Yes, sir. Well, as you know, poor Will was brought back in a terrible state and we thought for a day or two he was pretty well gone. He was out of his head and kept on calling out that he must go down to the church, but we put that down to the bell-ringing business. All the time he kept a sort of control over himself and never let out a word about Deacon, but one day, when Mary had gone out of the room, he clutched at my hand and said, "Don't let her know, Jim. Get him away." "Get who away?" I said. And he said, "In the belfry – bitter cold and starving." And then he sat up in bed and said, quite plain and clear, "My coat – give me my coat – I must have the keys and the money." I said, "All right, Will, I'll see to it" – thinking he was dreaming, and after a bit he seemed to forget about it and go off in a doze. But I thought it was queer, so I had a look in his coat, and there, sure enough, were the Rector's bunch of keys and a whole wad of money.

'Well, I began to think there might be something behind it, so I took the keys, and I thought, before I took them back, I'd just have a look round the church. I went in there – '

'Which day was this?'

'I reckon it was the 2nd of January. I went up into the belfry – right up to the bell-chamber, and – well! there he was!'

'He must have been pretty fed up with things by that time.'

'Fed up? He was dead and cold.'

'Starved to death?'

'Not he. There was a big bit of cheese beside him and near half a loaf of bread and two bottles of beer, one empty and one full. And he hadn't died of cold, neither, as you might expect. I've seen men that had died of exposure, and they died peaceful – curled up like kittens, mostly, as if they'd gone out in their sleep. No. He'd died on his feet, and whatever it was, he'd seen it coming to him. He'd struggled like a tiger against the ropes, working at them till he could get upright, and they had cut through the stuff off his jacket and through his socks. And his face! My God, sir, I've never seen anything like it. His eyes staring open and a look in them as if he'd looked down into hell. It fair shook me.

'I looked him over – and then I saw Will's old coat lying on the floor, thrown off, it might be, in his struggles – and that didn't look like dying of cold, neither. I couldn't tell what to make of it, for I didn't recognise him, you see. I had a look at his breast pocket, and found some papers. There was some made out in the name of Taylor and some in a French name that I've forgotten. I couldn't make head or tail of it. And then I had a look at his hands.'

'Ah!' said Wimsey, 'now we're coming to it.'

'Yes, my lord. You must remember that I knew Deacon. Not very well, but I knew him. And he carried a big scar on one hand, where he'd fallen down one day, carrying a tray with a glass jug on it. I'd seen that scar, and I'd never forget it. When I saw that, my lord, and knew who 'twas – well, there! I hadn't much doubt about what'd happened. Forgive me, Will – I thought you'd done him in, and as God's my witness, I couldn't blame you. Not that I hold with murder, and it came to me then that things could never be the same betwixt you and me – but I didn't blame you. Only I wished it had happened in a fair fight.'

'If it had happened, Jim, it would a-been in a fair fight. I might a-killed him, but I wouldn't a-killed him when he was tied up. You might a-known that.'

'Well, so I might. But it seemed to me at the time as there was no way out of it. I had to think quick what to do. I found some old boards and beams in a corner, and I stood them up in front of him, so as if anybody came in they might not notice him – not unless they were looking for something – and then I came away and thought hard. I kept the keys. I knew I'd be wanting them, and Rector is so absent minded, he'd probably think he'd mislaid them.

'I thought all that day – and then I remembered that Lady Thorpe's funeral was fixed for the Saturday. It seemed to me that I might put him in her grave and that he need never be found, baring accidents. I was due to leave on Saturday morning, and I thought I could fix things so as to have an alibi.

'I had a bad moment on Friday. Jack Godfrey told me they were going to ring a muffled peal for Lady Thorpe, and I was all of a shake, thinking he'd see him when he went up to put the leathers on the bells. By a big stroke of luck, he didn't go till after dark, and I suppose he never looked into that dark corner, or he'd have seen the planks had been moved.'

'We know what you did on Saturday,' said Parker. 'You needn't bother with that.'

'No, sir. I had an awful ride with the bike. The acetylene lamp worked none too well, and it was raining like the tropics. Still, I got there – much later than I meant, and I went to work. I cut him down – '

'You needn't tell us that, either. There was a witness on the top of that bell-chamber ladder all the time.'

'A witness?'

'Yes – and lucky for you, my lad, he was a highly respectable and gentlemanly burglar with the heart of a rabbit and a wholesome fear of bloodshed – otherwise you might be paying blackmail through the nose. But I will say for Nobby,' added Parker reflectively, 'that he would consider blackmail beneath him. You got the body down into the churchyard?'

'And glad I was to get it there. Rolling it down the ladders – it gave me the heebie-jeebies. And those bells! I was expecting all the time to hear them speak. I never have liked the sound of bells. There's something – you'd think they were alive, sometimes, and could talk. When I was a boy, I read a story in an old magazine about a bell that called out after a murderer. You'll think I'm soft, talking that way, but it made an impression on me and I can't forget it.'

'*The Rosamonde* – I know the story,' said Wimsey, gently. 'It called, 'Help Jehan! Help Jehan!' It gave me the grues, too.'

'That's the one, my lord. Anyhow, I got the body down, as I said. I opened the grave and was just going to put him in – '

'You used the sexton's spade, I suppose?'

'Yes, sir. The key of the crypt was on Rector's bunch. As I was saying, I was going to put it in, when I remembered that the grave *might* be opened and the body recognised. So I gave it some good, hard blows with the spade across the face – '

He shuddered.

'That was a bad bit, sir. And the hands. I'd recognised them, and so might other people. I got out my jack-knife, and I – well, there!'

'"With the big sugar-nippers they nipped off his flippers,"' quoted Wimsey, flippantly.

'Yes, my lord. I made them into a parcel with his papers and slipped it all in my pocket. But I put the ropes and his hat down the old well. Then I filled up the grave and put the wreaths back as tidily as I could, and cleaned the tools. But I can tell you, I didn't care about taking them back into the church. All those gold angels with their eyes open in the darkness – and old Abbot Thomas lying there on his tomb. When my foot crunched on a bit of coke behind the screen, my heart was in my mouth.'

'Harry Gotobed really ought to be more careful with the coke,' said Wimsey. 'It's not for want of telling.'

'That damned parcel of stuff was burning my pocket, too. I went up and had a look at the stoves, but they were all stoked up for the night, and the top nowhere near burnt through. I didn't dare put anything in there. Then I had to go up and clean down the belfry. There'd been beer spilt on the floor. Fortunately, Harry Gotobed had left a bucket of water in the coke-house, so I didn't have to draw any from the well, though I've often wondered if he noticed next day that the water had gone. I made everything as clean as I could, and stacked the planks up where I'd found them, and I took away the beer-bottles – '

'Two of them,' said Wimsey. 'There were three.'

'Were there? I couldn't see but the two. I locked up everything tight, and then I wondered what I'd better do with the keys. Finally I thought I'd best leave them in the vestry, as though Rector had forgotten them – all but the key of the porch, and I left that in the lock. It was the best I could think of.'

'And the parcel?'

'Ah! that. I kept the papers and a lot of money that was with them, but the – those other things – I threw into the Thirty-Foot, twelve miles off from Fenchurch, and the bottles with them. The papers and notes I burnt when I got back to London. There was a good fire – for a wonder – in the waiting-room at King's Cross and nobody much about. I didn't think anybody would look for them there. I didn't quite know what to do with Will's coat, but in the end I posted it back to him with a note. I just said, "Many thanks for the loan. I've put away what you left in the belfry." I couldn't be more open, you see, for fear Mary might undo the parcel and read the letter.'

'I couldn't write much to you, for the same reason,' said Will. 'I thought, you see, you had somehow got Deacon away. It never entered my head that he was dead. And Mary usually reads my letters through before they go, sometimes adding a bit of her own. So I just said: "Many thanks for all you've done for me" – which might a-been took to refer to you nursing me when I was ill. I see you hadn't took the £200, but I supposed you'd managed some fashion, so I just put that back in the bank where it came from. It was a queer thing to me that your letters had grown so short all of a sudden, but I understand it now?'

'I couldn't just feel the same, Will,' said Jim. 'I didn't blame you mind – but that rope stuck in my gullet. When did you find out what had happened?'

'Why, when the corpse came up. And – you'll have to forgive *me* Jim – but, naturally, I fancied you'd done the job yourself, and – why, there! I didn't rightly feel the same, neither. Only I kept on hoping, maybe he'd died natural.'

'He didn't do that,' said Parker, thoughtfully.

'Then who killed him?' demanded Jim.

'I'm sure you didn't, for one,' replied the detective. 'If you had, you'd have accepted the suggestion that he died of exposure. And somehow I'm inclined to believe your brother didn't do it either – though you're both accessories after the fact to Deacon's crimes, and you aren't clear of the other thing yet; don't think it. You'd have an awkward time with a prosecuting counsel, both of you. But personally I'm inclined to believe you both.'

'Thank you, sir.'

'How about Mrs Thoday? The truth, mind.'

'That's all right, sir. She was uneasy in her mind – I won't say she wasn't, seeing me so queer, especially after the body was found. But it was only when she saw Deacon's handwriting on that paper that the meaning of it all come to her. Then she asked me, and I told her part of the truth. I said I'd found out that the dead man was Deacon and that somebody – not me – must have killed him. And she guessed that Jim was mixed up in it. So I said, maybe, but we must stand together and not make trouble for Jim. And she agreed, only she said we must get married again, because we were living together in sin. She's a good woman, and I couldn't reason her out of it, so I gave in about that, and we'd fixed to get it all done quiet-like in London – only you found us out, sir.'

'Yes,' said Blundell, 'you've got to thank his lordship here for that. He seemed to know all about it, and very sorry he was to have to stop you, I must say. Seemed to think whoever put Deacon away ought to get the Wedding March out of Lohengrin and flowers all down the aisle.'

'Is there any reason why they shouldn't go on and get married now, Superintendent?'

'I don't know as there is,' grunted Mr Blundell. 'Not if these two are telling the truth. Proceedings there may be – you two ain't out of the wood yet, but as to getting married, I don't see no great harm in it. We've got their story, and I don't know as poor Mary can add very much to it.'

'Thank you very much, sir,' said Will again.

'But as to who *did* kill Deacon,' went on the Superintendent, we don't seem very much forrader. Unless it was Potty or Cranton, after all. I don't know if I ever heard anything queerer than this business. All these three, a-dodging in and out of that old belfry, one up t'other come on – there's something behind it yet that we don't understand. And you two' – he turned fiercely on the brothers – 'you keep your mouths shut about this. It'll have to come out some time, that's a certainty, but if you get talking and obstruct our duty of laying hands on the rightful murderer, you're *for* it. Understand?'

He ruminated, sucking his walrus moustache between his large yellow teeth.

'I'd better go down home and grill Potty, I suppose,' he muttered discontentedly. 'But if he done it, how did he do it? That's what beats me.'

PART 4

A FULL PEAL OF KENT TREBLE BOB MAJOR
(Three Parts)

5,376

By the Course Ends
6 5 4 3 2
3 4 5 6 2
2 3 6 4 5
3 5 6 4 2
4 2 3 5 6
8th the Observation.

Call her before, middle with a double, wrong with a double and home; wrong with a double and home with a double; middle with a double, wrong and home with a double; before, middle with a double, wrong and home with a double; before, middle with a double and wrong with a double. Twice repeated.

(J. WILDE)

THE FIRST PART

THE WATERS ARE CALLED OUT

Of clean beasts, and of beasts that are not clean, and of fowls, and of everything that creepeth upon the earth, there went in two and two unto Noah into the ark.

Genesis vii, 8, 9

The public memory is a short one. The affair of the Corpse in Country Churchyard was succeeded, as the weeks rolled on, by so many Bodies in Blazing Garages, Man-Hunts for Missing Murderers, Tragedies in West-End Flats, Suicide-Pacts in Lonely Woods, Nude Corpses in Caves, and Midnight shots in Fashionable Road-Houses that nobody gave it another thought, except Superintendent Blundell and the obscure villagers of Fenchurch St Paul. Even the discovery of the emeralds and the identity of the dead man had been successfully kept out of the papers, and the secret of the Thoday remarriage lay buried in the discreet breasts of the police, Lord Peter Wimsey and Mr Venables, none of whom had any inducement to make these matters known.

Potty Peake had been interrogated, but without much success. He was not good at remembering dates and his conversation, while full of strange hints and prophecies, had a way of escaping from the restraints of logic and playing gruesomely among the dangling bell-ropes. His aunt gave him an alibi, for what her memory and observation were worth, which was not a great deal. Nor did Mr Blundell feel any great enthusiasm about putting Potty Peake in the dock. It was a hundred to one that he would be pronounced unfit to plead, and the result, in any case, might be to lock him up in an institution. 'And you know, old lady,' said Mr Blundell to Mrs Blundell. 'I can't see Potty doing such a thing, poor chap.' Mrs Blundell agreed with him.

As regards the Thodays, the position was highly unsatisfactory. If either were charged separately, there would always be sufficient doubt about the other to secure an acquittal, while, if they were charged together, their joint story might well have the same effect upon the jury that it had already had upon the police. They would be acquitted and left under suspicion in the minds of their neighbours, and that would be unsatisfactory too. Or they might, of course, both be hanged – 'and between you and me, sir,' said Mr Blundell to the Chief Constable, 'I'd never be easy in my mind if they were.' The Chief Constable was uneasy too. 'You see, Blundell,' he observed, 'our difficulty is that we've no real proof of the murder. If you could only be sure what the fellow died of – '

So a period of inaction set in. Jim Thoday returned to his ship; Will Thoday, his marriage ceremony performed, went home and went on with his work. In time the parrot forgot its newly-learnt phrases – only coming out with them at long and infrequent intervals. The Rector carried on with his marryings, churching and baptisms, and Tailor Paul tolled out a knell or two, or struck her solemn blows as the bells hunted in their courses. And the River Wale, rejoicing in its new opportunity, and swollen by the heavy rains of a wet summer and autumn, ground out its channel inch by inch and foot by foot, nine feet deeper than before, so that the water came up brackish at high tide as far as the Great Leam and the Old Bank Sluices were set open to their full extent, draining the Upper Fen.

And it was needed; for in that summer the water lay on the land all through August and September, and the corn sprouted in the stocks, and the sodden ricks took fire and stank horribly, and the Rector of Fenchurch St Paul, conducting the Harvest Festival, had to modify his favourite sermon upon Thankfulness, for there was scarcely sound wheat enough to lay upon the altar and no great sheaves for the aisle windows or for binding about the stoves, as was customary. Indeed, so late was the harvest and so dark and chill the air, that the stoves were obliged to be lit for the evening service, whereby a giant pumpkin, left incautiously in the direct line of fire, was found to be part-roasted when the time came to send the kindly fruits of the earth to the local hospital.

Wimsey had determined that he would never go back to Fenchurch St Paul. His memories of it were disquieting, and he felt that there were one or two people in that parish who would be better pleased if they never saw his face again. But when Hilary Thorpe wrote to him and begged him to come and see her during her Christmas holidays, he felt bound to go. His position with regard to her was peculiar. Mr Edward Thorpe, as trustee under her father's will and her natural guardian, had rights which no court of law would gainsay; on the other hand Wimsey, as sole trustee to the far greater Wilbraham estate, held a certain advantage. He could, if he chose, make things awkward for Mr Thorpe. Hilary possessed evidence of her father's wishes about her education, and Uncle Edward could scarcely now oppose them on the plea of lack of funds. But Wimsey, holding the purse-strings, could refuse to untie them unless those wishes were carried out. If Uncle Edward chose to be obstinate, there was every prospect of a legal dogfight; but Wimsey did not believe that Uncle Edward would be obstinate to that point. It was in Wimsey's power to turn Hilary from an obligation into an asset for Uncle Edward, and it seemed very possible that he would pocket his principles and take the cash. Already he had shown signs of bowing to the rising sun; he had agreed to take Hilary down to spend Christmas at the Red House, instead of with him in London. It was, indeed, not Mr Thorpe's fault that the Red House was available; he had done his best to let it, but the number of persons desirous of tenanting a large house in ill-repair, situated in a howling desert and encumbered with a dilapidated and heavily mortgaged property, was not very large. Hilary had her way, and Wimsey, while heartily wishing that the whole business could have been settled in London, liked the girl for her determination to stick to the family estate. Here again, Wimsey was a power in the land. He could put the property in order if he liked and pay off the mortgages, and that would no doubt be a satisfaction to Mr Thorpe, who had no power to sell under the terms of his trust. A final deciding factor was that if Wimsey did not spend Christmas at Fenchurch, he would have no decent excuse for not spending it with his brother's family at Denver, and of all things in the world, a Christmas at Denver was most disagreeable to him.

Accordingly, he looked in at Denver for a day or two, irritated his sister-in-law and her guests as much as, and no more than, usual and thence, on Christmas Eve, made his way across country to Fenchurch St Paul.

'They seem,' said Wimsey, 'to keep a special brand of disgusting weather in these parts.' He thrust up his hand against the hood of the car, discharging a deluge of water. 'Last time it was snowing and now it's pelting cats and dogs. There's a fate in it, Bunter.'

'Yes, my lord,' said that long-suffering man. He was deeply attached to his master, but sometimes felt his determined dislike of closed cars to be a trifle unreasonable. 'A very inclement season, my lord.'

'Well, well, we must push on, push on. A merry heart goes all the way. You don't look very merry, Bunter, but then you're one of those Sphinx-like people. I've never seen you upset, except about that infernal beer-bottle.'

'No, my lord. That hurt my pride very much, if I may say so. A very curious circumstance, that, my lord.'

'Pure accident, I think, though it had a suspicious appearance at the time. Whereabouts are we now? Oh, yes, Lympsey, of course; we cross over the Geat Leam here by the Old Bank Sluice. We must be just coming to it. Yes, there it is. By Jove! some water coming through there!'

He pulled up the car beyond the bridge, got out and stood in the downpour staring at the sluice. Its five great gates were open, the iron ratchets on the bridge above drawn up to their full extent. Dark and menacing, the swollen flood-waters raced through the sluices, eddying and turning and carrying with them the brown reeds and broken willow-stems and here and there fragments of timber filched from the drowned lands of the Upper Fen. And even while he watched, there came a change. Angry little waves and gurgles ruffled the strong flow of the river, with an appearance as of repressed tumult and conflict. A man came out of the gate-house by the bridge and took up his position by the sluice, staring down into the river. Wimsey hailed him.

'Tide coming up?'

'Yes, sir. We has to watch her now if we don't want to get the water all across the causey. But she don't rise very far, not without there's an extraordinary high spring tide. She's just coming up to springs now, so we has to do a bit of manipulation, like.' He turned, and began to wind down the sluices.

'You see the idea, Bunter. If they shut his sluice, all the upland water has to go by the Old Leam, which has enough to do as it is. But if they leave it open and the tide's strong enough to carry the flood-water back with it through the sluice, they'll drown all the country above the sluice.'

'That's it, sir,' said the man with a grin. 'And if the floodwater carries the tide back, we might drown *you*. It all depends, you see.'

'Then we'll hope you manipulate things in our favour,' said Wimsey, cheerfully. The rush of water through the arches was slackening now with the lowering of the sluice-gates, the whirlpools became shallower, and the floating sticks and reeds began to eddy against the piles of the bridge. 'Just hold her back for a bit till we get to Fenchurch, there's a good fellow.'

'Oh, we'll keep her level, don't be afraid,' said the man, reassuringly. 'There ain't nothing wrong wi' *this* here sluice.'

He put such marked emphasis on the word 'this' that Wimsey looked sharply at him.

'How about Van Leyden's Sluice?'

The man shook his head.

'I dunno, sir, but I did hear as old Joe Massey down there was in a great taking about they old gates of his. There was three gentlemen went down yesterday to look at 'em – from the Conservancy or the Board of something o' that, I reckon. But you can't do nothing much for they gates in flood-time. Mebbe they'll hold, mebbe they won't. It's all according.'

'Well, that's jolly,' said Wimsey. 'Come on, Bunter. Have you made your will? We'd better go while the going's good.'

Their way this time lay along the south bank or Fenchurch side of the Thirty-Foot. Dyke and drain were everywhere abrim and here and there the water stood in the soaked fields as though they needed but little more to sink back into their ancient desolation of mere and fen. There was little movement on the long straight road. Here a shabby car met them, splashed with mud and squirting water from every pot-hole; here a slow farm cart plodded ahead with a load of mangel-wurzels, the driver huddled under the rough protection of a sodden sack, and deaf and blind to overtaking traffic! there a solitary labourer, bent with rheumatism, slouched homeward dreaming of fire and beer at the nearest pub. The air was so heavy with water, that not till they had passed Frog's Bridge did they hear the sweet, dull jangle of sound that told them that the ringers were practising their Christmas peal; it drifted through the streaming rain with an aching and intolerable melancholy, like the noise of the bells of a drowned city pulsing up through the overwhelming sea.

They turned the corner beneath the great grey tower and passed by the Rectory wall. As they neared the gate a blast of familiar toots smote upon their ears, and Wimsey slackened speed as the Rector's car came cautiously nosing its way into the road. Mr Venables recognised the Daimler immediately, and stopped his engine with the Morris halfway across the road. His hand waved cheerfully to them through the side-curtains.

'Here you are! Here you are again!' he cried in welcoming accents, as Wimsey got out and came forward to greet him. 'How lucky I am to have just caught you. I expect you heard me coming out. I always blow the horn before venturing into the roadway; the entrance is so very abrupt. How are you, my dear fellow, how are you? Just going along to the Red House, I expect. They are eagerly looking forward to your visit. You will come and see us often, I hope, while you're here. My wife and I are dining with you tonight. She will be so pleased to meet you again. I said to her, I wondered if I should meet you on the road. What terrible weather, is it not? I have to hurry off now to baptise a poor little baby at the end of Swamp Drove just the other side of Frog's Bridge. It's not likely to live, they tell me, and the poor mother is desperately ill, too, so I mustn't linger, because I expect I shall have to walk up the Drove with all this mud and it's nearly a mile and I don't walk as fast as I did. Yes, I am quite well, thank you, except for a slight cold. Oh, nothing at all – I got a little damp the other day taking a funeral for poor Watson at St Stephen – he's laid up with shingles, so painful and distressing, though not dangerous, I'm happy to say. Did you come through St Ives and Chatteris? Oh, you came direct from Denver. I hope your family are all quite well. I hear they've got the floods out all over the Bedford Level. There'll be skating on Bury Fen if we get any frosts after this – though it doesn't look like it at present, does it? They say a green winter makes a fat churchyard, but I always think extreme cold is really more trying for the old people. But I really must push on now. I beg your pardon? I didn't catch what you said. The bells are a little loud. That's why I blew my horn so energetically; it is difficult sometimes to hear while the ringing is going on. Yes, we're trying some Stedman's tonight. You don't ring Stedman's. I think. You must come along one day and have a try at them. Most fascinating. Wally Pratt is making great strides. Even Hezekiah says he isn't doing so badly. Will Thoday is ringing tonight. I turned over in my mind what you told me, but I saw no reason for excluding him. He did wrong, of course, but I feel convinced that he committed no *great* sin, and it would arouse so much comment in the village if he left the ringers. Gossip is such a wicked thing, don't you think? Dear me! I am neglecting my duties sadly in the pleasure of seeing you. That poor child! I *must* go. Oh, dear! I hope my engine won't give trouble, it is scarcely warmed up. Oh, please don't trouble. How very good of you. I'm ashamed to trespass on your – ah! she always responds at once to the starting-handle. Well, *au revoir, au revoir*! We shall meet this evening.'

He shugged off cheerfully, beaming round at them through the discoloured weather curtains and zigzagging madly across the road in his efforts to drive one way and look another. Wimsey and Bunter went on to the Red House.

THE SECOND PART

THE WATERS ARE CALLED HOME

Deep calleth unto deep at the noise of thy waterspouts: all the waves and thy billows are gone over me.
Psalm xlii 7

Christmas was over. Uncle Edward, sourly and reluctantly, had given way, and Hilary Thorpe's career was decided. Wimsey had exerted himself nobly in other directions. On Christmas Eve, he had gone out with the Rector and the Choir and sung 'Good King Wenceslas' in the drenching rain, returning to eat cold roast beef and trifle at the Rectory. He had taken no part in the Stedman's Triples, but had assisted Mrs Venables to tie wet bunches of holly and ivy to the font, and attended church twice on Christmas Day, and helped to bring two women and their infants to be churched and christened from a remote and muddy row of cottages two miles beyond the Drain.

On Boxing Day, the rain ceased, and was followed by what the Rector described as 'a tempestuous wind called Euroclydon'. Wimsey, taking advantage of a dry road and clear sky, ran over to see his friend at Walbeach and stayed the night, hearing great praises of the New Wash Cut and the improvement it had brought to the harbour and the town.

He returned to Fenchurch St Paul after lunch, skimming merrily along with Euroclydon bowling behind him. Turning across the bridge at Van Leyden's Sluice, he noticed how swift and angry the river ran through the weir, with flood-water and tide-water meeting the wind. Down by the sluice a gang of men were working on a line of barges, which were moored close against the gates and piled high with sandbags. One of the workmen gave a shout as the car passed over the bridge, and another man, seeing him point and gesticulate, came running from the sluice-head across the road, waving his arms. Lord Peter stopped and waited for him to come up. It was Will Thoday.

'My lord!' he cried, 'my lord! Thank God you are here! Go and warn them at St Paul that the sluice-gates are going. We've done what we can with sandbags and beams, but we can't do no more and there's a message come down from the Old Bank Sluice that the water is over the Great Leam at Lympsey, and they'll have to send it down here or be drowned themselves. She's held this tide, but she'll go the next with this wind and the tide at springs. It'll lay the whole country under water, my lord, and there's no time to lose.'

'All right,' said Wimsey. 'Can I send you more men?'

'A regiment of men couldn't do nothing now, my lord. They old gates is going, and there won't be a foot of dry land in the three Fenchurches six hours from now.'

Wimsey glanced at his watch. 'I'll tell 'em,' he said, and the car leapt forward.

The Rector was in his study when Wimsey burst in upon him with the news.

'Great Heavens!' cried Mr Venables. 'I've been afraid of this. I've warned the drainage authorities over and over again about those gates but they wouldn't listen. But it's no good crying over spilt milk. We must act quickly. If they open the Old Bank Sluice and Van Leyden's Sluice blows up, you see what will happen. All the Upper Water will be turned back up the Wale and drown us ten feet deep or more. My poor parishioners – all those outlying farms and cottages! But we mustn't lose our heads. We have taken our precautions. Two Sundays ago I warned the congregation what might happen and I put a note in the December Parish Magazine. And the Nonconformist minister has co-operated in the most friendly manner with us. Yes, yes. The first thing to do is to ring the alarm. They know what that means, thank God! they learnt it during the war. I never thought I should thank God for the war, but He moves in a mysterious way. Ring the bell for Emily, please. The church will be safe, whatever happens, unless we get a rise of over twelve feet, which is hardly likely. Out of the deep, O Lord, out of the deep. Oh, Emily, run and tell Hinkins that Van Leyden's Sluice is giving way. Tell him to fetch one of the other men and ring the alarm on Gaude and Tailor Paul at once. Here are the keys of the church and belfry. Warn your mistress and get all the valuables taken over to the church. Carry them up the tower. Now keep cool, there's a good girl. I don't think the house will be touched, but one cannot be too careful. Find somebody to help you with this chest – I've secured all the parish registers in it – and see that the church plate is taken up the tower as well. Now, where is my hat? We must get on the telephone to St Peter and St Stephen and make sure that they are prepared. And we will see what we can do with the people at the Old Bank Sluice. We haven't a moment to lose. Is your car here?'

They ran the car up to the village, the Rector leaning out perilously and shouting warnings to everyone they met. At the post office they called up the Fenchurches and then communicated with the keeper of the Old Bank Sluice. His report was not encouraging.

'Very sorry, sir, but we can't help ourselves. If we don't let the water through there'll be the best part of four miles o' the bank washed away. We've got six gangs a-working on it now, but they can't do a lot with all these thousands o' tons o' water coming down. And there's more to come, so they say.'

The Rector made a gesture of despair, and turned to the postmistress.

'You'd best get down to the church, Mrs West. You know what to do. Documents and valuables in the tower, personal belongings in the nave. Animals in the churchyard. Cats, rabbits and guinea-pigs in *baskets, please* – we can't have them running round loose. Ah! there go the alarm-bells. Good! I am more alarmed for the remote farms than for the village. Now, Lord Peter, we must go and keep order as best we can at the church.'

The village was already a scene of confusion. Furniture was being stacked on handcarts, pigs were being driven down the street, squealing; hens, squawking and terrified, were being bundled into crates. At the door of the school-house Miss Snoot was peering agitatedly out.

'When ought we to go, Mr Venables?'

'Not yet, not yet – let the people move their heavy things first. I will send you a message when the time comes, and then you will get the children together and march them down in an orderly way. You can rely on me. But keep them cheerful – reassure them and don't on any account let them go home. They are far safer here. Oh, Miss Thorpe! Miss Thorpe! I see you have heard the news.'

'Yes, Mr Venables. Can we do anything?'

'My dear, you are the very person! Could you and Mrs Gates see that the school-children are kept amused and happy, and give them tea later on if necessary? The urns are in the parish-room. Just a moment, I must speak to Mr Hensman. How are we off for stores, Mr Hensman?'

'Pretty well stocked, sir,' replied the grocer. 'We're getting ready to move as you suggested, sir.'

'That's fine,' said the Rector. 'You know where to go. The refreshment room will be in the Lady Chapel. Have you the key of the parish-room for the boards and trestles?'

'Yes, sir.'

'Good, good. Get a tackle rigged over the church well for your drinking-water, and be sure and remember to boil it first. Or use the Rectory pump, if it is spared to us. Now, Lord Peter, back to the church.'

Mrs Venables had already taken charge in the church. Assisted by Emily and some of the women of the parish, she was busily roping off areas – so many pews for the school-children, so many other pews near the stoves for the sick and aged, the area beneath the tower for furniture, a large placard on the par-close screen REFRESHMENTS. Mr Gotobed and his son, staggering under buckets of coke, were lighting the stoves. In the churchyard, Jack Godfrey and a couple of other farmers were making cattle-pens and erecting shelters among the tombs. Just over the wall which separated the consecrated ground from the bell-field, a squad of volunteer diggers were digging out a handsome set of sanitary trenches.

'Good Lord, sir,' said Wimsey, impressed, 'anybody would think you'd done this all your life.'

'I have devoted much prayer and thought to the situation in the last few weeks,' said Mr Venables. 'But my wife is the real manager. She has a marvellous head for organisation. Hinkins! right up to the bell-chamber with that plate – it'll be out of the way there. Alf! Alf Donnington! How about that beer?'

'Coming along, sir.'

'Splendid – into the Lady Chapel, please. You're bringing some of it bottled, I hope. It'll take two days for the casks to settle.'

'That's all right, sir. Tebbutt and me are seeing to that.'

The Rector nodded, and dodging past some of Mr Hensman's contingent, who were staggering in with cases of groceries, he went out to the gates, where he encountered P.C. Priest, stolidly directing the traffic.

'We're having all the cars parked along the wall, sir.'

'That's right. And we shall want volunteers with cars to run out to outlying places and bring in the women and sick people. Will you see to that?'

'Very good, sir.'

'Lord Peter, will you act as our Mercury between here and Van Leyden's Sluice? Keep us posted as to what is happening.'

'Right you are,' said Wimsey. 'I hope, by the way, that Bunter – where is Bunter?'

'Here, my lord. I was about to suggest that I might lend some assistance with the commissariat, if not required elsewhere.'

'Do, Bunter, do,' said the Rector.

'I understand, my lord, that no immediate trouble is expected at the Rectory, and I was about to suggest that, with the kind help of the butcher, sir, a sufficiency of hot soup might be prepared in the washhouse copper, and brought over in the wheeled watering tub – after the utensil had been adequately scalded, of course. And if there were such a thing as a paraffin stove anywhere – '

'By all means – but be careful with the paraffin. We do not want to escape the water to fall into the fire.'

'Certainly not, sir.'

'You can get paraffin from Wilderspin. Better send some more ringers up to the tower. Let them pull the bells as they like and fire them at intervals. Oh, here are the Chief Constable and Superintendent Blundell – how good of them to come over. We are expecting a little trouble here, Colonel.'

'Just so, just so. I see you are handling the situation admirably. I fear a lot of valuable property will be destroyed. Would you like any police sent over?'

'Better patrol the roads between the Fenchurches,' suggested Blundell. 'St Peter is greatly alarmed – they're afraid for the bridges. We are arranging a service of ferry-boats. They lie even lower than you do and are, I fear, not so well prepared as you sir.'

'We can offer them shelter here,' said the Rector. 'The church will hold nearly a thousand at a pinch, but they must bring what food they can. And their bedding, of course. Mrs Venables is arranging it all. Men's sleeping-quarters on the cantoris side, women and children on the decani side. And we can put the sick and aged people in the Rectory in greater comfort, if all goes well. St Stephen will be safe enough, I imagine, but if not, we must do our best for them too. And, dear me! We shall rely on you, Superintendent, to send us victuals by boat as soon as it can be arranged. The roads will be clear between Leamholt and the Thirty-Foot, and the supplies can be brought from there by water.'

'I'll organise a service,' said Mr Blundell.

'If the railway embankment goes, you will have to see to St Stephen as well. Good-day, Mrs Giddings, good-day to you! We are having quite an adventure, are we not? So glad to see you here in good time. Well, Mrs Leach! So here you are! How's baby? Enjoying himself, I expect. You'll find Mrs Venables in the church. Jack! Jackie Holliday! You must put that kitten in a basket. Run and ask Joe Hinkins to find you one. Ah, Mary! I hear your husband is doing fine work down at the sluice. We must see that he doesn't come to any harm. Yes, my dear, what is it? I am just coming.'

For three hours Wimsey worked among the fugitives – fetching and carrying, cheering and exhorting, helping to stall cattle and making himself as useful as he could. At length he remembered his duty as a messenger and extricating his car from the crowd made his way east along the Thirty-Foot. It was growing dark, and the road was thronged with carts and cattle, hurrying to the safety of Church Hill. Pigs and cattle impeded his progress.

'The animals went in two by two,' sang Wimsey, as he sped through the twilight, 'the elephant and the kangaroo. Hurrah!'

Down at the sluice, the situation looked dangerous. Barges had been drawn against both sides of the gates and an attempt had been made to buttress the sluice with beams and sandbags, but the piers were bulging dangerously and as fast as material was lowered into the water, it was swept down by the force of the current. The river was foaming over the top of the weir, and from the east, wind and tide were coming up in violent opposition.

'Can't hold her much longer, now, my lord,' gasped a man, plunging up the bank and shaking the water from him like a wet dog. 'She' going. God help us!'

The sluice-keeper was wringing his hands.

'I told 'em, I told 'em! What will become on us?'

'How long now?' asked Wimsey.

'An hour, my lord, if that.'

'You'd better all get away. Have you cars enough?'

'Yes, my lord, thank you.'

Will Thoday came up to him, his face white and working.

'My wife and children – are they safe?'

'Safe as houses, Will. The Rector's doing wonders. You'd better come back with me.'

'I'll hang on here till the rest go, my lord, thank you. But tell them to lose no time.'

Wimsey turned the car back again. In the short time that he had been away the organisation had almost completed itself. Men, women, children and household goods had been packed into the church. It was nearly seven o'clock and the dusk had fallen. The lamps were lit. Soup and tea were being served in the Lady Chapel, babies were crying, the churchyard resounded with the forlorn lowing of cattle and the terrified bleating of sheep. Sides of bacon were being carried in, and thirty wagon-loads of hay and corn were ranged under the church wall. In the only clear space amid the confusion the Rector stood behind the rails of the Sanctuary. And over all, the bells tumbled and wrangled, shouting their alarm across the country. Gaude, Sabaoth, John, Jericho, Jubilee, Dimity, Batty Thomas and Tailor Paul – awake! make haste! save yourselves! The deep waters have gone over us! They call with the noise of the cataracts!

Wimsey made his way up the altar-rail and gave his message. The Rector nodded. 'Get the men away quickly,' he said, 'tell them they must come at once. Brave lads! I know they hate to give in, but they mustn't sacrifice themselves uselessly. As you go through the village, tell Miss Snoot to bring the school-children down.' And as Wimsey turned to go, he called anxiously after him – 'And don't let them forget the other two tea-urns!'

The men were already piling into their waiting cars when Lord Peter again arrived at the sluice. The tide was coming up like a race, and in the froth and flurry of water he could see the barges flung like battering rams against the piers. Somebody shouted: 'Get out of it, lads, for your lives!' and was answered by a rending crash. The transverse beams that carried the footway over the weir, rocking and swaying upon the bulging piers, cracked and parted. The river poured over the tumult to meet the battering force of the tide. There was a cry. A dark figure, stepping hurriedly across the reeling barges, plunged and was gone. Another form dived after it, and a rush was made to the bank. Wimsey, flinging off his coat, hurled himself down to the water's edge. Somebody caught and held him.

'No good, my lord, they're gone! My God! did you see that?'

Somebody threw the flare of a headlight across the river. 'Caught between the barges and the pier – smashed like eggshells. Who is it? Johnnie Cross? Who went in after him? Will Thoday? That's bad, and him a married man. Stand back, my lord. We'll have no more lives lost. Save yourselves, lads, you can do them no good. Christ! the sluice gates are going. Drive like hell, men, it's all up!'

Wimsey found himself dragged and hurtled by strong hands to his car. Somebody scrambled in beside him. It was the sluicekeeper, still moaning, 'I told 'em, I told 'em!' Another thunderous crash brought down the weir across the Thirty-Foot, in a deluge of tossing timbers. Beams and barges were whirled together like straws, and a great spout of water raged over the bank and flung itself across the road. Then the sluice, that held the water back from the old Wale River, yielded, and the roar of the engines as the cars sped away was lost in the thunder of the meeting and overriding waters.

The banks of the Thirty-Foot held, but the swollen Wale, receiving the full force of the Upper Waters and the spring tide, gave at every point. Before the cars reached St Paul, the flood was rising and pursuing them. Wimsey's car – the last to start – was submerged to the axles. They fled through the dusk, and behind and on their left, the great silver sheet of water spread and spread.

In the church, the Rector, with the electoral roll-call of the parish in his hand, was numbering his flock. He was robed and stoled, and his anxious old face had taken on a look of great pastoral dignity and serenity.

'Eliza Giddings.'

'Here I am, Rector.'

'Jack Godfrey and his wife and family.'

'All here, sir.'

'Henry Gotobed and his family.'

'All here, sir.'

'Joseph Hinkins . . . Louisa Hitchcock . . . Obadiah Holliday . . . Miss Evelyn Holliday . . .'

The party from the sluice gathered awkwardly about the door. Wimsey made his way up to where the Rector stood on the chancel steps, and spoke in his ear.

'John Cross and Will Thoday? That is terrible. God rest them, poor, brave fellows. Will you be good enough to tell my wife and ask her to break the sad news to their people? Will went to try and rescue Johnnie? That is just what I should have expected of him. A dear, good fellow in spite of everything.'

Wimsey called Mrs Venables aside. The Rector's voice, shaking a little now, went on with his call:

'Jeremiah Johnson and his family . . . Arthur and Mary Judd . . . Luke Judson . . .'

Then came a long, wailing cry from the back of the church:

'Will! Oh, Will! He didn't want to live! Oh, my poor children – what shall we do?'

Wimsey did not wait to hear any more. He made his way down to the belfry door and climbed the stair to the ringing chamber. The bells were still sounding their frenzied call. He passed the sweating ringers and climbed again – up through the clock-chamber, piled with household goods, and up and on to the bell-chamber itself. As his head rose through the floor, the brazen fury of the bells fell about his ears like the blows from a thousand beating hammers. The whole tower was drenched and drunken with noise. It rocked and reeled with the reeling of the bells, and staggered like a drunken man. Stunned and shaken, Wimsey set his foot on the last ladder.

Halfway up he stopped, clinging desperately with his hands. He was pierced through and buffeted by the clamour. Through the brazen crash and clatter there went one high note, shrill and sustained, that was like a sword in the brain. All the blood of his body seemed to rush to his head, swelling it to bursting-point. He released his hold on the ladder and tried to shut out the uproar with his fingers, but such a sick giddiness overcame him that he swayed, ready to fall. It was not noise – it was brute pain, a grinding, bludgeoning, ran-dan, crazy, intolerable torment. He felt himself screaming, but could not hear his own cry. His eardrums were cracking; his senses swam away. It was infinitely worse than any roar of heavy artillery. That had beaten and deafened, but this unendurable shrill clangour was a raving madness, an assault of devils. He could move neither forward nor backwards though his failing wits urged him, 'I must get out – I must get out of this.' The belfry heaved and wheeled about him as the bells dipped and swung within the reach of an outstretched hand. Mouth up, mouth down, they brawled with their tongues of bronze, and through it all that shrill, high, sweet, relentless note went stabbing and shivering.

He could not go down, for his head dizzied and his stomach retched at the thought of it. With a last, desperate sanity, he clutched at the ladder and forced his tottering limbs upward. Foot by foot, rung by rung, he fought his way to the top. Now the trap-door was close above his head. He raised a leaden hand and thrust the bolt aside. Staggering, feeling as though his bones were turned to water, and with blood running from his nose and ears, he fell, rather than stepped, out upon the windy roof. As he flung the door to behind him, the demoniac clamour sank back into the pit, to rise again, transmuted to harmony, through the louvres of the belfry windows.

He lay for some minutes quivering upon the leads, while his senses slowly drifted back to him. At length he wiped the blood from his face, and pulled himself groaningly to his knees, hands fastened upon the fretwork of the parapet. An enormous stillness surrounded him. The moon had risen, and between the battlements the sullen face of the drowned fen showed like a picture in a shifting frame, like the sea seen through the porthole of a rolling ship, so widely did the tower swing to the relentless battery of the bells.

The whole world was lost now in one vast sheet of water. He hauled himself to his feet and gazed out from horizon to horizon. To the south-west, St Stephen's tower still brooded over a dark platform of land, like a broken mast upon a sinking ship. Every house in the village was lit up; St Stephen was riding out the storm. Westward, the thin line of the railway embankment stretched away to Little Dykesey, unvanquished as yet, but perilously besieged. Due south, Fenchurch St Peter, roofs and spire etched black against the silver, was the centre of a great mere. Close beneath the tower, the village of St Paul lay abandoned, waiting for its fate. Away to the east, a faint pencilling marked the course of the Potters Lode Bank, and while he watched it, it seemed to waver and vanish beneath the marching tide. The Wale River had sunk from sight in the spreading of the flood, but far beyond it, a dull streak showed where the land billowed up seaward, and thrust the water back upon the Fenchurches. Inward and westward the waters swelled relentlessly from the breach of Van Leyden's Sluice and stood level with the top of the Thirty-Foot Bank. Outward and eastward the gold cock on the weathervane stared and strained, fronting the danger, held to his watch by the relentless pressure of the wind from off the Wash. Somewhere amid that still surge of water, the broken bodies of Will Thoday and his mate drifted and tumbled with the wreckage of farm and field. The Fen had reclaimed its own.

One after another, the bells jangled into silence. Gaude, Sabaoth, John,

Jericho, Jubilee, Dimity and Batty Thomas lowered their shouting mouths and were at peace, and in their sudden stillness, Tailor Paul tolled out the Nine Tailors for two souls passed in the night. The notes of the organ rose solemnly.

Wimsey crept down from the tower. Into the ringing-chamber, where old Hezekiah still stood to his bell, streamed light and sound from the crowded church. The Rector's voice, musical and small, came floating up, past the wings of the floating cherubim:

'Lighten our darkness . . .'

THE THIRD PART

THE BELLS ARE RUNG DOWN

The bronze monster had struck him dead.
JULIAN SERMET:
The Rosamonde

For fourteen days and nights the Wale River ran backwards in its bed and the floods stood in the land. They lay all about Fenchurch St Stephen, a foot above the railway embankment, so that the trains came through snorting and slowly, sending up a wall of water right and left. St Peter suffered most, its houses being covered to the sills of the upper windows, and its cottages to the eaves. At St Paul, everything was flooded eight feet deep, except the mound where church and rectory stood.

The Rector's organisation worked brilliantly. Supplies were ample for three days, after which an improvised service of boats and ferries brought in fresh food regularly from the neighbouring towns. A curious kind of desert-island life was carried on in and about the church, which, in course of time, assumed a rhythm of its own. Each morning was ushered in by a short and cheerful flourish of bells, which rang the milkers out to the cowsheds in the graveyard. Hot water for washing was brought in wheeled water-butts from the Rectory copper. Bedding was shaken and rolled under the pews for the day; the tarpaulins dividing the men's side from the women's side of the church were drawn back and a brief service of hymns and prayer was held, to the accompaniment of culinary clinkings and odours from the Lady Chapel. Breakfast, prepared under Bunter's directions, was distributed along the pews by members of the Women's Institute, and when this was over, the duties of the day were in hand. Daily school was carried on in the south aisle; games and drill were organised in the Rectory garden by Lord Peter Wimsey; farmers attended to their cattle; owners of poultry brought the eggs to a communal basket; Mrs Venables presided over sewing-parties in the Rectory. Two possible wireless sets were available, one in the Rectory, the other in the church; these tirelessly poured out entertainment and instruction, the batteries being kept recharged by an ingenious device from the engine of Wimsey's Daimler, capably handled by the Wilderspins. Three evenings a week were devoted to concerts and lectures, arranged by Mrs Venables, Miss Snoot and the combined choirs of St Stephen and St Paul, with Miss Hilary Thorpe and Mr Bunter (comedian) assisting. On Sundays, the routine was varied by an Early Celebration, followed by an undenominational service conducted by the Church of England priests and the two Nonconformist ministers. A wedding, which happened to fall due in the middle of the fortnight, was made a gala occasion, and a baby, which also happened to fall due, was baptised 'Paul' (for the church) 'Christopher' (because St Christopher had to do with rivers and ferries), the Rector strenuously resisted the parents' desire to call it 'Van Leyden Flood'.

On the fourteenth day, Wimsey, passing early through the churchyard for a morning swim down the village street, noticed that the level of the water had shrunk by an inch, and returned, waving a handful of laurels from somebody's front garden, as the nearest substitute for an olive-branch. That day they rang a merry peal of Kent Treble Bob Major, and across the sundering flood heard the bells of St Stephen peal merrily back.

'The odour,' observed Bunter, gazing out on the twentieth day across the dismal strand of ooze and weed that had once been Fenchurch St Paul, 'is intensely disagreeable, my lord, and I should be inclined to consider it insanitary.'

'Nonsense, Bunter,' said his master. 'At Southend you would call it ozone and pay a pound a sniff for it.'

The women of the village looked rueful at the thought of the cleansing and drying that their homes would need, and the men shook their heads over the damage to rick and barn.

The bodies of Will Thoday and John Cross were recovered from the streets of St Stephen, whither the flood had brought them, and buried beneath the shadow of St Paul's tower, with all the solemnity of a muffled peal. It was only after they had been laid in the earth that Wimsey opened his mind to the Rector and to Superintendent Blundell.

'Poor Will,' he said, 'he died finely and his sins died with him. He meant no harm, but I think perhaps he guessed at last how Geoffrey Deacon died and felt himself responsible. But we needn't look for a murderer now.'

'What do you mean, my lord?'

'Because,' said Wimsey, with a wry smile, 'the murderers of Geoffrey Deacon are hanging already, and a good deal higher than Haman.'

'Murderers?' asked the Superintendent, quickly. 'More than one? Who were they?'

'Gaude, Sabaoth, John, Jericho, Jubilee, Dimity, Batty Thomas and Tailor Paul.'

There was an astonished silence. Wimsey added:

'I ought to have guessed. I believe it is at St Paul's Cathedral that it is said to be death to enter the bell-chamber when a peal is being rung. But I know that if I had stayed ten minutes in the tower that night when they rang the alarm, I should have been dead, too. I don't know exactly what of – stroke, apoplexy, shock – anything you like. The sound of a trumpet laid flat the walls of Jericho and the note of a fiddle will shatter a vessel of glass. I know that no human frame could bear the noise of the bells for more than fifteen minutes – and Deacon was shut up there, roped and tied there, for nine interminable hours between the Old Year and the New.'

'My God!' said the Superintendent. 'Why then, you were right, my lord, when you said that Rector, or you, or Hezekiah might have murdered him.'

'I was right,' said Wimsey. 'We did.' He thought for a moment and spoke again. 'The noise must have been worse that night than it was the other day – think how the snow choked the louvres and kept it pent up in the tower. Geoffrey Deacon was a bad man, but when I think of the helpless horror of his lonely and intolerable death-agony – '

He broke off, and put his head between his hands, as though instinctively seeking to shut out the riot of the bell-voices.

The Rector's mild voice came out of the silence.

'There have always,' he said, 'been legends about Batty Thomas. She has slain two other men in times past, and Hezekiah will tell you that the bells are said to be jealous of the presence of evil. Perhaps God speaks through those mouths of inarticulate metal. He is a righteous judge, strong and patient, and is provoked every day.'

'Well,' said the Superintendent, striking a note of cheerful commonplace, 'seems as if we didn't need to take any more steps in this matter. The man's dead, and the fellow that put him up there is dead too, poor chap, and that's all there is to it. I don't altogether understand about these bells, but I'll take your word for it, my lord. Matter of periods of vibration, I suppose. Yours seems the best solution, and I'll put it up to the Chief Constable. And that's all there is to it.'

He rose to his feet.

'I'll wish you good-morning, gentlemen,' he said, and went out.

The voice of the bells of Fenchurch St Paul: Gaude, Gaudy Domini in laude. Sanctus, sanctus, sanctus Dominus Deus Sabaoth. John Cole made me, John Presbyter paid me, John Evangelier aid me. From Jericho to John a-Groate there is no bell can better my note. Jubilate Deo. Nunc Dimittis, Domine. Abbot Thomas set me here and bad me ring both laud and clear. Paul is my name, honour that same.

Gaude, Sabaoth, John, Jericho, Jubilee, Dimity, Batty Thomas and Tailor Paul.

Nine Tailors Make a Man.

GIDEON'S DAY

JOHN CREASEY

The characters and situations in this book are entirely imaginary and bear no relation to any real person or actual happening

CHAPTER 1

GIDEON'S WRATH

The wrath of Gideon was remarkable to see and a majestic thing to hear. Among other things, it transformed Gideon himself. From a massive, slow-moving, pale man with a quiet voice and unassuming, almost modest manner, he became as a raging lion, cheeks reddening and voice bellowing. Such times did not come often; but as Gideon was a superintendent at New Scotland Yard, whenever it did, it made many people uneasy, and set them searching their consciences for evidence of things undone or badly done. All the sins of omission and commission noticed by Gideon but not used in evidence against his subordinates, became vivid in the recollection of the offenders; on any one of these, Gideon might descend. The first cause of the storm often suffered lightly compared with others. One consequence was inescapable; a shaking up. The thin, chill, sardonic reproof of the Assistant Commissioner, the curt disapproval of the Secretary, even the cold or hot wind created by the induction of a new Commissioner, were petty trials compared with the wrath of Gideon, for he was the Yard's senior superintendent, and regarded by many as its Grand Old Man.

Yet Gideon was not yet fifty.

On the occasion under discussion the first signs of the wrath to come were visible when Gideon drove too fast into the approaches to the Yard, swinging his new-looking black Wolseley off the Embankment at Flying Squad pace. He squeezed between the A.C.'s Daimler and Mr. Millington's Riley at fully twenty-five miles an hour and had only a foot to spare on one side and six inches on the other. He brought the car to a standstill with its bumper a bare inch off the wall, more by luck than judgment.

Quite evidently, this was going to be Gideon's day.

Five officers, all uniformed, read the signs.

By the time Gideon reached the foot of the stone steps leading to the main hall of the C.I.D. building, the news, in the form of a 'get everything under control, G.G.'s on the warpath' warning, was on its way through the Yard, via a one-armed lift attendant, two plainclothes sergeants and a telephone operator named Veronica (who was engaged to one of the Sergeants). It quivered along telephone lines, cut into large offices and small like a draught of cold wind; it reached the canteen, the divers departments from the laboratory to ballistics, and made the men on radio-control duty much brisker in the Information Room. In fact, by the time Gideon reached his own office, it had reached the ears of the Secretary, that almost anonymous personage who knew practically everything that went on.

The Secretary grinned.

Few others found it even slightly amusing, for even at the Yard a completely clear conscience is a rarity. Chief Inspector Lemaitre, who shared Gideon's office, had two minutes' notice of the storm. That was time in which to straighten his tie, put on his coat, empty the seven cigarette stubs out of his ashtray and then, for appearances' sake, pick up two and put them back. He also had time to stack the morning's reports on Gideon's desk, under three headings: *New Inquiries, Inquiries Proceeding,* and *Investigation Closed*. That done, he trundled back to his own desk, lifted the telephone and called 1B Division; he considered it wise to be on the telephone, for that would give him time to judge the likely effect of the tempest on him. Lemaitre was just a year younger than Gideon, a thin, lanky and laconic man, showing to all except Gideon a confidence which suggested that he was sure that he could never be wrong. In fact, he was prone to the mistakes which usually follow over-confidence.

He was holding on for the call when the door opened, banged back against the doorstep, and admitted Gideon. It was rather as if an elephant had changed its slow, stately progress for the furious speed of a gazelle; except that Gideon was not even remotely like a gazelle.

He looked round at Lemaitre, who raised a hand and gave a bright smile; and allowed it to freeze on his lantern cheeks, as if he had received no warning.

Gideon pushed the chair behind his own desk into position, so that it banged against the wall. He dropped into it, and stretched out for the telephone. He looked across at Lemaitre, his big, grey eyebrows thrust forward, his lined forehead narrowed in a scowl, hooked nose quivering slightly at the nostrils, as if under the influence of an unfamiliar smell. In his big way, Gideon was distinguished-looking, with his iron-grey hair, that nose, arched lips, a big, square chin. His looks would have been an asset in almost any profession from the law to politics, and especially in the Church; as a detective, they occasionally helped to impress a jury, especially when there were several women on it.

'Give me Foster,' he said into the telephone.

Lemaitre thought of a youngish, up-and-coming detective, spruce-looking, but unpopular. What had Foster done to cause such a storm as this? Lemaitre speculated hopefully; then his call came through but the man he wanted wasn't in. That was an advantage after all.

'I'd call him later,' he said, and rang off. He smiled brightly. 'Morning, George.'

Gideon nodded and grunted, but obviously was thinking of the telephone. A faint murmur came from it, and Gideon said:

'Come and see me, Foster, at once.'

He put down the receiver so heavily that the bell sounded. Then he placed both hands on his desk, fingers spread, and kept them very still as he looked at Lemaitre. The Chief Inspector probably had more experience of Gideon's wrath than anyone else at the Yard, and was quite sure that the cause of this was really serious. Gideon seldom if ever let himself go so utterly unless he had been given grim cause.

'What's up, George?' Lemaitre asked.

'Blurry fool,' Gideon said. 'Blurry crook, if it comes to that. I haven't felt as vicious as this for years. You get out, Lem, tell you about it afterwards. Get out as soon as he comes in.'

'Okay,' promised Lemaitre.

There was room for nothing else on Gideon's mind, another ominous sign; and when he talked of a C.I.D. man as a crook, it was more than ominous, it was alarming. Lemaitre felt uneasy for a deeper reason now.

The 'blurry' instead of 'bloody' meant nothing. When these two men had first met, nearly twenty-five years ago, Gideon had commanded the vocabulary of a trooper who had served his apprenticeship in Covent Garden market. He had always known exactly when to use it, and had first started toning it down precisely twenty years ago this spring.

He'd been a detective-sergeant then, with the same promise as young Foster. 'Blurry' had been his first substitution, uttered to Lemaitre's open-mouthed astonishment. Lemaitre, then also a detective-sergeant, hadn't been even slightly nervous of Gideon, although he had willingly conceded him best in most aspects of detective work.

'What's got into you?' he had asked. 'Toothache?'

'Toothache be *blowed*,' Gideon had said, and grinned fiercely. 'Sent young Tom to Sunday School yesterday for the first time, when he came back Kate and I asked him how he liked it. Know what he said? 'Bloody good,' he said, so we weighed into him about wicked words, and know what he said then? He said it was what *I'd* said after seeing a film the night before. I had, too. From now on, I've got to mind my language if I don't want trouble with Kate. The kid's too young to start, anyway.'

Lemaitre hadn't heard Gideon swear for many years.

He'd had good enough reason for watching his language, of course; young Tom had been the first of six and the youngest child was only eight now. Or was it ten? Lemaitre was not quite sure.

There was a tap at the door.'Come in,' Gideon called, and the door opened and Foster came in smartly. He dressed well, was tall, well-built, and had quite a name in amateur rugby and tennis circles. Aged about thirty, Lemaitre thought, and if he didn't think himself so clever and stopped putting on airs, he would be rated high.

Lemaitre stood up.

'Just going along to Records,' he said, 'won't be long.'

Gideon grunted.

Foster said: 'Good morning, sir,' in just about the right tone and manner. He did not look puzzled, apprehensive or guilty. Lemaitre even wondered whether the whisper of the wrath had reached him, he looked almost too bland for that. His dark hair was brushed flat down and straight back from his forehead; his rather bold eyes and nose told the discerning that he would be too interested in Number One. Lemaitre went out, reluctantly, and subdued the temptation to stand at the door and listen. He strolled off towards the canteen for a cup of tea, calling on Records *en route* in case Gideon telephoned him there. They would say that he'd been and gone. The fact that Lemaitre thought that a necessary precaution was an indication of the awe he felt at times for Gideon.

In the office, the detective-sergeant looked down at the Superintendent.

Gideon's hands were still on the desk, palms downwards, skin a leathery-looking brown, fingers and nails big and strong but not at all ugly. The cuffs of a clean white shirt showed. He wore a suit of navy blue and a blue and red spotted tie, all of good quality.

His eyes were slatey blue, big, with heavy, sleepy-looking lids – but there was nothing sleepy about them now. He was a man burning with anger. Foster, at first completely at ease, began to look less self-confident. That became worse because he had to stand in front of the desk like a schoolboy before an unpredictable master; after a few seconds he actually moistened his lips and broke the harsh silence.

'You – you sent for me, sir?'

'Yes,' Gideon said, very heavily. 'I sent for you, Foster. I sent for you to tell you a thing or two.' His voice was deep and rather husky; just now he gave the impression that he was trying not to raise it. 'I sent for you to tell you that you're a living disgrace to the C.I.D. and the Metropolitan Police Force generally. In all my years on the Force I've met some fools and a few knaves and here and there a rat, and you're one of the big rats. I ought to put you on a charge right away and make sure it sticks, and I'm not sure that I won't. We make mistakes here at the Yard, and occasionally let a rogue in, but you're the first of your kind I've come across, and I'd like to break your neck.'

All Foster's blandness had vanished. His thick, full lips were red and wet, where he kept licking them. His cheeks had no colour left, and his almost black eyes couldn't keep steady. When Gideon stopped talking, Foster gulped, tried to find words, but couldn't. Gideon sat there, motionless, damning, as if challenging him to say a word in his defence.

Foster gulped again and eased his collar.

'I – I think you ought to be – to be very careful about talking that way,' he said thinly. 'You've no right to –'

'I've sent Chief Inspector Lemaitre out of the office,' Gideon cut across the protest abruptly, 'so we can have this inverview between ourselves, without witnesses. But I can get all the witnesses I want to prove that you're a skunk. Only skunk isn't the best word. You're a renegade and you're a traitor, and if you were in the army you'd be shot and I'd be glad to pull the trigger.'

Now Foster went red.

'Who the hell do you think you're talking to?'

'At the moment to Detective-Sergeant Eric Foster, of the Criminal Investigation Department,' Gideon growled, 'but you won't be able to call yourself that for long.'

Foster still tried bluster.

'What's this all about? What are you accusing me of doing?'

'If you want it in simple words, I'm accusing you, as an officer of the Criminal Investigation Department, of accepting bribes and so deliberately failing to carry out your duty. I know who's been paying you and I know why, and I've a pretty good idea how much money you've had over the past three months. Like to know how I know?' The big hands didn't move, the gaze of the slatey-blue eyes didn't falter. 'Because an *honest* crook told me. He said that he didn't mind cracking a crib or doing a smash-and-grab job, but when it came to feeding dope to kids in their teens, he drew a line – and he thought I ought to, too.'

Foster exclaimed: 'He's lying! There was no dope –'

He broke off, and all his colour died away, leaving only his shiny dark eyes.

Gideon said heavily: 'That's right, say that you didn't know that they were selling reefers, or that one of them had a hypo and was selling shots of the muck for a guinea a time. Say you thought it was just a question of selling intoxicating liquor after hours – how much better policeman are you for that? You've got a job to do, and if you'd kept your eyes open you would have known what was going on. Even I can't believe that you knew about the dope. You –'

Of course I didn't,' Foster put in quickly. 'I – I didn't know about selling drink after hours, either.'

Gideon shook his head, slowly, deliberately, massively.

'Foster,' he said, 'you haven't even the sense not to lie about it. I suppose you've got to lie. It's the only way you might be able to save your skin. So you'll try.' Much of the power had gone from Gideon's voice, as if what had happened had exhausted him. 'And Chang will lie, too, because if he admitted it, he knows his club would be closed up and he wouldn't be allowed to open up again in London. I don't doubt that you're paid off in a dark corner, that no one sees you meet and no one else knows anything about it – or so you think. Or you *thought*.' The sneer was devastating. 'Well, now you know better. Now you know you can't get away with accepting bribes. From this day on, you'll know what it's like to realize that thanks to you, some kids have become cocaine addicts, and that it's ruined their whole lives.'

Foster said between clenched teeth: 'If kids want dope they'll find a way of getting it. And whoever told you that I've been taking bribes is a liar. You say you got a squeak – I want to know who from.' He paused. 'I know the kind who squeal about things like that. I know the kind who squeal to *you*, too.' Foster's sneer rivalled Gideon's; in fact, it was uglier. 'Old lags, blackguards who ought to be inside and would be if you did your job properly, but you let them keep out, so that you can get them to squeal on others. Think I don't know? Think I don't know that the name of Gideon stinks in the West End?'

When he stopped, it was almost fearfully, as if suddenly afraid that he had gone too far. But Gideon did not move; just looked at him as he might at something unclean. Foster ran his tongue along his lips.

'I – I'm sorry, sir, I didn't mean that. It's been a bit of a shock. I withdraw that remark, sir. But I assure you, you've been misinformed. I give you my word, Chang hasn't bribed me. I – er – I've been a bit too friendly with him, perhaps, but I think he's a decent chap at heart, and –'

'You'd better go, before I break your neck,' Gideon said. 'I don't think you're worth hanging for. As from this moment, you're relieved of all duties. You can protest to the Secretary or the Assistant Commissioner, but it won't make any difference. Stay in London, because we might want to see you at short notice.'

'Look here,' Foster said thickly, 'at least I've got the right to speak on my own behalf.'

'Every right,' Gideon conceded, 'and you'll get it, when the time comes. At the moment I know what you've done but I can't prove it in court. I'm going to look for proof at a time when I've a hundred other urgent jobs that need doing. I'm going to have to waste time in a job like this, and perhaps a murderer or two will get away as a result of it. That ought to make you feel happy.'

Foster said thinly: 'You can't prove what isn't true.'

'That's right, too,' said Gideon. He closed his eyes for a moment, as if he were very tired. 'All right, get out.'

Foster turned towards the door. With his fingers on the handle, he hesitated, and glanced over his shoulder. Gideon was no longer looking at him, but out of the window which overlooked the many windows of a wall on the other side of the rectangular yard.

But he spoke.

'Foster,' he asked, 'what made you do it?'

'I didn't do it,' Foster said, viciously angry. 'You'll be wasting your time all right. Be careful what you say, or I'll get you for defamation of character.'

He went out, and slammed the door.

CHAPTER 2

GIDEON WALKS

Lemaitre sat on the edge of his desk, bony legs crossed, cigarette drooping from his lips. All this was safe now, as the rage was spent. As he listened, he thought that Gideon was tired and showing signs of more years than forty-nine. It was always a strain, being a Yard officer, and Gideon took his responsibilities more to heart than most. He lived his job day and night, in the office, in London, in his home. They all did, up to a point, but few so thoroughly as Gideon.

'The filthy swine,' Lemaitre said, at last. 'I never did like him, he's always been too smooth. Can you pin it on him?'

'Not yet,' said Gideon. He was pulling at his empty pipe, a rough-surfaced cherry wood, which was almost a sign of affectation.

'Who put in the squeal?'

'Birdy.'

'Well,' Lemaitre said, 'you can trust Birdy.'

'That's right,' agreed Gideon, 'you can trust Birdy, especially on a job like this. His own daughter got to like reefers, and he buried her at nineteen. She'd been a pro for three years, and a dopey for two. That makes Birdy the most valuable contact man we've got in the Square Mile on all kinds of dope peddling, and we can't afford to lose him. So, I've put a man on to him, and had him warned that he must look out for trouble. Because Foster will tell Chang, and Chang will try to find out who squeaked. He may not have any luck, but if he does – well, we won't go any further than that. Chang will clean up the Chang Club, too, after this morning you'll be able to run a vacuum cleaner over it and not find a grain of marihuana or any kind of dope.'

'He'll do that,' agreed Lemaitre. 'That's what puzzles me, George. Why did you smack Foster down when you did? Why didn't you raid the place first? You might have picked Chang up and put him inside for ten years.' He looked puzzled, but he grinned. 'But being you, there's a reason, you cunning old so-and-so.' That he could talk so freely was conclusive proof that he felt sure that Gideon was his normal calm self again. 'After the suppliers?'

'Partly,' Gideon said. 'I went for Foster and took the chance of warning Chang because I want to drive Foster into doing something decisive. He'll have to go to Chang, if they're watched closely they'll probably be seen together. And we need proof.'

Lemaitre wrinkled his nose.

'Sounds more like me talking than you,' he remarked. 'Couldn't you have watched Foster, without telling him what you suspected?'

Gideon let himself smile, for the first time that day.

'I've had Foster watched for two months,' he said, 'and even you didn't know. Got nowhere. The thing that got me this morning was the dope. I can understand a man having his palm oiled, but –' he broke off, and ruminated. Then: 'I also think Chang's big time, and on his way to the top. I'd like to watch him now that he's had a smack, and see how he tries to cope.'

'Cunning as a fox,' Lemaitre mocked. 'I'd be inclined to put him away before he became big time.'

'That way, we wouldn't know who was climbing in his place,' said Gideon. Unexpectedly, he smiled again; it gave him the kind of look that all his children loved to see. 'You may be right, Lem, this could be one of my mistakes. I think I've started something, and I'd like to see where it goes.'

'Going to report Foster to the A.C.?'

'Unofficially,' Gideon said. 'We can't make a charge. Foster will soon discover that, and he's bound to resign. He's got the makings of a very bad man in him. Can't possibly give him a second chance, of course, if he won't go by himself, we'll have to find a way of getting rid of him, but I don't think that will cause any trouble. Now, what's in this morning?'

He turned to his desk and the three files.

All Scotland Yard knew that the wrath was past, having spent itself on the sleek head of Detective-Sergeant Foster; none found it in themselves to be sorry, because Foster, being a know-all, was without close friends. One or two casual friends tried to pump him, without success, and he left the Yard a little after eleven o'clock.

By that time Gideon had run through the three groups of cases. *Inquiries*

Proceeding held his attention more than either of the others, and he skimmed through the new cases quickly. Nothing seemed of exceptional interest. Inquiries into several robberies in central London looked like petering out, a jealous ex-lover had thrown vitriol over his love, a woman had been found murdered in Soho; the newspapers would make a sensation of it, but as far as a woman could ask for murder, she had. There was a forgery job building up; it might become very big before it was finished, but he needn't worry about that now.

The *Inquiries Proceeding* took most of his time, and the report he studied longest was one on the last mail van job, now ten days old. If the Yard had an Achilles' heel, it was that; mail van robberies had been going on for three years, and there was plenty of evidence to show that it was the work of one group of crooks; there was nothing about their identity. That worried Gideon because it had become a challenge to the Yard's prestige as well as to its skill.

It wasn't the only challenge.

There was the constant one, of drugs. Close up one distribution centre, and another would open. Judging from what he now knew, at least twelve were open all the time. None of them was big, none threatened to become extensive or to affect the lives of many people except those who were already on the fringe of crime; it was a kind of running sore. Sooner or later, a Duke's daughter or an M.P.'s son would become an addict, and then it would be made into a sensation; the Yard would be prodded from all sides, and Gideon would get as many of the prods as most. He seldom revolted against this form of injustice, for he knew well what some people seemed unable to grasp.

There was a never-ending war between the police and the criminals, a war fought with thoroughness, skill, patience and cunning on each side.

With a few exceptions, the big cases were not the important ones in this unending war. A man who had never committed a crime in his life might suddenly commit murder and his trial become a *cause célèbre*, but the chief impact upon the Yard would be to take detectives away from the daily struggle against vice and crime.

Now and again Gideon would say all this, earnestly, to a friend or to a new policeman or even a newspaper reporter, and shake his head a little sadly when he realized that they took very little notice.

There was dope, then; there were the mail van robberies; there were the thieves who worked as industriously as any man at his job or profession, taking the risk of a spell of prison life as another might take the risk of bankruptcy. Crime never stopped. Big robberies and little robberies, big thieves and the little sneaks, a few gangs but little violence, one fence sent to jail here, another discovered there – oh, the trouble with being an officer at Scotland Yard was that one lived in a tiny world, and found it hard to realize that ninety-nine per cent of the nation's citizens were wholly law-abiding. Gideon's greatest worry, and constant anxiety, was the formidable and increasing evidence that many law-abiding people would readily become law-breakers if they had a good chance and believed that they would not be found out.

Foster was a painful case in point. . . .

Inwardly, Gideon was worried in case he had been swayed too much by his fury when handling Foster. Ninety-nine times out of a hundred he would have waited to cool off before tackling the man; this time he hadn't been able to. Every now and again he erupted as he had this morning into a rage which perhaps only he knew was virtually uncontrollable.

Well, it was done. With twenty-odd years' experience of the Square Mile behind him, he could afford to play what some people would regard as a hunch – this time, that it was wise not to pull Chang in. It was policy to keep hunches even from Lemaitre and certainly from the Assistant Commissioner, although sometimes he thought that the A.C. knew.

The A.C. took the report on Foster very well. No eruption of shock and shame, just a calm acceptance of the fact that they'd picked a bad one when they'd taken Foster, and an almost casual:

'Sure of your facts, Gideon?'

'Yes.'

'All right, let me know if you think he's going to try to whitewash himself.' The A.C. didn't smile, but was almost bland. 'Nothing else outsize?'

'Not really,' said Gideon. 'Four of those mail bags were found floating in the Thames last night – from the Middlebury Road job, by the markings, where they stole the van and all. Ten days ago. Just a chance that we might be able to find out where they were thrown into the river, the River coppers are trying that now. Otherwise –' Gideon shrugged.

'If there's a job I want to finish before I get moved on, it's the mail van job,' the A.C. said quietly, 'but I needn't badger you about it, I know how you feel. All right, go off after your bad men.' This time he smiled, and then added as Gideon stood up 'How did that girl of yours get on with her examination?'

Gideon brightened perceptibly.

'Oh, she got through, thanks. She says she was lucky, she happened to know most of the questions, but –'

'Modest, like her father,' observed the A.C. 'Guildhall School of Music, wasn't it? I had a niece who used to think she could play the piano, too. Your girl a pianist?'

'Fiddler,' said Gideon. 'Can't say I'm a devotee of the violin, but she passed her exam. all right and can take a job to-morrow – if she can get one! Won't do her any harm to find that jobs don't grow on trees, though. Hard to believe that there's a musician in the family,' Gideon went on, with barely subdued pride, 'I can't sing a note without being flat, and my wife – well, never mind. Will you be in to-day, if I need you?'

'I'll be at lunch from twelve-thirty to three.'

Gideon kept a straight face. 'Right, sir, thanks.' He went out, letting the door close silently behind him, and shook his head. 'Two and a half hours for lunch, and I'll be lucky if I have time to get a bowl of soup and a sandwich from the canteen.' But he said it in no resentful mood; if changing incomes with the A.C. meant changing jobs, he would stay as he was. Nice of the old boy to remember Pru. Well done, Pru. Eighteen . . .

He remembered Birdy's daughter, buried at nineteen. He remembered how easy it was to become in need of reefers or of any drugs; you might have your first taste without knowing it, but you'd still be eager for a second, anxious for a third, desperate for a fourth – and there were precious few cures from addiction.

At half-past eleven, he was walking from the Yard into Parliament Street, soon to turn right towards Whitehall and Trafalgar Square. It was a crisp morning in April, no rain was about, the look of spring was upon London and the feel of spring was in Londoners. In a vague sort of way, Gideon knew that he loved London and after a fashion, loved Londoners. It wasn't just sentiment; he belonged to the hard pavements, the smell of petrol and oil, the rumble and the growl of traffic and the unending sound of footsteps, as some men belonged to the country. They could be said to love the soil. The only time that Gideon was really uneasy was when he had a job to handle outside London or one of the big cities. The country hadn't the same feel; he felt that it could cheat him, without him knowing it, whereas here in London the odds were always even.

He walked almost ponderously, six feet two in spite of slightly rounded shoulders, broad and striking enough to make most people look at him twice, and some turn and stare. He was sufficiently well-known for a dozen men to nudge their companions and say: 'There's Gideon of the Yard,' and sufficiently well-liked and trusted to get a grin and a 'Hi, Guv'nor!' from the newspaper sellers and one or two familiars who knew him in the way of business. Very few people disliked Gideon, even among those he put inside. That was one of the reassuring things, and it put the seal to his oneness with London. He supposed, in a way, that it was the common touch. He could think the same way as many of these men thought; they were as dependent on the throbbing heart of London as he.

Dope, gangs, thieves, murderers, prostitutes, pimps, ponces, forgers, blackmailers, coiners, con-men, big-time crooks and little squealers, frightened men and terrified women, vengeful old lags like Birdy who had suffered from the parasitic growth he had helped to put upon the body of London. Here they were, all together, practitioners of every kind of crime, side by side with every kind of goodness, clean crime and 'dirt', too. Somewhere, Foster was licking his wounds or talking to Chang or plotting revenge out of his hurt vanity.

Nothing happened that hadn't happened before.

Now, Gideon was going on his 'daily' rounds; in fact he could afford the time to do this only once or twice each week, and the years had taught him as well as those who employed him that the time he spent on his rounds was well-spent indeed. He was going without any specific purpose, and he didn't think about Foster or crooks all the time. Twice, a young girl he passed, bright with the beauty of youth and touched with the eagerness of innocence, reminded him of his Prudence. Once he told himself that he thought more of Pru than he did of Kate, and supposed that all couples who had been married for twenty-six years lost – something.

When he got back to the Yard, it was just after twelve. Except that he had shown himself to many people who needed reminding that he was about, it had not been an eventful morning. For the past hour he had hardly given Foster a thought, which meant that his fears of having used bad tactics didn't go very deep; it would be all right.

Two or three senior officers made cryptic remarks as he went along the wide corridors, but it was Lemaitre who waited with the stunning news.

'Hallo, George, you heard?'

Gideon put his hat on a corner peg. 'Heard what?'

'Foster's dead,' Lemaitre said. 'Run over by a car that didn't stop.'

CHAPTER 3

FOSTER'S SISTER

Gideon did not answer as he went round to his chair, moved it gently so that the back did not scrape against the wall, and sat down. He picked up his cold pipe, and ran his fingers over the corrugations in the cherry bark. Lemaitre waited until he was sitting back, before adding:

'They rang up from Great Marlborough Street, full of it.'

There was another long pause. Then: 'What beats me,' said Gideon, making himself keep very matter-of-fact, 'is that anyone could knock a chap down in London and drive off and get away with it. Or did anyone pick up the number of the car?'

'No,' said Lemaitre. 'Well, not yet.'

Gideon picked up a pencil, and spoke as he wrote down his first note, which read: 'General call for anyone who saw moving car near fatal spot.' Aloud: 'Was he killed instantaneously?'

'Pretty well.'

'Anything else?'

Lemaitre looked at a clock with big dark hands on the wall over the fireplace. It was ten past twelve.

'I should say it happened at eleven fifty-five,' he said. 'If you ask me –'

'In a minute, Lem,' Gideon said, and pulled a telephone towards him, then asked for the Chief Inspectors' room, then gave instructions: it was simply a call to find witnesses of the accident, all the usual routine; he said everything in a tone which was almost eager, suggesting that these hoary measures were fresh, interesting, even exciting. 'And let me know what you get, will you?' he added, and put the receiver down. 'What's that, Lem?'

'If you ask me,' repeated Lemaitre, 'Foster telephoned Chang, Chang got the wind up, and put him away. And don't tell me I'm romancing, they don't come any worse than Chang. Just because we've never been able to put him inside, it doesn't mean that he's a lily-white –'

'All right,' Gideon said, still feeling the rough bowl of the pipe, 'I know all about Chang. I'd like to find out if he did know about Foster being suspended – hmm. I think I'll go myself. Wonder what time Chang gets up.' He was muttering, might almost have forgotten that Lemaitre was still in the office with him. 'Hell of a thing to happen. Could have committed suicide, I suppose, or else been so steamed up that he didn't look where he was going. Car didn't stop, though. Looks ugly.' He stood up, thrusting both hands into the baggy pockets of his jacket, still holding the pipe in his left hand. 'Anything else in?'

'Nothing much. There was a go at a mail van in Liverpool Street at half-past ten, the railway police stopped their little game, but the three men involved got away.'

Gideon's interest in that seemed sharper than it had in the news of Foster's death.

'Description?'

'No. Masked, until they'd got away.'

'You know, Lem,' said Gideon, 'if we had as much nerve as some of these johnnies, maybe we'd get results quicker. They're quick, they're smart and they're full of guts. That the lot?'

'All that matters, I think,' said Lemaitre. 'There's a flash about a girl's body found in an apartment near Park Lane, nothing known yet – could be natural causes or accident. Patrol car flash, just before you came in.'

'Um,' said Gideon. 'Well, let me know.' He went to the door.

'George,' said Lemaitre, strongly.

'Yes?'

'Be careful with Chang.'

Gideon's slatey eyes lost their brooding look, and for a moment he smiled.

'Don't be a blurry fool,' he said, 'snow wouldn't melt in Chang's mouth to-day, never mind about butter!' He gave that quick, paternal smile again, and went out.

On his way for the morning perambulation, he had gone almost ponderously. Now he wasn't exactly brisk, but took long strides and passed three plainclothes men moving smartly towards the lift. He reached it first.

'Hear about that mail van attempt at Liverpool Street?' asked one of them, a middle-aged detective-inspector.

'Yes,' answered Gideon briefly.

A white-haired detective-sergeant said: 'I've got another six months in this cowshed, and if there's a job I'd like to see finished, it's the mail van job. How many robberies is it now?'

The D.I. said: 'Draw it mild. This wasn't one.'

'Not often they miss.'

'Thirty-nine in three years and two months,' said Gideon, 'and don't ask me whether they're all organized by the same man. I don't know. But I'll bet some of them are. Picked up some of the bags from the last job in the Thames,' he went on, in the way he had of talking freely to subordinates whenever it was possible. 'They make pretty sure we can't trace 'em back, don't they?'

'They'll slip up,' the D.I. prophesied.

Gideon rubbed his chin. 'It wouldn't worry me if we caught 'em before they slip up,' he said. 'Nice if our results weren't always governed by frailties on the part of the crooks, wouldn't it, boys?'

He sounded positively paternal.

The lift stopped, and the others made room for him to get out first.

'Thanks,' he murmured, and was walking towards the steps and his car a moment later, apparently forgetful of the others.

They watched him.

'Funny thing,' the elderly sergeant said, 'he came in on the rampage this morning, Foster went off with a flea in his ear, and now Foster's been run down. Next thing you know, Gee-Gee will be blaming himself for it.'

Gideon – his Christian name of George made Gee-Gee inevitable – squeezed into his shiny car, turned on the ignition and let in the clutch, reversed until he could swing clear, nodded to the men who saluted him, and drove at a moderate pace on to the Embankment. He turned right, heading for Whitehall, then Trafalgar Square, then Lower Regent Street – the main road route to Great Marlborough Street. Inside the car he looked massive, and rather dull. His driving was automatic, yet he wasn't careless and was usually a move ahead of other traffic; he changed gear smoothly, and gave no sign that he was thinking about Foster.

He was wondering whether this would have happened if he hadn't blown his top with Foster. The earlier, uneasy fears – that he might have done the wrong thing – were darker and heavier in one way, worrying him. In another, he was relieved. There was no longer the certainty of scandal, the newspaper headlines, sneers at the Yard, and God knew, things were difficult enough without that. Still, it was a worry. It did not harass him enough to make him careless, or forgetful of the main task: to find out whether Lemaitre's guess was anywhere near the truth. He found himself thinking of Lemaitre with a reluctant kind of disapproval. Over the years, Lem had made the same kind of mistakes, due to impetuosity. 'If you ask me, he telephoned Chang, Chang got the wind up, and put him away.' Lemaitre was still capable of talking like that without a tittle of evidence, of looking upon a possibility as if it were a probability. The years of being proved wrong hadn't cured him; it was why he would never become a Superintendent, either at the Yard or one of the Divisions.

Never mind Lem!

Gideon stopped at the police station in Great Marlborough Street, and had a word with the Divisional Superintendent by telephone from the duty sergeant's desk. Nothing more was known about Foster's accident, no news had come in about the car. The body was at the morgue attached to the police station.

'Want to have a look at him?' the Station Superintendent asked. It was on the tip of Gideon's tongue to say 'no', and then he changed his mind.

'Yes, thanks, mind if I go in on my own? I'm in a hurry.'

'Help yourself,' the other said.

There were two other bodies in the morgue; only one light was on, over a stone bench where one man lay and two others worked. Gideon moved among the stone-topped benches, until he reached the working men, and saw that Foster lay there. They'd almost finished, and didn't look up until one of them drew a white sheet over Foster's body, up as far as the chin. From where Gideon stood, he had a foreshortened view of Foster; he realized that he had been a strikingly good-looking man.

One of the others, a police-surgeon with black hair and a bald patch, looked up.

'Hallo, George.'

' 'Lo, Harry.'

'He went out as quick and clean as a whistle,' said the police-surgeon, 'it's always a help when you know that. Cracked the back of his head, and crushed his stomach, but the face is hardly damaged. Worked with you sometimes, didn't he?'

Gideon nodded.

'Married?' asked the police-surgeon.

'No,' said Gideon. 'One sister, no other close relatives.' Asked about any of the men who worked with him regularly, he could have given an answer as promptly and as accurately. 'Well, there we are.' He turned away, and walked with the police-surgeon towards the door of the morgue.

They didn't say much.

Back in his car, Gideon waited long enough to pack the pipe loosely with a mixture, and to light it. Two loose pipes in the morning, two in the afternoon and as much as he wanted in the evening, was his rule. He brushed a speck of glowing tobacco off his trousers, then moved off.

It wasn't far from there to Winter Street, Soho, where Chang had his club.

There was no room to park. Gideon drove round twice and then spotted a constable.

'I'm going to leave this here, double-parked,' he said. 'Keep an eye open, and if it blocks anyone who wants to get out, move it for me.' He took it for granted that he was recognized, handed over his ignition key, and walked towards Chang's, which was just round the corner.

For a district in the heart of the biggest city in the world, this was a disgrace and degradation. It was almost the only part of London Gideon disliked. The buildings were mostly dilapidated, none was impressive; it was like a shopping centre in the East End, except for the masses of cars parked bumper to bumper. Most of the shops looked closed. A laundry, a shop advertising: '*We make new collars from shirt tails*'; a butcher's shop open, with a woman with brassy hair and talon-like red nails smoking a cigarette and talking to the butcher, showed a glimpse of Soho life as it really was. Gideon knew the woman; she'd been up before the magistrate at Great Marlborough or Bow Street regularly for the past twenty years. She lived close by, and bought her groceries, her meat, her milk, all the things of daily life, from these small shops. Well, why not? She had to live somewhere. A corner shop was filled with dark-haired men and women, all shorter than the average Londoner; they were southern French, Italian or Spanish – and mostly Italian, Gideon knew. In the windows on the shelves were delicacies brought from the ends of the earth – literally from the ends of the earth. If you wanted a speciality of the Chinese, the Japanese, the Javanese, of India, Brazil, the south of Spain or the north of Italy, from Yugoslavia or from Russia, you could buy it here. Inside, everyone was chatting, all were dressed in black, and Gideon scented a funeral party preparing for the meal to come.

The pavements were dusty, the gutters littered with chaff, pieces of paper, cigarette ends, bus tickets. Dust carts and street sweepers could come through Soho half a dozen times a day without ridding it of this hint of squalor in the worst streets; and Winter Street was one of the worst.

By day, Chang's looked harmless.

The name, in mock-Chinese lettering, was on the fascia board, and the weather or years had worn it so badly that most of the 'h' and part of the 'g' were obliterated. Chang had been here a long time. It was a double-fronted shop, and the windows were blotted out with dirty-looking muslin curtains, but the *Bill of Fare*, showing what Chang had to offer in an English hand which would have suited a Billingsgate pub, looked clean enough. It was a restaurant by day and club by night.

Gideon went in.

He knew that he had been seen approaching; probably when he had driven past here he had been recognized. Word spread in Soho as quickly as it did to the Yard. He knew that the broad smile on the face of the diminutive Chinese who came towards him, hands covered in the folds of his snow-white apron, hair shiny with oil and expression one of friendliness and delight, could hide anything from thoughts of murder to honest curiosity.

'Goodday, sa, you like good lunch?'

'No, thanks,' Gideon said. 'Is Chang in?'

'Chang, sa?' The slit eyes widened, the hands performed strange gyrations, still beneath the apron. 'I find out, sa, name please?'

'Gideon,' said Gideon. 'Never mind, I'll find out for myself.'

He walked across the sawdusted boards, past several Chinese eating English food, a Malayan couple eating rice and an Indian woman in a pale pink sari, sitting in front of a metal tray with several metal dishes on it, and pushed open a door. Beyond was the kitchen; this was spotlessly clean, with two Chinese women working in the steamy heat. Beyond again was a staircase. Gideon went up the staircase, without hurrying. The boy would have warned Chang.

Gideon sniffed.

There was a strong smell of paint, and it became more noticeable as he approached the landing. The narrow stairs creaked. A strip of hair carpet ran in the middle of them, and along both passages at the top. One door, closed, was marked: '*Office*'. The other door, open, was marked: '*Club*'. 'Club' had never been more than a name used so as to obtain a late liquor licence, and until recently Chang had done nothing to invite being closed up.

Two painters were busy in the club-room, one lanky Englishman with a sniff, the other a sturdy, handsome youngster, obviously not English. 'A Pole,' Gideon thought, as he spoke to the lanky man.

'When did you start this job?'

Wary, watery eyes turned towards him.

'S'morning.'

'When did you get the order?'

The lanky man's eyes were now narrowed so tightly that they were nearly closed. The Pole was working steadily, using a small brush fat with crimson paint. The big clubroom stank of oil paint and distemper.

Gideon heard the other door open, although it made little sound.

'None-of-yer-bus'ness,' the lanky man drawled nasally.

Gideon didn't argue. 'I'll know you again,' he said, and turned round.

He wasn't surprised to see Chang in the office doorway. He was surprised to see the woman behind him, standing up and looking somehow unsure of herself, like someone who'd had an unpleasant surprise. She was quite a good-looker, and Gideon knew and had once danced with her at a police ball.

She was Foster's sister, and her name was Flo.

CHAPTER 4

CHANG

Chang was smiling diffidently.

Flo Foster wasn't really smiling at all, just looking bewildered. Gideon did not start guessing what she was doing here; it was better to find out for certain. He felt sure that something Chang had said, perhaps about his arrival, had startled her. She was not the type to look bewildered for long, and Gideon had another thought, the kind he would pigeon-hole and bring out for examination whenever he felt it necessary. Only a sharp shock would have affected her like this. She came from the same world and had much the same poise – over-confidence – as Foster himself. He did not know her well enough to wonder whether she had the same capacity for error as Foster. Error was one word! He judged that she was quite free from the taint of drugs, heavy drinking or any kind of debauchery; she looked not only handsome but wholesome and healthy. She was undoubtedly touched with arrogance.

All this took only a second or two to pass through Gideon's mind.

Chang was moving forward, hands held a little in front of his chest in a gesture which was already self-deprecatory. He had a big, wide forehead and a small, shallow chin, and his face tapered down in the proper proportions from his forehead. One first noticed that, which was smooth as yellowed alabaster, and then his small ears, which stuck out almost at right angles and seemed to thrust a way through his dark hair; hair, like that of most Chinese, as straight as a woman's in need of a perm. The rest of Chang was not, perhaps, important. He had the facial characteristics of the oriental, but only those who knew the Orient well could have said whether he was Chinese, Javanese, or one of the other races. His small mouth was faintly pink; a dirty pink. His eyes were dark and pinched a little at the corners; that didn't stop them from being blackly bright. His nose was slightly flattened and the nostrils were dark. For the rest, he was beautifully tailored in pale grey, with a discreet blue tie, a blue handkerchief making a triangle in his breast pocket and, almost certainly, blue socks to match.

He was not effusive. His English was good, with more inflection than accent. He had been born within five miles of this spot, and knew no other language; but he could use pidgin English effectively at times, and pretend not to know English fluently.

'Mr. Gideon,' he said, 'how unexpected. A pleasure indeed.' Now, his hands touched at the tips, and he gave the slightest of bows. 'You are most welcome. I was about to show my previous visitor the stairs, you will forgive me?'

'That's all right,' Gideon said.

'Perhaps you will wait here for me.' Chang thrust a hand, fingers crooked and palm upwards, towards his office, showing the natural grace so many of his kind had. His smile was not overdone.

'This way, please,' he said to Foster's sister, and stepped in front of Gideon, making no bones about wanting the woman to go.

Gideon showed no sign of recognition. Flo Foster now looked away from him, and moved quickly, as if anxious to get out of his sight. She looked good, but not necessarily in the sense of goodness. Her two-piece suit of rust-colour serge fitted well, and she had all black accessories – gloves, bag, shoes – with a touch of quality.

Gideon inclined his head, ponderously.

When Chang had started down the stairs with Flo Foster, Gideon went into the office. He left the door open. The lanky painter was staring at him, his brush hanging in the air; the Pole was still working, now on distemper with a big brush. Gideon didn't sit down, but stepped to the window and then to a spot out of sight from the surly painter. He touched nothing, but looked about him quickly and intently, missing little. Gideon was a man who, playing the parlour game of 'what were the articles on that tray' would invariably win, and would seldom miss even a single item. All he saw here were a few papers, neatly arranged, a big locked safe in one corner, a carved sandalwood box containing cigarettes. The desk was a cheap walnut pedestal one, with a tubular steel swivel chair behind it, and a square of brown carpet centred on the floor had a green linoleum surround.

Chang came back quietly, shut the door and hid the English painter. He smiled with the familiar reserve, and went round to his chair. His hand moved out again.

'Please sit down.'

'Thanks.' Gideon sat on an upright chair which looked and felt too flimsy for him. He did not say that he had recognized Foster's sister. Chang's expression was bland; his lips didn't close completely, and showed a glint of white teeth.

The silence and the protracted stare probably put him on edge, but nothing in this world was likely to make him show it.

'What can I do for you, Superintendent?'

'Has Foster been here to-day?' Gideon asked, flatly.

'Foster, Superintendent? Who is Foster?'

'You know,' said Gideon.

'I am afraid that I do not understand,' Chang declared. 'Foster, Foster.' He let the name float in the air, and so declared his tactics: flat denial of everything. He did not know Foster, he had never bribed Foster, he had not heard that day from anyone named Foster. At the end of this series of mute denials there was defiance, as evident although as mute: 'And you cannot prove that I know Foster.'

Gideon was convinced that Chang knew everything, now felt that he could go all the way with Lemaitre, although there was still no evidence. By his denials, Chang not only showed his hand but also made it clear that he did not think there was anything to worry about.

Confidence had always been his strong suit.

Over-confidence? Like Foster.

Gideon said: 'I mean Eric Foster, a detective-sergeant at New Scotland Yard, who's been taking money from you for some time, Chang.'

'It is some mistake,' said Chang, very smoothly. 'Perhaps you forget I am not the only Chang in Soho, Me. Superintendent.'

'No,' admitted Gideon, 'I don't forget.' He changed the subject but not his tone. 'What are you having the club-room painted for?'

'But *that*?' asked Chang, and smiled now with greater readiness; a stranger, seeing him for the first time, would have been greatly struck by his open face, the apparently friendly smile, the charm. 'I have many clients and I do very well, Mr. Superintendent, and so I am giving them something more pleasant than before.'

Gideon didn't answer. Chang did not wilt or even waver slightly under the ruthless scrutiny.

'Chang,' said Gideon, suddenly, heavily, 'I want to tell you a thing or two. In this country, crimes catch up with you. You ought to know that. Murderers get hanged, thieves get jailed, all criminals get punished sooner or later. We may miss them on one job but we always get them on another. Don't ever think you're safe. You've been doing some of the foulest things a man can do, and we're after you. That means we'll get you.'

Chang's smile became broader, although perhaps it grew a little tense.

'It is a pity,' he said carefully. 'I have always liked to be friends with the police. And I shall always be ready to be friends, Mr. Superintendent, but now you talk in hostile mysteries. How can *I* help?'

'You can't help yourself or us,' Gideon declared flatly. 'You've gone too far.' He got up and moved towards the door, wondering whether to use his only bullet or whether to keep it. He used it: 'Who was that woman in here just now?'

'My visitor?' Chang was not even slightly perturbed. 'A charming lady, one Mrs. Addinson. She is a painter who would have liked to paint the walls of the club but' – he gave a charming little shrug – 'she would also like too much money!' He moved towards Gideon, fingertips touching. 'So nice to have seen you again, Mr. Superintendent, I hope soon we shall be friends once more.'

The smell of paint was almost overpowering on the landing. The lanky painter had lit a fresh cigarette, and seemed to be pouring thinners into a tin of paint. The Pole was slapping distemper on to the ceiling, standing on a square packing case in order to reach up. Gideon didn't look at Chang again, but went deliberately downstairs, glanced into the kitchen, was escorted to the street door by the grinning youth, whose hands still hid themselves beneath the snow-white apron.

Gideon walked back to his car. The policeman was at hand eager to be of help.

'Have you seen Birdy Merrick about to-day?' asked Gideon.

'No, sir, haven't set eyes on him.'

'Well, if you do, tell him to keep out of Chang's reach for a bit,' said Gideon. 'Noticed anything unusual at Chang's to-day?'

'Well – in a way, sir.'

'What way?'

'He had a visitor – a nice-looking young lady, sir. He often has visitors, but not that kind and they don't usually come in the morning, they're nightbirds. Saw her at his window. She's left now, sir.'

'Hmm. Thanks. Anything else?'

'No, sir, but then I've been on my rounds most of the time.'

'Any friends round here who might know what's been going on at Chang's?'

'I think I could get someone to tell us, sir.'

'Get them to, will you? Who left Chang's place this morning after eleven o'clock, say. Especially anyone with a tough reputation. Chang knows plenty of them.'

The constable said worriedly: 'They *usually* come at night, sir. It's not easy to recognize them.'

'We're looking for the exception,' said Gideon, and smiled to encourage. 'Always worth trying. G'bye.'

He got in his car, but didn't drive off immediately. Instead, he picked up the radio-telephone, flicked it on, waited for the humming sound to tell him it was alive, then called the Yard. The man who answered from the Information Room knew his voice.

'Yes, sir, two messages for you. One of the three men who tried to rob a mail van at Liverpool Street Station this morning is under charge, being brought to the Yard now, sir – should be here in ten minutes or so. The child found dead in Hatherley Court, London, W.1 was murdered –

strangled and interfered with, sir. Chief Inspector Suter has gone over there, and will report as soon as he's had a look round. That's all, sir.'

Hmm,' said Gideon. His nose was wrinkled, his mouth turned down at the corners. Most men had a secret horror, his was of men who could first ravage and then kill a child. Nothing, not even the Changs with their dope and devilry, could make him see red so quickly, and as always, he distrusted himself when he saw red. 'All right, I'll come straight back.'

'Very good, sir.'

Gideon started off. At the corners, men and women loitered. The first of the pro's were beginning their ambling, more people were in the shops, a brewer's dray with a big engine instead of the horses of yesteryear stood outside a pub while barrels were dropped down the chute into the cellar. A normal enough scene.

Gideon began to feel angry about that child and sour because he couldn't go straight to see Florence Foster. She had to be told about her brother. The job would be left to the Yard, and he couldn't see anyone else doing it willingly. He found himself thinking again that if he hadn't torn Foster to shreds in the office, it might not have happened. It was that blurry bunch – the kind of thing he'd dress Lemaitre down for, but there it was. The Square Mile was his beat, and some pulsating sixth sense told him that this wasn't the time to go for Chang, but the time to start squeezing. When you squeezed a slug, it was surprising what oozed out. Chang with his diffident smile, his charm, his courtesy and grace, with as foul a mind –

Gideon slid through the traffic and began to argue with himself.

Half the trouble with men like Chang, whether they were Chinese, English or American – it didn't matter what nationality they were – was that they had no sense of doing wrong. They were as the slave traders had been a century ago, as the white slavers of North Africa were to-day. To them, nothing was sacred, nothing inviolate. He knew of a dozen men, respected, wealthy, perfectly honest by the legal codes, who rejected all moral values.

Foster had said the thing all these would say: if girls didn't get dope from Chang, they would get it from someone else. So, it was no crime to make money out of giving it to them. Orientals especially seemed to lack a sense of morality, but, hell, some of them were pretty strict in applying moral rules to their own families. That wasn't the point. The point, Gideon decided as he turned carefully into the gateway of Scotland Yard, was that most Eastern countries bred a lot of callousness, the people were fatalists, and if they came to England and turned against the law they were deadly because usually they had good minds and no scruples.

'Something,' Gideon said suddenly and aloud, 'in a Christian civilization.' And then he scowled. 'Still, what about Foster?'

He parked the car with more room to spare, and went up the steps. If he cared to count the number of times a week he went up those steps, he would be astounded. Some Superintendents spent most of their time at the desk; some people said he didn't spend enough. He didn't trouble about the lift, but went up the stairs two at a time, nodding at the many who passed him. His own office was empty, a disappointment. Before he sat down, he pressed a bell for a sergeant. Then he dropped heavily into his chair, and squinted down at a pencilled note Lemaitre had left:

'*Mail job man's talking, main waiting-room. Lem.*'

There was a tap at the door and a sergeant in plainclothes came in, absurdly young in Gideon's eyes.

'Yes, sir?'

'Get the Secretary's file on Detective-Sergeant Foster, will you? Put it on my desk. Check whether his sister, Florence, still lives with him. Lived. If she has a place of her own, find out where it is, find out where she worked, what she does. Don't take too much time about it. See if you can pick up anything from the other sergeants in Foster's office.'

'I could put up a bit myself, sir.'

Gideon, looking through other messages as he talked, glanced up into grey, eager eyes.

'All right, Miller, what?'

'Still lives – lived – with his sister, sir. I was on a job with him two days ago, he was moan – he was saying that he would have to get a place of his own, his sister didn't like his off duty hours. He was a bit tetchy. I gathered he'd had a row with her.'

'Hmm. Anything else?'

'They live Chelsea way.'

'Yes. Check everything you can. Thanks, Miller. If I'm wanted I'll be in the waiting-room with that mail van chap.' Gideon nodded and hurried out, thinking of the Fosters quarrelling and Flo Foster's (Addinson's) surprise, and a man who'd tried to rob a mail van being in talkative mood.

The main waiting-room was on the floor below. Gideon was there in thirty seconds, and opened the door briskly. He heard the words of a man speaking in a cultured voice:

'. . . I tell you that's all I know!'

The speaker was young, probably in his late teens. Take away his thin mouth, and he would be a nice-looking lad, with fair, curly hair, cornflower blue eyes, a look of innocence; full of a kind of charm, like Chang. As he stared at the door, he looked scared, and caught his breath sharply at sight of Gideon's burly figure. Lemaitre and two sergeants were in the room with the youth; one was from Liverpool Street, the other a

Yard man taking notes. The youth was neatly dressed, well-groomed.

'Anything?' asked Gideon.

'Nothing that won't bear repeating,' Lemaitre said, 'and I should say he's conveniently forgetting a hell of a lot.'

'That's a lie!' the youth burst out.

'All right, calm down,' said Gideon. He looked at the prisoner's fingers, stained dark with nicotine, then at the thin, unsteady mouth, and wondered when Lemaitre was going to grow up. He took out a fat, old-fashioned silver cigarette-case and proffered it; the youth grabbed, as some kids would grab a reefer. He snatched a lighter out of his pocket.

'Thanks.' He drew fiercely.

'That's all right,' said Gideon, 'no need to get steamed up, it won't make any difference, and if you play your cards right you'll probably get off more lightly than you deserve. Mind telling me all about it again?'

In the pause which followed, he glanced at the sergeant's notebook, and read the name: Lionel Tenby.

'Well, Tenby,' he went on, in an almost comforting way. 'What about it?'

'I've told them!' The words came with a rush, a spate followed. 'I don't know the names of the others, it was all laid on by telephone. They knew I could drive a damned sight better than most chaps, so they paid me twenty-five quid to do this job for them. All I had to do was to drive up in front of the van and wait until they told me to get a move on.'

'Payment in advance?' asked Gideon.

'Yes.' Tenby's gaze flickered towards a table where oddments lay in neat array; a pocket-watch, a comb, wallet, keys, silver coins, copper coins and a small wad of one pound notes.

Gideon's hopes began to fade; this wasn't the first time they'd caught a very small sprat.

'And you didn't know them?'

'No.'

'Pity. What else?'

'I asked them how they knew it would be worth doing, and they said that someone had tipped them the wink,' Tenby declared. The cigarette was nearly finished, and he seemed to look at it anxiously, as if nervous of what he would feel like when he had to stub it out.

'Tip from where?' asked Gideon.

'How the devil should I know?'

'Hmm,' said Gideon. Yes, it was disappointing. If things went on like this, it was going to be an unsatisfactory day. 'All right, get that statement typed out, sergeant, have Tenby read it and if he agrees that it's what he said, have him sign it.' He looked at Tenby patiently. 'But don't sign it and then start squealing to the magistrate that it isn't what you said. If you're not satisfied, write it out yourself in long-hand.'

Tenby winced – because the cigarette, now burned very low, stung his fingers.

Gideon gave him another.

'Throw the stub in the fireplace,' he said. 'You can have some cigarettes. It'll be deducted from any money belonging to you. Fix it, sergeant.'

'Yes, sir.'

'Anyone you want to know about this?' Gideon asked sharply.

Tenby's eyes glistened; he was very young and he wasn't one of the bad ones – just a young fool.

'No.'

'Girl-friend? Parents?'

'*No!*'

'Been in before on a charge?'

'No, I – I wish to God I'd never listened to those swine! I'd dropped a bit on the gees, and –' he broke off, biting his lips. Bring his mother into the room at this moment and he would burst into tears, Gideon surmised.

'Well, listen,' Gideon said, 'your relations have got to know, and it's better from us than from the Press, you won't get much change out of the Press. Let us tell your parents or the girl-friend, and have them –'

'*I said no!*'

'All right. Let him suffer. Come on, Lem,' Gideon said, and led the way out. 'Not much there,' he added almost absently. 'The story we've had a dozen times before. The P.O. people pick their drivers well. Like to know if it's directed by one man or not, there's a lot of similarity. When he's calmed down a bit, get repeat descriptions of the two men. Play him soft, though. Get hold of his people, if you can, and let them come and see him here. Mother, preferably. Blurry young fool.' He changed the subject but didn't alter his tone of voice. 'Hear about the Mayfair flat job?'

'Nine-year-old kid,' said Lemaitre. 'I could tell you what I'd do to them if I had my way.'

'Thing that worries me with those jobs is the risk of another,' Gideon said. 'We really want to bring the house down after the chap.'

'I'll say!'

'I'd better go along to the Back Room,' Gideon said, as if he wasn't quite sure. 'The Press will be on their toes. If they play up the child murder and the frustrated mail van robbery, they won't have much room for anything else.' They were at a corner, where they would go different ways. 'Saw Chang, by the way. Smooth as ever, denies everything.' He didn't say anything about Flo Foster (Addinson). 'And the club-room there is being redecorated. The smell of paint and distemper makes sure that no one with a sensitive nose could ever pick out the marihuana they've been smoking.'

'You know what you've done, don't you?' Lemaitre said, with a sniff.

'What?'

'Driven Chang somewhere else. It won't stop the kids from getting the weed, and –'

'Nearest thing I know to a certainty is that Chang won't do anything he shouldn't for some time,' Gideon asserted, marvelling that Lemaitre should think anything different. What limitations even able men had! 'We could draw all our dogs off him and he'd still behave like a learner priest, what-do-you-call-'em? Acolyte, isn't it? It's beginning to look as if he did hear from Foster, and got a move on. Might have had a row with Foster, though, and so made Foster walk across the road in a rage, not looking. Nobody ever thinks they could be knocked down in a street accident.'

'The car didn't stop,' Lemaitre insisted. 'Don't you want to believe that –'

Gideon was suddenly sharp; almost harsh.

'No,' he said bluntly. 'No, *I don't* want to believe that Chang had Foster killed. I don't want to think that Foster knew so much about Chang that it was worth killing him. But that's probably what happened, and if it is we'll get the killer and we'll get Chang!' He switched abruptly. 'Any news in?'

'We've picked up a girl typist who was looking out of the window and says she saw it happen. She was on her own, her boss was out, and when she saw someone come along the street to Foster's help, she just sat back.'

Gideon flashed: 'Any squeal of brakes?'

'Eh?'

'Did she hear – never mind, where is she?'

'On her way here.'

'Oh, good,' said Gideon, 'that's fine. By the way, there's a painter chap at Chang's, very thin, six feet one or two, big Adam's apple, watery eyes, probably blind or half-blind in the right, it's hazed over. Flat-footed, and pretty sly. I'd like his name and address and anything we can find out about him. There's a copper on duty over there, P.C. 10952. He seemed to have his head screwed on the right way and he's finding out if anything worth knowing happened at Chang's this morning. Send someone out to have a word with him about this painter.'

'Okay,' said Lemaitre.

They were outside the office. Lemaitre opened the door and Gideon went inside, looking at the carpet and giving a little frown, one more of preoccupation than of annoyance or worry.

'Well, we didn't get much out of the mail van chap,' Lemaitre said.

'Nearly always the same, if we do pick anyone up it's a young fool who doesn't know anything. But there was a tip-off again, that's the worrying thing, George, isn't it?'

'Hm?'

'A tip-off from the post office.'

'Oh, yes.'

'I'll tell you what's going to happen one of these days,' said Lemaitre. 'They're going to kill a copper or someone who tries to stop them and then our noses are going to be rubbed right in the dirt.' His own thin nose wrinkled disgustedly. 'Anything goes wrong, they blame us, but whose fault are these mail van jobs? We're understaffed, could do with dozens more at every station in London. The P.O. don't use half enough detectives – seem to think that every van is protected by some spirit.'

'Okay, Lem,' Gideon said. 'It's everybody's fault but ours, and we've got the job of stopping it.'

He sat down at his desk, grunting.

On it was a note – a pencilled report on an official buff form.

Telephone message received from 7Q Division 12.55 p.m.

Killer of nine-year-old Jennifer Gay Lee at Hatherley Court believed to be Arthur Sayer of 15, Warrender Street, Ealing. Ealing Division has been telephoned, general call asked for Sayer, description and photograph on way to us by special messenger.

Lemaitre was standing by the desk, looking down.

'What's this?'

'Old Tucker at 7Q thinks he can name the swine who killed that kid,' said Gideon. 'As soon as the photograph and description arrive, put out a general call, ports, airfields, everything, just for safety's sake. I wish –'

The telephone bell rang.

'Gideon,' he grunted into it, and then brightened. 'That's good. Keep her down there, the small waiting-room, I'll come and see her at once.' He put the receiver down. 'It's that typist who saw Foster knocked down. If she heard a squeal of brakes the driver tried to stop; if she didn't, there's the evidence you've been looking for.' He gave Lemaitre a quick but rather tired grin, and went out.

Two minutes later, there was a tap at the door. A constable in uniform, except that he was hatless, came in.

'Photograph and description from 7Q Division, sir.'

'Okay, I'll have 'em,' Lemaitre said. He stretched out a hand, and a moment later looked down at the glossy photograph of a man. 'So that's the brute, is it? Okay, ta.'

Lemaitre picked up a telephone and started to put out the general call for a certain Arthur Sayer, who was believed to have murdered the nine-year-old girl. As he talked into the telephone he skimmed the report of the murder, and his eyes frosted, even his tone changed, because it was a very, very ugly killing.

'. . . and get a move on,' he said. 'Once that kind's tasted blood you never know where they'll stop.'

The door opened, and Gideon came in, eyes bright, manner brisk, as if he were beginning to relish life.

'Seen her?' Lemaitre asked needlessly.

'Nice little kid, a bit scared, but reliable. There was no squeal of brakes, there's the pointer we want, Lem. Was probably intentional. Anything else in?'

That was like a refrain.

'No,' said Lemaitre, 'but that poor kid . . .' He was brief but graphic in his description of the mutilations on the child's body.

Gideon stood in the middle of the office, like a statue rough-hewn out of granite.

'Schools are closed for the Easter holidays,' he said abruptly. 'Sayer knew this child, and she trusted him. Better check on other children he knows, fast. All right. I'll talk to Ealing.'

He almost threw himself at the telephone on his desk.

CHAPTER 5

THE CHILD KILLER

Children swarmed over Clapham Common. Every square yard of grass was worn bare; every yard of the children's gravelled playground with its swings and seesaws, sliding chutes and vaulting horses, had a pair of feet – well shod, rough shod, badly shod, even three children who were bare-footed and wearing such rags that others looked at them askance, and some refused to play.

Clapham Common was one of the places where London breathed.

Now, at the tail-end of the Easter holidays, mothers were only too glad to shoo their offspring out. The morning had echoed with the same refrains in a thousand doorways and kitchens: 'Be careful crossing the road.' 'Don't go getting yourself dirty.' 'No fighting, mind.' 'Don't speak to any strange man, understand?' 'Look both ways.' The children had listened with half an ear, and found their way safely towards this breathing ground, soon racing, rushing, running, sprawling, giggling, laughing, crying, climbing, shouting, shrieking in the warm air of late spring.

Here, youths of recognized local renown chose sides at cricket or at football, coats went down for goal-posts or wickets, bats came out after a winter's storage, footballs looked flat and flabby and gave off a dull sound when kicked, and stubbed strong toes.

On the seats round the edges of the common, the old folk sat, mostly nice, pleasant, sleepy and indulgent, some with a packet of peppermints or toffees, most of the men with pipe and a little tobacco, all drowsy in the sun and the din. A few of these were nasty old men, but each was known by the common keepers, the local police, and by a few self-appointed guardians of the children.

'Nothing,' each harassed mother had said or thought when the children had gone flying down the road, 'can happen to them once they're on the common.' And most watched until the first roads were crossed and then went to wash-tub, sink, floors or bedrooms, or dressed hastily to go out shopping, gradually forgetting fears which would only return if the children were back late for the mid-day meal.

A few knew that their children might be late, most knew that hunger would bring them clattering home, a few minutes before one o'clock, or before half-past one; whichever was the regular meal time.

Of these, Mrs. Lucy Saparelli was one.

Mrs. Saparelli, at thirty-seven, was a red-cheeked, bright-eyed, wholesome-looking woman with a spruce figure and a seductive walk, although she had no idea that a few of the louts of the district called her Marilyn. Her husband was a commercial traveller away three or four nights out of the week's seven. He had only a vague notion that his forebears had been Spanish or Italian, and wasn't quite sure which. He could go back four generations of solid English ancestry, but was oddly proud of his unusual name. *Sap*-ar-elli.

He loved and trusted his wife and he was fiercely fond of Michael, his eldest child and as fond of Dorothy, his youngest – aged nine – although for some reason, Victor, the eleven-year-old who came in between, always managed to irritate him.

Victor did not irritate his mother, but if one of the apples of her eyes was brighter than the others, it was Dorothy. Boys drew away from their mother as the years passed, but Dorothy would always be with her. At nine, she was – just *lovely*. She had the looks, the plumpness, the *naïveté* and the natural gaiety which could make a child win approval from everyone. The hug that Lucy Saparelli gave Dorothy each night and each morning was born of the little extra delight the child gave her. Delight was the word which mattered, was the thing the girl child brought to Lucy, to Jim Saparelli, to the two boys.

Everyone loved Dorothy.

Arthur Sayer *loved* Dorothy.

Arthur Sayer knew the Saparellis well, because he had lodged with them some years ago, a schooldays acquaintance of Jim's who had been welcome when money had been short. It had soon become apparent that he was ever so nice, except for one thing: betting was his folly. Lucy had been heard to say, almost in tones of wonder, that he never said a word or put a finger out of place. He was rather odd, in some ways, a bit cissy, with long, silky, brown hair and a love of bright colours, but – well, nice.

Lucy was in her bedroom, scurrying round to make the beds and dust before going to the shops, when the front door bell rang.

'Damn!' she said, and looked out of the window, but saw no van; so it wasn't a tradesman. She peeked at herself in the mirror and straightened her hair as she hurried down the stairs, her skirt riding up over her pretty legs. The dress was a little too tight and one she only wore when doing the housework. She went quickly along the stained boards of the hall, seeing the dark shadow of a man against the coloured glass panels in the top of the door. She knew it was a man because of the shape of his hat.

It was then ten o'clock on Gideon's day; when Gideon was still at the Yard looking at reports.

Lucy opened the door.

'Why, Arthur!' she exclaimed, and annoyance faded in pleasure. 'Fancy seeing you at this hour of the morning. Come in, do.'

Arthur Sayer hesitated, and she stared at him intently.

He was almost one of the family, and more welcome than most of her in-laws. He looked pale, and his eyes glittered, as if his head ached badly; she remembered that he had often had severe headaches, needing absolute quiet to recover from them. He needed a shave, now, and his coat collar was turned up, although it was already warm.

'*You* look as if you've been up all night,' said Lucy forthrightly. 'You'd better let me make you a cup of tea and give you some aspirins.'

He moved forward.

'Thanks – thanks, Lucy. I've got one of my awful headaches.'

'Why on earth didn't you stay at home?'

He moistened his lips.

'I – I had a row with someone,' he said. 'Never mind about that now. I – I knew you'd let me rest here for a bit.'

'So I should think!' said Lucy. 'Look, you go in the front room, draw the blinds, and sit quiet until I bring you a cuppa.' She thrust open the door of the parlour. 'The only things in there are Dorothy's dolls, she's having her friends in to an exhibition. That child and her dolls! Now, sit you down, I won't be a couple of jiffs.'

She left him in the darkened room.

She frowned as she walked to the kitchen, every movement touched with throbbing vitality. She filled the kettle, put it on the gas, washed two cups and saucers from the pile waiting from breakfast, and then shook her head with a quick little gesture.

'The rest'll have to wait until after lunch. I can do all the washing-up together. Now he's come I can't get everything finished before I go out.' A pause. 'I suppose I *must* go out?'

She put the question aloud, but answered it silently. She gave Arthur very little thought as a person, just accepted him as she accepted the ups and downs of family life, the aches and pains of her children. Had Arthur been one of hers, she would have felt worried because he didn't look well; but she'd seen him almost as bad, it wasn't very important.

Jim would be home to-night, and she liked to have a good dinner for him, so she *must* go to the butcher's. If she had to go out she might just as well do all the week-end shopping and get it over. She would finish the bedrooms before she left. . . .

If Dorothy came back while she was out, Arthur could let her in, she wouldn't have to play in the street.

She bustled round, easy in her mind.

Arthur said very little when she took in the tea, but swallowed three aspirins obediently. His eyes were glittery, and she wondered if he was running a temperature. Dorothy always went pale when she had a temperature, and the boys were usually flushed.

'Sure you'll be all right on your own, Arthur?'

'Yes – yes, thank you.'

'Wouldn't like to see a doctor?'

'No!' He almost shouted the word. 'No, don't – don't tell anyone I'm here.'

'Look here,' said Lucy flatly, 'what's upset you, Art? You can confide in me, you know. What's the trouble?'

'Nothing! I – well, I – I owe some money, Lucy, I can get it back, but –'

'Why didn't you say so? It isn't as if it's the first time.' Lucy sniffed. 'I won't tell anyone you're here, and Jim's coming home to-night, perhaps he can suggest something to help. Now I've got to go to the shops. You needn't answer the door if you don't want to, but if Dorothy comes back I don't like her playing out in the street. Let her in, won't you?'

Arthur Sayer didn't answer.

'Art, you might at least answer me!'

'Oh,' said Sayer. 'What did – oh, yes. Yes, I'll let Dorothy in. Don't worry, Lucy.'

She left him alone, but was uneasy in her mind – although not because of Dorothy. That did not occur to her. He had helped to nurse Dorothy, was Uncle Art to her and would be for the rest of her life. She sensed that he was in serious trouble, and came of stock which was easily embarrassed by thought of any trouble which might warrant the interest of the police. Arthur had always been silly with money and that gambling, but –

She saw a bus coming along the main road as soon as she reached it, and rushed across to catch it. Some drivers would wait, some were *devils*.

She caught the bus. The only spare seat was next to a girl with a horse's tail tied with pink ribbon, who was reading the *Daily Mirror* . . .

Dorothy Saparelli stumbled away from the swing, and the hard wooden edge caught her a slight glancing blow on the shoulder. She turned and shook her fist at the bigger girl who had just grabbed the chain, and had made her get off. Nine years is not the age when one admits the justice of accusations of wrong-doing. She had used that swing for fifteen minutes and wanted it for another fifteen.

She brushed back some hair which had somehow escaped from one of the sleek wings which seemed to sweep from a centre parting. It was black, glossy hair, tied with scarlet ribbon. She wore a white blouse and a navy blue gym suit, her plimsolls were dusty but not dirty or torn.

'Mean pig!' she called shrilly, and looked disconsolate.

Three children were clinging to every place where there was room for one; on this playground Dorothy hadn't a chance of another toy. She sauntered over to a group of girls playing rounders, but they were in the early teens, and one snapped her fingers and ordered:

'You sheer off.'

Further afield, Victor was playing football. She couldn't see Michael, who was probably messing about at cricket. Disgruntled, a little tired and very thirsty, Dorothy made her way along a tarred path towards the roads leading to Micklem Street, where she lived. There was only one main road to worry about, but she could cope with that; when in doubt, wait until grown-ups were going to cross, and cross with them. That was so much part of training that a child's pride was never challenged; it simply wasn't safe to cross on one's own.

An old man, carrying a walking stick, was coming towards her.

She didn't like him, and moved off the path, but he stood and watched, raising his stick and smiling invitingly. He had no teeth, and a funny, straggly kind of moustache and beard. She saw him take a bag of peppermints out of his pocket, and it seemed as if her mother's voice was actually sounding in her ears.

'*Never stop and talk to strange men, even if they do offer you sweets.*'

She skipped past this old man. She wasn't really troubled, and the moment she was past him, he was forgotten, as a dog safely behind a gate would be. It did not occur to her that the uniformed policeman who started to hurry in the wake of the old man was doing so because of the little interlude.

One word of early warning could save a lot of distress.

Dorothy crossed the main road safely behind a woman with a push-chair.

She loitered on her way to the house.

She was happier here, her troubles quite forgotten, when a black-and-white spaniel puppy frisked up. She was almost outside her own house, Number 24, when she saw a sixpence glistening on the pavement.

A tanner!

She pounced.

Her delight, as she looked at it on the palm of her hand, was the absolute delight of a young child. Her whole world had changed. She held a fortune because this was money she had not dreamed she would have.

There was a corner sweet-shop, not far off.

She hesitated, wondering whether to go and spend her find, or whether to tell her mother. Mum would let her keep it, she was sure of that: findings keepings, if you really *had* found it. Seeing a few dirty marks on it, she began to rub the sixpence with the forefinger of her left hand. She looked at the front room window. The curtains were drawn, but there was a little gap in the middle.

She did not see Arthur Sayer looking at her.

She was *very* thirsty.

She went to the front door, at a hop, skip and jump pace, and banged on the iron knocker. She hoped Mum was in because she was so thirsty, but if she wasn't Mrs. Pommery next door would let her have a drink of water, or – should she buy a *lemonade*? Excitement rose again. She imagined the sharp sweetness of aerated lemonade on her cloyed mouth, and the temptation was so great that she wished she hadn't knocked. If Mum was out –

The door opened.

Arthur Sayer opened the door.

Dorothy stared, and then her eyes glowed.

'Why, Uncle Arthur!'

She went in gaily, and he closed the door behind her, heard her chattering, heard the story of the sixpence, followed her to the kitchen, watched her turn on the tap and put a cup under it . . .

She screamed three times.

Mercifully, that was all.

No one heard her, except Arthur Sayer.

Lucy Saparelli got off the bus with Mrs. Pommery, who lived next door, and was the only neighbour likely to have heard a sound from the Saparellis' kitchen. Each woman carried laden baskets; Lucy Saparelli had one in each hand. Yet they walked briskly, and a spotty youth, a nightworker, lounging against the porch of his home, watched Lucy's swaying hips and gave a silent whistle, then a whispered: 'Hi, Marilyn!' Lucy was talking, about the price of food, about Victor, about her Jim being a bit hard on Victor sometimes, about Dorothy's plan to have an exhibition of dolls, a kind of dolls' party, and wasn't it wonderful for a nine-year-old girl to think of such an idea on her own?

They turned the corner.

Lucy changed hands with the baskets, and wriggled her shoulders because of the strain.

Then she saw Victor and Michael, talking to another boy outside their home. She didn't give a thought to the possibility of – horror. Michael had torn his trousers, and Victor had a nasty scratch on the side of his face, but they looked clear-eyed and happy.

' 'Lo, mum!'

'Gosh, I'm hungry.'

'We'll have something to eat as soon as I've had time to look round,' said Lucy. 'Micky, take this bag for me, there's a dear. Victor, you can open the door for me, take the key out of my bag – oh, silly ass! Just knock, and Uncle Arthur will let us in.'

'What?' Michael took the laden bag. 'No one's in, Mum. I've knocked half a dozen times.'

'Well, that's *funny*,' said Lucy. 'Where's Dorothy, then?'

She didn't speak again, but opened her bag, took out the front door key, and went straight to the front door. She could not have told the others what had happened to her in that moment; she probably did not realize it herself. It was as if a shadow had fallen; a darkness, hiding something she was anxious to see. She did not consciously think of Dorothy. Afterwards, to her husband, she said in a stony voice that she thought Arthur might have done himself in.

She pushed the door open, strode in, and called: 'Arthur!'

There was no reply.

She looked inside the parlour, which was empty but for the dolls. She went briskly along the passage, high heels tapping on the stained boards, with Michael behind her and Victor just stepping across the front door mat.

Then she saw . . .

Then she *screamed*.

CHAPTER 6

MAN-HUNT

Gideon sat at his desk, in his shirt-sleeves, the big, blue and red spotted tie undone and ends hanging down, hair ruffled, face pale but forehead damp with sweat. He had a telephone at his ear, and was waving his left hand at Lemaitre, who came across.

'Someone saw him leave on foot, just before half-past twelve, so he didn't get far. Concentrate everything we've got on the south and south-west London area. Right.' He waved Lemaitre away, and grunted into the telephone: 'Yes, I've got all that, thanks.' He rang off, and plucked up another telephone. 'Back Room,' he demanded, and stretched his shoulders, leaning back so that his head touched the wall. Then, with his free hand, he picked up the first telephone again. 'Is Sergeant Miller back yet? . . . Yes I'll hold on.'

The Back Room Inspector spoke into the telephone at Gideon's right ear.

'Yes, George?'

'This Sayer chap,' Gideon said without preamble. 'Have a go at the evening paper chaps, ring up the news editors if necessary, ask them to make sure they run Sayer's picture in each edition, getting it in as soon as they can. And give 'em a picture of a girl . . . either of them will do . . . Yes, I've just had a word with the Old Man, he's okayed it. Thanks.' He rang off, spoke immediately into the other telephone. 'Hallo? . . . Good, send him in to me.'

He put that receiver down too, and took a deep breath.

Lemaitre was holding on to a telephone, but not speaking. He looked across and said:

'We won't get any more done if we starve. What about some grub? *Hallo*. Yes, all the men you can spare, pick up photographs of Sayer at 7Q, that's the quickest way.'

The door opened and the sergeant who had been instructed to find out what he could about Foster's sister, came in. He seemed touched by the vibrant excitement which affected the others. Neat as a new pin, he entered as if he were daring the lion's den, with Gideon the lion. But Gideon's expression was placid and his voice quiet, in spite of his pallor and the sweat on his forehead.

'Well, what have you got?' he asked.

'Miss Foster's at her home now,' the sergeant said. 'Incidentally, sir, she's married, and separated from her husband. She's a Mrs. Addinson. She does murals for cafés and night clubs, has a little studio in the Chelsea flat where they – she lives. As far as I know, she doesn't yet know what happened to Sergeant Foster.'

'Chelsea, yes,' said Gideon. 'Hmm.' He lived in Fulham, the adjoining borough. 'All right, thanks.' The sergeant put down some notes, and turned to go. 'Sergeant, send someone down to the canteen for some sandwiches and beer for both of us. Ham and beef all right, Lem?'

Lemaitre seemed to be listening to someone on his telephone; but he nodded.

'Beef well done, and plenty of salt,' ordered Gideon. 'Thanks.' He nodded and looked hard at the two telephones, as if he could not understand why they were silent; neither had rung for nearly five minutes. He wiped his forehead, then his neck, then made a gesture by tightening the knot of the tie, but he didn't do his shirt up at the neck. The once smooth, starched whiteness of the collar had wilted, and was damp near the neck.

Lemaitre said 'Oke' into a telephone, banged down the receiver, groped for a cigarette, lit it, and glanced at Gideon. 'Quiet all of a sudden, isn't it?'

'It's one of those days,' Gideon said. 'Two supers off duty, one ill, three out-of-town jobs taken our best C.I.'s. One of these days I'm going –'

One of his telephone bells rang.

He took it up slowly, almost gently.

'Superintendent Gideon here. Who? . . . Yes, yes, go on.' His eyes glistened, he grabbed a pencil and made waving signs in the air with it. He jotted down a couple of notes, and said: 'Yes, fine, thanks.' He let the receiver go down with a bang, and Lemaitre, looking at him, had an odd thought: that Gideon looked ten years younger than he had first thing that morning. 'The River boys say those mail bags were dropped into the Thames somewhere near Battersea Power Station. They've been out to look, and found another flapping around a submerged barge. It caught on a nail or something. Footprints near the spot, some tyre-marks, everything that might help us to get something. I can push that on to B2, pity it's near the Sayer job, but still . . .' He lifted a telephone. 'Give me B2 headquarters . . .' He waited, rubbing his forehead with the palm of his left hand. Then: 'Hallo, Superintendent Gillick? . . . Gideon here . . . No, not Sayer, but that's priority . . . Yes, he's a swine all right . . . Listen, Gil, the River boys think that some mail bags, part of that last post office job, were thrown in the river from a spot near Battersea Power Station last night. They've a launch standing by to guide your chaps, can you spare a couple? . . . Sure, sure, plaster casts, tyre-tracks, all the usual, and if we could have them this afternoon we might catch the beggars yet. We had a set of tyre-marks and some footprints from the Maida Vale job, you know, be interesting to see if they match up . . . Yes, thanks . . . Oh, fine, every one of them, noisy brats most of them . . .' He shook his head at Lemaitre, who was grinning broadly, and rolled his eyes. 'Yes, the oldest boy's working, thanks, doing nicely . . . Thanks a lot, Gil.'

He blew out a noisy breath as he put the receiver down.

'Champion talker on the Force,' Lemaitre said. 'Why don't you ring off when he starts gassing like that?'

'Might want some special help from him before this is over,' said Gideon philosophically, then looked up at a tap at the door. 'I'll swear at anyone short of the Old Man,' he declared, and barked: 'Come in!'

It was the uniformed but hatless constable, with a tray, sandwiches with ham and beef overlapping the bread, and two pint bottles of beer.

'And *wel*come!' grinned Lemaitre.

Downstairs in the Information Room, uniformed men were standing by the big maps spread out on tables in front of them, with tiny model cars and other models on the tables, and croupier's rakes to move them with. There was a continual chatter of low-pitched conversation, some men talking into radio-telephones, some into ordinary telephones, some to neighbours. No beehive would be busier on an early summer's day.

There were more men round one of the boards than any other – that depicting the south-west area. Here concentrations of model cars and of policemen and plainclothes men stuck on round wooden bases were continually being moved. A report would come by radio-telephone, a car would be moved; a report would come by telephone, and a man moved.

All the Divisional Police Stations and the sub-stations in the south-western area of London were reporting regularly. Police in uniform and in plainclothes were calling on shopkeepers throughout the huge area, with descriptions of Arthur Sayer. Photographs, some prints hardly dry, were already being distributed in large numbers. Special forces were watching spots like Clapham Common, Battersea Park and Tooting Bec – all places where children played.

In Clapham, a Divisional Inspector with a soft Devon burr in his voice was talking to Lucy Saparelli. Lucy seemed to have shrunk, her voice was a hoarse whisper. Michael and Victor were next door with the neighbour, and a sergeant – selected because he had boys of his own – was talking to them about Sayer.

The two o'clock radio programme on all wavelengths was interrupted with a description of the wanted man. The next evening newspaper editions carried his photographs as well as photographs of the first child victim, Jennifer Gay Lee. No minute, no second of time passed without someone showing another picture of Sayer, or asking if he'd been seen in the district.

Gradually the search narrowed. Sayer had been seen at Brixton, in the biggest shopping centre in the immediate neighbourhood.

A policeman who had been travelling on a bus recognized him. He did not give chase, but went swiftly to a nearby police box and telephoned his sub-station.

'Got off near the Forum,' he reported to his sergeant, 'same place as I did. Looked a bit dazed, if you know what I mean.'

'I'd daze him! Which way did he go?'

'Turned left – yes, that's right, left.'

'Well, that's something.' The sergeant picked up a telephone, and the message was flashed to the Yard. Instructions went out smoothly and swiftly for men to concentrate in the Brixton area, with the Forum cinema as a focal point.

Then a waitress at a busy café, shown the photograph by a plainclothes man, looked up at him eagerly.

'Why, he's been here!'

'Sure?'

' 'Course I'm sure, I served him, didn't I? Asked him if he had a headache, and he bit my head off. And a tuppenny tip! Not that I expect–'

'Which way did he go?'

'Well, I don't know that I noticed . . .'

'I know the one,' said the cashier, leaning out of her box. 'Wearing a light brown coat and grey flannels, and one of those pork pie hats. He turned left.'

'Sure?'

'Wouldn't say so if I wasn't.'

Shopkeepers, vanmen, road-sweepers, traffic duty police, newspaper sellers, newsagents – everyone between the café and the Forum was questioned quickly and comprehensively, and each revealed a little more of Sayer's trail. It always led the same way: to the Forum.

A commissionaire said: 'Let's have a better look.' He peered. 'D'you know, I think that chap's *inside*. Come in half an hour ago. I remember he looked over his shoulder as if he were scared of being followed, that's him all right. What's he done?'

A policeman explained.

'*What?*' The commissionaire looked sick.

A cashier said nervously: 'We only had about twenty in, and he was one of them. 'Course I'm sure.'

'That's him all right,' said the usherette on duty at the balcony entrance. 'Proper cissy he looked, and his hands was so cold you wouldn't believe . . . And don't you come it, copper – just happened to touch his hands while I was tearing his ticket in half, that's all.'

A sergeant in charge said: 'We'll cover all the exits, then telephone H.Q.'

The Superintendent at the Divisional H.Q. said: 'Good, but don't go in for him yet, I'll phone the Yard.'

Gideon was finishing his last sandwich when the telephone broke a glorious period of ten minutes' quiet. It rang sharply, with its oddly imperious notes. He swallowed hard, washed the bread and meat down with a gulp of beer, and snatched the receiver up; he moved quickly, as if feeling guilty at having been eating for ten minutes.

'Gideon . . .'

'Put him through!'

'Hallo, Gordie . . . The Forum, Brixton? . . . Fine . . . I don't know whether he'll put up a fight or not . . . Only weapon we know he's got is that knife . . . No, I won't come over myself, much rather your chaps handled him; if he's there I'm sure you won't miss him . . . Yes, please, the moment you have any news . . . Gordie, half a mo, and don't get me wrong, he might be deadly. He'll know that he hasn't a chance to save himself from hanging, and he could be right out of his mind. I – *God*!'

Gideon broke off.

Lemaitre actually jumped out of his seat.

'Get your men inside that place,' shouted Gideon, 'it'll be dark inside, and there might be some kids. I'm coming.'

CHAPTER 7

OLD WOMAN ALONE

At about the time that Gideon was shouting into the telephone in a kind of anguish, an old woman sat alone in the parlour behind her small shop in Islington, on the other side of London.

Her name was Mrs. Annie Sharp.

The Islington police, on the look-out for Arthur Sayer, were on the look-out for a lot of other people, too, although with less urgency. None of them suspected that there was any danger for the old woman in her shop. She had lived in the two rooms at the back for thirty years, and had never been known to have a holiday. Her husband had been killed early in the first world war, and since then she had managed alone. Now, her five children were married; those neighbours who knew her well knew that only two kept in touch with her, and one of those was now in Australia.

Annie Sharp was a good-natured, friendly soul, and although the shop did not make plenitude for her, it kept her from want. The counter was built so that she could move from the sweets and chocolate side to the tobacco, matches and cigarette side without trouble, and her small till was on the corner of the counter, immediately opposite the door leading to the parlour.

The upstairs flat was let to a man, his wife and three children, but these were all out. Annie Sharp knew that, but it did not worry her; thirty years without a frightening incident in the same place breeds a kind of confidence which has nothing to do with logic or probability. The district had its tough and its rough spots, but Annie Sharp's experience with crime was limited to a few small bad debts; and although she was a kindly and soft-hearted woman, some shrewd instinct warned her not to let anyone have more than a day or so's credit.

'*Don't ask for credit*,' said a little printed card in a fly-blown show-case, '*and you won't be refused*.' That hint was effective.

The two o'clock back-to-work hooter of a nearby factory had finished blowing some time ago. Everyone who came home for lunch had gone back now. Annie knew from experience that she was in for the quietest period of the day. Until about half-past three, when the women started out with their perambulators, the most she could expect was the odd casual customer for cigarettes; or the child who had succeeded in wheedling a few coppers from a parent who was probably feeling desperately anxious to have forty winks.

The shop door-bell would wake Annie up.

She settled down, with her feet up on an old, velour-covered pouffe, her thin grey hair awry, her head resting on the back of a comfortable old wing chair. She wore carpet slippers, worn shapeless by shuffling, but in spite of her seventy-two years she had a surprisingly tight little figure.

A tap, needing a new washer, dripped in the kitchen, but the sound did not disturb her. After a few seconds, she began to snore faintly. That and the continual dripping of the water into a saucepan made the only nearby sounds. Occasionally someone walked sharply along the pavement, or a car drove past, but these were distant sounds, and did not disturb Annie Sharp.

Then the bell at the shop door clanged.

Her eyes opened, and she clutched the arms of the chair in the same instant. She allowed herself a second or two to wake, then stood up. The shop door, on a black japanned spring fastener, closed slowly.

'Coming,' she called.

Then she heard a sound that worried her. It was as if the flap of the counter was being raised, and she allowed no one to come in here without being invited. A child, perhaps, trying to sneak sweets. What children were coming to . . .

She hurried to the doorway.

She saw the man.

He looked young, although it was hard to be sure of that, because he wore a cap pulled low over his eyes, and a brown scarf drawn up over the lower half of his face. He was at the till, and as she reached the door, it went *ting!* sharply.

'*Here*!' she cried, 'you get out of here!' She bustled forward, more angry than scared; but a little scared too. 'Go on, be off –'

'Shut up,' the youth said.

She saw his narrowed eyes, and didn't like them, but she was still more angry than scared, and snatched up a bottle of Coca-Cola from a case standing on a shelf.

'Be off!' she shouted.

He didn't speak again. His voice had sounded gruff and vague behind the scarf, but there was nothing vague about his spiteful eyes. She raised the bottle, and he struck her hand aside. The bottle dropped but didn't break. He had a piece of short iron piping in his other hand; Annie Sharp saw it and opened her mouth to scream.

He struck, savagely.

He struck again and a third time, but the third blow wasn't really necessary.

He dragged her behind the counter and then into the little back room. Two children went hurrying past, girl and boy. He pushed the old woman in a corner, where she lay, bleeding to death, and then made a quick search. He found twenty-five pounds in an old tea caddy, and a small bundle of notes which he didn't trouble to count, in a sewing basket. He muttered something under his breath, glanced at the woman, and then went into the shop.

The till was still open.

He took the few pound and ten-shilling notes from the back, grabbed a handful of silver and dropped it into his jacket pocket, then stepped through a gap in the counter, dropped the flap and went to the door.

He pulled down the scarf, bent his head, opened the door – and almost fell over a toddler standing and peering at the sweets, spittle-damp fingers making patterns on the window. He shoved the child aside. A woman, pushing a small-wheeled pram, was coming from the right. The man turned left. The woman stopped at the shop. The killer reached a corner and looked round; the woman was putting the brake on the pram and going into the shop.

He began to run.

Gideon, with a sergeant beside him, drove down Brixton High Street as if he were on a lap at Silverstone. He succeeded in scaring the sergeant, who until then had regarded himself as fit for the Flying Squad. He seemed to shoulder other cars aside, and had an impudent disregard of the giant buses, the throbbing of petrol and diesel engines, the wayward antics of cyclists, who thought themselves danger-proof. Seeing the Forum a little way ahead, the sergeant said:

'Nearly there, sir, slow down now.'

Gideon grunted.

He saw a gap in the cars parked outside the Forum, and performed a miracle of parking, getting into the space and then out of the car almost in one and the same movement.

Once out and on the pavement, the fury slackened.

A plainclothes man whom he recognized vaguely and two whom he didn't were coming out of the cinema. Several uniformed police were about them, like a blue-bottle bodyguard. Handcuffed to a man half a head taller than himself, was Arthur Sayer. His lips were parted and trembling, he was pulling against the plainclothes man, although a second man held his other arm and was helping him along.

Gideon saw the car they were heading for. He went to it. He would have confessed to no one in the world that his heart was thumping painfully, and that he hardly knew how to frame his question.

'Any more trouble?' he asked as they drew near.

The man he recognized said: 'Any more – oh, more kids? No. He was sitting just behind a couple, but hadn't started anything. I – you want to talk to him, sir?' The Divisional man suddenly realized who this was and what respect was due to Gideon.

Gideon wiped his forehead.

'Not now,' he said.'But we'll want him at the Yard. Better get him there at once, and have a doctor to him.' He looked at Arthur Sayer with eyes which had the hardness of diamonds. 'Don't stand any nonsense from him.'

'Take it from me we won't, sir!'

'All right,' said Gideon. He watched them squeezing into a police car, but hardly saw Sayer; he pictured two small girls, and two mothers and two fathers, some sisters and brothers. He trumpeted into his handkerchief, then turned to the sergeant whom he had scared. 'Do you know Micklem Street, Clapham, Sergeant?'

'Oh, yes, sir, near the Common.'

'We'll go there.'

'Yes, sir.'

'And this time,' said Gideon, without conceding a smile, 'I'll drive according to the Highway Code, you needn't hold on so tight.' He got up and shot a sideways glance at the embarrassed sergeant. 'Get the Yard on that radio, will you, and find out if there's anything in for me.'

'Yes, sir!'

Gideon drove as a benevolent bus driver might, with far, far more than average care. He heard the sergeant asking questions. He felt a sense of satisfaction from which anxiety wasn't altogether erased. They'd got Sayer, and with luck they'd hang him. The blurry psychological quacks would try to prove that he was insane, though. Gideon could see the shape of their case for the defence already.

He ought to have told that man what doctor to send for.

'Sergeant, tell them that Sayer is on his way –'

'I have, sir.'

'And will they keep all doctors away from him and hold off questioning until Dr. Page-Henderson or Dr. Julian Forsyth can examine him. Ask them to pass that request through to the Old – to the A.C.'

'Yes, sir.'

The sergeant obeyed, and then listened to the radio reports.

'Anything for me?' asked Gideon.

'They've got that tyre and footprint cast ready at B2 Division,' said the sergeant. 'Superintendent Gillick asked whether you'd happen to be passing, so that you could pop in and have a word with him.'

Gideon stifled a groan, and then said:

'I'll see.'

The sergeant directed him to the street where Lucy Saparelli lived. Judging from the crowds at either end, the throngs on the pavement, the cars parked in or near the street, more people were drawn here than by a street accident, and that was saying something. In spite of police help when they recognized him, Gideon couldn't drive right up to the house. When he squeezed out of the shiny car, a battery of newspapermen, many with cameras, came towards him like a moving phalanx. It was almost automatic: ask questions, take photographs with flashlights which brightened even the bright day, and then hurl more questions.

'All right,' Gideon said, 'we've got Sayer, you can go home and write your story.'

They flung their questions . . .

After two minutes, Gideon pushed his way through towards the front door of Lucy Saparelli's house. He had some idea of what he would find behind the door now closed and guarded by a policeman in uniform. He was not duty-bound to see the mother of the murdered child, yet something urged him to; as it had from the moment of seeing Sayer captured.

The constable had a key.

Gideon went in.

Two women were with Mrs. Saparelli, there were teapots and kettles and cups and saucers everywhere, untidy as a child's toys. People spoke to Gideon but he wasn't interested until he saw the mother. He stood, a giant in the small room, and looked at her, remembering. It was an old story and a long one, and it still hurt. Kate had asked him not to go on duty, but to telephone an excuse, because their second child was ill. He'd brushed the suggestion off, and told her to pull herself together.

The child had died during the night. One of seven, so six were left; but the gap was still there.

A mother, bereaved, looked like a woman robbed of hope. Kate had; Lucy Saparelli did.

'I just came to tell you,' Gideon said, looking into those strange lack-lustre eyes, 'that we've caught him.'

'Have you?' Her voice was strained; empty.

'Yes, Mrs. Saparelli. We made quite sure of that. Is there anything we can do to help? Your husband –'

'No,' she said, 'you've been ever so good, all of you police have, and Jim's on his way.' She didn't look at Gideon as she spoke. 'Ever so good,' she repeated, 'but there's nothing anyone can do, now, nothing anyone can do.'

Gideon knew that she wasn't going to cry. He knew that it was going to be much worse with her than with many women. Kate hadn't cried. He didn't know why, but he sensed a measure of self-reproach, of self-blame, in Mrs. Saparelli. He made a mental note to tell a police-surgeon to have a word with the woman's doctor about that, as he said good-bye.

It hadn't taken long but he was glad that he had been, even though it made him feel more vicious. It wasn't only the crime; the actual offence for which a man might hang or serve a long term of imprisonment, was not the really deadly thing. That, a living evil, was the effect on those who suffered. Mrs. Saparelli, with the long years of self-reproach ahead, was now living in the shadow of death, and thinking: 'If only I'd done this . . .'

It was always the same; there was so much suffering; that was why he hated killers.

The sergeant was at the side of his car, speaking into the walkie-talkie.

'Anything fresh?' asked Gideon, flatly.

'Old woman's been attacked, Islington way,' said the sergeant. He might have been reporting a case of shoplifting, judging from his voice. 'Alone in a shop – till robbed – she was battered to death.'

'Death?'

'Yes, sir.'

'Oh, hell,' breathed Gideon. 'Hell.' It was almost a groan.

'There was an attempted mail van robbery at Cannon Street station twenty minutes ago,' the sergeant went on in exactly the same voice. 'No one's been caught but there's a description of the driver of a van, and the car's been held.'

Gideon straightened his back. Something happened to him; something quite wonderful; as if he'd taken a tonic, which had instantaneous effect. His dull eyes brightened.

'Where? Cannon Street?'

'Yes, sir.'

'Well, well,' said Gideon. 'Two of the devils stopped in one day, eh? That's not so bad, not bad at all, we're improving.' The dark shadows vanished completely from his eyes, there was eager brightness in them as he rounded the nose of the car and took the wheel. 'Might get those beggars soon, after all.'

He was looking ahead; to Gillick, to the tyre and footprint casts, and to the time when he would be able to include in his report one murderer caught and two mail van robberies averted.

Behind him, there was grief.

About him, there were the crimes being plotted and the criminals preparing; the good and the bad. He did not always realize how wearying it was to deal almost exclusively with the bad.

Two young men whom Gideon did not know, and of whom he had never heard, were preparing to play a part in his life at the time that he left the Yard to visit Superintendent Gillick. Neither knew that they would cross Gideon's path, although one realized that there was a serious risk that he would run into trouble with the police.

The name of the first was Alec Fitzroy. He was twenty-seven years old, had a small West End flat, and a private income of about five hundred pounds a year which wasn't anything like enough for his expensive tastes or his gambling debts. For a long time he had pondered on ways and means of making a fortune quickly, and had come to the conclusion that the most likely way was by theft.

He had two cronies whose names don't matter.

The name of the second man was Julian Small. He too was twenty-seven years old, lived in two small rooms close to the church near the river, and not far from Shipham's Café, and also had a private income of about five hundred pounds a year. The stipend from his curacy at St. Mary's brought in an additional two hundred pounds a year. Of his total income he spent one-half on his personal needs, and the rest on the needs of the church and the needy of the parish, especially on the Youth Club. He had only been in the parish for a few months. The Vicar was venerable and frail, known to everyone in the district rather as a piece of furniture is known in a home. No one ever took any notice of him at all.

A great many people took notice of Julian Small. He was unhappily possessed of a long, thin nose which was always red. He looked weedy, too, and he took little trouble with his clothes. After the first few weeks, the boys with whom he had tried to cope had discovered that he was not gifted with the necessary authority. He was full of high hopes and good intentions, but was so easily guyed.

Many were cruel, and guyed him.

Julian Small had one thing in common with Alec Fitzroy: education. They had, in fact, been educated at the same school, and had left in the same year. Their background was as nearly identical as a background could be. One had a widowed mother, the other a widower-father.

In every other way they were almost unbelievably different; but they did have similar thoughts that day although the one was heavy-hearted and bitterly resigned, the other was vicious and determined at all costs to get the money he needed.

Julian Small, walking from his flat to the church, turned into the tiny churchyard and the headstones grimed by London's sooty atmosphere, and kicked against a piece of string tied to headstones and stretching across the path. He crashed down. He tried to save his nose, but couldn't; the blow on it was so painful that tears of pain sprang to his eyes. They were not only of pain as he picked himself up and walked blindly along the path towards the church doors. Shrill, cruel laughter followed him, and brought shame and despair to quicken the tears. He was a failure; nothing could ever alter the fact. There were times when he felt that he almost *hated* the people in the district; the children.

'Suffer the little children . . .'

Some of these were devils!

They shouted obscenities after him, and roared with laughter until the heavy door closed on him. They might go away. They might raid the churchyard. They might throw stones through the windows; the stained glass had long since been moved, for it wasn't safe. There was no end to the sacrileges that the children would commit and which many of their parents would condone.

Julian Small was probably the unhappiest man in the East End of London that morning, and when he looked into a small mirror and saw the blood welling up at the end of his nose, he raised clenched fists and shook them at the reflection that he hated as much as he hated the children.

Or some of them . . .

Alec Fitzroy wept no tears of pain or vexation. At the time when Small was pitching forward on to the asphalt of the churchyard path, Fitzroy was in the upper safe deposit of the Mid-Union Safe Deposit Company, in Wattle Street, E.C.3. He had rented a deed-box there a few months ago, when the plan he was expecting to put into operation to-night had first taken shape in his mind.

He had met a youngster, now one of his cronies, who had been fired by the Mid-Union for drinking when on night duty; and the idea had been born then. Since that night Fitzroy had learned all he could about the safe deposit, the upper room and the main vaults; and he had studied the system by which it was staffed and run at night. His crony had given him a great deal of help.

Fitzroy believed that his plot was almost foolproof. All it needed was a strong nerve. He had that; so had his two accomplices, one of them a man whom Fitzroy had met in the Air Force and who lived in much the same way as Fitzroy; lazily, lustfully, greedily.

Fitzroy telephoned each man to tell him that this was to be the night, and to lay everything on. That was the first direct move in the collision which was coming with Gideon.

Gideon was on his way across the river, to see Gillick.

CHAPTER 8

TYREPRINT

Gillick was a big block of a man with a heavy, thrusting jaw and a peculiarly small mouth with a short upper lip. When he talked, he appeared to be chewing, and to his cost Gideon knew that Gillick talked a lot. There was no better man on detail in the whole of London, including the Yard, and his failing was his touchiness. When annoyed, and it was easy to annoy him, he could and often would fall back on working strictly to regulation, and on no job in the world were go-slow tactics more exasperating. The days when the Yard asked for urgent information by open postcard had gone at last, but Gillick knew every regulation that he could use so as to be unhelpful.

His big, pedestal desk was so tidy that it didn't seem real. He stood up from it, navy blue reefer coat open and square corners brushing a single file of papers, a thick red hand held out.

'Hallo, Gee-Gee, haven't seen you for years! Well, months! Nice day.

Must say you're looking well. Got that child killer, I hear; quick work, good job we have a bit of luck sometimes. Pity about Foster, nasty job when a man like Foster gets knocked over. What was he doing – making an arrest, d'you think?'

Gillick paused; and his little brown eyes probed, obviously he thought he was on to something.

'Not been suggested, old man,' Gideon said comfortably.'I'll have another look at the reports, though. You might have something there.'

'Never know,' said Gillick warningly. 'Fresh mind often helps.' He went off again, each sentence short and the pause after each one barely noticeable. Any other man would have sounded breathless, but not Gillick. 'Two mail van jobs stopped to-day, I see – don't say we're really near at last. Talking about that, these prints. Footprints not much good. Look.'

Some white plaster of Paris casts stood on a trestle table against one wall. On each was a card, neatly typewritten, giving the details. There were seven casts of footprints, but only one of a complete toe, another of a complete heel. The card near the toe read:

> Footprint, man's right toe, found in mud on South Bank of River Thames, Battersea, spot identifiable as three hundred and fifty (350) yards from the main loading jetty of the Battersea Power Station. Note indentation showing sole sprigged (nailed) on, not sewn. Note smooth edge suggesting plenty of wear.

Gideon studied all these, well aware that Gillick was keeping the most important until the last.

'By the way, old man,' said Gillick, 'like a spot? Not too late? Oh, well, cuppa tea? Good, I'll send for it.' He picked up a telephone and gave orders as a martinet would. 'Won't be long.' He broke off and turned to the trestle. 'Tyreprint's better, now. See.' He picked up a large glossy print, showing the tyre-track, the footprints, other signs of activity on the river bank; it was an excellent photograph, and showed where a car or light van had driven over a soft patch of sandy soil; the mark of the tyre couldn't have been made more clearly in plaster of Paris itself. 'Michelin make, and that's something, they don't make a lot of small tyres, this was a 5.50 × 16. Almost new, too – see how sharp that impression is?'

He now turned to the prize exhibit – the moulded cast of the tyre. It was beautifully made, quite an artist's job.

'You've got a good chap on this stuff,' Gideon said.

'Training, my boy, that's the answer – training! Beat hell out of them every time they turn in a rough job, and they soon stop. It's really something, this is. Any other make of tyre and it would be needle in haystack, but Michelin of this size – eh?'

Gideon felt his pulse quickening, in spite of almost instinctive disagreement with anything that Gillick said.

'You're right, Gil,' he said, 'this may really be something. It doesn't square up with the other track we got, that was a Dunlop, but we can get a search made for this.' If there were a job in the calendar which really made him feel deeply at any given moment, it was the mail van job. Hope of results could always excite. 'How many photographs have you got?'

'Dozen. Twelve. To spare, I mean.'

'Casts?'

'Three. Two each for you, one for my own Black Museum.' Gillick grinned; his little mouth didn't stretch very widely.

There was a tap at the door.

'There's the tea,' Gillick said. 'Well, hope this bit of work gets us somewhere. Can't say we lost any time . . .'

Twenty minutes later, Gideon left the B2 Headquarters, with Gillick purring, and the casts loaded into the boot of Gideon's Wolseley. He had spoken to Lemaitre by telephone and details of the Michelin tyre were being teleprinted for attention by all London and Home Counties Stations; the quiet, methodical, thorough search for it would begin before dark and go on all to-morrow and for days on end; the eyes of every policeman would be cast down, and every Michelin tyre would be suspect. It wasn't really much; but the owners of cars with 5.50 × 16 Michelins could be watched, and their movements checked; and if a thousand, if ten thousand discreet inquiries proved fruitless and futile, there might be one which helped.

The Yard sergeant came hurrying out of the station, wiping his hand across the back of his mouth; there were two or three cake crumbs on his sleeve.

'You had any lunch?' Gideon asked abruptly.

'Just managed a bite, sir, I'm all right.'

'Hmm. Well, I'm going to look in at home for half an hour, hardly recognize the place when I do get there.'

The sergeant smiled, dutifully.

'So you drive back to the Yard, get this stuff unloaded, tell the boys to be careful with it, and then come back for me.'

'Yes, sir.'

They drove over Battersea Bridge, then turned left instead of right – which they would take for the Yard. Gideon took off his hat and enjoyed the cold wind stinging his forehead. He felt too hot in his serge coat and waistcoat; now he came to think, it had been getting hotter since mid-day and must be near the seventies.

He wondered if Kate would be in. He knew quite well that he wanted to have a cup of tea with her because of the look in Lucy Saparelli's eyes. He wondered whether Kate would be pleased to see him; the youngsters would – no, the youngsters wouldn't!

The three girls were out at a party – Prudence to play in the glow of her examination success, Priscilla to recite, no doubt – she was a wonderful mimic. Well, good. Penelope just to look pretty, and no one could do that more easily.

Pretty Penelope.

Pretty, dead Dorothy Saparelli and Jennifer Gay – what was the first dead girl's name? He couldn't call it to mind.

Prudence eighteen plus, Priscilla fifteen plus, Penelope twelve, with Pru younger than her years except in her playing, so they were all good friends. There was a greater disparity in the ages of the boys. Tom, the oldest, was twenty-six, Matthew was fourteen, Malcolm only just eight. Matthew would almost certainly be out playing – he'd probably gone as far as Putney Common, or even to Wimbledon. Malcolm was more likely to be at home with Kate – unless she had taken him out.

Well, at least he'd have looked in.

The sergeant got out of the car to open the door for him. 'Thanks,' said Gideon. He did not consciously make a note of the man's name or the way he'd behaved, but except for that attack of nerves when Gideon had been driving, he'd done very well. Shorter than most, wiry fair hair, slim waist and no hips to speak of, he was quick-moving, quiet, efficient; oh, yes, and his name was Wedderburn.

'Oh, come straight back. I've got another call to make.'

'Right, sir.'

Harringdon Street, Fulham, was on the 'classy' side, north of the Wandsworth Bridge Road, near Hurlingham – still an oddly exclusive district although bordered by some of the poorer neighbourhoods of south-west London. The solid houses were all of red brick, two storey plus attic, and most of the householders were sufficiently well off to keep them in good repair; painting the outside every third year was a matter of pride. This had been Gideon's third year, and the painting had been finished only a few weeks ago. It was still bright and shiny, black and white as Kate had wanted it, and made him look up with interest and satisfaction; one could still take pleasure in the appearance of one's house.

There were two stone steps, a shallow porch, and a solid oak door – the door put in by Gideon. Most front doors in Harringdon Street had coloured glass panels, open invitation to light-fingered gentry.

Not that wood would keep anyone out, if he wanted to get in.

There was a small front garden, neat and attractive, with a postage stamp lawn, two beds of vari-coloured wallflowers, daffodils out and tulips not yet in flower. No one was about; the street as well as the house looked empty. Gideon felt a twinge of disappointment, but it wasn't very strong.

They had come to live in the upstairs flat here when he and Kate had married, and over the years they had converted the flats to one house, reversing the usual process. Always handy with his tools and not so busy in those early days as he had been for the last ten years, he had worked on the attic so as to make a roomy playroom and cubicles for the boys. Now Tom had a small room to himself, and the younger boys the cubicles. A corner of the playroom was used for their books and homework.

Pru had now a tiny partitioned room to herself; the younger girls shared the other side of the partition.

Gideon took out his keys, opened the door, and wondered when he had last come back during daylight. Three Sundays ago, when all the family had been waiting for him since noon, a job had cropped up . . .

The hall was narrow but bright and fresh, and well-lit from a landing window.

'Anyone home?' he called, and was startled when he heard an immediate response; footsteps above his head, in his bedroom – and Kate's.

'George, is that you?'

'Yes, m'dear. Just looked in for a cup of tea.'

Kate's footsteps came clearly; he could picture her easy walk. Although she was getting rather heavy-breasted and thick at the waist, she was still graceful, and she didn't have to worry too much about her figure. She appeared at the head of the stairs, wearing a black skirt and a fresh white blouse, looking neat and wholesome; her hair was more grey than his, and she improved a natural wave deftly.

'You might as well shoot me as frighten me to death,' she said. 'I couldn't believe it was you when I heard the car, and when it drove off again –'

'Don't tell me you took any notice of a car pulling up outside!'

Kate had reached the foot of the stairs. With her broad forehead and high-bridged nose she was quite striking, and she used make-up well; more, these days, than she had a few years ago. Standing on the bottom stair, she was just an inch or two taller than he.

'Don't tell me you've just looked in for a cup of tea,' she scoffed. 'What did you leave behind?'

'Nothing, honest. I happened to be handy, and thought it would be a good idea to pop in.'

'Crime *must* be in a bad way,' Kate said.

It was only half serious, only half hurtful; in fact, hurtful was too strong a word. They had six children, the memory of a seventh, a certain kind of mutual dependence, and practically nothing else in common. In a queer way, one Gideon hadn't been aware of for a long time, he looked upon her as he might a stranger – Mrs. Lucy Saparelli, for instance.

'As a matter of fact,' he said, 'crime's flourishing. We've had a bad one to-day. Cleaned it up as well as it can be cleaned up, though.'

'Oh,' Kate moved, pushing past him, and their hands brushed; hers was very cool. 'Well, I don't suppose you've got long. Going to wait in the front room while I get it?'

'No, I'll come into the kitchen. Where's Malcolm?'

'Gone to the pictures with the Odlums,' Kate said. 'I think Mrs. Odlum knew all the others were out, and deliberately gave me an afternoon off. I was just going to do some window shopping.'

They reached the kitchen. It was spick-and-span, and more than that. Kate knew what she wanted, and went all out to get it; and to help she had a little money of her own. That had always made a big difference to them. The kitchen was fresh and bright in pale blue and white paint, pale blue cake tins, pale blue handles on the saucepans. A new kitchen cabinet was painted the same colour – the carpentry and paintwork by Tom and Matthew Gideon! Everything had a clean smell. The gas popped. Gideon sat back in an old bed-chair, one of those Heath Robinson contraptions which could be turned into a bed to sleep an extra one, if needs be.

It was Kate's passion for tidiness, contrasting with his habit of coming home and littering the place, that had first really come between them; really contrast of temperaments. Funny thing, to think like that about the mother of your six – seven – children. One married a girl, loved, lived; after a while the intimacies became almost habitual, and since Malcolm's arrival –

The only time he'd known Kate hysterical was when she had known for certain that Malcolm was coming. In this very room she had cried and screamed and shaken her clenched fists at him.

'I won't have it, I won't have another brat. It's all I ever do! Work, slave, *breed*, work, slave and *breed*. And for you! What do you care? You're never in, never got five minutes to spare, and – I tell you I won't have it! I'll get rid of it somehow.'

It had been a bad, even an ugly evening.

They had never really recovered from it, although oddly, she was passionately fond of Malcolm, and showed her affection more than she did with the others – showed it to Gideon that was; the children didn't know. If they did, it was because of some sixth sense that he knew nothing about.

'What kind of case was it?' asked Kate.

He sensed what she was feeling; as if this might be a chance to begin to get to know each other again. He'd made a gesture, she wanted to, too. She wasn't quite sure why he had come, and sitting back there and watching her, he wasn't sure either – except that one idea, which hadn't occurred to him before, came into his mind and wouldn't be dismissed. He had come home because he needed her, because the sight of little Dorothy Saparelli's mother had hurt him more than he knew.

The kettle was boiling.

Kate made the tea, and said, in a tighter voice: 'Or is that a forbidden subject?'

'No,' said Gideon. 'No, Kate. Just nasty. A sex maniac, two little girls, and the hell that it's caused to a couple of families. I've just come from one of the mothers. It – well, you know what it is. Sometimes it makes me sick. Sometimes I wish I were one of the average crowd, lost in anonymity, doing a job which didn't make me rub shoulders with all the beastliness and the brutality there is. A man kills a child – and the pain goes on and on and on. By hanging him you don't make it any less. I'm not even sure that you don't make it more.'

Kate was spooning sugar into his cup. The tea was very strong; sweet and strong, the way he liked it.

She took a big cake-tin out of the larder; the cake was already on a plate. Knives, plates and plastic mats appeared as if by sleight of hand.

'You look tired, George,' she said abruptly.

'Oh, I'm all right.'

'You can't give yourself a few hours off, I suppose?'

'Well – well, no, Kate. I wish I could.'

She didn't answer.

The fruit cake was rich, too, and good; it had that richness of flavour that made each mouthful something to enjoy and to remember, not just to eat. He had another piece.

'Window shopping where?' he asked.

'Oh, in town! Knightsbridge or Oxford Street.'

'How soon can you be ready?' asked Gideon. 'I've got the car coming back in twenty minutes or so. Could give you a lift.'

'Oh, that's lovely,' Kate said in a flash. 'All I need is five minutes. I must be back by half-past six, they'll start coming home soon after that – but it will give me a couple of hours to play truant in.'

Then Gideon remembered Foster's sister, in Chelsea; he had meant to call on her on the way back to the Yard. The fact came to the tip of his tongue, but he didn't utter it. Kate looked suddenly gay. She was bright-eyed and eager, her grey hair didn't make her look her age. It wouldn't take him long to drop her, and then come back to Chelsea and Miss Foster – *Mrs. Addinson.*

'Thanks a lot, George, that was lovely,' Kate said. 'You must drop in more often!' Her eyes were bright with excitement, and she was laughing at him; with the children and with others – and at one time with him – she had always laughed easily. She didn't let him get out, but slammed the door and walked off, tall and brisk, something to see in her black suit and white hat and gloves. Gideon was in at the kerb, forgetful of the fact that he was in the way of Oxford Street traffic. He picked up the radio-telephone.

Soon he was speaking to Lemaitre.

'Got something you want to see here, George – couple of good photographs of Foster, lying in the road.' Lemaitre paused; a note in his voice suggested that he had something up his sleeve. 'Going to be long?'

'Not long. Anything else?'

'Not to worry about. Sayer's made a clean breast of it, and the mystery of that kid in the tunnel out at Ealing isn't a mystery any longer. He did that, too. You know the job three weeks ago. Haven't got a clue on that Islington killer, except that the chap was medium height and wore a brown suit. Used iron piping, and gloves – no dabs, not very optimistic.' Lemaitre sucked his breath. 'Half a mo'.'

Gideon waited. Buses pulled up almost on the tail of his car, and then swung out. Traffic filtered past, a constable came up looking as if he had nothing in the world to do, bent down, and peered at him.

'Going to be here long, sir?' He bumped his helmet on the top of the window. 'Oo!' Praiseworthy self-control. 'Holding up the traffic, you know, very bad place to stop.'

'Yes. Sorry. Let me finish this talk to the Yard, and I'll move off.'

'To the –' There was a closer, sharper scrutiny. 'I didn't recognize you, sir! Sorry. Like me to make 'em give you a bit more lee room?'

Gideon chuckled. 'No, thanks, I'm all right.'

The constable did his best to salute so that the courtesy could be noticed, and moved off. There was the purr, the hum, the roar of engines, the swish of wheels on the tacky road, the perpetual motion of people weaving to and fro, the air heavy with petrol fumes. Gideon eased his collar; his neck was damp.

Lemaitre came again, almost bellowing:

'It's a flash from Waterloo. They've knocked off a van with thirty thousand quid in it. One of our chaps caught a packet. Three in one blasted day! Wonder if the others were dummy jobs – be seeing you.'

CHAPTER 9

THE MAIL VAN JOB

A small but well-set-up looking man in the early thirties, at the wheel of an Austin 10 saloon, cellulosed black, was drumming the steering wheel with the fingers of both hands, and watching a flow of traffic coming from the one-way street leading from Waterloo Road. Standing a few hundred yards away from him was another, younger man, dressed in drab grey and rather down at heel. He had a motor-cycle. Nearer the Austin was a short, stocky man who kept taking a cigarette out of his mouth, looking at it, then putting it back again.

All three had been there for ten minutes.

The stocky man near the Austin finished his cigarette, glanced up and down, and then stiffened; for a red mail van came in sight. It was on its own, clear of other traffic, and moving at a good speed.

The driver's hands stopped drumming. He started the engine. The others tensed, as if for action, although no one noticed them then.

The van didn't swing beneath the dark arches of the wide approach to Waterloo Station, but came straight on.

All three men relaxed; if relaxed was the word.

The stocky one came up to the car.

'You must have got it wrong.'

The driver said smoothly: 'I don't get things wrong.'

'It's late, nearly ten minutes –'

'That's your watch, it's fast,' the driver said. 'Beat it, Ted.'

'We can't stay around here any longer.'

'What's the matter, losing your nerve? We'll stay as long as we have to. I got the squeak, didn't I? There are thirty thousand quid in that van, being sent down to Bournemouth.'

'It'll have a cop tailing –'

'S'right,' the driver said, 'and we'll fix the cop and scram. Quit worrying. I'll see you at Shippy's, and –'

He stopped as another mail van came in sight. This time he didn't relax, for he read the registration number.

'That's it,' he whispered, and the stocky man shot away from him as the Austin's engine started; then roared.

The Austin 10 was on the move as the van swung towards the archway; as it turned left, the Austin swung right. That was normal enough, for there was access to traffic from both directions.

Behind the van was a Wolseley with two men in it. Anyone who knew a Yard car would recognize that there was something unmistakable about the look of the man at the wheel and his companion. They weren't in any mood of alarm – until the man in drab grey, astride his motor-bicycle, roared alongside and tossed a little, fragile glass tube through the driving window. It broke on the driver's forehead. Ammonia gas billowed, biting at both Yard men's eyes, mouths and noses. The driver grabbed at the gear lever and his foot went down on the brake, but he was going fast and was blinded before he could stop. The police car lurched across and smashed into the archway wall. The man by the driver's side gave a funny little grunting sound as the door buckled and squashed him.

The car was slewed across the road; no other traffic could get in and it was a one-way stretch.

The Austin, a hundred yards further on, screeched alongside the mail van. The scarlet of the van's cellulose, bright under the sun, was reflected on the black shine of the car. The post office driver and his mate glanced sideways nervously, sensing what was happening. Brakes went on, but the Austin forced the van to keep on the inside, drawing just ahead of it. The Austin driver pulled a gun. The post office men didn't move.

Two youths, bent low until then and wearing black cloth masks, jumped from the back of the Austin. They didn't wait for keys, didn't speak, smashed at the padlock at the back of the little red van and, as the doors swung open, grabbed the registered bags – all of green canvas.

They rushed back to the Austin.

Within ninety seconds they were being driven away at a furious but controlled pace, with the motor-cycle roaring after them. The post office men watched them go, and saw the registration plate of the saloon vanish. It had false plates; another would drop as soon as the robber car reached the Waterloo Road.

Back in the archway, cars were lined up behind the wreck. One Yard man was leaning against the wall, with tears still streaming down his face. Two men were pushing at the damaged car, so as to get at the driver's companion, who had slumped down in his seat; there was blood on his chin. Someone was calling for a doctor. Two uniformed policemen came hurrying.

The stocky youth, not needed to make a diversion after all, turned away and walked towards Whitehall, whistling.

Gideon switched off the radio-telephone and started his engine. He felt as if he were back where he had started; the all-pervading shadow of the mail van robberies had become blacker than ever. Whether the two earlier jobs had been to sell the police dummies or not, someone was bound to suggest that they had been, and two or three of the newspapers would have a smack at the Yard for it; and at him.

He was ten minutes' drive from the Yard.

He was fifteen minutes' drive from Foster's flat and his sister, Mrs. what-was-her-name? – Addinson.

'Can't prevent the damned hold-up now,' he said aloud and savagely, 'and if I don't see the woman soon I'll have to give the job to someone else.'

He swung round in the road, where there was a clear stretch, nodded to the watching constable, and drove through Hyde Park towards the south-west and Chelsea.

It was then four o'clock.

Florence Addinson, née Foster, opened the door. At the first moment, she was just an attractive young woman, with features – expression? – a little too bold perhaps, wearing a washed-out blue smock daubed here and there with paint, and poking red-lacquered fingers through her raven black hair. Her hair was untidy and piled up on top with one of those ring buns, or whatever they were called.

Then she recognized Gideon.

'Miss Foster,' Gideon said, and felt irritated with himself; why use the wrong name when he knew it was wrong?

'I – yes,' she said, as if she didn't think it worth contradicting him. 'Yes, aren't you –'

'Superintendent Gideon.'

'I thought you were.' She hadn't moved away from the door but held on to it tightly. Nervously? 'Weren't you at Mr. Chang's this morning?'

'Yes.'

'Superintendent Gideon, can you tell me –' she began, and then snatched her hand away from the door. 'Oh, what a fool I am! Won't you come in?'

'Thanks,' said Gideon.

'I've just been doing some sketching,' she said apologetically. 'A rush job.'

'For Chang?'

'No, he – he changed his mind.' She led the way into a long, narrow room overlooking the Embankment.

Had Gideon ever entered this room during Foster's life, he would soon have started wondering where the money came from. Detective-sergeants didn't usually live in luxurious apartments overlooking the Thames; or have dark, almost black oak furniture, *circa* 1600, in a room which was richly panelled and had several Dutch panels on the wall – each worth something more than three figures.

Had they family money?

The woman stood and faced him and the impression that she was nervous came back. She seemed younger than Gideon had thought, partly because she'd not made-up since morning, her cheeks had a scrubbed look. She no longer looked over-bold, nor so attractive, if you liked smoothness of line. The smock hid her figure, too, where her suit had emphasized it.

Her eyes were almost black; like Foster's.

'Superintendent, is my brother in any trouble?' The question came out swiftly, quickened by embarrassment.

'What makes you think he might be?' asked Gideon.

'I – I don't know. That doesn't matter. Is he?'

'Yes, Miss Foster –' Gideon glanced down at her left hand; she wasn't wearing a wedding ring – 'It would be pointless to lie to you, the papers have the story, I'm quite sure.' He really meant that it would be a mistake to come out with all the truth now, but if he questioned her first and afterwards told her what had happened, what would she think of him?

What did it matter what she thought? He had a job to do.

'I'd like to know the truth.' She was taut.

'Good. Do you mind telling me why you should think that he was in trouble?' When he chose to exert himself, Gideon could have the charm of a benevolent patriarch, and could inspire confidence even in people who ought to know better. 'It might help a lot, in the long run.'

She said abruptly: 'He seemed worried.'

'What about?'

'I don't know. I think –' she paused.

'I'll find out sooner or later, one way or the other,' Gideon said, 'and I've come myself because I thought it would help if you knew you were dealing with a senior officer.'

'Oh,' she said, and mechanically added: 'Yes, thank you. Well, it's – it's hard to say. I think he was being threatened. He –'

Gideon's big hand now held the fat cigarette-case. Foster's sister took a cigarette. He lit it, then shepherded her to a window seat. It was rather a fine view, especially with the sun shining on the broad Thames, the two bridges in sight just far enough away to look fragile, and the plane trees lining the embankment powdered with light green; husks of the buds were beginning to litter the road and pavement.

The story came out swiftly.

The girl was no fool, and obviously had been worried for some time. At heart, she said, she'd been worried for two years, since Foster had first started to buy new furniture. Some of this was their own, which they'd inherited, but some pieces were recent acquisitions. All the paintings had been bought in the last year or so. He said he bought them at wholesale prices, and she had never voiced her anxiety to him.

Lately, she knew that he'd been worried; he hadn't slept much, he had been at work all day and out too much at night. She had felt sure that he was being put under some kind of pressure.

'Did you suspect anybody?' Gideon asked bluntly.

She didn't answer.

'Nothing you say to me will be used,' Gideon said. 'I might be able to switch inquiries, that's all. *Did* you suspect anyone?'

She said hesitantly: 'Well – in a way. He – he knew that man Chang slightly, and I knew Chang had telephoned him. He always seemed more worried after that.'

'Why did you go to Chang's?' Gideon asked.

'I – I thought I might find out something,' she said. 'Oh, I know it was silly, but I was really anxious. There'd been some talk of mural paintings for the new club-room, and I got an agency to introduce me to Chang about it. That's why I was there. I could have dropped through the floor when you arrived.'

'You recognized me, didn't you?'

'You aren't a man to forget,' she said.

Unexpectedly, that pleased him; she seemed to know that it did, and for a moment she was more relaxed. Then she changed and her voice hardened.

'What *has* happened? I've tried to get Eric on the telephone several times, but couldn't, and a sergeant I spoke to was most evasive.'

'Hmm, yes,' Gideon commented. He didn't like what he had to do, and the dislike stiffened his voice. 'Rather ugly trouble, Mrs. Addinson. That's why I went to Chang's. I think Chang was bribing your brother to shut his eyes to certain offences.'

She exclaimed: 'Eric taking *bribes*?'

'Yes.'

'You can't be certain!'

'No,' agreed Gideon, 'I can't really be certain.'

'Where is Eric? What does he say?' She was flushed and very anxious.

'He denied it, of course,' Gideon said, and went on very heavily: 'Had you any reason to believe he was taking bribes?'

'No!'

Gideon thought: 'I don't believe her.' Then he began to wonder more about her; was her explanation of her visit to Chang the true one? Had she known Chang before? Was she involved? Were her present fears due to worry about the possibility of being caught out in some crime?

He saw her, now, just as another witness who might become a suspect. If Chang had warned her about Foster's danger from the Yard, it could explain much. The one thing that seemed certain was that she had not heard of the death of her brother.

'Mr. Gideon,' Florence Addinson said abruptly, 'will you please tell me where Eric is?'

'Yes,' said Gideon, 'although it's not a job I like, Mrs. Addinson. I hate bringing bad news of any kind.' He felt that it had all gone wrong, he wasn't breaking this gently; she was expecting to hear that her brother was under arrest.

He must get it over.

'He was run down by a car this morning,' he said, and stopped again.

He saw understanding dawning; surprise came first, because it was so unexpected, shock next; and the grief would come afterwards. He knew only too well that it was impossible to judge in advance how a woman would react to such news, but there was a one-in-four chance of a burst of hysteria. He let her have time to get used to the fear which he'd put into her mind, and then added quietly:

'It was over very quickly, I'm glad to say.'

'*Over*,' she ejaculated.

She sat on a cushioned window seat, back to the sun-gilt river, a few wisps of hair blowing slightly in the breeze from an open window. She didn't move. Sitting this way, the smock was drawn down tightly; she had the kind of figure Kate had had twenty years ago.

'*Over*,' she repeated hoarsely.

'I'm afraid that's it,' said Gideon, and liked the task less than ever. 'It's very distressing.'

'I can't – I can't believe it!'

It was going to be hysteria. She'd jump up in a minute and keep repeating that she couldn't believe it, and then she would probably call it murder, and she would look round for someone to blame. She was so young; middle twenties at most, thought Gideon. Then he realized that he was letting the emotional side gain the upper hand, he was seeing her as an attractive woman. He had to see her as the sister of a policeman who had accepted bribes, and probably had been murdered; as a witness who might lead him to Chang and beyond; to the distributors of drugs which corrupted and killed.

She jumped up, hands clenched.

'It can't be true! Why, he left here this morning, as fit as –'

She broke off.

Her colour was coming back, an angry red which seemed to be reflected in her eyes.

Gideon watched her, not quite dispassionately.

He would let the first blast pass over his head, then try to steady her, then he'd ring Lemaitre and have a couple of good men come along here, to start searching. There had to be a quick and thorough probe. She was on edge and likely to remain so; if they could find one little pointer that involved her, they would be justified in trying to make her crack. If she was in the clear, the sooner it was established the better.

He watched her fighting for her self-control. Admiration came back; it was impossible to rid himself of the curious sense of personal concern for her.

Then she said: 'I hope you'll tell me everything, Mr. Gideon. Everything, please.' She paused and then flung out: 'Did he kill himself?'

That startled Gideon.

'No,' he said. 'No, we've no reason to think so. Have you?'

'Just that he was worried. That man Chang. I –' she raised her hands, and let them fall. 'Anyhow, it's late to do anything to help Eric now.'

Very quietly, Gideon said: 'You may be able to help us, Mrs. Addinson. Will you try?'

'In every way I can,' she promised.

It was twenty to five when Gideon reached the Yard. He had waited there until Sergeants Wedderburn and Miller, the day's bright boys, had arrived at the flat. By then, Foster's sister had been completely composed, and he found doubts about her hard to retain. The two sergeants would go into figures, study all Foster's accounts, find out who the furniture was bought from, who sold Old Masters 'at wholesale prices'. It had all the makings of a nasty job, and Foster's game might have gone on for some time, but for Birdy.

Gideon had been thinking about the man who had really started his day. Birdy Merrick, at fifty-odd, had spent twenty years in jail. His was one of the worst records of any man in London for burglary and breaking and entering, but he had not been able to stand by and watch young girls become maddened with drugs. Good in every man? Certainly Birdy's love for his dead daughter had gone deep.

Gideon's office was empty.

He hung his hat with exemplary care on the peg in the corner, then took out his pipe and tobacco, next took off his coat, loosened his collar and, putting his right foot up on a chair, eased the lace of the shoe; the little toe was pinching a bit.

It was very warm. He sat down slowly, fingering the familiar roughness of his pipe and the smooth pouch at the same time, anticipating a smoke, feeling less tired than dispirited. That was partly due to Foster's sister. He thought of Kate asking him if he couldn't snatch a few hours off. It was so long since he had worked normal hours, and relaxed in the evening, that he had almost forgotten what it was like.

Lemaitre's hurriedly written notes were in front of him. There was one about a patrolman's report on the painter at Chang's; a man known to have a chip on his shoulder, but as far as was known, quite honest; he'd never worked for Chang before, and Chang had tried three decorators before getting one who had been able to come at once. So the painter was out; Chang's anxiety to get the club painted quickly was more firmly in.

Another showed negative results from the inquiry about anyone with a 'tough reputation' having left Chang's about eleven o'clock, and this confirmed, incidentally, that a decorating firm's foreman had been in to see Chang but had not been able to do an urgent job at the club. Chang, this report said, had wanted the decorating finished in time to open as usual that night.

The last report, at the bottom, made Gideon's teeth clench. Attached to it was a print of a photograph of Foster, lying dead in the road. He was face upwards. The photograph showed that the blood oozed from his head into the dust of the roadway. It was a brilliant picture – a bit macabre, perhaps, if that were the word, but as a photograph vivid and clear in every detail. Obviously the car had crushed his stomach.

There was death looking at Gideon –

In the kerb was a dark patch and shining surface; a puddle. It had rained early morning. There was something else, and Lemaitre had pointed a red-pencilled arrow towards it. Gideon looked closer, and then his heart began to beat fast, he felt the choking throb of excitement.

The arrow pointed to a tyre-track.

The tyre-track looked familiar; and was familiar. It was of a new Michelin tyre, and the size was probably 5.50 × 16.

Lemaitre had written hurriedly:

'Same make tyre as Gillick took a cast of, size and all, could be the same type, and if F. was bumped off by the mail v. boys – how about it?'

CHAPTER 10

FIND THAT TYRE

'The only thing that matters,' said Gideon to the Assistant Commissioner, who had come to his office, 'is to find that tyre. It's one of the first real mistakes they've made, and they probably don't know it. If we can find that tyre –'

The A.C. was tall, lean, grey-haired, sardonic when the mood took him, and just now sardonically amused.

'All right, George. I want them as much as you do, but we needn't get excited about it.'

'We needn't get –' began Gideon, explosively. He held his breath, then put his pipe down slowly. 'If you were Lemaitre, I'd have your hide for that remark! I don't mind telling you that there's just one job –'

He broke off.

They looked at each other uncertainly and grinned simultaneously.

'Seem to have heard that before somewhere,' said the A.C. 'Where's Lemaitre?'

'Waterloo.'

'He shouldn't have gone before you came back,' said the A.C. mildly. 'Drop him a hint that if he leaves the office empty I'll have *his* hide. I've just been looking through Sayer's statement. We've got a cold-blooded devil there.'

Gideon didn't speak.

'And that Islington job, the old woman in the sweetshop,' the Chief went on, 'that's a bad one, too. Haven't had a chance to look at it much, have you?'

'No.'

'More your cup of tea than anyone else's,' the A.C. said, 'and if it weren't, I've got to send Chatto to Portugal on that extradition job; he's the only one who can speak Portuguese well enough to get by in Lisbon, and I don't trust Portuguese English. Smith's still up to his eyes in the City fraud case, I don't want to take him off. Deering's cracked up –'

'Deering isn't the only one near cracking up,' Gideon said into a pause. 'I'm all right, and will be for a bit, but flesh and blood is flesh and blood. We're all being driven too hard, from sergeants up. Had a chap with me to-day. Discovered he was on until two o'clock this morning, back on duty at six, and still at it. That's the way we make mistakes, and that's the way we'll go on making mistakes. Hasn't any blurry fool got any idea how to get our recruits' strength up?'

'No,' said the A.C.

'I don't understand why it's so hard.'

'Want your boys to become C.I.D. men?' asked the A.C. dryly. 'Several years on the beat first at low pay with some danger, while there are plenty of good prospects elsewhere?'

'I wouldn't want my boys to become C.I.D. men if it made 'em millionaires,' said Gideon forcefully. 'Oh, I know what you mean, and I still think it's wrong recruiting methods. Bit more glamour, that's what we want. Well –' he broke off. 'What brought you in, sir?'

It was a casual, belated 'sir'; just as a matter of form.

'Islington,' said the A.C. 'Have a look at everything, will you, you've got X-ray eyes. And then there's the Moxley case. We don't want Moxley to get off, if ever a man deserved to be hanged he's the one. Sure the sergeant and the inspector you've briefed as witnesses are good enough?'

'As good as we'll get,' Gideon assured him. 'But don't count on a verdict. Moxley killed his wife all right, and he did it because of that tart who gets her face and fanny plastered all over the papers, but it's going to be tough. Not a thing more we can do about it, either. That rape job's up in Number 2 at the Old Bailey in the morning, too. We'll get those little baskets all right. Cor!'

The A.C. said: 'Seamy, isn't it?'

'What I want is to get away, have a nice clean breeze running through my hair for a bit,' said Gideon, 'but it won't be for a few months yet. I – excuse me.'

The telephone bell rang. He picked it up, sitting on a corner of the desk. The A.C., a tailor's dummy of a soldier in mufti, stood waiting. Gideon's expression told him nothing, Gideon's voice told him a lot.

'Hallo, Birdy,' said Gideon.

He listened . . .

'All right,' he said, 'I'll send it over to you in old notes . . . I don't know, but someone who'll recognize you. Then lie low for a bit, don't get yourself into trouble. . . . Unless you tell me anything more about Chang.'

He paused.

'Okay, Birdy,' he said and rang off.

He rubbed his hand across his forehead; both hand and forehead were damp.

'That's the squeaker on Chang and Foster, sir.' Here, if ever, was a time for formality. 'I'm paying him twenty-five pounds and it's cheap at the price. Two men are over at Foster's place now, I hope to have some kind of a report before I go off to-night.' He sniffed. 'Birdy says that there's a call out for him and he wants to get away.' Suddenly the two men, broadsword and rapier in contrast, were standing upright and looking squarely at each other; each with genuine respect. 'I don't like it, A.C. Foster was probably run down deliberately because once we found out what he was up to, he might have squealed.'

'But Chang –'

'Don't want to make it worse than it is,' said Gideon, 'but why assume that Chang was the only one he was taking bribes from? I don't say he wasn't, yet I can't see Chang paying out a fortune, and somehow Foster's cashed in pretty big money. Did you know that the tyre-mark near Foster's body might match up with the one at Battersea? – the car from which they threw those mail bags into the river.'

The A.C. said, 'No, I didn't.'

'Come'n have a look.' They pored over the photographs, Gideon's flat but well-shaped and clearly marked forefinger pointing at similarities. 'And that blakey settles it,' he said. 'See where it's embedded in the tyre – comes out in the cast and in the photograph clearly under magnification. Look.' He thrust a round magnifying glass into the A.C.'s hand.

The A.C. pursed his lips.

'. . . mmm I see what you mean. Well, I'll finish off where I came in – Find that Tyre!'

He went out.

Gideon wrote out a chit for twenty-five pounds. He charged it to the Information Account, rang for a plain clothes officer, and sent him along to cash it. When the man came back, Gideon was staring at the ceiling, and actually smoking; he owed himself an extra pipe, had only had one that morning.

'Thanks. Green, do you know Birdy Merrick?'

'Oh, yes, sir.'

'Sure?'

'Little chap with a chirruping voice and a little beak of a nose that's always red. Been inside –'

'That's the chap. Take this over to him – he'll be near the telephone kiosks at Aldgate Station by the time you get there. Don't let him put his hands on it until you've got his signature on the receipt. I like Birdy, but you can guess how far I'd trust him.'

Green, delighted at a chance to go out, chuckled with more than polite amusement.

When he'd gone, Gideon sat and pulled at his pipe and looked at a spot on the ceiling. It had been there for five years and he still didn't know how it had got there; a pale brownish spot about the size of half a crown. In it, he had seen many things and many faces. Leaning back in the swivel chair with the strong spring back at just the right angle, he could see it with complete comfort. He'd trained himself to lean back like this, a form of relaxation that was almost complete. In a minute, he would treat himself to a double whisky, then he would be set for a few hours.

He thought of Kate.

He thought of Foster's sister.

He had his whisky.

He thought of Lucy Saparelli. Those kids. Sayer. A little old woman with a battered head.

This was one of the bad days, but the newspapers would look much the same as usual next morning; half the headlines in the popular daily press were about major crimes. No one would be surprised. Now and again there was an outcry about unsolved crimes, and so there should be. Only one crime in two, not even as many as that some years, were ever solved. The miracle was that the Yard got so many results. Give them a ten per cent increase in staff –

The door opened, and Lemaitre came in, brand new trilby on and slightly at the back of his head, perky of feature and expression, grinning rather smugly.

'Hi!' he greeted.

'When you're going to leave the office empty again, make sure that the Old Man isn't coming in, will you?' Gideon said flatly.

Lemaitre's perkiness vanished; he positively sagged.

'You don't mean to say –'

'I do mean to say, and why you ask for trouble like that I don't know. Rule Number 1 – always have someone in the office. If we both *have* to be out, fetch in a sergeant.' Gideon grinned. 'But it's up to the Old Man to discipline you, you rebellious old so-and-so. Got anything from Waterloo?'

Lemaitre began to look less disconsolate. He took his hat off and twirled it round his forefinger, formed his mouth into a soundless whistle, and then said:

'Yes.'

That thumping started again at Gideon's chest.

'What?'

'Tyre-track, believe it or not. Patch of oil on the approach to the station, just where the van was held up. A lorry had a puncture there a few nights ago, and dripped a lot of engine oil. The rain had smoothed it out. One track as clear as a cucumber, unmistakable, too – but if I hadn't gone there it wouldn't have been noticed. All the photographs they took before I arrived were of the mail van. Five minutes more and they'd have trampled all over the oil patch. Now tell the Old Man –'

'No one said you shouldn't go out on a job sometimes, just be your age and make sure someone's here,' said Gideon. He had the patience of a schoolmaster with Lemaitre, who had one thing which no one else at the Yard had quite so well developed: a 'natural' sense of observation. Lemaitre's eyes did most of his work for him; he'd miss nothing out, and he could check another man's case brilliantly. If he could only restrain his impetuosity, he'd be a genius. 'So, what have we got?' Gideon asked.

'Three Michelin tyre-tracks,' Lemaitre said. 'One near Chang's – one at Battersea – the third at Waterloo. I know, I know, three different cars could –'

'They probably didn't. Anything else?'

'It was an Austin 10 with false number plates. The driver had black hair, and his cap was pulled low over his eyes, showing his hair from the crown downwards. *And*,' went on Lemaitre, voice rising in triumph, 'one of those post office johnnies kept his eyes open although he admits he was scared stiff. The black hair had a white mark in it – scar of some kind, starting just level with the right ear. Now we can look for the car, the tyre and the driver, and oh, boy –'

He broke off because a telephone bell rang on Gideon's desk.

'Yes,' said Gideon into it, and then repeated, although looking puzzled: 'Yes, put him through.' He glanced up at Lemaitre. 'It's Green, chap I sent to pay Birdy his blood money. Move your big head, I can't see the clock.' Lemaitre moved quickly. 'H'm. Five and twenty past six. Been gone twenty minutes.' He waited with the receiver at his ear. Then: 'Yes, Green?'

He listened.

He began to look very grim indeed.

'All right,' he said at last, 'stay there another twenty minutes, and if he hasn't turned up then, come back. 'Bye.'

Gideon rang off, scowled, looked at Lemaitre steadily, and said flatly: 'Someone sent a kid to tell Green we wouldn't be able to pay Birdy off to-night or any night. I don't like that at all.' He lifted the telephone, a mechanical action. 'Give me G5 headquarters,' he said, and added for Lemaitre's benefit, although he sounded as if he was talking to himself: 'Better get the Division to keep an eye open for him.'

'We can't afford to lose Birdy,' Lemaitre said, and meant it.

CHAPTER 11

BIRDY

'Birdy,' Birdy's wife said, 'they're after you.'

'Wife' was not strictly true, in the legal sense, but in all others it was. She was a small, faded woman, who had never been pretty, was balloon-breasted now, but still had small if work-torn hands – the fingers of her right hand were especially rough, for she was a seamstress. She also had beautifully shaped legs and feet. In spite of her weight and her top-heavy look, she moved very easily.

She had caught up with Birdy at the telephone boxes in the approach to Aldgate Station. The traffic in the wide main road was a hurtling, hooting, mass, choking the golden evening. Barrow boys with fruit stalls magnificently arranged shouted whether customers were near or not, news-boys droned. This great mouth of London's East End and the suburbia beyond throbbed with a vitality which it saw only once each day, always between half-past five and half-past six. All London seemed to be on the move.

Policemen walked; plodding, watchful, patient.

Thieves watched for their chances.

Pickpockets made theirs.

It isn't even remotely true that everyone in the East End, from Wapping to Rotherhithe, or from Bethnal Green to Whitechapel, is a criminal, or even criminally inclined. But ask any London policeman where crime and criminals flourish most, and he will unhesitatingly point to this part of the city. A few might say that at times there was a greater concentration of vice in the West End Square Mile, but very few are sure.

Most of this East End trouble area came within the jurisdiction of G5 Division. The Division had picked officers and picked men, and knew its job inside out. Like every other section of the London police it was understaffed, but it was more generously treated than most.

Every policeman in the Division knew Birdy, and most of them knew Birdy's 'wife'. An odd thing about Birdy was that he looked small, mean, sneaky and nasty altogether, yet he wasn't. He had a kind of morality. He had a kind of courage. He acted upon a kind of code. Take Birdy and his 'wife' – her name was Ethel – out of the slums where they lived and worked, out of the tiny, smelly hovel with its front door opening on to the pavement, put them in one of the clean sweet-smelling suburbs, and Birdy might be heard to say that his wife was the best woman in the world, and Ethel would certainly be heard to say that they didn't come any better than her Birdy.

He had a slightly hunched back, and was sparrow-thin, but very bright with a Cockney twang and a Cockney's swift repartee.

Now, he looked into Ethel's scared eyes.

' 'Ow'd you know?' he asked and caught his breath.

'Murphy's been around,' she said. 'Someone told me at Shippy's, so I went 'ome. 'E come to see me, wanted to know where to find you.'

'Murphy,' echoed Birdy, and licked his lips.

'Syd's at one corner, Hicky at another,' Ethel went on, 'waiting for you.'

'Syd,' echoed Birdy, 'and –' he didn't repeat 'Hicky'.

'Any – any of the kids in?'

'Dunno.'

'Look here,' said Birdy, and licked his lips again, 'we got to make sure they don't 'urt the kids. You better go rahnd to the Pie Shop, or git Dais to go, or telephone, see.'

'Okay, but what about you?'

Birdy said: 'I'll be okay.' He twisted his lips into a smile that called for a lot of courage, and did nothing to betray the suffocating fear which made his heart beat with a kind of sluggish reluctance. 'I'll lie low for a bit, don'chew worry.'

'But Birdy –' Ethel looked, felt and sounded anguished.

'You look arter yourself,' Birdy urged, 'and leave me to look arter myself, Ethel. Scram, ducky.' He gave her a slap, then turned away from the surging, growling traffic towards the bowels of the earth and the Underground that swallowed London's millions, gestated, and then spewed them up. A train was roaring down below. It stopped. A great surge of people, all eyes blinking, came up the wide stairs towards the welcoming light. Birdy was pressed against the wall, close to a colourful kiosk, where a shiny-haired woman began to serve as fast as she could.

Then the crowd passed and for a moment there was calm.

Birdy had only one idea; to get away from here. There was no safety in the East End. There was little safety anywhere, once 'they' came after him, or after anyone. He knew, because he had been on the run once before, and it had lasted for several weeks – until the police had cleaned up the gang that had come for him.

Now, he fingered the scar beneath his right eye; a vitriol scar. He still didn't know what had saved him from being blinded.

He reached the top of the stairs. A man wearing a purple choker, a lightweight, American-style coat with big stains on the wide lapels, was at the foot, grinning up at him. In the distance, another train rumbled.

Birdy missed a step when he saw the man. He did not reason, because panic came too close. The only sound he could hear now was the banging of his heart; painful, frightening. This meant that 'they' were out in strength. The Murphy Gang was the strongest in London at the moment, twenty or thirty strong. Like all the successful gangs, and those which flourished at all, it restricted its activities, worked mostly within the G5 boundary, and operated mostly against rival crooks. It had cannibal instincts. Its members were brutish, sadistic and utterly without scruple. It wasn't a gang in the sense that it had headquarters or acted in concert, but only in that it accepted Murphy's leadership. He got the jobs, paid the men off, gave them protection; he would hide them, get them alibis, do anything that was necessary to keep them safe from the law – and he would get his man. Now he had been given a job, and Birdy thought he knew who had given it to him.

Chang.

The job was simply to 'get' Birdy.

Birdy knew nothing at all beyond that. It might mean to kill him; it might mean to maim him; it might mean to torture him. There was no end to what it might mean, and that was one of the worst fears: the uncertainty. Only two weeks ago, 'they'd' gone after that poor little cove, Charlie Lin. Lin, half Chinese, half Cockney, was runner for a fence, and had kept more than his share of payment for a job. He had probably been cheated for years and driven to desperation, running the risks of taking money to the thief and the hot goods to the fence. He'd kept back a fiver, and the fence had hired Murphy.

One part of Birdy's mind told him that the fence wouldn't have done that if a fiver had been the only thing at stake. More likely, the fence was frightened in case Lin squealed.

Lin was in hospital being well looked-after. At least he wasn't frightened any more. They'd amputated his right leg and the fingers of his left hand, and there was some doubt whether he would ever be able to see again. He'd been found in a battered heap in a rubber warehouse, and there was no trace of the brutes who had done it, although the East End – including G5 Division – knew that it had been a Murphy job.

Murphy hadn't laid a hand on Lin.

No one knew who had – for Murphy would have given the order to four or five of the boys, who wouldn't talk except among themselves. One might have a drink too many and say what he shouldn't, but that didn't happen very often. Usually orders were given at a café in the Mile End Road – a place called Shippy's, after its owner, whose name was Shipham.

'Shippy's' was a byword.

Well, there was Lin.

There was the swaggering man with the broad grin at the foot of the steps.

Birdy turned away as a train rumbled in, another one from the West End. This would disgorge its hundreds, too. He hurried to get out of the station first and then saw Ali.

Ali was a lascar.

No one knew when Ali had last been aboard ship, and it didn't matter. He was a little Indian who spoke broken English, had smooth, dark skin, beautiful black eyes and beautiful, shiny black hair; a model for any painter. No one quite knew what went on in his mind, no one quite knew what he did with his days, but they knew him for a remarkably able knife artist. Ali could carve patterns on cheek or belly, arm or breast. He was lounging against the telephone kiosk, with his right hand in his pocket.

He was right-handed.

Birdy missed a step.

A policeman, big and genial, and hot in thick serge, came along, saw Ali, and lost his smile. Ali had never been inside and had never had his prints taken, and it was the oath of every man on the beat in the Division to get him. Ali stared back at the policeman. He didn't smile, either, but looked with an unmistakable impudence which could make a level-headed policeman lose his temper. The temptation to break Ali's neck was sometimes overpowering.

The train roared into the station.

Birdy waited. The policeman walked on, but took up a position, as if Ali's expression warned him of impending trouble and he meant to stop it. Then the crowd surged up the steps, caught up with Birdy and swept him out of the wide open mouth and past Ali. He caught a glimpse of Ali trying to breast the tide of humanity and keep level, but pilgrims bathing in the Holy Water of the Ganges could not have kept him away more successfully.

Birdy nipped across the road.

No member of Murphy's gang was in sight, as far as he could judge, but he didn't know all of Murphy's gang; no one did. That was another of the factors which made it unspeakable horror to be hunted by the gang. Birdy could go to the police and ask for protection, and he would get it for a while; only for a while. Once he did that he would cut off all hope for the future. The whole of the fraternity would turn against him, against Ethel and against the kids. They knew he squeaked sometimes, but they also knew that he squeaked only about dope, and that his daughter, by his first and real wife, had been an addict. They didn't blame Birdy for what he did, but if he stepped outside that one form of squeaking, they'd turn on him.

If he couldn't look after himself, they'd have no time for him either.

He was in this on his own and the heat was on. His hope was to get somewhere to lie low until it was off. The police might get Chang, and if Chang couldn't pay Murphy, Murphy wouldn't be interested. It was a matter of time.

Birdy turned down a narrow street leading towards Tower Hill. The East End was too hot for him, his best chance was down in the city, in one of the warehouses. One could live there for days, for weeks, without being seen, emerging only after dark, feeding at one of the little coffee stalls at Billingsgate. It would be dark in an hour and a half, if he could stay safe until after dark he would be all right.

There was another serious worry: Ethel.

Birdy was sweating.

Murphy would know that he wouldn't tell Ethel where he was going, wouldn't he? Murphy was bad, Murphy's gang didn't care whether they worked on a man or a woman, but they didn't waste their time. They'd be sure that he, Birdy, hadn't confided in Ethel –

Wouldn't they?

He reached the end of a narrow road which led to Tower Hill, and saw Lefty.

Lefty was a snowy-haired youth of nineteen, who looked cherubic enough for Leonardo. His strength was the broken beer bottle, thrust into a man's face and twisted. He was one of Murphy's gang.

Had he heard about the hunt for Birdy?

Birdy nipped back into a doorway, but didn't go fast enough. Lefty didn't smile, didn't change his expression, just sauntered towards Birdy. He wore a big, baggy, black jacket and there was a bulge, the kind of bulge likely to be made by a beer bottle with the neck smashed off. This was in his left-hand pocket. He was called Lefty for the obvious reason.

Birdy turned and ran.

Lefty didn't run; he whistled softly. It was only a matter of time.

Gideon looked at the clock; it was long after six. He yawned, but it was much too early to start yawning. This was a day which might last its full twenty-four hours. He knew himself well; what he needed now was a good meal, well-cooked vegetables and some good red meat, a pint of beer and forty winks. Once he'd put that inside him he would be all right, but he might not have time.

Lemaitre was out again.

The telephone bell rang.

'Gideon,' said Gideon. 'Oh, hallo, Fred, what's on?'

He listened, turned down his lips, made one or two notes, muttered an unenthusiastic thanks, and put the receiver down. He began to doodle on a blotting pad, and after a couple of minutes told himself that it was further evidence of the fact that he was running down and needed replenishing.

Lemaitre came in.

'George,' he said, as a man with a worry, 'I've just been downstairs to see my missus. Remember, I'm a married man? I forgot that I told her we'd go along for a snack to the Troc, and blow me, she's got tickets for the Arthur Askey show. If I can't go, *you've* got to tell her.' His anxiety was comical.

Gideon said: 'How long've you got?'

'She's come with the handcuffs,' Lemaitre said.

'About the only way they'll ever drag us away,' Gideon grunted. 'Wouldn't be a bad idea if we laid on a campaign. Now if Kate –' he drove the fanciful thought off. 'Okay, Lem, I don't know that there's anything to keep you.' What he did know was that this would keep him here until the small hours. 'Just had a word with Fred Hartley.'

' 'Bout Birdy?'

'Yes. The Murphy gang's out.'

Lemaitre said: 'Oh, gawd! Poor tick's had it now.'

'One day we'll get round to Murphy,' Gideon said. 'Anyway, Birdy's on the run. We're all looking out for him, and if our chaps find him first they'll pull him in on a charge. Not that Birdy'll want that. Still . . .' Gideon stood up, slowly. He felt very hungry, the kind of raw emptiness that affected one's nerves and muscles, made one sag, started the tight feeling at the back of the eyes. 'And Fred's worried about Birdy's woman and the two kids. So he's tipped off Black Jo, and Jo's looking after the family. Murphy won't risk a gang fight, I shouldn't think, but Black Jo won't lift a finger to help Birdy, although he'll help the woman. High Life in Civilized London!' He scratched his chin. 'Send for a sergeant, Lem, and then sort everything out so that it's in apple-pie order when I get back.'

'Okay. Where you going?'

'Across to the pub to get a square meal, and I'll tell Fifi about her good luck on the way.'

He was smiling when he went outside; he always smiled when he thought of Lemaitre's wife as Fifi, which was her real name. A French grandmother's influence – or was it grandfather? Skittish little blonde, no better than she ought to be, but then, Lem Lemaitre wasn't exactly a one-woman man. The frailty of human nature –

Fifi was in the main hall and there was an exceptionally good-looking constable on duty there. She was overdressed in a plum-coloured suit and a cherry-and-plum hat, and didn't look bored. Gideon told her Lem would be down in a few minutes, and then walked across the yard towards

Cannon Row and the convenient pub where he knew he could get a meal that any trencherman would enjoy. He could afford to relax for half an hour or so, too. It was easy to forget that the Yard didn't stop working, whatever he or anyone else did. Thousands of coppers were on the look-out for that Austin with a Michelin tyre, and there was just a chance that they'd have some luck to-night.

Odd thing, that tyre.

He thought about it a lot during the meal – roast saddle of mutton, mint sauce and new potatoes, with rich, fatty gravy – probably the potatoes came out of a tin, but they had the true Jersey flavour. He ploughed steadily through the meal, refusing to be hurried, making it clear that he didn't want to talk to the other Yard men, the reporters and a couple of sergeants from Cannon Row Police Station who were at the bar.

Chang – Foster – the Battersea riverside – the Waterloo Station job. If it were the same tyre, and there wasn't much doubt, this could really lead to something big. But it connected Chang with some of the post office robberies, and that was a very nasty possibility. The worst thing about the mail van jobs were the tips that the robbers had in advance. They always knew when a van would have a valuable load on, they knew when it would leave one place and was due at another; and of late, Yard men on duty at key points had been attacked and prevented from going to the rescue. To-day's two morning jobs had suggested a break in the system, but now –

Had Foster been one source of the leakage?

Foster wouldn't have known anything about the Waterloo job, would he?

The door opened, and King-Hadden, the Superintendent of *Fingerprints*, came in. If Gideon had a close friend at the Yard, as apart from a mass of good friends with mutual liking, it was King-Hadden. This man had succeeded one of the most brilliant fingerprint men the Yard had ever had, and he wasn't doing so badly. In fact, what King-Hadden didn't know about prints no one knew. He was a world authority, and in the middle-forties; he couldn't get any higher.

'Hallo, George.'

'Come and sit down, Nick.'

'Thanks.' The barmaid's help hovered. 'Bessie – double whisky and not too much soda, please.' He dropped down into a chair opposite Gideon. 'Got some good news for you, chum,' he said.

'Wassat?' Gideon's mouth was full of succulent roast potato, oozing fat.

King-Hadden grinned as he took a small envelope from his inside breast pocket. He was a big, plump, pale, rather shapeless man, whose intelligent eyes usually held a laugh. Coins chinked in the envelope. He opened it, and let three sixpences roll out on to the cloth; two of them were stained slightly, as if with brown wax.

Gideon knew a dried bloodstain when he saw it.

'Prints on two,' said King-Hadden, 'middle of the thumb, right index finger – could be the left. It depends on what pocket he had the money in.'

'Who and what money?'

'The Islington shop job.'

Gideon said sharply: 'No!'

'Yes. This was found on the pavement at a bus stop this afternoon. The kid who saw it was being watched by a copper. He recognized bloodstains. They fell out of the pocket of a man dressed in a brown suit, who was waiting for a bus at Islington Town Hall. That's five minutes' walk away from the shop where the old woman was killed. About the time of the job, too. The copper kept his wits about him, lot of good to be said for training some of the uniformed boys in C.I.D. work, whatever there is against it. He turned them into the Division.'

Gideon said: 'Any record?' as if it were too much to hope.

'Oh, yes,' said King-Hadden blandly, 'didn't I tell you?' He looked smug and his eyes glistened. 'Identified them as the prints of Arthur George Fessell, who's been inside twice for robbery with violence. The call's gone out for him. See – all we do is your work, while you sit gluttonizing!' He glanced up. 'Ta, Bessie, I'll drink your health.' He picked up a whisky and soda, sniffed it, and sipped. 'Ah, I needed that. Going home?'

'To-morrow, maybe!'

'Well, I'm off now,' said King-Hadden, 'I keep my department up to date. Cheers. By the way, there's another little thing that may amuse you. They've picked up that Austin with the Michelin tyre you've been making such a fuss about. Parked in Haymarket. Lemaitre's over there, waiting until the driver turns up for it, and his Fifi's giving him merry hell. Cheers,' King-Hadden repeated, and sipped again.

Bessie, flat-breasted and big-handed, approached them again.

'Want any sweet, Mr. Gideon?'

Gideon was rubbing his hands together and looking as pleased as a prizewinner schoolboy.

'I do, Bessie,' he said. 'Treacle pudding's on, isn't it? Plenty of treacle, remember. And after that a bit of Dorset Blue and some butter. This isn't such a bad day after all,' he confided in King-Hadden. 'We got Sayer, we've got a line on the Islington chap, Fessell you say? and now this tyre – not at *all* a bad day. Let me buy you a drink.'

'One's enough before I drive to the danger of the public,' said the flabby man. 'How's Kate?'

'Fine!'

'Must have a Sunday together again when the weather gets a bit better,' said King-Hadden. 'Might make it this week-end if it keeps like to-day. Meg'd like it. Well, good luck, hope you catch 'em all, but don't forget the day's only just started!' He sipped again. 'Be a funny thing if we could sit back now and know in advance what's going to happen to-night, wouldn't it? What's sure to happen? A dozen burglaries, a murder, dopies getting dopier, girls being laid for the first time, someone sitting back and plotting a coup for to-morrow, someone getting rid of the thirty thousand quid they picked up at Waterloo – who'd be a copper?' He finished his drink. 'So long, George.'

He went out.

Two minutes later Birdy's wife came in.

CHAPTER 12

TWO TALES OF JEWELLERY

Gideon recognized Ethel Merrick on the instant, long before she saw him. He judged from the expression on the faces of some of the other men that they also recognized her. She stood there, wearing a grey suit and a white blouse, a huge, frilly blouse which was stretched so tightly that it looked as if someone had stuffed it as sausage meat or sage and onions in a turkey. She had on a coat that was too small for her and strained open at the front. Her small red hat had a blue feather broken at the tip and her patent leather shoes had very high heels. No one could fail to see her distress, no one could miss the graceful shapeliness of those calves and ankles.

Then she saw Gideon, opened her mouth, gulped, and walked towards him.

He stood up.

No one else watched now.

'Hallo, Mrs. Merrick,' Gideon said, 'come and sit down.'

He could hear her agitated, bubbly breathing, almost as if she were asthmatic. She was pale, her forehead and upper lip were wet with sweat. Gideon pulled out a chair, and she licked her lips as she sat down, and then eased her coat under the right arm. Bessie, who had a wonderful sense of timing, appeared with the treacle pudding.

'What will you have, Mrs. Merrick?' asked Gideon.

'Oo, thanks ever so!' Ethel caught her breath. 'Could I – could I 'ave a gin and It, I need to buck meself up a bit.'

'Of course you can. Double gin and a splash of Italian, Bessie,' said Gideon. 'Cigarette, Mrs. Merrick?' The big case, with one side filled with cigarettes, the other half empty, was held out in front of her.

'Ta,' she breathed, and when she had settled down, added gustily: 'It's ever so good of you to make me feel at home like this, Mr. Gideon, I wouldn't have come if I wasn't so worried about Birdy.' Then her fear affected her words. 'They – they're *arter* him.'

Gideon said calmly: 'Who is, d'you know?'

'Why, Murphy's gang! Mr. Gideon, I know Birdy's done a lot of criminal things, but – oo, *ta*, dearie.' She almost snatched the glass out of Bessie's hand, for Bessie also had a trick of speed when it was necessary, and gulped. 'Oo, that's better. But he's not bad like some people, like that Murphy for instance. He –'

'Has Murphy threatened you?' asked Gideon hopefully.

'Well, no, not in so many words, but that don't count, do it? He come and asked where Birdy was, said he just had to see him, that's enough for me. Mr. Gideon, can't you pull Birdy in?'

'He's got a clean sheet these past few weeks, Mrs. Merrick.'

'Oh,' said Ethel Merrick, ' 'e 'as, 'as 'e?' She had given up the struggle with aspirates. 'Well, it's not that I like squealing on me own ole man, but don'chew believe it. Remember the Marshall Street jeweller's job? That was Birdy! Got some of the rings at home now, 'e – 'e 'id them,' she added hastily. 'I come across them by accident. Ain't that enough, Mr. Gideon?'

It was plenty.

She knew that if she appealed for police help against Murphy, it would do Birdy a lot of harm. She knew that she dared not go to the Division, because it would be reported. She also knew that if the police wanted Birdy for a 'job' it would be a different matter. He would get at least three years if he were sent down for the Marshall Street robbery, and she thought it worth sending him down; that was a measure of her fear.

Gideon didn't want Birdy inside, but he'd have to put him there.

'All right, Mrs. Merrick,' he said, 'I'll do what I can. We knew that Birdy was in trouble and we're looking out for him. Don't worry too much. This'll have to be done from the local station, you know that –'

'So long as you'll fix it,' Ethel pleaded.

Gideon went across to the Yard and 'fixed it'.

There was no news of Birdy. There was no further word from Lemaitre. Fifi was probably on her way to the theatre by herself, now – Gideon hoped she would not pick up a 'friend'. The only man at the Yard who didn't know most of what there was to know about Fifi was Lemaitre.

Gideon forgot that.

There was the fingerprint job that King-Hadden had done, and now that he saw photographs of the coins, enlarged to ten times their real size, he was able to marvel at the efficiency of King-Hadden's work; the fragment of the fingerprint on the bloodstained coins was so fractional that few men would have tried to identify it. With luck, it would hang Fessell, whose dossier was on Gideon's desk. It made ugly reading.

Gideon began to wonder wryly about King-Hadden's airy talk of the day 'just beginning'.

Dusk was falling, the day's brightness had quite gone, there were lights at some of the windows across the courtyards, and he could see lights on the cars and buses which passed along Parliament Street; he could see a few yards of the street from the window, too.

What was certain to happen? King-Hadden had asked.

Burglary; robbery with violence; murder – no, it wasn't as bad as that yet, murder was certain once or twice a week, but not once a day. There was the whole range of crimes, from major to minor. At this moment men were getting themselves into the toils of women who would never let go, blackmail was being nurtured, frightened people were blustering, there were young girls, perhaps completely innocent girls like Penelope, girls much younger than Pru, smoking their first reefer, feeling a terrific excitement and a tremendous kick and not knowing that they were on the way down to hell upon earth.

Somewhere men and women were out at dinner or at the pictures, who would go home and find their houses burgled. People were sitting at their own table at this very moment, not knowing that a thief had broken in and was even now raiding the woman's bedroom above their heads. It was a never-ending cycle. Gideon's one hope was that whatever happened, it would happen in such a way that he did not have to tackle anything new to-night.

His telephone rang.

'Gideon.'

'There's a Mrs. Addinson here, sir,' the hall sergeant told him. 'She would be glad if you could spare her a few minutes.'

Foster's sister had made up, and dressed for effect. Black suited her, the white blouse and cuffs gave a touch of purity. Nice-looking, wholesome woman. Only her eyes hinted at strain, and this eased when Gideon made her welcome and gave her a cigarette. No two women could contrast more sharply than Florence Addinson and Birdy's 'wife'.

'What can I do for you, Mrs. Addinson?' Gideon was almost casual.

'I've come because I think I can help you,' she said.

Gideon didn't show how that quickened his pulse.

'That's good. How?'

'I've been going over everything that Eric's been doing and saying,' she said 'We had a – a quarrel a night or two ago, because he was never in. He used to pretend he was always on duty, but I knew he wasn't. I said so, and – and he flared up.'

'I see,' Gideon said. He did not intend to help her; just to let it come. There was still the possibility that she was involved, even though her visit made that seem less likely.

'You may not think so, but I really want to help,' she said, a little sharply. 'I'm reconciled to the fact that Eric was – was doing wrong. I'd like to think that whoever made him do it suffers, too.'

Gideon relaxed.

'You don't want that any more than we do.' He looked almost eager. 'Really think you can help?'

'I'm not sure, but something he said might give you something to go on – unless you *know* who bribed him.' She added that so quickly and unexpectedly that it was possible to believe that it was the focal point of her visit; that she had really come to try to find out how much he knew.

Would Chang, would anyone, venture such tactics?

Gideon just couldn't be sure.

'We guess a lot,' he said, and left it at that. 'What was it that your brother said?'

'He was really talking to himself,' Foster's sister answered. 'As he was going out of the room, he said: "I'd be a damned sight better off living with Estelle." I didn't know whom he meant, I'd never heard him talk of a girl named Estelle. But a woman of that name telephoned me this evening.'

Now she really sparked Gideon's interest.

'Oh? What about? Eric?'

'Yes,' Foster's sister said wryly. 'She said that Eric had been murdered. She sounded quite hysterical, and rang off before I could get any more sense out of her.' Flo Addinson paused, eyeing Gideon very intently, before she went on: 'Was Eric murdered?'

Gideon answered bluntly: 'It's just possible.'

After a pause, Foster's sister said quietly: 'Thank you. I thought you might look for this woman, Estelle.'

'Believe me, we'll look for her,' Gideon promised. 'You've given us a lead which might be invaluable. If there's anything else –

'There's just one thing,' she said. 'I'd like to help actively, and I think I might be able to.'

Now, he was wary. 'How, Mrs. Addinson?'

'I could harass Chang,' she said. 'There's a picture of a dancer outside his office, and her name's Estelle. It could be the same one.'

How Lemaitre would benefit from some of her caution! 'I thought if I went to see Chang, asked him about what really happened, asked about Eric and Estelle –'

'No,' Gideon was abrupt, 'leave Estelle right out of it, you'd only warn Chang that we were interested in her. I'll check the dancer, though, that's most useful.'

He stopped.

'May I try to harass Chang?' she asked, and then added very quickly, almost fiercely: 'I don't think anything could keep me away, but if – if you could suggest how to handle him –'

Gideon chuckled.

'Not bad,' he said. 'Admire your honesty, Mrs. Addinson. I don't think you'll ever be able to shake Chang, but you might be able to try one angle.'

She leaned forward eagerly.

'If there was an association between Chang and your brother, and Chang thinks your brother confided in you, he'll be very edgy,' Gideon said. 'Edgy men make mistakes. Hm.' He hesitated. 'Hm, yes,' he repeated. 'Go along and see him, Mrs. Addinson, give him cause to think you know something. He'll probably try to square you, although he might conceivably try to harm –'

'Oh, he wouldn't dare *that*,' she exclaimed. 'Not if I told him you were having me followed.'

Gideon shook his head sagely.

'You've got a head for this kind of thing,' he conceded. 'We'll follow you, all right. Go home, Mrs. Addinson, and wait for word from us. We won't keep you long.'

They shook hands and he walked with her to the lift. As she went down, he watched and reflected that she was a very fine-looking, finely-built woman.

Five minutes later he'd laid on inquiries about the unknown Estelle, and made arrangements for Foster's sister to be followed. After that he was able to work for twenty minutes without being interrupted.

Perhaps it was going to be a quiet night, after all.

He knew nothing of Alec Fitzroy.

Fitzroy was in his West End flat, not very far from Chang's restaurant, but just outside the fringes of Soho. He stood in the tiny bathroom, shaving. His hand was absolutely steady; he was testing his nerve, making quite sure that it wouldn't let him down.

When he had finished shaving, he felt quite confident.

He left the bathroom, lit a cigarette, and looked at a decanter of whisky. He wanted a drink, but told himself that it might be a sign of weakness, and that he ought not to have one.

He put the temptation behind him by going into his bedroom. He sat on the side of the bed and went carefully through all the plans to rob the safe deposit in Wattle Street. Nothing was written down, and only he knew all the arrangements for the coup. He did not trust either of his cronies with everything, although they were reliable enough.

It would be necessary to start for the safe deposit building soon. The others, who had further to travel, were already on their way. The escape car was parked – a car which had been left near the Mid-Union Safe Deposit building nightly for several weeks, so there would be nothing unusual about it to-night – except that when it was driven off it would be carrying a fortune.

He checked over every single part of the plan and decided again that it was foolproof.

He jumped up, lit a cigarette, and went into the living-room. This time he didn't argue with himself but poured a tot of whisky and tossed it down. He felt angry because of the word 'foolproof'; he told himself that his attitude was completely realistic, and only a fool would call this a job which couldn't go wrong.

It wasn't likely to but it could.

If an inspector or official of the Mid-Union Company were to visit the safe deposit, he would be familiar with all the night staff and, seeing strangers, he would certainly try to raise an alarm. But he'd be bound to ask questions and so give his own identity away. He could be dealt with before doing any harm, like the other members of the night staff would be.

Perhaps it wasn't foolproof; but it certainly wasn't far short.

Fitzroy went back into the bedroom, knelt down in front of a dressing chest, opened the bottom drawer, and rummaged among the underclothes in it.

He drew out a gun and some ammunition. He loaded the gun, a .32 automatic, and slipped it into his pocket. Then he went and had another whisky. Then he left his flat.

The little widow with whom the Reverend Julian Small lodged watched him as he sat at the table that evening, toying with his food. She was a woman of mercifully few words, one of the few regular churchgoers in the district, and a familiar if faded figure at St. Mary's. She was fond of the new curate, but knew as well as he did that the task was too big for him; at least, he showed no sign that he would ever be able to handle it well.

He was far too gentle.

She was surprised by that in some ways. When his luggage had arrived a few months ago, and she had looked through it, she had found boxing gloves and other things to indicate that he was a dab at games and sports. So when the weedy-looking, rather timid man with the narrow nostrils had arrived on the doorstep, she hadn't realized that it was her lodger.

She had given up hope for him now.

Julian Small had almost given up hope for himself.

He had not properly recovered from the fall that morning. His nose was raw as well as red and painful whenever he touched it, which was often because he had a slight cold. His bitterness had gone, however, and in its place there was a sense of shame – that he should have betrayed his trust as he had; 'suffer little children –'

He could not find the way to their confidence or their friendship. It wasn't their fault, it was his.

He did not wholly convince himself of that, but he had one narrow wedge of hope; the Club to-night. It was officially the St. Mary's Club and twenty-odd years old, but when he had arrived there had been the bare hall, a few pieces of damaged furniture, a table-tennis top with the plywood warped and chipped, a dart-board so badly eaten away by the darts over the years that some holes showed right through. Small had put all this right. There were three new dart-boards, a regulation-size table-tennis top with trestles, draughts, dominoes, chess, a small library, and, what he regarded as more important than anything else, plenty of comfortable chairs. Thirty youngsters could sit in upholstered comfort and read books or magazines taken from the Club library. There was also a small bar, offering coffee, tea, soft drinks, cakes and biscuits. In fact, everything that a flourishing club of a hundred or so youths could revel in, and –

The Club had *eleven* members.

Usually, most of these failed to appear on Club nights: Mondays, Wednesdays, Fridays and Saturdays. No one had ever said so to the curate, but he believed that the others had been intimidated by youths who didn't come; or else made to feel ridiculous for having anything to do with him.

There was to be a special effort to-night; each member was to try to bring one new member. Until the string incident, Julian Small had told himself that it might be the turn of the tide, and, as he set out from his lodgings for the hall next to the church, he tried to induce a cheerful mood.

Twenty-two lads and lassies instead of one would make all the difference.

Lights were on in the hall.

It was very quiet.

He realized that this was partly due to the fact that the noises of cranes and derricks were missing. So were all the usual sounds which came from the docks by night. He didn't think much about this, but wondered how many would in fact turn up. Twenty-two was absurdly optimistic. Fifteen? Sixteen? He shivered with a kind of excitement as he drew nearer the hall; fifteen would make it a successful evening, and give him hope for the future.

He glanced across at a light fixed to the wall of a ruined warehouse nearby. Some movement by it caught his eye but he couldn't identify the movement. He took no notice until suddenly the warehouse wall light went out.

That made him miss a step.

Tight-lipped, he strode on to the hall. The door was open, light shone out from it, but he saw no one and heard nothing.

He reached it . . .

He stood quite still on the threshold, feeling almost choked. Nothing was in its proper place. The table-tennis top was in pieces, strewn about the floor; an axe had been used violently. Pieces of a dart-board were almost under his feet, as small as corks. Books were ripped open, pages strewed the scrubbed floor like pieces of giant confetti. And the chairs –

There wasn't a whole chair left.

He went in, falteringly. He looked round at this savage destruction of his hopes and at the shocking waste of money which he had needed for himself. He looked round, forgetful of his thin, bruised nose, aware only of disaster.

Then, slowly, he spoke to the deserted room.

'If I ever set my hands on them,' he said, 'I'll break their bloody necks.'

Suddenly, without having been given the slightest warning, he felt in a different mood from anything he had known before. He was savagely, viciously angry.

Also, unknown to Gideon, there was Rose Bray.

Rose, at sixteen, was in her first job, and although all of her friends had scoffed when she had said what she was going to do, she was revelling in it. She was a lady's maid. She had a modest but nice little home with her parents in Acton, and had been to school until she was nearly sixteen. She knew shorthand typing and was qualified for many other varieties of jobs, but chose to be a lady's maid.

She liked beautiful clothes.

It was not the kind of liking that creates envy. She was content just to see and handle them, to help dress Lady Muriel, who was nice and natural, not at all like she'd expected real ladies to be – so high falutin' and imperious. 'Imperious' was a word which Rose's boy friend had used with great scorn when she had told him what she was going to do.

'These rich people,' he had added smartingly, 'just a lot of wealthy tarts, that's all they are.' And after a moment's pause for research: 'Just a lot of *para*sites.'

Rose was thinking about her boy friend at the time that Gideon was looking up at the brown spot in the ceiling, without wondering how it had come there. She was thinking that if Dick only knew Lady Muriel and her husband – who wasn't a Lord or a Sir, she didn't quite understand the reason for that but accepted it – he would have an entirely different idea about the wealthy. Certainly they *were* rich. The diamond necklace which Lady Muriel had left on the dressing-table was worth at least fifteen *years'* wages for her father. The value did not intrigue Rose so much as the beauty, and Rose preferred coloured jewels to diamonds, which seemed to her so cold.

But more than precious stones, she loved the clothes; the rich satins, the smooth velvets, the tulles, the luxurious silks, the colours which were so beautiful that they often made her catch her breath. There were three large wardrobes, all filled with clothes, but Rose's favourites were in the dressing-room: the evening gowns and cocktail dresses.

Sometimes she would open the door, just to look at and to touch the materials.

Many things here had taken some getting used to; this room, for one. It had two doors, one opening into the passage, the other into the bedroom. And across the bedroom, with its two high beds, the rich, soft bedclothes and the twin canopies, each rather like a big baby's crib – was *his* dressing-room. Rose did not go in there much; just occasionally to get something if his valet, Forbes, was out.

Rose did not like Forbes. She could not have explained why, but she didn't trust him.

That evening, Lady Muriel and Mr. Simister were downstairs with friends. About a dozen in all; just a little informal cocktail party, Lady Muriel had said, as she had carelessly selected a dress which had cost over a hundred guineas. Rose was probably one of the few remaining people who could admire such an attitude towards money.

She stood looking at a rich, red velvet gown, and felt irresistibly drawn towards it, longing to smooth the pile of the velvet between her fingers.

She heard a sound in the bedroom.

It did not occur to her that anything was wrong, but she assumed that Lady Muriel had come upstairs for something she'd forgotten. The carpet on the floor of the dressing-room was thick, muffling the sound of her footsteps as she went towards the communicating door.

She actually began to open it and then saw the man.

He was crouching over the dressing-table. In his right hand was the diamond necklace. There were other jewels in the trinket box which he had taken out of a drawer; a drawer usually kept locked. He didn't look up. She couldn't see his face because of the brown scarf which was drawn up over his nose, but she saw that he wore gloves which looked skin tight.

After the first shock, Rose felt just one thing: fear. It made her want to run away crying for help. Her heart suddenly began to beat so fast that she felt as if she were choking. She knew that her cheeks went chalk-white. She watched, hypnotized, as the man thrust the jewels into a small bag – it looked rather like a chamois-leather, the kind window-cleaners used. She heard the hard stones grate against each other.

She knew what she had to do, if only she could make her legs do what she told them. It was difficult even to turn round. She let the door go, and managed to turn, then stood quite still; her legs simply would not move. Gradually, she made them. She reached the passage door, which was closed, turned the handle and pulled; the door scraped along the carpet and the sound seemed very loud to her.

If only Forbes would come.

She heard no other sound. The big house in Madeson Square overlooking beech and plane trees and a small grass plot where the people of the square aired and exercised their dogs, was solid and silent. A door closed out sound as well as sight.

The passage was carpeted.

She crept out of the dressing-room and now she found that her legs wanted to move too quickly, wanted to run. She dared not. She must go past that door and then downstairs to raise the alarm; if she shouted or if she ran she would warn the thief and he would get away.

Being out here, with the bedroom door closed, she felt safe; excitement replaced the panicky fear. Suddenly she saw herself as the heroine; the girl who had saved Lady Muriel's jewels. It would be easy! She tip-toed towards the door – yes, it was closed, just as it had been when she had passed. It wasn't far to the head of the stairs, and once she reached them she could hurry down.

She drew level with the door.

It opened and the thief grabbed at her.

CHAPTER 13

THE THIEF

Rose saw the door open, the grasping hand, the masked face, in the same awful moment of fear. She opened her mouth wide to scream, but the thief slapped her face. He hurt less than he terrified her. She choked back the scream. He shifted his grip, took her wrist and dragged her into the bedroom.

The door slammed.

'Don't make a sound or I'll break your neck,' he growled behind the mask.

She could not have made a sound then, even to save her neck. He was hurting her arm and pulled her across the room towards the beds. *Towards the beds*. Then he changed the direction, first pulled and then pushed her into a corner. She did not realize that here they were safe from the sight of anyone outside, especially the people on the other side of the square.

'Keep your voice low. Have you warned anyone?'

She couldn't get a word out, could only make the shape of the words: '*No, no, no!*'

'If you're lying to me, I'll –'

'*No, no, no!*'

'You'd better be telling the truth,' he said roughly. 'Turn round.'

'*No!*' That gasp came out.

'Turn round!' he said in a harsh whisper, and pulled at her shoulder. She gasped again and turned helplessly. Then something fell over her head; she started to scream until it reached her mouth, thick and muffling; then it was drawn tight, and she could hardly breathe. Next moment, she felt her hands seized, felt tightness at her wrists, and then realized that he had tied her wrists together behind her.

He spun her round again.

'Sit down,' he said, and before she could realize what the order meant, he bent down and picked her up, then dumped her heavily on the floor. With her hands behind her she couldn't get up easily. The scarf or whatever it was still forced itself into her mouth, and she was struggling for breath.

He left her.

He must have spent another three or four minutes at the dressing-table, cramming things into the wash-leather bag. Then he turned away, and took notice of her again. She had not recovered from the first fear and all this made it much, much worse.

'Now what am I going to do with you?' he said softly. 'If you raise the alarm –'

He came towards her slowly. She wanted to cry out that she wouldn't raise the alarm, if only he would go she'd never say a word to anyone; but she couldn't utter a sound of any kind. He stood looking down at her. He wasn't really very big, but from that angle he looked enormous, and she was absolutely in his power. All the stories of murder she had ever heard about seemed to flash through her mind.

'Get up,' he said, as if he had made up his mind what to do, and she cringed away from him. He bent down, took her waist, and pulled her to her feet. Then he pushed her towards the dressing-room. Her legs moved automatically, she thought she was bound to fall on her face.

The lovely clothes were in the wardrobe.

'Just the job,' he said, and hustled her forward. 'Get in.' He meant, 'get into the wardrobe with the clothes'. 'Go on, Rosie, get in, I won't hurt you!'

She was breathing through her nose, and felt as if she could never breathe freely again, was almost choked. And she was too frightened to believe what he said. Something made him change his mind, too. He stretched out an arm to her shoulder, turned her round, and loosened the scarf round her mouth; it dropped to her neck.

'My, my,' he said, 'you're quite something, pity we didn't meet some other place.'

Suddenly he pulled her to him and squeezed her. She felt his hard, lean body, the thudding of his heart. She felt the surge of desire in him, too, and a different fear began to choke her. She couldn't breathe, she felt his hands –

He let her go.

'Get inside,' he said harshly, 'and if you open your trap for the next five minutes, you'll wish you'd never been born.'

He thrust her back among the luxurious dresses, among thousands of pounds' worth of the most exclusive models by the world's great designers, and then closed the door. She heard the key in the lock. She leaned back against a velvet gown, slipping further and further down, still frightened, and also disturbed in a different way. She could not forget the hardness of his body against her.

Then she slipped down until she was almost full length on the floor. With her hands behind her, she could turn round. It was blackly dark. She felt herself breathing evenly, but fear soon began to catch up, like the sea sweeping over her in waves.

She shouted and the sound was muffled, she knew that it couldn't be heard.

She started to struggle and to shout, and was terrified. The blackness became thick, oily, choking, throttling; the blackness became peopled with strange shapes, strange, bright, dazzling, blinding colours. After a while she was screaming without knowing what she was doing . . .

Then the door opened:

'Good Lord!' exclaimed Lady Muriel's husband. 'What – here, Inspector, here's the maid, here she is!'

Rose felt much better.

Everyone had been very kind, especially Lady Muriel and Mr. Simister. The police had been quite nice, too. The man Mr. Simister called Inspector was ever so young, really. She'd had some hot coffee, very sweet, and then a weak whisky and water, and the doctor – Lady Muriel's own doctor – had been and examined her, and said that she wouldn't suffer much harm. Then the Inspector had started to question her, making her remember everything she had seen and everything that had been said. She didn't like it. Twice Lady Muriel asked him if it were really necessary, and in a firm but friendly way he said it was essential.

Then something he said made her remember that the thief had called her Rosie.

'Are you sure?' The Inspector's voice sharpened.

'Oh, yes! Of course I am.'

'How often did he use your name?'

'Well, only once, I remember . . .'

A few minutes afterwards, the Inspector spoke to Mr. Simister in a voice which Rose was supposed not to hear but which she heard quite clearly:

'If it's someone who knew the name of the maid, it suggests co-operation from your staff. And a key to the trinket box was used, remember. I think I'd better see the staff at once, Mr. Simister, especially anyone who knew this suite well.'

Lady Muriel said in a startled voice: 'Not *Forbes*.'

'Don't be silly, darling,' Mr. Simister said sharply.

There was a moment almost of conflict; then Lady Muriel turned to Rose.

'You look tired, Rose, and I'm sure the Inspector won't want you any more now.' Her glance at the Inspector suggested that he had better not. 'Come along to the morning room, and I'll get you something.'

She put a hand on Rose's arm.

It was rather wonderful, Rose thought, walking side by side with Lady Muriel, who was a head taller, very, *very* beautiful, and wearing that lovely cocktail gown which was full of rich colours. It was almost like walking alongside a friend.

Behind them, Mr. Simister was talking worriedly to the Inspector.

The office was stuffy. April was behaving oddly, you could usually rely on a chilly evening, but even with the windows open it was warm. Gideon had his coat off, his waistcoat open, his tie hanging down, his sleeves rolled up. For once his hair was ruffled. He was talking first into one telephone and then into another, putting down and lifting receivers as if he were juggling with Indian clubs. The smooth transition from one case to the next came much in the way that a brilliant linguist can change from one language to another without any apparent interruption in thought.

And Gideon made notes.

'That you, Adams – anything doing in the Madeson Square job? . . . Hmm . . . No, don't bring the valet over here unless you're pretty sure he's involved, no need to put a foot wrong. . . . Yes, old chap, watch him if you like. . . . How's the maid, what's her name? . . . Yes, Rose . . . Good. Any prints? . . . Hmm, looks as if the valet's the chief hope. 'Bye.'

There was hardly a pause before he turned to the other telephone, already in his left hand.

'Hallo, Lem, sorry to keep you. Any luck? . . .' He chuckled. 'And you stood Fifi up for this, you're going to know all about it! . . . I know it's not funny, calm down . . . Well, stay there if you like, we certainly want that chap. Think he's been along already and noticed that the car's being watched? . . . Who've you got with you?'

The other bell started to ring. Gideon lifted the receiver and switched to it swiftly: 'Hold on, please.' He went back to Lemaitre. 'Well, he doesn't look so much like a copper as some of 'em. Give it another hour. 'Bye.'

'Hallo . . .?'

'Oh, Fred, thanks for calling. Any news of Birdy? . . . Pity . . . Found that junk at his house, did you? Well, spread the story round, won't you, then if we pick him up his friends and neighbours will know it's because he's wanted; it won't look as if he came to us for protection. . . . No, I know he didn't. . . . So do I.'

There was a moment's lull.

'So do I,' he repeated, and meant that he hoped that the Divisional people found Birdy.

The hell of this was that a gang like Murphy's could act almost with impunity; *almost*.

He pulled his wad of notes towards him. These were the scribbled notes he had started to make from the moment he'd come in that morning. Everything that had been attended to he crossed off; only half a dozen items remained, and he wrote these out on a fresh slip of paper. They were mostly trifles, and among them was:

Check Basil B. about his evidence on the Moxley job.

He lifted a receiver.

'Know if Chief Inspector Boardman's in?' he said. 'Oh – ring his home for me, will you?' He put the receiver down and waited; the other bell rang. 'Hallo, Gideon here. Eh? . . . Good Lord!' He found himself chuckling, looked as if he were delighted. 'Nice work, glad they don't always get away with it.' He chuckled again, and then saw the office door open. 'Yes, I'll put some dynamite behind them, but King-Hadden's off duty to-night, it's never so quick when –'

The visitor was the Assistant Commissioner, his sleek grey suit changed to sleek dinner jacket, soft cream shirt, small bow-tie; a distinguished man indeed.

'. . . okay, Basil' Gideon said, and rang off and looked up smiling. 'didn't expect you back,' he remarked.

'I had a dinner date I couldn't miss,' the A.C. said, 'but wanted an excuse to cut the speeches. How are things going?'

'It's like rain,' said Gideon, and then corrected himself. 'Hailstorm, rather.'

'With an occasional rainbow – what's so funny?'

Gideon chuckled.

'Chap broke into a house in Maida Vale an hour ago, a six-footer apparently, and he had a gun. The woman of the house discovered him and chased him out with an umbrella. He dropped the gun! Empty. Evans was telling me, he can always make a story like that sound twice as funny as it is, but –' Gideon chuckled. 'Armed gunman chased by angry woman with umbrella – can't you see the headlines in the morning? It'll keep something off the front page.'

'The Waterloo job, I hope.'

'Not much chance of that.' Gideon grimaced and told what had happened.

'You've always thought that there was organization in these mail van jobs, haven't you?' the A.C. asked musingly.

'Some sort of,' agreed Gideon. 'The pattern's always pretty well the same, isn't it? I'd say that there's a clearing house for information, which always reaches the same chap. He passes it on to different people, and they give him a rake-off. First time I've ever been hopeful is to-day, if Chang –'

He broke off.

The A.C. lit a cigarette.

'I was wondering,' he said, sitting on the arm of the easy chair reserved for visitors. 'You've thought that it was worth giving Chang rope, haven't you? Any special reason?'

'You mean, when I heard about Foster from Birdy, why didn't I go for Chang straightaway?' Gideon pinched his nose. 'I don't know. Don't suppose I ever shall. I just felt it was the wrong thing to do, but I'm not so sure now. But see what's working out. Birdy squealed on Chang. Chang has put a finger on him, through Murphy. That gives a direct line between Chang and Murphy. Now we know that Murphy is nominal boss of a gang, and that among the people who do jobs for him there's every kind of crook, from killer to snatch artist. Well, if Chang is the man who gets the information about mail vans and passes it on to Murphy, Murphy might pass it further down. I don't say it is the answer, just that it could be. The one certain thing about Murphy's bunch is that they're tough and they're smart and they don't squeal. We've been trying to get Murphy for years, have never pulled him in on anything that counted, and haven't thought it worth while putting him inside for a couple of months. Now, we've got a half chance of picking up one of the men who did the Waterloo job to-day, and if we can lead back from him to Murphy we might really have something.'

Gideon paused.

'Yes, you would,' agreed the A.C. fervently.

'If we could get Murphy and hit him really hard it would do more good than we've done at one swipe for months,' said Gideon, as if he longed for exactly that. 'For *years*. Meanwhile, we've started a new line. I've sent out instructions for all known Murphy men to be checked and to find out if any of them have postmen among their friends. I'm having Chang's customers checked, too, to find out if there are any postmen among them. Or bank managers or clerks, for that matter. It's the first time we've thought of Chang or Murphy together or singly as in any way interested in the mail van jobs. Could be wrong now, but at least it's giving us a bit of pep for the time being.'

'George,' said the A.C., 'I have never suggested that you don't know your job.'

Gideon grinned.

'Thanks! Then there's another angle. Foster's sister had a telephone call from a hysterical woman who said that Foster had been murdered.' He deliberately ignored the A.C.'s start of surprise. Woman named Estelle, apparently a sweetie of Foster's. I started to check, and one of the girls who dance at Chang's club is named Estelle.'

'Well, well,' murmured the A.C. 'Talked to her yet?'

'Haven't found her. She digs in Chelsea, but hasn't been home since morning. As soon as we get a chance, we'll tackle her.'

A telephone bell rang, almost before he had finished.

'Excuse me,' he said, and plucked the receiver up. 'Gideon . . . *What?*' He bellowed the word, must have deafened the man at the other end of the line, and certainly startled the A.C. 'Bring him right over,' he said, only a little less boomingly, 'nice work, Lem! Wonderful!'

He put the receiver down. The Assistant Commissioner, who knew him in most moods, had seldom seen him show such obvious satisfaction; and that could only come from really good news.

Gideon appeared to want to savour it before passing it on.

'We've got the driver of the Austin with the Michelin tyre,' he said at last, and his expression said: 'How about *that*?' 'Young chap with a scar at the back of his head – the Waterloo post-office driver saw a chap like that, remember.' Gideon was more excited than the A.C. had seen him for years, but he fought against showing it. 'Lemaitre's bringing him over. Going to sit in on this interview, sir?' He grinned almost impudently.

The A.C. said: 'I think I will, George. That's fine.'

'But it's late to have that post-office driver in,' decided Gideon, and his pencil sped. 'We'll have an identification parade at ten o'clock in the morning. I wonder if this could be *the* day.' He got up to stretch his cramped limbs. 'I think a noggin's indicated here. Going to have one?'

'On principle and in office hours,' said the A.C., 'I disapprove. But thanks.' The telephone rang. 'All right, I'll get the whisky,' he said, and rounded the desk as Gideon picked up the receiver.

'Gideon here.'

'Oh . . .'

'Yes, all right. 'Bye.' Gideon rang off and kept a finger on the cradle of the telephone as the A.C. stooped to open a cupboard in one of the pedestals of his desk. 'Fire out at Mince Lane, a big fur warehouse. The fire chief thinks it might be arson. I'd better send Marjoribanks over.' He lifted a receiver. 'Detective-Inspector Marjoribanks, please. . . . Hallo, Marj, got nice job for you, Belinda Blue-eyes thinks that there's arson in Mince Lane – pretty well gutted a warehouse, I gather, have a go as soon as you can.'

'Thanks,' he added a minute later, and then put the receiver down and took a glass from the A.C., who held a syphon in his right hand. 'Splash more, I think' he said, and watched the soda water as it squirted and splashed. 'Whoa! Ta. Here's to getting a trail back from this to Chang or Murphy.' He ran his tongue along his lips. 'No more news of Birdy, I'm worried about that. I – oh, *damn the blurry telephone*!'

'If I were you,' said the A.C., 'I'd get out for a bit and leave a sergeant in here.'

'Blurry sergeants! . . . Gideon . . . Eh? . . . Oh, not bad, but he can keep until morning, hold him at Cannon Row, will you? It won't do him any harm to wriggle a bit. Yes, I'll hold on. It's Percival, from London Airport,' he told the A.C. offhandedly. 'That Foreign Office chap who pinched the diplomatic bag from the *sanctum sanctorum's* turned up, complete with bag. It's still full, so we do get results sometimes.' He scribbled. 'Must let the Press have that quickly, especially the *Globe*, it's been screaming about missing diplomats for two years. Or is it three?' Into the telephone he said, 'Violent, is he? Well, get some help, don't let him cut his throat. 'Bye.'

He rang off.

'You rather remind me,' said the A.C., sipping his whisky and soda, 'of a bulldozer which never stops moving.'

'Don't say that in anyone's hearing or I'll be the Bulldozer for the rest of my stay here, which I sometimes hope won't be long!'

Gideon grinned.

He rang the Back Room Inspector to tell them about the arrest of the diplomat.

He had time to light his pipe.

He picked up a telephone at the first ting of the bell.

'Gideon . . . Oh, yes . . . Oh, lor'. I hate those jobs. Can you handle it yourself? . . . Yes, you'll have to stop him, I suppose, fix it with the stations, ports and airports, but soft pedal a bit.' He rang off, forgetting to say ' 'bye'. 'That was about Eric Rosenthal – he and his wife have been having a tug-o'-war with their kid, remember. The wife got a court order for custody, and Rosenthal snatched her this evening. What will a thing like this do to a six-year-old girl?'

He shook his head.

He thought of Kate.

The telephone rang.

This time it was news with a vengeance. The man Fessell, wanted in connection with the murder of the old woman in the Islington sweet-shop, had been seen in Watford. He should be caught before long.

Then Gideon thought of Birdy Merrick.

He didn't think of a man named Fitzroy, for he had never heard of him.

CHAPTER 14

THE MURPHY GANG DRAWS CLOSE

Birdy stood in a dark doorway. Gaslight showed white and pure behind the glass of a lamp fastened to a wall by an iron bracket. Nearby, the ripple of the water of a backwater of the Thames sounded softly and insistently, as if someone were whispering to him. A long way off there was another whisper of sound: traffic on the Mile End and the Whitechapel Roads.

The river traffic was silent.

It was not often silent, like this; usually a tug chugged along or hooted; or cargo ships laden down to the Plimsoll line sent their short, urgent blasts to tell the Port of London Authority officials that they were on their way to distant lands. Or a police launch barked on its urgent, questing note, and a searchlight swept the dark, dirty water, looking for unexpected things; or else expected jetsam, such as floating bodies.

This silence was accursed. In it every little sound could be heard, and Birdy knew that two of Murphy's men were near him – listening. Their ears were as sensitive to the night sounds of London as a bushman's would be for the night sounds of the forest.

No cranes were working.

The silence was so deep that Birdy could have screamed; and screaming brought on death or whatever they planned for him.

Why weren't the cranes busy?

Birdy remembered: there was a strike. Not a full-blooded one, but a nasty, mean little strike – no overtime. Birdy had heard dockers talking about it, some for and some against; but they all obeyed. There was no trade union in crime, criminals were self-employed, uninsured and independent. Now, that awful hush fell upon dockland and upon Birdy. He had wormed his way here after seeing Lefty, and waited for the blessed fall of darkness. He had felt that he dared hope, and stood in the doorway, listening for protecting noises which would not come – and listening, too, for the stealthy sounds which might tell of Ali or the Snide.

The Snide was a knife artist, too.

Lefty was a broken bottle artist.

Down at the foot of the steps at Aldgate Station there had been – a razor artist. So Birdy had a good idea what to expect. They were going to cut him up. Chang had given the word because he had squealed, and now Murphy's gang were going to cut him up.

It would be better to kill himself.

He heard a soft, swift footfall.

His hands went up to his breast, clenched fearfully; his ears strained the quiet, his eyes tried to probe the darkness beyond the clear glow of the gas-lamp.

It came again – stealthy, nearer.

A voice whispered: '*Come on, Birdy, we've got you cornered.*'

That was the Snide. The Snide had once been an artist in making lead coins, sludge, snide, call it what you liked; but now he preferred that knife. He wasn't so good as Ali, but he was good.

The sneering, mocking whisper came again.

'*We've got you cornered.*'

Everything Birdy knew, everything he sensed, worked in him for his own protection now. Thirty years of East End slum life, most of it with one of the gangs or another – not a fighting member, just a hanger-on – had told him plenty. He knew London and Londoners and Ali and the Snide. That whisper was to work on his nerves, to lure him out of his doorway, to make him run *away* from the sound; and if he did that he would run into Ali. There might be others, too; he had been crouching here for ten minutes, plenty of time for reinforcements to creep up.

'*Give it up, Birdy.*'

'*What part of you shall we send home to Ethel, Birdy?*'

The Snide always tormented like this; he'd had an education and liked to demonstrate it.

'*Come on, Birdy –*'

Birdy fingered a sardine tin in his coat pocket; he'd picked it up from the kerb at dusk, and it was a weapon of sorts; not of attack but of defence by ruse. He nicked his finger on the torn edge. He didn't wince but flinched.

The Snide was very near.

Ali . . .?

In a moment or two they would rush him.

Birdy raised the sardine tin, moving it round in his fingers until he found a smooth section which he could grip. He made a few silent swinging motions with his arm and then tossed the can into the air. It made a funny little twittering noise, the others must wonder what it was. Then there was a hush; then the tin clanged upon the road on the other side of the street.

Birdy darted out of his cover.

In that split second the Snide would be distracted; at least he ought to be. He would look towards the sound and Ali would probably do the same thing. That would be Birdy's chance, his only one. He darted out of the doorway and was revealed for a moment in the white glow.

He saw the Snide, a thin face turned towards the sardine tin. He did not see Ali, but guessed that Ali was behind him.

He leapt forward.

The Snide swung round, the knife glittered. Birdy was very close. He felt the knife cut through his shoulder and then he drove his knee into the pit of the Snide's stomach with sickening force and with the accuracy of an expert. He heard the Snide give a groan that was torturing in its anguish, in its tale of sickening pain. The Snide slid away from him, and Birdy raced on towards the corner, the docks, the ships where he hoped to find refuge.

He heard Ali.

He looked over his shoulder and saw the dark shape of the lascar, and his long shadow cast by the gaslight.

Then he saw a man in front of him.

Lefty? . . .

Birdy's heart seemed to stop.

Lefty.

He swerved to one side. Lefty moved towards him with the extra speed of twenty-one to forty-one. Birdy was sure, then, that he hadn't a chance. He ran on blindly. He felt Lefty's outstretched hand pluck at his sleeve, but tore himself free. Now all he could do was to run until he fell in his tracks. There was no hope, but he had to go on until they fell upon him and carved him up – or tore him to pieces. Hounds after a fox. Hounds –

He became aware of a different, moving light, coming towards him, bright beams sweeping the street. A blue light showed at the top of the car, with the word *Police*. Birdy could just make out the shapes of the two men in the car.

He heard nothing behind him, but he knew that Lefty and Ali had turned away in fright. They might help the Snide or they might leave the Snide to be picked up.

Birdy waited until the car had passed him and then began to hurry towards the docks. He could get into a crane, or sneak aboard one of the ships; he might even swim across to the other side of the Thames. He'd done it before.

That was unless a Murphy man was watching him now; or waiting for him in the shadows ahead.

Gideon, his tie knotted loosely, coat on, shirt cuffs undone, bloodshot eyes obviously very tired, and hat on the back of his head, looked at the sergeant who had just come in. He had nothing against the sergeant; nothing against sergeants as a general rule. But you got the fool sometimes, and he had had two or three bright specimens that day: this seemed to be his moment of misfortune.

'Yes, put every message on paper,' he said, 'and make sure that anything that different sections ought to have, reaches them quickly.'

The tow-haired sergeant, who was old enough to know better, said timidly:

'What kind of things, sir?'

Gideon managed not to swear, tried to phrase what he meant simply, and was almost relieved that the telephone bell rang. He turned back to the desk to pick up the receiver, knowing that he ought to leave this call to the sergeant. Lemaitre and the others were downstairs with the prisoner with the scarred head; a man named Mazzioni. In a fury of checking, the Yard knew that Mazzioni had no record in London, and copies of his prints were being made to send to the Provinces. The A.C. was downstairs, waiting for Gideon, and a blockhead of a sergeant –

'Gideon . . . Oh, hallo, Fred.' This was the one call he was glad he'd taken, after all; and he was surprised that he felt really on edge. 'Anything?'

'Yes and no,' said the G5 Superintendent. 'One of my patrols picked up the Snide. He had a couple of knives in his pocket, with traces of blood on one –'

Gideon winced.

'– but Birdy got away,' the Superintendent went on. 'Our chaps saw him as he headed for the docks. He's as slippery as they come, and as frightened as hell.'

'I'd be frightened, in his shoes,' said Gideon heavily.

'Who wouldn't?'

'Well, thanks, Fred,' Gideon said. 'We picked up a chap in connection with the Waterloo job, by the way, and may have some luck.'

'Here's to it,' the other man said.

Gideon put the receiver down, and looked up at the sergeant, forgetting to glare; the man was at Lemaitre's desk, with a telephone in his hand. Gideon found himself chuckling.

He nodded and went out. Half-way along the passage he remembered that the sergeant seemed to be confident enough now, scribbling something in so fast that it must have been in shorthand. A job in hand was a fine nerve tonic.

Now for Mazzioni.

Mazzioni looked tough.

You could pick them out, and it was obvious from Lemaitre's manner that he had picked Mazzioni out, quickly enough. For the man was handcuffed with his hands in front of him. He was hatless, and swarthy – no, olive-skinned; not one of the good-looking Italians. He was either

Italian or of Italian extraction, Gideon knew, and when Italians came bad they were often very, very bad.

Mazzioni was shorter than medium height, and not particularly broad; really, a small man but very upright. It was obvious that he was physically fit; his poise somehow made that clear. He had a broad, flattened nose, obviously broken many years before, fine eyes, thick, jet black hair and jet black eyebrows. He needed a shave. His lips were parted and showed a glimpse of white teeth; he had that caged, criminal-at-bay look which the really vicious criminals had, and Gideon thought he had something else: the look of a dopey.

There was a nasty graze, bleeding a little, on his right temple.

Lemaitre said: 'He made a fight of it, that's where he got marked. Plenty of witnesses.'

Lemaitre no longer sounded cock-a-hoop; it was as if he knew that Mazzioni wasn't going to be a lot of help. There was the kind who would talk under pressure and the kind who wouldn't, and it was usually easy to pick these out, too. In Lemaitre's words as well as his manner there was a hint of frustration, and a thing which everyone at the Yard or on the Force anywhere suffered from: fear that they would be accused of exceeding their duty. A prisoner with a bruised face was a prisoner with an angry, vengeful counsel. Once convince a jury that a man had been ill-treated, and the odds against a conviction –

Gideon checked himself.

The A.C. wasn't here after all.

'When's the Old Man coming?' he asked.

'Just rang, won't be a minute,' Lemaitre answered.

Gideon nodded.

Mazzioni looked from him to Lemaitre and back again. He wasn't sure what to make of this or what they would make of him. He would be happier if either of them talked; this silence, this cold appraisal from the newcomer, was an unsettling, disturbing thing. And Gideon, looking like a great bear and glowering as if the bear were angry, didn't mind how much he worked on the prisoner's nerves.

Was he a dopey?

There was a tap at the door. A uniformed constable looked in.

'All okay, sir.'

'Thanks,' said Gideon.

That meant that the A.C. was in position, able to listen to what was being said, and looking into the room through a window which appeared to be opaque from the inside. They were ready to start.

But as he looked at Mazzioni, with his first question on his lips, Gideon felt suddenly hopeless, although it was hard to say why. It was partly because he was tired; not flogged out, as he was sometimes, but flagging badly; the day had caught up with him. It was partly because of the ugly look in Mazzioni's eyes, too, the certainty that this was a tough nut.

This interrogation was going to last a long time.

Lemaitre had his notebook out. Lemaitre, after his burst of triumph, felt much the same as Gideon; catching your man was only the beginning, and in this case it didn't look like the promising beginning they had hoped.

Lemaitre had been going to take his Fifi out.

He'd be lucky if he were home by midnight. So would Gideon.

The hell of it was that this was just another day.

Mazzioni didn't talk, but two things made Gideon very thoughtful. A police-surgeon said that he was certainly addicted to cocaine, and at Mazzioni's rooms in Bethnal Green the Divisional police found a packet of reefers and a small packet of cocaine.

CHAPTER 15

WORRIED MEN

Chang was worried.

He was in his office, with ledgers open in front of him, for his best love was to work over the figures of his business. Then the news of Mazzioni's capture reached him by telephone. It was a whispered statement, briefly made, as if the speaker were eager to get the message delivered and be off. He put the receiver down stealthily, and there was silence on the line and in Chang's office.

Chang now wore a dinner jacket, beautifully cut, a white shirt and a purple bow-tie. His sparse black hair glistened with brilliantine. The light in the ceiling cast soft shadows of his prominent eyebrows and his nose over his face, giving him an oddly sinister look. His lips were parted but not visible to anyone who happened to look at him. He sat quite still, a faintly yellow hand resting on the open pages of the ledger, in which he was keeping records of restaurant trade: or so the ledger's legend said. For tea, Chang read reefers; for deliveries of tea he read marihuana or hashish, whichever was available. Occasionally it was dagga from Africa, and the effect of this was much the same, with dagga perhaps more harsh than the others.

'Coffee' and cocaine were synonymous.

All this afforded Chang deep amusement most of the time, for he could safely allow the police to study these records. Until that morning, at all events, he had felt sure that there was no risk. With Foster at Scotland Yard, biddable under the twin pressures of greed and fear, with several key men in banks and post offices throughout London, and with his own carefully conceived plan to block every line of inquiry which might lead to him, he had felt that nothing could go wrong.

He was less sure now. Foster's telephone call, his sister's prying visit, Gideon's call and then a hysterical outburst from the dancer, Estelle, had combined to give him a very bad day. It was Estelle who had betrayed the fact that Birdy had found out and squealed. Now, Birdy was on the run, and so was the dancer.

Murphy was after them both.

Chang did not think Birdy could be dangerous, and knew that it had been a mistake to set Murphy on to the squealer. The police knew about it by now; and Murphy's contact men were unable to concentrate on the search for Estelle, whose knowledge could be deadly; could, in fact, hang him.

Chang had not realized that Estelle was in love with Foster.

Chang sat quite motionless in the small, warm office. No sound came from the café, although a radiogram was playing, soft, rhythmic music in there, and occasionally a crooner sang. No reefers were being sold, the soft drinks were not pepped up, yet any Yard man who came in, any doctor who knew the signs, and any victim of the dream-drugs, would know that half of the people here were dopies. From their bright eyes, they would have known that they had recently had a drag or a shot.

Chang did not think of these things.

Chang, in his way, was very like Gideon. He had the same kind of mind, the same tight grasp of situations and circumstances, the same unfailing memory and the same intentness. For Gideon, there was the reward of doing his job, for Chang the reward of making a fortune; but to each the actual task was the very pulse of life. In Gideon the chief thing was the task of seeking the criminal and hunting him down, of making sure that he could never strike again to hurt, to rob, to frighten or to maim. In Chang, the attraction was the plotting against the police, the moves in a game as in a game of chess or Mah Jong – wits against wits, and the amassing of a fortune.

The police had become his natural enemy.

They had suspected him for a long time, but with Foster in his pocket he had known that he was temporarily secure. Others were also in his pocket. He was ringed round with men, a few of whom knew that they served him, most of whom did not know that their instructions came from him. 'Instructions' was too often the wrong word. Hints, tip-offs, suggestions, help in emergency – all of these came through Chang, and for reward he received a share of whatever profit was made. His share was passed on to him. Sometimes it was handed over, in cash, at the café; or to other, smaller cafés where he had contacts in the East and West Ends, in Chelsea, in Bloomsbury.

There was Chang with supplies for his cafés, all legitimate business on the surface. Here was Chang, deeply worried. Estelle was anxiety enough, but he had trained himself to concentrate on one thing at a time, and the greatest anxiety was the captured Italian.

Chang knew Mazzioni personally and Mazzioni knew him; so he could betray him to the police. The Italian's record was good, because Chang had saved him from a charge several times, but reputations went for nothing once the police were working on you. Mazzioni might crack and talk to save himself.

Never trust anyone, Chang believed, unless you could compel them to serve faithfully.

Mazzioni was out of his reach.

Mazzioni's wife wasn't.

How should he deal with the Italian? Could he find a way of warning him of the consequences of failure?

No, Chang decided, not that; not yet. Mazzioni was tough and he would hold out for some time, he might hold out for a long time. He took an occasional sniff of snow, but could get along without it. The way to make sure of Mazzioni's loyalty was to promise him help. Help, for instance, for his pretty young wife; then help with the police.

Chang did not know how the Italian had been picked up. He knew that he had done the job at Waterloo, and that most of the money had already been safely salted away; but Mazzioni might have been caught with some of the money on him. The police might find indisputable evidence of his complicity, but they might be taking a chance. If Mazzioni had an alibi, it could make all the difference to the way the case went.

Chang lifted the telephone, dialled a number, and waited. He had to wait for a long time. *Brrr-brrr, brrr-brrr*. It was too long. Possessed of all the calm of his unknown ancestors, he began to bare his teeth; but then the call was answered, a man said breathlessly:

'Mayfair 29451.'

'Mr. Ledbetter,' Chang said softly, 'it is urgent that I should see you.'

'Who –'

'An old friend, Mr. Ledbetter.'

There was a moment's silence; then the man spoke again, in a voice less breathless but quite empty of pleasure.

'Oh, I know. Look, can't it wait? I have some friends here. In the morning –'

'I am sorry, Mr. Ledbetter, it is urgent. Meet me in Room 217 at the Occident Hotel, please.'

'But I can't –'

'It is very urgent, Mr. Ledbetter,' Chang said.

Ledbetter answered gruffly: 'Oh, all right.'

Chang rang off without another word. He lifted the receiver again, almost at once. His movement was quick yet graceful, very different from Gideon's grab; and his hand was half the size of Gideon's.

A woman answered.

'Mary,' Chang greeted, 'this afternoon, between two o'clock and four o'clock, where were you?'

'Hallo, Chin,' said the woman, in a deep, throaty voice. 'I was at Kingston. Didn't anyone tell you, I'm at Kingston every afternoon? It's one of the places where I work.' There was laziness and laughter in her voice, one would picture a big, hearty, fleshy woman, sensuous, good-hearted, quick-witted.

'Understand,' said Chang, 'you were at Kingston and a good friend of yours was there, also, with you. Mazzioni.'

'Maz? Why, he –'

'He was with you, please remember, all the time.'

The woman laughed.

'His little sweetie pie won't like that!'

'His little sweetie pie,' mimicked Chang, 'will not worry about it this time. Now, please understand. He arrived at two, he left at four, there is no mistake. Find one, find even two people to say that also.'

'Okay, Chin,' the woman said. 'Bad trouble?'

'It could be.'

'What I do for my men,' said the woman named Mary.

Chang rang off. He sat quite still again, until his left hand moved to the inside pocket of his beautifully cut coat. He took out a tiny lacquered snuff box, with a beautiful garden design, pressed, opened it, and took a tiny pinch of white snuff. He put this on to the back of his hand and sniffed it up each nostril; then he replaced the box slowly. He stood up, stretched for his hat, and went out of the office.

A girl was in the little cloakroom on the landing, and the radiogram was playing swing. Shuffling footsteps told of people dancing. The ordinary, clean smell of tobacco smoke wafted towards him.

'Has Estelle telephoned?'

'No, sir.'

'I will be back soon,' Chang said.

'Okay.'

He went downstairs, passing a coloured photograph of Estelle. She had long, rippling red hair and a big, white smile and quite beautiful legs. Chang only glanced in passing. Nodding to a flat-faced waiter, he turned into the spotless kitchen, where the Chinese staff looked at him without expression, and he behaved as if no one was there. He went out of the little back door and slipped swiftly along a passage towards Middle Street.

At Middle Street he had a shock.

A plainclothes man was on the other side of the road; and there was only one reason why he should be there.

Chang felt even more worried.

He smiled across at the man, and turned into Middle Street, then made his way towards Shaftesbury Avenue. He was followed, and was worried chiefly because the police were so interested. He would have to be very, very careful.

Had it been a mistake to run Foster down?

If so, it had been Mazzioni's mistake, too; that was the chief source of worry. Mazzioni had been at hand when Foster had telephoned. Foster had been scared, and had talked of squealing unless Chang promised help. In a quick flood of annoyance and alarm, Chang had made his mistake by telling Mazzioni what to do, and Mazzioni had acted too quickly, and too close to Soho.

Chang thought belatedly of other things that had turned out to be mistakes, too; letting Estelle know that Foster was in his pay, for instance; and forgetting that she had been here for a rehearsal, when he had given Mazzioni his orders.

At Piccadilly Circus, Chang slipped the sergeant who was on his tail, but knew that there might be others on the lookout for him. He was conspicuous, like any Chinese. Piccadilly Circus always had its policemen, its plainclothes men, its police spies, and if they had been told to watch for Chang it would be dangerous.

Chang got into a taxi. He did not think that he was followed as he was taken to the restaurant entrance of the Occident Hotel. There was not likely to be a detective lurking at this side, but there was sure to be a hotel dick if not a policeman in the foyer.

He went through a service door to service stairs and then up to Room 217. This was reserved in the name of Smith, and a Mr. Smith had come, signed the register, and left the hotel, sending the key to Chang. It would be a rendezvous for a week; then there would be another hotel, another room.

When Ledbetter came, he also looked worried. He was a big, lusty man with iron grey hair, quite distinguished in his way. He had a very good reputation, was an astute lawyer, and had made one mistake; a little matter of embezzlement. No one yet knew, except Chang and a clerk in Ledbetter's office who was aware that Chang liked that kind of information.

Chang looked very small beside him.

'Well, what is it?' Ledbetter didn't like Chinese, didn't like anyone whose skin was yellow or brown or black. He was as massive as Gideon, well-dressed, scowling, resentful. The furrows in his forehead added to the touch of distinction.

'There is a very urgent matter,' Chang said. He found it easy to smile, especially at men whom one disliked. 'A friend of mine, named Maro Mazzioni, has been arrested by the police. He is a very good friend, and it would be dangerous for many people if he were to be tried. It is believed that he was connected with the mail van robbery this afternoon, but that is ridiculous – he was at Kingston, with Mary Clayton. You know Mary.'

Ledbetter said: 'Did he do the job?'

'You have to see him,' said Chang, still smiling. 'Just see him, and tell him that he need not worry. Mary will tell the truth and say that he was with her from two o'clock until four. You understand?'

Ledbetter said: 'I don't like it, Chang. If the police can prove that he wasn't –'

'Then, Mary lied to you,' said Chang. 'Do not be foolish, Mr. Ledbetter. This is an urgent matter. See your friends at Scotland Yard at once, please.'

He smiled . . .

Ledbetter went out, obviously as worried as when he came in, much more resentful, but undoubtedly prepared to be obedient. Chang went to a telephone by the side of the bed. He looked very short. He hesitated for a moment, partly because he was thinking of Ledbetter. He knew that the solicitor regarded him as a yellow-skinned savage; he also knew that Ledbetter was in a very tight fix.

Chang telephoned Mazzioni's wife.

A man with a deep voice answered, almost certainly a policeman; in fact, Chang felt quite sure. He spoke promptly and in a deep voice from which he kept all trace of accent.

'Mrs. Mazzioni, please.'

'Who wants her?'

'A friend.'

There was a moment's pause; then the mutter of men's voices; then Mazzioni's wife came on the line. Chang knew her for a pretty, fluffy-haired blonde, with a jealous temperament.

She sounded scared.

'Who's that?'

'Of course, you know of the accident to your husband,' Chang said, still sounding 'English'. 'But it will be all right, my dear. You will find out that he was with Mary at Kingston all the afternoon. There is no need to worry at all. That is the perfect alibi, you see.'

'The perfect –'

'That is the police with you, I believe,' Chang said. 'They will ask who called. Say I am a friend, to tell you of what happened to Maz. And one other thing, little one – when the police ask if you know where Maz was this afternoon, be angry. Do you understand?' He paused, but only for a moment. 'Be *very* angry, say he was going to see that bitch Mary at Kingston.' Softly he repeated: 'You understand?'

'Sure,' said Mazzioni's wife, slowly. She was no fool, and she was cottoning on. 'Sure, I knew already.'

Chang rang off, unhurriedly.

He was still worried and uneasy; he did not like having to work at speed like this, and did not like having to do so much himself. But it began to look as if the real emergency was past. If only he could find Estelle.

He left the hotel, and twenty minutes later, entered the café in Middle Street again. The plainclothes man he had shaken off was back on duty. Chang smiled at him politely, but he didn't get a smile back.

In his office, Chang sat back, took another pinch of snuff, and glanced down at the figures in the book. It was silent again and he enjoyed the silence.

The telephone bell rang.

He lifted it and a man said: 'This is Murphy.'

Suddenly, Chang was acutely anxious; for Murphy never got in touch with him direct unless there was urgent news. Was this about Birdy Merrick or Estelle?

Had Estelle been found by the police? That was Chang's fear, that above all else.

Murphy was also an anxious man, although it took a great deal to get on his nerves. Most days, he told his cronies exactly what he thought of the police and how little they mattered to him; and most days he meant exactly that. The police had no terrors for him. He kept his nose clean, didn't he? He had committed no crime of any kind in the past two years except that of a little street corner betting, peddling some bad liquor, which was hardly a crime at all, and – inciting others to crime. No one named him as the instigator, so that did not count.

Yet Murphy was edgy.

It was worse, because there had been a long, long spell of freedom from fear. Everything had gone so smoothly that he had become dangerously complacent. He had given more orders himself than he should have done, instead of using messengers, and he had gone to see Birdy.

He would not have told anyone in the world, but he was frightened.

The sense of power which his habit of domination gave him, had betrayed him. He should not have gone to Birdy's house. Now, the Snide was in the hands of the police, and the Snide had been seen to attack Birdy. It would be all right if the police just handled Snide, but they might check on everyone who had been after Birdy that day.

They were out in strength in the district.

Murphy had that nasty, sickening kind of feeling that the police were out for a kill. It was Chang's doing. The orders to get Birdy had come from Chang, even if they'd travelled through three other people before reaching him. Murphy did not propose to handle this with go-betweens, he wanted to talk to Chang. There was the search for the red-haired dancer, too, which had got nowhere, and was wasting men.

So he telephoned the Chinese.

Chang lifted the receiver, heard who it was, and then very slowly shook his head. Murphy just reported, and asked if he should keep up the search for B. and the skirt. Chang was preparing to answer 'for the skirt only,' when there was an interruption.

It was entirely coincidence that at that moment the door burst open, but the sudden movement scared Chang, who actually jumped to his feet.

The door banged back.

Foster's sister came into the room with a scared-looking Chinese waiter behind her.

CHAPTER 16

SANCTUARY?

Chang looked up at Foster's sister. His eyes were lack-lustre; his mouth was set in long, thin lines.

'Yes, proceed, please,' he said into the telephone. 'Now I must go.' He rang off.

The woman had thrust her way past the waiter, outside, but Chang's expression stopped her, as a physical blow might do. She stood there, the sudden fear evident in her eyes, in the way her mouth opened and her teeth glinted. Behind her, the waiter hovered, hands rolling and rolling beneath his small white apron. Had Gideon seen the way he gazed at Chang, with silent supplication as to the Devil, Gideon would have hardened very much against Chang.

Then Chang spoke softly.

'Good evening, Mrs. Addinson. Please come in. Wen Li, please close the door.' As the waiter obeyed and as Flo Addinson moved forward, Chang brought a smile from the depths of his self-discipline, then stood up and rounded the desk.

'Please sit down,' he said. His voice was more sing-song than usual, as if he were fighting against showing his feelings. He touched the back of the easy chair and bowed. 'Can I get you a drink?'

'No,' she said. 'No, thank you.' She moved so that she could sit down. Chang bowed again and went back to his desk. Now the mask was on, but she had seen beneath it and she knew what was really there. When she had come in, she had been flushed, as with anger, actually with nervousness; now, she was very pale. Her eyes were bright, a shimmery kind of black, suggesting that she had a severe headache. She fumbled in her handbag, and Chang promptly stood up again and offered her cigarettes.

'Please smoke,' he said.

She hesitated and then accepted a cigarette. He smiled as he flicked a lighter for her, but it was the smile of a robot. It was a genuine cigarette, too, there was no drug in it, yet the temptation to give her marihuana had been almost overwhelming.

She still wore the good black suit.

'Thank you.'

'How can I help you, please?' murmured Chang.

'I came to – to ask you if you know what happened to my brother,' she said.

He was outwardly almost back to normal, suave, almost solemn, spreading his hands.

'I was informed this morning of what had happened. Such a sad accident. I am very sorry.'

'I'm not sure it was an accident,' Flo Addinson said.

'Oh,' said Chang, and his lips parted. Now he was in such complete command of himself that he folded his arms loosely across his narrow chest, and sat back in the chair. It was no indication of his feelings. 'I do not understand you. He was run down by a car, is that not so? The driver did not stop.'

Chang spread his hands.

'There are so many callous drivers –'

'Mr. Chang,' the woman said steadily, 'what association was there between my brother and you? Why did he see you so often? Why was he worried because of you?'

She had alarmed him, she knew; he could not hide it, even though he said:

'You are making mistakes, Mrs. Addinson, I cannot understand –'

'I must know what Eric had to do with you. The police kept asking me, they've followed me all day. Why is it? Do you know?'

Suavely, he insisted that he knew nothing, that he and her brother had just been acquaintances. But he questioned her tautly, trying to find out what she knew.

He learned little and soon she seemed tired.

'You have had a big shock,' Chang murmured, when she rose to go. 'Please allow me to send you home in my car, Mrs. Addinson. It is no trouble. Unless you would like to stay to have dinner here? As my guest. I shall be very happy.'

'No!' She jumped up. 'No, thank you, I'd rather walk. If you're sure you can't help –'

'If I could, Mrs. Addinson, I would, gladly.'

Chang pressed a bell, and the ringing sound could be heard faintly. In a moment, the door opened and the waiter appeared, big, flat, Mongolian face concealing his fear now.

'Show Mrs. Addinson downstairs,' Chang said. He rounded the desk. 'My very deep condolences, I assure you. I was very fond of Mr. Foster.' He did not offer to shake hands, but bowed; and waited until the door closed on her.

Then he moved to his desk, swift as a flash, picked up a telephone, and was answered almost at once.

'The woman now downstairs,' Chang said swiftly, 'you will follow her and see if she is followed by the police. You understand?'

A man said, 'Yes, sir.'

Chang rang off. He didn't sit down, but went to the door and opened it. The music from the radiogram had started again, a fox-trot that sounded rather sensuous and slow. The landing light fell on Chang's black hair. He waited until the waiter came up the stairs, and the man with the flat Mongolian face could no longer hide his fear.

No one should have reached Chang's room without a warning preceding them; he had been panicked into forgetting to press a bell.

His feet dragged on the last two steps.

Chang waited until he was close to him, and then struck him across the face. The man swayed right and left under the impact of the savage blows, but didn't try to evade them. Chang did not speak, but turned back to his office. The waiter stumbled towards the narrow stairs. The fox-trot moaned on and the shuffling sound of dancing feet came clearly. Outside, a car horn tooted.

Outside, Flo Addinson walked towards Shaftesbury Avenue, was followed by a small man in a shabby suit, and by a plainclothes man detailed to follow her.

In his report to the Yard, this man said that Chang had had Mrs. Addinson followed almost to her door.

'You stay and keep an eye on her,' he was ordered.

A few miles away from Soho, in a line which cut through the throbbing, cosmopolitan heart of the West End, through the dead City, and into the shadowy ill-lit streets of the East End, Murphy sat at a table in the front room of his house. For a man in his position, virtually boss of a powerful gang, he lived very humbly. The house was small, and the rooms tiny; only a twenty-inch television set, and bottles of every conceivable kind of drink standing on a cheap oak sideboard, suggested a man of means. That – and his wife. Murphy's wife wore diamonds when she wore rings or jewellery at all, and she aped a refinement which, in this part of London, made her quite the lady.

She was watching the television and the light reflected from the screen shimmered on the engagement ring.

Murphy, a big, vague figure at the table, was looking at a small man who had only one arm, his left sleeve dangled empty by his side. The screen flickered, a man talked.

'That's right,' Murphy said, 'you tell 'em all to call it off, leave Birdy alone, see. And don't lose no time.'

'Okay, but –'

'Scram,' growled Murphy.

'Red,' protested his wife, as if her mouth were full, 'why don't you shut up or go in the other room?'

'You heard,' Murphy said to the one-armed man.

'But Red –'

'Get out, I said.'

Murphy got up from the table. The one-armed man hesitated, then went out. He closed the door softly. Murphy moved across to his wife's chair, which was placed immediately in front of the big television. She had a box of chocolates open at her side, and Murphy took one. Paper rustled. She put her hand over his, and squeezed. He whispered: 'It's okay,' and began to caress her. They watched the big screen, and listened to the deep voice coming from the set.

Meanwhile, the one-armed man sent the word round to call off the hunt.

What he had wanted to say was that just before he had been called in to Murphy, he'd been given a message saying that Ali and Lefty had cornered Birdy. It was next door to impossible to draw the hunt off in time.

Birdy did not find sanctuary in a ship, or in the docks, although he had run there believing that he could. A shadowy figure had appeared from behind some crates waiting for loading and turned him away.

Now he was back in his own native ground; in the narrow streets, among the towering warehouses, within sight of the silent river and the silent docks. Some kind of homing instinct had brought him here, after the sickening failure to get clear away on less familiar ground. He knew every inch of this, every hiding-place, every hole and cellar; and he now tried to believe that he had more chance to save himself here.

He did not know if he was being closely watched.

He tried to persuade himself that this was his lucky night; the police car had saved him, he'd seen Lefty just in time, he'd beaten the Snide. But there was something else which filled him with terror. He'd left the Snide writhing in pain on the ground, where the police would pick him up. That would fill the others, especially Ali and Lefty, with a vindictive hatred.

He'd hurt one of the gang; in a way, had shopped him. Now it was more than a job for money, it was a vendetta.

In this narrow street it was very dark. That worried Birdy more than anything else. There should be a light on, jutting from a warehouse wall. Had it been broken? Had Ali put it out, so that he could confuse the hunted man?

Birdy moved furtively towards a corner. Round it, there was the ruin of a warehouse destroyed by fire; it was no use as a hiding-place because it was the first spot where the others would look. But beyond the warehouse was a church.

Birdy worked his way towards this.

He knew the church, as everyone did, but he had never been inside. He knew people who had; among them his daughter, before her death. He knew the elderly vicar whose chin was always on his chest as he walked about the parish, as if the dirt, the squalor, the crime, the vice, all the evil incarnate in man and so visible there, had weighed him down and sickened him, so that he served God only on sufferance and with a heavy heart. Birdy also knew the curate by sight, a spindly, unimpressive young man with a pointed nose, already a victim of catcalls and stink-bombs, a man likely to be led a hell of a life in his parish.

Birdy was very near the church. He had only to pass the ruins of the warehouse to reach it.

He had been hunted before but never like this, never to feel in deadly danger. That was why he saw the church as a very different thing; he saw it as a sanctuary, for no one would expect him to go there.

It offered him life and it was only a few yards away. The doors would be open as always. No ordinary criminal would go in and break open the offertory boxes, that was a crime which only perverts committed.

There was a yellow light at one window, at the far end of the church.

Birdy wondered who was there.

He reached the yawning entrance to the ruined warehouse, and, as he did so, a figure leapt at him.

It came from the warehouse; a dark figure with arms raised like a great bat. There was a sliding sound, a deadly rush of footsteps. Birdy knew that they had him; both of them were here. His terror seemed to explode inside him.

He screamed.

He leapt forward and kicked against an outstretched leg and pitched forward. The fall drove the wind out of him. He banged his head so painfully that tears stung his eyes. He heard the thudding of his own heart, which was swelling and pounding with great fear. He saw pictures: Ethel, Murphy, Gideon, Ethel; *Ethel.*

He felt the sharp, searing pain of a razor cut in his cheeks; in one wrist.

He felt a man kneeling on his back, knee grinding into the vertebrae, agonizing, and enough to break his back. But he couldn't think about that, only about razors and knives. He tried to twist round but couldn't.

Suddenly, he felt the pressure relax.

That was only for a moment.

Lefty, the bottle artist, caught Birdy's right wrist, twisted him, and turned him over so that he now lay on his back. He stamped his heel into Birdy's stomach, so as to paralyse him. Birdy felt hands at his wrists, pinioning him to the ground. These hands belonged to Ali, and they were coming for his face; his throat . . .

Unbelievably, the pressure at his wrist relaxed.

The awful thrust didn't come.

He heard other sounds, gasping, thudding, grunting. He realized that men were fighting, and thought that the police had come again. He rolled over but couldn't get up; his back felt as if it had been broken.

He groaned and sobbed.

Then he heard the engine of a car, and although his eyes were only open a fraction of an inch, saw the swaying beams of headlamps. Had he been able to see properly, he would also have seen Lefty reeling back against the warehouse wall, and Ali and another man locked together, gasping and struggling.

He did not recognize the spindly curate.

The police car screamed up, men jumped out, a door slammed, a police whistle blew.

Every instinct Birdy had was to try to get away, but he could not even roll over. He was vaguely aware of footsteps and of a man running. Then came sharp, authoritative voices; next, sharp metallic sounds – the click of handcuffs. A man bent over him and the light of a torch fell into his face.

'Better get a doctor,' said the man behind the torch.

'You take it easy, padre,' said another man gruffly. 'I've radioed for an ambulance.'

Birdy didn't know . . .

Lefty had escaped, but Ali was handcuffed and already inside the police car. The ambulance was on the way. The unhappy curate of the church had saved Birdy's life, and risked his own; the news of that would spread, his stature would rise; he might be hated but he had a chance to win respect.

Birdy just didn't know any of this.

He lost consciousness before the ambulance arrived, and while the policeman was giving him first aid for nasty cuts in his wrist and cheeks.

Gideon, looking solid, stolid and unimaginative, was still in the waiting-room with Lemaitre, but he knew that it was virtually a waste of time. Mazzioni had not said a word that mattered. Occasionally he said 'no' to a leading question, but the main burden of what he said was simple: he wanted a lawyer.

He'd been charged with complicity in the Waterloo raid, and had every right to legal representation.

The A.C., behind that window, might now have some idea of the frustration that the law itself created for the police. They had a man they were quite sure was guilty of a crime of violence and of highway robbery, and all they could do was to ask him *questions*; there was no way to make him answer, no way to get past that silent, sullen front.

Then a sergeant came in.

'Can you spare a moment, Mr. Gideon?'

'Yes, what is it?'

'Outside, sir, if it's convenient.'

'All right,' Gideon said. He looked at Mazzioni, who was sneering up into his face. The Italian's fingers were stained dark brown with nicotine, but he hadn't tried to take out cigarettes, and Gideon hadn't offered him one. Gideon had an intuitive feeling that he was looking at someone really evil; one who could kill and maim remorselessly, who seemed to have no redeeming feature. Nothing in Mazzioni's manner suggested that he was worth a moment's compunction; or a cigarette.

Gideon went out.

The A.C. was coming out of the room from which he had been watching, and the sergeant glanced at him, then back at Gideon.

'Sorry to interrupt, sir, but there's a Mr. Ledbetter at the main hall, asking for – er – Mr. Mazzioni. He asked whether it's true that Mazzioni is on a charge, and insisted on seeing you personally, sir.'

Gideon echoed: '*Ledbetter*.'

'Yes, sir.'

'Hmm,' said Gideon heavily. 'All right, tell him I'll see him in a few minutes.' He waited for the man to walk briskly along the corridor. 'Well, they didn't lose much time, did they?'

'Who?' asked the A.C.

'Ledbetter's already done two jobs for Chang, or friends of Chang,' Gideon said. 'I don't trust him an inch. Hard to say why. Good solicitor, done some first-class work, until a year or two ago there was nothing rumoured against him, but now – how did he get to know about the arrest, unless Mazzioni has friends who passed it on? That's what I'd like to know more than anything else. *How* did Ledbetter get to know?'

The A.C. didn't speak.

'Can't stop him from seeing the Italian,' Gideon went on gloomily. 'I could stall, but it'd be a waste of time. Better let them meet. There ought,' added Gideon with feeling, 'to be a law against allowing accused and his solicitor to have a *tête-à-tête*.'

He looked and sounded tired and disappointed.

He was much more disappointed, twenty minutes later, when he heard about the 'alibi'. More; he was angry, feeling quite sure that the alibi was faked. He sensed a hidden nervousness in Ledbetter's manner, too.

He could have used an alternative charge, of being in unlawful possession of dangerous drugs, but he didn't; he could hold it over Mazzioni's head, and it might help in the next day or two. Mazzioni 'cleared' of the mail van job was better free to meet his cronies than on a charge.

Gideon tried to bluff by holding the Italian for the night.

'I take the strongest exception to that,' Ledbetter said decisively. 'There is nothing to prevent you from asking the witness whether she can offer supporting evidence, and if she can, then it's up to you to check it at once. My client was miles away at the time of the crime you've charged him with. I'm sorry you've made a mistake, but I'm more sorry for my client than I am for you.'

Gideon looked at him thoughtfully.

'I don't know whom I'm most sorry for,' he said. 'Yet.'

Ledbetter coloured . . .

When he and Mazzioni had gone, the A.C. looked in on Gideon, approved the decision to hold over the dangerous drugs charge, and asked:

'Think you can make Mazzioni crack in time?'

'Dunno,' said Gideon frankly. 'More than anything else, I want that dancer, Estelle.'

'Any news?'

'Not yet,' Gideon said.

The A.C. went off as glum as Gideon, and Gideon sat back and studied transcripts of Mazzioni's statements, and the record of the woman who'd given him an alibi. He wanted to talk to her, but –

Before he could even think about visiting her, he had to check what reports were coming in. He hadn't yet heard about the night's biggest job, at the Mid-Union Safe Deposit in the City.

CHAPTER 17

THE BIGGEST JOB . . .

Every part of London had known its moments of crisis that night, every Division received its urgent call for help. The placid men in the Information Room had taken call after call to 999 without fuss, quietly reassuring agitated callers, extracting the necessary information, passing it through to the Flying Squad, the Patrol Cars or the Divisions for action.

The Yard seemed more alive by night than by day.

The reports were on Gideon's desk, in a thick sheaf of notes written in a bold, legible hand and a welcome economy of phrase; and the sergeant stood looking at Gideon as if he hoped the Superintendent would make a favourable comment.

There were the burglaries; dozens of them. Attacks on women alone in the streets, smash-and-grab jobs, two club raids with fifty-seven names taken. Great Marlborough Street was overflowing with the so-called flower of the aristocracy, most of whom took a raid on a gambling club for a joke, or pretended to.

There was the inevitable crop of charges of soliciting, there were two men accused of attempting to murder their wives. One was still belligerent after being stopped from thrashing his wife, the other cowed and frightened, so much so that it was hard to believe that he had ever been brandishing a knife, as if ready to kill.

Three men had been picked up in the Occident Hotel for passing sludge, or forged money. A man who had already served two sentences for fraud was held on suspicion of trying to earn his third sentence; crimes of all kinds and all varieties were committed in the few hours that were left of Gideon's day, but there was only one which held dynamite.

The note read: *City Police glad if you will call them, suspected burglary Mid-Union Safe Deposit.*

'Oh no,' grunted Gideon.

He skimmed through the other notes, and then the telephone bell rang. The sergeant could have answered it, but Gideon's hand was already on the smooth black surface.

'Gideon here.'

He listened.

'Are you *sure*?' His voice rose, his face brightened.

'Oh, that's fine,' he said. 'How badly hurt? . . . Well, he'll get over it. Tell his wife, won't you?' He rang off and looked up at the door as it opened, and Lemaitre came in, very subdued. 'Thought you'd gone home,' he said.

'Daren't,' said Lemaitre gloomily.

Gideon chuckled.

'What's pleased you?' demanded Lemaitre. 'The last I saw of you, you looked –'

'They've picked up Birdy.'

'That so?' Lemaitre brightened. 'Okay?'

'Cuts on his right wrist and his cheeks and some nasty bruising on his back and stomach, but an X-ray showed nothing to worry about,' said Gideon. 'They got Ali, too.'

'You mean that little lascar swine?'

'He's being held – was caught with the knife on him and in the act of using it. Actually a curate over there stopped it, young chap who's new to the district.'

Lemaitre whistled.

'If he hadn't been new, he wouldn't have interfered! Ali would have knifed him as soon as look at him. That's a bit better, anyhow. We've still got the chance of getting somewhere through the Snide and Ali. One of them will probably squeal, and if we could tuck Murphy away for a few years it would be something. What do you think of that crook, Led –'

'Okay, sergeant,' Gideon interrupted, 'I'll call you when I want you. Thanks – very good job.'

'Thank you, sir.' The sergeant hurried out.

'Hell, what would it have mattered if I had told him what I thought of Ledbetter?' growled Lemaitre. 'And to think what I've done for this night's work – proper mucked things up with Fifi. If you'd seen the way she looked when I told her I had to stand her up.'

'Go home, wake her up, and tell her you love her,' said Gideon, 'and blame me for standing her up.'

'Strewth!' exclaimed Lemaitre, 'it's bad enough when I wake her if I just get home late. Anything much in?'

'The City chaps want me,' said Gideon. 'Some trouble at the Mid-Union Safe Deposit. Better call them.' He stifled a yawn. 'And then come hell or high water, I'm going *home*.'

He felt flat again as he spoke. The temporary stimulant of the news about Birdy had faded in fresh gloom about Mazzioni. Ledbetter's part depressed him, too; there were plenty of unreliable solicitors, but they didn't grow on trees. Few of them were crooked for the sake of it, usually they drifted, some were blackmailed.

'I wouldn't mind a bit of action,' Lemaitre said. 'Got anything?'

He really funked going home.

'Go and see this woman,' Gideon said, and tapped the card with the name and address of Mazzioni's 'alibi'. 'Try to shake her about where she was and who she was with this afternoon.'

'Oke,' Lemaitre promised.

Gideon called the City Police.

Earlier in the evening, the night staff of the Mid-Union Safe Deposit Company had settled down to the usual quiet night's work. Most of this would be keeping records. There would be some business in the early hours of the morning, when the really sensible, who had taken out jewels for wear, brought them back instead of taking them home. That 'rush' would last for an hour, and after it there would be nothing until the morning staff took over. Only three men were on duty; a fourth, usually present, was on sick-leave.

Three could cope.

The building of the Mid-Union Safe Deposit Company was a large stone-faced one, in narrow Wattle Street, and was sandwiched between a block of offices let to a hundred different firms – from lawyers to tea brokers, rubber merchants to shipping companies, accountants and insurance brokers – and the Head offices of one of the largest insurance companies. Mid-Union actually owned the building, but let off the ground and upper floors, retaining a basement office and two big vaults, each below basement level. The entrance was through Wattle Street and past a wide doorway which was protected, when necessary, by a strong steel door.

This was always open.

No one could step through the doorway without sending two warnings through to the officials on the floor below; one warning was electric, the other was by secret ray; neither rang a bell, but each flashed a light which would be seen at once by the men on duty.

These were behind a strong grille, heavily protected, and entrance could be gained only through a small doorway which was kept locked and unlocked for every fresh customer. No customer was allowed in the vaults by himself – neither the one at first level, where the more frequently needed deposits were stored, nor the deep vault. An armed official always accompanied him. By night, it was sometimes necessary to keep customers waiting, but if they wished they could drop their packets into a night safe – much on the bank system – and this would be put in a community safe until they came to put it in their own box.

The staff took the daily and nightly handling of valuables for granted. On really busy days, a million pounds' worth of precious stones would be brought in or taken out, and no one thought twice about it.

Except Fitzroy . . .

About the time that Gideon had finished his dinner one of the three members of the staff had gone into the bottom vaults, to check some entries. That was regular enough, and he should be gone for about half an hour. In fact, he was longer. Neither of the others was worried about this, for some jobs were difficult to estimate.

All the men on duty carried guns, but in the forty-nine years of its existence, the Mid-Union had never had an attempted robbery. This did not make anyone careless; the warning system was perfect, and each night-duty official was trained in the use of his gun. They were selected men with brilliant war records. No one over forty-five was employed by night.

The big general office behind the reception desk was empty by night, too.

When the first man had been gone for forty minutes – by then, Gideon had seen Ledbetter – one of the others went to look for him, leaving only the night-manager behind the grille.

The second man didn't come back either.

The night-manager, a youthful forty-one, knew his staff well and was quite sure that they were reliable. He was going to find out what was keeping them, when two customers came in. Both were men, both wanted to deposit jewels. They were regular customers, the night-manager could not offend them, and he took them downstairs to the first vault, one at a time.

In all, that job took him twelve minutes.

He locked the reception desk door on the two customers, and hurried to the narrow stone steps which led to the lower vault.

Half-way down, he stopped.

Ought he to telephone the police, and make sure that if anything were wrong –

It was too late.

A man appeared at the foot of the steps, holding an automatic pistol. The night-manager felt as if death had suddenly knocked loudly at his door. The man with the gun was masked, tall, lean, leathery-looking. The gun was very steady. He started up the stairs and the manager backed a step, but didn't move far. He was in between two alarm bells that would call the police, and his hope of getting to one was to turn and rush up the steps.

The eyes of Fitzroy, the man with the gun, discouraged notions of heroism.

'Take it easy,' Fitzroy said. 'You won't get hurt if you do what you're told, but if you try any tricks, you'll get hurt badly. *And* you might not recover.'

The manager licked his lips.

Fitzroy was within two yards of him.

If he jumped –

He jumped.

As he moved, he had an awful sense of failure, of doom. He saw the gunman draw to one side, saw a long leg shoot out. He could not avoid it and fell headlong down the stairs.

Another masked man appeared at the foot of them and picked him up. Dazed and bruised, he could only think of the gun.

Fitzroy spoke brightly:

'Just do what you're told, and you won't get hurt. Let's have your keys for a start.'

'No. No, I –'

The second man struck the manager sharply across the face and spun him round. The keys were fastened to a thick leather belt running round his waist. The second man used a pair of wire-cutters to cut the belt, then pushed the manager towards the lower vault. The manager was too frightened to think clearly, but a thought flashed into his mind.

These men seemed to know their way about.

Entrance must have been forced from *below*. That wasn't possible, it –

He was pushed into the large bottom vault, where big, solid safes and rows of metal boxes lined the walls from floor to ceiling. On the floor, lying on their backs, were the two clerks. In one wall was a hole nearly two feet square, and by it was a heap of dirt and debris, chippings of cement, everything to show how the 'impossible' had been achieved.

Then a man thrust a cloth over the manager's head, tied it at the back, seized his hands and bound them, and then laid him down.

He did not know what was happening; all he knew was that he was alive. Fitzroy looked at him and grinned, then turned to the two men with him, pulling off his mask.

'I'm going up to the office to look after the customers.' He chuckled again. 'They won't know how safe their baubles are!' He went off, moving easily and outwardly confident, and he whistled softly as he took the place of the manager.

The odds had been nicely calculated.

He knew that the fourth member of the night staff was away. He knew that the hour for late deposits was almost past, and that even if there were more, they would only be for the upper floor. He could lock himself in with the depositor, see the goods put in the box, and wish the man 'good night'. His two assistants were expert safebreakers, and if they managed to open only two of the safes and two or three dozen of the metal boxes, the haul would be sensational. So he whistled as he sat at the desk, and made a show of working when he heard footsteps.

A young man came down and stopped short at sight of him.
'Evening, sir,' said Fitzroy, getting up.
'Good evening. Isn't Mr. Ilott here?'
'Downstairs at the moment,' said Fitzroy glibly, 'but I can send for him if you really want him.'
'Well –'
'Or I can help you, sir.' Fitzroy looked so brisk and friendly, smiled so amiably, and spoke with such conviction, that the depositor gave way. He had his own key. Fitzroy let him into the upper deposit vault, escorted him to his box, and watched him deposit a diamond ring and two diamond drop earrings.
'I always feel safer when they're locked away,' said the depositor.
'I bet you do,' said Fitzroy warmly. 'I would if they were mine, too. I'll tell Mr. Ilott that you've been, sir.'
'Thanks,' the depositor said, and left with a hearty 'Good night'.
Fitzroy went back to his desk, and whistled under his breath until the man's footsteps had faded; then he lit a cigarette, and took out a newspaper folded to the crossword puzzle. Now and again he perked his head up, and listened; he had heard imagined sounds from the street.
Down below, the others were working quickly and with great skill.
Two safes were open, and cash, diamonds, jewellery of all kinds and a little bullion, were loaded into canvas mail van sacks. One man was working at a third safe, the other was beginning on the steel boxes. He had a tool which pierced them at the edges, and, working rather like wire cutters or tin openers, tore a big hole. He made some noise, but it did not travel even up the narrow stone steps to Fitzroy.
He opened box after box.
The other man forced the door of his third safe, and, hardly troubling to examine the jewellery in it, dropped it into another sack.
The first man had emptied twenty-one boxes.
'About all we can manage,' he said, looking round the vault regretfully. 'I hope we haven't missed any juicy ones. They could tell us!' He grinned across at the three prisoners, but didn't go towards them.
He went up to the main floor, and, without showing himself in the office whispered:
'You there, Fitz?'
Fitz called immediately: 'Yes.'
'We're going.'
'Nice haul?'
'Plenty.' There was an echo of satisfaction in the man's voice; an echo of excitement, too. Fitzroy got up and went to the head of the stairs, leaving the reception desk untenanted for a moment. He was pulling at a cigar-

ette, and excitement showed in the brightness of his eyes; the other man showed his with a slight quiver of the lips and the hands. 'Wouldn't like to guess how much, but not less than a couple of hundred thousand.'

'*Nice* work! Off you go.'

'How long will you stay?'

'Ten minutes,' said Fitzroy, 'and then I'll lock the front doors, and any customers will be annoyed!' The shrillness of his laugh was another betrayal of his taut nerves.

He went back to the reception desk. He didn't hear a car stop outside, but for some reason went suddenly tense.

Below, his companions were taking the loot out through the hole they had made.

A man and woman came hurrying down the steps, the man in evening dress, the woman wearing a long dress and a mink wrap. The man produced his key and his card, and said briskly:

'Don't want to rush you, but I'm in a hurry.'

'All right,' said Fitzroy. 'I'll be as quick as I can.'

There was no reason at all why they should suspect that anything was wrong; no reason for them to believe that anything was. They looked natural, happy. The woman was little more than a girl, and she had a glow in her eyes which suggested that she was not used to hanging on to this particular arm.

Number 413 – close to the head of the stairs leading to the lower vault.

Fitzroy, all right then, became slow-moving, in spite of the impatience of the man; he was drawing attention to himself by his slowness.

He unlocked the door. He knew that it was a matter of custom for the depositor to come in alone, but the girl was like a limpet. A brunette, rather nice, low-bosomed dress, everything. Fitzroy looked at her and swallowed hard. This was where he could easily make a fool of himself.

He forced a smile.

'Depositor only, please.'

'Won't be a jiff, dear,' said the young man, and prised himself free.

Fitzroy's fists, clenched until then, unclenched as he closed and locked the door. It seemed a very long way to Number 413, and it seemed as if the man had eyes that could see through the brick walls. Fitzroy's body was a-quiver, it was a good thing that the depositor had to unlock his own box.

He did so, took out a string of pearls, left everything else in, locked the box again, and was back at the grille ahead of Fitzroy. Fitzroy breathed rather hissingly. It was over and he'd kept his head.

After that it was easy.

He did not give a thought to the three prisoners.

It did not occur to him that trouble might lie ahead.

CHAPTER 18

THE TUNNEL

Gideon heard the voice of the City Superintendent, warm and friendly, broad in its Scots accent. Gideon was not thinking deeply about this call yet, for he was still preoccupied, although beginning to warn himself that he must go home and get some rest. Only the countless loose ends which came at the very end of every day were left undone.

'Hallo, Alec,' he said, 'what can I do for you?'

'George, man, I'm puzzled a wee bit,' the Superintendent said. 'You know the Mid-Union place? They keep half the valuables of London there, which is a slight exaggeration but you know what I mean.'

'I ken,' said Gideon, straight-faced.

'Stop your joking, man. One of the regular customers went there a while ago and said that he didn't recognize the official at the reception desk. The official seemed to know his way about all right, but he didn't have anyone with him. And that's a curious thing, George, under the regulations there are always two men on duty at the desk. I've never known it any different. So I told my man to keep a sharp look-out, and just this minute he's telephoned to say that the doors are locked. Now that's not done any night in the year, the Mid-Union is always open. So I'm putting a cordon round the place. I thought you'd like to know.'

Gideon said very slowly: 'Thanks, Alec, that's good of you.' He was thinking more deeply now; worriedly. The City man had probably exaggerated, but the valuables in that safe deposit were worth a fabulous sum. The City police did not want to handle it on their own, and hadn't lost any time asking for help. 'All right, I'll put word round and have some support sent along.' Gideon went on: 'Are you going there yourself?'

'Aye, I think so.'

'I'll see you there,' promised Gideon.

He still did not, could not, understand how important the job was; but it might be very big indeed. The drive to Wattle Street in the night air would wake him up a bit. If this fizzled out, he could go straight home.

'Lem, hand everything over to Cartwright, will you?' he said. 'And then go home. Better forget Estelle, she'll have to keep till morning. Take a chance on getting kicked out of bed.'

Lemaitre grimaced and moved to his telephone.

Gideon went out.

He was in a curiously unsatisfied mood. He could not really complain about the day, and the capture of Sayer had been of first importance. A lot had gone right, too. At heart, he knew that two things had gone very deep: the discovery of Foster's duplicity, and his death; and the face of Mrs. Saparelli. These made the finding of Estelle more urgent, but it would all take time. There were the drugs at Mazzioni's, too – the Italian didn't know they'd been found. He'd probably make a slip –

Gideon telephoned orders to the Flying Squad C.O. to have all available squad cars concentrated on the City area, and then hurried out. Few policemen were about. A squad car was waiting ready for an emergency call, with two men sitting in front. His own car shone darkly under a lamp immediately above it.

Big Ben boomed eleven.

Gideon got into the Wolseley, slammed the door, and then, for some reason, remembered Kate. There was an added cause for his discontent. He could picture her running down the stairs to him, almost eagerly. *Eagerly*. He could picture her bright eyes and attractive face as she had sat next to him on the way to Oxford Street, and the jaunty grace of her walk as she had left him. She hadn't looked back. She'd obviously been pleased that he had taken the trouble to drop in, and to give her the lift. It would have been all right had he been able to go home early, but here it was eleven o'clock, and even if this turned out to be a false alarm, it would be midnight before he was home.

He didn't hurry.

Two squad cars passed him, on their way to the City.

Fitzroy finished locking the door at the top of the narrow steps, and, still whistling, hurried down them to the brightly-lit reception desk. The street door was closed and they were safe. He opened a drawer and found some loose change and a few one pound and ten shilling notes. He stuffed these into his pocket, saluted the drawer, and then looked round quickly, making sure that he hadn't left anything behind. The stubs of three cigarettes were in an ashtray; he emptied this into a piece of paper, screwed it up, and thrust it into his pocket.

Whistling, he went down the next flight of steps to the main deposit room. The three prisoners lay stretched out, and one of them was wriggling.

'You'll soon feel better, chum, don't worry,' Fitzroy said, and then hurried towards the lower vault and the hole in the wall.

He saw one of the others coming back into the vault, *out* of the hole. The man was treading on bits of cement and dirt.

When he saw this, Fitzroy stood stock still and open-mouthed. No shock could have been greater. He had pictured his accomplices already driving through London to the safety of obscurity. It was like seeing the ghost of a living man. But this was no ghost; it was a youth in the early twenties, looking badly scared.

'What the hell's this?' Fitzroy demanded in a squeaky voice.

'We – we can't get out,' the man said, as thinly.

Fitzroy just would not believe it.

'Don't talk a lot of bull! We can –'

'Police are – are in Hay Court,' the man announced.

Fitzroy didn't speak.

The light was good and he had not put on his mask again. He had pleasant features, an open face, and smiling blue eyes; only they were not smiling now. A new light came into them, cold and ugly.

'We've got to get out,' he said 'Where's Jem?'

'Keeping watch.'

'Come on,' said Fitzroy.

He had to bend almost double, to get through the hole. He took a torch out of his pocket, and it showed the gap they had made in days of patient labour. Now they made grating noises as they moved along, and once or twice Fitzroy bumped his head painfully on the uneven roof; but he didn't stop. Soon, bright light glowed.

He reached the cellar of the building next door, one used for storing old files and documents. The night watchman of the building was in his, Fitzroy's pay; he did not know what they were doing in the cellar, just turned a blind eye and did not come beyond the first cellar level.

The steps leading to that cellar were of stone, crumbling away. Fitzroy went up them slowly. He moved with great caution, while the full significance of what was happening gradually caught up with him.

He reached the ground floor.

There were two ways out of this building; the big, massive front door, which was barred and bolted to prevent anyone from coming in; and a small doorway at the back, leading to a little courtyard and, by a narrow alley, to Milchester Street. It should have been so easy. The only problem was to get the sacks through the alley to the small car which was parked nearby, in a little private parking place. They had studied the time of the police patrols in the district, and had judged the right moment.

Fitzroy went through the deserted building, his footsteps making little sound on the stone floor of the hall; then on linoleum over wide boards; finally over tiles. Soon, he saw the faint light against a window. He could not make out the figure of the third burglar, Jem, but heard the faint whisper.

'How many outside?'

'Dunno.'

Fitzroy moved towards the window. He shone his torch so that the beam fell upon a chair which he knew one of the others had put into position. He climbed up, and could now peer through a window into the courtyard.

He saw *three* uniformed policemen.

He got down. His heart was thumping, but he told himself that he wasn't really frightened. He had been in tough spots before, and had got out of them. He slid his right hand into his hip pocket; the steel of an automatic pistol felt very cold.

'How many in Wattle Street?'

'Several,' Jem muttered. He was the tallest of the three. 'Tell you what –'

'What?'

'We could go up to the first floor, and climb up, then –'

'Carrying what?' Fitzroy asked sneeringly.

Jem didn't answer.

'We've got a fortune,' Fitzroy said, 'and we're going to keep it. Stay here a minute.'

He turned back towards the front entrance. He would not have admitted it to anyone, but he did not really know what to do. He had been so sure that this way of escape would be left open, because it didn't affect Mid-Union. He began to ask himself what had gone wrong, but gave that up as futile. He could see the street lights showing against the huge fanlight, but if he went into one of the offices . . .

He tried a door handle; and the door opened.

He stepped into an office. This had frosted glass half-way up the window, but through the top he could see the dark shape of a lamp standard; as he went in, the light outside grew brighter and the engine of a car sounded. The car swept along the street, the driver changed gear and turned a corner.

A desk stood close to the window.

Fitzroy climbed up and peered cautiously over the frosted glass into the street.

Two cars were parked a little way along. Men in uniform and in plainclothes were outside the entrance to the Mid-Union Building. It wasn't surprising that the police should concentrate on that, but –

How could he get out?

He climbed down and went away from the window as another car arrived and stopped.

He began to sweat.

They had to get out, now. If the police forced their way into the building next door, they would find the hole in five minutes, would be in this building in ten; squeezed between the two forces, Fitzroy and his companions wouldn't have a chance.

'Jem,' he said, when back in the rear hall.

'Yes?'

'Any reinforcements out there?'

'No.'

'Okay. I'm going to open the door. I'll keep them busy. I'll take a few sparklers with me, that'll fool them. I'll draw them off and when I've done that, you two get to the car. Take a sack each and make it snappy.'

'But –'

'Think of anything better?' Fitzroy demanded angrily.

'No, but –'

'Then quit crabbing.'

'Fitz,' the other man said, in a whisper which was hardly audible, 'you won't go killing?'

'Who said anything about killing?'

'That gun?'

'What a gutless pair to work with,' Fitzroy growled. 'Okay, if you want to spend the next ten years in jail, I don't. Do it my way.' He didn't give them a chance to answer, but went to the door.

He heard one of them breathing very heavily, then heard the rustle as he picked up the bag.

He opened the door a fraction, mildly surprised that it did open. He knew that the police would be watching intently, and that they hoped that whoever was inside would come out without realizing that anyone was lying in wait.

The light shone on the paving stones of the courtyard; on the frosted glass of the window of offices surrounding it; on a grating; on a drain pipe down which water gurgled. Apart from that there was no sound.

He opened the door wider.

He saw nothing.

He called in a whisper: 'Looks as if they've gone.' At heart he did not believe that, but he was desperately anxious to get away, and wishful thinking fooled him for a few dazzling seconds. 'Come on.'

He stepped into the courtyard.

No one was in sight and there were no shadows. Somewhere, high up, the wind whistled, but in this yard all was still. Perhaps they hadn't realized that the door was opening. Perhaps they had gone to reinforce men at the Mid-Union building, not this.

He tiptoed across the courtyard to the end of the alley.

The others were in the courtyard now.

He carried the gun in front of him, but with the passing of every second, the palpitations grew less, for the chances of success were obviously greater. The car wasn't far away, he would lead the way to it, and keep cover while they got in.

Then he heard a gasp:

'Fitz!' a man cried.

Fitzroy spun round, saw one of his accomplices stagger, and saw a policeman jumping *down* from a window just above the door.

Other police appeared at first floor windows, a whistle shrilled out along the alley.

Fitzroy fired at the falling policeman, did not wait to see if he had scored a hit, but turned towards the alley and ran. All hope of loot was gone, escape was his one purpose – escape, with the determination to shoot himself to safety.

CHAPTER 19

THE ESCAPE

Gideon reached the offices of the Mid-Union Company when two police cars and a small crowd of policemen were outside. He slowed down and a uniformed man wearing the helmet of the City Police came forward, recognized him, and said:

'Superintendent Cameron's in Hay Court, sir.'

'Hay Court? Where – oh, I know. Thanks. All quiet?'

'Someone inside there as shouldn't be,' the constable said emphatically. 'The manager's on the way with another set of keys.'

'Good,' said Gideon. 'Thanks.' He drove on, not travelling fast, looking for the narrow turning which would take him to Hay Court. He knew the City almost as well as he knew his own Square Mile, but not quite as well. In the West End he could have found his way about blindfolded; here, he wasn't sure, until he saw another tall City policeman at a corner. The man put out an arm to stop the car; a silent, immutable force, showing all the confidence in the world.

Gideon poked his head through the window.

'I'm Gideon. Is Superintendent Cameron here?'

'Just along here, sir, but I shouldn't take the car if I were you. We've put a barricade up.'

'Oh. Thanks. I'll park along here.' Gideon drove on a few yards and climbed out.

The night air was fresh but by no means cold. The sky had a clearness and the stars a brightness which were more common to winter than to spring. Gideon felt not so much tired now as relaxed.

He walked briskly and with hardly a sound towards Hay Court. At the end of this narrow, cobbled road, he saw a row of galvanized dustbins beneath a gas light and grinned at the form of the barricade. Two policemen stood on duty, one peered at and recognized him and saluted. Gideon passed between two dustbins, unpleasantly aware of the smell of rotting vegetables.

There was a small square, surrounded by high buildings, and with two recesses holding the doorways to small buildings, and one lane, which led towards Fenchurch Street. He remembered it well now. He saw two policemen climbing up the side of one office building and watched them in the semi-darkness. They were making for a window sill above a door which was closed, and edged their way along.

He saw shadowy figures at one of the windows.

Cameron came up.

'Hallo, George,' he greeted, 'good to see you.' They shook hands. Cameron was a man of medium size; even in this light his fair features and sharp, pointed nose were evident. 'We think they'll come out this way, a door opened a few minutes ago. And there's a car waiting not far away, often parked there late, I'm told.'

'Any idea who it is?'

'No.' Cameron whispered a few other details: that he had telephoned the manager of the Mid-Union Company and been told that the top gates should not be locked. An observant constable had really started this, and a puzzled customer taken it a step further.

Cameron was in a mood for rejoicing; so was Gideon. Usually they were called after the job was done, when the men and the loot were miles away, and the whole resources of the Force had to be called on, straining the men almost beyond endurance. This should be a short, sharp case, and –

'Look!' whispered Cameron.

In the faint light they saw the doorway open. Then a man appeared and looked round cautiously. Had he looked up, he must have seen the policemen poised above him. He hesitated, then went back into the building.

Gideon's big hand closed round Cameron's arm, and gave a silent message. Cameron breathed:

'*Aye, a gun.*'

Gideon felt his mood changing to one of acute wariness. He wanted to shout a warning to everyone else within earshot, but dare not. He sensed Cameron's increased tension. Then the man with the gun came forward, other dark figures emerged from the doorway.

One of the policemen jumped.

The movement, the gasp and the scuffle of footsteps came quickly and then the first man swung round, and Gideon saw him raise his arm.

'*Look out!*' roared Gideon.

But the shot came before his words. He saw the policeman falling and heard a kind of squeal. Then the men who had come from the doorway all moved together, but it was impossible to tell one from another. A heavy weight fell. Policemen closed with one man, and then torch lights shone out, carving Hay Court into sections of bright light and darkness, showing the pallor of frightened faces, the darkness of clothes, the gun, struggling feet, a big sack.

Gideon concentrated on the gunman.

Fitzroy was free of police for a split second, but another was running at him, and Cameron moved, too. Fitzroy fired, point-blank.

'. . . swine,' Gideon muttered under his breath.

He waited, like a footballer ready to go into the tackle, swaying from side to side. The policeman fell back, then crumpled up.

Fitzroy was free of him – and Fitzroy saw another policeman coming at him.

He fired again.

The policeman swayed to one side, and Fitzroy made a wild leap, passed him, and reached the end of the alley. The gun was waving as he ran.

Only one big man in plainclothes was in his path.

'Now, drop that,' Gideon said. He was surprised that his own voice was level and intelligible. 'Don't be a fool.'

For a second, a long, frightening, deathly second, neither man moved.

Gideon knew that words were useless, only one thing would save him.

He plunged forward, hands outstretched to clutch the gunman's ankles. It was impossible to tell whether the other would shoot at him or not; if he pointed the gun downwards and fired, he couldn't miss.

Gideon felt the cloth of the man's trousers in his fingers. He tried to grab the ankles, but missed. A foot cracked against his temple, and there was an explosive sound inside his head; he wasn't sure whether it came from a shot or the kick. He drew his hands in instinctively to protect his head. The thief jumped over him and the sharp crack of another shot came.

Gideon began to pick himself up drunkenly.

No one came to help him.

He got to one knee. There was a nasty throbbing in his ears, but he knew that he hadn't been shot, because there was no blood. He felt light-headed. Sounds came as if from a long way off. On his feet, he staggered until he came up against the wall.

Someone said: 'You all right, sir?'

'Yes. Yes, don't worry about –' he didn't finish, but tried to focus his gaze. The light in the court was brighter and clearer now, coming from rooms in the nearby offices as well as the torches. It was a strange, almost a frightening sight. Men bent over two policemen who lay on the ground, one of them grunting, moaning. Two men, each handcuffed to a policeman, were standing quite still. Sacks near the doorway told their own story.

Then, from some way off, came the bark of another shot.

'I've got a nasty feeling,' Gideon said, 'that that brute's going to get away.'

'You all right, George?' Cameron demanded.

'Yes, thanks.'

'What've you done to your head?'

'Just a kick.'

'We'll get him,' Cameron said, 'we'll get him if –'

He didn't finish. Words were futile, rage with himself as well as with the prisoner who had escaped was just as futile. The simple truth was that the man had shot his way out of the ambush and, in doing so, wounded three policemen, one of whom seemed to be in a bad way.

Ambulances had been summoned.

A general call had gone out for the gunman, and at least they knew his name and had a description; one of the prisoners had talked freely; words had spilled out with fear.

It had all happened ten minutes ago and it seemed like hours. Gideon, his head aching but no longer giddy, had sent out the instructions by radio-telephone, but he felt sick. It wasn't because of the kick or the fall – it was because of the failure.

Could one call it failure?

Already he was beginning to ask himself questions about it and his own part in it. Cameron had been in charge, but he needn't have left so much to the City man. The truth was that he had taken this too casually, almost like an exercise; 'trapped men cannot get away' had been his axiom, and he hadn't allowed for a killer shooting his way to freedom. Failure as such wasn't the only bad thing. It meant that the Yard and all the Divisions would have to screw themselves up to a high-powered effort, and tension was never-ending. If all three men had been captured, the police could have breathed more easily; only routine jobs need have worried them, jobs like this seldom came up more than once in two or three weeks.

Well, it had to be done.

The night duty man at the Yard would be doing much the same as he had been doing all day, every policeman in London would be steeling himself. Gideon couldn't explain why, but it was a fact that if a policeman were shot and injured, especially if one were killed, something seemed to be infused into the rest of the Force. They became killer-minded. They would work until they dropped and they would get this man, Fitzroy. But that wasn't the beginning or the end. They could only do one job at a time, and the little crooks who worked by night were quick to sense when the police had a big job on. This was a night when the graph of London's crime would shoot upwards sharply. In temporary, perhaps in false security, the sneak-thieves would be out like vultures ready to peck and tear at an unprotected carcase.

Gideon knew all this.

He knew, too, that if he had grabbed an inch closer to the gunman's ankles, he would have brought the man down, and there would have been no need for the great hunt. That was one cause of his bitterness. He of all men knew how tightly the police were stretched; and he could have eased the burden for a little while, but had failed.

There it was.

He heard a bell ringing, shrilly; an ambulance was on its way. In the distance, another sounded. Then men came from Wattle Street. Next Gideon and Cameron went through the building next to Mid-Union, and found the hole which had been made into the lower vault.

Gideon's lips turned down.

'They didn't do that in a hurry,' he said.

'Dunno,' said Cameron, and bent down to pick up a small electric drill. 'Home-made job and it wouldn't make much noise.' He paused. 'You can't get through there, can you?'

'No,' said Gideon.

'See you the other side.' Cameron was already on his knees, ready to climb through.

Gideon walked back into Hay Court, along the narrow cobbled road into Wattle Street. The door was being unlocked, policemen were waiting warily, in case other gunmen lay in wait. None did. Gideon and a scared, worried manager who had hurried from his home in Hampstead, led the way down the stairs. The empty reception office, the narrow stairs, the ordinary strong-room – and the three members of the staff were found, stretched out, two of them struggling with their bonds, the other unconscious.

Outside, the hunt for Fitzroy went on.

Gideon yawned.

It was half-past twelve, exactly fifteen hours since he had stepped into his office that morning, an age ago. He was by himself for a few minutes, sitting in his car. No word had come in of Fitzroy's capture and the hunt might go on for days. The ambulances had carried off the wounded policemen and one of the Mid-Union staff, who was suffering badly from shock and fright. None of the victims was likely to die: that was one relief. The accomplices had told their story without defiance, as if they had realized that nothing else could help them.

They were amateurs who'd adapted army-acquired knowledge to the safe-breaking. If they were to be believed and Gideon thought that they were, the idea had been Fitzroy's. But neither of them had raised any strenuous objections and they had come in of their own free will. These were the kind who really worried Gideon most. The old lags, the regulars, the confidence tricksters, the blackmailers, even the dope distributors – all of them were within Gideon's range. He could understand them and he could calculate what they were likely to do. Amateurs were different and their methods were different. They were likely to be more reckless and so more deadly. A man like Fitzroy saw this as a great adventure, as well as a chance of making a fortune. A man like Chang saw it as a game to be played with great precision and Chang would never take such risks as Fitzroy, would never shoot his way out. If he killed, it would be cunningly – as he had killed Foster.

Gideon found his lips twisting in a wry, almost bitter smile.

If Lemaitre had said that, he would have jumped on him. It was still a guess. It might not be a wild guess, there might be some reason for making it, but it was still a guess. He didn't *know* that Chang had killed Foster, tried to kill Birdy, was hunting Estelle down. He could not be sure that Foster had not served some other master, too, whom Chang did not know.

That was the trouble; not knowing.

If only he had known at the beginning of the day what he knew now, how much could have been prevented and how much done. If he'd handled Foster differently, Foster might be alive now, and willingly co-operating.

The thought of that hit Gideon with savage force, and suddenly he understood why he had been so easily depressed during the day.

He hadn't liked Foster and that was partly why his temper had broken. With almost any other man at the Yard – the sergeant who'd been so nervous and yet so efficient, for instance – he could have talked reasonably, almost as a friend. He began to go over in his mind the things he should have said to Foster, and the line he should have taken.

His head ached.

He wished Cameron would hurry up with whatever he was doing.

He wondered if they'd catch Fitzroy.

He worried about red-haired Estelle.

He heard the radio-telephone buzz, looked at the instrument without enthusiasm, picked it up, and flicked it on:

'Gideon speaking.'

'How you doing, George?' This was Lemaitre, speaking direct; and Lemaitre with a lilt in his voice as if his Fifi and his fears were all forgotten. Lemaitre speaking like that was a tonic in itself; cold water in Gideon's face. 'Like to meet me over at Shippy's place, Whitechapel?'

'Why, what's on?'

'We've made quite a find,' Lemaitre said smugly. 'See you there!'

He banged his receiver down.

Gideon fought down the momentary annoyance. In some ways Lemaitre would never grow up, and his attitude now was rather like a boy's. But he was highly pleased with himself and that might mean anything.

Anything.

Gideon was getting up when the telephone rang again, was tempted to go out and ignore it, but conquered temptation.

He had never been more glad.

'Gillick here, G.G.,' said Gillick, spitting his words out. 'Now I really have got some news for us, trust B2. Eh, old boy? All right, I'll get to the point. We've picked up that chap Fessell you're after, the Islington sweet-shop job. One of my chaps thought he saw him earlier in the evening, and kept a look-out. He was in a hotel, dabs make it certain. Shall we keep him here for the night?'

CHAPTER 20

END OF THE DAY

Gideon drove through the deserted streets of the City towards the East End, munching a ham sandwich which Cameron had laid on. Cameron was looking after everything at the Mid-Union now, and Gideon wasn't needed any more. Gideon wasn't sure that he had ever been needed, but at least he knew all about it.

Depression at the knowledge that Fitzroy was still at large had gone. Fessell's capture was a fresh triumph, and there was the titillating promise of Lemaitre's manner.

Shippy's was a café nearly of ill-repute in the Whitechapel area, not far from the Mile End Road. It was known to be the rendezvous of most of the really bad types in the East End. Murphy used it and most of the men who worked in liaison with Murphy. Many ugly crimes were plotted there. Yet outwardly it was reputable and Shippy, the man who ran it, looked like a citizen *par excellence*. As a café it was not only good, it was spotlessly clean. Shippy, or Luke Shipham, was a thin man who always wore a new white apron, a stiff white collar and a grey tie, whose hair was smartly groomed and brushed to a high quiff. He had never been inside, but had been interviewed a hundred times, and always presented the same bland story and the same bland face:

'Nothing wrong happens in my café, Mr. Gideon. I can't refuse to serve men because they might be criminal, can I?'

Most people prophesied that Shippy would slip up one day. Gideon wasn't so sure.

Whitechapel was dimly lit, the wide streets seemed derelict, the unlighted houses were drab, deserted hovels. A few neon advertising signs burned in the High Street, but there was a long gap in them, broken when Gideon came within sight of Shippy's. The name was emblazoned in white neon across the front of the double-fronted café. As Gideon pulled up outside he was impressed, as he had often been, by the smart appearance of the place. Put it in Oxford Street, and it would compare favourably with most restaurants.

A blue sign declared: '*Open Day & Night.*'

A squad car was outside, and two uniformed policemen walking up and down. They came closer to see who it was and then touched their helmets.

Gideon felt a quickening sense of excitement as he pushed open the double doors.

The big room with cream-painted walls, blue and red tables and chairs, and the brightly shining urn at the long counter, struck warm. There was a smell of ground coffee. Sandwiches in a glass showcase looked more succulent than those which Gideon had been given by Cameron, and far superior to anything ever supplied by the Yard. A youth stood behind the counter and two plainclothes men of the Flying Squad were sitting at a table, eating and drinking; they jumped up when Gideon appeared.

'All right,' Gideon said, 'so long as you pay for it. Mr. Lemaitre here?'

One man grinned; the other said, 'Yes, sir,' and nodded towards the open door leading to the kitchen and the room at the back of the restaurant. Gideon found himself thinking of Chang; and restaurants generally; and the restaurants Chang supplied with tea and other goods.

Shippy, looking correct and aloof, was standing in one corner of the room. A uniformed policeman was watching him. Lemaitre, hat and coat off, sleeves rolled up over those big, swelling arms, sat at a desk with another Yard man, and on a big, deal-topped table there were wads and wads of one-pound notes.

Gideon caught his breath.

'Mr. Gideon, sir,' Shippy said quickly. 'I didn't know anything about it. A gentleman asked if he could leave his luggage here, and I obligingly said that he could. Mr. Lemaitre is being extremely rude, and –'

Lemaitre looked up, grinning so broadly that Gideon was infected by a kind of gaiety.

'Hark at him,' Lemaitre scoffed. 'White as blurry snow! Know what we've found, Geo – Superintendent?'

Gideon said slowly and with great, choking relish: 'I've got a good idea, Chief Inspector.'

'The notes from the Waterloo Station job,' said Lemaitre, unable to repress his bubbling elation. 'Exactly the same number of packages, and I've counted five, each with five hundred quid in it. Found them in three suitcases.' He chuckled. 'I'll tell you more when Mr. Shipham isn't with us.'

'Mr. Gideon –' Shipham had a walrus-shaped moustache and sad-looking eyes, but they were scared, too, as if he knew that he was really in trouble at last. 'I assure you that I knew nothing about it, and I must ask –'

'Just a minute,' Gideon said. 'Have you made any charge, Chief Inspector?'

'Not yet.'

'All right.' Gideon was brisk. 'You'll have your chance to tell us all about it,' he told Shipham. 'Now I'm charging you with being in possession of a quantity of treasury notes, knowing them to have been stolen.

Anything you say may be taken down and used as evidence. Constable –'

'It's just not right,' Shipham protested. 'I don't know a thing, Mr. Gideon. In the name of fair play, I appeal to you.'

Gideon looked at him coldly.

'Shippy,' he said, 'in these mail van jobs, three people have been seriously injured, one of them crippled for life. A man was injured at Waterloo this afternoon. That's only one angle. You'll get your chance to say what you like to the magistrate in the morning, and if you want a solicitor, you can send for him. But not until we've got you at the Yard. Constable, ask one of the officers outside to come in, will you?'

'Yes, sir.'

'But my business –' began Shippy fearfully.

'You won't be doing any more business to-night, and in the morning your wife can open, if we've finished searching,' Gideon declared.

Shipham didn't argue any more.

Lemaitre finished a count and then leaned back, taking cigarettes out of the pocket of the coat hanging on the back of the chair. The other man said:

'Five hundred here, too.'

'Oh, it's the same stuff,' Lemaitre said emphatically. 'Every penny of it, George. What a bit of blurry luck!'

It was almost too good to be true.

'How'd we get it?'

'When we picked up the Snide he was in a bad way,' said Lemaitre. 'Knocked silly, you know. He said he must get to Shippy's. No one took much notice of it; it's a meeting place for the mob, but it was reported and I noticed it. So I got G5 to keep an eye on Shippy's. Half an hour before I called you on the r.t. another of Murphy's boys came here empty-handed and went out with a case. The G5 chap stopped him. There was a hell of a schemozzle, and three others tried to get the case away. Then Lady Luck looked in, because a squad car was coming along.' Lemaitre chuckled and rubbed his hands jubilantly. 'Now we've got a busy day to-morrow, George!'

Gideon smiled faintly.

He picked up one of the bundles of notes. Fingerprint men had already been over them, he could see the traces of powder. Prints didn't show up on the edges of a bundle of notes, but a few might have been handled top and bottom. Shippy would probably crack when he knew that they'd be able to send him down. Was it worth trying to work on him now?

Gideon went into a tiny office behind the shop and ran through the papers – bills, invoices, receipts, delivery orders. Then, he began to feel a fresh and tingling excitement; there were several invoices from Chang's restaurant, mostly for tea; yet other big packages marked TEA had a blender's name and address.

Gideon had a funny, choky feeling.

Small packets with a different label were also marked TEA. One was open at the end. Gideon took it off a shelf and looked inside.

There were cigarettes.

He stared blankly – and then began to smile slowly, tensely, unbelievingly. He took out a cigarette, broke it, and sniffed.

These were loaded with marihuana; these were reefers! If he could trace this 'TEA' to Chang –

Gideon laid on a raid before Chang could get warning of Shippy's arrest.

Chang wasn't at the restaurant.

The 'tea' was.

Gideon drove home through this dark, quiet London, and the events of the day flitted through his mind. It had been a wonderful day; the day of a lifetime; never to be forgotten.

Chang was under a charge. Mazzioni had been picked up again, and there was a chance of breaking Murphy's power, too, although that would take some time.

Thoughts of the Saparelli family, especially the mother, quietened his jubilation, but the police had done all that anyone could, and time would help, wouldn't it?

He thought of Foster's sister; of Estelle who was no longer in danger. They hadn't got the man who'd stolen Lady Muriel's jewels, a dozen, a hundred crimes had been committed that day which were still unsolved; some would remain so for weeks and some for ever.

They'd have to find Fitzroy, and there was a case all right. Red-handed prisoners, no problem, just routine.

That was how he liked them.

Gideon turned into Harringdon Street and saw a light on at the first floor bedroom window of his house. He ran the car into the wooden garage at the corner, and hurried back, suddenly anxious; was one of the youngsters ill?

He let himself in quietly, hurried upstairs, saw a light beneath the door of his room, but nowhere else. So Kate was awake. He called out softly:

'Only me.'

He opened the door.

Kate was sitting up in bed with a pink angora wool bed-jacket round her shoulders, a book open in front of her. She looked tired, but her colour was good, and her hair neat in a net he sensed rather than saw.

'What's this?' he asked. 'Can't you sleep?'

'Malcolm ran a little temperature,' Kate said, 'and he hasn't been settled for long. I rang the Yard, and they said you were on your way, so I thought you might like a cup of tea.' She glanced at a tray on a bedside table, and the kettle on the bedroom gas-ring. Under a silver dish cover, Gideon was sure, were sandwiches.

Kate hadn't worried to do anything like this for years.

'Nothing I'd like more,' he said, and went to light the gas. But she slid out of bed.

'I'll do it. You look tired out. And what's that nasty bruise on your temple?'

'Oh, nothing,' said Gideon. 'All in the day's work.'

He began to undress, and to talk as he did so, only vaguely understanding that it was a long time since he had talked about the day's work with Kate. It was as if the years had been bridged, so that they were together again. He did not think of that in so many words, he just felt that it was good to be home.

FUZZ

ED
McBAIN

This is for my father-in-law,
HARRY MELNICK,
who inspired The Heckler,
and who must therefore take
at least partial blame for this one

The city in these pages is imaginary.
The people, the places are all fictitious.
Only the police routine is based on established
investigatory technique.

CHAPTER 1

Oh boy, what a week.

Fourteen muggings, three rapes, a knifing on Culver Avenue, thirty-six assorted burglaries, and the squadroom was being painted.

Not that the squadroom didn't *need* painting.

Detective Meyer Meyer would have been the first man to admit that the squadroom definitely needed painting. It merely seemed idiotic for the city to decide to paint it now, at the beginning of March, when everything outside was rotten and cold and miserable and dreary, and when you had to keep the windows shut tight because you never could get enough damn heat up in the radiators, and as a result had the stink of turpentine in your nostrils all day long, not to mention two painters underfoot and overhead, both of whom never would have made it in the Sistine Chapel.

'Excuse me,' one of the painters said, 'could you move that thing?'

'What thing?' Meyer said.

'That thing.'

'*That* thing,' Meyer said, almost blowing his cool, 'happens to be our Lousy File. *That* thing happens to contain information on known criminals and trouble-makers in the precinct, and *that* thing happens to be invaluable to the hard-working detectives of this squad.'

'Big deal,' the painter said.

'Won't he move it?' the other painter asked.

'You move it,' Meyer said. 'You're the painters, *you* move it.'

'We're not supposed to move nothing,' the first painter said.

'We're only supposed to paint,' the second painter said.

'I'm not supposed to move things, either,' Meyer said. 'I'm supposed to detect.'

'OK, so don't move it,' the first painter said, 'it'll get all full of green paint.'

'Put a dropcloth on it,' Meyer said.

'We got our dropcloths over there on those desks there,' the second painter said, 'that's all the dropcloths we got.'

'Why is it I always get involved with vaudeville acts?' Meyer asked.

'Huh?' the first painter said.

'He's being wise,' the second painter said.

'All I know is I don't plan to move that filing cabinet,' Meyer said. 'In fact, I don't plan to move *any*thing. You're screwing up the whole damn squadroom, we won't be able to find anything around here for a week after you're gone.'

'We do a thorough job,' the first painter said.

'Besides, we didn't ask to come,' the second painter said. 'You think we got nothing better to do than shmear around up here? You think this is an interesting job or something? This is a *boring* job, if you want to know.'

'It is, huh?' Meyer said.

'Yeah, it's boring,' the second painter said.

'It's boring, that's right,' the first painter agreed.

'Everything apple green, you think that's interesting? The ceiling apple green, the walls apple green, the stairs apple green, that's some interesting job, all right.'

'We had a job last week at the outdoor markets down on Council Street, *that* was an interesting job.'

'That was the most interesting job we ever had,' the second painter said. 'Every stall was a different pastel colour, you know those stalls they got? Well, every one of them was a different pastel colour, *that* was a *good* job.'

'*This* is a *crappy* job,' the first painter said.

'It's boring and it's crappy,' the second painter agreed.

'I'm still not moving that cabinet,' Meyer said, and the telephone rang. '87th Squad, Detective Meyer,' he said into the receiver.

'Is this Meyer Meyer in person?' the voice on the other end asked.

'Who's this?' Meyer asked.

'First please tell me if I'm speaking to Meyer Meyer himself?'

'This is Meyer Meyer himself.'

'Oh God, I think I may faint dead away.'

'Listen, who . . .'

'This is Sam Grossman.'

'Hello, Sam, what's . . .'

'I can't tell you how thrilled I am to be talking to such a famous person,' Grossman said.

'Yeah?'

'Yeah.'

'OK, what is it? I don't get it.'

'You mean you don't know?'

'No, I don't know. What is it I'm supposed to know?' Meyer asked.

'I'm sure you'll find out,' Grossman said.

'There's nothing I hate worse than a mystery,' Meyer said, 'so why don't you just tell me what you're talking about and save me a lot of trouble?'

'Ah-ha,' Grossman said.

'You I need today,' Meyer said, and sighed.

'Actually, I'm calling about a man's sports jacket, size thirty-eight, colour red-and-blue plaid, label Tom's Town and Country, analysis of suspect stain on left front flap requested. Know anything about it?'

'I requested the test,' Meyer said.

'You got a pencil handy?'

'Shoot.'

'Blood negative, semen negative. Seems to be an ordinary kitchen stain, grease or oil. You want us to break it down?'

'No, that won't be necessary.'

'This belong to a rape suspect?'

'We've had three dozen rape suspects in here this week. We also have two painters.'

'I beg your pardon?'

'Forget it. Is that all?'

'That's all. It certainly was a pleasure talking to you, Mr Meyer Meyer, you have no idea how thrilled I am.'

'Listen, what the hell . . . ?' Meyer started, but Grossman hung up. Meyer held the receiver in his hand a moment longer, looking at it peculiarly, and then put it back on to the cradle. He noticed that there were several spatters of apple green paint on the black plastic. 'Goddam slobs,' he muttered under his breath, and one of the painters said, 'What?'

'Nothing.'

'I thought you said something.'

'Listen, what department are you guys from, anyway?' Meyer asked.

'Public Works,' the first painter said.

'Maintenance and Repair,' the second painter said.

'Whyn't you come paint this damn place last summer, instead of now when all the windows are closed?'

'Why? What's the matter?'

'It stinks in here, that's what's the matter,' Meyer said.

'It stunk in here even before we got here,' the first painter said, which was perhaps true. Meyer sniffed disdainfully, turned his back on the two men, and tried to locate the filing cabinet containing last week's DD reports, which cabinet seemed to have vanished from sight.

If there was one thing (and there were *many* things) Meyer could not abide, it was chaos. The squadroom was in a state of utter, complete, and total chaos. Stepladders, dropcloths, newspapers, closed paint cans, open paint cans, used paint brushes, clean paint brushes, cans of turpentine and cans of thinner, mixing sticks, colour samples (all in various lovely shades of apple green), rollers, rolling trays, rolls of masking tape, coveralls, stained rags were strewn, thrown, draped, scattered, leaning against, lying upon, spread over and balanced precariously on desks, cabinets, floors, walls, water coolers, window-sills, and anything inanimate. (Yesterday, the painters had almost thrown a dropcloth over the inert form of Detective Andy Parker who was, as usual, asleep in the swivel chair behind his desk, his feet propped up on an open drawer.) Meyer stood in the midst of this disorder like the monument to patience he most certainly was, a sturdy man with china blue eyes and a bald head, speckled now (he didn't even realize it) with apple green paint. There was a pained look on his round face, his shoulders slumped with fatigue, he seemed disoriented and discombobulated, and he didn't know where the hell anything *was*! Chaos, he thought, and the telephone rang again.

He was standing closest to Carella's desk, so he groped around under the dropcloth for the ringing telephone, came away with a wide apple green stain on his jacket sleeve, and bounded across the room to the phone on his own desk. Swearing, he lifted the receiver.

'87th Squad, Detective Meyer,' he said.

'Parks Commissioner Cowper will be shot to death tomorrow night unless I receive five thousand dollars before noon,' a man's voice said. 'More later.'

'What?' Meyer said.

The line went dead.

He looked at his watch. It was 4.15 pm.

At four-thirty that afternoon, when Detective Steve Carella got to the squadroom, Lieutenant Byrnes asked him to come into his office for a moment. He was sitting behind his desk in the two-windowed room, puffing on a cigar and looking very much like a boss (which he was) in his grey pin-striped suit, a shade darker than his close-cropped hair, a black-and-gold silk rep tie on his white shirt (tiny spatter of apple green on one cuff), college ring with maroon stone on his right ring finger, wedding band on his left. He asked Carella if he wanted a cup of coffee, and Carella said yes, and Byrnes buzzed Miscolo in the Clerical Office and asked him to bring in another cup of coffee, and then asked Meyer to fill Carella in on the telephone call. It took Meyer approximately ten seconds to repeat the content of the conversation.

'Is that it?' Carella asked.

'That's it.'

'Mmm.'

'What do you think, Steve?' Byrnes asked.

Carella was sitting on the edge of Byrnes' scarred desk, a tall slender man who looked like a vagrant at the moment because as soon as it got dark he would take to the streets, find himself an alley or a doorway and lie there reeking of wine and hoping somebody would set fire to him. Two weeks ago, a *real* vagrant had been set ablaze by some fun-loving youngsters, and last week another bum had supplied fuel for a second bonfire, a fatal one this time. So Carella had been spending his nights lying in assorted doorways simulating drunkenness and wishing for arson. He had not shaved for three days. There was a bristly stubble on his jaw, the same colour as his brown hair, but growing sparsely and patchily and giving his face a somewhat incomplete look, as though it had been hastily sketched by an inexpert artist. His eyes were brown (he liked to think of them as penetrating), but they appeared old and faded now through association with the scraggly beard and the layers of unadulterated dirt he had allowed to collect on his forehead and his cheeks. What appeared to be a healing cut ran across the bridge of his nose, collodion and vegetable dye skilfully applied to resemble congealing blood and pus and corruption. He also looked as if he had lice. He made Byrnes a little itchy. He made everybody in the room a little itchy. He blew his nose before answering the lieutenant's question, and the handkerchief he took from the back pocket of his greasy pants looked as if it had been fished from a nearby sewer. He blew his nose fluidly (There's such a thing as carrying an impersonation *too* far, Meyer thought), replaced the handkerchief in his trouser pocket, and then said, 'He ask to talk to anyone in particular?'

'Nope, just began talking the minute I said who I was.'

'Could be a crank,' Carella said.

'Could be.'

'Why *us*?' Byrnes said.

It was a good question. Assuming the man was *not* a crank, and assuming he *did* plan to kill the commissioner of parks unless he got his five thousand dollars by noon tomorrow, why call the Eight-Seven? There were a great many squadrooms in this fair city, none of which (it was safe to assume) were in the midst of being painted that first week in March, all of which contained detectives every bit as hard-working and determined as the stalwart fellows who gathered together now to sip their afternoon beverages and while away the deepening hours, all of whom doubtless knew the commissioner of parks as intimately as did these very minions of the law – so why the Eight-Seven?

A good question. Like most good questions, it was not immediately answered. Miscolo came in with a cup of coffee, asked Carella when he planned to take a bath, and then went back to his clerical duties. Carella picked up the coffee cup in a filth-encrusted hand, brought it to his cracked and peeling lips, sipped at it, and then said, 'We ever have anything to do with Cowper?'

'How do you mean?'

'I don't know. Any special assignments, anything like that?'

'Not to my recollection,' Byrnes said. 'Only thing I can think of is when he spoke at that PBA thing, but every cop in the city was invited to that one.'

'It must be a crank,' Carella said.
'Could be,' Meyer said again.
'Did he sound like a kid?' Carella asked.
'No, he sounded like a grown man.'
'Did he say when he'd call again?'
'No. All he said was "More later".'
'Did he say when or where you were supposed to deliver the money?'
'Nope.'
'Did he say where you were supposed to *get* it?'
'Nope.'
'Maybe he expects us to take up a collection,' Carella said.
'Five grand is only five hundred and fifty dollars less than I make in a year,' Meyer said.
'Sure, but he's undoubtedly heard how generous the bulls of the 87th are.'
'I admit he sounds like a crank,' Meyer said. 'Only one thing bothers me about what he said.'
'What's that?'
'Shot to death. I don't like that, Steve. Those words scare me.'
'Yeah. Well,' Carella said, 'why don't we see if he calls again, OK? Who's relieving?'
'Kling and Hawes should be in around five.'
'Who's on the team?' Byrnes asked.
'Willis and Brown. They're relieving on post.'
'Which case?'
'Those car snatches. They're planted on Culver and Second.'
'You think it's a crank, Meyer?'
'It could be. We'll have to see.'
'Should we call Cowper?'
'What for?' Carella said. 'This may turn out to be nothing. No sense alarming him.'
'OK,' Byrnes said. He looked at his watch, rose, walked to the hat rack in the corner, and put on his overcoat. 'I promised Harriet I'd take her shopping, the stores are open late tonight. I should be home around nine if anybody wants to reach me. Who'll be catching?'
'Kling.'
'Tell him I'll be home around nine, will you?'
'Right.'
'I hope it's a crank,' Byrnes said, and went out of the office.
Carella sat on the edge of the desk, sipping his coffee. He looked very tired. 'How does it feel to be famous?' he asked Meyer.
'What do you mean?'

Carella looked up. 'Oh, I guess you don't know yet.'
'Don't know *what* yet?'
'About the book.'
'What book?'
'Somebody wrote a book.'
'So?'
'It's called *Meyer Meyer*.'
'What?'
'Yeah. *Meyer Meyer*. It was reviewed in today's paper.'
'Who? What do you mean? Meyer *Meyer*, you mean?'
'It got a nice review.'
'Meyer Meyer?' Meyer said. 'That's *my* name.'
'Sure.'
'He can't do that!'
'She. A woman.'
'Who?'
'Her name's Helen Hudson.'
'She can't do that!'
'She's already done it.'
'Well, she *can't*. I'm a *person*, you can't go naming some character after a *person*.' He frowned and then looked at Carella suspiciously. 'Are you putting me on?'
'Nope, God's honest truth.'
'Is this guy supposed to be a cop?'
'No, I think he's a teacher.'
'A *teacher*, Jesus Christ!'
'At a university.'
'She can't do that!' Meyer said again. 'Is he bald?'
'I don't know. He's short and plump, the review said.'
'Short and plump! She can't use my name for a short plump person. I'll sue her.'
'So sue her,' Carella said.
'You think I won't? Who published that goddamn book?'
'Dutton.'
'OK!' Meyer said, and took a pad from his jacket pocket. He wrote swiftly on a clean white page, slammed the pad shut, dropped it to the floor as he was putting it back into his pocket, swore, stooped to pick it up, and then looked at Carella plaintively and said, 'After all, *I* was here first.'

The second call came at ten minutes to eleven that night. It was taken by Detective Bert Kling, who was catching, and who had been briefed on the earlier call before Meyer left the squadroom.

'87th Squad,' he said, 'Kling here.'

'You've undoubtedly decided by now that I'm a crank,' the man's voice said. 'I'm not.'

'Who is this?' Kling asked, and motioned across the room for Hawes to pick up the extension.

'I was quite serious about what I promised,' the man said. 'Parks Commissioner Cowper will be shot to death some time tomorrow night unless I receive five thousand dollars by noon. This is how I want it. Have you got a pencil?'

'Mister, why'd you pick on *us*?' Kling asked.

'For sentimental reasons,' the man said, and Kling could have sworn he was smiling on the other end of the line. 'Pencil ready?'

'Where do you expect us to get five thousand dollars?'

'Entirely your problem,' the man said. '*My* problem is killing Cowper if you fail to deliver. Do you want this information?'

'Go ahead,' Kling said, and glanced across the room to where Hawes sat hunched over the other phone. Hawes nodded.

'I want the money in singles, need I mention they must be unmarked?'

'Mister, do you know what extortion is?' Kling asked suddenly.

'I know what it is,' the man said. 'Don't try keeping me on the line. I plan to hang up long before you can effect a trace.'

'Do you know the penalty for extortion?' Kling asked, and the man hung up.

'*Son* of a bitch,' Kling said.

'He'll call back. We'll be ready next time,' Hawes said.

'We can't trace it through automatic equipment, anyway.'

'We can try.'

'*What'd* he say?'

'He said "sentimental reasons".'

'That's what I thought he said. What's that supposed to mean?'

'Search me,' Hawes said, and went back to his desk, where he had spread a paper towel over the dropcloth, and where he had been drinking tea from a cardboard container and eating a cheese Danish before the telephone call interrupted him.

He was a huge man, six feet two inches tall and weighing two hundred pounds, some ten pounds more than was comfortable for him. He had blue eyes, and a square jaw with a cleft chin. His hair was red, except for a streak over his left temple where he had once been knifed and where the hair had curiously grown in white after the wound healed. He had a straight unbroken nose, and a good mouth with a wide lower lip. Sipping his tea, munching his Danish, he looked like a burly Captain Ahab who had somehow been trapped in a civil service job. A gun butt protruded from the holster under his coat as he leaned over the paper towel and allowed the Danish crumbs to fall on to it. The gun was a big one, as befitted the size of the man, a Smith & Wesson .357 Magnum, weighing forty-four and a half ounces, and capable of putting a hole the size of a baseball on your head if you happened to cross the path of Cotton Hawes on a night when the moon was full. He was biting into the Danish when the telephone rang again.

'87th Squad, Kling here.'

'The penalty for extortion,' the man said, 'is imprisonment not exceeding fifteen years. Any other questions?'

'Listen . . .' Kling started.

'*You* listen,' the man said. 'I want five thousand dollars in unmarked singles. I want them put into a metal lunch pail, and I want the pail taken to the third bench on the Clinton Street footpath into Grover Park. More later,' he said, and hung up.

'We're going to play Fits and Starts, I see,' Kling said to Hawes.

'Yeah. Shall we call Pete?'

'Let's wait till we have the whole picture,' Kling said, and sighed and tried to get back to typing up his report. The phone did not ring again until eleven-twenty. When he lifted the receiver, he recognized the man's voice at once.

'To repeat,' the man said, 'I want the lunch pail taken to the third bench on the Clinton Street footpath into Grover Park. If the bench is watched, if your man is not alone, the pail will not be picked up, and the commissioner will be killed.'

'You want five grand left on a park bench?' Kling asked.

'You've got it,' the man said, and hung up.

'You think that's all of it?' Kling asked Hawes.

'I don't know,' Hawes said. He looked up at the wall clock. 'Let's give him till midnight. If we don't get another call by then, we'll ring Pete.'

'OK,' Kling said.

He began typing again. He typed hunched over the machine, using a six-finger system that was uniquely his own, typing rapidly and with a great many mistakes, overscoring or erasing as the whim struck him, detesting the paperwork that went into police work, wondering why anyone would want a metal pail left on a park bench where any passing stranger might pick it up, cursing the decrepit machine provided by the city, and then wondering how anyone could have the unmitigated gall to demand five thousand dollars *not* to commit a murder. He frowned as he worked, and because he was the youngest detective on the squad, with a face comparatively unravaged by the pressures of his chosen profession, the only wrinkle in evidence was the one caused by the frown, a deep cutting ridge across his smooth forehead. He was a blond man, six feet tall, with hazel eyes and an open countenance. He wore a yellow sleeveless pullover, and his brown sports jacket was draped over the back of his chair. The Colt .38 Detective's Special he usually wore clipped to his belt was in its holster in the top drawer of his desk.

He took seven calls in the next half-hour, but none of them was from the man who had threatened to kill Cowper. He was finishing his report, a routine listing of the persons interrogated in a mugging on Ainsley Avenue, when the telephone rang again. He reached for the receiver automatically. Automatically, Hawes lifted the extension.

'Last call tonight,' the man said. 'I want the money before noon tomorrow. There are more than one of us, so don't attempt to arrest the man who picks it up or the commissioner will be killed. If the lunch pail is empty, or if it contains paper scraps or phoney bills or marked bills, or if for any reason or by any circumstance the money is not on that bench before noon tomorrow, the plan to kill the commissioner will go into effect. If you have any questions, ask them now.'

'You don't really expect us to hand you five thousand dollars on a silver platter, do you?'

'No, in a lunch pail,' the man said, and again Kling had the impression he was smiling.

'I'll have to discuss this with the lieutenant,' Kling said.

'Yes, and he'll doubtless have to discuss it with the parks commissioner,' the man said.

'Is there any way we can reach you?' Kling asked, taking a wild gamble, thinking the man might hastily and automatically reveal his home number or his address.

'You'll have to speak louder,' the man said. 'I'm a little hard of hearing.'

'I said is there any way . . .'

And the man hung up.

The bitch city can intimidate you sometimes by her size alone, but when she works in tandem with the weather she can make you wish you were dead. Cotton Hawes wished he was dead on that Tuesday, March 5th. The temperature as recorded at the Grover Park Lane at 7 am that morning was twelve degrees above zero, and by 9 am – when he started on to the Clinton Street footpath – it had risen only two degrees to stand at a frigid fourteen above. A strong harsh wind was blowing off the River Harb to the north, racing untrammelled through the narrow north-south corridor leading directly to the path. His red hair whipped fitfully about his hatless head, the tails of his overcoat were flat against the backs of his legs. He was wearing gloves and carrying a black lunch pail in his left hand. The third button of his overcoat, waist high, was open, and the butt of his Magnum rested just behind the gaping flap, ready for a quick right-handed, spring-assisted draw.

The lunch pail was empty.

They had awakened Lieutenant Byrnes at five minutes to twelve the night before, and advised him of their subsequent conversations with the man they now referred to as The Screwball. The lieutenant had mumbled a series of grunts into the telephone and then said, 'I'll be right down,' and then asked what time it was. They told him it was almost midnight. He grunted again, and hung up. When he got to the squadroom, they filled him in more completely, and it was decided to call the parks commissioner to appraise him of the threat against his life, and to discuss any possible action with him. The parks commissioner looked at his bedside clock the moment the phone rang and immediately informed Lieutenant Byrnes that it was half past midnight, wasn't this something that could wait until morning?

Byrnes cleared his throat and said, 'Well, someone says he's going to shoot you.'

The parks commissioner cleared his throat and said, 'Well, why didn't you say so?'

The situation was ridiculous.

The parks commissioner had never heard of a more ridiculous situation, why this man had to be an absolute maniac to assume anyone would pay him five thousand dollars on the strength of a few phone calls. Byrnes agreed that the situation was ridiculous, but that none the less a great many crimes in this city were committed daily by misguided or unprincipled people, some of whom were doubtless screwballs, but sanity was not a prerequisite for the successful perpetration of a criminal act.

The situation was unthinkable.

The parks commissioner had never heard of a more unthinkable situation, he couldn't even understand why they were bothering him with what were obviously the rantings of some kind of lunatic. Why didn't they simply forget the entire matter?

'Well,' Byrnes said, 'I hate to behave like a television cop, sir, I would really *rather* forget the entire thing, as you suggest, but the possibility exists that there *is* a plan to murder you, and in all good conscience I cannot ignore that possibility, not without discussing it first with you.'

'Well, you've discussed it with me,' the parks commissioner said, 'and I say forget it.'

'Sir,' Byrnes said, 'we would like to try to apprehend the man who picks up the lunch pail, and we would also like to supply you with police protection tomorrow night. Had you planned on leaving the house tomorrow night?'

The parks commissioner said that Byrnes could do whatever he thought fit in the matter of apprehending the man who picked up the lunch pail, but that he did indeed plan on going out tomorrow night, was in fact invited by the mayor to attend a performance of Beethoven's *Eroica* given by the Philharmonic at the city's recently opened music and theatre complex near Remington Circle, and he did not want or need police protection.

Byrnes said, 'Well, sir, let's see what results we have with the lunch pail, we'll get back to you.'

'Yes, get back to me,' the parks commissioner said, 'but not in the middle of the night again, OK?' and hung up.

At 5 am on Tuesday morning, while it was still dark, Detectives Hal Willis and Arthur Brown drank two fortifying cups of coffee in the silence of the squadroom, donned foul-weather gear requisitioned from an Emergency Squad truck, clipped on their holsters, and went out on to the arctic tundra to begin a lonely surveillance of the third bench on the Clinton Street footpath into Grover Park. Since most of the park's paths meandered from north to south and naturally had entrances on either end they thought at first there might be some confusion concerning the Clinton Street footpath. But a look at the map on the precinct wall showed that there was only one entrance to this particular path, which began on Grover Avenue, adjacent to the park, and then wound through the park to end at the band shell near the lake. Willis and Brown planted themselves on a shelf of rock overlooking the suspect third bench, shielded from the path by a stand of naked elms. It was very cold. They did not expect action, of course, until Hawes dropped the lunch pail where specified, but they could hardly take up posts after the events, and so it had been Byrnes' brilliant idea to send them out before anyone watching the bench might observe them. They did windmill exercises with their arms, they stamped their feet, they continuously pressed the palms of their hands against portions of their faces that seemed to be going, the telltale whiteness of frostbite appearing suddenly and frighteningly in the bleak early morning hours. Neither of the two men had ever been so cold in his life.

Cotton Hawes was almost, but not quite, as cold when he entered the park at 9 am that morning. He passed two people on his way to the bench. One of them was an old man in a black overcoat, walking swiftly towards the subway kiosk on Grover Avenue. The other was a girl wearing a mink coat over a long pink nylon nightgown that flapped dizzily about her ankles, walking a white poodle wearing a red wool vest. She smiled at Hawes as he went by with his lunch pail.

The third bench was deserted.

Hawes took a quick look around and then glanced up and out of the park to the row of apartment buildings on Grover Avenue. A thousand windows reflected the early morning sun. Behind any one of these windows, there might have been a man with a pair of binoculars and a clear unobstructed view of the bench. He put the lunch pail on one end of the bench, moved it to the other end, shrugged, and relocated it in the exact centre of the bench. He took another look around, feeling really stupid, and then walked out of the park and back to the office. Detective Bert Kling was sitting at his desk, monitoring the walkie-talkie operated by Hal Willis in the park.

'How you doing down there?' Kling asked.

'We're freezing our asses off,' Willis replied.

'Any action yet?'

'You think anybody's crazy enough to be out in this weather?' Willis said.

'Cheer up,' Kling said, 'I hear the boss is sending you both to Jamaica when this is over.'

'Fat Chance Department,' Willis said. 'Hold it!'

There was silence in the squadroom. Hawes and Kling waited. At last, Willis' voice erupted from the speaker on Kling's box.

'Just a kid,' Willis said. 'Stopped at the bench, looked over the lunch pail, and then left it right where it was.'

'Stay with it,' Kling said.

'We have to stay with it,' Brown's voice cut in. 'We're frozen solid to this goddamn rock.'

There were people in the park now.

They ventured into the bitch city tentatively, warned by radio and television forecasters, further cautioned by the visual evidence of thermometers outside apartment windows, and the sound of the wind whipping beneath the eaves of old buildings, and the touch of the frigid blast that attacked any exploratory hand thrust outdoors for just an instant before a window slammed quickly shut again. They dressed with no regard to the dictates of fashion, the men wearing ear muffs and bulky mufflers, the women bundled into layers of sweaters and fur-lined boots, wearing woollen scarves to protect their heads and ears, rushing at a quick trot through the park, barely glancing at the bench or the black lunch pail sitting in the centre of it. In a city notorious for its indifference, the citizens were more obviously withdrawn now, hurrying past each other without so much as eyes meeting, insulating themselves, becoming tight private cocoons that defied the cold. Speech might have made them more vulnerable, opening the mouth might have released the heat they had been storing up inside, commiseration would never help to diminish the wind that tried to cut them down in the streets, the sabre-slash wind that blew in off the river and sent newspapers wildly soaring into the air, fedoras wheeling into the gutter. Speech was a precious commodity that cold March day.

In the park, Willis and Brown silently watched the bench.

The painters were in a garrulous mood.

'What have you got going, a stakeout?' the first painter asked.

'Is that what the walkie-talkie's for?' the second painter asked.

'Is there gonna be a bank holdup?'

'Is that why you're listening to that thing?'

'Shut up,' Kling said encouragingly.

The painters were on their ladders, slopping apple green paint over everything in sight.

'We painted the DA's office once,' the first painter said.

'They were questioning this kid who stabbed his mother forty-seven times.'

'Forty-*seven* times.'

'In the belly, the head, the breasts, every place.'

'With an ice-pick.'

'He was guilty as sin.'

'He said he did it to save her from the Martians.'

'A regular bedbug.'

'Forty-*seven* times.'

'How could that save her from the Martians?' the second painter asked.

'Maybe Martians don't like ladies with ice-pick holes in them,' the first painter said, and burst out laughing. The second painter guffawed with him. Together, they perched on their ladders, helpless with laughter, limply holding brushes that dripped paint on the newspapers spread on the squadroom floor.

The man entered the park at 10 am.

He was perhaps twenty-seven years old, with a narrow cold-pinched face, his lips drawn tight against the wind, his eyes watering. He wore a beige car coat, the collar pulled up against the back of his neck, buttoned tight around a green wool muffler at his throat. His hands were in the slash pockets of the coat. He wore brown corduroy trousers, the wale cut diagonally, and brown high-topped workman's shoes. He came on to the Clinton Street footpath swiftly, without looking either to the right or the left, walked immediately and directly to the third bench on the path, picked up the lunch pail, tucked it under his arm, put his naked hand back into his coat pocket, wheeled abruptly, and was starting out of the park again, when a voice behind him said, 'Hold it right there, Mac.'

He turned to see a tall burly Negro wearing what looked like a blue astronaut's suit. The Negro was holding a big pistol in his right hand. His left hand held a wallet which fell open to reveal a gold and blue shield.

'Police officer,' the Negro said. 'We want to talk to you.'

CHAPTER 2

Miranda-Escobedo sounds like a Mexican bullfighter.

It is not.

It is the police shorthand for two separate Supreme Court decisions. These decisions, together, lay down the ground rules for the interrogation of suspects, and cops find them a supreme pain in the ass. There is not one working cop in the United States who thinks Miranda-Escobedo is a good idea. They are all fine Americans, these cops, and are all very concerned with the rights of the individual in a free society, but they do not like Miranda-Escobedo because they feel it makes their job more difficult. Their job is crime prevention.

Since the cops of the 87th had taken a suspect into custody and intended to question him, Miranda-Escobedo immediately came into play. Captain Frick, who was in charge of the entire precinct, had issued a bulletin to his men shortly after the Supreme Court decision in 1966, a flyer printed on green paper and advising every cop in the precinct, uniformed and plainclothes, on the proper interrogation of criminal suspects. Most of the precinct's uniformed cops carried the flyer clipped inside their notebooks, where it was handy for reference whenever they needed it.

The detectives, on the other hand, normally questioned more people than their uniformed colleagues, and had committed the rules to memory. They used them now with easy familiarity, while continuing to look upon them with great distaste.

'In keeping with the Supreme Court decision in *Miranda v. Arizona*,' Hal Willis said, 'we're required to advise you of your rights, and that's what I'm doing now. First, you have the right to remain silent if you choose, do you understand that?'

'I do.'

'Do you also understand that you need not answer any police questions?'

'I do.'

'And do you also understand that if you *do* answer questions, your answers may be used as evidence against you?'

'Yes, I understand.'

'I must also inform you that you have the right to consult with an attorney before or during police questioning, do you understand that?'

'I understand.'

'And if you decide to exercise that right but do not have the funds with which to hire counsel, you are entitled to have a lawyer appointed without cost, to consult with him before or during the questioning. Is that also clear?'

'Yes.'

'You understand all of your rights as I have just explained them to you?'

'I do.'

'Are you willing to answer questions without the presence of an attorney?'

'Gee, I don't know,' the suspect said. 'Should I?'

Willis and Brown looked at each other. They had thus far played Miranda-Escobedo by the book, warning the suspect of his privilege against self-incrimination, and warning him of his right to counsel. They had done so in explicit language, and not by merely making references to the Fifth Amendment. They had also made certain that the suspect understood his rights before asking him whether or not he wished to waive them. The green flyer issued by Captain Frick had warned that it was not sufficient for an officer simply to give the warnings and then proceed with an interrogation. It was necessary for the prisoner to *say* he understood, and that he was willing to answer questions without counsel. Only then would the court find that he had waived his constitutional rights.

In addition, however, the flyer had warned all police officers to exercise great care in avoiding language which could later be used by defence attorneys to charge that the officer had 'threatened, tricked, or cajoled' the defendant into waiving. The officer was specifically cautioned against advising the suspect not to bother with a lawyer, or even implying that he'd be better off without a lawyer. He was, in short, supposed to inform the defendant of his privilege against self-incrimination and his right to counsel, period. Both Willis and Brown knew that they could not answer the suspect's question. If either of the two had advised him to answer questions without an attorney present, any confession they thereafter took would be inadmissible in court. If, on the other hand, they advised him *not* to answer questions, or advised him to consult with an attorney, their chances of getting a confession would be substantially lessened.

So Willis said, 'I've explained your rights, and it would be improper for me to give you any advice. The decision is yours.'

'Gee, I don't know,' the man said.

'Well, think it over,' Willis said.

The young man thought it over. Neither Willis nor Brown said a word. They knew that if their suspect refused to answer questions, that was it, the questioning would have to stop then and there. They also knew that if he began answering questions and suddenly decided he didn't want to go on with the interrogation, they would have to stop immediately, no matter what language he used to express his wishes – 'I claim my rights,' or 'I don't want to say nothing else,' or 'I demand a mouthpiece.'

So they waited.

'I got nothing to hide,' the young man said at last.

'Are you willing to answer questions without the presence of an attorney?' Willis asked again.

'I am.'

'What's your name?' Willis asked.

'Anthony La Bresca.'

'Where do you live, Anthony?'

'In Riverhead.'

'Where in Riverhead, Anthony?' Brown said.

Both detectives had automatically fallen into the first-name basis of interrogation that violated only human dignity and not human rights, having nothing whatever to do with Miranda-Escobedo, but having everything in the world to do with the psychological unsettling of a prisoner. Call a man by his first name without allowing him the return courtesy and:

(a) you immediately make him a subordinate; and

(b) you instantly rob the familiarity of any friendly connotation, charging its use with menace instead.

'Where in Riverhead, Anthony?' Willis said.

'1812 Johnson.'

'Live alone?'

'No, with my mother.'

'Father dead?'

'They're separated.'

'How old are you, Anthony?'

'Twenty-six.'

'What do you do for a living?'

'I'm unemployed at the moment.'

'What do you normally do?'

'I'm a construction worker.'

'When's the last time you worked?'

'I was laid off last month.'

'Why?'

'We completed the job.'

'Haven't worked since?'

'I've been looking for work.'

'But didn't have any luck, right?'

'That's right.'

'Tell us about the lunch pail.'

'What about it?'

'Well, what's *in* it, first of all?'

'Lunch, I guess,' La Bresca said.

'Lunch, huh?'

'Isn't that what's usually in lunch pails?'

'We're asking *you*, Anthony.'

'Yeah, lunch,' La Bresca said.

'Did you call this squadroom yesterday?' Brown asked.

'No.'

'How'd you know where that lunch pail would be?'

'I was told it would be there.'

'Who told you?'

'This guy I met.'

'What guy?'

'At the employment agency.'

'Go on,' Willis said, 'let's hear it.'

'I was waiting on line outside this employment agency on Ainsley, they handle a lot of construction jobs, you know, and that's where I got my last job from, so that's where I went back today. And this guy is standing on line with me, all of a sudden he snaps his fingers and says, "Jesus, I left my lunch in the park." So I didn't say nothing, so he looks at me and says, "How do you like that, I left my lunch on a park bench." So I said that's a shame, and all, I sympathized with him, you know. What the hell, poor guy left his lunch on a park bench.'

'So then what?'

'So he tells me he would run back into the park to get it, except he has a bum leg. So he asks me if I'd go get it for him.'

'So naturally you said yes,' Brown said. 'A strange guy asks you to walk all the way from Ainsley Avenue over to Grover and into the park to pick up his lunch pail, so naturally you said yes.'

'No, naturally I said no,' La Bresca said.

'Then what were you doing in the park?'

'Well, we got to talking a little, and he explained how he got his leg hurt in World War II fighting against the Germans, picked up shrapnel from a mortar explosion, he had a pretty rough deal, you know?'

'So naturally you decided to go for the lunch pail after all.'

'No, naturally I still didn't decide to do nothing.'

'So how *did* you finally end up in the park?'

'That's what I've been trying to tell you.'

'You took pity on this man, right? Because he had a bum leg, and because it was so cold outside, right?' Willis said.

'Well, yes, and no.'

'You didn't want him to have to walk all the way to the park, right?' Brown said.

'Well, yes and no. I mean, the guy was a stranger, why the hell should I care if he walked to the park or not?'

'Look, Anthony,' Willis said, beginning to lose his temper, and trying to control himself, reminding himself that it was exceptionally difficult to interrogate suspects these days of Miranda-Escobedo when a man could simply refuse to answer at any given moment, Sorry, boys, no more questions, must shut your dear little flatfoot mouths or run the risk of blowing your case. 'Look, Anthony,' he said more gently, 'we're only trying to find out how *you* happened to walk to the park and go directly to the third bench to pick up that lunch pail.'

'I know,' La Bresca said.

'You met a disabled war veteran, right?'

'Right.'

'And he told you he left his lunch pail in the park.'

'Well, he didn't say lunch *pail* at first. He just said *lunch*.'

'When did he say lunch *pail*?'

'After he gave me the five bucks.'

'Oh, he offered you five dollars to go get his lunch pail, is that it?'

'He didn't *offer* it to me, he *handed* it to me.'

'He handed you five bucks and said, 'Would you go get my lunch pail for me?'

'That's right. And he told me it would be on the third bench in the park, on the Clinton Street footpath. Which is right where it was.'

'What were you supposed to do with this lunch pail after you got it?'

'Bring it back to him. He was holding my place in line.'

'Mm-huh,' Brown said.

'What's so important about that lunch pail, anyway?' La Bresca asked.

'Nothing,' Willis said. 'Tell us about this man. What did he look like?'

'Ordinary-looking guy.'

'How old would you say he was?'

'Middle thirties, thirty-five, something like that.'

'Tall, short, or average?'

'Tall. About six feet, I would say, give or take.'
'What about his build? Heavy, medium, or slight?'
'He was built nice. Good shoulders.'
'Heavy?'
'Husky, I would say. A good build.'
'What colour was his hair?'
'Blond.'
'Was he wearing a moustache or a beard?'
'No.'
'What colour were his eyes, did you notice?'
'Blue.'
'Did you notice any scars or identifying marks?'
'No.'
'Tattoos?'
'No.'
'What sort of voice did he have?'
'Average voice. Not too deep. Just average. A good voice.'
'Any accent or regional dialect?'
'No.'
'What was he wearing?'
'Brown overcoat, brown gloves.'
'Suit?'
'I couldn't see what he had on under the coat. I mean, he was wearing pants, naturally, but I didn't notice what colour they were, and I couldn't tell you whether they were part of a suit or whether . . .'
'Fine, was he wearing a hat?'
'No hat.'
'Glasses?'
'No glasses.'
'Anything else you might have noticed about him?'
'Yeah,' La Bresca said.
'What?'
'He was wearing a hearing aid.'

The employment agency was on the corner of Ainsley Avenue and Clinton Street, five blocks north of the entrance to the park's Clinton Street footpath. On the off-chance that the man wearing the hearing aid would still be waiting for La Bresca's return, they checked out a sedan and drove over from the station house. La Bresca sat in the back of the car, willing and eager to identify the man if he was still there.

There was a line of men stretching halfway around the corner of Clinton, burly men in work clothes and caps, hands thrust into coat pockets, faces white with cold, feet moving incessantly as they shuffled and jigged and tried to keep warm.

'You'd think they were giving away dollar bills up there,' La Bresca said. 'Actually, they charge you a whole week's pay. They got good jobs, though. The last one they got me paid real good, and it lasted eight months.'

'Do you see your man anywhere on that line?' Brown asked.

'I can't tell from here. Can we get out?'

'Yeah, sure,' Brown said.

They parked the car at the kerb. Willis, who had been driving, got out first. He was small and light, with the easy grace of a dancer and the steady cold gaze of a blackjack dealer. He kept slapping his gloved hands together as he waited for Brown. Brown came out of the car like a rhinoceros, pushing his huge body through the door frame, slamming the door behind him, and then pulling his gloves on over big-knuckled hands.

'Did you throw the visor?' Willis asked.

'No. We'll only be a minute here.'

'You'd better throw it. Goddamn eager beavers'll give us a ticket sure as hell.'

Brown grunted and went back into the car.

'Boy, it's cold out here,' La Bresca said.

'Yeah,' Willis said.

In the car, Brown lowered the sun visor. A hand-lettered cardboard sign was fastened to the visor with rubber bands. It read:

POLICE DEPARTMENT VEHICLE

The car door slammed again. Brown came over and nodded, and together they began walking towards the line of men standing on the sidewalk. Both detectives unbuttoned their overcoats.

'Do you see him?' Brown asked La Bresca.

'Not yet,' La Bresca said.

They walked the length of the line slowly.

'Well?' Brown asked.

'No,' La Bresca said. 'He ain't here.'

'Let's take a look upstairs,' Willis suggested.

The line of job seekers continued up a flight of rickety wooden steps to a dingy second-floor office. The lettering on a frosted glass door read

MERIDIAN EMPLOYMENT AGENCY
Jobs Our Speciality

'See him?' Willis asked.

'No,' La Bresca said.

'Wait here,' Willis said, and the two detectives moved away from him, towards the other end of the corridor.

'What do you think?' Brown asked.

'What can we hold him on?'

'Nothing.'

'So *that's* what I think.'

'Is he worth a tail?'

'It depends on how serious the loot thinks this is.'

'Why don't you ask him?'

'I think I will. Hold the fort.'

Brown went back to La Bresca. Willis found a pay phone around the bend in the corridor, and dialled the squadroom. The lieutenant listened carefully to everything he had to report, and then said, 'How do you read him?'

'I think he's telling the truth.'

'You think there really *was* some guy with a hearing aid?'

'Yes.'

'Then why'd he leave before La Bresca got back with the pail?'

'I don't know, Pete. I just don't make La Bresca for a thief.'

'Where'd you say he lived?'

'1812 Johnson. In Riverhead.'

'What precinct would that be?'

'I don't know.'

'I'll check it out and give them a ring. Maybe they can spare a man for a tail. Christ knows we can't.'

'So shall we turn La Bresca loose?'

'Yeah, come on back here. Give him a little scare first, though, just in case.'

'Right,' Willis said, and hung up, and went back to where La Bresca and Brown were waiting.

'OK, Anthony,' Willis said, 'you can go.'

'Go? Who' *going* any place? I got to get back on that line again. I'm trying to get a job here.'

'And remember, Anthony, if anything happens, we know where to find you.'

'What do you mean? What's gonna happen?'

'Just remember.'

'Sure,' La Bresca said. He paused and then said, 'Listen, you want to do me a favour?'

'What's that?'

'Get me up to the front of the line there.'

'How can we do that?'

'Well, you're cops, ain't you?' La Bresca asked, and Willis and Brown looked at each other.

When they got back to the squadroom, they learned that Lieutenant Byrnes had called the 115th in Riverhead and had been informed they could not spare a man for the surveillance of Anthony La Bresca. Nobody seemed terribly surprised.

That night, as Parks Commissioner Cowper came down the broad white marble steps outside Philharmonic Hall, his wife clinging to his left arm, swathed in mink and wearing a diaphanous white scarf on her head, the commissioner himself resplendent in black tie and dinner jacket, the mayor and his wife four steps ahead, the sky virtually starless, a bitter brittle dryness to the air, that night as the parks commissioner came down the steps of Philharmonic Hall with the huge two-storey-high windows behind him casting warm yellow light on to the windswept steps and pavement, that night as the commissioner lifted his left foot preparatory to placing it on the step below, laughing at something his wife said in his ear, his laughter billowing out of his mouth in puffs of visible vapour that whipped away on the wind like comic strip balloons, that night as he tugged on his right-hand glove with his already gloved left hand, that night two shots cracked into the plaza, shattering the wintry stillness, and the commissioner's laugh stopped, the commissioner's hand stopped, the commissioner's foot stopped, and he tumbled headlong down the steps, blood pouring from his forehead and his cheek, and his wife screamed, and the mayor turned to see what was the matter, and an enterprising photographer on the sidewalk caught the toppling commissioner on film for posterity.

He was dead long before his body rolled to a stop on the wide bottom step.

CHAPTER 3

Concetta Esposita La Bresca had been taught only to dislike and distrust all Negroes. Her brothers, on the other hand, had been taught to dismember them if possible. They had learned their respective lessons in a sprawling slum ghetto affectionately and sarcastically dubbed Paradiso by its largely Italian population. Concetta, as a growing child in this dubious garden spot, had watched her brothers and other neighbourhood boys bash in a good many Negro skulls when she was still just a *piccola ragazza*. The mayhem did not disturb her. Concetta figured if you were stupid enough to come wandering into Paradiso, why then you deserved to have your fool black head split wide open every now and then.

Concetta had left Paradiso at the age of nineteen, when the local iceman, a fellow *Napolitano* named Carmine La Bresca moved his business to Riverhead and asked the youngest of the Esposito girls to marry him. She readily accepted because he was a handsome fellow with deep brown eyes and curly black hair, and because he had a thriving business of which he was the sole owner. She also accepted because she was pregnant at the time.

Her son was born seven months later, and he was now twenty-seven years old, and living alone with Concetta in the second-floor apartment of a two-family house on Johnson Street. Carmine La Bresca had gone back to Pozzuoli, fifteen miles outside Naples, a month after Anthony was born. The last Concetta heard of him was a rumour that he had been killed during World War II, but, knowing her husband, she suspected he was king of the icemen somewhere in Italy, still fooling around with young girls and getting them pregnant in the icehouse, as was her own cruel misfortune.

Concetta Esposita La Bresca still disliked and distrusted all Negroes, and she was rather startled – to say the least – to find one on her doorstep at 12.01 am on a starless, moonless night.

'What is it?' she shouted. 'Go away.'

'Police officer,' Brown said, and flashed the tin, and it was then that Concetta noticed the other man standing with the Negro, a white man, short, with a narrow face and piercing brown eyes, *madonna mia*, it looked as if he was giving her the *malocchio*.

'What do you want, go away,' she said in a rush, and lowered the shade on the glass-panelled rear door of her apartment. The door was at the top of a rickety flight of wooden steps (Willis had almost tripped and broken his neck on the third one from the top) overlooking a back yard in which there was a tar-paper-covered tree. (Doubtless a fig tree, Brown remarked on their way up the steps.) A clothes-line stiff with undergarments stretched from the tiny back porch outside the glass-panelled door to a pole set diagonally at the other end of the yard. The wind whistled around the porch and did its best to blow Willis off and down into the grape arbour covering the outside patio below. He knocked on the door again, and shouted, 'Police officers, you'd better open up, lady.'

'*Sta zitto!*' Concetta said, and unlocked the door. 'You want to wake the whole neighbour? *Ma che vergogna!*'

'Is it all right to come in, lady?' Willis asked.

'Come in, come in,' Concetta said, and stepped back into the small kitchen, allowing Willis and then Brown to pass her.

'So what you want two o'clock in the morning?' Concetta said, and closed the door against the wind. The kitchen was narrow, the stove, sink, and refrigerator lined up against one wall, an enamel-topped table on the opposite wall. A metal cabinet, its door open to reveal an array of breakfast cereals and canned foods, was on the right-angled wall, alongside a radiator. There was a mirror over the sink and a porcelain dog on top of the refrigerator. Hanging on the wall over the radiator was a picture of Jesus Christ. A light bulb with a pull chain and a large glass globe hung in the centre of the kitchen. The faucet was dripping. An electric clock over the range hummed a steady counterpoint.

'It's only midnight,' Brown said. 'Not two o'clock.'

There was an edge to his voice that had not been there on the long ride up to Riverhead, and Willis could only attribute it to the presence of Mrs La Bresca, if indeed that was who the lady was. He wondered for perhaps the hundredth time what radar Brown possessed that enabled him to pinpoint unerringly any bigot within a radius of a thousand yards. The woman was staring at both men with equal animosity, it seemed to Willis, her long black hair pinned into a bun at the back of her head, her brown eyes slitted and defiant. She was wearing a man's bathrobe over her nightgown, and he saw now that she was barefoot.

'Are you Mrs La Bresca?' Willis asked.

'I am Concetta La Bresca, who wants to know?' she said.

'Detectives Willis and Brown of the 87th Squad,' Willis said. 'Where's your son?'

'He's asleep,' Concetta said, and because she was born in Naples and raised in Paradiso, immediately assumed it was necessary to provide him with an alibi. 'He was here with me all night,' she said, 'you got the wrong man.'

'You want to wake him up, Mrs La Bresca?' Brown said.

'What for?'

'We'd like to talk to him.'

'What for?'

'Ma'am, we can take him into custody, if that's what you'd like,' Brown said, 'but it might be easier all around if we just asked him a few simple questions right here and now. You want to go fetch him, ma'am?'

'I'm up,' La Bresca's voice said from the other room.

'You want to come out here, please, Mr La Bresca?' Willis said.

'Just a second,' La Bresca said.

'He was here all night,' Concetta said, but Brown's hand drifted none the less towards the revolver holstered at his waist, just in case La Bresca had been out pumping two bullets into the commissioner's head instead. He was a while coming. When he finally opened the door and walked into the kitchen, he was carrying nothing more lethal in his hand than the sash of his bathrobe, which he knotted about his waist. His hair was tousled, and his eyes were bleary.

'What now?' he asked.

Since this was a field investigation, and since La Bresca couldn't conceivably be considered 'in custody', neither Willis nor Brown felt it necessary to advise him of his rights. Instead, Willis immediately said, 'Where were you tonight at eleven thirty?'

'Right here,' La Bresca said.

'Doing what?'

'Sleeping.'

'What time'd you go to bed?'

'About ten.'

'You always hit the sack so early?'

'I do when I gotta get up early.'

'You getting up early tomorrow?'

'Six am,' La Bresca said.

'Why?'

'To get to work.'

'We thought you were unemployed.'

'I got a job this afternoon, right after you guys left me.'

'What kind of a job?'

'Construction work. I'm a labourer.'

'Meridian get you the job?'

'That's right.'

'Who with?'

'Erhard Engineering.'

'In Riverhead?'

'No, Isola.'

'What time'd you get home tonight?' Brown asked.

'I left Meridian, it musta been about one o'clock, I guess. I went up the pool hall on South Leary and shot a few games with the boys. Then I came home here, it musta been about five or six o'clock.'

'What'd you do then?'

'He ate,' Concetta said.

'Then what?'

'I watched a little TV, and got into bed,' La Bresca said.

'Can anybody besides your mother verify that story?'

'Nobody was here, if that's what you mean.'

'You get any phone calls during the night?'

'No.'

'Just your word then, right?'

'And *mine*,' Concetta said.

'Listen, I don't know what you guys want from me,' La Bresca said, 'but I'm telling you the truth, I mean it. What's going on, anyway?'

'Did you happen to catch the news on television?'

'No, I musta fell asleep before the news went on. Why? What happened?'

'I go in his room and turn off the light at ten thirty,' Concetta said.

'I wish you guys would believe me,' La Bresca said. 'Whatever it is you've got in mind, I didn't have nothing to do with it.'

'I believe you,' Willis said. 'How about you, Artie?'

'I believe him, too,' Brown said.

'But we have to ask questions,' Willis said, 'you understand?'

'Sure, I understand,' La Bresca said, 'but I mean, it's the middle of the night, you know? I gotta get up tomorrow morning.'

'Why don't you tell us about the man with the hearing aid again,' Willis suggested gently.

They spent at least another fifteen minutes questioning La Bresca and at the end of that time decided they'd either have to pull him in and charge him with something, or else forget him for the time being. The man who'd called the squadroom had said, 'There are more than one of us,' and this information had been passed from Kling to the other detectives on the squad, and it was only this nagging knowledge that kept them there questioning La Bresca long after they should have stopped. A cop can usually tell whether he's on to real meat or not, and La Bresca did not seem like a thief. Willis had told the lieutenant just that only this afternoon, and his opinion hadn't changed in the intervening hours. But if there *was* a gang involved in the commissioner's murder, wasn't it possible that La Bresca was one of them? A lowly cog in the organization, perhaps, the gopher, the slob who was sent to pick up things, the expendable man who ran the risk of being caught by the police if anything went wrong? In which case, La Bresca was lying.

Well, if he was lying, he did it like an expert, staring out of his baby blues and melting both those hardhearted cops with tales of the job he was anxious to start tomorrow morning, which is why he'd gone to bed so early and all, got to get a full eight hours' sleep, growing mind in a growing body, red-blooded second-generation American, and all that crap. Which raised yet another possibility. If he *was* lying – and so far they hadn't been able to trip him up, hadn't been able to budge him from his description of the mystery man he'd met outside Meridian, hadn't been able to find a single discrepancy between the story he'd told that afternoon and the one he was telling now – but if he *was* lying, then wasn't it possible the caller and La Bresca were one and the same person? *Not* a gang at all, that being a figment of his own imagination, a tiny falsehood designed to lead the police into believing this was a well-organized group instead of a single ambitious hood trying to make a killing. And if La Bresca and the caller were one and the same, then La Bresca and the man who'd murdered the commissioner were also one and the same. In which case, it would be proper to take the little liar home and book him for murder. Sure, and then try to find something that would stick, *anything* that would stick, they'd be laughed out of court right at the preliminary hearing.

Some nights you can't make a nickel.

So after fifteen minutes of some very fancy footwork designed to befuddle and unsettle La Bresca, with Brown utilizing his very special logically persistent method of questioning while Willis sniped and jabbed around the edges, they knew nothing more than they had known that afternoon. The only difference was that now the commissioner was dead. So they thanked Mrs La Bresca for the use of the hall, and they shook hands with her son and apologized for having pulled him out of bed, and they wished him luck at his new job, and then they both said goodnight again and went out of the house and heard Mrs La Bresca locking the kitchen door behind them, and went down the rickety wooden steps, and down the potholed driveway, and across the street to where they had parked the police sedan.

Then Willis started the car, and turned on the heater, and both men talked earnestly and softly for several moments and decided to ask the lieutenant for permission to bug La Bresca's phone in the morning.

Then they went home.

It was cold and dark in the alley where Steve Carella lay on his side huddled in a tattered overcoat. The late February snow had been shovelled and banked against one brick alley wall, soiled now with the city's grime, a thin layer of soot crusted on to its surface. Carella was wearing two pairs of thermal underwear and a quilted vest. In addition, a hand warmer was tucked into one pocket of the vest, providing a good steady heat inside the threadbare overcoat. But he was cold.

The banked snow opposite him only made him colder. He did not like snow. Oh yes, he could remember owning his own sled as a boy, and he could remember belly-whopping with joyous abandon, but the memory seemed like a totally fabricated one in view of his present very real aversion to snow. Snow was cold and wet. If you were a private citizen, you had to shovel it, and if you a were a Department of Sanitation worker, you had to truck it over to the River Dix to get rid of it. Snow was a pain in the arse.

This entire stakeout was a pain in the arse.

But it was also very amusing.

It was the amusing part of it that kept Carella lying in a cold dark alley on a night that wasn't fit for man or beast. (Of course, he had also been *ordered* to lie in a cold dark alley by the lieutenant for whom he worked, nice fellow name of Peter Byrnes, *he* should come lie in a cold dark alley some night.) The amusing part of this particular stakeout was that Carella wasn't planted in a bank hoping to prevent a multimillion dollar robbery, nor was he planted in a candy store some place, hoping to crack an international ring of narcotics peddlers, nor was he even hidden in the bathroom of a spinster lady's apartment, hoping to catch a mad rapist. He was lying in a cold dark alley, and the amusing part was that two vagrants had been set on fire. That wasn't so amusing, the part about being set on fire. That was pretty serious. The amusing part was that the victims had been vagrants. Ever since Carella could remember, the police had been waging an unremitting war against this city's vagrants, arresting them, jailing them, releasing them, arresting them again, on and on *ad infinitum*. So now the police had been presented with two benefactors who were generously attempting to rid the streets of any and all bums by setting them aflame, and what did the police do? The police promptly dispatched a valuable man to a cold dark alley to lie on his side facing a dirty snowbank while hoping to catch the very fellows who were in charge of incinerating bums. It did not make sense. It was amusing.

A lot of things about police work were amusing.

It was certainly funnier to be lying here freezing than to be at home in bed with a warm and loving woman; oh God, that was so amusing it made Carella want to weep. He thought of Teddy alone in bed, black hair spilling all over the pillow, half-smile on her mouth, nylon gown pulled back over curving hip, God, I could freeze to death right here in this goddamn alley, he thought, and my own wife won't learn about it till morning. My own passionate wife! She'll read about it in the papers! She'll see my name on page four! She'll –

There were footsteps at the other end of the alley.

He felt himself tensing. Beneath the overcoat, his naked hand moved away from the warmer and dropped swiftly to the cold steel butt of his service revolver. He eased the gun out of its holster, lay hunched on his side with the gun ready, and waited as the footsteps came closer.

'Here's one,' a voice said.

It was a young voice.

'Yeah,' another voice answered.

Carella waited. His eyes were closed, he lay huddled in the far corner of the alley, simulating sleep, his finger curled inside the trigger guard now, a hair's-breadth away from the trigger itself.

Somebody kicked him.

'Wake up!' a voice said.

He moved swiftly, but not swiftly enough. He was shoving himself off the floor of the alley, yanking the revolver into firing position, when the liquid splashed on to the front of his coat.

'Have a drink!' one of the boys shouted, and Carella saw a match flare into life, and suddenly he was in flames.

His reaction sequence was curious in that his sense of smell supplied the first signal, the unmistakable aroma of petrol fumes rising from the front of his coat, and then the flaring match, shocking in itself, providing a brilliant tiny explosion of light in the nearly black alley, more shocking in combination with the smell of petrol. Warning slammed with physical force into his temples, streaked in a jagged electric path to the back of his skull, and suddenly there were flames. There was no shock coupled with the fire that leaped up towards his face from the front of his coat. There was only terror.

Steve Carella reacted in much the same way Cro-Magnon must have reacted the first time he ventured too close to a raging fire and discovered that the flames can cook people as well as sabre-toothed tigers. He dropped his weapon, he covered his face, he whirled abruptly, instinctively rushing for the soot-crusted snowbank across the alley, forgetting his attackers, only vaguely aware that they were running, laughing, out of the alley and into the night, thinking only in a jagged broken pattern fire run burn fire out fire fire and hurled himself full length on to the snow. His hands were cupped tightly to his face, he could feel the flames chewing angrily at the backs of them, could smell the terrifying stench of burning hair and flesh, and then heard the sizzle of fire in contact with the snow, felt the cold and comforting snow, was suddenly enveloped in a white cloud of steam that rose from the beautiful snow, rolled from shoulder to shoulder in the glorious marvellous soothing beneficial white and magnificent snow, and found tears in his eyes, and thought nothing, and lay with his face pressed to the snow for a long while, breathing heavily, and still thinking nothing.

He got up at last and painfully retrieved his discarded revolver and walked slowly to the mouth of the alley and looked at his hands in the light of the street lamp. He caught his breath, and then went to the call box on the next corner. He told Sergeant Murchison at the desk that the fire bugs had hit, and that his hands had been burned and he would need a meat wagon to get him over to the hospital. Murchison said, 'Are you all right?' and Carella looked at his hands again, and said, 'Yes, I'm all right, Dave.'

CHAPTER 4

Detective Bert Kling was in love, but nobody else was.

The mayor was not in love, he was furious. The mayor called the police commissioner in high dudgeon and wanted to know what kind of a goddamn city this was when a man of the calibre of Parks Commissioner Cowper could be gunned down on the steps of Philharmonic Hall, what the hell kind of a city was this, anyway?

'Well, sir,' the police commissioner started, but the mayor said, 'Perhaps you can tell me why adequate police protection was not provided for Commissioner Cowper when his wife informs me this morning that the police *knew* a threat had been made on his life, perhaps you can tell me that,' the mayor shouted into the phone.

'Well, sir,' the police commissioner started, but the mayor said, 'Or perhaps you can tell me why you still haven't located the apartment from which those shots were fired, when the autopsy has already revealed the angle of entrance and your ballistics people have come up with a probable trajectory, perhaps you can tell me that.'

'Well, sir,' the police commissioner started, but the mayor said, 'Get me some results, do you want this city to become a laughing-stock?'

The police commissioner certainly didn't want the city to become a laughing-stock, so he said, 'Yes, sir, I'll do the best I can,' and the mayor said, 'You had better,' and hung up.

There was no love lost between the mayor and the police commissioner that morning. So the police commissioner asked his secretary, a tall wan blond man who appeared consumptive and who claimed his constant hacking cough was caused by smoking three packs of cigarettes a day in a job that was enough to drive anyone utterly mad, the police commissioner asked his secretary to find out what the mayor had meant by a threat on the parks commissioner's life, and report back to him immediately. The tall wan blond secretary got to work at once, asking around here and there, and discovering that the 87th Precinct had indeed logged several telephone calls from a mysterious stranger who had threatened to kill the parks commissioner unless five thousand dollars was delivered to him by noon yesterday. When the police commissioner received this information, he said, 'Oh, *yeah*?' and immediately dialled Frederick 7–8024, and asked to talk to Detective-Lieutenant Peter Byrnes.

Detective-Lieutenant Peter Byrnes had enough headaches that morning, what with Carella in the hospital with second-degree burns on the backs of both hands, and the painters having moved from the squadroom into his own private office, where they were slopping up everything in sight and telling jokes on their ladders. Byrnes was not over fond of the police commissioner to begin with, the commissioner being a fellow who had been imported from a neighbouring city when the new administration took over, a city which, in Byrnes' opinion, had an even larger crime rate than this one. Nor was the new commissioner terribly fond of Lieutenant Byrnes, because Byrnes was the sort of garrulous Irishman who shot off his mouth at Police Benevolent Association and Emerald Society functions, letting anyone within earshot know what he thought of the mayor's recent whiz-kid appointee. So there was hardly any sweetness and light oozing over the telephone wires that morning between the commissioner's office at Headquarters downtown on High Street, and Byrnes' paint-spattered corner office on the second floor of the grimy station house on Grover Avenue.

'What's this all about, Byrnes?' the commissioner asked.

'Well, sir,' Byrnes said, remembering that the *former* commissioner used to call him Pete, 'we received several threatening telephone calls from an unidentified man yesterday, which telephone calls I discussed with Parks Commissioner Cowper.'

'What did you do about those calls, Byrnes?'

'We placed the drop site under surveillance, and apprehended the man who made the pick-up.'

'So what happened?'

'We questioned him and released him.'

'Why?'

'Insufficient evidence. He was also interrogated after the parks commissioner's murder last night. We did not have ample grounds for an arrest. The man is still free, but a telephone tap went into effect this morning, and we're ready to move in if we monitor anything incriminating.'

'Why wasn't the commissioner given police protection?'

'I offered it, sir, and it was refused.'

'Why wasn't your suspect put under surveillance *before* a crime was committed?'

'I couldn't spare any men, sir, and when I contacted the 115th in Riverhead, where the suspect resides, I was told they could not spare any men either. Besides, as I told you, the commissioner did not *want* protection. He felt we were dealing with a crackpot, sir, and I must tell you that was our opinion here, too. Until, of course, recent events proved otherwise.'

'Why hasn't that apartment been found yet?'

'What apartment, sir?'

'The apartment from which the two shots were fired that killed Parks Commissioner Cowper.'

'Sir, the crime was not committed in our precinct. Philharmonic Hall, sir, is in the 53rd Precinct and, as I'm sure the commissioner realizes, a homicide is investigated by the detectives assigned to the squad in the precinct in which the homicide was committed.'

'Don't give me any of that bullshit, Byrnes,' the police commissioner said.

'That is the way we do it in this city, sir,' Byrnes said.

'This is your case,' the commissioner answered. 'You got that, Byrnes?'

'If you say so, sir.'

'I say so. Get some men over to the area, and find that goddamn apartment.'

'Yes, sir.'

'And report back to me.'

'Yes, sir,' Byrnes said, and hung up.

'Getting a little static, huh?' the first painter said.

'Getting your arse chewed out, huh?' the second painter said.

Both men were on their ladders, grinning and dripping apple green paint on the floor.

'Get the hell out of this office!' Byrnes shouted.

'We ain't finished yet,' the first painter said.

'We don't leave till we finish,' the second painter said.

'That's our orders,' the first painter said.

'We don't work for the Police Department, you know.'

'We work for the Department of Public Works.'

'Maintenance and Repair.'

'And we don't quit a job till we finish it.'

'Stop dripping paint all over my goddamn floor!' Byrnes shouted, and stormed out of the office. 'Hawes!' he shouted. 'Kling! Willis! Brown! Where the hell *is* everybody?' he shouted.

Meyer came out of the men's room, zipping up his fly. 'What's up, Skipper?' he said.

'Where were you?'

'Taking a leak. Why, what's up?'

'Get somebody over to the area!' Byrnes shouted.

'What area?'

'Where the goddamn commissioner got shot!'

'Okay, sure,' Meyer said. 'But why? That's not our case.'

'It is now.'

'Oh?'

'Who's catching?'

'I am.'

'Where's Kling?'

'Day off.'

'Where's Brown?'

'On that wire tap.'

'And Willis?'

'He went to the hospital to see Steve.'

'And Hawes?'

'He went down for some Danish.'

'What the hell am I running here, a resort in the mountains?'

'No, sir. We . . .'

'Send Hawes over there! Send him over the minute he gets back. Get on the phone to Ballistics. Find out what they've got. Call the ME's office and get that autopsy report. Get cracking, Meyer!'

'Yes, *sir*!' Meyer snapped, and went immediately to the telephone.

'This goddamn racket drives me crazy,' Byrnes said, and started to storm back into his office, remembered that the jolly green painters were in there slopping around, and stormed into the Clerical Office instead.

'Get these files in order!' he shouted. 'What the hell do you do in here all day, Miscolo, make coffee?'

'Sir?' Miscolo said, because that's exactly what he was doing at the moment.

Bert Kling was in love.

It was not a good time of the year to be in love. It is better to be in love when flowers are blooming and balmy breezes are wafting in off the river, and strange animals come up to lick your hand. There's only one good thing about being in love in March, and that's that it's better to be in love in March than not to be in love at all, as the wise man once remarked.

Bert Kling was madly in love.

He was madly in love with a girl who was twenty-three years old, full-breasted and wide-hipped, her blonde hair long and trailing midway down her back or sometimes curled into a honey conch shell at the back of her head, her eyes a cornflower blue, a tall girl who came just level with his chin when she was wearing heels. He was madly in love with a scholarly girl who was studying at night for her master's degree in psychology, while working during the day conducting interviews for a firm downtown on Shepherd Street; a serious girl who hoped to go on for her PhD, and then pass the state boards, and then practise psychology; a nutty girl who was capable of sending to the squadroom a six-foot high heart cut out of plywood and painted red and lettered in yellow with the words Cynthia Forrest Loves Detective 3rd/Grade Bertram Kling, So Is That A Crime?, as she had done on St Valentine's Day just last month (and which Kling had still not heard the end of from all his comical colleagues); an emotional girl who could burst into tears at the sight of a blind man playing an accordion on The Stem, to whom she gave a five-dollar bill, merely put the bill silently into the cup, soundlessly, it did not even make a rustle, and turned away to weep into Kling's shoulder; a passionate girl who clung to him fiercely in the night and who woke him sometimes at six in the morning to say, 'Hey, Cop, I have to go to work in a few hours, are you interested?' to which Kling invariably answered, 'No, I am not interested in sex and things like that,' and then kissed her until she was dizzy and afterwards sat across from her at the kitchen table in her apartment, staring at her, marvelling at her beauty and once caused her to blush when he said, 'There's a woman who sells *pidaguas* on Mason Avenue, her name is Iluminada, she was born in Puerto Rico. Your name should be Iluminada, Cindy. You fill the room with light.'

Boy, was he in love.

But, it being March, and the streets still banked high with February snow, and the winds howling, and the wolves growling and chasing civilians in troikas who cracked whips and huddled in bear rugs, it being a bitter cold winter which seemed to have started in September and showed no signs of abating till next August, when possibly, but just possibly, all the snow might melt and the flowers would bloom – it being that kind of a treacherous winter, what better to do than discuss police work? What better to do than rush along the frozen street on Cindy's lunch hour with her hand clutched tightly in the crook of his arm and the wind whipping around them and drowning out Kling's voice as he tried to tell her of the mysterious circumstances surrounding the death of Parks Commissioner Cowper.

'Yes, it *sounds* very mysterious,' Cindy said, and brought her hand out of her pocket in an attempt to keep the wind from tearing her kerchief from her head. 'Listen, Bert,' she said, 'I'm really very tired of winter, aren't you tired of it?'

'Yeah,' Kling said. 'Listen, Cindy, you know who I hope this isn't?'

'Hope who isn't?' she said.

'The guy who made the calls. The guy who killed the commissioner. You know who I hope we're not up against?'

'*Who?*' Cindy said.

'The deaf man,' he said.

'What?' she said.

'He was a guy we went up against a few years back, it must have been maybe seven, eight years ago. He tore this whole damn city apart trying to rob a bank. He was the smartest crook we ever came up against.'

'*Who?*' Cindy said.

'The deaf man,' Kling said again.

'Yes, but what's his name?'

'We don't know his name. We never caught him. He jumped in the river and we thought he drowned, but maybe he's back now. Like Frankenstein.'

'Like Frankenstein's monster, you mean,' Cindy said.

'Yeah, like him. Remember he was supposed to have died in that fire, but he didn't.'

'I remember.'

'That was a scary picture,' Kling said.

'I wet my pants when I saw it,' Cindy said. 'And that was on television.'

'You wet your pants on *television*?' Kling said. 'In front of forty million *people*?'

'No, I saw *Frankenstein* on television,' Cindy said, and grinned and poked him.

'The deaf man,' Kling said. 'I hope it's not him.'

It was the first time any man on the squad had voiced the possibility that the commissioner's murderer was the man who had give them so much trouble so many years ago. The thought was somewhat numbing. Bert Kling was a young man, and not a particularly philosophical one, but he intuitively understood that the deaf man (who had once signed a note L. Sordo, very comical, El Sordo meaning 'The Deaf One' in Spanish) was capable of manipulating odds with computer accuracy, of spreading confusion and fear, of juggling permutations and combinations in a manner calculated to upset the strict and somewhat bureaucratic efficiency of a police precinct, making law enforcers behave like bumbling Keystone cops in a yellowing ancient film, knew instinctively and with certainty that if the commissioner's murderer was indeed the deaf man, they had not heard the end of all this. And because the very thought of what the deaf man might and *could* do was too staggering to contemplate, Kling involuntarily shuddered, and he knew it was not from the cold.

'I hope it isn't him,' he said, and his words were carried away on the wind.

'Kiss me,' Cindy said suddenly, 'and then buy me a hot chocolate, you cheapskate.'

The boy who came into the muster room that Wednesday afternoon was about twelve years old.

He was wearing his older brother's hand-me-down ski parka which was blue and three sizes too large for him. He had pulled the hood of the parka up over his head, and had tightened the drawstrings around his neck, but the hood was still too big, and it kept falling off. He kept trying to pull it back over his head as he came into the station house carrying an envelope in the same hand with which he wiped his runny nose. He was wearing high-topped sneakers with the authority of all slum kids who wear sneakers winter and summer, all year round, despite the warnings of paediatrists. He walked to the muster desk with a sneaker-inspired bounce, tried to adjust the parka hood again, wiped his dripping nose again, and then looked up at Sergeant Murchison and said, 'You the desk sergeant?'

'I'm the desk sergeant,' Murchison answered without looking up from the absentee slips he was filling out from that morning's muster sheet. It was 2.10 pm, and in an hour and thirty-five minutes the afternoon shift of uniformed cops would be coming in, and there'd be a new roll call to take, and new absentee slips to fill out, a regular rat race, he should have become a fireman or a postman.

'I'm supposed to give you this,' the kid said, and reached up to hand Murchison the sealed envelope.

'Thanks,' Murchison said, and accepted the envelope without looking at the kid, and then suddenly raised his head and said, 'Hold it just a second.'

'Why, what's the matter?'

'Just hold it right there a second,' Murchison said, and opened the envelope. He unfolded the single sheet of white paper that had been neatly folded in three equal parts, and he read what was on the sheet, and then he looked down at the kid again and said, 'Where'd you get this?'

'Outside.'

'Where?'

'A guy gave it to me.'

'What guy?'

'A tall guy outside.'

'Outside where?'

'Near the park there. Across the street.'

'Gave you this?'

'Yeah.'

'What'd he say?'

'Said I should bring it in here and give it to the desk sergeant.'

'You know the guy?'

'No, he gave me five bucks to bring it over here.'

'What'd he look like?'

'A tall guy with blond hair. He had a thing in his ear.'

'What kind of a thing?'

'Like he was deaf,' the kid said, and wiped his hand across his nose again.

That was what the note read.

So they studied the note, being careful not to get any more fingerprints on it than Sergeant Murchison had already put there, and then they stood around a runny-nosed twelve-year-old kid wearing a blue ski parka three sizes too large for him, and fired questions at him as though they had captured Jack the Ripper over from London for the weekend.

They got nothing from the kid except perhaps his cold.

He repeated essentially what he had told Sergeant Murchison, that a tall blond guy wearing a thing in his ear (A hearing aid, you mean, kid?) yeah, a thing in his ear, had stopped him across the street from the police station and offered him five bucks to carry an envelope in to the desk sergeant. The kid couldn't see nothing wrong with bringing an envelope into the police station, so he done it, and that was all, he didn't even know who the guy with the thing in his ear was (You mean a hearing aid, kid?) yeah, a thing in his ear, he didn't know who he was, never even seen him around the neighbourhood or nothing, so could he go home now because he had to make a stop at Linda's Boutique to pick up some dresses for his sister who did sewing at home for Mrs Montana? (He was wearing a hearing aid, huh, kid?) Yeah, a thing in his ear, the kid said.

So they let the kid go at two thirty without even offering him an ice-cream cone or some gumdrops, and then they sat around the squad-room handling the suspect note with a pair of tweezers and decided to send it over to Lieutenant Sam Grossman at the police lab. in the hope that he could lift some latent prints that did not belong to Sergeant Murchison.

None of them mentioned the deaf man.

Nobody likes to talk about ghosts.

Or even *think* about them.

'Hello, Bernice,' Meyer said into the telephone, 'is your boss around? Yeah, sure, I'll wait.'

Patiently, he tapped a pencil on his desk and waited. In a moment, a bright perky voice materialized on the line.

'Assistant District Attorney Raoul Chabrier,' the voice insisted.

'Hello, Rollie, this is Meyer Meyer up here at the 87th,' Meyer said. 'How's every little thing down there on Chelsea Street?'

'Oh, pretty good, pretty good,' Chabrier said, 'what have you got for us, a little homicide up there perhaps?'

'No, nothing like that Rollie,' Meyer said.

'A little axe murder perhaps?' Chabrier said.

'No, as a matter of fact, this is something personal,' Meyer said.

'Oh-*ho*!' Chabrier said.

'Yeah. Listen, Rollie, what can you do if somebody uses your name?'

'What do you mean?' Chabrier asked.

'In a book.'

'Oh-*ho*!' Chabrier said. 'Did somebody use your name in a book?'

'Yes.'

'In a book about the workings of the police department?'

'No.'

'Were you mentioned specifically?'

'No. Well, yes *and* no. What do you mean?'

'Did the book specifically mention Detective 3rd/Grade Meyer . . .'

'Detective *2nd*/Grade,' Meyer corrected.

'It specifically mentioned Detective 2nd/Grade Meyer Meyer of the . . .'

'No.'

'It *didn't* mention you?'

'No. Not that way.'

'I thought you said somebody used your name.'

'Well, they did. She did.'

'Meyer, I'm a busy man,' Chabrier said. 'I've got a case load here that would fell a brewer's horse, now would you please tell me what's on your mind?'

'A novel,' Meyer said. 'It's a novel named *Meyer Meyer*.'

'That is the title of the novel?' Chabrier asked.

'Yes, Can I sue?'

'I am a criminal lawyer,' Chabrier said.

'Yes, but . . .'

'I am not familiar with the law of literary property.'

'Yes, but . . .'

'Is it a good book?'

'I don't know,' Meyer said. 'You see,' he said, 'I'm a *person*, and this book is about some college professor or something, and he's a short plump fellow . . .'

'I'll have to read it,' Chabrier said.

'Will you call me after you've read it?'

'What for?'

'To advise me.'

'On what?'

'On whether I can sue or not.'

'I'll have to read the law,' Chabrier said. 'Do I owe you a favour, Meyer?'

'You owe me *six* of them,' Meyer said somewhat heatedly, 'as for example the several times I could have got you out of bed at three o'clock in the morning when we had real meat here in the squadroom and at great risk to myself I held the suspect until the following morning so you could get your beauty sleep on nights when you had the duty. Now, Rollie, I'm asking a very tiny favour, I don't want to go to the expense of getting some fancy copyright lawyer or whatever the hell, I just want to know whether I can sue somebody who used my name that's on record in the Department of Health on a birth certificate, can I sue this person who uses my name as the title of a novel, and for a *character* in a novel, when here I am a real *person*, for Christ's sake!'

'OK, don't get excited,' Chabrier said.

'Who's excited?' Meyer said.

'I'll read the law and call you back.'

'When?'

'Sometime.'

'Maybe if we get somebody in the squadroom sometime when you've got the duty, I'll fly in the face of Miranda-Escobedo again and hold off till morning so you can peacefully snore the night . . .'

'OK, OK, I'll get back to you tomorrow.' Chabrier paused. 'Don't you want to know what *time* tomorrow?'

'What time tomorrow?' Meyer asked.

The landlady had arthritis, and she hated winter, and she didn't like cops too well, either. She immediately told Cotton Hawes that there had been other policemen prowling around ever since that big mucky-muck got shot last night, why couldn't they leave a lady alone? Hawes, who had been treated to similar diatribes from every landlady and superintendent along the street, patiently explained that he was only doing his job, and said he knew she would want to cooperate in bringing a murderer to justice. The landlady said the city was rotten and corrupt, and as far as she was concerned they could shoot *all* those damn big mucky-mucks, and she wouldn't lose no sleep over any of them.

Hawes had thus far visited four buildings in a row of identical slum tenements facing the glittering glass and concrete structure that was the city's new Philharmonic Hall. The building, a triumph of design (the acoustics weren't so hot, but what the hell) could be clearly seen from any one of the tenements, the wide marble steps across the avenue offering an unrestricted view of anyone who happened to be standing on them, or coming down them, or going up them. The man who had plunked two rifle slugs into Cowper's head could have done so from *any* of these buildings. The only reason the police department was interested in the exact source of the shots was that the killer may have left some evidence behind him. Evidence is always nice to have in a murder case.

The first thing Hawes asked the landlady was whether she had rented an apartment or a room recently to a tall blond man wearing a hearing aid.

'Yes,' the landlady said.

That was a good start. Hawes was an experienced detective, and he recognized immediately that the landlady's affirmative reply was a terribly good start.

'Who?' he asked immediately. 'Would you know his name?'

'Yes.'

'What's his name?'

'Orecchio. Mort Orecchio.'

Hawes took out his pad and began writing. 'Orecchio,' he said, 'Mort. Would you happen to know whether it was Morton or Mortimer or exactly what?'

'Just Mort,' the landlady said. 'Mort Orecchio. He was Eye-talian.'

'How do you know?'

'Anything ending in O is Eye-talian.'

'You think so? How about Shapiro?' Hawes suggested.

'What are you, a wise guy?' the landlady said.

'This fellow Orecchio, which apartment did you rent him?'

'A *room*, not an apartment,' the landlady said. 'Third floor front.'

'Facing Philharmonic?'

'Yeah.'

'Could I see the room?'

'Sure, why not? I got nothing else to do but show cops rooms.'

They began climbing. The hallway was cold and the air shaft windows were rimed with frost. There was the commingled smell of garbage and urine on the stairs, a nice clean old lady this landlady. She kept complaining about her arthritis all the way up to the third floor, telling Hawes the cortisone didn't help her none, all them big mucky-muck doctors making promises that didn't help her pain at all. She stopped outside a door with the brass numerals 31 on it, and fished into the pocket of her apron for a key. Down the hall, a door opened a crack and then closed again.

'Who's that?' Hawes asked.

'Who's who?' the landlady said.

'Down the hall there. The door that just opened and closed.'

'Musta been Polly,' the landlady said, and unlocked the door at 31.

The room was small and cheerless. A three-quarter bed was against the wall opposite the door, covered with a white chenille bedspread. A framed print was over the bed. It showed a logging mill and a river and a sheepdog looking up at something in the sky. A standing floor lamp was on the right of the bed. The shade was yellow and soiled. A stain, either whisky or vomit, was on the corner of the bedspread where it was pulled up over the pillows. Opposite the bed, there was a single dresser with a mirror over it. The dresser had cigarette burns all the way around its top.

The mirror was spotted and peeling. The sink alongside the dresser had a big rust ring near the drain.

'How long was he living here?' Hawes asked.

'Took the room three days ago.'

'Did he pay by cheque or cash?'

'Cash. In advance. Paid for a full week. I only rent by the week, I don't like none of these one-night stands.'

'Naturally not,' Hawes said.

'I know what you're thinking. You're thinking it ain't such a fancy place, I shouldn't be so fussy. Well, it may not be fancy,' the landlady said, 'but it's clean.'

'Yes, I can see that.'

'I mean it ain't got no *bugs*, mister.'

Hawes nodded and went to the window. The shade was torn and missing its pull cord. He grabbed the lower edge in his gloved hand, raised the shade and looked across the street.

'You hear any shots last night?'

'No.'

He looked down at the floor. There were no spent cartridge cases anywhere in sight.

'Who else lives on this floor?'

'Polly down the hall, that's all.'

'Polly who?'

'Malloy.'

'Mind if I look through the dresser and the closet?'

'Go right ahead. I got all the time in the world. The way I spend my day is I conduct guided tours through the building.'

Hawes went to the dresser and opened each of the drawers. They were all empty, except for a cockroach nestling in the corner of the bottom drawer.

'You missed one,' Hawes said, and closed the drawer.

'Huh?' the landlady said.

Hawes went to the closet and opened it. There were seven wire hangers on the clothes bar. The closet was empty. He was about to close the door when something on the floor caught his eye. He stooped for a closer look, took a pen light from his pocket, and turned it on. The object on the floor was a dime.

'If that's money,' the landlady said, 'it belongs to me.'

'Here,' Hawes said, and handed her the dime. He did so knowing full well that even if the coin *had* belonged to the occupant of the room, it was as impossible to get latent prints from money as it was to get re-imbursed by the city for petrol used in one's private car on police business.

'Is there a john in here?' he asked.
'Down the hall. Lock the door behind you.'
'I only wanted to know if there was another room, that's all.'
'It's clean, if that's what you're worrying about.'
'I'm sure it's spotless,' Hawes said. He took another look around. 'So this is it, huh?'
'This is it.'
'I'll be sending a man over to dust that sill,' Hawes said.
'Why?' the landlady said. 'It's clean.'
'I mean for fingerprints.'
'Oh.' The landlady stared at him. 'You think that big mucky-muck was shot from this room?'
'It's possible,' Hawes said.
'Will that mean trouble for me?'
'Not unless you shot him,' Hawes said, and smiled.
'You got some sense of humour,' the landlady said.
They went out of the apartment. The landlady locked the door behind her. 'Will that be all,' she asked, 'or did you want to see anything else?'
'I want to talk to the woman down the hall,' Hawes said, 'but I won't need you for that. Thank you very much, you were very helpful.'
'It breaks the monotony,' the landlady said, and he believed her.
'Thank you again,' he said, and watched her as she went down the steps. He walked to the door marked 32 and knocked. There was no answer. He knocked again and said, 'Miss Malloy?'
The door opened a crack.
'Who is it?' a voice said.
'Police officer. May I talk to you?'
'What about?'
'About Mr Orecchio.'
'I don't know any Mr Orecchio,' the voice said.
'Miss Malloy . . .'
'It's *Mrs* Malloy, and I don't know any Mr Orecchio.'
'Could you open the door, ma'am?'
'I don't want any trouble.'
'I won't . . .'
'I know a man got shot last night, I don't want any trouble.'
'Did you hear the shots, Miss Malloy?'
'*Mrs* Malloy.'
'Did you?'
'No.'
'Would you happen to know if Mr Orecchio was in last night?'
'I don't know who Mr Orecchio is.'

'The man in 31.'

'I don't know him.'

'Ma'am, could you please open the door?'

'I don't want to.'

'Ma'am, I can come back with a warrant, but it'd be a lot easier . . .'

'Don't get me in trouble,' she said. 'I'll open the door, but please don't get me in trouble.'

Polly Malloy was wearing a pale green cotton wrapper. The wrapper had short sleeves. Hawes saw the hit marks on her arms the moment she opened the door, and the hit marks explained a great deal about the woman who was Polly Malloy. She was perhaps twenty-six years old, with a slender youthful body and a face that would have been pretty if it were not so clearly stamped with knowledge. The green eyes were intelligent and alert, the mouth vulnerable. She worried her lip and held the wrapper closed about her naked body, and her fingers were long and slender, and the hit marks on her arms shouted all there was to shout.

'I'm not holding,' she said.

'I didn't ask.'

'You can look around if you like.'

'I'm not interested,' Hawes said.

'Come in,' she said.

He went into the apartment. She closed and locked the door behind him.

'I don't want trouble,' she said. 'I've had enough trouble.'

'I won't give you any. I only want to know about the man down the hall.'

'I know somebody got shot. Please don't get me involved in it.'

They sat opposite each other, she on the bed, he on a straight-backed chair facing her. Something shimmered on the air between them, something as palpable as the tenement stink of garbage and piss surrounding them. They sat in easy informality, comfortably aware of each other's trade, Cotton Hawes detective, Polly Malloy addict. And perhaps they knew each other better than a great many people ever get to know each other. Perhaps Hawes had been inside too many shooting galleries not to understand what it was like to be this girl, perhaps he had arrested too many hookers who were screwing for the couple of bucks they needed for a bag of shit, perhaps he had watched the agonized writhings of too many cold turkey kickers, perhaps his knowledge of this junkie or any junkie was as intimate as a pusher's, perhaps he had seen too much and knew too much. And perhaps the girl had been collared too many times, had protested too many times that she was clean, had thrown too many decks of heroin under bar stools or down sewers at the approach of a cop, had been in too many different squadrooms and handled by too many different bulls, been offered the Lexington choice by too many different magistrates, perhaps her knowledge of the law as it applied to narcotics addicts was as intimate as any assistant district attorney's, perhaps she too had seen too much and knew too much. Their mutual knowledge was electric, it generated a heat lightning of its own, ascertaining the curious symbiosis of lawbreaker and enforcer, affirming the interlocking subtlety of crime and punishment. There was a secret bond in that room, an affinity – almost an empathy. They could talk to each other without any bullshit. They were like spent lovers whispering on the same pillow.

'Did you know Orecchio?' Hawes asked.

'Will you keep me clean?'

'Unless you had something to do with it.'

'Nothing.'

'You've got my word.'

'A cop?' she asked, and smiled wanly.

'You've got my word, if you want it.'

'I need it, it looks like.'

'You need it, honey.'

'I knew him.'

'How?'

'I met him the night he moved in.

'When was that?'

'Two, three nights ago.'

'Where'd you meet?'

'I was hung up real bad, I needed a fix. I just got out of Caramoor, *that* sweet hole, a week ago. I haven't had time to get really connected yet.'

'What were you in for?'

'Oh, hooking.'

'How old are you, Polly?'

'Nineteen. I look older, huh?'

'Yes, you look older.'

'I got married when I was sixteen. To another junkie like myself. Some prize.'

'What's he doing now?'

'Time at Castleview.'

'For what?'

Polly shrugged. 'He started pushing.'

'OK, what about Orecchio next door?'

'I asked him for a loan.'

'When was this?'

'Day before yesterday.'

'Did he give it to you?'

'I didn't actually ask him for a loan. I offered to turn a trick for him. He was right next door, you see, and I was pretty sick, I swear to God I don't think I coulda made it to the street.'

'Did he accept?'

'He gave me ten bucks. He didn't take nothing from me for it.'

'Sounds like a nice fellow.'

Polly shrugged.

'Not a nice fellow?' Hawes asked.

'Let's say not my type,' Polly said.

'Mm-huh.'

'Let's say a son of a bitch,' Polly said.

'What happened?'

'He came in here last night.'

'When? What time?'

'Musta been about nine, nine-thirty.'

'After the symphony started,' Hawes said.

'Huh?'

'Nothing, I was just thinking out loud. Go on.'

'He said he had something nice for me. He said if I came into his room, he would give me something nice.'

'Did you go?'

'First I asked him what it was. He said it was something I wanted more than anything else in the world.'

'But did you get into his room?'

'Yes.'

'Did you see anything out of the ordinary?'

'Like what?'

'Like a high-powered rifle with a telescopic sight.'

'No, nothing like that.'

'All right, what was this "something nice" he promised you?'

'Hoss.'

'He had heroin for you?'

'Yes.'

'And that's why he asked you to come into his room? For the heroin?'

'That's what he said.'

'He didn't attempt to sell it to you, did he?'

'No. But . . .'

'Yes?'

'He made me beg for it.'

'What do you mean?'

'He showed it to me, and he let me taste it to prove that it was real stuff, and then he refused to give it to me unless I . . . begged for it.'

'I see.'

'He . . . teased me for . . . I guess for . . . for almost two hours. He kept looking at his watch and making me . . . do things.'

'What kind of things?'

'Stupid things. He asked me to sing for him. He made me sing "White Christmas", that was supposed to be a joke, you see, because the shit is white and he knew how bad I needed a fix, so he made me sing "White Christmas" over and over again, I musta sung it for him six or seven times. And all the while he kept looking at his watch.'

'Go ahead.'

'Then he . . . he asked me to strip, but . . . I mean, not just take off my clothes, but . . . you know, do a strip for him. And I did it. And he began . . . he began making fun of me, of the way I looked, of my body. I . . . he made me stand naked in front of him, and he just went on and on about how stupid and pathetic I looked, and he kept asking me if I really wanted the heroin, and then looked at his watch again, it was about eleven o'clock by then, I kept saying Yes, I want it, please let me have it, so he asked me to dance for him, he asked me to do the waltz, and then he asked me to do the shag, I didn't know what the hell he was talking about, I never even heard of the shag, have you ever heard of the shag?'

'Yes, I've heard of it,' Hawes said.

'So I did all that for him, I would have done anything for him, and finally he told me to get on my knees and explain to him why I felt I really needed the bag of heroin. He said he expected me to talk for five minutes on the subject of the addict's need for narcotics, and he looked at his watch and began timing me, and I talked. I was shaking by this time, I had the chills, I needed a shot more than . . .' Polly closed her eyes. 'I began crying. I talked and I cried, and at last he looked at his watch and said, "Your five minutes are up. Here's your poison, now get the hell out of here." And he threw the bag to me.'

'What time was this?'

'It musta been about ten minutes after eleven. I don't have a watch, I hocked it long ago, but you can see the big electric numbers on top of the Mutual Building from my room, and when I was shooting up later it was eleven fifteen, so this musta been about ten after or thereabouts.'

'And he kept looking at his watch all through this, huh?'

'Yes. As if he had a date or something.'

'He did,' Hawes said.

'Huh?'

'He had a date to shoot a man from his window. He was just amusing himself until the concert broke. A nice fellow, Mr. Orecchio.'

'I got to say one thing for him,' Polly said.

'What's that?'

'It was good stuff.' A wistful look came on to her face and into her eyes. 'It was some of the best stuff I've had in years. I wouldn't have heard a *cannon* if it went off next door.'

Hawes made a routine check of all the city's telephone directories, found no listing for an Orecchio – Mort, Morton, or Mortimer – and then called the Bureau of Criminal Identification at four o'clock that afternoon. The BCI, fully automated, called back within ten minutes to report that they had nothing on the suspect. Hawes then sent a teletype to the FBI in Washington, asking them to check their voluminous files for any known criminal named Orecchio, Mort or Mortimer or Morton. He was sitting at his desk in the paint-smelling squadroom when Patrolman Richard Genero came up to ask whether he had to go to court with Kling on the collar they had made jointly and together the week before. Genero had been walking his beat all afternoon, and he was very cold, so he hung around long after Hawes had answered his question, hoping he would be offered a cup of coffee. His eye happened to fall on the name Hawes had scribbled on to his desk pad when calling the BCI, so Genero decided to make a quip.

'Another Italian suspect, I see,' he said.

'How do you know?' Hawes asked.

'Anything ending in O is Italian,' Genero said.

'How about Munro?' Hawes asked.

'What are you, a wise guy?' Genero said, and grinned. He looked at the scribbled name again, and then said, 'I got to admit *this* guy has a very funny name for an Italian.'

'Funny how?' Hawes asked.

'Ear,' Genero said.

'What?'

'Ear. That's what Orecchio means in Italian. Ear.'

Which when coupled with Mort, of course, could mean nothing more or less than Dead Ear.

Hawes tore the page from the pad, crumpled it into a ball, and threw it at the wastebasket, missing.

'I said something?' Genero asked, knowing he'd never get his cup of coffee now.

CHAPTER 5

The boy who delivered the note was eight years old, and he had instructions to give it to the desk sergeant. He stood in the squadroom now surrounded by cops who looked seven feet tall, all of them standing around him in a circle while he looked up with saucer-wide blue eyes and wished he was dead.

'Who gave you this note?' one of the cops asked.

'A man in the park.'

'Did he pay you to bring it here?'

'Yeah. Yes. Yeah.'

'How much?'

Five dollars.'

'What did he look like?'

'He had yellow hair.'

'Was he tall?'

'Oh, yeah.'

'Was he wearing a hearing aid?'

'Yeah. A *what*?'

'A thing in his ear.'

'Oh, yeah,' the kid said.

Everybody tiptoed around the note very carefully, as though it might explode at any moment. Everybody handled the note with tweezers or white cotton gloves. Everybody agreed it should be sent at once to the police lab. Everybody read it at least twice. Everybody studied it and examined it. Even some patrolmen from downstairs came up to have a look at it. It was a very important document. It demanded at least an hour of valuable police time before it was finally encased in a celluloid folder and sent downtown in a manilla envelope.

Everybody decided that what this note meant was that the deaf man (who they now reluctantly admitted was once again in their midst) wanted fifty thousand dollars in lieu of killing the deputy mayor exactly as he had killed the parks commissioner. Since fifty thousand dollars was considerably more than the previous demand for five thousand dollars, the cops of the 87th were quite rightfully incensed by the demand. Moreover, the audacity of this criminal somewhere out there was something beyond the ken of their experience. For all its resemblance to a kidnapping, with its subsequent demand for ransom, this case was *not* a kidnapping. No one had been abducted, there was nothing to ransom. No, this was very definitely extortion, and yet the extortion cases they'd dealt

Look! A whole new

price.

$ 50,000.

with over the years had been textbook cases involving a 'wrongful use of force or fear' in an attempt to obtain 'property from another'. The key word was 'another'. 'Another' was invariably the person against whom mayhem had been threatened. In this case, though, their extortionist didn't seem to care *who* paid the money so long as someone did. *Any*one. Now how were you supposed to deal with a maniac like that?

'He's a maniac,' Lieutenant Byrnes said. 'Where the hell does he expect us to get fifty thousand dollars?'

Steve Carella, who had been released from the hospital that afternoon and who somewhat resembled a boxer about to put on gloves, what with assorted bandages taped around his hands, said, 'Maybe he expects the deputy mayor to pay it.'

'Then why the hell didn't he *ask* the deputy mayor?'

'We're his intermediaries,' Carella said. 'He assumes his demand will carry more weight if it comes from law enforcement officers.'

Byrnes looked at Carella.

'Sure,' Carella said. 'Also, he's getting even with us. He's sore because we fouled up his bank-robbing scheme eight years ago. This is his way of getting back.'

'He's a maniac,' Byrnes insisted.

'No, he's a very smart cookie,' Carella said. 'He knocked off Cowper after a measly demand for five thousand dollars. Now that we know he can do it, he's asking ten times the price not to shoot the deputy mayor.'

'Where does it say "shoot"?' Hawes asked.

'Hmmm?'

'He didn't say anything about *shooting* Scanlon. The note yesterday just said "Deputy Mayor Scanlon Goes Next." '

'That's right,' Carella said. 'He can poison him or bludgeon him or stab him or . . .'

'Please,' Byrnes said.

'Let's call Scanlon,' Carella suggested. 'Maybe he's got fifty grand lying around he doesn't know what to do with.'

They called Deputy Mayor Scanlon and advised him of the threat upon his life, but Deputy Mayor Scanlon did not have fifty grand lying around he didn't know what to do with. Ten minutes later, the phone on Byrnes' desk rang. It was the police commissioner.

'All right, Byrnes,' the commissioner said sweetly, 'what's this latest horseshit?'

'Sir,' Byrnes said, 'we have had two notes from the man we suspect killed Parks Commissioner Cowper, and they constitute a threat upon the life of Deputy Mayor Scanlon.'

'What are you doing about it?' the commissioner asked.

'Sir,' Byrnes said, 'we have already sent both notes to the police laboratory for analysis. Also, sir, we have located the room from which the shots were fired last night, and we have reason to believe we are dealing with a criminal known to this precinct.'

'Who?'

'We don't know.'

'I thought you said he was known . . .'

'Yes, sir, we've dealt with him before, but to our knowledge, sir, he is unknown.'

'How much money does he want this time?'

'Fifty thousand dollars, sir.'

'When is Scanlon supposed to be killed?'

'We don't know, sir.'

'When does this man want his money?'

'We don't know, sir.'

'Where are you supposed to deliver it?'

'We don't know, sir.'

'What the hell *do* you know, Byrnes?'

'I know, sir, that we are doing our best to cope with an unprecedented situation, and that we are ready to put our entire squad at the deputy mayor's disposal, if and when he asks for protection. Moreover, sir, I'm sure I can persuade Captain Frick who, as you may know, commands this entire precinct . . .'

'What do you mean, *as* I may know, Byrnes?'

'That is the way we do it in this city, sir.'

'That is the way they do it in *most* cities, Byrnes.'

'Yes, sir, of course. In any case, I'm sure I can persuade him to release some uniformed officers from their regular duties, or perhaps to call in some off-duty officers, if the commissioner feels that's necessary.'

'I feel it's necessary to protect the life of the deputy mayor.'

'Yes, of course, sir, we all feel that,' Byrnes said.

'What's the matter, Byrnes, don't you like me?' the commissioner asked.

'I try to keep personal feelings out of my work, sir,' Byrnes said. 'This is a tough case. I don't know about you, but I've never come up against anything like it before. I've got a good team here, and we're doing our best. More than that, we can't do.'

'Byrnes,' the commissioner said, 'you may *have* to do more.'

'Sir . . .' Byrnes started, but the commissioner had hung up.

Arthur Brown sat in the basement of Junior High School 106, with a pair of earphones on his head and his right hand on the start button of a tape recorder. The telephone at the La Bresca house diagonally across the street from the school had just rung for the thirty-second time that day, and as he waited for Concetta La Bresca to lift the receiver (as she had done on thirty-one previous occasions) he activated the recorder and sighed in anticipation of what was to come.

It was very clever of the police to have planted a bug in the La Bresca apartment, that bug having been installed by a plainclothes cop from the lab. who identified himself as a telephone repairman, did his dirty work in the La Bresca living-room, and then strung his overhead wires from the roof of the La Bresca house to the telephone pole outside, and from there to a pole on the school sidewalk, and from there to the roof of the school building, and down the side wall, and into a basement window, and across the basement floor to a tiny room containing stacked textbooks and the school's old sixteen-millimetre sound projector, where he had set up Arthur Brown's monitoring station.

It was also very clever of the police to have assigned Arthur Brown to this eavesdropping plant because Brown was an experienced cop who had conducted wiretaps before and who was capable of separating the salient from the specious in any given telephone conversation.

There was only one trouble.

Arthur Brown did not understand Italian, and Concetta La Bresca spoke to her friends exclusively in Italian. For all Brown knew, they might have plotted anything from abortion to safe cracking thirty-one times that day, and for all he knew were about to plot it yet another time. He had used up two full reels of tape because he hadn't understood a word that was said, and he wanted each conversation recorded so that someone – probably Carella – could later translate them.

'Hello,' a voice said in English.

Brown almost fell off his stool. He sat erect, adjusted the headset, adjusted the volume on the tape recorder, and began listening.

'Tony?' a second voice asked.

'Yeah, who's this?' The first voice belonged to La Bresca. Apparently he had just returned home from work. The second voice . . .

'This is Dom.'

'Who?'

'Dominick.'

'Oh, hi, Dom, how's it going?'

'Great.'

'What's up, Dom?'

'Oh, nothing,' Dom said. 'I was just wondering how you was, that's all.'

There was silence on the line. Brown tilted his head and brought his hand up to cover one of the earphones.

'I'm fine,' La Bresca said at last.

'Good, good,' Dom said.

Again, there was silence.

'Well, if that was all you wanted,' La Bresca said, 'I guess . . .'

'Actually, Tony, I was wondering . . .'

'Yeah?'

'I was wondering if you could lend me a couple of bills till I get myself organized here.'

'Organized doing what?' La Bresca asked.

'Well, I took a big loss on that fight two weeks ago, you know, and I still ain't organized.'

'You never been organized in your life,' La Bresca said.

'That ain't true, Tony.'

'OK, it ain't true. What *is* true is I ain't got a couple of bills to lend you.'

'Well, I heard different,' Dom said.

'Yeah? What'd you hear?'

'The rumble is you're coming into some very big loot real soon.'

'Yeah? Where'd you hear *that* shit?'

'Oh, I listen around here and there, I'm always on the earie.'

'Well, this time the rumble is wrong.'

'I was thinking maybe just a few C-notes to tide me over for the next week or so. Till I get organized.'

'Dom, I ain't seen a C-note since Hector was a pup.'

'Tony . . .'

There was a slight hesitation, only long enough to carry the unmistakable weight of warning. Brown caught the suddenly ominous note and listened expectantly for Dom's next words.

'I *know*,' Dom said.

There was another silence on the line. Brown waited. He could hear one of the men breathing heavily.

'*What* do you know?' La Bresca asked.

'About the caper.'

'*What* caper?'

'Tony, don't let me say it on the phone, huh? You never know who's listening these days.'

'What the hell are you trying to do?' La Bresca asked. 'Shake me down?'

'No, I'm trying to borrow a couple of hundred is all. Until I get organized. I'd hate like hell to see all your planning go down the drain, Tony. I'd really hate to see that happen.'

'You blow the whistle, pal, and we'll know just who done it.'

'Tony, if *I* found out about the caper, there's lots of other guys also know about it. It's all over the street. You're lucky the fuzz aren't on to you already.'

'The cops don't even know I exist,' La Bresca said. 'I never took a fall for nothing in my life.'

'What you took a fall for and what you done are two different things, right, Tony?'

'Don't bug me, Dom. You screw this up . . .'

'I ain't screwing nothing up. I'm asking for a loan of two hundred bucks, now yes or no, Tony, I'm getting impatient here in this goddamn phone booth. Yes or no?'

'You're a son of a bitch,' La Bresca said.

'Does that mean yes?'

'Where do we meet?' La Bresca asked.

Lying in the alleyway that night with his bandaged hands encased in woollen gloves, Carella thought less often of the two punks who had burned him, and also burned him up, than he did about the deaf man.

As he lay in his tattered rags and mildewed shoes, he was the very model of a modern major derelict, hair matted, face streaked, breath stinking of cheap wine. But beneath that torn and threadbare coat, Carella's gloved right hand held a .38 Detective's Special. The right index finger of the glove had been cut away to the knuckle, allowing Carella to squeeze the finger itself inside the trigger guard. He was ready to shoot, and this time he would not allow himself to be cold-cocked. Or even pan-broiled.

But whereas his eyes were squinted in simulated drunken slumber while alertly he watched the alley mouth and listened for tandem footsteps, his thoughts were on the deaf man. He did not like thinking about the deaf man because he could remember with painful clarity the shotgun blast fired at him eight years ago, the excruciating pain in his shoulder, the numbness of his arm and hand, and then the repeated smashing of the shotgun's stock against his face until he fell senseless to the floor. He did not like thinking about how close he had come to death at the hands of the deaf man. Nor did he enjoy thinking of a criminal adversary who was really quite smarter than any of the detectives on the 87th Squad, a schemer, a planner, a brilliant bastard who juggled life and death with the dexterity and emotional sang-froid of a mathematician. The deaf man – somewhere out there – was a machine, and Carella was terrified of things that whirred with computer precision, logical but unreasoning, infallible and aloof, cold and deadly. He dreaded the thought of going up against him once again, and yet he knew this stakeout was small potatoes, two punks itching to get caught, two punks who *would* be caught because they assumed all their intended victims were defenceless and did not realize that one of them could be a detective with his finger curled around the trigger of a deadly weapon. And once they were caught, he would move from the periphery of the deaf man case into the very nucleus of the case itself. And perhaps, once again, come face to face with the tall blond man who wore the hearing aid.

He thought it oddly coincidental and perfectly ironic that the person he loved most in the world was a woman named Teddy Carella, who happened to be his wife, and who also happened to be a deaf mute, whereas the person who frightened him the most as a cop and as a man was also deaf, or at least purported to be so, advertised it blatantly – or was this only another subterfuge, a part of the overall scheme? The terrifying thing about the deaf man was his confident assumption that he was dealing with a bunch of nincompoops. Perhaps he was. That was *another* terrifying thing about him. He moved with such certainty that his assumptions took on all the aspects of cold fact. If he said that all flatfoots were fools, then by God that's exactly what they must be – better pay the man whatever he wants before he kills off every high-ranking official in the city. If he could outrageously outline a murder scheme and then execute it before the startled eyes of the city's finest, how could he possibly be stopped from committing the *next* murder, or the one after that, or the one after that?

Carella did not enjoy feeling like a fool.

There were times when he did not necessarily enjoy police work (like right now, freezing his arse off in an alley) but there were never times when he lacked respect for what he did. The concept of law enforcement was simple and clear in his mind. The good guys against the bad guys. He was one of the good guys. And whereas the bad guys in this day and age won often enough to make virtue seem terribly unfashionable sometimes, Carella none the less felt that killing people (for example) was not a very nice thing. Nor was breaking into someone's dwelling-place in the night-time over considerate. Nor was pushing dope quite thoughtful. Nor were mugging, or forging, or kidnapping, or pimping (or spitting on the sidewalk, for that matter) civilized acts designed to uplift the spirit or delight the soul.

He was a cop.

Which meant that he was stuck with all the various images encouraged by countless television shows and motion pictures: the dim-witted public servant being outsmarted by the tough private eye; the overzealous jerk inadvertently blocking the attempts of the intelligent young advertising executive in distress; the insensitive dolt blindly encouraging the young to become criminals. Well, what're you gonna do? You got an image, you got one. (He wondered how many television writers were lying in an alley tonight waiting for two hoods to attack.) The damn thing about the deaf man, though, was that he made all these stereotypes seem true. Once he appeared on the scene, every cop on the squad *did* appear dim-witted and bumbling and inefficient.

And if a man could do that merely by making a few phone calls or sending a few notes, what would happen if –

Carella tensed.

The detective assigned to the surveillance of Anthony La Bresca was Bert Kling, whom he had never seen before. Brown's call to the squadroom had advised the lieutenant that La Bresca had admitted he was involved in a forthcoming caper, and this was reason enough to put a tail on him. So

Kling took to the sub-zero streets, leaving the warmth and generosity of Cindy's apartment, and drove out to Riverhead, where he waited across the street from La Bresca's house, hoping to pick up his man the moment he left to meet Dominick. Brown had informed the lieutenant that the pair had arranged a meeting for ten o'clock that night, and it was now 9.07 by Kling's luminous dial, so he figured he had got here good and early, just in time to freeze solid.

La Bresca came down the driveway on the right of the stucco house at ten minutes to ten. Kling stepped into the shadows behind his parked car. La Bresca began walking east, towards the elevated train structure two blocks away. Just my luck, Kling thought, he hasn't got a car. He gave him a lead of half a block, and then began following him. A sharp wind was blowing west off the wide avenue ahead. Kling was forced to lift his face to its direct blast every so often because he didn't want to lose sight of La Bresca, and he cursed for perhaps the fifty-seventh time that winter the injustice of weather designed to plague a man who worked outdoors. Not that he worked outdoors all of the time. Part of the time, he worked at a desk typing up reports in triplicate or calling victims or witnesses. But *much* of the time (it was fair to say much of the time) he worked outdoors, legging it here and there all over this fair city, asking questions and compiling answers and this was the worst son of a bitch winter he had ever lived through in his life. I hope you're going some place nice and warm, La Bresca, he thought. I hope you're going to meet your friend at a Turkish bath or some place.

Ahead, La Bresca was climbing the steps to the elevated platform. He glanced back at Kling only once, and Kling immediately ducked his head, and then quickened his pace. He did not want to reach the platform to discover that La Bresca had already boarded a train and disappeared.

He need not have worried. La Bresca was waiting for him near the change booth.

'You following me?' He asked.

'What?' Kling said.

'I *said* are you following me?' La Bresca asked.

The choices open to Kling in that moment were severely limited. He could say, 'What are you out of your mind, why would I be following you, you're so handsome or something?' Or he could say, 'Yes, I'm following you, I'm a police officer, here's my shield and my ID card,' those were the open choices. Either way, the tail was blown.

'You looking for a rap in the mouth?' Kling said.

'What?' La Bresca said, startled.

'I said what are you, some kind of paranoid nut?' Kling said, which wasn't what he had said at all. La Bresca didn't seem to notice the discrepancy. He stared at Kling in honest surprise, and then started to mumble something, which Kling cut short with a glowering, menacing, thoroughly frightening look. Mumbling himself, Kling went up the steps to the uptown side of the platform. The station stop was dark and deserted and windswept. He stood on the platform with his coat-tails flapping about him, and waited until La Bresca came up the steps on the downtown side. La Bresca's train pulled in not three minutes later, and he boarded it. The train rattled out of the station. Kling went downstairs again and found a telephone booth. When Willis picked up the phone at the squadroom, Kling said, 'This is Bert. La Bresca made me a couple of blocks from his house. You'd better get somebody else on him.'

'How long you been a cop?' Willis asked.

'It happens to the best of us,' Kling said. 'Where'd Brown say they were meeting?'

'A bar on Crawford.'

'Well, he boarded a downtown train just a few minutes ago, you've got time to plant somebody there before he arrives.'

'Yeah, I'll get O'Brien over there right away.'

'What do you want me to do, come back to the office or what?'

'How the hell did you manage to get spotted?'

'Just lucky, I guess,' Kling said.

It was one of those nights.

They came into the alley swiftly, moving directly towards Carella, both of them boys of about seventeen or eighteen, both of them brawny, one of them carrying a large tin can, the label gone from it, the can catching light from the street lamp, glinting in the alleyway as they approached, that's the can of petrol, Carella thought.

He started to draw his gun and for the first time ever in the history of his career as a cop, it snagged.

It snagged somewhere inside his coat. It was supposed to be a gun designed for negligible bulk, it was not supposed to catch on your goddamn clothing, the two-inch barrel was not supposed to snag when you pulled it, here we go, he thought, the Keystone cops, and leaped to his feet. He could not get the damn gun loose, it was tangled in the wool of his slipover sweater, the yarn pulling and unravelling, he knew the can of petrol would be thrown into his face in the next moment, he knew a match or a lighter would flare into life, this time they'd be able to smell burning flesh away the hell back at the squadroom. Instinctively, he brought his left hand down as straight and as rigid as a steel pipe, slammed it down on to the forearm of the boy with the can, hitting it hard enough to shatter bone, hearing the scream that erupted from the boy's mouth as he dropped the can, and then feeling the intense pain that rocketed into his head and almost burst from his own lips as his burned and bandaged hand reacted. This is great, he thought, I have no hands, they're going to beat the shit out of me, which turned out to be a fairly good prediction because that's exactly what they did.

There was no danger from the petrol now, small consolation, at least they couldn't set fire to him. But his hands were useless, and his gun was snagged somewhere inside there on his sweater – he tried ripping the tangled yarn free, ten seconds, twenty seconds, a millennium – and his attackers realized instantly that they had themselves a pigeon, so they all jumped on him, all forty guys in the alley, and then it was too late. They were very good street fighters, these boys. They had learned all about punching to the Adam's apple, they had learned all about flanking operations, one circling around to his left and the other coming up behind him to clout him on the back of the head with the neatest rabbit's punch he had ever taken, oh, they were nice fighters, these boys, he wondered whether the coffin would be metal or wood. While he was wondering this, one of the boys who had learned how to fight in some clean friendly slum, kicked him in the groin, which can hurt. Carella doubled over, and the other clean fighter behind him delivered a second rabbit punch, rabbit punches doubtless being his speciality, while the lad up front connected with a good hard-swinging uppercut that almost tore off his head. So now he was down on the alley floor, the alley covered with refuse and grime and not a little of his own blood, so they decided to stomp him, which is of course what you must necessarily do when your opponent falls down, you kick him in the head and the shoulders and the chest and everywhere you can manage to kick him. If he's a live one, he'll squirm around and try to grab your feet, but if you happen to be lucky enough to get a pigeon who was burned only recently, why you can have an absolute field day kicking him at will because his hands are too tender to grab at *anything*, no less feet. That's why guns were invented, Carella thought, so that if you happen to have second-degree burns on your hands you don't have to use them too much, all you have to do is squeeze a trigger, it's a shame the gun snagged. It's a shame, too, that Teddy's going to be collecting a widow's dole tomorrow morning, he thought, but these guys are going to kill me unless I do something pretty fast. The trouble is I'm a bumbling goddamn cop, the deaf man is right. The kicks landed now with increasing strength and accuracy, nothing encourages a stomper more than an inert and increasingly more vulnerable victim. I'm certainly glad the petrol, he thought, and a kick exploded against his left eye. He thought at once he would lose the eye, he saw only a blinding flash of yellow, he rolled away, feeling dizzy and nauseous, a boot collided with his rib, he thought he felt it crack, another kick landed on the kneecap of his left leg, he tried to get up, his hands, 'You fucking fuzz,' one of the boys said, Fuzz, he thought, and was suddenly sick, and another kick crashed into the back of his skull and sent him falling face forward into his own vomit.

He lost consciousness.

He might have been dead, for all he knew.

It was one of those nights.

Bob O'Brien got a flat tyre on the way to the Erin Bar & Grill on Crawford Avenue, where Tony La Bresca was to meet the man named Dom.

By the time he changed his flat, his hands were numb, his temper was short, the time was 10.32, and the bar was still a ten-minute drive away. On the off-chance that La Bresca and his fair-weather friend would still be there, O'Brien drove downtown, arriving at the bar at ten minutes to eleven. Not only were both gone already, but the bartender said to O'Brien the moment he bellied up, 'Care for something to drink, Officer?'

It was one of those nights.

CHAPTER 6

On Friday morning, March 8th, Detective-Lieutenant Sam Grossman of the Police Laboratory called the squadroom and asked to talk to Cotton Hawes. He was informed that Hawes, together with several other detectives on the squad, had gone to Buena Vista Hospital to visit Steve Carella. The man answering the telephone was Patrolman Genero, who was holding the fort until one of them returned.

'Well, do *you* want this information or what?' Grossman asked.

'Sir, I'm just supposed to record any calls till they get back,' Genero said.

'I'm going to be tied up later,' Grossman said, 'why don't I just give this to you?'

'All right, sir,' Genero said, and picked up his pencil. He felt very much like a detective. Besides, he was grateful not to be outside on another miserable day like this one. 'Shoot,' he said, and quickly added, 'Sir.'

'It's on these notes I received.'

'Yes, sir, what notes?'

' "Deputy Mayor Scanlon goes next",' Grossman quoted, 'and "Look! A whole new", et cetera.'

'Yes, sir,' Genero said, not knowing what Grossman was talking about.

'The paper is Whiteside Bond, available at any stationery store in the city. The messages were clipped from national magazines and metropolitan dailies. The adhesive is rubber cement.'

'Yes, sir,' Genero said, writing frantically.

'Negative on latent prints. We got a whole mess of smeared stuff, but nothing we could run a make on.'

'Yes, sir.'

'In short,' Grossman said, 'you know what you can do with these notes.'

'What's that, sir?' Genero asked.

'We only run the tests,' Grossman said. '*You* guys are supposed to come up with the answers.'

Genero beamed. He had been included in the phrase 'You guys' and felt himself to be a part of the élite. 'Well, thanks a lot,' he said, 'we'll get to work on it up here.'

'Right,' Grossman said. 'You want these notes back?'

'No harm having them.'

'I'll send them over,' Grossman said, and hung up.

Very interesting, Genero thought, replacing the receiver on its cradle. If he had owned a deerstalker hat, he would have put it on in that moment.

'Where's the john?' one of the painters asked.

'Why?' Genero said.

'We have to paint it.'

'Try not to slop up the urinals,' Genero said.

'We're Harvard men,' the painter said. 'We never slop up the urinals.'

The other painter laughed.

The third note arrived at eleven o'clock that morning.

It was delivered by a high school drop-out who walked directly past the muster desk and up to the squadroom where Patrolman Genero was evolving an elaborate mystery surrounding the rubber cement that had been used as an adhesive.

'What's everybody on vacation?' the kid asked. He was seventeen years old, his face sprinkled with acne. He felt very much at home in the squadroom because he had once been a member of a street gang called The Terrible Ten, composed of eleven young men who had joined together to combat the Puerto Rican influx into their turf. The gang had disbanded just before Christmas, not because the Puerto Ricans had managed to demolish them, but only because seven of the eleven called The Terrible Ten had finally succumbed to an enemy common to Puerto Rican and white Anglo-Saxon alike: narcotics. Five of the seven were hooked, two were dead. Of the remaining three, one was in prison for a gun violation, another had got married because he'd knocked up a little Irish girl, and the last was carrying an envelope into a detective squadroom, and feeling comfortable enough there to make a quip to a uniformed cop.

'What do you want?' Genero asked.

'I was supposed to give this to the desk sergeant, but there's nobody at the desk. You want to take it?'

'What is it?'

'Search me,' the kid said. 'Guy stopped me on the street and give me five bucks to deliver it.'

'Sit down,' Genero said. He took the envelope from the kid and debated opening it, and then realized he had got his fingerprints all over it. He dropped it on the desk. In the toilet down the hall, the painters were singing. Genero was only supposed to answer the phone and take down messages. He looked at the envelope again, severely tempted. 'I said sit down,' he told the kid.

'What for?'

'You're going to wait here until one of the detectives gets back, that's what for.'

'Up yours, fuzz,' the kid said, and turned to go.

Genero drew his service revolver. 'Hey,' he said, and the boy glanced over his shoulder into the somewhat large bore of a .38 Police Special.

'I'm hip to Miranda-Escobedo,' the kid said, but he sat down none the less.

'Good, that makes two of us,' Genero said.

Cops don't like other cops to get it. It makes them nervous. It makes them feel they are in a profession that is not precisely white collar, despite the paperwork involved. It makes them feel that at any moment someone might hit them or kick them or even shoot them. It makes them feel unloved.

The two young sportsmen who had unloved Carella so magnificently had broken three of his ribs and his nose. They had also given him such a headache, due to concussion caused by a few well-placed kicks in the medulla oblongata. He had gained consciousness shortly after being admitted to the hospital and he was conscious now, of course, but he didn't look good, and he didn't feel good, and he didn't feel much like talking. So he sat with Teddy beside the bed, holding her hand and breathing shallowly because the broken ribs hurt like hell. The detectives did most of the talking, but there was a cheerlessness in their banter. They were suddenly face to face with violence of a most personal sort, not the violence they dealt with every working day of their lives, not an emotionless confrontation with broken mutilated strangers, but instead a glimpse at a friend and colleague who lay in battered pain on a hospital bed while his wife held his hand and tried to smile at their feeble jokes. The four detectives left the hospital at twelve noon. Brown and Willis walked ahead of Hawes and Kling, who trailed behind them silently.

'Man, they got him good,' Brown said.

The seventeen-year old drop-out was beginning to scream Miranda-Escobedo, quoting rights like a lawyer. Genero kept telling him to shut up, but he had never really understood the Supreme Court decision too well, despite the flyers issued to every cop in the precinct, and he was afraid now that the kid knew something he didn't know. He was overjoyed to hear the ring of footsteps on the recently painted iron-runged steps leading to the squadroom. Willis and Brown came into view on the landing first. Kling and Hawes were behind them. Genero could have kissed them all.

'These the bulls?' the drop-out asked, and Genero said, 'Shut up.'

'What's up?' Brown asked.

'Tell your friend here about Miranda-Escobedo,' the kid said.

'Who're you?' Brown asked.

'He delivered an envelope,' Genero said.

'Here we go,' Hawes said.

'What's your name, kid?'

'Give me some advice on my rights,' the kid said.

'Tell me your name, or I'll kick your arse in,' Brown said. 'How do you like *that* advice?' He had just witnessed what a pair of young hoods had done to Carella, and he was in no mood to take nonsense from a snotnose.

'My name is Michael McFadden, and I won't answer no questions without a lawyer here,' the kid said.

'Can you afford a lawyer?' Brown asked.

'No.'

'Get him a lawyer, Hal,' Brown said, bluffing.

'Hey, wait a minute, what is this?' McFadden asked.

'You want a lawyer, we'll get you a lawyer,' Brown said.

'What do I need a lawyer for? All I done was deliver an envelope.'

'*I* don't know why you need a lawyer,' Brown said. '*You're* the one who said you wanted one. Hal, call the DA's office, get this suspect here a lawyer.'

'Suspect?' McFadden said. '*Suspect*? What the hell did *I* do?'

'I don't know, kid,' Brown said, 'and I can't find out because you won't let me ask any questions without a lawyer here. You getting him that lawyer, Hal?'

Willis, who had lifted the phone receiver and was listening to nothing more vital than a dial tone, said, 'Tie-line's busy, Art.'

'OK, I guess we'll just have to wait then. Make yourself comfortable, kid, we'll get a lawyer up here for you as soon as we can.'

'Look, what the hell,' McFadden said, 'I don't need no lawyer.'

'You said you wanted one.'

'Yeah, but, I mean, like if this is nothing serious . . .'

'We just wanted to ask you some questions about that envelope, that's all.'

'Why? What's in it?'

'Let's open the envelope and show the kid what's in it, shall we do that?' Brown said.

'All I done was deliver it,' McFadden said.

'Well, let's see what's inside it, shall we?' Brown said. He folded his handkerchief over the envelope, slit it open with a letter opener, and then used a tweezer to yank out the folded note.

'Here, use these,' Kling said, and took a pair of white cotton gloves from the top drawer of his desk. Brown put on the gloves, held his hands widespread alongside his face, and grinned.

'Whuffo does a chicken cross de road, Mistuh Bones?' he said, and burst out laughing. The other cops all laughed with him. Encouraged, McFadden laughed too. Brown glowered at him, and the laugh died in his throat. Gingerly, Brown unfolded the note and spread it flat on the desk top.

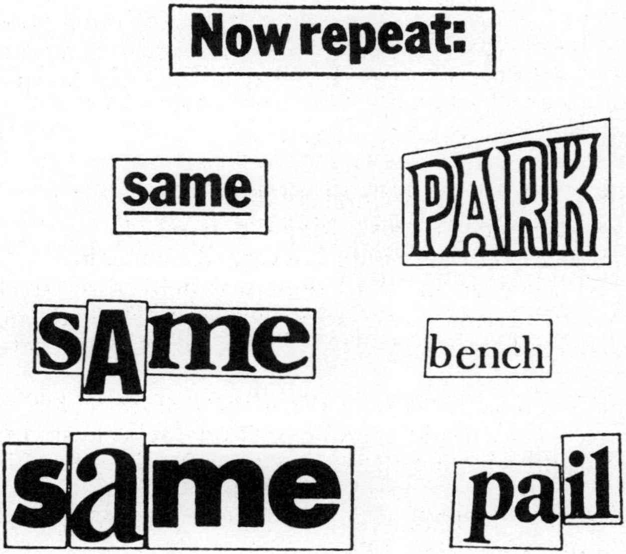
Now repeat:

same PARK

sAme bench

same pail

before NOON tomorrow

OR ELSE

same ASSASSINS

'What's that supposed to mean?' McFadden asked.

'You tell us,' Brown said.

'Beats me.'

'Who gave you this note?'

'A tall blond guy wearing a hearing aid.'

'You know him?'

'Never saw him before in my life.'

'He just came up to you and handed you the envelope, huh?'

'No, he came up and offered me a fin to take it in here.'

'Why'd you accept?'

'Is there something wrong with bringing a note in a police station?'

'Only if it's an extortion note,' Brown said.

'What's extortion?' McFadden asked.

'You belong to The Terrible Ten, don't you?' Kling asked suddenly.

'The club broke up,' McFadden said.

'But you *used* to belong.'

'Yeah, how do you know?' McFadden asked, a trace of pride in his voice.

'We know every punk in this precinct,' Willis said. 'You finished with him, Artie?'

'I'm finished with him.'

'Goodbye, McFadden.'

'What's extortion?' McFadden asked again.

'Goodbye,' Willis said again.

The detective assigned to tailing Anthony La Bresca was Meyer Meyer. He was picked for the job because detectives aren't supposed to be bald, and it was reasoned that La Bresca, already gun shy, would never tip to him. It was further reasoned that if La Bresca was really involved in a contemplated caper, it might be best not to follow him from his job to wherever he was going, but instead to be waiting for him there when he arrived. This presented the problem of second-guessing where he might be going, but it was recalled by one or another of the detectives that La Bresca had mentioned frequently a pool hall on South Leary, and so this was where Meyer stationed himself at four o'clock that afternoon.

He was wearing baggy corduroy trousers, a brown leather jacket, and a brown watch cap. He looked like a longshoreman or something. Actually, he didn't know what he looked like, he just hoped he didn't look like a cop. He had a matchstick in his mouth. He figured that was a nice touch, the matchstick. Also because criminal types have an uncanny way of knowing when somebody is heeled, he was not carrying a gun. The only weapon on his person was a longshoreman's hook tucked into the waistband of his trousers. If anyone asked him about the hook, he would say he needed it on the job, thereby establishing his line of work at the same time. He hoped he would not have to use the hook.

He wandered into the pool hall, which was on the second floor of a dingy brick building, said 'Hi,' to the man sitting behind the entrance booth, and then said, 'You got any open tables?'

'Pool or billiards?' the man said. He was chewing on a matchstick, too.

'Pool,' Meyer said.

'Take Number Four,' the man said, and turned to switch on the table lights from the panel behind him. 'You new around here?' he asked, his back to Meyer.

'Yeah, I'm new around here,' Meyer said.

'We don't dig hustlers,' the man said.

'I'm no hustler,' Meyer answered.

'Just make sure you ain't.'

Meyer shrugged and walked over to the lighted table. There were seven other men in the pool hall, all of them congregated around a table near the windows, where four of them were playing and the other three were kibitzing. Meyer unobtrusively took a cue from the rack, set up the balls, and began shooting. He was a lousy player. He kept mentally calling shots and missing. Every now and then he glanced at the door. He was playing for perhaps ten minutes when one of the men from the other table sauntered over.

'Hi,' the man said. He was a burly man wearing a sports jacket over a woollen sports shirt. Tufts of black hair showed above the open throat of the shirt. His eyes were a deep brown, and he wore a black moustache that seemed to have leaped from his chest on to the space below his nose. The hair on his head was black too. He looked tough and he looked menacing, and Meyer immediately made him for the local cheese.

'You play here before?' the man asked.

'Nope,' Meyer said without looking up from the table.

'I'm Tino.'

'Hello, Tino,' Meyer said, and shot.

'You missed,' Tino said.

'That's right, I did.'

'You a hustler?' Tino said.

'Nope.'

'We break hustlers' arms and throw them down the stairs,' Tino said.

'The arms or the whole hustler?' Meyer asked.

'I got no sense of humour,' Tino said.

'Me, neither. Buzz off, you're ruining my game.'

'Don't try to take nobody, mister,' Tino said. 'This's a friendly neighbourhood pool hall.'

'Yeah, you sure make it sound very friendly,' Meyer said.

'It's just we don't like hustlers.'

'I got your message three times already,' Meyer said. 'Eight ball in the side.' He shot and missed.

'Where'd you learn to shoot pool?' Tino said.

'My father taught me.'

'Was he as lousy as you?'

Meyer didn't answer.

'What's that in your belt there?'

'That's a hook,' Meyer said.

'What's it for?'

'I use it,' Meyer said.

'You work on the docks?'

'That's right.'

'Where?'

'On the docks,' Meyer said.

'Yeah, *where* on the docks?'

'Look, friend,' Meyer said, and put down the pool cue and stared at Tino.

'Yeah?'

'What's it your business where I work?'

'I like to know who comes in here.'

'Why? You own the joint?'

'My brother does.'

'OK,' Meyer said. 'My name's Stu Levine, I'm working the Leary Street docks right now, unloading the SS *Agda* out of Sweden. I live downtown on Ridgeway, and I happened to notice there was a pool hall here, so I decided to come in and run off a few racks before heading home. You think that'll satisfy your brother, or do you want to see my birth certificate?'

'You Jewish?' Tino asked.

'Funny I don't look it, right?'

'No, you *do* look it.'

'So?'

'So nothing. We get some Jewish guys from around the corner in here every now and then.'

'I'm glad to hear it. Is it OK to shoot now?'

'You want company?'

'How do I know *you're* not a hustler?'

'We'll play for time, how's that?'

'You'll win,' Meyer said.

'So what? It's better than playing alone, ain't it?'

'I came up here to shoot a few balls and enjoy myself,' Meyer said. 'Why should I play with somebody better than me? I'll get stuck with the time, and you'll be doing all the shooting.'

'You could consider it a lesson.'

'I don't need lessons.'

'You need lessons, believe me,' Tino said. 'The way you shoot pool, it's a disgrace.'

'If I need lessons, I'll get Minnesota Fats.'

'There ain't no real person named Minnesota Fats,' Tino said, 'he was just a guy they made up,' which reminded Meyer that someone had named a fictitious character after him, and which further reminded him that he had not yet heard from Rollie Chabrier down at the DA's office.

'Looks like I'll never get to shoot, anyway,' he said, 'if you're gonna stand here and gab all day.'

'OK?' Tino said.

'Go ahead, take a cue,' Meyer said, and sighed. He felt he had handled the encounter very well. He had not seemed too anxious to be friendly, and yet he had succeeded in promoting a game with one of the pool hall regulars. When La Bresca walked in, if indeed he ever did, he would find Tino playing with his good old buddy Stu Levine from the Leary Street docks. Very good, Meyer thought, they ought to up me a grade tomorrow morning.

'First off, you hold your cue wrong,' Tino said. 'Here's how you got to hold it if you expect to sink anything.'

'Like this?' Meyer said, trying to imitate the grip.

'You got arthritis or something?' Tino asked, and burst out laughing at his own joke, proving to Meyer's satisfaction that he really did not have a sense of humour.

Tino was demonstrating the proper English to put on the cue ball in order to have it veer to the left after contact, and Meyer was alternately watching the clock and the door when La Bresca walked in some twenty minutes later. Meyer recognized him at once from the description he'd been given, but turned away immediately, not wanting to seem at all interested, and listened to Tino's explanation, and then listened to the meagre joke Tino offered, something about the reason it's called English is because if you hit an Englishman in the balls with a stick, they'll turn white just like the cue ball on the table, get it? Tino laughed, and Meyer laughed with him, and that was what La Bresca saw as he approached the table, Tino and his good old buddy from the Leary Street docks, laughing it up and shooting a friendly game of pool in the friendly neighbourhood pool hall.

'Hi, Tino,' La Bresca said.

'Hi, Tony.'

'How's it going?'

'So-so. This here is Stu Levine.'

'Glad to meet you,' La Bresca said.

'Same here,' Meyer said, and extended his hand.

'This here is Tony La Bresca. He shoots a good game.'

'Nobody shoots as good as you,' La Bresca said.

'Stu here shoots the way Angie used to. You remember Angie who was crippled? That's the way Stu here shoots.'

'Yeah, I remember Angie,' La Bresca said, and both men burst out laughing. Meyer laughed with them, what the hell.

'Stu's father taught him,' Tino said.

'Yeah? Who taught his father?' La Bresca said, and both men burst out laughing again.

'I hear you got yourself a job,' Tino said.

'That's right.'

'You just getting through?'

'Yeah, I thought I'd shoot a game or two before supper. You see Calooch around?'

'Yeah, he's over there by the windows.'

'Thought maybe I'd shoot a game with him.'

'Why'nt you join us right here?' Tino said.

'Thanks,' La Bresca said, 'but I promised Calooch I'd shoot a game with him. Anyway, you're too much of a shark.'

'A shark, you hear that, Stu?' Tino said. 'He thinks I'm a shark.'

'Well, I'll see you,' La Bresca said, and walked over to the window table. A tall thin man in a striped shirt was bent over the table, angling for a shot. La Bresca waited until he had run off three or four balls, and then they both went up to the front booth. The lights suddenly came on over a table across the hall. La Bresca and the man named Calooch went to the table, took sticks down, racked up the balls, and began playing.

'Who's Calooch?' Meyer asked Tino.

'Oh, that's Pete Calucci,' Tino said.

'Friend of Tony's?'

'Oh, yeah, they know each other a long time.'

Calooch and La Bresca were doing a lot of talking. They weren't doing too much playing, but they sure were talking a lot. They talked, and then one of them took a shot, and then they talked some more, and after a while the other one took a shot, and it went like that for almost an hour. At the end of the hour, both men put up their sticks, and shook hands. Calooch went back to the window table, and La Bresca went up front to settle for the time. Meyer looked up at the clock and said, 'Wow, look at that, already six o'clock. I better get home, my wife'll murder me.'

'Well, Stu, I enjoyed playing with you,' Tino said. 'Stop in again sometime.'

'Yeah, maybe I will,' Meyer said.

The street outside was caught in the pale grey grasp of dusk, empty, silent except for the keening of the wind, bitterly cold, forbidding. Anthony La Bresca walked with his hands in the pockets of his beige car coat, the collar raised, the green muffler wound about his neck and flapping in the fierce wind. Meyer stayed far behind him, mindful of Kling's embarrassing encounter the night before and determined not to have the same thing happen to an old experienced workhorse like himself. The cold weather and the resultant empty streets did not help him very much. It was comparatively simple to tail a man on a crowded street, but when there are only two people left alive in the world, the one up front might suddenly turn at the sound of a footfall or a tail-of-the-eye glimpse of something or someone behind him. So Meyer kept his distance and utilized every doorway he could find, ducking in and out of the street, grateful for the frantic activity that helped ward off the cold, convinced he would not be spotted, but mindful of the alternate risk he was running: if La Bresca turned a corner suddenly, or entered a building unexpectedly, Meyer could very well lose him.

The girl was waiting in a Buick.

The car was black, Meyer made the year and make at once, but he could not read the licence plate because the car was too far away, parked at the kerb some two blocks up the street. The engine was running. The exhaust threw grey plumes of carbon monoxide into the grey and empty street. La Bresca stopped at the car, and Meyer ducked into the closest doorway, the windowed alcove of a pawnshop. Surrounded by saxophones and typewriters, cameras and tennis rackets, fishing rods and loving cups, Meyer looked diagonally through the joined and angled windows of the shop and squinted his eyes in an attempt to read the licence plate of the Buick. He could not make out the numbers. The girl had blonde hair, it fell loose to the base of her neck, she leaned over on the front seat to open the door for La Bresca.

La Bresca got into the car and slammed the door behind him.

Meyer came out of the doorway just as the big black Buick gunned away from the kerb.

He still could not read the licence plate.

CHAPTER 7

Nobody likes to work on Saturday.

There's something obscene about it, it goes against the human grain. Saturday is the day before the day of rest, a good time to stomp on all those pressures that have been building Monday to Friday. Given a nice blustery rotten March day with the promise of snow in the air and the city standing expectantly monolithic, stoic, and solemn, given such a peach of a Saturday, how nice to be able to start a cannel coal fire in the fireplace of your three-room apartment and smoke yourself out of the joint. Or, lacking a fireplace, what better way to utilize Saturday than by pouring yourself a stiff hooker of bourbon and curling up with a blonde or a book, spending your time with *War and Peace* or *Whore and Piece*, didn't Shakespear invent some of his best puns on Saturday, drunk with a wench in his first best bed?

Saturday is a quiet day. It can drive you to distraction with its prospects of leisure time, it can force you to pick at the coverlet wondering what to do with all your sudden freedom, it can send you wandering through the rooms in search of occupation while moodily contemplating the knowledge that the loneliest night of the week is fast approaching.

Nobody likes to work on Saturday because nobody else is working on Saturday.

Except cops.

Grind, grind, grind, work, work, work, driven by a sense of public-mindedness and dedication to humanity, law enforcement officers are forever at the ready, alert of mind, swift of body, noble of purpose.

Andy Parker was asleep in the swivel chair behind his desk.

'Where is everybody?' one of the painters said.

'What?' Parker said. 'Huh?' Parker said, and sat bolt upright, and glared at the painter and then washed his huge hand over his face and said, 'What the hell's the matter with you, scaring a man that way?'

'We're leaving,' the first painter said.

'We're finished,' the second painter said.

'We already got all our gear loaded on the truck, and we wanted to say goodbye to everybody.'

'So where is everybody?'

'There's a meeting in the lieutenant's office,' Parker said.

'We'll just pop in and say goodbye,' the first painter said.

'I wouldn't advise that,' Parker said.

'Why not?'

'They're discussing homicide. It's not wise to pop in on people when they're discussing homicide.'

'Not even to say goodbye?'

'You can say goodbye to *me*,' Parker said.

'It wouldn't be the same thing,' the first painter said.

'So then hang around and say goodbye when they come out. They should be finished before twelve. In fact, they *got* to be finished before twelve.'

'Yeah, but *we're* finished *now*,' the second painter said.

'Can't, you find a few things you missed?' Parker suggested. 'Like, for example, you didn't paint the typewriters, or the bottle on the water cooler, or our guns. How come you missed our guns? You got green all over everything else in the goddamn place.'

'You should be grateful,' the first painter said. 'Some people won't work on Saturday *at all*, even at time and a half.'

So both painters left in high dudgeon, and Parker went back to sleep in the swivel chair behind his desk.

'I don't know what kind of a squad I'm running here,' Lieutenant Byrnes said, 'when two experienced detectives can blow a surveillance, one by getting made first crack out of the box, and the other by losing his man; that's a pretty good batting average for two experienced detectives.'

'I was told the suspect didn't have a car,' Meyer said. 'I was told he had taken a train the night before.'

'That's right, he did,' Kling said.

'I had no way of knowing a woman would be waiting for him in a car,' Meyer said.

'So you lost him,' Byrnes said, 'which might have been all right if the man had gone home last night. But O'Brien was stationed outside the La Bresca house in Riverhead, and the man never showed, which means we don't know where he is today, now do we? We don't know where a prime suspect is on the day the deputy mayor is supposed to get killed.'

'No, sir,' Meyer said, 'we don't know where La Bresca is.'

'Because *you* lost him.'

'I guess so, sir.'

'Well, how would you revise that statement, Meyer?'

'I wouldn't, sir. I lost him.'

'Yes, very good, I'll put you in for a commendation.'

'Thank you, sir.'

'Don't get flip, Meyer.'

'I'm sorry, sir.'

'This isn't a goddamn joke here, I don't want Scanlon to wind up with two holes in his head the way Cowper did.'

'No, sir, neither do I.'

'OK, then learn for Christ's sake how to tail a person, will you?'

'Yes, sir.'

'Now what about this other man you say La Bresca spent time with in conversation, what was his name?'

'Calucci, sir. Peter Calucci.'

'Did you check him out?'

'Yes, sir, last night before I went home. Here's the stuff we got from BCI.'

Meyer placed a manilla envelope on Byrnes' desk, and then stepped back to join the other detectives ranged in a military line before the desk. None of the men was smiling. The lieutenant was in a lousy mood, and somebody was supposed to come up with fifty thousand dollars before noon, and the possibility existed that the deputy mayor would soon be dispatched to that big City Hall in the sky, so nobody was smiling. The lieutenant reached into the envelope and pulled out a photocopy of a fingerprint card, glanced at it cursorily, and then pulled out a photocopy of Calucci's police record.

Byrnes read the sheet, and then said, 'When did he get out?'

'He was a bad apple. He applied for parole after serving a third of the sentence, was denied, and applied every year after that. He finally made it in seven.'

Byrnes looked at the sheet again.

'What's he been doing?' Byrnes asked.

'Construction work.'

'That how he met La Bresca?'

IDENTIFICATION BUREAU

NAME Peter Vincent Calucci

IDENTIFICATION JACKET NUMBER P 421904

ALIAS "Calooch" "Cooch" "Kook"

COLOR White

RESIDENCE 336 South 91st Street, Isola

DATE OF BIRTH October 2, 1938 **AGE** 22

BIRTHPLACE Isola

HEIGHT 5'9" **WEIGHT** 156 **HAIR** Brown **EYES** Brown

COMPLEXION Swarthy **OCCUPATION** Construction worker

SCARS AND TATTOOS Appendectomy scar, no tattoos.

ARRESTED BY: Patrolman Henry Butler

DETECTIVE DIVISION NUMBER: 63-R1-1605-1960

DATE OF ARREST 3/14/60 **PLACE** 812 North 65 St., Isola

CHARGE Robbery

BRIEF DETAILS OF CRIME Calucci entered gasoline station at 812 North 65 Street at or about midnight, threatened to shoot attendant if he did not open safe. Attendant said he did not know combination, Calucci cocked revolver and was about to fire when patrolman Butler of 63rd Precinct came upon scene and apprehended him.

PREVIOUS RECORD None

INDICTED Criminal Courts, March 15, 1960.

FINAL CHARGE Robbery in first degree, Penal Law 2125

DISPOSITION Pleaded guilty 7/8/60, sentenced to ten years at Castleview Prison.

'Calucci's parole officer reports that his last job was with Abco Construction, and a call to the company listed La Bresca as having worked there at the same time.'

'I forget, does this La Bresca have a record?'

'No, sir.'

'Has Calucci been clean since he got out?'

'According to his parole officer, yes, sir.'

'Now who's this person "Dom" who called La Bresca Thursday night?'

'We have no idea, sir.'

'Because La Bresca tipped to your tailing him, isn't that right, Kling?'

'Yes, sir, that's right, sir.'

'Is Brown still on that phone tap?'

'Yes, sir.'

'Have you tried any of our stoolies?'

'No, sir, not yet.'

'Well, when the hell do you propose to get moving? We're supposed to deliver fifty thousand dollars by twelve o'clock. It's now a quarter after ten, when the hell . . .'

'Sir, we've been trying to get a line on Calucci. His parole officer gave us an address, and we sent a man over, but his landlady says he hasn't been there since early yesterday morning.'

'Of course not!' Byrnes shouted. 'The two of them are probably shacked up with that blonde woman, whoever the hell *she* was, planning how to murder Scanlon when we fail to deliver the payoff money. Get Danny Gimp or Fats Donner, find out if they know a fellow named Dom who dropped a bundle on a big fight two weeks ago. Who the hell was fighting two weeks ago, anyway? Was that the champion fight?'

'Yes, sir.'

'All right, get cracking. Does anybody use Gimp besides Carella?'

'No, sir.'

'Who uses Donner?'

'I do, sir.'

'Then get to him right away, Willis.'

'If he's not in Florida, sir. He usually goes south in the winter.'

'Goddamn stool pigeons go south,' Byrnes grumbled, 'and we're stuck here with a bunch of maniacs trying to kill people. All right, go on, Willis, get moving.'

'Yes, sir,' Willis said, and left the office.

'Now what about this other possibility, this deaf man thing? Jesus Christ, I hope it's not him. I hope this is La Bresca and Calucci and the blonde bimbo who drove him clear out of sight last night, Meyer . . .'

'Yes, sir . . .'

' . . . and not that deaf bastard again. I've talked to the commissioner on this, and I've also talked to the deputy mayor *and* the mayor, and we're agreed that paying fifty thousand dollars is out of the question. We're to try apprehending whoever picks up that lunch pail and see if we can't get a lead this time. And we're to provide protection for Scanlon and that's all for now. So I want you two to arrange the drop, and saturation coverage of that bench, and I want a suspect brought in here today, and I want him questioned till he's blue in the face, have a lawyer ready and waiting for him in case he screams Miranda-Escobedo, I want a *lead* today, have you got that?'

'Yes, sir,' Meyer said.

'Yes, sir,' Kling said.

'You think you can set up the drop and cover without fouling it up like you fouled up the surveillance?'

'Yes, sir, we can handle it.'

'All right, then get going, and bring me some meat on this goddamn case.'

'Yes, sir,' Kling and Meyer said together, and then went out of the office.

'Now what's this about a junkie being in that room with the killer?' Byrnes asked Hawes.

'That's right, sir.'

'Well, what's your idea, Cotton?'

'My idea is he got her in there to make sure she'd be stoned when he started shooting, that's my idea, sir.'

'That's the stupidest idea I've ever heard in my life,' Byrnes said. 'Get the hell out of here, go help Meyer and Kling, go call the hospital, find out how Carella's doing, go set up another plant for those two punks who beat him up, go do *something*, for Christ's sake!'

'Yes, sir,' Hawes said, and went out into the squadroom.

Andy Parker, awakened by the grumbling of the other men, washed his hand over his face, blew his nose, and then said, 'The painters said to tell you goodbye.'

'Good riddance,' Meyer said.

'Also, you got a call from the DA's office.'

'Who from?'

'Rollie Chabrier.'

'When was this?'

'Half-hour ago, I guess.'

'Why didn't you put it through?'

'While you were in there with the loot? No, sir.'

'I've been waiting for this call,' Meyer said, and immediately dialled Chabrier's number.

'Mr Chabrier's office,' a bright female voice said.

'Bernice, this is Meyer Meyer up at the 87th. I hear Rollie called me a little while ago.'

'That's right,' Bernice said.

'Would you put him on, please?'

'He's gone for the day,' Bernice said.

'Gone for the day? It's only a little after ten.'

'Well,' Bernice said, 'nobody likes to work on Saturday.'

The black lunch pail containing approximately fifty thousand scraps of newspaper was placed in the centre of the third bench on the Clinton Street footpath into Grover Park by Detective Cotton Hawes, who was wearing thermal underwear and two sweaters and a business suit and an overcoat and ear muffs. Hawes was an expert ski-er, and he had ski-ed on the days the temperature at the base was four below zero and the temperature at the summit was thirty below, had ski-ed on the days when his feet went and his hands went and he boomed the mountain non-stop not for fun or sport but just to get near the fire in the base lodge before he shattered into a hundred brittle pieces. But he had never been this cold before. It was bad enough to be working on Saturday, but it was indecent to be working when the weather threatened to gelatinize a man's blood.

Among the other people who were braving the unseasonable winds and temperatures that Saturday were:

(1) A pretzel salesman at the entrance to Clinton Street footpath.

(2) Two nuns saying their beads on the second bench into the park.

(3) A passionate couple necking in a sleeping bag on the grass behind the third bench.

(4) A blind man sitting on the fourth bench, patting his seeing-eye German shepherd and scattering bread crumbs to the pigeons.

The pretzel salesman was a detective named Stanley Faulk, recruited from the 88th across the park, a man of fifty-eight who wore a grey handlebar moustache as his trademark. The moustache made it quite simple to identify him when he was working in his own territory, thereby diminishing his value on plants. But it also served to strike terror into the hearts of hoods near and wide, in much the same way that the green-and-white colour combination of a radio motor patrol car is supposed to frighten criminals and serve as a deterrent. Faulk wasn't too happy about being called into service for the 87th on a day like this one, but he was bundled up warmly in several sweaters over which was a black cardigan-type candy store-owner sweater over which he had put on a white apron.

He was standing behind a cart that displayed pretzels stacked on long round sticks. A walkie-talkie was set into the top of the cart.

The two nuns saying their beads were Detectives Meyer Meyer and Bert Kling, and they were really saying what a son of a bitch Byrnes had been to bawl them out that way in front of Hawes and Willis, embarrassing them and making them feel very foolish.

'I feel very foolish right now,' Meyer whispered.

'How come?' Kling whispered.

'I feel like I'm in drag,' Meyer whispered.

The passionate couple assignment had been the choice assignment, and Hawes and Willis had drawn straws for it. The reason it was so choice was that the other half of the passionate couple was herself quite choice, a police-woman named Eileen Burke, with whom Willis had worked on a mugging case many years back. Eileen had red hair and green eyes, Eileen had long legs, sleek and clean, full-calved, tapering to slender ankles, Eileen had very good breasts, and whereas Eileen was much taller than Willis (who only barely scraped past the five-foot-eight height requirement), he did not mind at all because big girls always seemed attracted to him, and vice versa.

'We're supposed to be kidding,' he said to Eileen, and held her close in the warm sleeping bag.

'My lips are getting chapped,' she said.

'Your lips are very nice,' he said.

'We're supposed to be here on business,' Eileen said.

'Mmm,' he answered.

'Get your hand off my behind,' she said.

'Oh, is that your behind?' he asked.

'Listen,' she said.

'I hear it,' he said. 'Somebody's coming. You'd better kiss me.'

She kissed him. Willis kept one eye on the bench. The person passing was a governess wheeling a baby carriage. God knew who would send an infant out on a day when the glacier was moving south. The woman and the carriage passed. Willis kept kissing Detective 2nd/Grade Eileen Burke.

'Mm frick sheb bron,' Eileen mumbled.

'Mmm?' Willis mumbled.

Eileen pulled her mouth away and caught her breath. 'I *said* I think she's gone.'

'What's that?' Willis asked suddenly.

'Do not be afraid, *guapa*, it is only my pistol,' Eileen said, and laughed.

'I meant on the path. Listen.'

They listened.

Someone else was approaching the bench.

From where Patrolman Richard Genero sat in plainclothes on the fourth bench, wearing dark glasses and patting the head of the German shepherd at his feet, tossing crumbs to the pigeons, wishing for summer, he could clearly see the young man who walked rapidly to the third bench, picked up the lunch pail, looked swiftly over his shoulder, and began walking not *out* of the park, but deeper *into* it.

Genero didn't know quite what to do at first.

He had been pressed into duty only because there was a shortage of available men that afternoon (crime prevention being an arduous and difficult task on any given day, but especially on Saturday), and he had been placed in the position thought least vulnerable, it being assumed the man who picked up the lunch pail would immediately reverse direction and head out of the park again, on to Grover Avenue, where Faulk the pretzel man and Hawes, parked in his own car at the curb, would immediately collar him. But the suspect was coming into the park instead, heading for Genero's bench, and Genero was a fellow who didn't care very much for violence, so he sat there wishing he was home in bed with his mother serving him hot minestrone and singing old Italian arias.

The dog at his feet had been trained for police work, and Genero had been taught a few hand signals and voice signals in the squadroom before heading out for his vigil on the fourth bench, but he was also afraid of dogs, especially big dogs, and the idea of giving this animal a kill command that might possibly be misunderstood filled Genero with fear and trembling. Suppose he gave the command and the dog leaped for his *own* jugular rather than for the throat of the young man who was perhaps three feet away now and walking quite rapidly, glancing over his shoulder every now and again? Suppose he did that and this beast tore him to shreds, what would his mother say to that? *che bella cosa*, you hadda to become a police, hah?

Willis, in the meantime, had slid his walkie-talkie up between Eileen Burke's breasts and flashed the news to Hawes, parked in his own car on Grover Avenue, good place to be when your man is going the other way. Willis was now desperately trying to lower the zipper on the bag, which zipper seemed to have become somehow stuck. Willis didn't mind being stuck in a sleeping bag with someone like Eileen Burke, who wiggled and wriggled along with him as they attempted to extricate themselves, but he suddenly fantasied the lieutenant chewing him out the way he had chewed out Kling and Meyer this morning and so he really *was* trying to lower that damn zipper while entertaining the further fantasy that Eileen Burke was beginning to enjoy all this adolescent tumbling. Genero, of course, didn't know that Hawes had been alerted, he only knew that the suspect was abreast of him now, and passing the bench now, and moving swiftly beyond the bench now, so he got up and first took off the sun-glasses, and then unbuttoned the third button of his coat the way he had seen detectives do on television, and then reached in for his revolver and then shot himself in the leg.

The suspect began running.

Genero fell to the ground and the dog licked his face.

Willis got out of the sleeping bag and Eileen Burke buttoned her blouse and her coat and then adjusted her garters, and Hawes came running into the park and slipped on a patch of ice near the third bench and almost broke his neck.

'Stop, police!' Willis shouted.

And, miracle of miracles, the suspect stopped dead in his tracks and waited for Willis to approach him with his gun in his hand and lipstick all over his face.

The suspect's name was Alan Parry.

They advised him of his rights and he agreed to talk to them without a lawyer, even though a lawyer was present and waiting for him in case he demanded one.

'Where do you live, Alan?' Willis asked.

'Right around the corner. I know you guys. I see you guys around all the time. Don't you know me? I live right around the corner.'

'You make him?' Willis asked the other detectives.

They all shook their heads. They were standing around him in a loose circle, the pretzel man, two nuns, the pair of lovers, and the big redhead with a white streak in his hair and a throbbing ankle in his thermal underwear.

'Why'd you run, Alan?' Willis asked.

'I heard a shot. In this neighbourhood, when you hear shooting, you run.'

'Who's your partner?'

'What partner?'

'The guy who's in this with you.'

'In *what* with me?'

'The murder plot.'

'The *what*?'

'Come on, Alan, you play ball with us, we'll play ball with you.'

'Hey, man, you got the wrong customer,' Parry said.

'How were you going to split the loot, Alan?'

'What loot?'

'The loot in that lunch pail.'

'Listen, I never seen that lunch pail before in my life.'

'There's thirty thousand dollars in that lunch pail,' Willis said, 'now come on, Alan, you know that, stop playing it cosy.'

Parry either avoided the trap, or else did not know there was supposed to be *fifty* thousand dollars in the black pail he had lifted from the bench. He shook his head and said, 'I don't know nothing about no loot, I was asked to pick up the pail, and I done it.'

'Who asked you?'

'A big blond guy wearing a hearing aid.'

'Do you expect me to believe that?' Willis said.

The cue was one the detectives of the 87th had used many times before in interrogating suspects, and it was immediately seized upon by Meyer, who said, 'Take it easy, Hal,' the proper response, the response that told Willis they were once again ready to assume antagonistic roles. In the charade that would follow, Willis would play the tough bastard out to hang a phoney rap on poor little Alan Parry, while Meyer would play the sympathetic father figure. The other detectives (including Faulk of the 88th, who was familiar with the ploy and had used it often enough himself in his own squadroom) would serve as a sort of nodding Greek chorus, impartial and objective.

Without even so much as a glance at Meyer, Willis said, 'What do you mean, take it easy? This little punk has been lying from the minute we got him up here.'

'Maybe there really *was* a tall blond guy with a hearing aid,' Meyer said. 'Give him a chance to tell us, will you?'

'Sure, and maybe there was a striped elephant with pink polka dots,' Willis said. 'Who's your partner, you little punk?'

'I don't *have* no partner!' Parry said. Plaintively, he said to Meyer, 'Will you please tell this guy I ain't *got* a partner?'

'Calm down, Hal, will you?' Meyer said. 'Let's hear it, Alan.'

'I was on my way home when . . .'

'From where?' Willis snapped.

'Huh?'

'Where were you coming from?'

'From my girl's house.'

'Where?'

'Around the corner. Right across the street from my house.'

'What were you doing there?'

'Well, you know,' Parry said.

'No, we *don't* know,' Willis said.

'For God's sake, Hal,' Meyer said, 'leave the man a little something personal and private, will you please?'

'Thanks,' Parry said.

'You went to see your girl-friend,' Meyer said. 'What time was that, Alan?'

'I went up there around nine thirty. Her mother goes to work at nine. So I went up around nine thirty.'

'You unemployed?' Willis snapped.

'Yes, sir,' Parry said.

'When's the last time you worked?'

'Well, you see . . .'

'Answer the question!'

'Give him a chance, Hal!'

'He's stalling!'

'He's trying to answer you.' Gently, Meyer said, 'What happened, Alan?'

'I had this job, and I dropped the eggs.'

'What?'

'At the grocery store on Eightieth. I was working in the back and one day we got all these crates of eggs, and I was taking them to the refrigerator, and I dropped two crates. So I got fired.'

'How long did you work there?'

'From when I got out of high school.'

'When was that?' Willis asked.

'Last June.'

'Did you graduate?'

'Yes, sir, I have a diploma,' Parry said.

'So what have you been doing since you lost the job at the grocery?'

Parry shrugged. 'Nothing,' he said.

'How old are you?' Willis asked.

'I'll be nineteen . . . what's today?'

'Today's the ninth.'

'I'll be nineteen next week. The fifteenth of March.'

'You're liable to be spending your birthday in jail,' Willis said.

'Now cut it out,' Meyer said, 'I won't have you threatening this man. What happened when you left your girl-friend's house, Alan?'

'I met this guy.'

'Where?'

'Outside the Corona.'

'The what?'

'The Corona. You know the movie house that's all boarded up about three blocks from here, you know the one?'

'We know it,' Willis said.

'Well, there.'

'What was he doing there?'

'Just standing. Like as if he was waiting for somebody.'

'So what happened?'

'He stopped me and said was I busy? So I said it depended. So he said would I like to make five bucks? So I asked him doing what? He said there was a lunch pail in the park and if I picked it up for him, he'd give me five bucks. So I asked him why he couldn't go for it himself, and he said he was waiting there for somebody, and he was afraid if he left the guy might show up and think he'd gone. So he said I should get the lunch pail for him and bring it back to him there outside the theatre so he wouldn't miss his friend. He was supposed to meet him outside the Corona, you see. You know the place? A cop got shot outside there once.'

'I told you we know it,' Willis said.

'So I asked him what was in the lunch pail, and he said just his lunch, but he said he also had a few other things in there with his sandwiches, so I asked him like what and he said do you want this five bucks or not? So I took the five and went to get the pail for him.'

'He gave you the five dollars?'

'Yeah.'

'*Before* you went for the pail?'

'Yeah.'

'Go on.'

'He's lying,' Willis said.

'That is the truth, I swear to God.'

'What'd you think was in that pail?'

Parry shrugged. 'Lunch. And some other little things. Like he said.'

'Come on,' Willis said. 'Do you expect us to buy that?'

'Kid what'd you *really* think was in that pail?' Meyer asked gently.

'Well . . . look . . . you can't do nothing to me for what I *thought* was in there, right?'

'That's right,' Meyer said. 'If you could lock up a man for what he's thinking, we'd *all* be in jail, right?'

'Right,' Parry said, and laughed.

Meyer laughed with him. The Greek chorus laughed too. Everybody laughed except Willis, who kept staring stonefaced at Parry. 'So what'd you *think* was in that pail?' Meyer said.

'Junk,' Parry said.

'You a junkie?' Willis asked.

'No, sir, never touch the stuff.'

'Roll up your sleeve.'

'I'm not a junkie, sir.'

'Let's see your arm.'

Parry rolled up his sleeve.

'OK,' Willis said.

'I told you,' Parry said.

'OK, you told us. What'd you plan to do with that lunch pail?'

'What do you mean?'

'The Corona is three blocks *east* of here. You picked up that pail and started heading *west*. What were you planning?'

'Nothing.'

'Then why were you heading *away* from where the deaf man was waiting?'

'I wasn't heading anyplace.'

'You were heading *west*.'

'No, I musta got mixed up.'

'You got so mixed up you forgot how you came into the park, right? You forgot that the entrance was *behind* you, right?'

'No, I didn't forget where the entrance was.'

'Then why'd you head deeper into the park?'

'I told you. I musta got mixed up.'

'He's a lying little bastard,' Willis said. 'I'm going to book him, Meyer, no matter *what* you say.'

'Now hold it, just hold it a minute,' Meyer said. 'You know you're in pretty serious trouble if there's junk in that pail, don't you, Alan?' Meyer said.

'Why? Even if there *is* junk in there, it ain't mine.'

'Well, *I* know that, Alan, *I* believe you, but the law is pretty specific about possession of narcotics. I'm sure you must realize that every pusher we pick up claims somebody must have planted the stuff on him, he doesn't know how it got there, it isn't his, and so on. They all give the same excuses, even when we've got them dead to rights.'

'Yeah, I guess they must,' Parry said.

'So you see, I won't be able to help you much if there really *is* junk in that pail.'

'Yeah, I see,' Parry said.

'He knows there's no junk in that pail. His partner sent him to pick up the money,' Willis said.

'No, no,' Parry said, shaking his head.

'You didn't know anything about the thirty thousand dollars, is that right?' Meyer asked gently.

'Nothing,' Parry said, shaking his head. 'I'm telling you, I met this guy outside the Corona and he gave me five bucks to get his pail.'

'Which you decided to steal,' Willis said.

'Huh?'

'Were you going to bring that pail back to him?'

'Well . . .' Parry hesitated. He glanced at Meyer. Meyer nodded encouragingly. 'Well, no,' Parry said. 'I figured if there was junk in it, maybe I could turn a quick buck, you know. There's lots of guys in this neighbourhood'll pay for stuff like that.'

'Like what's in the pail,' Parry said.

'Open the pail, kid,' Willis said.

'No' Parry shook his head. 'No, I don't want to.'

'Why not?'

'If it's junk, I don't know nothing about it. And if it's thirty Gs, I got nothing to do with it. I don't know nothing. I don't want to answer no more questions, that's it.'

'That's it.'

'That's it, Hal,' Meyer said.

'Go on home, kid,' Willis said.

'I can go?'

'Yeah, yeah, you can go,' Willis said wearily.

Parry stood up quickly, and without looking back headed straight for the gate in the slatted railing that divided the squadroom from the corridor outside. He was down the hallway in a wink. His footfalls clattered noisily on the iron-runged steps leading to the street floor below.

'What do you think?' Willis said.

'I think we did it arse-backwards,' Hawes said. 'I think we should have followed him out of the park instead of nailing him. He would have led us straight to the deaf man.'

'The lieutenant didn't think so. The lieutenant figured nobody would be crazy enough to send a stranger after fifty thousand dollars. The lieutenant figured the guy who made the pick-up *had* to be a member of the gang.'

'Yeah, well the lieutenant was wrong,' Hawes said.

'You know what I think?' Kling said.

'What?'

'I think the deaf man *knew* there'd be nothing in that lunch pail. That's why he could risk sending a stranger for it. He *knew* the money wouldn't be there, and he *knew* we'd pick up whoever he sent.'

'If that's the case . . .' Willis started.

'He *wants* to kill Scanlon,' Kling said.

The detectives all looked at each other. Faulk scratched his head and said, 'Well, I better be getting back across the park, unless you need me some more.'

'No, thanks a lot, Stan,' Meyer said.

'Don't mention it,' Faulk said, and went out.

'I enjoyed the plant,' Eileen Burke said, and glanced archly at Willis, and then swivelled towards the gate and out of the squadroom.

'Can it be the breeze . . .' Meyer sang.

'That fills the trees . . .' Kling joined in.

'Go to hell,' Willis said, and then genuflected and piously added, 'Sisters.'

If nobody in the entire world likes working on Saturdays, even less people like working on Saturday night.

Saturday night, baby, is the night to howl. Saturday night is the night to get out there and hang ten. Saturday night is when you slip into your satin slippers and your Pucci dress, put on your shirt with the monogram on the cuff, spray your navel with cologne, and laugh too loud.

The bitch city is something different on Saturday night, sophisticated in black, scented and powdered, but somehow not as unassailable, shiveringly beautiful in a dazzle of blinking lights. Reds and oranges, electric blues and vibrant greens assault the eye incessantly, and the resultant turn-on is as sweet as a quick fix in the penthouse pad, a liquid cool that conjures dreams of towering glass spires and enamelled minarets. There is excitement in this city on Saturday night, but it is tempered by romantic expectancy. She is not a bitch, this city. Not on Saturday night.

Not if you will love her.

Nobody likes to work on Saturday night, and so the detectives of the 87th Squad should have been pleased when the police commissioner called Byrnes to say that he was asking the DA's Squad to assume the responsibility of protecting Deputy Mayor Scanlon from harm. If they'd had any sense at all, the detectives of the 87th would have considered themselves fortunate.

But the commissioner's cut was deeply felt, first by Byrnes, and then by every man on the squad when he related the news to them. They went their separate ways that Saturday night, some into the streets to work, others home to rest, but each of them felt a corporate sense of failure. Not one of them realized how fortunate he was.

The two detectives from the DA's Squad were experienced men who had handled special assignments before. When the deputy mayor's personal chauffeur arrived to pick them up that night, they were waiting on the sidewalk outside the Criminal Courts Building, just around the corner from the District Attorney's office. It was exactly 8 pm. The deputy mayor's chauffeur had picked up the Cadillac sedan at the municipal garage a half-hour earlier. He had gone over the upholstery with a whisk broom, passed a dust rag over the hood, wiped the windows with a chamois cloth, and emptied all the ashtrays. He was now ready for action, and he was pleased to note that the detectives were right on time; he could not abide tardy individuals.

They drove up to Smoke Rise, which was where the deputy mayor lived, and one of the detectives got out of the car and walked to the front door, and rang the bell, and was ushered into the huge brick house by a maid in a black uniform. The deputy mayor came down the long white staircase leading to the centre hall, shook hands with the detective from the DA's Squad, apologized for taking up his time this way on a Saturday night, made some comment about the 'damn foolishness of it all', and then called up to his wife to tell her the car was waiting. His wife came down the steps, and the deputy mayor introduced her to the detectives from the DA's Squad, and then they all went to the front door.

The detective stepped outside first, scanned the bushes lining the driveway, and then led the deputy mayor and his wife to the car. He opened the door and allowed them to precede him into the automobile. The other detective was stationed on the opposite side of the car, and as soon as the deputy mayor and his wife were seated, both detectives got into the automobile and took positions facing them on the jump seats.

The dashboard clock read 8.30 pm.

The deputy mayor's personal chauffeur set the car in motion, and the deputy mayor made a few jokes with the detectives as they drove along the gently winding roads of exclusive Smoke Rise on the edge of the city's northern river, and then on to the service road leading to the River Highway. It had been announced in the newspapers the week before that the deputy mayor would speak at a meeting of the B'nai Brith in the city's largest synagogue at nine o'clock that night. The deputy mayor's home in Smoke Rise was only fifteen minutes away from the synagogue, and so the chauffeur drove slowly and carefully while the two detectives from the DA's Squad eyed the automobiles that moved past on either side of the Cadillac.

The Cadillac exploded when the dashboard clock read 8.45 pm.

The bomb was a powerful one.

It erupted from somewhere under the hood, sending flying steel into the car, tearing off the roof like paper, blowing the doors into the highway. The car screeched out of control, lurched across two lanes, rolled on to its side like a ruptured metal beast and was suddenly ablaze.

A passing convertible tried to swerve around the flaming Cadillac. There was a second explosion. The convertible veered wildly and crashed into the river barrier.

When the police arrived on the scene, the only person alive in either car was a bleeding seventeen-year-old girl who had gone through the windshield of the convertible.

CHAPTER 8

On Sunday morning the visiting hours at Beuna Vista Hospital were from ten to twelve. It was a busy day, busier than Wednesday, for example, because Saturday night encourages broken arms and legs, bloody pates and shattered sternums. There is nothing quite so hectic as the Emergency Room of a big city hospital on a Saturday night. And on Sunday morning it's only natural for people to visit the friends and relatives who were unfortunate enough to have met with assorted mayhem the night before.

Steve Carella had met with assorted mayhem on Thursday night, and here it was Sunday morning, and he sat propped up in bed expecting Teddy's arrival and feeling gaunt and pale and unshaven even though he had shaved himself not ten minutes ago. He had lost seven pounds since his admission to the hospital (it being singularly difficult to eat and breathe at the same time when your nose is taped and bandaged) and he still ached everywhere, seemed in fact to discover new bruises every time he moved, which can make a man feel very unshaven.

He had had a lot of time to do some thinking since Thursday night, and as soon as he had got over feeling, in sequence, foolish, angry, and murderously vengeful, he had decided that the deaf man was responsible for what had happened to him. That was a good way to feel, he thought, because it took the blame away from two young punks (for Christ's sake, how could an experienced detective get smeared that way by two young punks?) and put it squarely on to a master criminal instead. Master criminals are very handy scapegoats, Carella reasoned, because they allow you to dismiss your own inadequacies. There was an old Jewish joke Meyer had once told him, about the mother who says to her son, '*Trombenik*, go get a job,' and the son answers, 'I can't, I'm a *trombenik*.' The situation now was similar, he supposed, with the question being altered to read, 'How can you let a master criminal do this to you?' and the logical answer being, 'It's easy, he's a master criminal.'

Whether or not the deaf man was a master criminal was perhaps a subject for debate. Carella would have to query his colleagues on the possibility of holding a seminar once he got back to the office. This, according to the interns who'd been examining his skull like phrenologists, should be by Thursday, it being their considered opinion that unconsciousness always meant concussion and concussion always carried with it the possibility of internal haemorrhage with at least a week's period of observation being *de rigueur* in such cases, go argue with doctors.

Perhaps the deaf man wasn't a master criminal at all. Perhaps he was simply smarter than any of the policemen he was dealing with, which encouraged some pretty frightening conjecture. Given a superior intelligence at work, was it even *possible* for inferior intelligences to second-guess whatever diabolical scheme was afoot? Oh, come on now, Carella thought, diabolical indeed! Well, *yeah*, he thought, diabolical. It is diabolical to demand five thousand dollars and then knock off the parks commissioner, and it *is* diabolical to demand fifty thousand dollars and then knock off the deputy mayor, and it is staggering to imagine what the next demand might be, or who the next victim would be. There most certainly would be another demand which, if not met, would doubtless lead to yet another victim. Or would it? How can you second-guess a master criminal? You can't, he's a master criminal.

No, Carella thought, he's only a human being, and he's counting on several human certainties. He's hoping to establish a pattern of warning and reprisal, he's hoping we'll fail, forcing him to carry out his threat. Which means that the two early extortion tries were only preparation for the big caper. And since he seems to be climbing the municipal government ladder, and since he multiplied his first demand by ten, I'm willing to bet his next declared victim will be James Martin Vale, the mayor himself, and that he'll ask for ten times what he asked for the last time: five hundred thousand dollars. This is a lot of strawberries.

Or am I only second-guessing a master criminal?

Am I *supposed* to be second-guessing him?

Is he really preparing the ground for a big killing, or is there quite another diabolical (there we go again) plan in his mind?

Teddy Carella walked into the room at that moment.

The only thing Carella had to second-guess was whether he would kiss her first or vice versa. Since his nose was in plaster, he decided to let her choose the target, which she did with practised ease, causing him to consider some wildly diabolical schemes of his own, which if executed would have resulted in his never again being permitted inside Buena Vista Hospital.

Not even in a private room.

Patrolman Richard Genero was in the same hospital that Sunday morning, but his thoughts were less erotic than they were ambitious.

Despite a rather tight official security lid on the murders, an enterprising newspaperman had only this morning speculated on a possible connection between Genero's leg wound and the subsequent killing of Scanlon the night before. The police and the city officials had managed to keep all mention of the extortion calls and notes out of the newspapers thus far, but the reporter for the city's leading metropolitan daily wondered in print whether or not the detectives of 'an uptown precinct bordering the park' hadn't in reality possessed foreknowledge of an attempt to be made on the deputy mayor's life, hadn't in fact set up an elaborate trap that very afternoon, 'a trap in which a courageous patrolman was destined to suffer a bullet wound in the leg while attempting to capture the suspected killer.' Wherever the reporter had dug up his information, he had neglected to mention that Genero had inflicted the wound upon himself, due to a fear of dogs and criminals, and due to a certain lack of familiarity with shooting at fleeing suspects.

Genero's father, who was a civil service employee himself, having worked for the Department of Sanitation for some twenty years now, was not aware that his son had accidentally shot himself in the leg. All he knew was that his son was a hero. As befitted a hero, he had brought a white carton of *cannoli* to the hospital, and now he and his wife and his son sat in the semi-private stillness of a fourth-floor room and demolished the pastry while discussing Genero's almost certain promotion to Detective 3rd/Grade.

The idea of a promotion had not occurred to Genero before this, but as his father outlined the heroic action in the park the day before, Genero began to visualize himself as the man who had made the capture possible. Without him, without the warning shot he had fired into his own leg, the fleeing Alan Parry might never have stopped. The fact that Parry had turned out to be a wet fuse didn't matter at all to Genero. It was all well and good to realize a man wasn't dangerous *after* the fact, but where were all those detectives when Parry was running straight for Genero with a whole lunch pail full of God-knew-what under his arm, where were they *then*, while Genero was courageously drawing his pistol, that Parry would turn out to be only another innocent dupe, nossir it had been impossible to tell.

'You were brave,' Genero's father said, licking pot cheese from his lips. 'It was *you* who tried to stop him.'

'That's true,' Genero said, because it *was* true.

'It was *you* who risked your life.'

'That's right,' Genero said, because it *was* right.

'They should promote you.'

'They should,' Genero said.

'I will call your boss,' Genero's mother said.

'No, I don't think you should, Mama.'

'*Perchè no?*'

'*Perchè* . . . Mama, please don't talk Italian, you know I don't understand Italian so well.'

'*Vergogna*,' his mother said, 'an Italian doesn't understand his own tongue. I will call your boss.'

'No, Mama, that isn't the way it's done.'

'Then how *is* it done?' his father asked.

'Well, you've got to hint around.'

'Hint? To who?'

'Well, to people.'

'Which people?'

'Well, Carella's upstairs in this same hospital, maybe . . .'

'*Ma chi è questa Carella?*' his mother said.

'Mama, please.'

'Who is this Carella?'

'A detective on the squad.'

'Where you work, *si*?'

'*Si*. Please, Mama.'

'He is your boss?'

'No, he just works up there.'

'He was shot, too?'

'No, he was beat up.'

'By the same man who shot you?'

'No, not by the same man who shot me,' Genero said, which was also the truth.

'So what does he have to do with this?'

'Well, he's got influence.'

'With the boss?'

'Well, no. You see, Captain Frick runs the entire precinct, he's actually the boss. But Lieutenant Byrnes is in charge of the detective squad, and Carella is a detective/2nd, and him and the lieutenant are like this, so maybe if I talk to Carella he'll see how I helped them grab that guy yesterday, and put in a good word for me.'

'Let her call the boss,' Genero's father said.

'No, it's better this way,' Genero said.

'How much does a detective make?' Genero's mother asked.

'A fortune,' Genero said.

Gadgets fascinated Detective-Lieutenant Sam Grossman, even when they were bombs. Or perhaps especially when they were bombs. There was no question in anyone's mind (how much question *could* there have been, considering the evidence of the demolished automobile and its five occupants?) that someone had put a bomb in the deputy mayor's car. Moreover, it was mandatory to assume that someone had set the bomb to go off at a specific time, rather than using the ignition wiring of the car as an immediate triggering device. This aspect of the puzzle pleased Grossman enormously because he considered ignition-trigger bombs to be rather crude devices capable of being wired by any gangland ape. *This* bomb was a time bomb. But it was a very special time bomb. It was a time bomb that had not been wired to the automobile clock.

How did Grossman know this?

Ah-ha, the police laboratory never sleeps, not even on Sunday. And besides, his technicians had found two clock faces in the rubble of the automobile.

One of the faces had been part of the Cadillac's dashboard clock. The other had come from a nationally advertised, popular-priced electric alarm clock. There was one other item of importance found in the rubble: a portion of the front panel of a DC-to-AC inverter, part of its brand name still showing where it was stamped into the metal.

These three parts lay on the counter in Grossman's laboratory like three key pieces to a jigsaw puzzle. All he had to do was fit them together and come up with a brilliant solution. He was feeling particularly brilliant this Sunday morning because his son had brought home a 92 on a high-school chemistry exam only two days ago; it always made Grossman feel brilliant when his son achieved anything. Well, let's see, he thought brilliantly. I've got three parts of a time bomb, or rather *two* parts because I think I can safely eliminate the car's clock except as a reference point. Whoever wired the bomb undoubtedly refused to trust his own wrist watch since a difference of a minute or two in timing might have proved critical – in a minute, the deputy mayor could have been out of the car already and on his way into the synagogue. So he had set the electric clock with the time showing on the dashboard clock. Why an *electric* clock? Simple. He did not want a clock that *ticked*. Ticking might have attracted attention, especially if it came from under the hood of a purring Cadillac. OK, so let's see what we've got. We've got an electric alarum clock, and we've got a DC-to-AC inverter, which means someone wanted to translate direct current to alternating current. The battery in a Cadillac would *have* to be 12-volts DC, and the electric clock would doubtless be wired for alternating current. So perhaps we can reasonably assume that someone wanted to wire the clock to the battery and needed an inverter to make this feasible. Let's see.

He'd have to run a positive lead to the battery and a negative lead to any metal part of the automobile, since the car itself would have served as a ground, right? So now we've got a power source to the clock, and the clock is running. OK, right, the rest is simple, he'd have had to use an electric blasting cap, sure, there'd have been enough power to set one off, most commercial electric detonators can be fired by passing a continuous current of 0.3 to 0.4 amperes through the bridge wire. OK, let's see, hold it now, let's look at it.

The battery provides our source of power . . .

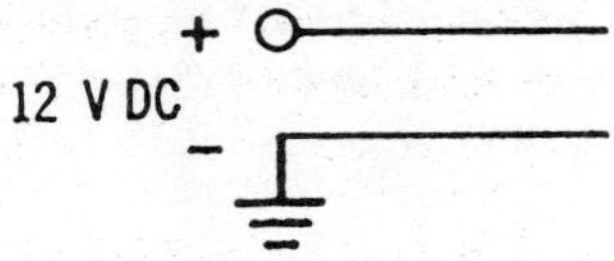

. . . to the inverter . . .

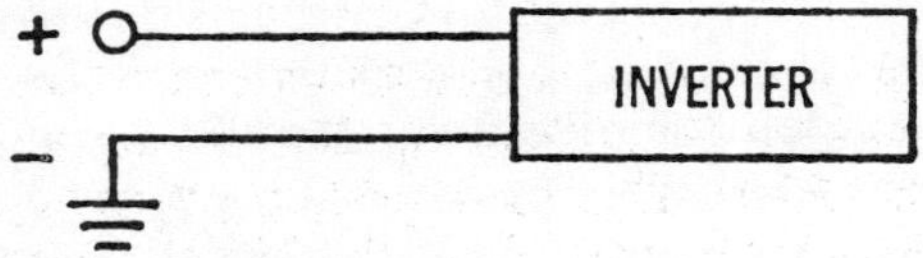

. . . and runs the electric clock . . .

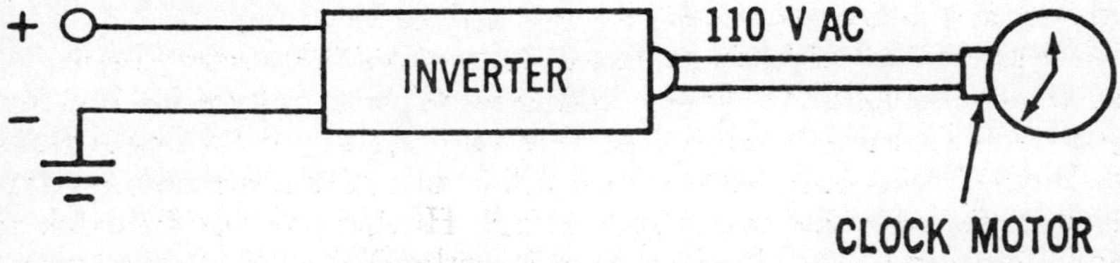

. . . which is in turn set for a specific time, about eight, wasn't it? He'd have had to monkey around with the clock so that instead of the alarum ringing, a switch would close. That would complete the circuit, let's see, he'd have needed a lead running back to the battery, another lead running to the blasting cap, and a lead from the blasting cap to any metal part of the car. So that would look like . . .

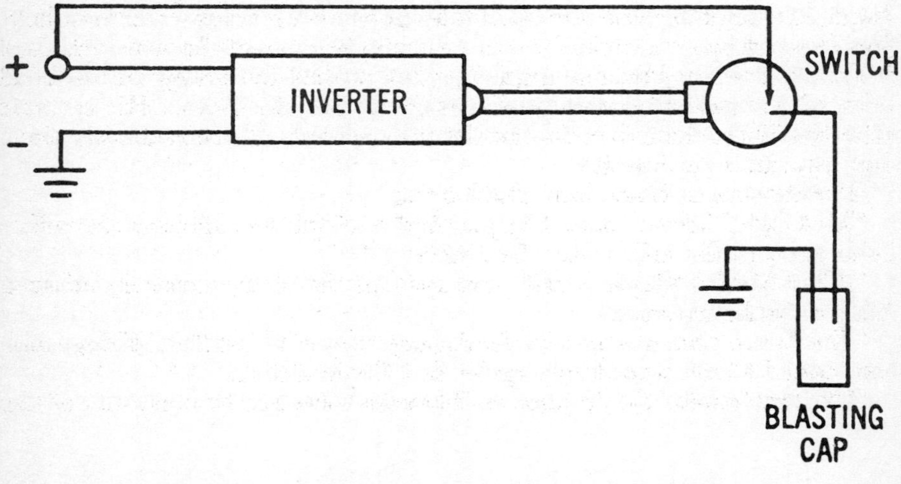

And that's it.

He could have assembled the entire package at home, taken it with him in a tool box, and wired it to the car in a very short time – making certain, of course, that all his wires were properly insulated, to guard against a stray current touching off a premature explosion. The only remaining question is how he managed to get access to the car, but happily that's not my problem.

Whistling brilliantly, Sam Grossman picked up the telephone and called Detective Meyer Meyer at the 87th.

The municipal garage was downtown on Dock Street, some seven blocks from City Hall. Meyer Meyer picked up Bert Kling at ten thirty. The drive down along the River Dix took perhaps twenty minutes. They parked on a meter across the street from the big concrete and tile structure, and Meyer automatically threw the visor sign, even though this was Sunday and parking regulations were not in force.

The foreman of the garage was a man named Spencer Coyle.

He was reading Dick Tracy and seemed less impressed by the two detectives in his midst than by the fictional exploits of his favourite comic strip sleuth. It was only with a great effort of will that he managed to tear himself away from the newspaper at all. He did not rise from his chair, though. The chair was tilted back against the tiled wall of the garage. The tiles, a vomitous shade of yellow, decorated too many government buildings all over the city, and it was Meyer's guess that a hefty hunk of graft had influenced some purchasing agent back in the thirties, either that or the poor bastard had been colour-blind. Spencer Coyle leaned back in his chair against the tiles, his face long and grey and grizzled, his long legs stretched out in front of him, the comic section still dangling from his right hand, as though he were reluctant to let go of it completely even though he had stopped lip-reading it. He was wearing the greenish-brown overalls of a Transportation Division employee, his peaked hat sitting on his head with all the rakish authority of a major in the Air Force. His attitude clearly told the detectives that he did not wish to be disturbed at *any* time, but especially on Sunday.

The detectives found him challenging.

'Mr Coyle,' Meyer said, 'I've just had a telephone call from the police laboratory to the effect that the bomb . . .'

'What bomb?' Coyle asked, and spat on the floor, narrowly missing Meyer's polished shoe.

'The bomb that was put in the deputy mayor's Cadillac,' Kling said, and hoped Coyle would spit again, but Coyle didn't.

'Oh, *that* bomb,' Coyle said, as if bombs were put in every one of the city's Cadillacs regularly, making it difficult to keep track of all the bombs around. 'What *about* that bomb?'

'The lab says it was a pretty complicated bomb, but that it couldn't have taken too long to wire to the car's battery, provided it had been assembled beforehand. Now, what we'd like to know . . .'

'Yeah, I'll bet it was complicated,' Coyle said. He did not look into the faces of the detectives, but instead seemed to direct his blue-eyed gaze at a spot somewhere across the garage. Kling turned to see what he was staring at, but the only thing he noticed was another yellow tile wall.

'Would you have any idea who installed that bomb, Mr Coyle?'

'*I* didn't,' Coyle said flatly.

'Nobody suggested that you did,' Meyer said.

'Just so we understand each other,' Coyle said. 'All I do is run this garage, make sure the cars are in working order, make sure they're ready to roll when ever somebody up there wants one, that's all I'm in charge of.'

'How many cars do you have here?' Meyer asked.

'We got two dozen Caddys, twelve used on a regular basis, and the rest when ever we get visiting dignitaries. We also got fourteen buses and eight motorcycles. And there's also some vehicles that are kept here by the Department of Parks, but that's a courtesy because we got the space.'

'Who services the cars?'

'Which ones?'

'The Caddys.'

'Which one of the Caddys?' Coyle said, and spat again.

'Did you know, Mr Coyle,' Kling said, 'that spitting on the sidewalk is a misdemeanour?'

'This ain't a sidewalk, this is my garage,' Coyle said.

'This is city property,' Kling said, 'the equivalent of a sidewalk. In fact, since the ramp comes in directly from the street outside there, it could almost be considered an extension of the sidewalk.'

'Sure,' Coyle said. 'You going to arrest me for it, or what?'

'You going to keep giving us a hard time?' Kling asked.

'Who's giving you a hard time?'

'We'd like to be home reading the funnies too,' Kling said, 'instead of out busting our arses on a bombing. Now how about it?'

'None of our mechanics put a bomb in that car,' Coyle said flatly.

'How do you know?'

'Because I know all the men who work for me, and none of them put a bomb in that car, that's how I know.'

'Who was here yesterday?' Meyer asked.

'I was.'

'You were here alone?'

'No, the men were here too.'

'Which men?'

'The mechanics.'

'How many mechanics?'

'Two.'

'Is that how many you usually have on duty?'

'We usually have six, but yesterday was Saturday, and we were working with a skeleton crew.'

'Anybody else here?'

'Yeah, some of the chauffeurs were either picking up cars or bringing them back, they're in and out all the time. Also, there was supposed to be an outdoor fishing thing up in Grover Park, so we had a lot of bus drivers in. They were supposed to pick up these slum kids and take them to the park where they were going to fish through the ice on the lake. It got called off.'

'Why?'

'Too cold.'

'When were the bus drivers here?'

'They reported early in the morning, and they hung around till we got word it was called off.'

'You see any of them fooling around near that Cad?'

'Nope. Listen, you're barking up the wrong tree. All those cars got checked out yesterday, and they were in A-number-One shape. That bomb must've been put in there *after* the car left the garage.'

'No, that's impossible, Mr Coyle.'

'Well, it wasn't attached here.'

'You're sure of that, are you?'

'I just told you the cars were inspected, didn't I?'

'Did you inspect them personally, Mr Coyle?'

'No, I got other things to do besides inspecting two dozen Caddys and fourteen buses and eight motorcycles.'

'Then who *did* inspect them, Mr Coyle? One of your mechanics?'

'No, we had an inspector down from the Bureau of Motor Vehicles.'

'And he said the cars were all right?'

'He went over them from top to bottom, every vehicle in the place. He gave us a clean bill of health.'

'Did he look under the hoods?'

'Inside, outside, transmission, suspension, everything. He was here almost six hours.'

'So he would have found a bomb if one was there, is that right?'

'That's right.'

'Mr Coyle, did he give you anything in writing to the effect that the cars were inspected and found in good condition?'

'Why?' Coyle asked. 'You trying to get off the hook?'

'No, we're . . .'

'You trying to pass the buck to Motor Vehicles?'

'We're trying to find out how he could have missed the bomb that was undoubtedly under the hood of that car, that's what we're trying to do.'

'It *wasn't*, that's your answer.'

'Mr Coyle, our lab reported . . .'

'I don't care what your lab reported or didn't report. I'm telling you all these cars were gone over with a fine-tooth comb yesterday, and there couldn't have been a bomb in the deputy mayor's car when it left this garage. Now that's *that*,' Coyle said, and spat on the floor again, emphatically.

'Mr Coyle,' Kling said, 'did you personally see the deputy mayor's car being inspected?'

'I personally saw it being inspected.'

'You personally saw the hood being raised?'

'I did.'

'And you'd be willing to swear that a thorough inspection was made of the area under the hood?'

'What do you mean?'

'Did you actually *see* the inspector checking the area under the hood?'

'Well, I didn't stand around looking over his shoulder, if that's what you mean.'

'Where were you, actually, when the deputy mayor's car was being inspected?'

'I was right here.'

'On this exact spot?'

'No, I was inside the office there. But I could see out into the garage. There's a glass panel in there.'

'And you saw the inspector lifting the hood of the deputy mayor's car?'

'That's right.'

'There are two dozen Caddys here. How'd you know that one was the deputy mayor's car?'

'By the licence plate. It has DMA on it, and then the number. Same as Mayor Vale's car has MA on it for "mayor", and then the number. Same as the . . .'

'All right, it was clearly his car, and you definitely saw . . .'

'Look, that guy spent a good half-hour on each car, now don't tell *me* it wasn't a thorough inspection.'

'Did he spend a half-hour on the deputy mayor's car?'

'Easily.'

Meyer sighed. 'I guess we'll have to talk to him personally,' he said to Kling. He turned again to Coyle. 'What was his name, Mr Coyle?'

'Who?'

'The inspector. The man from Motor Vehicles.'

'I don't know.'

'He didn't give you his name?' Kling asked.

'He showed me his credentials, and he said he was here to inspect the cars, and that was that.'

'What kind of credentials?'

'Oh, printed papers. You know.'

'Mr Coyle,' Kling asked, 'when was the last time a man from Motor Vehicles came to inspect?'

'This was the first time,' Coyle said.

'They've never sent an inspector down before?'

'Never.'

Slowly, wearily, Meyer said, 'What did this man look like, Mr Coyle?'

'He was a tall blond guy wearing a hearing aid,' Coyle answered.

Fats Donner was a mountainous stool pigeon with a penchant for warmer climates and the complexion of an Irish virgin. The complexion, in fact, over-reached the boundaries of common definition to extend to every part of Donner's body; he was white all over, so sickly pale that sometimes Willis suspected him of being a junkie. Willis couldn't have cared less. On any given Sunday, a conscientious cop could collar seventy-nine junkies in a half-hour, seventy-eight of whom would be holding narcotics in some quantity. It was hard to come by a good informer, though, and Donner was one of the best around, *when* he was around. The difficulty with Donner was that he was likely to be found in Vegas or Miami Beach or Puerto Rico during the winter months, lying in the shade with his Buddha-like form protected against even a possible reflection of the sun's rays, quivering with delight as the sweat poured from his body.

Willis was surprised to find him in the city during the coldest March on record. He was not surprised to find him in a room that was suffocatingly hot, with three electric heaters adding their output to the two banging radiators. In the midst of this thermal onslaught, Donner sat in overcoat and gloves wedged into a stuffed armchair. He was wearing two pairs of woollen socks, and his feet were propped up on the radiator. There was a girl in the room with him. She was perhaps fifteen years old, and she was wearing a flowered bra and bikini panties over which she had put on a silk wrapper. The wrapper was unbelted. The girl's near-naked body showed when ever she moved, but she seemed not to mind the presence of a strange man. She barely glanced at Willis when he came in, and then went about the room straightening up, never looking at either of the men as they whispered together near the window streaming wintry sunlight.

'Who's the girl?' Willis asked.

'My daughter,' Donner said, and grinned.

He was not a nice man, Fats Donner, but he was a good stoolie, and criminal detection sometimes made strange bed-fellows. It was Willis' guess that the girl was hooking for Donner, a respectable stoolie sometimes being in need of additional income which he can realize, for example, by picking up a little girl straight from Ohio and teaching her what it's all about and then putting her on the street, there are more things in heaven and earth, Horatio. Willis was not interested in Donner's possible drug habit, nor was Willis interested in hanging a prostitution rap on the girl, nor in busting Donner as a 'male person living on the proceeds of prostitution', Section 1148 of the Penal Law. Willis was interested in taking off his coat and hat and finding out whether or not Donner could give him a line on a man named Dom.

'Dom who?' Donner asked.

'That's all we've got.'

'How many Doms you suppose are in this city?' Donner asked. He turned to the girl, who was puttering around rearranging food in the refrigerator, and said, 'Mercy, how many Doms you suppose are in this city?'

'I don't know,' Mercy replied without looking at him.

'How many Doms you know personally?' Donner asked her.

'I don't know any Doms,' the girl said. She had a tiny voice, tinged with an unmistakably Southern accent. Scratch Ohio, Willis thought, substitute Arkansas or Tennessee.

'She don't know any Doms,' Donner said, and chuckled.

'How about you, Fats? You know any?'

'That's all you're giving me?' Donner asked. 'Man, you're really generous.'

'He lost a lot of money on the championship fight two weeks ago.'

'Everybody I *know* lost a lot of money on the championship fight two weeks ago.'

'He's broke right now. He's trying to promote some scratch,' Willis said.

'Dom, huh?'

'Yeah.'

'From this part of the city?'

'A friend of his lives in Riverhead,' Willis said.

'What's the friend's name?'

'La Bresca. Tony La Bresca.'

'What about *him*?'

'No record.'

'You think this Dom done time?'

'I've got no idea. He seems to have tipped to a caper that's coming off.'

'Is that what you're interested in? The caper?'

'Yes. According to him, the buzz is all over town.'

'There's always some buzz or other that's all over town,' Donner said. 'What the hell are you doing there, Mercy?'

'Just fixing things,' Mercy said.

'Get the hell away from there, you make me nervous.'

'I was just fixing things in the fridge,' Mercy said.

'I hate that Southern accent,' Donner said. 'Don't you hate Southern accents?' he asked Willis.

'I don't mind them,' Willis said.

'Can't even understand her half the time. Sounds as if she's got marbles in her mouth.'

The girl closed the refrigerator door and went to the closet. She opened the door and began moving around empty hangers.

'*Now* what're you doing?' Donner asked.

'Just straightening things,' she said.

'You want me to kick you out in the street bare-arsed?' Donner asked.

'No,' she said softly.

'Then cut it out.'

'All right.'

'Anyway, it's time you got dressed.'

'All right.'

'Go on, go get dressed. What time is it?' he asked Willis.

'Almost noon,' Willis said.

'Sure, go get dressed,' Donner said.

'All right,' the girl said, and went into the other room.

'Damn little bitch,' Donner said, 'hardly worth keeping around.'

'I thought she was your daughter,' Willis said.

'Oh, is that what you thought?' Donner asked, and again he grinned.

Willis restrained a sudden impulse. He sighed and said, 'So what do you think?'

'I don't think nothing yet, man. Zero so far.'

'Well, you want some time on it?'

'How much of a sweat are you in?'

'We need whatever we can get as soon as we can get it.'

'What's the caper sound like?'

'Maybe extortion.'

'Dom, huh?'

'Dom,' Willis repeated.

'That'd be for Dominick, right?'

'Yes.'

'Well, let me listen around, who knows?'

The girl came out of the other room. She was wearing a mini-skirt and white mesh stockings, a low-cut purple blouse. There was a smear of bright red lipstick on her mouth, green eyeshadow on her eyelids.

'You going down now?' Donner asked.

'Yes,' she answered.

'Put on your coat.'

'All right,' she said.

'And take your bag.'

'I will.'

'Don't come back empty, baby,' Donner said.

'I won't,' she said, and moved towards the door.

'I'm going too,' Willis said.

'I'll give you a buzz.'

'OK, but try to move fast, will you?' Willis said.

The girl was on the hallway steps, below Willis, walking down without any sense of haste, buttoning her coat, slinging her bag over her shoulder. Willis caught up with her and said, 'Where are you from, Mercy?'

'Ask Fats,' she answered.

'I'm asking *you*.'

'You fuzz?'

'That's right.'

'Georgia,' she said.

'When'd you get up here?'

'Two months ago.'

'How old are you?'

'Sixteen.'

'What the hell are you doing with a man like Fats Donner?' Willis asked.

'I don't know,' she said. She would not look into his face. She kept her head bent as they went down the steps to the street. As Willis opened the door leading outside, a blast of frigid air rushed into the hallway.

'Why don't you get out?' he said.

The girl looked up at him.

'Where would I go?' she asked, and then left him on the stoop, walking up the street with a practised swing, the bag dangling from her shoulder, her high heels clicking along the pavement.

At two o'clock that afternoon, the seventeen-year-old girl who had been in the convertible that crashed the river barrier died without gaining consciousness.

The Buena Vista Hospital record read simply: Death secondary to head injury.

CHAPTER 9

The Squadroom phone began jangling early Monday morning.

The first call was from a reporter on the city's austere morning daily. He asked to speak to whoever was in charge of the squad and, when told that Lieutenant Byrnes was not in at the moment, asked to speak to whoever was in command.

'This is Detective 2nd/Grade Meyer Meyer,' he was told. 'I suppose I'm in command at the moment.'

'Detective Meyer,' the reporter said, 'this is Carlyle Butterford, I wanted to check out a possible story.'

At first, Meyer thought the call was put-on, nobody had a name like Carlyle Butterford. Then he remembered that *everybody* on this particular morning newspaper had names like Preston Fingerlaver, or Clyde Masterfield, or Aylmer Coopermere. 'Yes, Mr Butterford,' he said, 'what can I do for you?'

'We received a telephone call early this morning . . .'

'From whom, sir?'

'An anonymous caller,' Butterford said.

'Yes?'

'Yes, and he suggested that we contact the 87th Precinct regarding certain extortion calls and notes that were received before the deaths of Parks Commissioner Cowper and Deputy Mayor Scanlon.'

There was a long silence on the line.

'Detective Meyer, is there any truth in this allegation?'

'I suggest that you call the Public Relations Officer of the Police Department,' Meyer said, 'his name is Detective Glenn, and he's downtown at Headquarters. The number is Centre 6–0800.'

'Would he have any knowledge of these alleged extortion calls and notes?' Butterford asked.

'I guess you'd have to ask him,' Meyer said.

'Do *you* have any knowledge of these alleged . . .?'

'As I told you,' Meyer said, 'the lieutenant is out at the moment, and he's the one who generally supplies information to the press.'

'But would *you*, personally, have any information . . .?'

'I have information on a great many things,' Meyer said. 'Homicides, muggings, burglaries, robberies, rapes, extortion attempts, all sorts of things. But, as I'm sure you know, detectives are public servants and it has been the department's policy to discourage us from seeking personal aggrandizement. If you wish to talk to the lieutenant, I suggest you call back at around ten o'clock. He should be in by then.'

'Come on,' Butterford said, 'give me a break.'

'I'm sorry, pal, I can't help you.'

'I'm a working stiff, just like you.'

'So's the lieutenant,' Meyer said, and hung up.

The second call came at nine thirty. Sergeant Murchison, at the switchboard, took the call and immediately put it through to Meyer.

'This is Cliff Savage,' the voice said. 'Remember me?'

'Only too well,' Meyer said. 'What do you want, Savage?'

'Carella around?'

'Nope.'

'Where is he?'

'Out,' Meyer said.

'I wanted to talk to him.'

'He doesn't want to talk to you,' Meyer said. 'You almost got his wife killed once with your goddamn yellow journalism. You want my advice, keep out of his sight.'

'I guess I'll have to talk to you, then,' Savage said.

'I'm not too fond of you myself, if you want the truth.'

'Well, thank you,' Savage said, 'but that's not the truth I'm after.'

'What *are* you after?'

'I got a phone call this morning from a man who refused to identify himself. He gave me a very interesting piece of information.' Savage paused. 'Know anything about it?'

Meyer's heart was pounding, but he very calmly said, 'I'm not a mind reader, Savage.'

'I thought you might know something about it.'

'Savage, I've given you the courtesy of five minutes of valuable time already. Now if you've got something to say . . .'

'OK, OK. The man I spoke to said the 87th Precinct had received several threatening telephone calls preceding the death of Parks Commissioner Cowper, and three extortion notes preceding the death of Deputy Mayor Scanlon. Know anything about it?'

'Telephone company'd probably be able to help you on any phone calls you want to check, and I guess the Documents Section of the Public Library . . .'

'Come on, Meyer, don't stall me.'

'We're not permitted to give information to reporters,' Meyer said. 'You know that.'

'How much?' Savage asked.

'Huh?'

'How much do you want, Meyer?'

'How much can you afford?' Meyer asked.

'How does a hundred bucks sound?'

'Not so good.'

'How about two hundred?'

'I get more than that just for protecting our friendly neighbourhood pusher.'

'Three hundred is my top offer,' Savage said.

'Would you mind repeating the offer for the benefit of the tape recorder?' Meyer said. 'I want to have evidence when I charge you with attempting to bribe a police officer.'

'I was merely offering you a loan,' Savage said.

'Neither a borrower nor a lender be,' Meyer said, and hung up.

This was not so good. This was, in fact, bad. He was about to dial the lieutenant's home number, hoping to catch him before he left for the office, when the telephone on his desk rang again.

'87th Squad,' he said, 'Detective Meyer.'

The caller was from one of the two afternoon papers. He repeated essentially what Meyer had already heard from his two previous callers, and then asked if Meyer knew anything about it. Meyer, loath to lie lest the story eventually broke and tangentially mentioned that there had been a police credibility gap, suggested that the man try the lieutenant later on in the day. When he hung up, he looked at the clock and decided to wait for the next call before trying to contact the lieutenant. Fortunately, there were now only four daily newspapers in the city, the leaders of the various newspaper guilds and unions having decided that the best way to ensure higher wages and lifetime employment was to make demands that would kill off the newspapers one by one, leaving behind only scattered goose feathers and broken golden egg shells. Meyer did not have to wait long. The representative of the fourth newspaper called within five minutes. He had a bright chirpy voice and an ingratiating style. He got nothing from Meyer, and he finally hung up in cheerful rage.

It was now five minutes to ten, too late to catch Byrnes at home.

While he waited for the lieutenant to arrive, Meyer doodled a picture of a man in a fedora shooting a Colt .45 automatic. The man looked very much like Meyer, except that he possessed a full head of hair. He tried to remember when. It was probably when he was ten years old. He was smiling painfully over his own joke when Byrnes came into the squad-room. The lieutenant looked dyspeptic this morning. Meyer surmised that he missed the painters. Everyone on the squad missed the painters. They had added humanity to the joint, and richness, a spirit of gregarious joy, a certain *je ne sais quoi*.

'We got trouble,' Meyer said, but before he could relate the trouble to the lieutenant, the phone rang again. Meyer lifted the receiver, identified himself, and then looked at Byrnes.

'It's the Chief of Detectives,' he said, and Byrnes sighed and went into his office to take the call privately.

Thirty-three telephone calls were exchanged that morning as police and city government officials kept the wires hot between their own offices and Lieutenant Byrnes', trying to decide what to do about this latest revolting development. The one thing they did not need on this case was publicity that would make them all appear foolish. And yet, if there really *had* been a leak about the extortion attempts, it seemed likely that the full story might come to light at any moment, in which case it might be best to level with the papers *before* they broke the news. At the same time, the anonymous caller might only have been speculating, without any real evidence to back up his claim of extortion, in which case a premature release to the newspapers would only serve to breach a danger that was not truly threatening. What to do, oh, what to do?

The telephones rang, and the possibilities multiplied. Heads swam and tempers flared. The mayor, James Martin Vale himself, postponed a walking trip from City Hall to Grover Park and personally called Lieutenant Byrnes to ask his opinion on 'the peril of the situation'. Lieutenant Byrnes passed the buck to the Chief of Detectives, who in turn passed it back to Captain Frick of the 87th, who referred JMVs secretary to the police commissioner, who for reasons unknown said he must first consult with the traffic commissioner, who in turn referred the police commissioner to the Bridge Authority who somehow got on to the city comptroller, who in turn called JMV himself to ask what this was all about.

At the end of two hours of dodging and wrangling, it was decided to take the bull by the horns and release transcripts of the telephone conversations, as well as photocopies of the three notes, to all four city newspapers. The city's liberal blue-headline newspaper (which was that week running an exposé on the growth of the numbers racket as evidenced by the prevalence of nickel and dime betters in kindergarten classes) was the first paper to break the story, running photos of the three notes side by side on its front page. The city's other afternoon newspaper, recently renamed the

Pierce-Arrow-Universal-International-Bugle-Chronicle-Clarion or something, was next to feature the notes on its front page, together with transcripts of the calls in 24-point Cheltenham Bold.

That night, the early editions of the two morning newspapers carried the story as well. This meant that a combined total of four million readers now knew all about the extortion threats.

The next move was anybody's.

Anthony La Bresca and his pool hall buddy, Peter Vincent Calucci (alias Calooch, Cooch, or Kook) met in a burlesque house on a side street off The Stem at seven o'clock that Monday night.

La Bresca had been tailed from his place of employment, a demolition site in the city's downtown financial district, by three detectives using the ABC method of surveillance. Mindful of the earlier unsuccessful attempts to keep track of him, nobody was taking chances any more – the ABC method was surefire and foolproof.

Detective Bob O'Brien was 'A', following La Bresca while Detective Andy Parker, who was 'B' walked behind O'Brien and kept him constantly in view. Detective Carl Kapek was 'C', and he moved parallel with La Bresca, on the opposite side of the street. This meant that if La Bresca suddenly went into a coffee shop or ducked around the corner, Kapek could instantly swap places with O'Brien, taking the lead 'A' position while O'Brien caught up, crossed the street, and manoeuvred into the 'C' position. It also meant that the men could use camouflaging tactics at their own discretion, changing positions so that the combination became BCA or CBA or CAB or whatever they chose, a scheme that guaranteed La Bresca would not recognize any one man following him over an extended period of time.

Wherever he went, La Bresca was effectively contained. Even in parts of the city where the crowds were unusually thick, there was no danger of losing him. Kapek would merely cross over on to La Bresca's side of the street and begin walking some fifteen feet *ahead* of him, so that the pattern read C, La Bresca, A, and B. In police jargon, they were 'sticking like a dirty shirt', and they did their job well and unobtrusively, despite the cold weather and despite the fact that La Bresca seemed to be a serendipitous type who led them on a jolly excursion halfway across the city, apparently trying to kill time before his seven-o'clock meeting with Calucci.

The two men took seats in the tenth row of the theatre. The show was in progress, two baggy-pants comics relating a traffic accident one of them had had with a car driven by a voluptuous blonde.

'You mean she crashed right into your tail pipe?' one of the comics asked.

'Hit me with her headlights,' the second one said.

'Hit your tail pipe with her headlights?' the first one asked.

'Almost broke it off for me,' the second one said.

Kapek, taking a seat across the aisle from Calucci and La Bresca, was suddenly reminded of the squadroom painter and realized how sorely he missed their presence. O'Brien had moved into the row behind the pair, and was sitting directly back of them now. Andy Parker was in the same row, two seats to the left of Calucci.

'Any trouble getting here?' Calucci whispered.

'No,' La Bresca whispered back.

'What's with Dom?'

'He wants in.'

'I thought he just wanted a couple of bills.'

'That was last week.'

'What's he want now?'

'A three-way split.'

'Tell him to go screw,' Calucci said.

'No. He's hip to the whole thing.'

'How'd he find out?'

'I don't know. But he's hip, that's for sure.'

There was a blast from the trumpet section of the four-piece band in the pit. The overhead leikos came up purple, and a brilliant follow spot hit the curtain stage left. The reed section followed the heraldic trumpet with a saxophone obbligato designed to evoke memory or desire or both. A gloved hand snaked its way around the curtain. 'And now,' a voice said over the loudspeaker system while one half of the rhythm section started a snare drum roll, 'and *now*, for the first time in America, direct from Brest, which is where the little lady comes from . . . exhibiting her titillating terpsichoreal skills for your pleasure, we are happy to present Miss . . . Freida Panzer!'

A leg appeared from behind the curtain.

It floated disembodied on the air. A black high-heeled pump pointed, wiggled, a calf muscle tightened, the knee bent, and then the toe pointed again. There was more of the leg visible now, the black nylon stocking shimmered in the glow of the lights, ribbed at the top where a vulnerable white thigh lay exposed, black garter biting into the flesh, fetishists all over the theatre thrilled to the sight, not to mention a few detectives who weren't fetishists at all. Freida Panzer undulated on to the stage bathed in the glow of the overhead purple leikos, wearing a long purple gown slit up each leg to the waist, the black stockings and taut black garters revealed each time she took another long-legged step across the stage.

'Look at them legs,' Calucci whispered.

'Yeah,' La Bresca said.

O'Brien sitting behind them, looking at the legs. They were extraordinary legs.

'I hate to cut anybody else in on this,' Calucci whispered.

'Me neither,' La Bresca said, 'but what else can we do? He'll run screaming to the cops if we don't play ball.'

'Is that what he said?'

'Not in so many words. He just hinted.'

'Yeah, the son of a bitch.'

'So what do you think?' La Bresca asked.

'Man, there's big money involved here,' Calucci said.

'You think I don't know?'

'Why cut him in after we done all the planning?'

'What else can we do?'

'We can wash him,' Calucci whispered.

The girl was taking off her clothes.

The four-piece ensemble in the orchestra pit rose to heights of musical expression, a heavy bass drum beat accentuating each solid bump as purple clothing fell like aster petals, a triple-tongued trumpet winding up with each pelvic grind, a saxophone wail climbing the girl's flanks in accompaniment with her sliding hands, a steady piano beat banging out the rhythm of each long-legged stride, each tassel-twirling, fixed-grin, sexy-eyed, contrived and calculated erotic move. 'She's got some tits,' Calucci whispered, and La Bresca whispered back, 'Yeah.'

The men fell silent.

The music rose in earsplitting crescendo. The bass drum beat was more insistent now, the trumpet shrieked higher and higher, a C above high C reached for and missed, the saxophone trilled impatiently, the piano pounded in the upper register, a tinny insistent honky-tonk rhythm, cymbals clashed, the trumpet reached for the screech note again, and again missed. The lights were swirling now, the stage was inundated in colour and sound. There was the stink of perspiration and lust in that theatre as the girl ground out her coded message in a cipher broken long ago on too many similar stages, pounded out her promises of ecstasy and sin, Come and get it, baby, Come and get it, Come and come and come and come.

The stage went black.

In the darkness, Calucci whispered. 'What do you think?'

One of the baggy-pants comics came on again to do a bit in a doctor's office accompanied by a pert little blonde with enormous breasts who explained that she thought she was stagnant because she hadn't fenestrated in two months.

'I hate the idea of knocking somebody off,' La Bresca whispered.

'If it's necessary, it's necessary.'

'Still.'

'There's lots of money involved here, don't forget it.'

'Yeah, but at the same time, there's enough to split three ways, ain't there?' La Bresca said.

'Why should we split it three ways when we can split it down the middle?'

'Because Dom'll spill the whole works if we don't cut him in. Look, what's the sense going over this a hundred times? We *got* to cut him in.'

'I want to think about it.'

'You ain't got that much time to think about it. We're set for the fifteenth. Dom wants to know right away.'

'OK, so tell him he's in. Then we'll decide whether he's in or out. And I mean *really* out, the little son of a bitch.'

'And now, ladies and gentlemen,' the loudspeaker voice said, 'it gives us great pleasure to present the rage of San Francisco, a young lady who thrilled the residents of that city by the Golden Gate, a young lady whose exotic dancing caused the pious officials of Hong Kong to see Red . . . it is with bursting pride that we turn our stage over to Miss . . . *Anna . . . May . . . Zong*!'

The house lights dimmed. The band struck up a sinuous version of *Limehouse Blues*. A swish cymbal echoed on the air, and a sloe-eyed girl wearing mandarin garb came into the spotlight with mincing steps, hands together in an attitude of prayer, head bent.

'I dig these Chinks,' Calucci said.

'You guys want to stop talking?' a bald-headed man in the row ahead said. 'I can't see the girls with all that gabbing behind me.'

'Fuck off, Baldy,' La Bresca said.

But both men fell silent. O'Brien leaned forward in his seat. Parker bent sideways over the armrest. There was nothing further to hear. Kapek, across the aisle, could not have heard anything anyway, so he merely watched the Chinese girl as she took off her clothes.

At the end of the act, La Bresca and Calucci rose quietly from their seats and went out of the theatre. They split up outside. Parker followed Calucci to his house, and Kapek followed La Bresca to his. O'Brien went back to the squadroom to type up a report.

The detectives did not get together again until eleven o'clock that night, by which time La Bresca and Calucci were both hopefully asleep. They met in a diner some five blocks from the squadroom. Over coffee and crullers, they all agreed that the only thing they'd learned from their eavesdropping was the date of the job La Bresca and Calucci were planning: March the fifteenth. They also agreed that Freida Panzer had much larger breasts than Anna May Zong.

In the living-room of a luxurious apartment on Harbourside Oval, overlooking the river, a good three miles from where Detectives O'Brien, Parker, and Kapek were speculating on the comparative dimensions of the two strippers, the deaf man sat on a sofa facing sliding glass doors, and happily sipped at a glass of scotch and soda. The drapes were open, and the view of warm and glowing lights strung on the bridge's cables, the distant muted reds and ambers blinking on the distant shore gave the night a deceptively springtime appearance; the thermometer on the terrace outside read ten degrees above zero.

Two bottles of expensive scotch, one already dead, were on the coffee table before the sofa upholstered in rich black leather. On the wall opposite the sofa, there hung an original Rouault, only a gouache to be sure, but none the less quite valuable. A grand piano turned its wide curve into the room, and a petite brunette, wearing a miniskirt and a white crocheted blouse, sat at the piano playing *Heart and Soul* over and over again.

The girl was perhaps twenty-three years old, with a nose that had been recently bobbed, large brown eyes, long black hair that fell to a point halfway between her waist and her shoulder blades. She was wearing false eyelashes. They fluttered whenever she hit a sour note, which was often. The deaf man seemed not to mind the discord that rose from the piano. Perhaps he really *was* deaf, or perhaps he had consumed enough scotch to have dimmed his perception. The two other men in the room didn't seem to mind the cacophony either. One of them even tried singing along with the girl's treacherous rendition – until she hit another sour note and began again from the top.

'I can't seem to get it,' she said, pouting.

'You'll get it, honey,' the deaf man said. 'Just keep at it.'

One of the men was short and slender, with the dust-coloured complexion of an Indian. He wore narrow black tapered trousers and a white shirt over which was an open black vest. He was sitting at a drop-leaf desk, typing. The other man was tall and burly, with blue eyes, red hair, and a red moustache. There were freckles spattered over his cheeks and his forehead, and his voice, as he began singing along with the girl again, was deep and resonant. He was wearing tight jeans and a blue turtleneck sweater.

As the girl continued to play *Heart and Soul*, a feeling of lassitude spread through the deaf man. Sitting on the couch, watching the second phase of his scheme as it became a reality, he mused again on the beauty of his plan, and then glanced at the girl, and then smiled when she hit the same sour note (an E flat where it should have been a natural E) and then looked again to where Ahmad was typing.

'The beauty of this phase,' he said aloud, 'is that none of them will believe us.'

'They will believe,' Ahmad offered, and smiled thinly.

'Yes, but not at this phase.'

'No, only later,' Ahmad said, and sipped at his scotch, and glanced at the girl's thighs, and went back to his typing.

'How much is this mailing going to cost us?' the other man asked.

'Well, Buck,' the deaf man said, 'we're sending out a hundred pieces of first-class mail at five cents postage per envelope, so that comes to a grand total of five dollars – if my arithmetic is correct.'

'Your arithmetic is *always* correct,' Ahmad said, and smiled.

'*This* is the damn part I can't get,' the girl said, and struck the same note over and over again, as though trying to pound it into her memory.

'Keep at it, Rochelle,' the deaf man said. 'You'll get it.'

Buck lifted his glass, discovered it was empty, and went to the coffee table to refill it, moving with the economy of an athlete, back ramrod stiff, hands dangling loosely at his sides, as though he were going back for the huddle after having executed a successful line plunge.

'Here, let me help you,' the deaf man said.

'Not too heavy,' Buck said.

The deaf man poured a liberal shot into Buck's extended glass. 'Drink,' he said. 'You deserve it.'

'Well, I don't want to get crocked.'

'Why not? You're among friends,' the deaf man said, and smiled.

He was feeling particularly appreciative of Buck's talent tonight, because without it this phase of the scheme would never have become a reality. Oh yes, a primitive bomb *could* have been assembled and hastily wired to the ignition switch, but such sloppiness, such dependency on chance, had never appealed to the deaf man. The seriousness with which Buck had approached the problem had been truly heart-warming. His development of a compact package (the inverter had weighed a mere twenty-two pounds and measured only ten by ten by five) that could be easily transported and wired in a relatively short period of time, his specific demand for an inverter with a regulated sine-wave output (costing a bit more, yes, $64.95, but a negligible output in terms of the hoped-for financial realization), his insistence on a briefing session to explain the proper handling of the dynamite and the electric blasting cap, all were admirable, admirable. He was a good man, Buck, a demolition expert who had worked on countless legitimate blasting jobs, a background essential to the deaf man's plan; in this state, you were not allowed to buy explosives without a permit and insurance, both of which Buck possessed. The deaf man was very pleased indeed to have him in his employ.

Ahmad, too, was indispensable. He had been working as a draughtsman at Metropolitan Power & Light, earning $150 a week in the Bureau of Maps and Records, when the deaf man first contacted him. He had readily appreciated the huge rewards to be reaped from the scheme, and had enthusiastically supplied all of the information so necessary to its final phase. In addition, he was a meticulous little man who had insisted that all of these letters be typed on high-quality bond paper, with each of the hundred men receiving an original rather than a carbon or a photocopy, a touch designed to allay any suspicion that the letter was a practical joke. The deaf man knew that the difference between success and failure very often depended on such small details, and he smiled at Ahmad in appreciation now, and sipped a little more of his scotch, and said, 'How many have you typed so far?'

'Fifty-two.'

'We'll be toiling long into the night, I'm afraid.'

'When are we going to mail these?'

'I had hoped by Wednesday.'

'I will finish them long before then,' Ahmad promised.

'Will you really be working here all night?' Rochelle asked, pouting again.

'You can go to bed if you like, dear,' the deaf man said.

'What good's bed without you?' Rochelle said, and Buck and Ahmad exchanged glances.

'Go on, I'll join you later.'

'I'm not sleepy.'

'Then have a drink, and play us another song.'

'I don't know any other songs.'

'Read a book then,' the deaf man suggested.

Rochelle looked at him blankly.

'Or go into the den and watch some television.'

'There's nothing on but old movies.'

'Some of those old films are very instructive,' the deaf man said.

'Some of them are very crappy, too,' Rochelle replied.

The deaf man smiled. 'Do you feel like licking a hundred envelopes?' he asked.

'No, I don't feel like licking envelopes,' she answered.

'I didn't think so,' the deaf man said.

'So what should I do?' Rochelle asked.

'Go get into your nightgown, darling,' the deaf man said.

'Mmm?' she said, and looked at him archly.

'Mmm,' he replied.

'OK,' she said, and rose from the piano stool. 'Well, goodnight, fellas,' she said.

'Goodnight,' Buck said.

'Goodnight, miss,' Ahmad said.

Rochelle looked at the deaf man again, and then went into the other room.

'Empty-headed little bitch,' he said.

'I think she's dangerous to have around,' Buck said.

'On the contrary,' the deaf man said, 'she soothes the nerves and eases the daily pressures. Besides, she thinks we're respectable businessmen promoting some sort of harebrained scheme. She hasn't the vaguest notion of what we're up to.'

'Sometimes *I* don't have the vaguest notion either,' Buck said, and pulled a face.

'It's really very simple,' the deaf man said. 'We're making a direct-mail appeal, a tried-and-true method of solicitation pioneered by businessmen all over this bountiful nation. *Our* mailing, of course, is a limited one. We're only sending out a hundred letters. But it's my hope that we'll get a highly favourable response.'

'And what if we don't?'

'Well, Buck, let's assume the worst. Let's assume we get a one-per-cent return, which is the generally expected return on a direct-mail piece. Our entire outlay thus far has been $86.95 for a lever-action carbine; $3.75 for a box of cartridges; $64.95 for your inverter; $7.00 for the electric clock; $9.60 for a dozen sticks of dynamite at eighty cents a stick; sixty cents for the blasting cap; $10.00 for the stationery; and $5.00 for the postage. If my addition is correct . . .' (He paused here to smile at Ahmad.) '. . . that comes to $187.85. Our future expenses – for the volt-ohm meter, the pressure-sensitive letters, the uniform, and so on – should be negligible. Now, if we get only one-per-cent return on our mailing, if only *one* person out of the hundred comes through, we'll *still* be reaping a large profit on our initial investment.'

'Five thousand dollars seems like pretty small change for two murders,' Buck said.

'*Three* murders,' the deaf man corrected.

'Even better,' Buck said, and pulled a face.

'I assure you I'm expecting much more than a one-per-cent return. On Friday, we execute – if you'll pardon the pun – the final phase of our plan. By Saturday morning, there'll be no disbelievers.'

'How many of them do you think'll come through?'

'Most of them. If not all of them.'

'And what about the fuzz?'

'What about them? They *still* don't know who we are, and they'll never find out.'

'I hope you're right.'

'I *know* I'm right.'

'I worry about fuzz,' Buck said. 'I can't help it. I've been conditioned to worry about them.'

'There's nothing to worry about. Don't you realize *why* they're called fuzz?'

'No. Why?'

'Because they're fuzzy and fussy and antiquated and incompetent. Their investigatory technique is established and routine, designed for effectiveness in an age that no longer exists. The police in this city are like wind-up toys with keys sticking out of their backs, capable of performing only in terms of their own limited design, tiny mechanical men clattering along the sidewalk stiff-legged, scurrying about in aimless circles. But put an obstacle in their path, a brick wall or an orange crate, and they unwind helplessly in the same spot, arms and legs thrashing but taking them nowhere.' The deaf man grinned, 'I, my friend, am the brick wall.'

'Or the orange crate,' Buck said.

'No,' Ahmad said intensely. 'He is the brick wall.'

CHAPTER 10

The first break in the case came at ten o'clock the next morning, when Fats Donner called the squadroom.

Until that time, there were still perhaps two thousand imponderables to whatever La Bresca and Calucci were planning. But aside from such minor considerations as *where* the job would take place, or at exactly what *time* on March fifteenth, there were several unknown identities to contend with as well, such as Dom (who so far had no last name) and the long-haired blonde girl who had given La Bresca a lift last Friday night. It was the police supposition that if either of these two people could be located, the nature of the impending job might be wrung from one or the other of them. Whether or not the job was in any way connected with the recent murders would then become a matter for further speculation, as would the possibility that La Bresca was in some way involved with the deaf man. There were a lot of questions to be asked if only they could find somebody to ask them to.

Donner was put through immediately.

'I think I got your Dom,' he said to Willis.

'Good,' Willis said. 'What's his last name?'

'Di Fillippi. Dominick Di Fillippi. Lives in Riverhead near the old Coliseum, you know the neighbourhood?'

'Yeah. What've you got on him?'

'He's with The Coaxial Cable.'

'Yeah?' Willis said.

'Yeah.'

'Well, what's that?' Willis said.

'What's *what*?'

'What's it supposed to *mean*?'

'What's *what* supposed to mean?'

'What you just said. Is it some kind of code or something?'

'Is what some kind of code?' Donner asked.

'The coaxial cable.'

'No, it's a group.'

'A group of *what*?'

'A group. Musicians,' Donner said.

'A band, you mean?'

'That's right, only today they call them groups.'

'Well, what's the coaxial cable got to do with it?'

'That's the name of the group. The Coaxial Cable.'

'You're putting me on,' Willis said.

'No, that's the name, I mean it.'

'What does Di Fillippi play?'

'Rhythm guitar.'

'Where do I find him?'

'His address is 365 North Anderson.'

'That's in Riverhead?'

'Yeah.'

'How do you know he's our man?'

'Well, it seems he's a big bullshit artist, you know?' Donner said. 'He's been going around the past few weeks saying he dropped a huge bundle on the championship fight, made it sound like two, three Gs. It turns out all he lost was fifty bucks, that's some big bundle, huh?'

'Yeah, go ahead.'

'But he's also been saying recently that he knows about a big caper coming off.'

'Who'd he say this to?'

'Well, one of the guys in the group is a big hophead from back even before it got stylish. That's how I got my lead on to Di Fillippi. And the guy said they were busting some joints together maybe three, four days ago, and Di Fillippi came on about this big caper he knew about.'

'Did he say what the caper was?'

'No.'

'And they were smoking pot?'

'Yeah, busting a few joints, you know, social.'

'Maybe Di Fillippi was out of his skull.'

'He probably was. What's that got to do with it?'

'He might have dreamt up the whole thing.'

'I don't think so.'

'Did he mention La Bresca at all?'

'Nope.'

'Did he say when the job would be coming off?'

'Nope.'

'Well, it's not much, Fats.'

'It's worth half a century, don't you think?'

'It's worth ten bucks,' Willis said.

'Hey, come on, man, I had to do some real hustling to get this for you.'

'Which reminds me,' Willis said.

'Huh?'

'Get rid of your playmate.'

'Huh?'

'The girl. Next time I see you, I want her out of there.'

'Why?'

'Because I thought it over, and I don't like the idea.'

'I kicked her out twice already,' Donner said. 'She always comes back.'

'Then maybe you ought to use this ten bucks to buy her a ticket back to Georgia.'

'Sure. Maybe I ought to contribute another ten besides to the Salvation Army,' Donner said.

'Just get her out of there,' Willis said.

'When'd you get so righteous?' Donner asked.

'Just this minute.'

'I thought you were a businessman.'

'I am. Here's my deal. Let the girl go, and I forget whatever else I know about you, and whatever I might learn in the future.'

'Nobody learns nothing about me,' Donner said. 'I'm The Shadow.'

'No,' Willis said. 'Only Lamont Cranston is The Shadow.'

'You serious about this?'

'I want the girl out of there. If she's still around next time I see you, I throw the book.'

'And lose a valuable man.'

'Maybe,' Willis said. 'In which case, we'll have to manage without you somehow.'

'Sometimes I wonder why I bother helping you guys at all,' Donner said.

'I'll *tell* you why sometime, if you have a minute,' Willis said.

'Never mind.'

'Will you get the girl out of there?'

'Yeah, yeah. You're going to send me fifty, right?'

'I said ten.'

'Make it twenty.'

'For the birdseed you just gave me?'

'It's a lead, ain't it?'

'That's all it is.'

'So? A lead is worth at least twenty-five.'

'I'll send you fifteen,' Willis said, and hung up.

The phone rang again almost the instant he replaced it on the cradle. He lifted the receiver and said, '87th, Willis speaking.'

'Hal, this is Artie over at the school.'

'Yep.'

'I've been waiting for Murchison to put me through. I think I've got something.'

'Shoot.'

'La Bresca talked to his mother on the phone about five minutes ago.'

'In English or Italian?'

'English. He told her he was expecting a call from Dom Di Fillippi. That could be our man, no?'

'Yeah, it looks like he is,' Willis said.

'He told his mother to say he'd meet Di Fillippi in his lunch hour at the corner of Cathedral and Seventh.'

'Has Di Fillippi called yet?'

'Not yet. This was just five minutes ago, Hal.'

'Right. What time did he say they'd meet?'

'Twelve thirty.'

'Twelve thirty, corner of Cathedral and Seventh.'

'Right,' Brown said.

'We'll have somebody there.'

'I'll call you back,' Brown said. 'I've got another customer.'

In five minutes, Brown rang the squadroom again. 'That was Di Fillippi,' he said. 'Mrs La Bresca gave him the message. Looks like pay dirt at last, huh?'

'Maybe,' Willis said.

From where Meyer and Kling sat in the Chrysler sedan parked on Cathedral Street, they could clearly see Tony La Bresca waiting on the corner near the bus stop sign. The clock on top of the Catholic church dominating the intersection read twelve twenty. La Bresca was early and apparently impatient. He paced the pavement anxiously, lighting three cigarettes in succession, looking up at the church clock every few minutes, checking the time against his own wrist watch.

'This has got to be it,' Kling said.

'The payoff of the burley joint summit meeting,' Meyer said.

'Right. La Bresca's going to tell old Dom he's in for a three-way split. Then Calooch'll decide whether or not they're going to dump him in the river.'

'Six-to-five old Dom gets the cement block.'

'I'm not a gambling man,' Kling said.

The church clock began tolling the half-hour. The chimes rang out over the intersection. Some of the lunch-hour pedestrians glanced up at the bell tower. Most of them hurried past with their heads ducked against the cold.

'Old Dom seems to be late,' Meyer said.

'Look at old Tony,' Kling said. 'He's about ready to take a fit.'

'Yeah,' Meyer said, and chuckled. The car heater was on, and he was snug and cosy and drowsy. He did not envy La Bresca standing outside on the windy corner.

'What's the plan?' Kling said.

'As soon as the meeting's over, we move in on old Dom.'

'We ought to pick up *both* of them,' Kling said.

'Tell me what'll stick.'

'We heard La Bresca planning a job, didn't we? That's Conspiracy to Commit, Section 580.'

'Big deal. I'd rather find out what he's up to and then catch him in the act.'

'If he's in with the deaf man, he's *already* committed two crimes,' Kling said. 'And very big ones at that.'

'*If* he's in with the deaf man.'

'You think he is?'

'No.'

'I'm not sure,' Kling said.

'Maybe old Dom'll be able to tell us.'

'If he shows.'

'What time is it?'

'Twenty to,' Kling said.

'Mmm,' Meyer said.

They kept watching La Bresca. He was pacing more nervously now, slapping his gloved hands against his sides to ward off the cold. He was wearing the same beige car coat he had worn the day he'd picked up the lunch pail in the park, the same green muffler wrapped around his throat, the same thick-soled workman's shoes.

'Look,' Meyer said suddenly.

'What is it?'

'Across the street. Pulling up to the kerb.'

'Huh?'

'It's the blonde girl, Bert. In the same black Buick!'

'How'd *she* get into the act?'

Meyer started the car. La Bresca had spotted the Buick and was walking towards it rapidly. From where they sat, the detectives could see the girl toss her long blonde hair and then lean over to open the front door for him. La Bresca got into the car. In a moment, it gunned away from the kerb.

'What do we do now?' Kling asked.

'We follow.'

'What about Dom?'

'Maybe the girl's taking La Bresca to see him.'

'And maybe not.'

'What can we lose?' Meyer asked.

'We can lose Dom,' Kling said.

'Just thank God they're not walking,' Meyer said, and pulled the Chrysler out into traffic.

This was the oldest part of the city. The streets were narrow, the buildings crowded the sidewalks and gutters, pedestrians crossed at random, ignoring the lights, ducking around moving vehicles with practised ease, nonchalant to possible danger.

'Like to give them all tickets for jaywalking,' Meyer mumbled.

'Don't lose that Buick,' Kling cautioned.

'You think I'm new in this business, Sonny?'

'You lost that same car only last week,' Kling said.

'I was on *foot* last week.'

'They're making a left turn,' Kling said.

'I see them.'

The Buick had indeed made a left turn, coming out on to the wide tree-lined esplanade bordering the River Dix. The river was icebound shore to shore, a phenomenon that had happened only twice before in the city's history. Devoid of its usual busy harbour traffic, it stretched towards Calm's Point like a flat Kansas plain, a thick cover of snow uniformly hiding the ice below. The naked trees along the esplanade bent in the strong wind that raced across the river. Even the heavy Buick seemed struggling to move through the gusts, its nose swerving every now and again as the blonde fought the wheel. At last, she pulled the car to the kerb and killed the engine. The esplanade was silent except for the roaring of the wind. Newspapers flapped into the air like giant headless birds. An empty wicker-wire trash barrel came rolling down the centre of the street.

A block behind the parked Buick, Meyer and Kling sat and looked through the windshield of the unmarked police sedan. The wind howled around the automobile, drowning out the calls that came from the radio. Kling turned up the volume.

'What now?' he asked.

'We wait,' Meyer said.

'Do we pick up the girl when they're finished talking?' Kling asked.

'Yep.'

'You think she'll know anything?'

'I hope so. She must be in on it, don't you think?'

'I don't know. Calucci was talking about splitting the take up the middle. If there're three people in it already . . .'

'Well, then maybe she's old Dom's girl.'

'Substituting for him, you mean?'

'Sure. Maybe old Dom suspects they're going to dump him. So he sends his girl to the meeting while he's safe and sound somewhere, strumming his old rhythm guitar.'

'That's possible,' Kling said.

'Sure, it's possible,' Meyer said.

'But then, *anything's* possible.'

'That's a very mature observation,' Meyer said.

'Look,' Kling said, 'La Bresca's getting out of the car.'

'Short meeting,' Meyer said. 'Let's hit the girl.'

As La Bresca went up the street in the opposite direction, Meyer and Kling stepped out of the parked Chrysler. The wind almost knocked them off their feet. They ducked their heads against it and began running, not wanting the girl to start the car and take off before they reached her, hoping to prevent a prolonged automobile chase through the city. Up ahead, Meyer heard the Buick's engine spring to life.

'Let's *go*!' he shouted to Kling, and they sprinted the last five yards to the car, Meyer fanning out into the gutter, Kling pulling open the door on the kerb side.

The blonde sitting behind the wheel was wearing slacks and a short grey coat. She turned to look at Kling as he pulled open the door, and Kling was surprised to discover that she wasn't wearing make-up and that her features were rather heavy and gross. As he blinked at her in amazement, he further learned that she was sporting what looked like a three-day-old beard stubble on her chin and on her cheeks.

The door on the driver's side snapped open.

Meyer took one surprised look at the 'girl' behind the wheel and then immediately said, 'Mr Dominick Di Fillippi, I presume?'

Dominick Di Fillippi was very proud of his long blond hair.

In the comparative privacy of the squadroom, he combed it often and explained to the detectives that guys belonging to a group had to have an image, you dig? Like all the guys in his group, they all looked different, you dig? Like the drummer wore these Ben Franklin eyeglasses, and the lead guitar player combed his hair down in bangs over his eyes, and the organist wore red shirts and red socks, you dig, all the guys had a different image. The long blond hair wasn't exactly his own idea, there were lots of guys in other groups who had long hair, which is why he was growing the beard to go with it. His beard was a sort of reddish-blond, he explained, he figured it would look real tough once it grew in, give him his own distinct image, you dig?

'Like what's the beef,' he asked, 'what am I doing inside a police station?'

'You're a musician, huh?' Meyer asked.

'You got it, man.'

'That's what you do for a living, huh?'

'Well, like we only recently formed the group.'

'How recently?'

'Three months.'

'Play any jobs yet?'

'Yeah. Sure.'

'When?'

'Well, we had like auditions.'

'Have you ever actually been *paid* for playing anywhere?'

'Well, no, man, not yet. Not actually. I mean, man, even The Beatles had to start *some place*, you know.'

'Yeah.'

'Like, man, they were playing these crumby little cellar joints in Liverpool, man, they were getting maybe a farthing a night.'

'What the hell do you know about farthings?'

'Like it's a saying.'

'OK, Dom, let's get away from the music business for a little while, OK? Let's talk about *other* kinds of business, OK?'

'Yeah, let's talk about why I'm here, OK?'

'You'd better read him the law,' Kling said.

'Yeah,' Meyer said, and went through the Miranda-Escobedo bit. Di Fillippi listened intently. When Meyer was finished, he nodded his blond locks and said, 'I can get a lawyer if I want one, huh?'

'Yes.'

'I want one,' Di Fillippi said.

'Have you got anyone special in mind, or do you want us to get one for you?'

'I got somebody in mind,' Di Fillippi said.

While the detectives back at the squadroom fuzzily and fussily waited for Di Fillippi's lawyer to arrive, Steve Carella, now ambulatory, decided to go down to the fourth floor to visit Patrolman Genero.

Genero was sitting up in bed, his wounded leg bandaged and rapidly healing. He seemed surprised to see Carella.

'Hey,' he said, 'this is a real honour, I mean it. I'm really grateful to you for coming down here like this.'

'How's it going, Genero?' Carella asked.

'Oh, so-so. It still hurts. I never thought getting shot could hurt. In the movies, you see these guys get shot all the time, and they just fall down, but you never get the impression it hurts.'

'It hurts, all right,' Carella said, and smiled. He sat on the edge of Genero's bed. 'I see you've got a television in here,' he said.

'Yeah, it's the guy's over in the next bed.' Genero's voice fell to a whisper. 'He never watches it. He's pretty sick, I think. He's either sleeping all the time or else moaning. I don't think he's going to make it, I'll tell you the truth.'

'What's wrong with him?'

'I don't know. He just sleeps and moans. The nurses are in here day and night, giving him things, sticking him with needles, it's a regular railroad station, I'm telling you.'

'Well, that's not so bad,' Carella said.

'What do you mean?'

'Nurses coming in and out.'

'Oh, no, that's *great*!' Genero said. 'Some of them are pretty good-looking.'

'How'd this happen?' Carella asked, and nodded towards Genero's leg.

'Oh, you don't know, huh?' Genero said.

'I only heard you were shot.'

'Yeah,' Genero said, and hesitated. 'We were chasing this suspect, you see. So as he went past me, I pulled my revolver to fire a warning shot.' Genero hesitated again. 'That was when I got it.'

'Tough break,' Carella said.

'Well, you got to expect things like that, I suppose. If you expect to make police work your life's work, you got to expect things like that in your work,' Genero said.

'I suppose so.'

'Well, sure, look what happened to you,' Genero said.

'Mmm,' Carella said.

'Of course, you're a detective,' Genero said.

'Mmm,' Carella said.

'Which is sort of understandable.'

'What do you mean?'

'Well, you expect detectives to get in trouble more than ordinary patrolmen, don't you? I mean, the ordinary patrolman, the run-of-the-mill patrolman who doesn't expect to make police work his life's work, well, you don't *expect* him to risk his life trying to apprehend a suspect, do you?'

'Well,' Carella said, and smiled.

'Do you?' Genero persisted.

'Everybody starts out as a patrolman,' Carella said gently.

'Oh, sure. It's just you think of a patrolman as a guy directing traffic or helping kids cross the street or taking information when there's been an accident, things like that, you know? You never figure he's going to risk his life, the run-of-the-mill patrolman, anyway.'

'Lots of patrolmen get killed in the line of duty,' Carella said.

'Oh, sure, I'm sure. I'm just saying you don't *expect* it to happen.'

'To your*self*, you mean.'

'Yeah.'

The room was silent.

'It sure hurts,' Genero said. 'I hope they let me out of here soon, though. I'm anxious to get back to duty.'

'Well, don't rush it,' Carella said.

'When are *you* getting out?'

'Tomorrow, I think.'

'You feel OK?'

'Oh yeah, I feel fine.'

'Broke your ribs, huh?'

'Yeah, three of them.'

'Your nose, too.'

'Yeah.'

'That's rough,' Genero said. 'But, of course, you're a detective.'

'Mmm,' Carella said.

'I was up the squadroom the other day,' Genero said, 'filling in for the guys when they came here to visit you. This was before the shooting. Before I got it.'

'How'd you like that madhouse up there?' Carella said, and smiled.

'Oh, I handled it OK, I guess,' Genero said. 'Of course, there's a lot to learn, but I suppose that comes with actual practice.'

'Oh, sure,' Carella said.

'I had a long talk with Sam Grossman . . .'

'Nice fellow, Sam.'

'. . . yeah, at the lab. We went over those suspect notes together. Nice fellow, Sam,' Genero said.

'Yeah.'

'And then some kid came in with another one of those notes, and I held him there till the guys got back. I guess I handled it OK.'

'I'm sure you did,' Carella said.

'Well, you've got to be conscientious about it if you expect to make it your life's work,' Genero said.

'Oh, sure,' Carella said. He rose, winced slightly as he planted his weight, and then said, 'Well, I just wanted to see how you were getting along.'

'I'm fine, thanks. I appreciate your coming down.'

'Oh, well,' Carella said, and smiled, and started for the door.

'When you get back,' Genero said, 'give my regards, huh?' Carella looked at him curiously. 'To all the guys,' Genero said. 'Cotton, and Hal, and Meyer and Bert. All of us who were on the plant together.'

'Oh, sure.'

'And thanks again for coming up . . .'

'Don't mention it.'

'. . . Steve,' Genero ventured as Carella went out.

Di Fillippi's lawyer was a man named Irving Baum.

He arrived at the squadroom somewhat out of breath and the first thing he asked was whether the detectives had advised his client of his rights. When assured that Di Fillippi had been constitutionally protected, he nodded briefly, took off his brown Homburg and heavy brown overcoat, placed both neatly across Meyer's desk, and then asked the detectives what it was all about. He was a pleasant-looking man, Baum, with white hair and moustache, sympathetic brown eyes, and an encouraging manner of nodding when anyone spoke, short little nods that seemed to be signs of agreement. Meyer quickly told him that it was not the police intention to book Di Fillippi for anything, but merely to solicit information from him. Baum could see no reason why his client should not cooperate to the fullest extent. He nodded to Di Fillippi and then said, 'Go ahead, Dominick, answer their questions.'

'OK, Mr Baum,' Di Fillippi said.

'Can we get your full name and address?' Meyer said.

'Dominick Americo Di Fillippi, 365 North Anderson Street, Riverhead.'

'Occupation.'

'I already told you. I'm a musician.'

'I beg your pardon,' Baum said. 'Were you questioning him *before* I arrived?'

'Steady, counsellor,' Meyer said. 'All we asked him was what he did for a living.'

'Well,' Baum said, and tilted his head to one side as though considering whether there had been a miscarriage of justice. 'Well,' he said, 'go on, please.'

'Age?' Meyer asked.

'Twenty-eight.'

'Single? Married?'

'Single.'

'Who's your nearest living relative?'

'I beg your pardon,' Baum said, 'but if you merely intend to solicit information, why do you need these statistics?'

'Mr Baum,' Willis said, 'you're a lawyer, and you're here with him, so stop worrying. He hasn't said anything that'll send him to jail. Not yet.'

'This is routine, counsellor,' Meyer said. 'I think you're aware of that.'

'All right, all right, go on,' Baum said.

'Nearest living relative?' Meyer repeated.

'My father. Angelo Di Fillippi.'

'What's he do?'

'He's a stonemason.'

'Hard to find good stonemasons today,' Meyer said.

'Yeah.'

'Dom,' Willis said. 'What's your connection with Tony La Bresca?'

'He's a friend of mine.'

'Why'd you meet with him today?'

'Just friendly.'

'It was a very short meeting,' Willis said.

'Yeah, I guess it was.'

'Do you always go all the way downtown just to talk to someone for five minutes?'

'Well, he's a friend of mine.'

'What'd you talk about?'

'Uh music,' Di Fillippi said.

'What about music?'

'Well uh he's got a cousin who's gonna get married soon, so he wanted to know about our group.'

'What'd you tell him?'

'I told him we were available.'

'When's this wedding coming off?'

'The uh sometime in June.'

'When in June?'

'I forget the exact date.'

'Then how do you know you'll be available?'

'Well, we ain't got no jobs for June, so I know we'll be available.'

'Are you the group's business manager?'

'No.'

'Then why'd La Bresca come to you?'

'Because we're friends, and he heard about the group.'

'So that's what you talked about. His cousin's wedding.'

'Yes, that's right.'

'How much did you tell him it would cost?'

'I said uh it uh seventy dollars.'

'How many musicians are there in the group?'

'Five.'

'How much is that a man?' Meyer asked.

'It's uh seventy uh divided by five.'

'Which is how much?'

'That's uh well five into seven is one and carry the two, five into twenty is uh four, so that comes to fourteen dollars a man.'

'But you didn't know that when you asked for the seventy, did you?'

'Yes, sure I knew it.'

'Then why'd you have to do the division just now?'

'Just to check it, that's all.'

'So you told La Bresca you'd be available, and you told him it would cost seventy dollars, and then what?'

'He said he'd ask his cousin, and he got out of the car.'

'That was the extent of your conversation with him?'

'That was the extent of it, yes.'

'Couldn't you have discussed this on the telephone?'

'Sure, I guess so.'

'Then why didn't you?'

'Well, I like to see Tony every now and then, he's a good friend of mine.'

'So you drove all the way downtown to see him.'

'That's right.'

'How much did you lose on that championship fight?'

'Oh, not much.'

'*How* much?'

'Ten bucks or so. How do *you* know about that?'

'Wasn't it more like fifty?'

'Well, maybe, I don't remember. How do you know this?' He turned to Baum. 'How do they know this?' he asked the lawyer.

'How do you know this?' Baum asked.

'Well, counsellor, if it's all right with you,' Meyer said, '*we'll* ask the questions, unless you find something objectionable.'

'No, I think everything's been proper so far, but I *would* like to know where you're going.'

'I think that'll become clear,' Meyer said.

'Well, Detective Meyer, I think I'd like to know right *now* what this is all about, or I shall feel compelled to advise my client to remain silent.'

Meyer took a deep breath. Willis shrugged in resignation.

'We feel your client possesses knowledge of an impending crime,' Meyer said.

'What crime?'

'Well, if you'll permit us to question him . . .'

'No, not until you answer me,' Baum said.

'Mr Baum,' Willis said, 'we can book him for Compounding, Section 570 of the Penal Law, or we can book him for . . .'

'Just a moment, young man,' Baum said. 'Would you mind explaining that?'

'Yes, sir, we have reason to believe that your client has been promised money or other property to conceal a crime. Now that's either a felony or a misdemeanour, sir, depending on what the crime is he's agreed to conceal. I think you know that, sir.'

'And what's this crime he's agreed to conceal?'

'We might also be able to book him for Conspiracy, Section 580, if he's actually *involved* in this planned crime.'

'Do you have definite knowledge that a crime is to take place?' Baum asked.

'We have reasonable knowledge, sir, yes, sir.'

'You realize, do you not, that no agreement amounts to a conspiracy unless some act *beside* such agreement is done to effect the object thereof?'

'Look, Mr Baum,' Meyer said, 'this isn't a court of law, so let's not argue the case right here and now, OK? We're not going to book your client for anything provided he cooperates a little and answers . . .'

'I hope I didn't detect a threat in that statement,' Baum said.

'Oh, for Christ's sake,' Meyer said, 'we know that a man named Anthony La Bresca and another man named Peter Calucci are planning to commit a crime, misdemeanour or felony we don't know which, on March fifteenth. We also have very good reason to believe that your client here knows *exactly* what they're up to and has demanded money from them to keep such knowledge or information from reaching the police. Now, Mr Baum, we don't want to pull in La Bresca and Calucci for conspiracy because (*a*) it wouldn't stick without that "act" you were talking about, and (*b*) we might end up with only a misdemeanour, depending on what they've cooked up. As I'm sure you know, if they've planned the crime of murder, kidnapping, robbery One, selling narcotics, arson, or extortion, and if they've committed some act other than their agreement to pull the job, each of them is guilty of a felony. And as I'm sure you also know, some very big officials in this city were recently murdered, and the possibility exists that La Bresca and Calucci are somehow involved and that this crime they've planned may have to do with extortion or murder, or both, which would automatically make the conspiracy a felony. As you can see, therefore, we're not after your client *per se*, we're merely trying to prevent a crime. So can we cut all the legal bullshit and get a little cooperation from you, and especially from him?'

'It seems to me he's been cooperating splendidly,' Baum said.

'It seems to me he's been lying splendidly,' Meyer said.

'Considering what's involved here . . .' Baum started.

'Mr Baum, could we please . . .?'

'. . . I think you had better charge Mr Di Fillippi with whatever it is you have in mind. We'll let the courts settle the matter of his guilt or innocence.'

'While two hoods pull off their job, right?'

'I'm not interested in the entrapment of two hoodlums,' Baum said. 'I'm advising my client to say nothing further, in accordance with the rights granted to him under . . .'

'Thanks a lot, Mr Baum.'

'Are you going to book him, or not?'

'We're going to book him' Meyer said.

'For what?'

'Compounding a crime, Section 570 of the Penal Law.'

'Very well, I suggest you do that with reasonable dispatch,' Baum said. 'It seems to me he's been held in custody an extremely long time as it is. I know you're aware . . .'

'Mr Baum, we're aware of it inside out and backwards. Take him down, Hal. Charge him as specified.'

'Hey, wait a minute,' Di Fillippi said.

'I suggest that you go with them,' Baum said. 'Don't worry about a thing. Before you're even arraigned, I'll have contacted a bail bondsman.

You'll be back on the street . . .'

'Hey, wait one goddamn minute,' Di Fillippi said. 'What if those two guys go ahead with . . .'

'Dominick, I advise you to remain silent.'

'Yeah? What can I get for this "compounding", whatever the hell it is?'

'Depends on what they do,' Meyer said.

'Dominick . . .'

'If they commit a crime punishable by death or by life imprisonment, you can get five years. If they commit . . .'

'What about a hold-up?' Di Fillippi asked.

'Dominick, as your attorney, I must again strongly advise you . . .'

'What about a hold-up?' Di Fillippi said again.

'Is that what they've planned?' Meyer said.

'You didn't answer me.'

'If they commit a robbery, and you take money from them to conceal the crime, you can get three years in prison.'

'Mmm,' Di Fillippi said.

'Will you answer some questions for us?'

'Will you let me go if I do?'

'Dominick, you don't have to . . .'

'Do *you* want to go to prison for three years?' Di Fillippi asked.

'They have no case, they're . . .'

'No? Then how do they know the job's coming off on March fifteenth? Where'd they get *that*? Some little birdie whisper it in their ear?'

'We've levelled with you, Dominick,' Willis said, 'and believe me, we wouldn't have brought any of this out in the open if we didn't have plenty to go on. Now you can either help us or we can book you and take you down for arraignment and you'll have an arrest record following you for the rest of your life. What do you want to do?'

'That's coercion!' Baum shouted.

'It may be coercion, but it's also fact,' Willis said.

'I'll tell you everything I know,' Di Fillippi said.

He knew a lot, and he told it all.

He told them that the hold-up was set for eight o'clock on Friday night, and that the victim was to be the owner of a tailor shop on Culver Avenue. The reason the hit had been scheduled for that particular night and time was that the tailor, a man named John Mario Vicenzo, usually packed up his week's earnings then and took them home with him in a small metal box, which box his wife Laura carried to the Fiduciary Trust early Saturday morning. The Fiduciary Trust, as it happened, was the only bank in the neighbourhood that was open till noon on Saturday, bank employees being among those who did not like to work on weekends.

John Mario Vicenzo (or John the Tailor as he was known to the people along Culver Avenue) was a man in his early seventies, an easy mark. The take would be enormous, Di Fillippi explained, with more than enough for everyone concerned even if split three ways. The plan was to go into the shop at ten minutes to eight, just before John the Tailor drew the blinds on the plate glass window fronting the street. La Bresca was to perform that task instead, and then he was to lock the front door while Calucci forced John the Tailor at gun point into the back room, where he would tie him and leave him bound and helpless on the floor near the pressing machine. They would then empty the cash register of the money that had been piling up there all week long, and take off. John the Tailor would be left dead or alive depending on how cooperative he was.

Di Fillippi explained that he'd overheard all this one night in the piazzeria on South Third, La Bresca and Calucci sitting in a booth behind him and not realizing they were whispering a little too loud. At first he'd been annoyed by the idea of two Italians knocking over a place owned by another Italian, but then he figured What the hell, it was none of his business; the one thing he'd never done in his life was rat on anybody. But that was before the fight, and the bet that had left him broke. Desperate for a little cash, he remembered what he'd heard them discussing and figured he'd try to cut himself in. He didn't think there'd be too much static from them because the take, after all, was a huge one, and he figured they'd be willing to share it.

'Just how much money is involved here?' Willis asked.

'Oh, man,' Di Fillippi said, rolling his eyes, 'there's at least four hundred bucks involved here, maybe even more.'

CHAPTER 11

A lot of things happened on Wednesday.

It was discovered on Wednesday, for example, that somebody had stolen the following items from the squadroom:

A typewriter.
Six ballpoint pens.
An electric fan.
A thermos jug.
A can of pipe tobacco, and
Four bars of soap.

Nobody could figure out who had done it.

Not even Carella, who had been released from the hospital and who was very delicately walking around with his ribs taped, could figure out who had done it. Some of the squadroom wits suggested that Carella, being an invalid and all, should be assigned to the Great Squadroom Mystery, but Lieutenant Byrnes decided it would be better to assign him to the tailor shop stakeout instead, together with Hal Willis. At twelve noon that Wednesday, the pair headed crosstown to John the Tailor's shop.

But before then a lot of other things happened, it was certainly a busy Wednesday.

At 8 am, for example, a patrolman walking his beat called in to report that he had found a stiff in a doorway and that it looked to him as if the guy had been burned to death. Which meant that the two fire bugs had struck again sometime during the night, and that something was going to have to be done about them pretty soon before they doused every bum in the city with petrol. Kling, who took the call, advised the patrolman to stay with the body until he could get a meat wagon over, and the patrolman complained that the doorway and the entire street stank to high heaven and Kling told him that was tough, he should take the complaint to Captain Frick.

At 9.15 am, Sadie the Nut came up to tell Willis about the rapist who had tried to steal her virginity the night before. Sadie the Nut was seventy-eight years old, a wrinkled toothless crone who had been protecting her virginity for close to fourscore years now, and who unfailingly reported to the squadroom every Wednesday morning, either in person or by phone, that a man had broken into her tenement flat the night before and tried to tear off her nightgown and rape her. The first time she'd reported this crime some four years back, the police had believed her, figuring they had another Boston Strangler on their hands, only this time right on their own back yard. They immediately initiated an investigation, going as far as to plant Detective Andy Parker in the old lady's apartment. But the following Wednesday morning, Sadie came to the squadroom again to report a second rape attempt – even though Parker had spent an uneventful Tuesday night alert and awake in her kitchen. The squadroom comedians speculated that perhaps Parker himself was the rape artist, a premise Parker found somewhat less than amusing. They all realized by then, of course, that Sadie was a nut, and that they could expect frequent visits or calls from her. They did not realize that the visits or calls would come like clockwork every Wednesday morning, nor that Sadie's fantasy was as fixed and as unvaried as the squadroom itself. Her rapist was always a tall swarthy man who somewhat resembled Rudolph Valentino. He was always wearing a black cape over a tuxedo, white dress shirt, black bow tie, black satin dancing slippers. His pants had buttons on the fly. Five buttons. He always unbuttoned his fly slowly and teasingly, warning Sadie not to scream, he was not going to hurt her, he was (in Sadie's own words) 'only going to rapage her'. Sadie invariably waited until he had unbuttoned each of the five buttons and taken out his 'thing' before she screamed. The rapist would then flee from the apartment, leaping on to the fire escape like Douglas Fairbanks, and swinging down into the back yard.

Her story this Wednesday was the same story she had been telling every Wednesday for the past four years. Willis took down the information and promised they would do everything in their power to bring this insane womanizer to justice. Sadie the Nut left the squadroom pleased and excited, doubtless anticipating next week's nocturnal visit.

At a quarter to ten that morning, a woman came in to report that her husband was missing. The woman was perhaps thirty-five years old, an attractive brunette wearing a green overcoat that matched her Irish eyes. Her face was spanking pink from the cold outside, and she exuded health and vitality even though she seemed quite upset by her husband's disappearance. Upon questioning her, though, Meyer learned that the missing man wasn't her husband at all, he was really the husband of her very best friend who lived in the apartment next door to her on Ainsley Avenue. And upon further questioning, the green-eyed lady explained to Meyer that she and her very best friend's husband had been having 'a relationship' (as she put it) for three years and four months, with never a harsh word between them, they were that fond of each other. But last night, when the green-eyed lady's best friend went to play Bingo at the church, the green-eyed lady and the husband had had a violent argument because he had wanted to 'do it' (as she again put it) right there in his own apartment on the living-room couch with his four children asleep in the other room, and she had refused, feeling it would not be decent, and he had put on his hat and coat and gone out into the cold. He had not yet returned, and whereas the green-eyed lady's best friend figured he was out having himself a toot, the husband apparently being something of a drinking man, the green-eyed lady missed him sorely and truly believed he had vanished just to spite her, had she known he would do something like that she certainly would have let him have his way, you know how men are.

Yes, Meyer said.

So whereas the wife felt it would not be necessary to report him missing and thereby drag policemen into the situation, the green-eyed lady feared he might do something desperate, having been denied her favours, and was therefore asking the law's assistance in locating him and returning him to the bosom of his family and loved ones, you know how men are.

Yes, Meyer said again.

So he took down the information, wondering when it was that he'd last attempted to lay Sarah on the living-room couch with his own children asleep in their respective rooms, and realized that he had *never* tried to lay Sarah on the living-room couch. He decided that he would try to do it tonight when he got home, and then he assured the green-eyed lady that they would do everything in their power to locate her best friend's husband, but that probably there was nothing to worry about, he had probably gone to spend the night with a friend.

Yes, that's *just* what I'm worried about, the green-eyed lady said.

Oh, Meyer said.

When the green-eyed lady left, Meyer filed the information away for future use, not wanting to bug the Bureau of Missing Persons prematurely. He was beginning to type up a report on a burglary when Detective Andy Parker came into the squadroom with Lewis the Pickpocket. Parker was laughing uncontrollably, but Lewis did not seem too terribly amused. He was a tall slender man with a bluish cast to his jowls, small sharp penetrating blue eyes, thinning sandy-coloured hair. He was wearing a beige trench coat and brown leather gloves, and he carried an umbrella in the crook of his arm and scowled at everyone in the squadroom as Parker continued laughing uproariously.

'Look who I got!' Parker said, and burst into a choking gasping fit.

'What's so special?' Meyer said. 'Hello, Lewis, how's business?'

Lewis scowled at Meyer. Meyer shrugged.

'Best pickpocket in the precinct!' Parker howled. 'Guess what happened?'

'What happened?' Carella asked.

'I'm standing at the counter in Jerry's, you know? The luncheonette?'

'Yeah?'

'Yeah, with my back to the door, you know? So guess what?'

'What?'

'I feel somebody's hand in my pocket, fishing around for my wallet. So I grab the hand by the wrist, and I whip around with my gun in my other hand, and guess who it is?'

'Who is it?'

'It's Lewis!' Parker said, and began laughing again. 'The best pickpocket in the precinct, he chooses a *detective* for a mark!'

'I made a mistake,' Lewis said, and scowled.

'Oh, man, you made a *big* mistake!' Parker bellowed.

'You had your back to me,' Lewis said.

'Lewis, my friend, you are going to prison,' Parker said gleefully, and then said, 'Come on down, we're going to book you before you try to pick Meyer's pocket there.'

'I don't think it's funny,' Lewis said, and followed Parker out of the squadroom, still scowling.

'*I* think it's pretty funny,' Meyer said.

A man appeared at the slatted rail divider just then, and asked in hesitant English whether any of the policemen spoke Italian. Carella said that he did, and invited the man to sit at his desk. The man thanked him in Italian and took off his hat, and perched it on his knees when he sat, and then began telling Carella his story. It seemed that somebody was putting garbage in his car.

'*Rifiuti?*' Carella asked.

'*Si, rifiuti*,' the man said.

For the past week now, the man went on, someone had been opening his car at night and dumping garbage all over the front seat. All sorts of garbage. Empty tin cans and dinner leftovers and apple cores and coffee grounds, everything. All over the front seat of the car.

'*Perchè non lo chiude a chiave?*' Carella asked.

Well, the man explained, he *did* lock his car every night, but it didn't do any good. Because the way the garbage was left in it the first time was that *quello porco* broke the side vent and opened the door that way in order to do his dirty work. So it didn't matter if he continued to lock the car, the befouler continued to open the door by sticking his hand in through the broken flap window, and then he dumped all his garbage on the front seat, the car was beginning to stink very badly.

Well, Carella said, do you know of anyone who might want to put garbage on your front seat?

No, I do not know of anyone who would do such a filthy thing, the man said.

Is there anyone who has a grudge against you? Carella asked.

No, I am loved and respected everywhere in the world, the man said.

Well, Carella said, we'll send a man over to check it out.

'*Per piacere*,' the man said, and put on his hat, and shook hands with Carella, and left the squadroom.

The time was 10.33 am.

At 10.35 am, Meyer called Raoul Chabrier down at the district attorney's office, spent a delightful three minutes chatting with Bernice, and was finally put through to Chabrier himself.

'Hello, Rollie,' Meyer said, 'what'd you find out?'

'About what?' Chabrier said.

'About the book I called to . . .'

'Oh.'

'You forgot,' Meyer said flatly.

'Listen,' Chabrier said, 'have *you* ever tried handling two cases at the same time?'

'Never in my life,' Meyer said.

'Well, it isn't easy, believe me. I'm reading law on one of them and trying to get a brief ready on the other. You expect me to worry about some goddamn novel at the same time?'

'Well . . .' Meyer said.

'I know, I know, I know,' Chabrier said, 'I promised.'

'Well . . .'

'I'll get to it. I promise you again, Meyer. I'm a man who never breaks his word. Never. I promised you, and now I'm promising you again. What was the title of the book?'

'*Meyer Meyer*,' Meyer said.

'Of course, *Meyer Meyer*, I'll look into it immediately. I'll get back to you, I promise. Bernice,' he shouted, 'make a note to get back to Meyer!'

'When?' Meyer said.

That was at 10.39.

At five minutes to eleven, a tall blond man wearing a hearing aid and carrying a cardboard carton walked into the Hale Street Post Office downtown. He went directly to the counter, hefted the carton on to it, and shoved it across to the mail clerk. There were a hundred sealed and stamped envelopes in the carton.

'These all going to the city?' the clerk asked.

'Yes,' the deaf man replied.

'First class?'

'Yes.'

'All got stamps?'

'Every one of them'

'Right,' the clerk said, and turned the carton over, dumping the envelopes on to the long table behind him. The deaf man waited. At 11 am, the mail clerk began running the envelopes through the cancellation machine.

The deaf man went back to the apartment, where Rochelle met him at the door.

'Did you mail off your crap?' she asked.

'I mailed it,' the deaf man said, and grinned.

John the Tailor wasn't having any of it.

'I no wanna cops in my shop,' he said flatly and unequivocally and in somewhat fractured English.

Carella patiently explained, in English, that the police had definite knowledge of a planned hold-up to take place on Friday night at eight o'clock but that it was the lieutenant's idea to plant two men in the rear of the shop starting tonight in case the thieves changed their minds and decided to strike earlier. He assured John the Tailor that they would unobtrusively take up positions behind the hanging curtain that divided the front of the shop from the rear, out of his way, quiet as mice, and would move into action only if and when the thieves struck.

'*Lei è pazzo!*' John the Tailor said in Italian, meaning he thought Carella was crazy. Whereupon Carella switched to speaking Italian, which he had learned as a boy and which he didn't get much chance to practise these days except when he was dealing with people like the man who had come in to complain about the garbage in his car, or people like John the Tailor, who was suddenly very impressed with the fact that Carella, like himself, was Italian.

John the Tailor had once written a letter to a very popular television show, complaining that too many of the Italians on that show were crooks. He had seventy-four people in his immediate family, all of them living here in the United States, in this city, for most of their lives, and none of them were criminals, all of them were honest, hard-working people. So why should the television make it seem that all Italians were thieves? He had received a letter written by some programming assistant, explaining that not all the criminals on the show were Italians, some of them were Jews and Irish, too. This had not mollified John the Tailor, since he was quite intelligent and capable of understanding the basic difference between the two statements *Not all Italians are criminals* and *Not all criminals are Italians*. So it was very pleasant to have an Italian cop in his shop, even if it meant having to put up with strangers in the back behind the curtain. John the Tailor did not like strangers, even if they were Italian cops. Besides, the other stranger, the short one, definitely was *not* Italian, God knew what *he* was!

The tailor shop did a very thriving business, though Carella doubted it brought in anything near four hundred dollars a week, which was apparently La Bresca's and Calucci's estimate of the take. He wondered why either of the two men would be willing to risk a minimum of ten and a maximum of thirty years in prison, the penalty for first-degree robbery, when all they could hope to gain for their efforts was four hundred dollars. Even granting them the minimum sentence, and assuming they'd be out on parole in three-and-a-half, that came to about a hundred and fifteen dollars a year, meagre wages for *any* occupation.

He would never understand the criminal mind.

He could not, for example, understand the deaf man at all.

There seemed to be something absolutely lunatic about the enormous risk he had taken, a gamble pitting fifty thousand dollars against possible life imprisonment. Now surely a man of his intelligence and capabilities must have known that the city wasn't going to reach into its treasury and plunk down fifty thousand dollars solely because someone threatened murder. The odds against such a payoff were staggering, and any shrewd manipulator of odds would have realized this. The deaf man, then, had not *expected* to be paid, he had *wanted* to kill the deputy mayor, as he had earlier killed the parks commissioner. But why? Whatever else the deaf man happened to be, Carella did not figure him for a thrill killer. No, he was a hardheaded businessman taking a calculated risk. And businessmen don't take risks unless there's at least some hope of a payoff. The deaf man had asked for five grand at first, and been refused, and committed murder. He had next asked for fifty grand, knowing full well he'd be refused again, and had again committed murder. He had then advised the newspapers of his unsuccessful extortion attempts and had since remained silent.

So where was the payoff?

It was coming, baby, of that Carella was sure.

In the meantime, he sat in the back of John the Tailor's shop and wondered how much a good pressing-machine operator earned.

CHAPTER 12

Mr. Carl Wahler
1121 Marshall Avenue
Isola

Dear Mr. Wahler:

If you treat this letter as a joke, you will die.

These are the facts. Read them carefully. They can save your life.
1) Parks Commissioner Cowper ignored a warning and was killed.
2) Deputy Mayor Scanlon ignored a warning and was killed.
3) JMV is next. He will be killed this Friday night.

What does all this have to do with you?

1) This is your warning. It is your only warning. There will be no further warnings. Remember that.

2) You are to withdraw five thousand dollars in small, unmarked bills from your account.
3) You will be contacted by telephone sometime within the next week. The man you speak to will tell you how and when and where the money is to be delivered.
4) If you fail to meet this demand, you too will be killed. Without warning.

Do not entertain false hopes!

The police could not save Cowper or Scanlon, although sufficiently forewarned. They will not be able to save JMV, either. What chance will you have unless you pay? What chance will you have when we strike without warning?

Get the money. You will hear from us again. Soon.

The letters were delivered to a hundred homes on Thursday. The deaf man was very cheerful that morning. He went whistling about his apartment, contemplating his scheme again and again, savouring its more refined aspects, relishing the thought that one hundred very wealthy individuals would suddenly be struck with panic come Saturday morning.

By five o'clock tonight, he could reasonably assume that most of the men receiving his letter would have read it and formed at least some tentative opinion about it. He fully expected some of them to glance cursorily at it, crumple it into a ball, and immediately throw it into the garbage. He also expected a handful, the paranoid fringe, to call the police at once, or perhaps even visit their local precinct, letter in hand, indignantly demanding protection. *That* part of his plan was particularly beautiful, he felt. The mayor was being warned, yes, but oh so indirectly. He would learn about the threat on his life only because some frightened citizens would notify the police.

And tomorrow night, forewarned, the mayor would none the less die.

Six months ago when the deaf man had begun the preliminary work on his scheme, several rather interesting pieces of information had come to light. To begin with, he had learned that anyone desiring to know the exact location of the city's underground water pipes need only apply to the Department of Water Supply in Room 1720 of the Municipal Building, where the maps were available for public scrutiny. Similarly, maps of the city's underground sewer system were obtainable at the Department of Public Works in the main office of that same building. The deaf man, unfortunately, was not interested in either water pipes or sewers. He was interested in electricity. And he quickly learned that detailed maps of the underground power lines were *not*, for obvious reasons, open to the public for inspection. Those maps were kept in the Maps and Records Bureau of the Metropolitan Light & Power Company, worked on by an office staffed largely by draughtsmen. Ahmad had been one of those draughtsmen.

The first map he delivered to the deaf man was titled '60 Cycle Network Area Designations and Boundaries Lower Isola', and it showed the locations of all the area substations in that section of the city. The area that specifically interested the deaf man was the one labelled 'Cameron Flats'. The mayor's house was on the corner of South Meridian and Vanderhof, in Cameron Flats. The substation serving South Meridian and Vanderhof was marked with a cross in a circle, and was designated 'No. 3 South Meridian'. Into this substation ran high-voltage supply cables ('They're called feeders,' Ahmad said) from a switching station elsewhere on the transmission system. It would be necessary to destroy those supply cables if the mayor's house was to be thrown into darkness on the night of his murder.

The second map Ahmad delivered was titled 'System Ties' and was a detailed enlargement of the feeder systems supplying any given substation. The substation on the first map had been labelled 'No. 3 South Meridian'. By locating this on the more detailed map the deaf man was able to identify the number designation of the feeder: 65CA3. Which brought him to the third pilfered map, simply and modestly titled '65CA3', and subtitled 'Location South Meridian Substation'. This was a rather long, narrow diagram of the route the feeder travelled below the city's streets, with numbers indicating the manholes that provided access to the cables. 65CA3 passed through eleven manholes on its meandering underground travels from the switching station to the substation. The deaf man chose a manhole approximately a half-mile from the mayor's house and wrote down its number: M3860–120'SSC-CENT.

The last map, the crucial one, was titled 'Composite Feeder Plate' and it pinpointed the manhole exactly. M3860 was located on Faxon Drive, a hundred and twenty feet south of the southern curb of Harris, in the centre of the street – hence the 120'SSC-CENT. The high-voltage cables passing through that concrete manhole were five feet below the surface of the street protected by a three-hundred pound manhole cover.

Tomorrow night, Ahmad, Buck, and the deaf man would lift that cover, and one of Buck's bombs would effectively take care of the cables.

And then . . .

Ahhh, then . . .

The really beautiful part was still ahead, and the deaf man smiled as he contemplated it.

He could visualize the mayor's house at 10 pm tomorrow night, surrounded by policemen and detectives on special assignment, all there to protect the honourable JMV from harm. He could see himself driving a black sedan directly to the curb in front of the darkened brick structure, a police flashlight picking out the gold lettering on the front door, Metropolitan Light & Power Company (pressure-sensitive letters expertly applied by Ahmad to both front doors of the car, cost eight cents per letter at Studio Art Supply, total expenditure $4.80). He could see the car doors opening. Three men step out of it. Two of them are wearing workmen's overalls (Sears, Roebuck, $6.95 a pair). The third is wearing the uniform of a police sergeant, complete with a citation ribbon pinned over the shield on the left breast (Theatrical Arts Rental, $10.00 per day, plus a $75.00 deposit) and the yellow sleeve patch of the Police Department's Emergency Service ($1.25 at the Civic Equipment Company, across the street from Headquarters).

'Who's there?' the policeman on duty asks. His flashlight scans the trio. Buck, in the sergeant's uniform, steps forward.

'It's all right,' Buck says. 'I'm Sergeant Pierce, Emergency Service. These men are from the electric company. They're trying to locate that power break.'

'OK, Sergeant,' the cop answers.

'Everything quiet in there?' Buck asks.

'So far, Sarge.'

'Better check out their equipment,' Buck says. 'I don't want any static on this later.'

'Good idea,' the cop says. He swings his flashlight around. Ahmad opens the tool box. There is nothing in it but electrician's tools: a test light, a six foot rule, a brace, four screwdrivers, a Stillson wrench, a compass saw, a hacksaw, a hammer, a fuse puller, wire skinners, wire cutters, gas pliers, Allen wrenches, friction tape, rubber tape . . . 'OK,' the cop says, and turns to the deaf man. 'What's that you're carrying?'

'A volt-ohm meter,' the deaf man answers.

'Want to open it for me?'

'Sure,' the deaf man says.

The testing equipment is nothing more than a black leather case perhaps twelve inches long by eight inches wide by five inches deep. When the deaf man unclasps and raises the lid, the flashlight illuminates an instrument panel set into the lower half of the case, level with the rim. Two large dials dominate the panel, one marked 'Volt-Ohm Meter', the other marked 'Ammeter'. There are three knobs spaced below the dials. Factory-stamped lettering indicates their use: the two end knobs are marked 'Adjuster', and the one in the middle is marked 'Function'. Running vertically down the left-hand side of the panel are a series of jacks respectively marked 600V, 300V, 150V, 75V, 30V, and Common. Flanking the dials on the right-hand side of the plate there are similar jacks marked 60 Amps, 30 Amps, 15 Amps, 7.5 Amps, 3 Amps, and Common. Another jack and a small bulb are below the second adjuster knob, and they are collectively marked 'Leakage Indicator'. In bold factory-stamped lettering across the length of the tester are the words 'Industrial Analyser'.

'OK,' the cop says, 'you can close it.'

The deaf man snaps the lid of the case shut, fastens the clasp again.

'I'll take them inside,' Buck says.

'Right, Sarge,' the cop says, and the trio go up the walk to the house, where they are stopped by a detective at the front door.

'Sergeant Pierce, Emergency Service,' Buck says. 'These men are from the electric company, here to check that power failure.'

'Right,' the detective says.

'I'll stick with them,' Buck says, 'but I don't want no other responsibility.'

'What do you mean?'

'Well, if the mayor trips and breaks his ankle while they're on the premises, I don't want no static from my captain.'

'We'll keep the mayor far away from you,' the detective says, and smiles.

'OK, where you guys want to start?' Buck asks. 'The basement?'

They go into the house. There are battery-powered lights set up, but for the most part the house is dim, the figures moving through it are uncertainly defined. The three men start in the basement, going through the motions of checking out circuits. They go through every room of the house, never once seeing the mayor in the course of their inspection. In the master bedroom, the deaf man shoves the testing equipment under the huge double bed, ostensibly searching for a leak at the electrical outlet. When he walks out of the room, he is no longer carrying anything. The 'Industrial Analyser' is on the floor under the mayor's bed.

That analyser, with its factory-sleek assortment of dials, knobs, jacks, and electrical terminology is real – but none the less fake. There *is* no testing equipment behind those meters, the interior of the box has been stripped bare. Hidden below the instrument panel, set to go off at 2 am, there is only another of Buck's bombs.

Tomorrow night, the mayor would die.

And on Saturday morning, the uncommitted would commit. They would open their newspapers and read the headlines, and they would know the letter was for real, no opportunist could have accurately predicted the murder without having engineered it and executed it himself. They would take the letter from where they had casually put it, and they would read it once again, and they would fully comprehend its menace now, fully realize the absolute terror inherent in its words. When one was faced with the promise of unexpected death, was five thousand dollars really so much to invest? Not a man on that list of one hundred earned less than $200,000 a year. They had all been carefully researched, the original list of four hundred and twenty names being cut and revised and narrowed down to only those who seemed the most likely victims, those to whom losing five thousand dollars at a Las Vegas crap table meant nothing, those who were known to have invested in speculative stocks or incoming Broadway plays – those, in short, who would be willing to gamble five thousand dollars in hope of salvation.

They will pay us, the deaf man thought.

Oh, not all of them, certainly not all of them. But enough of them. Perhaps a few more murders are in order, perhaps some of those sleek fat cats on the list will have to be eliminated before the rest are convinced, but they *will* be convinced, and they *will* pay.

After the murder tomorrow night, after that, when they know we're not fooling, they will pay.

The deaf man suddenly smiled.

There should be a very large crowd around City Hall starting perhaps right this minute, he thought.

It will be an interesting weekend.

'You hit the nail right on the head,' Lieutenant Byrnes said to Steve Carella. 'He's going for the mayor next.'

'He'll never get away with it,' Hawes said.

'He'd better *not* get away with it,' Byrnes said. 'If he succeeds in knocking off the mayor, he'll be picking up cash like its growing in the park. How many of these letters do you suppose he's mailed?'

'Well, let's try to figure it,' Carella said. 'First he warned the parks commissioner and demanded five thousand dollars. Next the deputy mayor, and a demand for fifty thousand. Now he tells us he'll kill the mayor this Friday night. So if the escalation carries through, he should be bucking for ten times fifty thousand, which is five hundred thousand. If we divide that by –'

'Forget it,' Byrnes said.

'I'm only trying to figure out the mathematics.'

'What's mathematics got to do with JMV getting killed?'

'I don't know,' Carella said, and shrugged. 'But it seems to me if we can figure out the progression, we can also figure out what's *wrong* with the progression.'

Byrnes stared at him.

'I'm just trying to say it just isn't enough for this guy to knock off the mayor,' Carella said.

'It isn't, huh? Knocking off the mayor seems like *more* than enough to me.'

'Yeah, but not for somebody like the deaf man. He's too proud of his own cleverness.' Carella looked at the letter again. 'Who's this man Carl Wahler?' he asked.

'A dress manufacturer, lives downtown in Stewart City, 17th Precinct. He brought the letter in there this morning. Captain Bundy thought we'd want to see it. Because of our involvement with the previous murders.'

'It seems to fit right in with the pattern, doesn't it?' Hawes said. 'He announced the other murders, too.'

'Yes, but there's something missing,' Carella said.

'What?'

'The personal angle. He started this in the 87th, a little vendetta for fouling him up years ago, when he was planting bombs all over the goddamn city to divert attention from his bank job. So why's he taking it *out* of the 87th all at once? If he knocks off the mayor, nobody looks foolish but the special police assigned to his protection. *We're* off the hook, home free. And that's what I can't understand. That's what's wrong with the pattern.'

'The pattern seems pretty clear to me,' Byrnes said. 'If he can get to JMV after advertising it, what chance will anybody have *without* warning? Look at how many times he says that in his letter. Without warning, without warning.'

'It still bothers me,' Carella said.

'It shouldn't,' Byrnes said. 'He's spelled it out in black and white. The man's a goddamn *fiend*.'

The instant reaction of both Hawes and Carella was to laugh. You don't as a general rule hear cops referring to criminals as 'fiends', even when they're child molesters and mass murderers. That's the sort of language reserved to judges or politicians. Nor did Byrnes usually express himself in such colourful expletives. But whereas both men felt a definite impulse to laugh out loud, one look at Byrne's face stifled any such urge. The lieutenant was at his wit's end. He suddenly looked very old and very tired. He sighed heavily, and said, 'How do we stop him, guys?' and he sounded for all the world like a freshman quarterback up against a varsity team with a three-hundred-pound line.

'We pray,' Carella said.

Although James Martin Vale, the mayor himself, was a devout Episcopalian, he decided that afternoon that he'd best do a lot more than pray if his family was to stay together.

So he called a top-level meeting in his office at City Hall (a meeting to which Lieutenant Byrnes was not invited), and it was decided that every precaution would be taken starting right then to keep 'the deaf man' (as the men of the 87th insisted on calling him) from carrying out his threat. JMV was a man with a charming manner and a ready wit, and he managed to convince everyone in the office that he was more concerned about the people of his city than he was about his own safety. 'We've got to save my life only so that this man won't milk hard-earned dollars from the people of this great city,' he said. 'If he gets away with this, they'll allow themselves to be extorted. That's why I want protection.'

'Your Honour,' the district attorney said, 'if I may suggest, I think we should extend protection beyond the Friday night deadline. I think if this man succeeds in killing you any time in the near future, the people of this city'll think he's made good his threat.'

'Yes, I think you're right,' JMV said.

'Your Honour,' the city comptroller said, 'I'd like to suggest that you cancel all personal appearances at least through April.'

'Well, I don't think I should go into complete seclusion, do you?' JMV asked, mindful of the fact that this was an election year.

'Or at least *curtail* your personal appearances,' the comptroller said, remembering that indeed this was an election year, and remembering, too, that he was on the same ticket as His Honour the Mayor JMV.

'What do you think, Slim?' JMV asked the police commissioner.

The police commissioner, a man who was six feet four inches tall and weighed two hundred and twenty-five pounds, shifted his buttocks in the padded leather chair opposite His Honour's desk, and said, 'I'll cover you with cops like fleas,' a not particularly delicate simile, but one which made its point none the less.

'You can count on however many men you need from my squad,' the district attorney said, mindful that two of his most trusted detectives had been blown to that big Police Academy in the sky only days before.

'I would like to suggest,' the city's medical examiner said, 'that you undergo a complete physical examination as soon as this meeting is concluded.'

'Why?' JMV asked.

'Because the possibility exists, Your Honour, that you've already been poisoned.'

'Well,' JMV said, 'that sounds a bit far-fetched.'

'Your Honour,' the medical examiner said, 'an accumulation of small doses of poison administered over a period of time can result in death. Since we're dealing with a man who has obviously evolved a long-term plan . . .'

'Yes, of course,' JMV said, 'I'll submit to examination as soon as you wish. Maybe you can clear up my cold at the same time,' he said charmingly, and grinned charmingly.

'Your Honour,' the president of the city council said, 'I suggest we have each of the city's vehicles inspected thoroughly and at once. I am remembering, sir, the bomb placed in . . .'

'Yes, we'll have that done at once,' the district attorney said hastily.

'Your Honour,' the mayor's press secretary said, 'I'd like to suggest that we suppress all news announcements concerning your whereabouts, your speaking engagements, and so on, until this thing blows over.'

'Yes, that's a good idea,' JMV said, 'but of course I won't be venturing too far from home in any case, will I, Stan?' he said, and grinned charmingly at the district attorney.

'No, sir, I'd advise your becoming a homebody for the next month or so,' the district attorney said.

'Of course, there may be a bomb in this office right this minute,' the police commissioner said tactlessly, causing everyone to fall suddenly silent. Into the silence came the loud ticking of the wall clock, which was a little unnerving.

'Well,' JMV said charmingly, 'perhaps we ought to have the premises searched, as well as my home. If we're to do this right, we'll have to take every precaution.'

'Yes, sir,' the district attorney said.

'And, of course, we'll have to do everything in our power meanwhile to locate this man, this deaf man.'

'Yes, sir, we're doing everything in our power right now,' the police commissioner said.

'Which is what?' JMV asked, charmingly.

'He's got to make a mistake,' the police commissioner said.

'And if he doesn't?'

'He's *got* to.'

'But in the meantime,' JMV asked, 'do you have any leads?'

'Police work,' the commissioner said, 'is a combination of many seemingly unconnected facets that suddenly jell,' and frowned, suspecting that his metaphor hadn't quite come off. 'There are a great many accidents involved in police work, and we consider these accidents a definite contributing factor in the apprehension of criminals. We will, for example, arrest a man on a burglary charge, oh, six or seven months from now, and discover in questioning him that he committed a homicide during the commission of another crime, oh, four or five months ago.'

'Well,' JMV said charmingly, 'I hope we're not going to have to wait six or seven months for our man to make a mistake while committing another crime.'

'I didn't mean to sound so pessimistic,' the commissioner said. 'I was merely trying to explain, Your Honour, that a lot of police work dovetails past and present and future. I have every confidence that we'll apprehend this man within a reasonable length of time.'

'Hopefully before he kills me,' JMV said, and grinned charmingly. 'Well,' he said, 'if there's nothing further to discuss, perhaps we can set all these precautionary measures into motion. I'll be happy to see your doctor, Herb, whenever you want to send him in.'

'Meanwhile, I'll get in touch with the Bomb Squad,' the police commissioner said, rising.

'Yes, that's probably the first thing to do,' JMV said, rising. 'Gentlemen, thank you for your time and your valuable suggestions. I'm sure everything will work out fine.'

'You'll have men here in the next two or three minutes,' the district attorney promised.

'Thank you, Stan,' the mayor said, 'I certainly appreciate your concern.'

The men filed out of the mayor's office, each of them assuring him once again that he would be amply protected. The mayor thanked each of them charmingly and individually, and then sat in the big padded leather chair behind his desk and stared at the ticking wall clock.

Outside, it was beginning to snow.

The snow was very light at first.

It drifted from the sky lazily and uncertainly, dusting the streets and sidewalks with a thin fluffy powder. By 8 pm that night, when Patrolman Richard Genero was discharged from Buena Vista Hospital, the snow was beginning to fall a bit more heavily, but it presented no major traffic problems as yet, especially if – like Genero's father – one had snow tyres on one's automobile. Their ride home was noisy but uneventful. Genero's mother kept urging her son to talk to the captain, and Genero's father kept telling her to shut up. Genero himself felt healthy and strong and was anxious to get back to work, even though he'd learned he would start his tour of duty on the four-to-midnight tomorrow. He had also learned, however, that Captain Frick, in consideration for his recent wound, was not asking him to walk a beat for the next week or so. Instead, he would be riding shotgun in one of the RMP cars. Genero considered this a promotion.

Of sorts.

The snow continued to fall.

CHAPTER 13

Friday.

The city was a regular tundra, you never saw so much snow in your life unless you happened to have been born and raised in Alaska, and then probably not. There was snow on everything. There was snow on roofs and walls and sidewalks and streets and garbage cans and automobiles and flowerpots, and even on people. Boy, what a snowfall. It was worse than the Blizzard of '88, people who didn't remember the Blizzard of '88 were saying. His Honour the Mayor JMV, as if he didn't have enough headaches, had to arrange with the Sanitation Department for the hiring of 1,200 additional temporary employees to shovel and load and dump the snow into the River Dix, a job estimated to cost five hundred and eight thousand four hundred dollars and to consume the better part of a full week – if it didn't snow again.

The men began working as soon as the snow stopped. It did not stop until 3.30 pm, fifteen minutes before Genero began riding the RPM car, an hour and a half before Willis and Carella took their posts in the rear of the tailor shop. The city had figured on working their snow people in three continuous shifts, but they hadn't figured on the numbing cold that followed the storm and lowered the rate of efficiency, a biting frigid wave that had come down from Canada or some place. Actually, nobody cared *where* it had come from, they merely wished it would continue going, preferably out to sea, or down to Bermuda, or even all the way to Florida; do it to *Julia*, everyone was thinking.

There was no doing it to Julia that day.

The cold gripped the city and froze it solid. Emergency snow regulations had gone into effect at noon, and by 4 pm the city seemed deserted. Most large business offices were closed, with traffic stalled to a standstill and buses running only infrequently. Alternate-side-of-the-street parking had been suspended, but stranded automobiles blocked intersections, humped with snow like igloos on an arctic plain. The temporary snowmen fought the cold and the drifted snow, huddled around coal fires built in empty petrol drums, and then manned their shovels again while waiting dump trucks idled, exhaust pipes throwing giant white plumes into the bitter dusk. The lamp-post lights came on at 5 pm, casting isolated amber circles on the dead white landscape. A fierce relentless wind howled across the avenue and street as the leaden sky turned dark and darker and black.

Sitting cosy and warm in the back room of John the Tailor's shop, playing checkers with Hal Willis (and losing seven games in a row since it turned out that Willis had belonged to the checkers club in high school, an elite group calling itself *The Red and The Black*), Carella wondered how he would get home after La Bresca and Calucci hit the shop.

He was beginning to doubt that they would hit at all. If there was one thing he did not understand, of course, it was the criminal mind, but he was willing to venture a guess that no self-respecting crook would brave the snow and the cold outside on a night like this. It would be different if the job involved a factor that might change in a day or so, like say ten million dollars of gold bullion to be delivered at a precise moment on a specific day, making it necessary to combine pinpoint timing with insane daring, but no such variable was involved in this penny-ante stick-up. The men had cased the shop and learned that John the Tailor carried his week's earning home in a metal box every Friday night after closing. He had doubtless been performing this same chore every Friday night for the past seven thousand years and would continue to do it without variation for the next thousand. So if not *this* Friday night, what are you doing *next* Friday, John? Or, better yet, why not wait until May, when the trees are budding and the birds are singing, and a man can pull off a little felony without the attendant danger of frostbite?

But assuming they did hit tonight, Carella thought as he watched Willis double-jump two of his kings, assuming they *did* hit, and assuming he and Willis behaved as expected, made the capture and then called in for a squad car with chains, how would he get home to his wife and children after La Bresca and Calucci were booked and put away for the night? His own car had snow tyres, but not chains, and he doubted if the best snow tyres made would mean a damn on that glacier out there. A possibility, of course, was that Captain Frick would allow one of the RMPs to drive him home to Riverhead, but using city property for transporting city employees was a practice heavily frowned upon especially in these days of strife when deaf people were running around killing officials.

'King me,' Willis said.

Carella snorted and kinged him. He looked at his watch. It was seven twenty. If La Bresca and Calucci hit as expected, there was little more than a half-hour to go.

In Pete Calucci's rented room on North Sixteenth, he and La Bresca armed themselves. John the Tailor was seventy years old, a slight stooped man with greying hair and failing eyes, but they were not taking any chances with him that night. Calucci's gun was a Colt Government Model .45, weighing thirty-nine ounces and having a firing capacity of seven, plus one in the chamber. La Bresca was carrying a Walther P-38, which he had bought from a fence on Dream Street, with eight slugs in the magazine and another in the chamber. Both guns were automatics. The Walther was classified as a medium-powered pistol whereas the Colt, of course, was a heavy gun with greater power. Each was quite capable of leaving John the Tailor enormously dead if he gave them any trouble. Neither man owned a holster. Calucci put his pistol into the right-hand pocket of his heavy overcoat. La Bresca tucked his into the waistband of his trousers.

They had agreed beween them that they would not use the guns unless John the Tailor began yelling. It was their plan to reach the shop by ten minutes to eight, surprise the old man, leave him bound and gagged in the back room, and then return to Calucci's place. The shop was only five minutes away, but because of the heavy snow, and because neither man owned an automobile, they set out at seven twenty-five.

They both looked very menacing, and they both felt quite powerful with their big guns. It was a shame nobody was around to see how menacing and powerful they looked and felt.

In the warm snug comfort of the radio motor patrol car, Patrolman Richard Genero studied the bleak and windswept streets outside, listening to the clink of the chains on the rear wheel tyres, hearing the two-way short-wave radio spewing its incessant dialogue. The man driving the RMP was a hair bag named Phillips, who had been complaining constantly from the moment they'd begun their shift at 3.45 pm. It was now seven thirty, and Phillips was still complaining, telling Genero he'd done a Dan O'Leary this whole past week, not a minute's breather, man had to be crazy to become a cop, while to his right the radio continued its oblivious spiel, Car Twenty-one. Signal thirteen, This is Twenty-one, Wilco, Car Twenty-eight, signal . . .

'This reminds me of Christmas,' Genero said.

'Yeah, some Christmas,' Phillips said. 'I *worked* on Christmas day, you know that?'

'I meant, everything white.'

'Yeah, everything white,' Phillips said. 'Who needs it?'

Genero folded his arms across his chest and tucked his gloved hands into his armpits. Phillips kept talking. The radio buzzed and crackled. The skid chains clinked like sleigh bells.

Genero felt drowsy.

Something was bothering the deaf man.

No, it was not the heavy snow which had undoubtedly covered manhole number M3860, a hundred and twenty feet south of the southern curb of Harris, in the centre of Faxon Drive, no, it was not that. He had prepared for the eventuality of inclement weather, and there were snow shovels in the trunk of the black sedan idling at the kerb downstairs. The snow would merely entail some digging to get at the manhole, and he was allowing himself an extra hour for that task, no, it was not the snow, it was definitely not the snow.

'What is it?' Buck whispered. He was wearing his rented police sergeant's uniform, and he felt strange and nervous inside the blue garment.

'I don't know,' Ahmad answered. 'Look at the way he's pacing.'

The deaf man was indeed pacing. Wearing electrician's coveralls, he walked back and forth past the desk in one corner of the room, not quite muttering, but certainly wagging his head like an old man contemplating the sorry state of the world. Buck, perhaps emboldened by the bravery citation on his chest, finally approached him and said, 'What's bothering you?'

'The 87th,' the deaf man replied once.

'What?'

'The 87th, the 87th,' he repeated impatiently. 'What difference will it make if we kill the mayor? Don't you see?'

'No.'

'They get away clean,' the deaf man said. 'We kill JMV, and *who* suffers, will you tell me that?'

'Who?' Buck asked.

'*Not* the 87th, that's for sure.'

'Look,' Buck said gently, 'We'd better get started. We've got to dig down to that manhole, we've got to . . .'

'So JMV dies, so what?' the deaf man asked. 'Is money everything in life? Where's the pleasure?'

Buck looked at him.

'Where's the *pleasure*?' the deaf man repeated. 'If JMV –' He suddenly stopped, his eyes widening. 'JMV,' he said again, his voice a whisper. 'JMV!' he shouted excitedly, and went to the desk, and opened the middle drawer, and pulled out the Isola telephone directory. Quickly, he flipped to the rear section of the book.

'What's he doing?' Ahmad whispered.

'I don't know,' Buck whispered.

'*Look* at this!' the deaf man shouted. 'There must be hundreds of them, *thousands* of them!'

'Thousands of what?' Buck asked.

The deaf man did not reply. Hunched over the directory, he kept turning pages, studying them, turning more pages. 'Here we are,' he mumbled, 'no, that's no good . . . let's see . . . here's another one . . . no, no . . . just a second . . . ahhh, good . . . no that's all the way downtown . . . let's see, let's see . . . here . . . no . . .' mumbling to himself as he continued to turn pages, and finally shouting 'Culver Avenue, *that's* it, that'll do it!' He picked up a pencil, hastily scribbled on to the desk pad, tore the page loose, and stuffed it into the pocket of his coveralls. 'Let's go!' he said.

'You ready?' Buck asked.

'I'm ready,' the deaf man said, and picked up the volt-ohm meter. 'We promised to get JMV, didn't we?' he asked.

'We sure did.'

'Okay,' he said, grinning. 'We're going to get *two* JMV's – and one of them's in the 87th Precinct!'

Exuberantly, he led them out of the apartment.

The two young men had been prowling the streets since dinnertime. They had eaten in a delicatessen off Ainsley and then had stopped to buy a half-gallon of petrol in the service station on the corner of Ainsley and Fifth. The taller of the two young men, the one carrying the open can of petrol, was cold. He kept telling the shorter one how cold he was. The shorter one said *everybody* was cold on a night like this, what the hell did he expect on a night like this?

The taller one said he wanted to go home. He said they wouldn't find nobody out on a night like this, anyway, so what was the use walking around like this in the cold? His feet were freezing, he said. His hands were cold too. Why don't *you* carry this fuckin' gas a while? he said.

The shorter one told him to shut up.

The shorter one said this was a perfect night for what they had to do because they could probably find maybe two guys curled up together in the same hallway, didn't that make sense?

The taller one said he wished *he* was curled up in a hallway someplace.

They stood on the street corner arguing for a few minutes, each of them yelling in turn, and finally the taller one agreed to give it another ten minutes, but that was all. The shorter one said Let's try it for another half-hour, we bound to hit pay dirt, and the taller one said No, ten minutes and that's it, and the shorter one said You fuckin' idiot, I'm telling you this is a good night for it, and the taller one saw what was in his eyes, and became afraid again and said, OK, OK, but only a half-hour, I mean it, Jimmy, I'm really cold, really.

You look like you're about to start crying, Jimmy said.

I'm cold, the other one said, that's all.

Well, come on, Jimmy said, we'll find somebody and make a nice fire, huh? A nice warm fire.

The two young men grinned at each other.

Then they turned the corner and walked up the street towards Culver Avenue as Car Seventeen, bearing Phillips and Genero, clinked by on its chained tyres sounding like sleigh bells.

It was difficult to tell who was more surprised, the cops or the robbers.

The police commissioner had told His Honour the Mayor JMV that 'a lot of police work dovetails past and present and future', but it was fairly safe to assume he had nothing too terribly philosophical in mind. That is, he probably wasn't speculating on the difference between illusion and reality, or the overlap of the dream state and the workaday world. That is, he probably wasn't explaining time continua or warps, or parallel universes, or coexisting systems. He was merely trying to say that there are a lot of accidents involved in police work, and that too many cases would never get solved if it weren't for those very accidents. He was trying to tell His Honour the Mayor JMV that sometimes cops get lucky.

Carella and Willis got very lucky on that night of March fifteenth at exactly ten minutes to eight.

They were watching the front of the shop because Dominick Di Fillippi (who had never ratted on anybody in his life) had told them the plan was to go into the shop at ten minutes to eight, just before John the Tailor drew the blinds on the plate glass window fronting the street. La Bresca was to perform that task instead, Di Fillippi had further said, and then he was to lock the front door while Calucci forced John the Tailor at gun point into the back room. In Di Fillippi's ardent recital, there had been a lot of emphasis real or imagined, on the *front* of the shop. So everyone had merely assumed (as who wouldn't?) that La Bresca and Calucci would come in through the front door, open the door, ting-a-ling would go the bell, shove their guns into John the Tailor's face, and then go about their dirty business. It is doubtful that the police even *knew* there was a back door to the shop.

La Bresca and Calucci knew there was a back door.

They kicked that door in at precisely seven fifty, right on schedule, kicked it in noisily and effectively, not caring whether or not they scared John the Tailor out of ten years' growth, knowing he would rush to the back of the shop to see what the hell was happening, knowing he would run directly into two very large pistols.

The first thing they saw was two guys playing checkers.

The first thing La Bresca said was, 'Fuzz!'

He knew the short guy was fuzz because he had been questioned by him often enough. He didn't know who the other guy was, but he reasoned that if you saw *one* mouse you probably had fifty, and if you saw one *cop* you probably had a thousand, so the place was probably crawling with cops, they had stepped into a very sweet little trap here – and that was when the curtain shot back and the front door of the shop burst open.

It was also when all the overlapping confusion started, the past, present, and future jazz getting all mixed up so that it seemed for a tense ten seconds as if seven movies were being projected simultaneously on the same tiny screen. Even later, much later, Carella couldn't quite put all the pieces together; everything happened too fast and too luckily, and he and Willis had very little to do with any of it.

The first obvious fact that crackled up Carella's spine and into his head was that he and Willis had been caught cold. Even as he rose from his chair, knocking it over backwards, even as he shouted, 'Hal, behind you!' and reached for his revolver, he knew they'd been caught cold, they were staring into the open muzzles of two high calibre guns and they would be shot dead on the spot. He heard one of the men shout, 'Fuzz!' and then he saw both guns come up level at the same time, and too many last thoughts crowded into his head in the tick of a second. Willis whirled, knocking checkerboard and checkers to the floor, drawing his gun, and suddenly John the Tailor threw back the curtain separating the rear of the shop from the front, and the front door of the shop burst open in the same instant.

John the Tailor later said he had run back to see what the noise was, throwing the curtain between the two rooms, and then whirling to see what Carella only later saw, three men standing in the front doorway of his shop, all of them holding pistols.

This was what La Bresca and Calucci must have seen as well, looking through the now open curtain directly to the front door. And whereas they must have instantly known they had caught the back-room cops cold, they now recognized the threat of the three other cops standing in the front door, all of them with pistols in their fists and kill looks on their faces. The three men weren't cops, but La Bresca and Calucci didn't know that. The sergeant standing in the doorway shouted, 'Fuzz!' meaning he thought La Bresca and Calucci were fuzz, but La Bresca and Calucci merely thought he was announcing his own arrival. So they began shooting. The three men in the door, facing what they too thought was a police trap, opened fire at the same time. John the Tailor threw himself to the floor. Carella and Willis, recognizing a good healthy crossfire when they saw one, tried to flatten themselves against the wall. In the flattening process, Willis slipped on one of the fallen checkers and went tumbling to the floor, bullets spraying over his head.

Carella's gun was in his hand now. He levelled it at the front door because he had taken a good look at one of the men standing there firing into the back room, and whereas the man was not wearing his aid, he was tall and blond and Carella recognized him at once. He aimed carefully and deliberately. The gun bucked in his hand when he pulled off the shot. He saw the deaf man clutch for his shoulder and then half-stumble, half-turn towards the open doorway. Someone screamed behind Carella, and he turned to see La Bresca falling over the pressing machine, spilling blood on to the white padding, and then four more shots exploded in the tiny shop and someone grunted, and there were more shots, Willis was up and firing, and then there was only smoke, heavy smoke that hung on the air in layers, the terrible nostril-burning stink of cordite, and the sound of John the Tailor on the floor, praying softly in Italian.

'Outside!' Carella shouted, and leaped the counter dividing the shop, slipping in a pool of blood near the sewing machine, but regaining his footing and running coatless into the snow.

There was no one in sight.

The cold was numbing.

It hit his naked gun hand immediately, seemed to wed flesh to steel.

A trail of blood ran from the shop door across the white snow stretching endlessly into the city.

Carella began following it.

The deaf man ran as fast as he could, but the pain in his shoulder was intolerable.

He could not understand what had happened.

Was it possible they had figured it out? But no, they couldn't have. And yet, they'd been there, waiting. How *could* they have known? How could they *possibly* have known when he *himself* hadn't known until fifteen minutes ago?

There had been at least twenty-five pages of 'V' listings in the Isola directory, with about 500 names to a page, for a combined total of some 12,500 names. He had not counted the number of first names beginning with the letter 'J', but there seemed to be at least twenty or thirty on every page, and he had actually gone through *eleven* names with the initials 'JMV', the same initials as His Honour the Mayor James Martin Vale, before coming to the one on Culver Avenue.

How could they have known? How could they have pinpointed the tailor shop of John Mario Vicenzo, the final twist of the knife, a JMV located within the very confines of the 87th? It's impossible, he thought. I left nothing to chance, it should have worked, I should have got them both, there were no wild cards in the deck, it should have worked.

There were *still* some wild cards in the deck.

'Look,' Jimmy said.

The taller boy, the one carrying the petrol can, lifted his head, squinted against the wind, and then ducked it immediately as a fiercer gust attacked his face. He had seen a tall blond man staggering off the pavement and into the centre of the snow-bound street.

'Drunk as a pig,' Jimmy said beside him. 'Let's get him, Baby.'

The one called Baby nodded bleakly. Swiftly, they ran towards the corner. The wind was stronger there, it struck them with gale force as they turned on to the wide avenue. The vag was nowhere in sight.

'We lost him,' Baby said. His teeth were chattering, and he wanted to go home.

'He's got to be in one of these hallways,' Jimmy said. 'Come on, Baby, it's fire time.'

From where Genero sat in the RMP car, he could see the empty windswept avenue through a frost-free spot on the windshield, snow devils ascending with each fresh gust of wind, hanging signs clanging and flapping, an eerie graveyard sound rasping at the windows of the automobile. The avenue was deserted, the snow locked the street from sidewalk to sidewalk, lights burned behind apartment windows like warming fires in a primeval night.

'What's that?' he said suddenly.

'What's what?' Phillips asked.

'Up ahead. Those two guys.'

'Huh?' Phillips said.

'They're trying doors,' Genero said. 'Pull over.'

'Huh?'

'Pull over and cut your engine!'

He could hear them talking on the sidewalk outside, he could hear their voices coming closer and closer. He lay in the hallway with his shoulder oozing blood, knowing he had to climb those steps and get to the roof, get from this building to the next one, jump rooftops all night long if he had to, but first rest, just rest, just rest a little, rest before they opened the door and found him, how had they got to him so fast? Were there policemen all over this damn city?

There were too many things he did not understand.

He listened as the voices came closer, and then he saw the doorknob turning.

'Hold it right there!' Genero shouted.

The boys turned immediately.

'Fuzz!' Baby shouted, and dropped the petrol can, and began running. Genero fired a warning shot over his head, and then belatedly yelled,

'Police! Stop or I'll shoot!' and then fired another warning shot. Up the street, where he had parked the RMP at the kerb, Phillips was opening the door on the driver's side and unholstering his revolver. Genero fired again, surprised when he saw the running boy drop to the snow. I *got* him! he thought, and then whirled to see the second boy running in the opposite direction, Holy Jesus, he thought, I'm busting up a *robbery* or something! 'Halt!' he shouted. 'Stop!' and fired into the air, and saw the boy rounding the corner, and immediately ran after him.

He chased Jimmy for three blocks in the snow, pushing through knee-deep drifts, slipping on icy patches, the wind a constant adversary, and finally caught up with him as he was scaling a back-alley fence.

'Hold it right there, Sonny,' Genero said, 'or I'll put one right up your ass.'

Jimmy hesitated astride the fence, debating whether to swing his legs up and over it, or to get down before this trigger-happy bastard really carried out his threat.

Sighing, he dropped to the ground at Genero's feet.

'What seems to be the trouble, Officer?' he asked.

'*Trouble* is right,' Genero said. 'Get your hands up.'

Phillips came puffing into the alley just then. He walked up to Genero like the hair bag he was, shoved him aside, and then pushed Jimmy against the fence while he frisked him. Genero was smart enough to make certain *his* handcuffs were the ones they put on the kid, though there was a moment there when it seemed like a touch-and-go race with Phillips.

By the time they got the kid back to the squad car, by the time they went up the street to ascertain that the other kid was still alive, though barely, by the time they located the hallway door the kids were about to open, by the time they opened that door themselves and flashed their lights into the foyer, all they saw was a puddle of blood on the floor.

The blood continued up the steps.

They followed the spatters to the top floor, directly to the open door of the roof. Genero stepped outside and threw the beam of his flash across the snow.

Bloodstains and footprints led in an erratic trail to the edge of the roof, and from there to the roof beyond, and from there to the rest of the city, or perhaps the rest of the world.

Two blocks away, they found Steve Carella wandering coatless in the snow like Dr Zhivago or somebody.

CHAPTER 14

The clean up in the tailor shop was a gruesome job.

La Bresca and Calucci were both dead. The big red-headed man named Buck was also dead. Ahmad was alive and breathing when they carted him off in the meat wagon, but he had taken two slugs in the chest from Calucci's .45, and another in the stomach from La Bresca's Walther. He was gushing blood, and spitting blood, and shivering and mumbling, and they doubted very much if he'd make it to the hospital alive.

Carella was shivering a little himself.

He stood near the radiator in the tailor shop, wrapped in his overcoat, his teeth chattering, and asked John the Tailor how much money there was in the metal box he was taking home.

'*Due cento tre dollari*,' John the Tailor said.

Two hundred and three dollars.

Ahmad knew the deaf man's name.

'Orecchio,' he said, and the nurse wiped blood from his lips. 'Mort Orecchio.'

'That's not his real name,' Willis told him. 'Do you know him by any other name?'

'Orecchio,' Ahmad repeated. 'Mort Orecchio.'

'Is there anyone who *might* know his real name?'

'Orecchio,' Ahmad repeated.

'Was there anyone else in this with you?'

'The girl,' Ahmad said.

'What girl?'

'Rochelle,' he said.

'Rochelle what?'

Ahmad shook his head.

'Where can we find her?'

'Three . . . three . . . eight . . . Ha . . . Ha . . . Ha . . .' he said, and died.

He had not died laughing.

He was trying to say 338 Harbourside.

They found in Buck's pants pocket a letter addressed to him at 338 Harbourside Oval. His full name was Andrew Buckley, and the letter was addressed to him c/o Mr Mort Orecchio. Carella and Willis hit the apartment and found a pretty brunette girl in lounging pyjamas, sitting at the piano playing *Heart and Soul*. They waited while she got dressed and then took her to the squadroom, where they questioned her for a half-hour in the presence of a lawyer. The girl told them her name was Rochelle Newell and that she had known the deaf man for only a short time, two or three months. She insisted his name was Mort Orecchio.

'That's not his name,' Carella said.

'Yes, that's his name.'

'What'd *you* call him?'

'Mort,' the girl said.

'What'd you call him in *bed*?' Willis asked suddenly, hoping to surprise her.

'Sweetie,' the girl answered.

Jimmy could not stop giggling.

They had just told him that his friend Baby was dead, and yet he could not stop giggling.

'You know the kind of trouble you're in, son?' Meyer asked.

'No, what kind?' Jimmy said, and giggled.

'We're going to book you for homicide.'

'It won't stick,' Jimmy said, and giggled.

'It'll stick, son,' Meyer said. 'We got a dying confession from your pal, and it was taken in the presence of a lawyer, and we've got a cop outside who you tried to kill and who'll make a positive identification of both of you. It'll stick, believe me.'

'Naw, it won't stick,' Jimmy said, and kept giggling.

Meyer figured he was crazy.

Meyer figured Rollie Chabrier was crazy too.

He called at close to midnight.

'This is kind of late, isn't it?' Meyer said. 'I was just about to head home.'

'Well, I'm still working here at the goddamn office,' Chabrier said. 'You guys have it easy.'

'Well, what is it?' Meyer said.

'About this book,' Chabrier said.

'Yeah?'

'You want my advice?'

'Sure, I want your advice. Why do you think I contacted you?'

'My advice is forget it.'

'That's some advice.'

'Has Steve Carella ever had a book named after him?'

'No, but . . .'

'Has Bert Kling?'

'No.'

'Or Cotton Hawes? Or Hal Willis? Or Arthur Brown? Or . . .'

'Look, Rollie . . .'

'You should be flattered,' Chabrier said. 'Even *I* have never had a book named after me.'

'Yeah, but . . .'

'You know how many people go their entire lives and never have books named after them?'

'How many?'

'Millions! You should be flattered.'

'I should?'

'Sure. Somebody named a book after you! You're famous!'

'I am?'

'Absolutely. From now to the very end of time, people will be able to go into libraries all over the world and see your name on a book, Meyer, think of it. On a *book*. Meyer Meyer,' he said grandly, and Meyer could almost visualize him spreading his hands as though conjuring marquee lights. 'God, Meyer, you should be thrilled to death.'

'Yeah?' Meyer said.

'I envy you, Meyer. I truly and honestly envy you.'

'Gee,' Meyer said. 'Thanks. Thanks a lot, Rollie. Really. Thanks a lot.'

'Don't mention it,' Chabrier said, and hung up.

Meyer went into the men's room to look at himself in the mirror.

Andy Parker brought the morning papers into the squadroom at 2 am.

'You want to read how smart we are?' he said, and dropped the papers on Kling's desk.

Kling glanced at the headlines.

'Sure,' Parker said, 'we busted the whole thing wide open. Nobody can lick *this* team, pal.'

Kling nodded, preoccupied.

'Everybody can rest easy now,' Parker said. 'The papers tell all about the scheme, and how the ring is busted, and how none of those hundred marks have to worry any more. And all because of the brilliant bulls of the 87th.' He paused and then said, 'I bet Genero gets a promotion out of this. His name's all over the paper.'

Kling nodded and said nothing.

He was pondering the latest development in the Great Squadroom Mystery. The stolen electric fan, it seemed, had turned up in a hockshop downtown. There had been an apple green fingerprint on its base.

'Now who do you suppose . . .' he started, but Parker had already stretched out in the swivel chair behind his desk, with one of the newspapers over his face.

THE BIG SLEEP

RAYMOND CHANDLER

THE BIG SLEEP
The characters and situations in this work are wholly fictional and imaginary and do no portray and are not intended to portray any actual persons or parties.

CHAPTER 1

It was about eleven o'clock in the morning, mid October, with the sun not shining and a look of hard wet rain in the clearness of the foothills. I was wearing my powder-blue suit, with dark blue shirt, tie and display handkerchief, black brogues, black wool socks with dark blue clocks on them. I was neat, clean, shaved and sober, and I didn't care who knew it. I was everything the well-dressed private detective ought to be. I was calling on four million dollars.

The main hallway of the Sternwood place was two stories high. Over the entrance doors, which would have let in a troop of Indian elephants, there was a broad stained-glass panel showing a knight in dark armour rescuing a lady who was tied to a tree and didn't have any clothes on but some very long and convenient hair. The knight had pushed the vizor of his helmet back to be sociable, and he was fiddling with the knots on the ropes that tied the lady to the tree and not getting anywhere. I stood there and thought that if I lived in the house, I would sooner or later have to climb up there and help him. He didn't seem to be really trying.

There were French doors at the back of the hall, beyond them a wide sweep of emerald grass to a white garage, in front of which a slim dark young chauffeur in shiny black leggings was dusting a maroon Packard convertible. Beyond the garage were some decorative trees trimmed as carefully as poodle dogs. Beyond them a large greenhouse with a domed roof. Then more trees and beyond everything the solid, uneven, comfortable line of the foothills.

On the east side of the hall a free staircase, tile-paved, rose to a gallery with a wrought-iron railing and another piece of stained-glass romance. Large hard chairs with rounded red plush seats were backed into the vacant spaces of the wall round about. They didn't look as if anybody had ever sat in them. In the middle of the west wall there was a big empty fireplace with a brass screen in four hinged panels, and over the fireplace a marble mantel with cupids at the corners. Above the mantel there was a large oil portrait, and above the portrait two bullet-torn or moth-eaten cavalry pennants crossed in a glass frame. The portrait was a stiffly posed job of an officer in full regimentals of about the time of the Mexican War. The officer had a neat black imperial, black mustachios, hot hard coal-black eyes, and the general look of a man it would pay to get along with. I thought this might be General Sternwood's grandfather. It could hardly be the General himself, even though I had heard he was pretty far gone in years to have a couple of daughters still in the dangerous twenties.

I was still staring at the hot black eyes when a door opened far back under the stairs. It wasn't the butler coming back. It was a girl.

She was twenty or so, small and delicately put together, but she looked durable. She wore pale blue slacks and they looked well on her. She walked as if she were floating. Her hair was a fine tawny wave cut much shorter than the current fashion of pageboy tresses curled in at the bottom. Her eyes were slate-grey, and had almost no expression when they looked at me. She came over near me and smiled with her mouth and she had little sharp predatory teeth, as white as fresh orange pith and as shiny as porcelain. They glistened between her thin too taut lips. Her face lacked colour and didn't look too healthy.

'Tall, aren't you?' she said.

'I didn't mean to be.'

Her eyes rounded. She was puzzled. She was thinking. I could see, even on that short acquaintance, that thinking was always going to be a bother to her.

'Handsome too,' she said. 'And I bet you know it.'

I grunted.

'What's your name?'

'Reilly,' I said. 'Doghouse Reilly.'

'That's a funny name.' She bit her lip and turned her head a little and looked at me along her eyes. Then she lowered her lashes until they almost cuddled her cheeks and slowly raised them again, like a theatre curtain. I was to get to know that trick. That was supposed to make me roll over on my back with all four paws in the air.

'Are you a prizefighter?' she asked, when I didn't.

'Not exactly. I'm a sleuth.'

'A – a—' She tossed her head angrily, and the rich colour of it glistened in the rather dim light of the big hall. 'You're making fun of me.'

'Uh-uh.'

'What?'

'Get on with you,' I said. 'You heard me.'

'You didn't say anything. You're just a big tease.' She put a thumb up and bit it. It was a curiously shaped thumb, thin and narrow like an extra finger, with no curve in the first joint. She bit it and sucked it slowly, turning it around in her mouth like a baby with a comforter.

'You're awfully tall,' she said. Then she giggled with secret merriment. Then she turned her body slowly and lithely, without lifting her feet. Her hands dropped limp at her sides. She tilted herself towards me on her toes. She fell straight back into my arms. I had to catch her or let her crack her head on the tessellated floor. I caught her under her arms and she went rubber-legged on me instantly. I had to hold her close to hold her up. When her head was against my chest she screwed it around and giggled at me.

'You're cute,' she giggled. 'I'm cute too.'

I didn't say anything. So the butler chose that convenient moment to come back through the French doors and see me holding her.

It didn't seem to bother him. He was a tall thin silver man, sixty or close to it or a little past it. He had blue eyes as remote as eyes could be. His skin was smooth and bright and he moved like a man with very sound muscles. He walked slowly across the floor towards us and the girl jerked away from me. She flashed across the room to the foot of the stairs and went up them like a deer. She was gone before I could draw a long breath and let it out.

The butler said tonelessly: 'The General will see you now, Mr Marlowe.'

I pushed my lower jaw up off my chest and nodded at him. 'Who was that?'

'Miss Carmen Sternwood, sir.'

'You ought to wean her. She looks old enough.'

He looked at me with grave politeness and repeated what he had said.

CHAPTER 2

We went out at the French doors and along a smooth red-flagged path that skirted the far side of the lawn from the garage. The boyish-looking chauffeur had a big black and chromium sedan out now and was dusting that. The path took us along to the side of the greenhouse and the butler opened a door for me and stood aside. It opened into a sort of vestibule that was about as warm as a slow oven. He came in after me, shut the outer door, opened an inner door and we went through that. Then it was really hot. The air was thick, wet, steamy and larded with the cloying smell of tropical orchids in bloom. The glass walls and roof were heavily misted and big drops of moisture splashed down on the plants. The light had an unreal greenish colour, like light filtered through an aquarium tank. The plants filled the place, a forest of them, with nasty meaty leaves and stalks like the newly washed fingers of dead men. They smelled as overpowering as boiling alcohol under a blanket.

The butler did his best to get me through without being smacked in the face by the sodden leaves, and after a while we came to a clearing in the middle of the jungle, under the domed roof. Here, in a space of hexagonal flags, an old red Turkish rug was laid down and on the rug was a wheel chair, and in the wheel chair an old and obviously dying man watched us come with black eyes from which all fire had died long ago, but which still had the coal-black directness of the eyes in the portrait that hung above the mantel in the hall. The rest of his face was a leaden mask, with the bloodless lips and the sharp nose and the sunken temples and the outward-turning ear-lobes of approaching dissolution. His long narrow body was wrapped – in that heat – in a travelling rug and a faded red bathrobe. His thin clawlike hands were folded loosely on the rug, purple-nailed. A few locks of dry white hair clung to his scalp, like wild flowers fighting for life on a bare rock.

The butler stood in front of him and said: 'This is Mr Marlowe, General.'

The old man didn't move or speak, or even nod. He just looked at me lifelessly. The butler pushed a damp wicker chair against the backs of my legs and I sat down. He took my hat with a deft scoop.

Then the old man dragged his voice up from the bottom of a well and said: 'Brandy, Norris. How do you like your brandy, sir?'

'Any way at all,' I said.

The butler went away among the abominable plants. The General spoke again, slowly, using his strength as carefully as an out-of-work showgirl uses her last good pair of stockings.

'I used to like mine with champagne. The champagne as cold as Valley Forge and about a third of a glass of brandy beneath it. You may take your coat off, sir. It's too hot in here for a man with blood in his veins.'

I stood up and peeled off my coat and got a handkerchief out and mopped my face and neck and the backs of my wrists. St Louis in August had nothing on that place. I sat down again and felt automatically for a cigarette and then stopped. The old man caught the gesture and smiled faintly.

'You may smoke, sir. I like the smell of tobacco.'

I lit the cigarette and blew a lungful at him and he sniffed at it like a terrier at a rat-hole. The faint smile pulled at the shadowed corners of his mouth.

'A nice state of affairs when a man has to indulge his vices by proxy,' he said dryly. 'You are looking at a very dull survival of a rather gaudy life, a cripple paralysed in both legs and with only half of his lower belly. There's very little that I can eat and my sleep is so close to waking that it is hardly worth the name. I seem to exist largely on heat, like a newborn spider, and the orchids are an excuse for the heat. Do you like orchids?'

'Not particularly,' I said.

The general half closed his eyes. 'They are nasty things. Their flesh is too much like the flesh of men. And their perfume has the rotten sweetness of a prostitute.'

I stared at him with my mouth open. The soft wet heat was like a pall around us. The old man nodded, as if his neck was afraid of the weight of his head. Then the butler came pushing back through the jungle with a tea-wagon, mixed me a brandy and soda, swathed the copper ice bucket with a damp napkin, and went softly away among the orchids. A door opened and shut behind the jungle.

I sipped the drink. The old man licked his lips watching me, over and over again, drawing one lip slowly across the other with a funereal absorption, like an undertaker dry-washing his hands.

'Tell me about yourself, Mr Marlowe. I suppose I have a right to ask?'

'Sure, but there's very little to tell. I'm thirty-three years old, went to college once and can still speak English if there's any demand for it. There isn't much in my trade. I worked for Mr Wilde, the District Attorney, as an investigator once. His chief investigator, a man named Bernie Ohls, called me and told me you wanted to see me. I'm unmarried because I don't like policemen's wives.'

'And a little bit of a cynic,' the old man smiled. 'You didn't like working for Wilde?'

'I was fired. For insubordination. I test very high on insubordination, General.'

'I always did myself, sir. I'm glad to hear it. What do you know about my family?'

'I'm told you are a widower and have two young daughters, both pretty and both wild. One of them has been married three times, the last time to an ex-bootlegger, who went in the trade by the name of Rusty Regan. That's all I heard, General.'

'Did any of it strike you as peculiar?'

'The Rusty Regan part, maybe. But I always got along with bootleggers myself.'

He smiled his faint economical smile. 'It seems I do too. I'm very fond of Rusty. A big curly-headed Irishman from Clonmel, with sad eyes and a smile as wide as Wilshire Boulevard. The first time I saw him I thought he might be what you are probably thinking he was, an adventurer who happened to get himself wrapped up in some velvet.'

'You must have liked him,' I said. 'You learned to talk the language.'

He put his thin bloodless hands under the edge of the rug. I put my cigarette stub out and finished my drink.

'He was the breath of life to me – while he lasted. He spent hours with me, sweating like a pig, drinking brandy by the quart, and telling me stories of the Irish revolution. He had been an officer in the I.R.A. He wasn't even legally in the United States. It was a ridiculous marriage of course, and it probably didn't last a month, as a marriage. I'm telling you the family secrets, Mr Marlowe.'

'They're still secrets,' I said 'What happened to him?'

The old man looked at me woodenly. 'He went away, a month ago.

Abruptly, without a word to anyone. Without saying good-bye to me. That hurt a little, but he had been raised in a rough school. I'll hear from him one of these days. Meantime I am being blackmailed again.'

I said: 'Again?'

He brought his hands from under the rug with a brown envelope in them. 'I should have been very sorry for anybody who tried to blackmail me while Rusty was around. A few months before he came – that is to say about nine or ten months ago – I paid a man named Joe Brody five thousand dollars to let my younger daughter Carmen alone.'

'Ah,' I said.

He moved his thin white eyebrows. 'That means what?'

'Nothing,' I said.

He went on staring at me, half frowning. Then he said: 'Take this envelope and examine it. And help yourself to the brandy.'

I took the envelope off his knees and sat down with it again. I wiped off the palms of my hands and turned it around. It was addressed to General Guy Sternwood, 3765 Alta Brea Crescent, West Hollywood, California. The address was in ink, in the slanting printing engineers use. The envelope was slit. I opened it up and took out a brown card and three slips of stiff paper. The card was of thin brown linen, printed in gold: 'Mr Arthur Gwynn Geiger.' No address. Very small in the lower lefthand corner: 'Rare Books and De Luxe Editions.' I turned the card over. More of the slanted printing on the back. 'Dear Sir: In spite of the legal uncollectibility of the enclosed, which frankly represent gambling debts, I assume you might wish them honoured. Respectfully, A. G. Geiger.'

I looked at the slips of stiffish white paper. They were promissory notes filled out in ink, dated on several dates early in the month before, September. 'On Demand I promise to pay to Arthur Gwynn Geiger or Order the sum of One Thousand Dollars ($1000.00) without interest. Value Received. Carmen Sternwood.'

The written part was in a sprawling moronic handwriting with a lot of fat curlicues and circles for dots. I mixed myself another drink and sipped it and put the exhibit aside.

'Your conclusions?' the General asked.

'I haven't any yet. Who is this Arthur Gwynn Geiger?'

'I haven't the faintest idea.'

'What does Carmen say?'

'I haven't asked her. I don't intend to. If I did, she would suck her thumb and look coy.'

I said: 'I met her in the hall. She did that to me. Then she tried to sit in my lap.'

Nothing changed in his expression. His clasped hands rested peacefully on the edge of the rug, and the heat, which made me feel like a New England boiled dinner, didn't seem to make him even warm.

'Do I have to be polite?' I asked. 'Or can I just be natural?'

'I haven't noticed that you suffer from many inhibitions, Mr Marlowe.'

'Do the two girls run around together?'

'I think not. I think they go their separate and slightly divergent roads to perdition. Vivian is spoiled, exacting, smart and quite ruthless. Carmen is a child who likes to pull wings off flies. Neither of them has any more moral sense than a cat. Neither have I. No Sternwood ever had. Proceed.'

'They're well educated, I suppose. They know what they're doing.'

'Vivian went to good schools of the snob type and to college. Carmen went to half a dozen schools of greater and greater liberality, and ended up where she started. I presume they both had, and still have, all the usual vices. If I sound a little sinister as a parent, Mr Marlowe, it is because my hold on life is too slight to include any Victorian hypocrisy.' He leaned his head back and closed his eyes, then opened them again suddenly. 'I need not add that a man who indulges in parenthood for the first time at the age of fifty-four deserves all he gets.'

I sipped my drink and nodded. The pulse in his lean grey throat throbbed visibly and yet so slowly that it was hardly a pulse at all. An old man two-thirds dead and still determined to believe he could take it.

'Your conclusions?' he asked suddenly.

'I'd pay him.'

'Why?'

'It's a question of a little money against a lot of annoyance. There has to be something behind it. But nobody's going to break your heart, if it hasn't been done already. And it would take an awful lot of chisellers an awful lot of time to rob you of enough so that you'd even notice it.'

'I have pride, sir,' he said coldly.

'Somebody's counting on that. It's the easiest way to fool them. That or the police. Geiger can collect on these notes, unless you can show fraud. Instead of that he makes you a present of them and admits they are gambling debts, which gives you a defence, even if he had kept the notes. If he's a crook, he knows his onions, and if he's an honest man doing a little loan business on the side, he ought to have his money. Who was this Joe Brody you paid the five thousand dollars to?'

'Some kind of gambler. I hardly recall. Norris would know. My butler.'

'Your daughters have money in their own right, General?'

'Vivian has, but not a great deal. Carmen is still a minor under her mother's will. I give them both generous allowances.'

I said: 'I can take this Geiger off your back, General, if that's what you want. Whoever he is and whatever he has. It may cost you a little money, besides what you pay me. And, of course, it won't get you anything. Sugaring them never does. You're already listed on their book of nice names.'

'I see.' He shrugged his wide sharp shoulders in the faded red bathrobe. 'A moment ago you said pay him. Now you say it won't get me anything.'

'I mean it might be cheaper and easier to stand for a certain amount of squeeze. That's all.'

'I'm afraid I'm rather an impatient man, Mr Marlowe. What are your charges?'

'I get twenty-five a day and expenses – when I'm lucky.'

'I see. It seems reasonable enough for removing morbid growths from people's backs. Quite a delicate operation. You realize that, I hope. You'll make your operation as little of a shock to the patient as possible? There might be several of them, Mr Marlowe.'

I finished my second drink and wiped my lips and my face. The heat didn't get any less hot with the brandy in me. The General blinked at me and plucked at the edge of his rug.

'Can I make a deal with this guy, if I think he's within booting distance of being on the level?'

'Yes. The matter is now in your hands. I never do things by halves.'

'I'll take him out,' I said. 'He'll think a bridge fell on him.'

'I'm sure you will. And now I must excuse myself. I am tired.' He reached out and touched the bell on the arm of his chair. The cord was plugged into a black cable that wound along the side of the deep dark green boxes in which the orchids grew and festered. He closed his eyes, opened them again in a brief bright stare, and settled back among his cushions. The lids dropped again and he didn't pay any more attention to me.

I stood up and lifted my coat off the back of the damp wicker chair and went off with it among the orchids, opened the two doors and stood outside in the brisk October air getting myself some oxygen. The chauffeur over by the garage had gone away. The butler came along the red path with smooth light steps and his back as straight as an ironing board. I shrugged into my coat and watched him come.

He stopped about two feet from me and said gravely: 'Mrs Regan would like to see you before you leave, sir. And in the matter of money the General has instructed me to give you a cheque for whatever seems desirable.'

'Instructed you how?'

He looked puzzled, then he smiled. 'Ah, I see, sir. You are, of course, a detective. By the way he rang his bell.'

'You write his cheques?'

'I have that privilege.'

'That ought to save you from a pauper's grave. No money now, thanks. What does Mrs Regan want to see me about?'

His blue eyes gave me a smooth level look. 'She has a misconception of the purpose of your visit, sir.'

'Who told her anything about my visit?'

'Her windows command the greenhouse. She saw us go in. I was obliged to tell her who you were.'

'I don't like that,' I said.

His blue eyes frosted. 'Are you attempting to tell me my duties, sir?'

'No. But I'm having a lot of fun trying to guess what they are.'

We stared at each other for a moment. He gave me a blue glare and turned away.

CHAPTER 3

This room was too big, the ceiling was too high, the doors were too tall, and the white carpet that went from wall to wall looked like a fresh fall of snow at Lake Arrowhead. There were full-length mirrors and crystal doodads all over the place. The ivory furniture had chromium on it, and the enormous ivory drapes lay tumbled on the white carpet a yard from the windows. The white made the ivory look dirty and the ivory made the white look bled out. The windows stared towards the darkening foothills. It was going to rain soon. There was pressure in the air already.

I sat down on the edge of a deep soft chair and looked at Mrs Regan. She was worth a stare. She was trouble. She was stretched out on a modernistic chaise-longue with her slippers off, so I stared at her legs in the sheerest silk stockings. They seemed to be arranged to stare at. They were visible to the knee and one of them well beyond. The knees were dimpled, not bony and sharp. The calves were beautiful, the ankles long and slim and with enough melodic line for a tone poem. She was tall and rangy and strong-looking. Her head was against an ivory satin cushion. Her hair was black and wiry and parted in the middle and she had hot black eyes of the portrait in the hall. She had a good mouth and a good chin. There was a sulky droop to her lips and the lower lip was full.

She had a drink. She took a swallow from it and gave me a cool level stare over the rim of the glass.

'So you're a private detective,' she said. 'I didn't know they really existed, except in books. Or else they were greasy little men snooping around hotels.'

There was nothing in that for me, so I let it drift with the current. She put her glass down on the flat arm of the chaise-longue and flashed an emerald and touched her hair. She said slowly: 'How did you like Dad?'

'I liked him,' I said.

'He liked Rusty. I suppose you know who Rusty is?'

'Uh-huh.'

'Rusty was earthy and vulgar at times, but he was very real. And he was a lot of fun for Dad. Rusty shouldn't have gone off like that. Dad feels very badly about it, although he won't say so. Or did he?'

'He said something about it.'

'You're not much of a gusher, are you, Mr Marlowe? But he wants to find him, doesn't he?'

I stared at her politely through a pause. 'Yes and no,' I said.

'That's hardly an answer. Do you think you can find him?'

'I didn't say I was going to try. Why not try the Missing Persons Bureau? They have the organization. It's not a one-man job.'

'Oh, Dad wouldn't hear of the police being brought into it.' She looked at me smoothly across her glass again, emptied it, and rang a bell. A maid came into the room by a side door. She was a middle-aged woman with a long yellow gentle face, a long nose, no chin, large wet eyes. She looked like a nice old horse that had been turned out to pasture after long service. Mrs Regan waved the empty glass at her and she mixed another drink and handed it to her and left the room, without a word, without a glance in my direction.

When the door shut Mrs Regan said: 'Well, how will you go about it then?'

'How and when did he skip out?'

'Didn't Dad tell you?'

I grinned at her with my head on one side. She flushed. Her hot black eyes looked mad. 'I don't see what there is to be cagey about,' she snapped. 'And I don't like your manners.'

'I'm not crazy about yours,' I said. 'I didn't ask to see you. You sent for me. I don't mind your ritzing me or drinking your lunch out of a Scotch bottle. I don't mind your showing me your legs. They're very swell legs and it's a pleasure to make their acquaintance. I don't mind if you don't like my manners. They're pretty bad. I grieve over them during the long winter evenings. But don't waste your time trying to cross-examine me.'

She slammed her glass down so hard that it slopped over on an ivory cushion. She swung her legs to the floor and stood up with her eyes sparking fire and her nostrils wide. Her mouth was open and her bright teeth glared at me. Her knuckles were white.

'People don't talk like that to me,' she said thickly.

I sat there and grinned at her. Very slowly she closed her mouth and looked down at the spilled liquor. She sat down on the edge of the chaise-longue and cupped her chin in one hand.

'My God, you big dark handsome brute! I ought to throw a Buick at you.'

I snicked a match on my thumbnail and for once it lit. I puffed smoke into the air and waited.

'I loathe masterful men,' she said. 'I simply loathe them.'

'Just what is it you're afraid of, Mrs Regan?'

Her eyes whitened. Then they darkened until they seemed to be all pupil. Her nostrils looked pinched.

'That wasn't what he wanted with you at all,' she said in a strained voice that still had shreds of anger clinging to it. 'About Rusty. Was it?'

'Better ask him.'

She flared up again. 'Get out! Damn you, get out!'

I stood up. 'Sit down!' she snapped. I sat down. I flicked a finger at my palm and waited.

'Please,' she said. 'Please. You could find Rusty – if Dad wanted you to.'

That didn't work either. I nodded and asked: 'When did he go?'

'One afternoon a month back. He just drove away in his car without saying a word. They found the car in a private garage somewhere.'

'They?'

She got cunning. Her whole body seemed to go lax. Then she smiled at me winningly. 'He didn't tell you then.' Her voice was almost gleeful, as if she had outsmarted me. Maybe she had.

'He told me about Mr Regan, yes. That's not what he wanted to see me about. Is that what you've been trying to get me to say?'

'I'm sure I don't care what you say.'

I stood up again. 'Then I'll be running along.' She didn't speak. I went over to the tall white door I had come in at. When I looked back she had her lip between her teeth and was worrying it like a puppy at the fringe of a rug.

I went out, down the tile staircase to the hall, and the butler drifted out of somewhere with my hat in his hand. I put it on while he opened the door for me.

'You made a mistake,' I said. 'Mrs Regan didn't want to see me.'

He inclined his silver head and said politely: 'I'm sorry, sir. I make many mistakes.' He closed the door against my back.

I stood on the step breathing my cigarette smoke and looking down a succession of terraces with flowerbeds and trimmed trees to the high iron fence with gilt spears that hemmed in the estate. A winding driveway dropped down between retaining walls to the open iron gates. Beyond the fence the hill sloped for several miles. On this lower level faint and far off I could just barely see some of the old wooden derricks of the oilfield from which the Sternwoods had made their money. Most of the field was public park now, cleaned up and donated to the city by General Sternwood. But a little of it was still producing in groups of wells pumping five or six barrels a day. The Sternwoods, having moved up the hill, could no longer smell the stale sump water or the oil, but they could still look out of their front windows and see what had made them rich. If they wanted to. I don't suppose they would want to.

I walked down a brick path from terrace to terrace, followed along inside the fence and so out of the gates to where I had left my car under a pepper tree on the street. Thunder was cracking in the foothills now and the sky above them was purple-black. It was going to rain hard. The air had the damp foretaste of rain. I put the top up on my convertible before I started down-town.

She had lovely legs. I would say that for her. They were a couple of pretty smooth citizens, she and her father. He was probably just trying me out; the job he had given me was a lawyer's job. Even if Mr Arthur Gwynn Geiger, 'Rare Books and De Luxe Edition', turned out to be a blackmailer, it was still a lawyer's job. Unless there was a lot more to it than met the eye. At a casual glance I thought I might have a lot of fun finding out.

I drove down to the Hollywood public library and did a little superficial research in a stuffy volume called *Famous First Editions*. Half an hour of it made me need my lunch.

CHAPTER 4

A. G. Geiger's place was a store frontage on the north side of the boulevard near Las Palmas. The entrance door was set far back in the middle and there was a copper trim on the windows, which were backed with Chinese screens, so I couldn't see into the store. There was a lot of Oriental junk in the windows. I didn't know whether it was any good, not being a collector of antiques, except unpaid bills. The entrance door was plate glass, but I couldn't see much through that either, because the store was very dim. A building entrance adjoined it on one side and on the other was a glittering credit jewellery establishment. The jeweller stood in his entrance, teetering on his heels and looking bored, a tall handsome white-haired Jew in lean dark clothes, with about nine carats of diamond on his right hand. A faint knowing smile curved his lips when I turned into Geiger's store. I let the door close softly behind me and walked on a thick blue rug that paved the floor from wall to wall. There were blue leather easy chairs with smoke stands beside them. A few sets of tooled leather bindings were set out on narrow polished tables, between book ends. There were more tooled bindings in glass cases on the walls. Nice-looking merchandise, the kind a rich promoter would buy by the yard and have somebody paste his bookplate in. At the back there was a grained wood partition with a door in the middle of it, shut. In the corner made by the partition and one wall a woman sat behind a small desk with a carved wooden lantern on it.

She got up slowly and swayed towards me in a tight black dress that didn't reflect any light. She had long thighs and she walked with a certain something I hadn't often seen in bookstores. She was an ash blonde with greenish eyes, beaded lashes, hair waved smoothly back from ears in which large jet buttons glittered. Her fingernails were silvered. In spite of her getup she looked as if she would have a hall bedroom accent.

She approached me with enough sex appeal to stampede a businessmen's lunch and tilted her head to finger a stray, but not very stray, tendril of softly glowing hair. Her smile was tentative, but could be persuaded to be nice.

'Was it something?' she inquired.

I had my horn-rimmed sun-glasses on. I put my voice high and let a bird twitter in it. 'Would you happen to have a *Ben Hur* 1860?'

She didn't say: 'Huh?' but she wanted to. She smiled bleakly. 'A first edition?'

'Third,' I said. 'The one with the erratum on page 116.'

'I'm afraid not – at the moment.'

'How about a *Chevalier Audubon* 1840 – the full set, of course?'

'Er – not at the moment,' she said harshly. Her smile was now hanging by its teeth and eyebrows and wondering what it would hit when it dropped.

'You *do* sell books?' I said in my polite falsetto.

She looked me over. No smile now. Eyes medium to hard. Pose very straight and stiff. She waved silver finger-nails at the glassed-in shelves. 'What do they look like – grapefruit?' she inquired tartly.

'Oh, that sort of thing hardly interests me, you know. Probably has duplicate sets of steel engravings, tuppence coloured and a penny plain. The usual vulgarity. No. I'm sorry. No.'

'I see.' She tried to jack the smile back upon her face. She was as sore as an alderman with the mumps. 'Perhaps Mr Geiger – but he's not in at the moment.' Her eyes studied me carefully. She knew as much about rare books as I knew about handling a flea circus.

'He might be in later?'

'I'm afraid not until late.'

'Too bad,' I said. 'Ah, too bad. I'll sit down and smoke a cigarette in one of these charming chairs. I have rather a blank afternoon. Nothing to think about but my trigonometry lesson.'

'Yes,' she said. 'Ye–es, of course.'

I stretched out in one and lit a cigarette with the round nickel lighter on the smoking stand. She still stood, holding her lower lip with her teeth, her eyes vaguely troubled. She nodded at last, turned slowly and walked back to her little desk in the corner. From behind the lamp she stared at me. I crossed my ankles and yawned. Her silver nails went out to the cradle phone on the desk, didn't touch it, dropped and began to tap on the desk.

Silence for about five minutes. The door opened and a tall hungry-looking bird with a cane and a big nose came in neatly, shut the door behind him against the pressure of the door-closer, marched over to the desk and placed a wrapped parcel on the desk. He took a pin-seal wallet with gold corners from his pocket and showed the blonde something. She pressed a button on the desk. The tall bird went to the door in the panelled partition and opened it barely enough to slip through.

I finished my cigarette and lit another. The minutes dragged by. Horns tooted and grunted on the boulevard. A big red interurban car grumbled past. A traffic light gonged. The blonde leaned on her elbow and cupped a hand over her eyes and stared at me behind it. The partition door opened and the tall bird with the cane slid out. He had another wrapped parcel, the shape of a large book. He went over to the desk and paid money. He left as he had come, walking on the balls of his feet, breathing with his mouth open, giving me a sharp side glance as he passed.

I got to my feet, tipped my hat to the blonde and went out after him. He walked west, swinging his cane in a small tight arc just above his right shoe. He was easy to follow. His coat was cut from a rather loud piece of horse robe with shoulders so wide that his neck stuck up out of it like a celery stalk and his head wobbled on it as he walked. We went a block and a half. At the Highland Avenue traffic signal I pulled up beside him and let him see me. He gave me a casual, then a suddenly sharpened side glance, and quickly turned away. We crossed Highland with the green light and made another block. He stretched his long legs and had twenty yards on me at the corner. He turned right. A hundred feet up the hill he stopped and hooked his cane over his arm and fumbled a leather cigarette-case out of an inner pocket. He put a cigarette in his mouth, dropped his match, looked back when he picked it up, saw me watching him from the corner, and straightened up as if somebody had booted him from behind. He almost raised dust going up the block, walking with long gawky strides and jabbing his cane into the pavement. He turned left again. He had at least half a block on me when I reached the place where he had turned. He had me wheezing. This was a narrow tree-lined street with a retaining wall on one side and three bungalow courts on the other.

He was gone. I loafed along the block peering this way and that. At the second bungalow court I saw something. It was called The La Baba, a quiet dim place with a double row of tree-shaded bungalows. The central walk was lined with Italian cypresses trimmed short and chunky, something the shape of the oil jars in *Ali Baba and the Forty Thieves*. Behind the third jar a loud-patterned sleeve edge moved.

I leaned against a pepper tree in the parkway and waited. The thunder in the foothills was rumbling again. The glare of lightning was reflected on piled-up black clouds off to the south. A few tentative raindrops splashed down on the pavement and made spots as large as nickels. The air was as still as the air in General Sternwood's orchid house.

The sleeve behind the tree showed again, then a big nose and one eye and some sandy hair without a hat on it. The eye stared at me. It disappeared. Its mate reappeared like a woodpecker on the other side of the tree. Five minutes went by. It got him. His type are half nerves. I heard a match strike and then whistling started. Then a dim shadow slipped along the grass to the next tree. Then he was out on the walk coming straight towards me, swinging the cane and whistling. A sour whistle with jitters in it. I stared vaguely at the dark sky. He passed within ten feet of me and didn't give me a glance. He was safe now. He had ditched it.

I watched him out of sight and went up the central walk of The La Baba and parted the branches of the third cypress. I drew out a wrapped book and put it under my arm and went away from there. Nobody yelled at me.

CHAPTER 5

Back on the boulevard I went into a drugstore phone booth and looked up Mr Arthur Gwynn Geiger's residence. He lived on Laverne Terrace, a hillside street off Laurel Canyon Boulevard. I dropped my nickel and dialled his number just for fun. Nobody answered. I turned to the classified section and noted a couple of bookstores within blocks of where I was.

The first I came to was on the north side, a large lower floor devoted to stationery and office supplies, a mass of books on the mezzanine. It didn't look the right place. I crossed the street and walked two blocks east to the other one. This was more like it, a narrowed cluttered little shop stacked with books from floor to ceiling and four or five browsers taking their time putting thumb marks on the new jackets. Nobody paid any attention to them. I shoved on back into the store, passed through a partition and found a small dark woman reading a law book at a desk.

I flipped my wallet open on her desk and let her look at the buzzer pinned to the flap. She looked at it, took her glasses off and leaned back in her chair. I put the wallet away. She had the fine-drawn face of an intelligent Jewess. She stared at me and said nothing.

I said: 'Would you do me a favour, a very small favour?'

'I don't know. What is it?' She had a smoothly husky voice.

'You know Geiger's store across the street, two blocks west?'

'I think I may have passed it.'

'It's a bookstore,' I said. 'Not your kind of bookstore. You know darn well.'

She curled her lips slightly and said nothing. 'You know Geiger by sight?' I asked.

'I'm sorry. I don't know Mr Geiger.'

'Then you couldn't tell me what he looks like?'

Her lips curled some more. 'Why should I?'

'No reason at all. If you don't want to, I can't make you.'

She looked out through the partition door and leaned back again. 'That was a sheriff's star, wasn't it?'

'Honorary deputy. Doesn't mean a thing. It's worth a dime cigar.'

'I see.' She reached for a pack of cigarettes and shook one loose and reached for it with her lips. I held a match for her. She thanked me, leaned back again and regarded me through smoke. She said carefully:

'You wish to know what he looks like and you don't want to interview him?'

'He's not there,' I said.

'I presume he will be. After all, it's his store.'

'I don't want to interview him just yet,' I said.

She looked out through the open doorway again. I said: 'Know anything about rare books?'

'You could try me.'

'Would you have a *Ben Hur,* 1860, third edition, the one with the duplicated line on page 116?'

She pushed her yellow law book to one side and reached a fat volume up on the desk, leafed it through, found her page, and studied it. 'Nobody would,' she said without looking up. 'There isn't one.'

'Right.'

'What in the world are you driving at?'

'The girl in Geiger's store didn't know that.'

She look up. 'I see. You interest me. Rather vaguely.'

'I'm a private dick on a case. Perhaps I ask too much. It didn't seem much to me somehow.'

She blew a soft grey smoke ring and poked her finger through. It came to pieces in frail wisps. She spoke smoothly, indifferently. 'In his early forties, I should judge. Medium height, fattish. Would weigh about a hundred and sixty pounds. Fat face, Charlie Chan moustache, thick soft neck. Soft all over. Well dressed, goes without a hat, affects a knowledge of antiques and hasn't any. Oh yes. His left eye is glass.'

'You'd make a good cop,' I said.

She put the reference book back on an open shelf at the end of her desk, and opened the law book in front of her again. 'I hope not,' she said. She put her glasses on.

I thanked her and left. The rain had started. I ran for it, with the wrapped book under my arm. My car was on a side street pointing at the boulevard almost opposite Geiger's store. I was well sprinkled before I got there. I tumbled into the car and ran both windows up and wiped my parcel off with my handkerchief. Then I opened it up.

I knew about what it would be, of course. A heavy book, well bound, handsomely printed in handset type on fine paper. Larded with full-page arty photographs. Photos and letterpress were alike of an indescribable filth. The book was not new. Dates were stamped on the front endpaper, in and out dates. A rent book. A lending library of elaborate smut.

I re-wrapped the book and locked it up behind the seat. A racket like that, out in the open on the boulevard, seemed to mean plenty of protection. I sat there and poisoned myself with cigarette smoke and listened to the rain and thought about it.

CHAPTER 6

Rain filled the gutters and splashed knee-high off the pavement. Big cops in slickers that shone like gun barrels had a lot of fun carrying giggling girls across the bad place. The rain drummed hard on the roof of the car and the burbank top began to leak. A pool of water formed on the floorboards for me to keep my feet in. It was too early in the fall for that kind of rain. I struggled into a trench coat and made a dash for the nearest drugstore and bought myself a pint of whisky. Back in the car I used enough of it to keep warm and interested. I was long overparked, but the cops were too busy carrying girls and blowing whistles to bother about that.

In spite of the rain, or perhaps even because of it, there was business done at Geiger's. Very nice cars stopped in front and very nice-looking people went in and out with wrapped parcels. They were not all men.

He showed about four o'clock. A cream-coloured coupé stopped in front of the store and I caught a glimpse of the fat face and the Charlie

Chan moustache as he dodged out of it and into the store. He was hatless and wore a belted green leather raincoat. I couldn't see his glass eye at that distance. A tall and very good-looking kid in a jerkin came out of the store and rode the coupé off around the corner and came back walking, his glistening black hair plastered with rain.

Another hour went by. It got dark and the rain-clouded lights of the stores were soaked up by the black street. Street-car bells jangled crossly. At around five-fifteen the tall boy in the jerkin came out of Geiger's with an umbrella and went after the cream-coloured coupé. When he had it in front Geiger came out and the tall boy held the umbrella over Geiger's bare head. He folded it, shook it off and handed it into the car. He dashed back into the store. I started my motor.

The coupé went west on the boulevard, which forced me to make a left turn and a lot of enemies, including a motorman who stuck his head out into the rain to bawl me out. I was two blocks behind the coupé before I got in the groove. I hoped Geiger was on his way home. I caught sight of him two or three times and then made him turning north into Laurel Canyon Drive. Half-way up the grade he turned left and took a curving ribbon of wet concrete which was called Laverne Terrace. It was a narrow street with a high bank on one side and a scattering of cabin-like houses built down the slope on the other side, so that their roofs were not very much above road level. Their front windows were masked by hedges and shrubs. Sodden trees dripped all over the landscape.

Geiger had his lights on and I hadn't. I speeded up and passed him on a curve, picked a number off a house as I went by and turned at the end of the block. He had already stopped. His car lights were tilted in at the garage of a small house with a square box hedge so arranged that it masked the front door completely. I watched him come out of the garage with his umbrella up and go in through the hedge. He didn't act as if he expected anybody to be tailing him. Light went on in the house. I drifted down to the next house above it, which seemed empty but had no signs out. I parked, aired out the convertible, had a drink from my bottle, and sat. I didn't know what I was waiting for, but something told me to wait. Another army of sluggish minutes dragged by.

Two cars came up the hill and went over the crest. It seemed to be a very quiet street. At a little after six more bright lights bobbed through the driving rain. It was pitch-black by then. A car dragged to a stop in front of Geiger's house. The filaments of its lights glowed dimly and died. The door opened and a woman got out. The small slim woman in a vagabond hat and a transparent raincoat. She went in through the box maze. A bell rang faintly, light through the rain, a closing door, silence.

I reached a flash out of my car pocket and went down-grade and looked at the car. It was a Packard convertible, maroon or dark brown. The left window was down. I felt for the licence-holder and poked light at it. The registration read: Carmen Sternwood, 3765 Alta Brea Crescent, West Hollywood. I went back to my car again and sat and sat. The top dripped on my knees and my stomach burned from the whisky. No more cars came up the hill. No light went on in the house before which I was parked. It seemed like a nice neighbourhood to have bad habits in.

At seven-twenty a single flash of hard white light shot out of Geiger's house like a wave of summer lightning. As the darkness folded back on it and ate it up a thin tinkling scream echoed out and lost itself among the rain-drenched trees. I was out of the car and on my way before the echoes died.

There was no fear in the scream. It had a sound of half-pleasurable shock, an accent of drunkenness, an overtone of pure idiocy. It was a nasty sound. It made me think of men in white and barred windows and hard narrow cots with leather wrist and ankle straps fastened to them. The Geiger hideaway was perfectly silent again when I hit the gap in the hedge and dodged around the angle that masked the front door. There was an iron ring in a lion's mouth for a knocker. I reached for it, I had hold of it. At that exact instant, as if somebody had been waiting for the cue, three shots boomed in the house. There was a sound that might have been a long harsh sigh. Then a soft messy thump. And then rapid footsteps in the house – going away.

The door fronted on a narrow run, like a footbridge over a gully, that filled the gap between the house wall and the edge of the bank. There was no porch, no solid ground, no way to get around to the back. The back entrance was at the top of a flight of wooden steps that rose from the alley-like street below. I knew this because I heard a clatter of feet on the steps, going down. Then I heard the sudden roar of a starting car. It faded swiftly into the distance. I thought the sound was echoed by another car, but I wasn't sure. The house in front of me was as silent as a vault. There wasn't any hurry. What was in there was in there.

I straddled the fence at the side of the runway and leaned far out to the draped but unscreened French window and tried to look in at the crack where the drapes came together. I saw lamplight on a wall and one end of a bookcase. I got back on the runway and took all of it and some of the hedge and gave the front door the heavy shoulder. This was foolish. About the only part of a California house you can't put your foot through is the front door. All it did was hurt my shoulder and make me mad. I climbed over the railing again and kicked the French window in, used my hat for a glove and pulled out most of the lower small pane of glass. I could now reach in and draw a bolt that fastened the window to the sill. The rest was easy. There was no top bolt. The catch gave. I climbed in and pulled the drapes off my face.

Neither of the two people in the room paid any attention to the way I came in, although only one of them was dead.

CHAPTER 7

It was a wide room, the whole width of the house. It had a low beamed ceiling and brown plaster walls decked out with strips of Chinese embroidery, and Chinese and Japanese prints in grained wood frames. There were low bookshelves, there was a thick pinkish Chinese rug in which a gopher could have spent a week without showing his nose above the nap. There were floor cushions, bits of odd silk tossed around, as if whoever lived there had to have a piece he could reach out and thumb. There was a broad low divan of old rose tapestry. It had a wad of clothes on it, including lilac-coloured silk underwear. There was a big carved lamp on a pedestal, two other standing lamps with jade-green shades and long tassels. There was a black desk with carved gargoyles at the corners and behind it a yellow satin cushion on a polished black chair with carved arms and back. The room contained an odd assortment of odours, of which the most emphatic at the moment seemed to be the pungent aftermath of cordite and the sickish aroma of ether.

On a sort of low dais at one end of the room there was a high-backed teakwood chair in which Miss Carmen Sternwood was sitting on a fringed orange shawl. She was sitting very straight, with her hands on the arms of the chair, her knees close together, her body stiffly erect in the pose of an Egyptian goddess, her chin level, her small bright teeth shining between her parted lips. Her eyes were wide open. The dark slate colour of the iris had devoured the pupil. They were mad eyes. She seemed to be unconscious, but she didn't have the pose of unconsciousness. She looked as if, in her mind, she was doing something very important and making a fine job of it. Out of her mouth came a tinny chuckling noise which didn't change her expression or even move her lips.

She was wearing a pair of long jade earrings. They were nice earrings and had probably cost a couple of hundred dollars. She wasn't wearing anything else.

She had a beautiful body, small, lithe, compact, firm, rounded. Her skin in the lamplight had the shimmering lustre of a pearl. Her legs didn't quite have the raffish grace of Mrs Regan's legs, but they were very nice. I looked her over without either embarrassment or ruttishness. As a naked girl she was not there in that room at all. She was just a dope. To me she was always just a dope.

I stopped looking at her, and looked at Geiger. He was on his back on the floor, beyond the fringe of the Chinese rug, in front of a thing that looked like a totem pole. It had a profile like an eagle and its wide round eye was a camera lens. The lens was aimed at the naked girl in the chair. There was a blackened flash bulb clipped to the side of the totem pole. Geiger was wearing Chinese slippers with thick felt soles, and his legs were in black satin pyjamas and the upper part of him wore a Chinese embroidered coat, the front of which was mostly blood. His glass eye shone brightly up at me and was by far the most lifelike thing about him. At a glance none of the three shots I heard had missed. He was very dead.

The flash bulb was the sheet lightning I had seen. The crazy scream was the doped and naked girl's reaction to it. The three shots had been somebody else's idea of how the proceedings might be given a new twist. The idea of the lad who had gone down the back steps and slammed into a car and raced away. I could see merit in his point of view.

A couple of fragile gold-veined glasses rested on a red lacquer tray on the end of the black desk, beside a pot-bellied flagon of brown liquid. I took the stopper out and sniffed at it. It smelled of ether and something else, possibly laudanum. I had never tried the mixture but it seemed to go pretty well with the Geiger *ménage*.

I listened to the rain hitting the roof and the north windows. Beyond was no other sound, no cars, no siren, just the rain beating. I went over to the divan and peeled off my trench coat and pawed through the girl's clothes. There was a pale green rough wool dress of the pull-over type, with half sleeves. I thought I might be able to handle it. I decided to pass up her underclothes, not from feelings of delicacy, but because I couldn't see myself putting her pants on and snapping her brassiére. I took the dress over to the teak chair on the dais. Miss Sternwood smelled of ether also, at a distance of several feet. The tinny chuckling noise was still coming from her and a little froth oozed down her chin. I slapped her face. She blinked and stopped chuckling. I slapped her again.

'Come on,' I said brightly. 'Let's be nice. Let's get dressed.'

She peered at me, her slaty eyes as empty as holes in a mask. 'Gugugoterell,' she said.

I slapped her around a little more. She didn't mind the slaps. They didn't bring her out of it. I set to work with the dress. She didn't mind that either. She let me hold her arms up and she spread her fingers out wide, as if that was cute. I got her hands through the sleeves, pulled the dress down over her back, and stood her up. She fell into my arms giggling. I set her back in the chair and got her stockings and shoes on her.

'Let's take a little walk,' I said. 'Let's take a nice little walk.'

We took a little walk. Part of the time her earrings banged against my chest and part of the time we did the splits in unison, like adagio dancers. We walked over to Geiger's body and back. I had her look at him. She thought he was cute. She giggled and tried to tell me so, but she just bubbled. I walked her over to the divan and spread her out on it. She hiccuped twice, giggled a little and went to sleep. I stuffed her belongings into my pockets and went over behind the totem pole thing. The camera was there all right, set inside it, but there was no plateholder in the camera. I looked around on the floor, thinking he might have got it out before he was shot. No plateholder. I took hold of his limp chilling hand and rolled him a little. No plateholder. I didn't like this development.

I went into a hall at the back of the room and investigated the house. There was a bathroom on the right and a locked door, a kitchen at the back. The kitchen window had been jimmied. The screen was gone and the place where the hook had pulled out showed on the sill. The back door was unlocked. I left it unlocked and looked into a bedroom on the left side of the hall. It was neat, fussy, womanish. The bed had a flounced cover. There was perfume on the triple-mirrored dressing-table, beside a handkerchief, some loose money, a man's brushes, a keyholder. A man's clothes were in the closet and a man's slippers under the flounced edge of the bed cover. Mr Geiger's room. I took the keyholder back to the living-room and went through the desk. There was a locked steel box in the deep drawer. I used one of the keys on it. There was nothing in it but a blue leather book with an index and a lot of writing in code, in the same slanting printing that had written to General Sternwood. I put the notebook in my pocket, wiped the steel box where I had touched it, locked the desk up, pocketed the keys, turned the gas logs off in the fireplace, wrapped myself in my coat and tried to rouse Miss Sternwood. It couldn't be done. I crammed her vagabond hat on her head and swathed her in her coat and carried her out to her car. I went back and put all the lights out and shut the front door, dug her keys out of her bag and started the Packard. We went off down the hill without lights. It was less than ten minutes' drive to Alta Brea Crescent. Carmen spent them snoring and breathing ether in my face. I couldn't keep her head off my shoulder. It was all I could do to keep it out of my lap.

CHAPTER 8

There was dim light behind narrow leaded panes in the side door of the Sternwood mansion. I stopped the Packard under the *porte-cochère* and emptied my pockets out on the seat. The girl snored in the corner, her hat tilted rakishly over her nose, her hands hanging limp in the folds of the raincoat. I got out and rang the bell. Steps came slowly, as if from a long dreary distance. The door opened and the straight, silvery butler looked out at me. The light from the hall made a halo of his hair.

He said: 'Good evening, sir' politely and looked past me at the Packard. His eyes came back to look at my eyes.

'Is Mrs Regan in?'

'No, sir.'

'The General is asleep, I hope?'

'Yes. The evening is his best time for sleeping.'

'How about Mrs Regan's maid?'

'Mathilda? She's here, sir.'

'Better get her down here. The job needs the woman's touch. Take a look in the car and you'll see why.'

He took a look in the car. He came back. 'I see,' he said. 'I'll get Mathilda.'

'Mathilda will do right by her,' I said.

'We all try to do right by her,' he said.

'I guess you'll have had practice,' I said.

He let that one go. 'Well, good night,' I said. 'I'm leaving it in your hands.'

'Very good, sir. May I call you a cab?'

'Positively not,' I said. 'As a matter of fact I'm not here. You're just seeing things.'

He smiled then. He gave me a duck of his head and I turned and walked down the driveway and out of the gates.

Ten blocks of that, winding down curved rainswept street, under the steady drip of trees, past lighted windows in big houses in ghostly enormous grounds, vague clusters of eaves and gables and lighted windows high on the hillside, remote and inaccessible, like witch houses in a forest. I came out at a service station glaring with wasted light, where a bored attendant in a white cap and a dark blue windbreaker sat hunched on a stool, inside the steamed glass, reading a paper. I started in, then kept going. I was as wet as I could get already. And on a night like that you can grow a beard waiting for a taxi. And taxi drivers remember.

I made it back to Geiger's house in something over half an hour of nimble walking. There was nobody there, no car on the street except my own car in front of the next house. It looked as dismal as a lost dog. I dug my bottle of rye out of it and poured half of what was left down my throat and got inside to light a cigarette. I smoked half of it, threw it away, got out again and went down to Geiger's. I unlocked the door and stepped into the still warm darkness and stood there, dripping quietly on the floor and listening to the rain. I groped to a lamp and lit it.

The first thing I noticed was that a couple of strips of embroidered silk were gone from the wall. I hadn't counted them, but the spaces of brown plaster stood out naked and obvious. I went a little farther and put another lamp on. I looked at the totem pole. At its foot, beyond the margin of the Chinese rug, on the bare floor another rug had been spread. It hadn't been there before. Geiger's body had. Geiger's body was gone.

That froze me. I pulled my lips back against my teeth and leered at the glass eye in the totem pole. I went through the house again. Everything was exactly as it had been. Geiger wasn't in his flounced bed or under it or in his closet. He wasn't in the kitchen or the bathroom. That left the locked door on the right of the hall. One of Geiger's keys fitted the lock. The room inside was interesting, but Geiger wasn't in it. It was interesting because it was so different from Geiger's room. It was a hard bare masculine bedroom with a polished wood floor, a couple of small throw rugs in an Indian design, two straight chairs, a bureau in dark grained wood with a man's toilet set and two black candles in foot-high brass candlesticks. The bed was narrow and looked hard and had a maroon batik cover. The room felt cold. I locked it up again, wiped the knob off with my handkerchief, and went back to the totem pole. I knelt down and squinted along the nap of the rug to the front door. I thought I could see two parallel grooves pointing that way, as though heels had dragged. Whoever had done it had meant business. Dead men are heavier than broken hearts.

It wasn't the law. They would have been there still, just about getting warmed up with their pieces of string and chalk and their cameras and dusting powders and their nickel cigars. They would have been very much there. It wasn't the killer. He had left too fast. He must have seen the girl. He couldn't be sure she was too batty to see him. He would be on his way to distant places. I couldn't guess the answer, but it was all right with me if somebody wanted Geiger missing instead of just murdered. It gave me a chance to find out if I could tell it leaving Carmen Sternwood out. I locked up again, choked my car to life and rode off home to a shower, dry clothes and a late dinner. After that I sat around in the apartment and drank too much hot toddy trying to crack the code in Geiger's blue indexed notebook. All I could be sure of was that it was a list of names and addresses probably of the customers. There were over four hundred of them. That made it a nice racket, not to mention any blackmail angles, and there were probably plenty of those. Any name on the list might be a prospect as the killer. I didn't envy the police their job when it was handed to them.

I went to bed full of whisky and frustration and dreamed about a man in a bloody Chinese coat who chased a naked girl with long jade earrings while I ran after them and tried to take a photograph with an empty camera.

CHAPTER 9

The next morning was bright, clear and sunny. I woke up with a motorman's glove in my mouth, drank two cups of coffee and went through the morning papers. I didn't find any reference to Mr Arthur Gwynn Geiger in either of them. I was shaking the wrinkles out of my damp suit when the phone rang. It was Bernie Ohls, the DA's chief investigator, who had given me the lead to General Sternwood.

'Well, how's the boy?' he began. He sounded like a man who had slept well and didn't owe too much money.

'I've got a hangover,' I said.

'Tsk, tsk.' He laughed absently and then his voice became a shade too casual, a cagey cop voice. 'Seen General Sternwood yet?'

'Uh-huh.'

'Done anything for him?'

'Too much rain,' I answered, if that was an answer.

'They seem to be a family things happen to. A big Buick belonging to one of them is washing about in the surf off Lido fish pier.'

I held the telephone tight enough to crack it. I also held my breath.

'Yeah,' Ohls said cheerfully. 'A nice new Buick sedan all messed up with sand and sea water. . . . Oh, I almost forgot. There's a guy inside it.'

I let my breath out so slowly that it hung on my lips. 'Regan?' I asked.

'Huh? Who? Oh, you mean the ex-legger the eldest girl picked up and went and married. I never saw him. What would he be doing down there?'

'Quit stalling. What would anybody be doing down there?'

'I don't know, pal. I'm dropping down to look-see. Want to go along?'

'Yes.'

'Snap it up,' he said. 'I'll be in my hutch.'

Shaved, dressed and lightly breakfasted I was at the Hall of Justice in less than an hour. I rode up to the seventh floor and went along to the group of small offices used by the DA's men. Ohls's was no larger than the others, but he had it to himself. There was nothing on his desk but a blotter, a cheap pen set, his hat and one of his feet. He was a medium-sized blondish man with stiff white eyebrows, calm eyes and well-kept teeth. He looked like anybody you would pass on the street. I happened to know he had killed nine men – three of them when he was covered, or somebody thought he was.

He stood up and pocketed a flat tin of toy cigars called Entractes, jiggled the one in his mouth up and down and looked at me carefully along his nose, with his head thrown back.

'It's not Regan,' he said. 'I checked. Regan's a big guy, as tall as you and a shade heavier. This is a young kid.'

I didn't say anything.

'What made Regan skip out?' Ohls asked. 'You interested in that?'

'I don't think so,' I said.

'When a guy out of the liquor traffic marries into a rich family and then waves good-bye to a pretty dame and a couple million legitimate bucks – that's enough to make even me think. I guess you thought that was a secret.'

'Uh-huh.'

'Okey, keep buttoned, kid. No hard feelings.' He came around the desk tapping his pockets and reaching for his hat.

'I'm not looking for Regan,' I said.

He fixed the lock on his door and we went down to the official parking lot and got into a small blue sedan. We drove out Sunset, using the siren once in a while to beat a signal. It was a crisp morning, with just enough snap in the air to make life seem simple and sweet, if you didn't have too much on your mind. I had.

It was thirty miles to Lido on the coast highway, the first ten of them through traffic. Ohls made the run in three-quarters of an hour. At the end of that time we skidded to a stop in front of a faded stucco arch and I took my feet out of the floorboards and we got out. A long pier railed with white two-by-fours stretched seaward from the arch. A knot of people leaned out at the far end and a motor-cycle officer stood under the arch keeping another group of people from going out on the pier. Cars were parked on both sides of the highway, the usual ghouls, of both sexes. Ohls showed the motorcycle officer his badge and we went out on the pier, into a loud fish smell which one night's hard rain hadn't even dented.

'There she is – on the power barge,' Ohls said, pointing with one of his toy cigars.

A low black barge with a wheelhouse like a tug's was crouched against the pilings at the end of the pier. Something that glistened in the morning sunlight was on its deck, with hoist chains still around it, a large black and chromium car. The arm of the hoist had been swung back into position and lowered to deck level. Men stood around the car. We went down slippery steps to the deck.

Ohls said hello to a deputy in green khaki and a man in plain clothes. The barge crew of three men leaned against the front of the wheelhouse and chewed tobacco. One of them was rubbing at his wet hair with a dirty bathtowel. That would be the man who had gone down into the water to put the chains on.

We looked the car over. The front bumper was bent, one headlight smashed, the other bent up but the glass still unbroken. The radiator shell had a big dent in it, and the paint and nickel were scratched up all over the car. The upholstery was sodden and black. None of the tyres seemed to be damaged.

The driver was still draped around the steering post with his head at an unnatural angle to his shoulders. He was a slim dark-haired kid who had been good-looking not so long ago. Now his face was bluish white and his eyes were a faint dull gleam under the lowered lids and his open mouth had sand in it. On the left side of his forehead there was a dull bruise that stood out against the whiteness of the skin.

Ohls backed away, made a noise in his throat and put a match to his little cigar. 'What's the story?'

The uniformed man pointed up at the rubbernecks on the end of the pier. One of them was fingering a place where the white two-by-fours had been broken through in a wide space. The splintered wood showed yellow and clean, like fresh-cut pine.

'Went through there. Must have hit pretty hard. The rain stopped early down here, around 9 p.m. The broken wood's dry inside. That puts it after the rain stopped. She fell in plenty of water not to be banged up worse, not more than half tide or she'd have drifted farther, and not more than half tide going out or she'd have crowded the piles. That makes it around ten last night. Maybe nine-thirty, not earlier. She shows under the water when the boys come down to fish this morning, so we get the barge to hoist her out and we find the dead guy.'

The plain-clothes man scuffed at the deck with the toe of his shoe. Ohls looked sideways along his eyes at me, and twitched his little cigar like a cigarette.

'Drunk?' he asked, of nobody in particular.

The man who had been towelling his head went over to the rail and cleared his throat in a loud hawk that made everyone look at him. 'Got some sand,' he said, and spat. 'Not as much as the boy friend got – but some.'

The uniformed man said: 'Could have been drunk. Showing off all alone in the rain. Drunks will do anything.'

'Drunk, hell,' the plain-clothes man said. 'The hand throttle's set halfway down and the guy's been sapped on the side of the head. Ask me and I'll call it murder.'

Ohls looked at the man with the towel. 'What do you think, buddy?'

The man with the towel looked flattered. He grinned. 'I say suicide, Mac. None of my business, but you ask me, I say suicide. First off the guy ploughed an awful straight furrow down that pier. You can read his tread marks all the way nearly. That puts it after the rain like the Sheriff said. Then he hit the pier hard and clean or he don't go through and land right side up. More likely turned over a couple of times. So he had plenty of speed and hit the rail square. That's more than half-throttle. He could have done that with his hand falling and he could have hurt his head falling too.'

Ohls said: 'You got eyes, buddy. Frisked him?' he asked the deputy. The deputy looked at me then, at the crew against the wheelhouse. 'Okey, save that,' Ohls said.

A small man with glasses and a tired face and a black bag came down the steps from the pier. He picked out a fairly clean spot on the deck and put the bag down. Then he took his hat off and rubbed the back of his neck and stared out to sea, as if he didn't know where he was or what he had come for.

Ohls said: 'There's your customer, Doc. Dived off the pier last night. Around nine to ten. That's all we know.'

The small man looked in at the dead man morosely. He fingered the head, peered at the bruise on the temple, moved the head around with both hands, felt the man's ribs. He lifted a lax dead hand and stared at the fingernails. He let it fall and watched it fall. He stepped back and opened his bag and took out a printed pad of DOA forms and began to write over a carbon.

'Broken neck's the apparent cause of death,' he said, writing. 'Which means there won't be much water in him. Which means he's due to start getting stiff pretty quick now he's out in the air. Better get him out of the car before he does. You won't like doing it after.'

Ohls nodded. 'How long dead, Doc?'

'I wouldn't know.'

Ohls looked at him sharply and took the little cigar out of his mouth and looked at that sharply. 'Pleased to know you, Doc. A coroner's man that can't guess within five minutes has me beat.'

The little man grinned sourly and put his pad in his bag and clipped his pencil back on his waistcoat. 'If he ate dinner last night, I'll tell you – if I know what time he ate it. But not within five minutes.'

'How would he get that bruise – falling?'

The little man looked at the bruise again. 'I don't think so. That blow came from something covered. And it had already bled subcutaneously while he was alive.'

'Blackjack, huh?'

'Very likely.'

The little ME's man nodded, picked his bag off the deck and went back up the steps to the pier. An ambulance was backing into position outside the stucco arch. Ohls looked at me and said: 'Let's go. Hardly worth the ride, was it?'

We went back along the pier and got into Ohls's sedan again. He wrestled it around on the highway and drove back towards town along a three-lane highway washed clean by the rain, past low rolling hills of yellow-white sand terraced with pink moss. Seaward a few gulls wheeled and swooped over something in the surf and far out a white yacht looked as if it was hanging in the sky.

Ohls cocked his chin at me and said: 'Know him?'

'Sure. The Sternwood chauffeur. I saw him dusting that very car out there yesterday.'

'I don't want to crowd you, Marlowe. Just tell me, did the job have anything to do with him?'

'No. I don't even know his name.'

'Owen Taylor. How do I know? Funny about that. About a year or so back we had him in the cooler on a Mann Act rap. It seems he run Sternwood's hotcha daughter, the young one, off to Yuma. The sister ran after them and brought them back and had Owen heaved into the icebox. Then next day she comes down to the DA and gets him to beg the kid off with the US 'cutor. She says the kid meant to marry her sister and wanted to, only the sister can't see it. All *she* wanted was to kick a few high ones off the bar and have herself a party. So we let the kid go and then darned if they don't have him come back to work. And a little later we get the routine report on his prints from Washington, and he's got a prior back in Indiana, attempted hold-up six years ago. He got off with a six months in the county jail, the very one Dillinger bust out of. We hand that to the Sternwoods and they keep him on just the same. What do you think of that?'

'They seem to be a screwy family,' I said. 'Do they know about last night?'

'No. I gotta go up against them now.'

'Leave the old man out of it, if you can.'

'Why?'

'He has enough troubles and he's sick.'

'You mean Regan?'

I scowled. 'I don't know anything about Regan, I told you. I'm not looking for Regan. Regan hasn't bothered anybody that I know of.'

Ohls said: 'Oh,' and stared thoughtfully out to sea and the sedan nearly went off the road. For the rest of the drive back to town he hardly spoke. He dropped me off in Hollywood near the Chinese Theatre and turned back west to Alta Brea Crescent. I ate lunch at a counter and looked at an afternoon paper and couldn't find anything about Geiger in it.

After lunch I walked east on the boulevard to have another look at Geiger's store.

CHAPTER 10

The lean black-eyed credit jeweller was standing in his entrance in the same position as the afternoon before. He gave me the same knowing look as I turned in. The store looked just the same. The same lamp glowed on the small desk in the corner and the same ash blonde in the same black suéde-like dress got up from behind it and came towards me with the same tentative smile on her face.

'Was it—?' she said and stopped. Her silver nails twitched at her side. There was an overtone of strain in her smile. It wasn't a smile at all. It was a grimace. She just thought it was a smile.

'Back again,' I said airily, and waved a cigarette. 'Mr Geiger in today?'

'I'm – I'm afraid not. No – I'm afraid not. Let me see – you wanted—?'

I took my dark glasses off and tapped them delicately on the inside of my left wrist. If you can weigh a hundred and ninety pounds and look like a fairy, I was doing my best.

'That was just a stall about those first editions,' I whispered. 'I have to be careful. I've got something he'll want. Something he's wanted for a long time.'

The silver finger-nails touched the blonde hair over one small jet-buttoned ear. 'Oh, a salesman,' she said. 'Well – you might come in tomorrow. I think he'll be here tomorrow.'

'Drop the veil,' I said. 'I'm in the business too.'

Her eyes narrowed until they were a faint greenish glitter, like a forest pool far back in the shadow of trees. Her fingers clawed at her palm. She stared at me and chopped off a breath.

'Is he sick? I could go up to the house,' I said impatiently. 'I haven't got for ever.'

'You – a – you – a –' her throat jammed. I thought she was going to fall on her nose. Her whole body shivered and her face fell apart like a bride's pie crust. She put it together again slowly, as if lifting a great weight, by sheer will power. The smile came back, with a couple of corners badly bent.

'No,' she said. 'No. He's out of town. That – wouldn't be any use. Can't you – come in – tomorrow?'

I had my mouth open to say something when the partition door opened a foot. The tall dark handsome boy in the jerkin looked out, pale-faced and tight-lipped, saw me, shut the door quickly again, but not before I had seen on the floor behind him a lot of wooden boxes lined with newspapers and packed loosely with books. A man in very new overalls was fussing with them. Some of Geiger's stock was being moved out.

When the door shut I put my dark glasses on again and touched my hat. 'Tomorrow, then. I'd like to give you a card but you know how it is.'

'Ye – es. I know how it is.' She shivered a little more and made a faint sucking noise between her bright lips. I went out of the store and west on the boulevard to the corner and north on the street to the alley which ran behind the stores. A small black truck with wire sides and no lettering on it was backed up to Geiger's place. The man in the very new overalls was just heaving a box up on the tailboard. I went back to the boulevard and along the block next to Geiger's and found a taxi standing at a fireplug. A fresh-faced kid was reading a horror magazine behind the wheel. I leaned in and showed him a dollar: 'Tail job?'

He looked me over. 'Cop?'

'Private.'

He grinned. 'My meat, Jack.' He tucked the magazine over his rear-view mirror and I got into the cab. We went around the block and pulled up across from Geiger's alley, beside another fireplug.

There were about a dozen boxes on the truck when the man in overalls closed the screened doors and hooked the tailboard up and got in behind the wheel.

'Take him,' I told my driver.

The man in overalls gunned his motor, shot a glance up and down the alley and ran away fast in the other direction. He turned left out of the alley. We did the same. I caught a glimpse of the truck turning east on Franklin and told my driver to close in a little. He didn't or couldn't do it. I saw the truck two blocks away when we got to Franklin. We had it in sight to Vine and across Vine and all the way to Western. We saw it twice after Western. There was a lot of traffic and the fresh-faced kid tailed from too far back. I was telling him about that without mincing words when the truck, now far ahead, turned north again. The street at which it turned was called Britanny Place. When we got to Britanny Place the truck had vanished.

The fresh-faced kid made comforting sounds at me through the panel and we went up the hill at four miles an hour looking for the truck behind bushes. Two blocks up, Britanny Place swung to the east and met Randall Place in a tongue of land on which there was a white apartment house with its front on Randall Place and its basement garage opening on Britanny. We were going past that and the fresh-faced kid was telling me the truck couldn't be far away when I looked through the arched entrance of the garage and saw it back in the dimness with its rear doors open again.

We went around to the front of the apartment house and I got out. There was nobody in the lobby, no switchboard. A wooden desk was pushed back against the wall beside a panel of gilt mailboxes. I looked the names over. A man named Joseph Brody had Apartment 405. A man named Joe Brody had received five thousand dollars from General Sternwood to stop playing with Carmen and find some other little girl to play with. It could be the same Joe Brody. I felt like giving odds on it.

I went around an elbow of wall to the foot of tiled stairs and the shaft of the automatic elevator. The top of the elevator was level with the floor. There was a door beside the shaft lettered 'Garage'. I opened it and went down narrow steps to the basement. The automatic elevator was propped open and the man in new overalls was grunting hard as he stacked heavy boxes in it. I stood beside him and lit a cigarette and watched him. He didn't like my watching him.

After a while I said: 'Watch the weight, bud. She's only tested for half a ton. Where's the stuff going?'

'Brody, four-o-five,' he said. 'Manager?'

'Yeah. Looks like a nice lot of loot.'

He glared at me with pale white-rimmed eyes. 'Books,' he snarled. 'A hundred pounds a box, easy, and me with a seventy-five pound back.'

'Well, watch the weight,' I said.

He got into the elevator with six boxes and shut the doors. I went back up the steps to the lobby and out to the street and the cab took me down-town again to my office building. I gave the fresh-faced kid too much money and he gave me a dog-eared business card which for once I didn't drop into the majolica jar of sand beside the elevator bank.

I had a room and a half on the seventh floor at the back. The half-room was an office split in two to make reception-rooms. Mine had my name on it and nothing else, and that only on the reception-room. I always left this unlocked, in case I had a client, and the client cared to sit down and wait.

I had a client.

CHAPTER 11

She wore brownish speckled tweeds, a mannish shirt and tie, hand-carved walking shoes. Her stockings were just as sheer as the day before, but she wasn't showing as much of her legs. Her black hair was glossy under a brown Robin Hood hat that might have cost fifty dollars and looked as if you could have made it with one hand out of a desk blotter.

'Well, you *do* get up,' she said, wrinkling her nose at the faded red settee, the two odd semi-easy chairs, the net curtains that needed laundering and the boy's size library table with the venerable magazines on it to give the place a professional touch. 'I was beginning to think perhaps you worked in bed, like Marcel Proust.'

'Who's he?' I put a cigarette in my mouth and stared at her. She looked a little pale and strained, but she looked like a girl who could function under a strain.

'A French writer, a connoisseur in degenerates. You wouldn't know him.'

'Tut, tut,' I said. 'Come into my boudoir.'

She stood up and said: 'We didn't get along very well yesterday. Perhaps I was rude.'

'We were both rude,' I said. I unlocked the communicating door and held it for her. We went into the rest of my suite, which contained a rust-red carpet, not very young, five green filing cases, three of them full of California climate, an advertising calendar showing the Quins rolling around on a sky-blue floor, in pink dresses, with seal-brown hair and sharp black eyes as large as mammoth prunes. There were three near-walnut chairs, the usual desk with the usual blotter, pen set, ashtray and telephone, and the usual squeaky swivel chair behind it.

'You don't put on much of a front,' she said, sitting down at the customer's side of the desk.

I went over to the mail slot and picked up six envelopes, two letters and four pieces of advertising matter. I hung my hat on the telephone and sat down.

'Neither do the Pinkertons,' I said. 'You can't make much money at this trade, if you're honest. If you have a front, you're making money – or expect to.'

'Oh – are you honest?' she asked and opened her bag. She picked a cigarette out of a French enamel case, lit it with a pocket lighter, dropped case and lighter back into the bag and left the bag open.

'Painfully.'

'How did you ever get into this slimy kind of business then?'

'How did you come to marry a bootlegger?'

'My God, let's not start quarrelling again. I've been trying to get you on the phone all morning. Here and at your apartment.'

'About Owen?'

Her face tightened sharply. Her voice was soft. 'Poor Owen,' she said. 'So you know about that.'

'A DA's man took me down to Lido. He thought I might know something about it. But he knew much more than I did. He knew Owen wanted to marry your sister – once.'

She puffed silently at her cigarette and considered me with steady black eyes. 'Perhaps it wouldn't have been a bad idea,' she said quietly. 'He was in love with her. We don't find much of that in our circle.'

'He had a police record.'

She shrugged. She said negligently: 'He didn't know the right people. That's all a police record means in this rotten crime-ridden country.'

'I wouldn't go that far.'

She peeled her right glove off and bit her index finger at the first joint, looking at me with steady eyes. 'I didn't come to see you about Owen. Do you feel yet that you can tell me what my father wanted to see you about?'

'Not without his permission.'

'Was it about Carmen?'

'I can't even say that.' I finished filling a pipe and put a match to it. She watched the smoke for a moment. Then her hand went into her open bag and came out with a thick envelope. She tossed it across the desk.

'You'd better look at it anyway,' she said.

I picked it up. The address was typewritten to Mrs Vivian Regan, 3765 Alta Brea Crescent, West Hollywood. Delivery had been by messenger service and the office stamp showed 8.35 a.m. as the time out. I opened the envelope and drew out the shiny 4¼ by 3¼ photo that was all there was inside.

It was Carmen sitting in Geiger's high-backed teakwood chair on the dais, in her earrings and her birthday suit. Her eyes looked even a little crazier than as I remembered them. The back of the photo was blank. I put it back in the envelope.

'How much do they want?' I asked.

'Five thousand – for the negative and the rest of the prints. The deal has to be closed tonight, or they give the stuff to some scandal sheet.'

'The demand came how?'

'A woman telephoned me, about half an hour after this thing was delivered.'

'There's nothing in the scandal sheet angle. Juries convict without leaving the box on that stuff nowadays. What else is there?'

'Does there have to be something else?'

'Yes.'

She stared at me, a little puzzled. 'There is. The woman said there was a police jam connected with it and I'd better lay it on the line fast, or I'd be talking to my little sister through a wire screen.'

'Better,' I said. 'What kind of jam?'

'I don't know.'

'Where is Carmen now?'

'She's at home. She was sick last night. She's still in bed, I think.'

'Did she go out last night?'

'No. I was out, but the servants say she wasn't. I was down at Las Olindas, playing roulette at Eddie Mars's Cypress Club. I lost my shirt.'

'So you like roulette. You would.'

She crossed her legs and lit another cigarette. 'Yes. I like roulette. All the Sternwoods like losing games, like roulette and marrying men that walk out on them and riding steeplechases at fifty-eight years old and being rolled on by a jumper and crippled for life. The Sternwoods have money. All it has bought them is a rain cheque.'

'What was Owen doing last night with your car?'

'Nobody knows. He took it without permission. We always let him take a car on his night off, but last night wasn't his night off.' She made a wry mouth. 'Do you think—?'

'He knew about this nude photograph? How would I be able to say? I don't rule him out. Can you get five thousand in cash right away?'

'Not unless I tell Dad – or borrow it. I could probably borrow it from Eddie Mars. He ought to be generous with me, Heaven knows.'

'Better try that. You may need it in a hurry.'

She leaned back and hung an arm over the back of the chair. 'How about telling the police?'

'It's a good idea. But you won't do it.'

'Won't I?'

'No. You have to protect your father and your sister. You don't know what the police might turn up. It might be something they couldn't sit on. Though they usually try in blackmail cases.'

'Can you do anything?'

'I think I can. But I can't tell you why or how.'

'I like you,' she said suddenly. 'You believe in miracles. Would you have a drink in the office?'

I unlocked my deep drawer and got out my office bottle and two pony glasses. I filled them and we drank. She snapped her bag shut and pushed her chair back.

'I'll get the five grand,' she said. 'I've been a good customer of Eddie

Mars. There's another reason why he should be nice to me, which you may not know.' She gave me one of those smiles the lips have forgotten before they reach the eyes. 'Eddie's blonde wife is the lady Rusty ran away with.'

I didn't say anything. She stared tightly at me and added: 'That doesn't interest you?'

'It ought to make it easier to find him – if I was looking for him. You don't think he's in this mess, do you?'

She pushed her empty glass at me. 'Give me another drink. You're the hardest guy to get anything out of. You don't even move your ears.'

I filled the little glass. 'You've got all you wanted out of me – a pretty good idea I'm not looking for your husband.'

She put the drink down very quickly. It made her gasp – or gave her an opportunity to gasp. She let a breath out slowly.

'Rusty was no crook. If he had been, it wouldn't have been for nickels. He carried fifteen thousand dollars, in bills. He called it his mad money. He had it when I married him and he had it when he left me. No – Rusty's not in on any cheap blackmail racket.'

She reached for the envelope and stood up. 'I'll keep in touch with you,' I said. 'If you want to leave me a message, the phone girl at my apartment house will take care of it.'

We walked over to the door. Tapping the white envelope against her knuckles, she said: 'You still feel you can't tell me what Dad—'

'I'd have to see him first.'

She took the photo out and stood looking at it, just inside the door. 'She has a beautiful little body, hasn't she?'

'Uh-huh.'

She leaned a little towards me. 'You ought to see mine,' she said gravely.

'Can it be arranged?'

She laughed suddenly and sharply and went half-way through the door, then turned her head to say coolly: 'You're as cold-blooded a beast as I ever met, Marlowe. Or can I call you Phil?'

'Sure.'

'You can call me Vivian.'

'Thanks, Mrs Regan.'

'Oh, go to hell, Marlowe.' She went on out and didn't look back.

I let the door shut and stood with my hand on it, staring at the hand. My face felt a little hot. I went back to the desk and put the whisky away and rinsed out the two pony glasses and put them away.

I took my hat off the phone and called the DA's office, and asked for Bernie Ohls.

He was back in his cubby-hole. 'Well, I let the old man alone,' he said. 'The butler said he or one of the girls would tell him. This Owen Taylor lived over the garage and I went through his stuff. Parents at Dubuque, Iowa. I wired the Chief of Police there to find out what they want done. The Sternwood family will pay for it.'

'Suicide?' I asked.

'No can tell. He didn't leave any notes. He had no leave to take the car. Everybody was home last night but Mrs Regan. She was down at Las Olindas with a playboy named Larry Cobb. I checked on that. I know a lad on one of the tables.'

'You ought to stop some of that flash gambling,' I said.

'With the syndicate we got in this county? Be your age, Marlowe. That sap mark on the boy's head bothers me. Sure you can't help me on this?'

I liked his putting it that way. It let me say no without actually lying. We said good-bye and I left the office, bought all three afternoon papers and rode a taxi down to the Hall of Justice to get my car out of the lot. There was nothing in any of the papers about Geiger. I took another look at his blue notebook, but the code was just as stubborn as it had been the night before.

CHAPTER 12

The trees on the upper side of Laverne Terrace had fresh green leaves after the rain. In the cool afternoon sunlight I could see the steep drop of the hill and the flight of steps down which the killer had run after his three shots in the darkness. Two small houses fronted on the street below. They might or might not have heard the shots.

There was no activity in front of Geiger's house or anywhere along the block. The box hedge looked green and peaceful and the shingles on the roof were still damp. I drove past slowly, gnawing at an idea. I hadn't looked in the garage the night before. Once Geiger's body slipped away I hadn't really wanted to find it. It would force my hand. But dragging him to the garage, to his own car and driving that off into one of the hundred-odd lonely canyons around Los Angeles would be a good way to dispose of him for days or even for weeks. That supposed two things: a key to his car and two in the party. It would narrow the sector of search quite a lot, especially as I had had his personal keys in my pocket when it happened.

I didn't get a chance to look at the garage. The doors were shut and padlocked and something moved behind the hedge as I drew level. A woman in a green and white check coat and a small button of a hat on soft blonde hair stepped out of the maze and stood looking wild-eyed at my car, as if she hadn't heard it come up the hill. Then she turned swiftly and dodged back out of sight. It was Carmen Sternwood, of course.

I went on up the street and parked and walked back. In the daylight it seemed an exposed and dangerous thing to do. I went in through the hedge. She stood there straight and silent against the locked front door. One hand went slowly up to her teeth and her teeth bit at her funny thumb. There were purple smears under her eyes and her face was gnawed white by nerves.

She half smiled at me. She said: 'Hello,' in a thin, brittle voice. 'What–what—?' That tailed off and she went back to the thumb.

'Remember me?' I said. 'Doghouse Reilly, the man that grew too tall. Remember?'

She nodded and a quick jerky smile played across her face.

'Let's go in,' I said. 'I've got a key. Swell, huh?'

'Wha–wha—?'

I pushed her to one side and put the key in the door and opened it and pushed her in through it. I shut the door again and stood there sniffing. The place was horrible by daylight. The Chinese junk on the walls, the rug, the fussy lamps, the teakwood stuff, the sticky riot of colours, the totem pole, the flagon of ether and laudanum – all this in the daytime had a stealthy nastiness, like a fag party.

The girl and I stood looking at each other. She tried to keep a cute little smile on her face but her face was too tired to be bothered. It kept going blank on her. The smile would wash off like water off sand and her pale skin had a harsh granular texture under the stunned and stupid blankness of her eyes. A whitish tongue licked at the corners of her mouth. A pretty, spoiled and not very bright little girl who had gone very, very wrong, and nobody was doing anything about it. To hell with the rich. They made me sick. I rolled a cigarette in my fingers and pushed some books out of the way and sat on the end of the black desk. I lit my cigarette, puffed a plume of smoke and watched the thumb and tooth act for a while in silence. Carmen stood in front of me, like a bad girl in the principal's office.

'What are you doing here?' I asked her finally.

She picked at the cloth of her coat and didn't answer.

'How much do you remember of last night?'

She answered that – with a foxy glitter rising at the back of her eyes. 'Remember what? I was sick last night. I was home.' Her voice was a cautious throaty sound that just reached my ears.

'Like hell you were.'

Her eyes flicked up and down very swiftly.

'Before you went home,' I said. 'Before I took you home. Here. In that chair' – I pointed to it – 'on that orange shawl. You remember all right.'

A slow flush crept up her throat. That was something. She could blush. A glint of white showed under the clogged grey irises. She chewed hard on her thumb.

'You – were the one?' she whispered.

'Me. How much of it stays with you?'

She said vaguely: 'Are you the police?'

'No. I'm a friend of your father's.'

'You're not the police?'

'No.'

She let out a thin sigh. 'Wha–what do you want?'

'Who killed him?'

Her shoulders jerked, but nothing more moved in her face. 'Who else – knows?'

'About Geiger? I don't know. Not the police, or they'd be camping here. Maybe Joe Brody.'

It was a stab in the dark but it got her. 'Joe Brody! Him!'

Then we were both silent. I dragged at my cigarette and she ate her thumb.

'Don't get clever, for God's sake,' I urged her. 'This is a spot for a little old-fashioned simplicity. Did Brody kill him?'

'Kill who?'

'Oh, Christ,' I said.

She looked hurt. Her chin came down an inch. 'Yes,' she said solemnly. 'Joe did it.'

'Why?'

'I don't know.' She shook her head, persuading herself that she didn't know.

'Seen much of him lately?'

Her hands went down and made small white knots. 'Just once or twice. I hate him.'

'Then you know where he lives.'

'Yes.'

'And you don't like him any more?'

'I hate him!'

'Then you'd like him for the spot.'

A little blank again. I was going too fast for her. It was hard not to. 'Are you willing to tell the police it was Joe Brody?' I probed.

Sudden panic flamed all over her face. 'If I can kill the nude photo angle, of course,' I added soothingly.

She giggled. That gave me a nasty feeling. If she had screeched or wept or even nose-dived to the floor in a dead faint, that would have been all right. She just giggled. It was suddenly a lot of fun. She had had her photo taken as Isis and somebody had swiped it and somebody had bumped Geiger off in front of her and she was drunker than a Legion convention, and it was suddenly a lot of nice clean fun. So she giggled. Very cute. The giggles got louder and ran around the corners of the room like rats behind the wainscoting. She started to go hysterical. I slid off the desk and stepped up close to her and gave her a smack on the side of the face.

'Just like last night,' I said. 'We're a scream together. Reilly and Sternwood, two stooges in search of a comedian.'

The giggles stopped dead, but she didn't mind the slap any more than last night. Probably all her boy friends got around to slapping her sooner or later. I could understand how they might. I sat down on the end of the black desk again.

'Your name isn't Reilly,' she said seriously. 'It's Philip Marlowe. You're a private detective. Viv told me. She showed me your card.' She smoothed the cheek I had slapped. She smiled at me, as if I was nice to be with.

'Well, you do remember,' I said. 'And you came back to look for that photo and you couldn't get into the house. Didn't you?'

Her chin ducked down and up. She worked the smile. I was having the eye put on me. I was being brought into camp. I was going to yell 'Yippee!' in a minute and ask her to go to Yuma.

'The photo's gone,' I said. 'I looked last night, before I took you home. Probably Brody took it with him. You're not kidding me about Brody?'

She shook her head earnestly.

'It's a pushover,' I said. 'You don't have to give it another thought. Don't tell a soul you were here, last night or today. Not even Vivian. Just forget you were here. Leave it to Reilly.'

'Your name isn't—' she began, and then stopped and shook her head vigorously in agreement with what I had said or with what she had just thought of. Her eyes became narrow and almost black and as shallow as enamel on a cafeteria tray. She had had an idea. 'I have to go home now,' she said, as if we had been having a cup of tea.

'Sure.'

I didn't move. She gave me another cute glance and went on towards the front door. She had her hand on the knob when we both heard a car coming. She looked at me with questions in her eyes. I shrugged. The car stopped, right in front of the house. Terror twisted her face. There were steps and the bell rang. Carmen stared back at me over her shoulder, her hand clutching the door knob, almost drooling with fear. The bell kept on ringing. Then the ringing stopped. A key tickled at the door and Carmen jumped away from it and stood frozen. The door swung open. A man stepped through it briskly and stopped dead, staring at us quietly, with complete composure.

CHAPTER 13

He was a grey man, all grey, except for his polished black shoes and two scarlet diamonds in his grey satin tie that looked like the diamonds on roulette layouts. His shirt was grey and his double-breasted suit of soft, beautifully cut flannel. Seeing Carmen he took a grey hat off and his hair underneath it was grey and as fine as if it had been sifted through gauze. His thick grey eyebrows had that indefinably sporty look. He had a long chin, a nose with a hook to it, thoughtful grey eyes that had a slanted look because the fold of skin over his upper lid came down over the corner of the lid itself.

He stood there politely, one hand touching the door at his back, the other holding the grey hat and flapping it gently against his thigh. He looked hard, not the hardness of the tough guy. More like the hardness of a well-weathered horseman. But he was no horseman. He was Eddie Mars.

He pushed the door shut behind him and put that hand in the lap-seamed pocket of his coat and left the thumb outside to glisten in the rather dim light of the room. He smiled at Carmen. He had a nice easy smile. She licked her lips and stared at him. The fear went out of her face. She smiled back.

'Excuse the casual entrance,' he said. 'The bell didn't seem to rouse anybody. Is Mr Geiger around?'

I said: 'No. We don't know just where he is. We found the door a little open. We stepped inside.'

He nodded and touched his long chin with the brim of his hat. 'You're friends of his, of course?'

'Just business acquaintances. We dropped by for a book.'

'A book, eh?' He said that quickly and brightly and, I thought, a little slyly, as if he knew all about Geiger's books. Then he looked at Carmen again and shrugged.

I moved towards the door. 'We'll trot along now,' I said. I took hold of her arm. She was staring at Eddie Mars. She liked him.

'Any message – if Geiger comes back?' Eddie Mars asked gently.

'We won't bother you.'

'That's too bad,' he said, with too much meaning. His grey eyes twinkled and then hardened as I went past him to open the door. He added in a casual tone: 'The girl can dust. I'd like to talk to you a little, soldier.'

I let go of her arm. I gave him a blank stare. 'Kidder, eh?' he said nicely. 'Don't waste it. I've got two boys outside in a car that always do just what I want them to.'

Carmen made a sound at my side and bolted through the door. Her steps faded rapidly downhill. I hadn't seen her car, so she must have left it down below. I started to say: 'What the hell—!'

'Oh, skip it,' Eddie Mars sighed. 'There's something wrong around here. I'm going to find out what it is. If you want to pick lead out of your belly, get in my way.'

'Well, well,' I said, 'a tough guy.'

'Only when necessary, soldier.' He wasn't looking at me any more. He was walking around the room, frowning, not paying any attention to me. I looked out above the broken pane of the front window. The top of a car showed over the hedge. Its motor idled.

Eddie Mars found the purple flagon and the two gold-veined glasses on the desk. He sniffed at one of the glasses, then at the flagon. A disgusted smile wrinkled his lips. 'The lousy pimp,' he said tonelessly.

He looked at a couple of books, grunted, went on around the desk and stood in front of the little totem pole with the camera eye. He studied it, dropped his glance to the floor in front of it. He moved the small rug with his foot, then bent swiftly, his body tense. He went down on the floor with one grey knee. The desk hid him from me partly. There was a sharp exclamation and he came up again. His arm flashed under his coat and a black Luger appeared in his hand. He held it in long brown fingers, not pointing it at me, not pointing it at anything.

'Blood,' he said. 'Blood on the floor there, under the rug. Quite a lot of blood.'

'Is that so?' I said, looking interested.

He slid into the chair behind the desk and hooked the mulberry-coloured phone towards him and shifted the Luger to his left hand. He frowned sharply at the telephone, bringing his thick grey eyebrows close together and making a hard crease in the weathered skin at the top of his hooked nose. 'I think we'll have some law,' he said.

I went over and kicked at the rug that lay where Geiger had lain. 'It's old blood,' I said. 'Dried blood.'

'Just the same we'll have some law.'

'Why not?' I said.

His eyes went narrow. The veneer had flaked off him, leaving a well-dressed hard boy with a Luger. He didn't like my agreeing with him.

'Just who the hell are you, soldier?'

'Marlowe is the name. I'm a sleuth.'

'Never heard of you. Who's the girl?'

'Client. Geiger was trying to throw a loop on her with some blackmail. We came to talk it over. He wasn't here. The door being open we walked in to wait. Or did I tell you that?'

'Convenient,' he said. 'The door being open. When you didn't have a key.'

'Yes. How come *you* had a key?'

'Is that any of your business, soldier?'

'I could make it my business.'

He smiled tightly and pushed his hat back on his grey hair. 'And I could make your business my business.'

'You wouldn't like it. The pay's too small.'

'All right, bright eyes. I own this house. Geiger is my tenant. Now what do you think of that?'

'You know such lovely people.'

'I take them as they come. They come all kinds.' He glanced down at the Luger, shrugged and tucked it back under his arm. 'Got any good ideas, soldier?'

'Lots of them. Somebody gunned Geiger. Somebody got gunned by Geiger, who ran away. Or it was two other fellows. Or Geiger was running a cult and made blood sacrifices in front of that totem pole. Or he had chicken for dinner and liked to kill his chickens in the front parlour.'

The grey man scowled at me.

'I give up,' I said. 'Better call your friends down-town.'

'I don't get it,' he said. 'I don't get your game here.'

'Go ahead, call the buttons. You'll get a big reaction from it.'

He thought that over without moving. His lips went back against his teeth. 'I don't get that, either,' he said tightly.

'Maybe it just isn't your day. I know you, Mr Mars. The Cypress Club at Las Olindas. Flash gambling for flash people. The local law in your pocket and a well-greased line into LA. In other words, protection. Geiger was in a racket that needed that too. Perhaps you spared him a little now and then, seeing he's your tenant.'

His mouth became a hard white grimace. 'Geiger was in what racket?'

'The smut book racket.'

He stared at me for long level minute. 'Somebody got to him,' he said softly. 'You know something about it. He didn't show at the store today. They don't know where he is. He didn't answer the phone here. I came up to see about it. I find blood on the floor, under a rug. And you and a girl here.'

'A little weak,' I said. 'But maybe you can sell the story to a willing buyer. You missed a little something, though. Somebody moved his books out of the store today – the nice books he rented out.'

He snapped his fingers sharply and said: 'I should have thought of that, soldier. You seem to get around. How do you figure it?'

'I think Geiger was rubbed. I think that is his blood. And the books being moved out gives a motive for hiding the body for a while. Somebody is taking over the racket and wants a little time to organize.'

'They can't get away with it,' Eddie Mars said grimly.

'Who says so? You and a couple of gunmen in your car outside? This is a big town now, Eddie. Some very tough people have checked in here lately. The penalty of growth.'

'You talk too damned much,' Eddie Mars said. He bared his teeth and whistled twice, sharply. A car door slammed outside and running steps came through the hedge. Mars flicked the Luger out again and pointed it at my chest. 'Open the door.'

The knob rattled and a voice called out. I didn't move. The muzzle of the Luger looked like the mouth of the Second Street tunnel, but I didn't move. Not being bullet-proof is an idea I had had to get used to.

'Open it yourself, Eddie. Who the hell are you to give me orders? Be nice and I might help you out.'

He came to his feet rigidly and moved around the end of the desk and over to the door. He opened it without taking his eyes off me. Two men tumbled into the room, reaching busily under their arms. One was an obvious pug, a good-looking pale-faced boy with a bad nose and one ear like a club steak. The other man was slim, blond, deadpan, with close-set eyes and no colour in them.

Eddie Mars said: 'See if this bird is wearing any iron.'

The blond flicked a short-barrelled gun out and stood pointing it at me. The pug sidled over flatfooted and felt my pockets with care. I turned around for him like a bored beauty modelling an evening gown.

'No gun,' he said in a burry voice.

'Find out who he is.'

The pug slipped a hand into my breast pocket and drew out my wallet. He flipped it open and studied the contents. 'Name's Philip Marlowe, Eddie. Lives at the Hobart Arms on Franklin. Private licence, deputy's badge and all. A shamus.' He slipped the wallet back in my pocket, slapped my face lightly and turned away.

'Beat it,' Eddie Mars said.

The two gunmen went out again and closed the door. There was the sound of them getting back into the car. They started its motor and kept it idling once more.

'All right. Talk,' Eddie Mars said. The peaks of his eyebrows made sharp angles against his forehead.

'I'm not ready to give out. Killing Geiger to grab his racket would be a dumb trick and I'm not sure it happened that way, assuming he has been killed. But I'm sure that whoever got the books knows what's what, and I'm sure that the blonde lady down at his store is scared batty about something or other. And I have a guess who got the books.'

'Who?'

'That's the part I'm not ready to give out. I've got a client, you know.'

He wrinkled his nose. 'That—' he chopped it off quickly.

'I expected you would know the girl,' I said.

'Who got the books, soldier?'

'Not ready to talk, Eddie. Why should I?'

He put the Luger down on the desk and slapped it with his open palm. 'This,' he said. 'And I might make it worth your while.'

'That's the spirit. Leave the gun out of it. I can always hear the sound of money. How much are you clinking at me?'

'For doing what?'

'What did you want done?'

He slammed the desk hard. 'Listen, soldier. I ask you a question and you ask me another. We're not getting anywhere. I want to know where Geiger is, for my own personal reasons. I didn't like his racket and I didn't protect him. I happen to own this house. I'm not so crazy about that right now. I can believe that whatever you know about all this is under glass, or there would be a flock of johns squeaking sole leather around this dump. You haven't got anything to sell. My guess is you need a little protection yourself. So cough up.'

It was a good guess, but I wasn't going to let him know it. I lit a cigarette and blew the match out and flicked it at the glass eye of the totem pole. 'You're right,' I said. 'If anything has happened to Geiger, I'll have to give what I have to the law. Which puts it in the public domain and doesn't leave me anything to sell. So with your permission I'll just drift.'

His face whitened under the tan. He looked mean, fast and tough for a moment. He made a movement to lift the gun. I added casually: 'By the way, how is Mrs Mars these days?'

I thought for a moment I had kidded him a little too far. His hand jerked at the gun, shaking. His face was stretched out by hard muscles. 'Beat it,' he said quite softly. 'I don't give a damn where you go or what you do when you get there. Only take a word of advice, soldier. Leave me out of your plans or you'll wish your name was Murphy and you lived in Limerick.'

'Well, that's not so far from Clonmel,' I said. 'I hear you had a pal came from there.'

He leaned down on the desk, frozen-eyed, unmoving. I went over to the door and opened it and looked back at him. His eyes had followed me, but his lean grey body had not moved. There was hate in his eyes. I went out and through the hedge and up the hill to my car and got into it. I turned it around and drove up over the crest. Nobody shot at me. After a few blocks I turned off, cut the motor and sat for a few moments. Nobody followed me either. I drove back into Hollywood.

CHAPTER 14

It was ten minutes to five when I parked near the lobby entrance of the apartment house on Randall Place. A few windows were lit and radios were bleating at the dusk. I rode the automatic elevator up to the fourth floor and went along a wide hall carpeted in green and panelled in ivory. A cool breeze blew down the hall from the open screened door to the fire escape.

There was a small ivory pushbutton beside the door marked '405'. I pushed it and waited what seemed a long time. Then the door opened noiselessly about a foot. There was a steady, furtive air in the way it opened. The man was long-legged, long-waisted, high-shouldered and he had dark brown eyes in a brown expressionless face that had learned to control its expressions long ago. Hair like steel wool grew far back on his head and gave him a great deal of domed brown forehead that might at a careless glance have seemed a dwelling-place for brains. His sombre eyes probed at me impersonally. His long thin brown fingers held the edge of the door. He said nothing.

I said: 'Geiger?'

Nothing in the man's face changed that I could see. He brought a cigarette from behind the door and tucked it between his lips and drew a little smoke from it. The smoke came towards me in a lazy, contemptuous puff and behind it words in a cool, unhurried voice that had no more inflection than the voice of a faro dealer.

'You said what?'

'Geiger. Arthur Gwynn Geiger. The guy that has the books.'

The man considered that without any haste. He glanced down at the tip of his cigarette. His other hand, the one that had been holding the door, dropped out of sight. His shoulder had a look as though his hidden hand might be making motions.

'Don't know anybody by that name,' he said. 'Does he live around here?'

I smiled. He didn't like the smile. His eyes got nasty. I said: 'You're Joe Brody?'

The brown face hardened. 'So what? Got a grift, brother – or just amusing yourself?'

'So you're Joe Brody,' I said. 'And you don't know anybody named Geiger. That's very funny.'

'Yeah? You got a funny sense of humour maybe. Take it away and play on it somewhere else.'

I leaned against the door and gave him a dreamy smile. 'You got the books, Joe. I got the sucker list. We ought to talk things over.'

He didn't shift his eyes from my face. There was a faint sound in the room behind him, as though a metal curtain ring clicked lightly on a metal rod. He glanced sideways into the room. He opened the door wider.

'Why not – if you think you've got something?' he said coolly. He stood aside from the door. I went past him into the room.

It was a cheerful room with good furniture and not too much of it. French windows in the end wall opened on a stone porch and looked across the dusk at the foothills. Near the windows a closed door in the west wall and near the entrance door another door in the same wall. This last had a plush curtain drawn across it on a thin brass rod below the lintel.

That left the east wall, in which there were no doors. There was a davenport backed against the middle of it, so I sat down on the davenport. Brody shut the door and walked crab-fashion to a tall oak desk studded with square nails. A cedarwood box with gilt hinges lay on the lower leaf of the desk. He carried the box to an easy chair midway between the other two doors and sat down. I dropped my hat on the davenport and waited.

'Well, I'm listening,' Brody said. He opened the cigar box and dropped his cigarette stub into a dish at his side. He put a long thin cigar in his mouth. 'Cigar?' He tossed one at me through the air.

I reached for it. Brody took a gun out of the cigar box and pointed it at my nose. I looked at the gun. It was a black Police ·38. I had no argument against it at the moment.

'Neat, huh?' Brody said. 'Just kind of stand up a minute. Come forward just about two yards. You might grab a little air while you're doing that.' His voice was the elaborately casual voice of the tough guy in pictures. Pictures have made them all like that.

'Tsk, tsk,' I said, not moving at all. 'Such a lot of guns around town and so few brains. You're the second guy I've met within hours who seems to think a gat in the hand means a world by the tail. Put it down and don't be silly, Joe.'

His eyebrows came together and he pushed his chin at me. His eyes were mean.

'The other guy's name is Eddie Mars,' I said. 'Ever heard of him?'

'No.' Brody kept the gun pointed at me.

'If he ever gets wise to where you were last night in the rain, he'll wipe you off the way a check raiser wipes a check.'

'What would I be to Eddie Mars?' Brody asked coldly. But he lowered the gun to his knee.

'Not even a memory,' I said.

We stared at each other. I didn't look at the pointed black slipper that showed under the plush curtain on the doorway to my left.

Brody said quietly: 'Don't get me wrong. I'm not a tough guy – just careful. I don't know hell's first whisper about you. You might be a lifetaker for all I know.'

'You're not careful enough,' I said. 'That play with Geiger's books was terrible.'

He drew a long slow breath and let it out silently. Then he leaned back and crossed his long legs and held the Colt on his knee.

'Don't kid yourself I won't use this heat, if I have to,' 'What's your story?'

'Have your friend with the pointed slippers come on in. She gets tired of holding her breath.'

Brody called out without moving his eyes off my stomach. 'Come on in, Agnes.'

The curtain swung aside and the green-eyed, thigh-swinging ash blonde from Geiger's store joined us in the room. She looked at me with a kind of mangled hatred. Her nostrils were pinched and her eyes had darkened a couple of shades. She looked very unhappy.

'I knew damn well you were trouble,' she snapped at me. 'I told Joe to watch his step.'

'It's not his step, it's the back of his lap he ought to watch,' I said.

'I suppose that's funny,' the blonde said.

'It has been,' I said. 'But it probably isn't any more.'

'Save the gags,' Brody advised me. 'Joe's watchin' his step plenty. Put some light on so I can see to pop this guy, if it works out that way.'

The blonde snicked on a light in a big square standing lamp. She sank down into a chair beside the lamp and sat stiffly, as if her girdle was too tight. I put my cigar in my mouth and bit the end off. Brody's Colt took a close interest in me while I got matches out and lit the cigar. I tasted the smoke and said:

'The sucker list I spoke of is in code. I haven't cracked it yet, but there are about five hundred names. You got twelve boxes of books that I know of. You should have at least five hundred books. There'll be a bunch more out on loan, but say five hundred is the full crop, just to be cautious. If it's a good active list and you could run it even fifty per cent down the line, that would be one hundred and twenty-five thousand rentals. Your girl friend knows all about that. I'm only guessing. Put the average rental as low as you like, but it won't be less than a dollar. That merchandise costs money. At a dollar a rental you take one hundred and twenty-five grand and you still have your capital. I mean, you still have Geiger's capital. That's enough to stop a guy for.'

The blonde said: 'You're crazy, you goddam egg-headed—!'

Brody put his teeth sideways at her and snarled: 'Pipe down, for Chrissake. Pipe down!'

She subsided into an outraged mixture of slow anguish and bottled fury. Her silvery nails scraped on her knees.

'It's no racket for bums,' I told Brody almost affectionately. 'It takes a smooth worker like you, Joe. You've got to get confidence and keep it. People who spend their money for secondhand sex jags are as nervous as dowagers who can't find the rest-room. Personally I think the blackmail angles are a big mistake. I'm for shedding all that and sticking to legitimate sales and rentals.'

Brody's dark brown stare moved up and down my face. His Colt went on hungering for my vital organs. 'You're a funny guy,' he said tonelessly. 'Who has this lovely racket?'

'*You* have,' I said. 'Almost.'

The blonde choked and clawed her ear. Brody didn't say anything. He just looked at me.

'What?' the blonde called. 'You sit there and try to tell us Mr Geiger ran that kind of business right down on the main drag? You're nuts!'

I leered at her politely. 'Sure I do. Everyone knows the racket exists. Hollywood's made to order for it. If a thing like that has to exist, then right out on the street is where all practical coppers want it to exist. For the same reason they favour red light districts. They know where to flush the game when they want to.'

'My God,' the blonde said. 'You let this cheese-head sit there and insult me, Joe? You with a gun in your hand and him holding nothing but a cigar and his thumb?'

'I like it,' Brody said. 'The guy's got good ideas. Shut your trap and keep it shut, or I'll slap it shut for you with this.' He flicked the gun around in an increasingly negligent manner.

The blonde gasped and turned her face to the wall. Brody looked at me and said cunningly: '*How* have I got that lovely racket?'

'You shot Geiger to get it. Last night in the rain. It was dandy shooting weather. The trouble is he wasn't alone when you whiffed him. Either you didn't notice that, which seems unlikely, or you got the wind up and lammed. But you had nerve enough to take the plate out of his camera and you had nerve enough to come back later on and hide his corpse, so you could tidy up on the books before the law knew it had a murder to investigate.'

'Yah,' Brody said contemptuously. The Colt wobbled on his knee. His brown face was as hard as a piece of carved wood. 'You take chances, mister. It's kind of goddamned lucky for you I *didn't* bop Geiger.'

'You can step off for it just the same,' I told him cheerfully. 'You're made to order for the rap.'

Brody's voice went rough. 'Think you got me framed for it?'

'Positive.'

'How come?'

'There's somebody who'll tell it that way. I told you there was a witness. Don't go simple on me, Joe.'

He exploded then. 'That goddamned little hot pants!' he shouted. 'She would, goddamn her! She would – just that!'

I leaned back and grinned at him. 'Swell. I thought you had those nude photos of her.'

He didn't say anything. The blonde didn't say anything. I let them chew on it. Brody's face cleared slowly, with a sort of greyish relief. He put his Colt down on the end table beside his chair but kept his right hand close to it. He knocked ash from his cigar on the carpet and stared at me with eyes that were a tight shine between narrowed lids.

'I guess you think I'm dumb,' Brody said.

'Just average, for a grifter. Get the pictures.'

'What pictures?'

I shook my head. 'Wrong play, Joe. Innocence gets you nowhere. You were either there last night, or you got the nude photo from somebody that was there. You know *she* was there because you had your girl friend threaten Mrs Regan with a police rap. The only ways you could know enough to do that would be by seeing what happened or by holding the photo and knowing where and when it was taken. Cough up and be sensible.'

'I'd have to have a little dough,' Brody said. He turned his head a little to look at the green-eyed blonde. Not now green-eyed and only superficially a blonde. She was as limp as a fresh-killed rabbit.

'No dough,' I said.

He scowled bitterly. 'How d'you get to me?'

I flicked my wallet out and let him look at my buzzer. 'I was working on Geiger – for a client. I was outside last night, in the rain. I heard the shots. I crashed in. I didn't see the killer. I saw everything else.'

'And kept your lip buttoned,' Brody sneered.

I put my wallet away. 'Yes,' I admitted. 'Up till now. Do I get the photos or not?'

'About these books,' Brody said. 'I don't get that.'

'I tailed them here from Geiger's store. I have a witness.'

'That punk kid?'

'What punk kid?'

He scowled again. 'The kid that works at the store. He skipped out after the truck left. Agnes don't even know where he flops.'

'That helps,' I said, grinning at him. 'That angle worried me a little. Either of you ever been in Geiger's house – before last night?'

'Not even last night,' Brody said sharply. 'So she says I gunned him, eh?'

'With the photos in hand I might be able to convince her she was wrong. There was a little drinking being done.'

Brody sighed. 'She hates my guts. I bounced her out. I got paid, sure, but I'd have had to do it anyway. She's too screwy for a simple guy like me.' He cleared his throat. 'How about a little dough? I'm down to nickels. Agnes and me gotta move on.'

'Not from my client.'

'Listen—'

'Get the pictures, Brody.'

'Oh, hell,' he said. 'You win.' He stood up and slipped the Colt into his side pocket. His left hand went up inside his coat. He was holding it there, his face twisted with disgust, when the door buzzer rang and kept on ringing.

CHAPTER 15

He didn't like that. His lower lip went in under his teeth, and his eyebrows drew down sharply at the corners. His whole face became sharp and foxy and mean.

The buzzer kept up its song. I didn't like it either. If the visitors should happen to be Eddie Mars and his boys, I might get chilled off just for being there. If it was the police, I was caught with nothing to give them but a smile and a promise. And if it was some of Brody's friends – supposing he had any – they might turn out to be tougher than he was.

The blonde didn't like it. She stood up in a surge and chipped at the air with one hand. Nerve tension made her face old and ugly.

Watching me, Brody jerked a small drawer in the desk and picked a bone-handled automatic out of it. He held it at the blonde. She slid over to him and took it, shaking.

'Sit down next to him,' Brody said. 'Hold it on him low down, away from the door. If he gets funny use your own judgement. We ain't licked yet, baby.'

'Oh, Joe,' the blonde wailed. She came over and sat next to me on the davenport and pointed the gun at my leg artery. I didn't like the jerky look in her eyes.

The door buzzer stopped humming and a quick impatient rapping on the wood followed it. Brody put his hand in his pocket, on his gun, and walked over to the door and opened it with his left hand. Carmen Sternwood pushed him back into the room by putting a little revolver against his lean brown lips.

Brody backed away from her with his mouth working and an expression of panic on his face. Carmen shut the door behind her and looked neither at me nor at Agnes. She stalked Brody carefully, her tongue sticking out a little between her teeth. Brody took both hands out of his pockets and gestured placatingly at her. His eyebrows designed themselves into an odd assortment of curves and angles. Agnes turned the gun away from me and swung it at Carmen. I shot my hand out and closed my fingers down hard over her hand and jammed my thumb on the safety catch. It was already on. I kept it on. There was a short silent tussle, to which neither Brody nor Carmen paid any attention whatever. I had the gun. Agnes breathed deeply and shivered the whole length of her body. Carmen's face had a bony scraped look and her breath hissed. Her voice said without tone:

'I want my pictures, Joe.'

Brody swallowed and tried to grin. 'Sure, kid, sure.' He said it in a small flat voice that was as much like the voice he had used to me as a scooter is like a ten-ton truck.

Carmen said: 'You shot Arthur Geiger. I saw you. I want my pictures.' Brody turned green.

'Hey, wait a minute, Carmen,' I called.

Blonde Agnes came to life with a rush. She ducked her head and sank her teeth in my right hand. I made more noises and shook her off.

'Listen, kid,' Brody said. 'Listen a minute—'

The blonde spat at me and threw herself on my leg and tried to bite that. I cracked her on the head with the gun, not very hard, and tried to stand up. She rolled down my legs and wrapped her arms around them. I fell back on the davenport. The blonde was strong with the madness of love or fear, or a mixture of both, or maybe she was just strong.

Brody grabbed for the little revolver that was so close to his face. He missed. The gun made a sharp rapping noise that was not very loud. The bullet broke glass in a folded-back French window. Brody groaned horribly and fell down on the floor and jerked Carmen's feet from under her. She landed in a heap and the little revolver went skidding off into a corner.

Brody jumped up on his knees and reached for his pocket.

I hit Agnes on the head with less delicacy than before, kicked her off my feet, and stood up. Brody flicked his eyes at me. I showed him the automatic. He stopped trying to get his hand into his pocket.

'Christ!' he whined. 'Don't let her kill me!'

I began to laugh. I laughed like an idiot, without control. Blonde Agnes was sitting up on the floor with her hands flat on the carpet and her mouth wide open and a wick of metallic blonde hair down over her right eye. Carmen was crawling on her hands and knees, still hissing. The metal of her little revolver glistened against the baseboard over in the corner. She crawled towards it relentlessly.

I waved my share of the guns at Brody and said: 'Stay put. You're all right.'

I stepped past the crawling girl and picked the gun up. She looked at me and began to giggle. I put her gun in my pocket and patted her on the back. 'Get up, angel. You look like a Pekinese.'

I went over to Brody and put the automatic against his midriff and reached his Colt out of his side pocket. I now had all guns that had been exposed to view. I stuffed them into my pockets and held my hand out to him.

'Give.'

He nodded, licking his lips, his eyes still scared. He took a fat envelope out of his breast pocket and gave it to me. There was a developed plate in the envelope and five glossy prints.

'Sure these are all?'

He nodded again. I put the envelope in my own breast pocket and turned away. Agnes was back on the davenport, straightening her hair. Her eyes ate Carmen with a green distillation of hate. Carmen was up on her feet too, coming towards me with her hand out, still giggling and hissing. There was a little froth at the corners of her mouth. Her small white teeth glinted close to her lips.

'Can I have them now?' she asked me with a coy smile.

'I'll take care of them for you. Go on home.'

'Home?'

I went to the door and looked out. The cool night breeze was blowing peacefully down the hall. No excited neighbour hung out of doorways. A small gun had gone off and broken a pane of glass, but noises like that don't mean much any more. I held the door open and jerked my head at Carmen. She came towards me, smiling uncertainly.

'Go on home and wait for me,' I said soothingly.

She put her thumb up. Then she nodded and slipped past me into the hall. She touched my cheek with her fingers as she went by. 'You'll take care of Carmen, won't you?' she said.

'Check.'

'You're cute.'

'What you see is nothing,' I said. 'I've got a Bali dancing girl tattooed on my right thigh.'

Her eyes rounded. She said: 'Naughty,' and wagged a finger at me. Then she whispered: 'Can I have my gun?'

'Not now. Later. I'll bring it to you.'

She grabbed me suddenly around the neck and kissed me on the mouth. 'I like you,' she said. 'Carmen likes you a lot.' She ran off down the hall as gay as a thrush, waved at me from the stairs and ran down the stairs out of my sight.

I went back into Brody's apartment.

CHAPTER 16

I went over to the folded-back French window and looked at the small broken pane in the upper part of it. The bullet from Carmen's gun had smashed the glass like a blow. It had not made a hole. There was a small hole in the plaster which a keen eye would find quickly enough. I pulled the drapes over the broken pane and took Carmen's gun out of my pocket. It was a Banker's Special, ·22 calibre, hollow point cartridges. It had a pearl grip, and a small round silver plate set into the butt was engraved: 'Carmen from Owen'. She made saps of all of them.

I put the gun back in my pocket and sat down close to Brody and stared into his bleak brown eyes. A minute passed. The blonde adjusted her face by the aid of a pocket mirror. Brody fumbled around with a cigarette and jerked: 'Satisfied?'

'So far. Why did you put the bite on Mrs Regan instead of the old man?'

'Tapped the old man once. About six, seven months ago. I figured maybe he gets sore enough to call in some law.'

'What made you think Mrs Regan wouldn't tell him about it?'

He considered that with some care, smoking his cigarette and keeping his eyes on my face. Finally he said: 'How well you know her?'

'I've met her twice. You must know her a lot better to take a chance on that squeeze with the photo.'

'She skates around plenty. I figure maybe she has a couple of soft spots she don't want the old man to know about. I figure she can raise five grand easy.'

'A little weak,' I said. 'But pass it. You're broke, eh?'

'I been shaking two nickels together for a month, trying to get them to mate.'

'What you do for a living?'

'Insurance. I got desk rooms in Puss Walgreen's office, Fulwider Building, Western and Santa Monica.'

'When you open up, you open up. The books here in your apartment?'

He snapped his teeth and waved a brown hand. Confidence was oozing back into his manner. 'Hell, no. In storage.'

'You had a man bring them here and then you had a storage outfit come and take them away again right afterwards?'

'Sure. I don't want them moved direct from Geiger's place, do I?'

'You're smart,' I said admiringly. 'Anything incriminating in the joint right now?'

He looked worried again. He shook his head sharply.

'That's fine,' I told him. I looked across at Agnes. She had finished fixing her face and was staring at the wall, blank-eyed hardly listening. Her face had the drowsiness which strain and shock induce, after their first incidence.

Brody flicked his eyes warily. 'Well?'

'How'd you come by the photo?'

He scowled. 'Listen, you got what you came after, got it plenty cheap. You done a nice neat job. Now go peddle it to your top man. I'm clean. I don't know nothing about any photo, do I, Agnes?'

The blonde opened her eyes and looked at him with vague but uncomplimentary speculation. 'A half-smart guy,' she said with a tired sniff. 'That's all I ever draw. Never once a guy that's smart all the way around the course. Never once.'

I grinned at her. 'Did I hurt your head much?'

'You and every other man I ever met.'

I looked back at Brody. He was pinching his cigarette between his fingers, with a sort of twitch. His hand seemed to be shaking a little. His brown poker face was still smooth.

'We've got to agree on a story,' I said. 'For instance, Carmen wasn't here. That's very important. She wasn't here. That was a vision you saw.'

'Huh!' Brody sneered. 'If you say so, pal, and if—' he put his hand out palm up and cupped the fingers and rolled the thumb gently against the index and middle fingers.

I nodded. 'We'll see. There might be a small contribution. You won't count it in grands, though. Now where did you get the picture?'

'A guy slipped it to me.'

'Uh-huh. A guy you just passed in the street. You wouldn't know him again. You never saw him before.'

Brody yawned. 'It dropped out of his pocket,' he said.

'Uh-huh. Got an alibi for last night, poker pan?'

'Sure. I was right here. Agnes was with me. Okay, Agnes?'

'I'm beginning to feel sorry for you again,' I said.

His eyes flicked wide and his mouth hung loose, the cigarette balanced on his lower lip.

'You think you're smart and you're so goddamned dumb,' I told him. 'Even if you don't dance off up in Quentin, you have such a bleak long lonely time ahead of you.'

His cigarette jerked and dropped ash on his waistcoat.

'Thinking about how smart you are,' I said.

'Take the air,' he growled suddenly. 'Dust. I got enough chinning with you. Beat it.'

'Okey.' I stood up and went over to the tall oak desk and took his two guns out of my pockets, laid them side by side on the blotter so that the barrels were exactly parallel. I reached my hat off the floor beside the davenport and started for the door.

Brody called: 'Hey!'

I turned and waited. His cigarette was jiggling like a doll on a coiled spring. 'Everything's smooth, ain't it?' he asked.

'Why, sure. This is a free country. You don't have to stay out of jail, if you don't want to. That is, if you're a citizen. Are you a citizen?

He just stared at me, jiggling the cigarette. The blonde Agnes turned her head slowly and stared at me along the same level. Their glances contained almost the exact same blend of foxiness, doubt and frustrated anger. Agnes reached her silvery nails up abruptly and yanked a hair out of her head and broke it between her fingers with a bitter jerk.

Brody said tightly: 'You're not going to any cops, brother. Not if it's the Sternwoods you're working for. I've got too much stuff on that family. You got your pictures and you got your hush. Go and peddle your papers.'

'Make your mind up,' I said. 'You told me to dust, I was on my way out, you hollered at me and I stopped, and now I'm on my way out again. Is that what you want?'

'You ain't got anything on me,' Brody said.

'Just a couple of murders. Small change in your circle.'

He jumped more than an inch, but it looked like a foot. The white cornea showed all around the tobacco-coloured iris of his eyes. The brown skin of his face took on a greenish tinge in the lamplight.

Blonde Agnes let out a low animal wail and buried her head in a cushion on the end of the davenport. I stood there and admired the long line of her thighs.

Brody moistened his lips slowly and said: 'Sit down, pal. Maybe I have a little more for you. What's that crack about two murders mean?'

I leaned against the door. 'Where were you last night about seven-thirty, Joe?'

His mouth drooped sulkily and he stared down at the floor. 'I was watching a guy, a guy who had a nice racket I figured he needed a partner in. Geiger. I was watching him now and then to see had he any tough connections. I figure he has friends or he don't work the racket as open as he does. But they don't go to his house. Only dames.'

'You didn't watch hard enough,' I said. 'Go on.'

'I'm there last night on the street below Geiger's house. It's raining hard and I'm buttoned up in my coupé and I don't see anything. There's a car in front of Geiger's and another car a little way up the hill. That's why I stay down below. There's a big Buick parked down where I am and after a while I go over and take a gander into it. It's registered to Vivian Regan. Nothing happens, so I scram. That's all.' He waved his cigarette. His eyes crawled up and down my face.

'Could be,' I said. 'Know where that Buick is now?'

'Why would I?'

'In the Sheriff's garage. It was lifted out of twelve feet of water off Lido fish pier this morning. There was a dead man in it. He had been sapped and the car pointed out the pier and the hand throttle pulled down.'

Brody was breathing hard. One of his feet tapped restlessly. 'Jesus, guy, you can't pin that one on me,' he said thickly.

'Why not? This Buick was down back of Geiger's according to you. Well, Mrs Regan didn't have it out. Her chauffeur, a lad named Owen Taylor, had it out. He went over to Geiger's place to have words with him, because Owen Taylor was sweet on Carmen, and he didn't like the kind of games Geiger was playing with her. He let himself in the back way with a jimmy and a gun and he caught Geiger taking a photo of Carmen without any clothes on. So his gun went off, as guns will, and Geiger fell down dead and Owen ran away, but not without the photo negative Geiger had just taken. So you ran after him and took the photo from him. How else would you have got hold of it?'

Brody licked his lips. 'Yeah,' he said. 'But that don't make me knock him off. Sure, I heard the shots and saw this killer come slamming down the back steps into the Buick and off. I took out after him. He hit the bottom of the canyon and went west on Sunset. Beyond Beverly Hills he skidded off the road and had to stop and I came up and played copper. He had a gun but his nerve was bad and I sapped him down. So I went through his clothes and found out who he was and I lifted the plateholder, just out of curiosity. I was wondering what it was all about and getting my neck wet when he came out of it all of a sudden and knocked me off the car.

He was out of sight when I picked myself up. That's the last I saw of him.'

'How did you know it was Geiger he shot?' I asked gruffly.

Brody shrugged. 'I figure it was, but I can be wrong. When I had the plate developed and saw what was on it, I was pretty damn sure. And when Geiger didn't come down to the store this morning and didn't answer his phone I was plenty sure. So I figure it's a good time to move his books out and make a quick touch on the Sternwoods for travel money and blow for a while.'

I nodded. 'That seems reasonable. Maybe you didn't murder anybody at that. Where did you hide Geiger's body?'

He lifted his eyebrows. Then he grinned. 'Nix, nix. Skip it. You think I'd go back there and handle him, not knowing when a couple carloads of law would come tearing around the corner? Nix.'

'Somebody hid the body,' I said.

Brody shrugged. The grin stayed on his face. He didn't believe me. While he was still not believing me the door buzzer started to ring again. Brody stood up sharply, hardeyed. He glanced over at his guns on the desk.

'So she's back again,' he growled.

'If she is, she doesn't have her gun,' I comforted him. 'Don't you have any other friends?'

'Just about one,' he growled. 'I got enough of this puss-in-the-corner game.' He marched to the desk and took the Colt. He held it down at his side and went to the door. He put his left hand to the knob and twisted it and opened the door a foot and leaned into the opening, holding the gun tight against his thigh.

A voice said: 'Brody?'

Brody said something I didn't hear. The two quick reports were muffled. The gun must have been pressed tight against Brody's body. He tilted forward against the door and the weight of his body pushed it shut with a bang. He slid down the wood. His feet pushed the carpet away behind him. His left hand dropped off the knob and the arm slapped the floor with a thud. His head was wedged against the door. He didn't move. The Colt clung to his right hand.

I jumped across the room and rolled him enough to get the door open and crowd through. A woman peered out of a door almost opposite. Her face was full of fright and she pointed along the hall with a clawlike hand.

I raced down the hall and heard thumping feet going down the tile steps and went down after the sound. At the lobby level the front door was closing itself quietly and running feet slapped the pavement outside. I made the door before it was shut, clawed it open again and charged out.

A tall hatless figure in a leather jerkin was running diagonally across the street between the parked cars. The figure turned and flame spurted from it. Two heavy hammers hit the stucco wall beside me. The figure ran on, dodged between two cars, vanished.

A man came up beside me and asked: 'What happened?'

'Shooting going on,' I said.

'Jesus!' He scuttled into the apartment house.

I walked quickly down the pavement to my car and got in and started it. I pulled out from the kerb and drove down the hill, not fast. No other car started up on the other side of the street. I thought I heard steps, but I wasn't sure about that. I rode down the hill a block and a half, turned at the intersection and started to back up. The sound of a muted whistling came to me faintly along the pavement. Then steps. I double parked and slid between two cars and went down low. I took Carmen's little revolver out of my pocket.

The sound of the steps grew louder, and the whistling went on cheerfully. In a moment the jerkin showed. I stepped out between the two cars and said: 'Got a match, buddy?'

The boy spun towards me and his right hand darted up to go inside the jerkin. His eyes were a wet shine in the glow of the round electroliers. Moist dark eyes shaped like almonds, and a pallid handsome face with wavy black hair growing low on the forehead in two points. A very handsome boy indeed, the boy from Geiger's store.

He stood there looking at me silently, his right hand on the edge of the jerkin, but not inside it yet. I held the little revolver down at my side.

'You must have thought a lot of that queen,' I said.

'Go — yourself,' the boy said softly, motionless between the parked cars and the five-foot retaining wall on the inside of the pavement.

A siren wailed distantly coming up the long hill. The boy's head jerked towards the sound. I stepped in close and put my gun into his jerkin.

'Me or the cops?' I asked him.

His head rolled a little sideways as if I had slapped his face. 'Who are you?' he said.

'Friend of Geiger's.'

'Get away from me, you son of a bitch.'

'This is a small gun, kid. I'll give it you through the navel and it will take three months to get you well enough to walk. But you'll get well. So you can walk to the nice new gas chamber up in Quentin.'

He said: 'Go — yourself.' His hand moved inside the jerkin. I pressed harder on his stomach. He let out a long soft sigh, took his hand away from the jerkin and let it fall limp at his side. His wide shoulders sagged. 'What you want?' he whispered.

I reached inside the jerkin and plucked out the automatic. 'Get into my car, kid.'

He stepped past me and I crowded him from behind. He got into the car.

'Under the wheel, kid. You drive.'

He slid under the wheel and I got into the car beside him. I said: 'Let the prowl car pass up the hill. They'll think we moved over when we heard the siren. Then turn her downhill and we'll go home.'

I put Carmen's gun away and leaned the automatic against the boy's ribs. I looked back through the window. The whine of the siren was very loud now. Two red lights swelled in the middle of the street. They grew larger and blended into one and the car rushed by in a wild flurry of sound.

'Let's go,' I said.

The boy swung the car and started off down the hill.

'Let's go home,' I said. 'To Laverne Terrace.'

His smooth lips twitched. He swung the car west on Franklin. 'You're a simple-minded lad. What's you name?'

'Carol Lundgren,' he said lifelessly.

'You shot the wrong guy, Carol, Joe Brody didn't kill your queen.'

He spoke three words to me and kept on driving.

CHAPTER 17

A moon half gone from the full glowed through a ring of mist among the high branches of the eucalyptus trees on Laverne Terrace. A radio sounded loudly from a house low down the hill. The boy swung the car over to the box hedge in front of Geiger's house, killed the motor and sat looking straight before him with both hands on the wheel. No light showed through Geiger's hedge.

I said: 'Anybody home, son?'

'You ought to know.'

'How would I know?'

'Go — yourself.'

'That's how people get false teeth.'

He showed me his in a tight grin. Then kicked the door open and got out. I scuttled out after him. He stood with his fists on his hips, looking silently at the house above the top of the hedge.

'All right,' I said. 'You have a key. Let's go on in.'

'Who said I had a key?'

'Don't kid me, son. The fag gave you one. You've got a nice clean manly little room in there. He shooed you out and locked it up when he had lady visitors. He was like Caesar, a husband to women and a wife to men. Think I can't figure people like him and you out?'

I still held his automatic more or less pointed at him, but he swung on me just the same. It caught me flush on the chin. I backstepped fast enough to keep from falling, but I took plenty of the punch. It was meant to be a hard one, but a pansy has no iron in his bones, whatever he looks like.

I threw the gun down at the kid's feet and said: 'Maybe you need this.'

He stooped for it like a flash. There was nothing slow about his movements. I sank a fist in the side of his neck. He toppled over sideways, clawing for the gun and not reaching it. I picked it up again and threw it in the car. The boy came up on all fours, leering with his eyes too wide open. He coughed and shook his head.

'You don't want to fight,' I told him. 'You're giving away too much weight.'

He wanted to fight. He shot at me like a plane from a catapult, reaching for my knees in a diving tackle. I sidestepped and reached for his neck and took it into chancery. He scraped the dirt hard and got his feet under him enough to use his hands on me where it hurt. I twisted him around and heaved him a little higher. I took hold of my right wrist with my left hand and turned my right hipbone into him and for a moment it was a balance of weights. We seemed to hang there in the misty moonlight, two grotesque creatures whose feet scraped on the road and whose breath panted with effort.

I had my right forearm against his windpipe now and all the strength of both arms in it. His feet began a frenetic shuffle and he wasn't panting any more. He was ironbound. His left foot sprawled off to one side and the knee went slack. I held on half a minute longer. He sagged on my arm, an enormous weight I could hardly hold up. Then I let go. He sprawled at my feet, out cold. I went to the car and got a pair of handcuffs out of the glove compartment and twisted his wrists behind him and snapped them on. I lifted him by the armpits and managed to drag him in behind the hedge, out of sight from the street. I went back to the car and moved it a hundred feet up the hill and locked it.

He was still out when I got back. I unlocked the door, dragged him into the house, shut the door. He was beginning to gasp now. I switched a lamp on. His eyes fluttered open and focused on me slowly.

I bent down, keeping out of the way of his knees and said: 'Keep quiet or you'll get the same and more of it. Just lie quiet and hold your breath. Hold it until you can't hold it any longer and then tell yourself that you have to breathe, that you're black in the face, that your eyeballs are popping out, and that you're going to breathe right now, but that you're sitting strapped in the chair in the clean little gas chamber up in San Quentin and when you take that breath you're fighting with all your soul not to take it, it won't be air you'll get, it will be cyanide fumes. And that's what they call humane execution in our state now.'

'Go — yourself,' he said with a soft stricken sigh.

'You're going to cop a plea, brother, don't ever think you're not. And you're going to say just what we want you to say and nothing we don't want you to say.'

'Go — yourself.'

'Say that again and I'll put a pillow under your head.'

His mouth twitched. I left him lying on the floor with his wrists shackled behind him and his cheek pressed into the rug and an animal brightness in his visible eye. I put on another lamp and stepped into the hallway at the back of the living-room. Geiger's bedroom didn't seem to have been touched. I opened the door, not locked now, of the bedroom across the hall from it. There was a dim flickering light in the room and a smell of sandalwood. Two cones of incense ash stood side by side on a small brass tray on the bureau. The light came from the two tall black candles in the foot-high candlesticks. They were standing on straight-backed chairs, one on either side of the bed.

Geiger lay on the bed. The two missing strips of Chinese tapestry made a St Andrew's Cross over the middle of his body, hiding the blood-smeared front of his Chinese coat. Below the cross his black-pyjama'd legs lay stiff and straight. His feet were in the slippers with thick white felt soles. Above the cross his arms were crossed at the wrists and his hands lay flat against his shoulders, palms down, fingers close together and stretched out evenly. His mouth was closed and his Charlie Chan moustache was as unreal as a toupee. His broad nose was pinched and white. His eyes were almost closed, but not entirely. The faint glitter of his glass eye caught the light and winked at me.

I didn't touch him. I didn't go very near him. He would be as cold as ice and as stiff as a board.

The black candles guttered in the draught from the open door. Drops of black wax crawled down their sides. The air of the room was poisonous and unreal. I went out and shut the door again and went back to the living-room. The boy hadn't moved. I stood still, listening for sirens. It was all a question of how soon Agnes talked and what she said. If she talked about Geiger, the police would be there any minute. But she might not talk for hours. She might even have got away.

I looked down at the boy. 'Want to sit up, son?'

He closed his eyes and pretended to go to sleep. I went over to the desk and scooped up the mulberry-coloured phone and dialled Bernie Ohls's office. He had left to go home at six o'clock. I dialled the number of his home. He was there.

'This is Marlowe,' I said. 'Did your boys find a revolver on Owen Taylor this morning?'

I could hear him clearing his throat and then I could hear him trying to keep the surprise out of his voice. 'That would come under the heading of police business,' he said.

'If they did, it had three empty shells in it.'

'How the hell did you know that?' Ohls asked quietly.

'Come over to 7244 Laverne Terrace, off Laurel Canyon Boulevard. I'll show you where the slugs went.'

'Just like that, huh?'

'Just like that.'

Ohls said: 'Look out the window and you'll see me coming round the corner. I thought you acted a little cagey on that one.'

'Cagey is no word for it,' I said.

CHAPTER 18

Ohls stood looking down at the boy. The boy sat on the couch leaning sideways against the wall. Ohls looked at him silently, his pale eyebrows bristling and stiff and round like the little vegetable brushes the Fuller Brush man gives away.

He asked the boy: 'Do you admit shooting Brody?'

The boy said his favourite three words in a muffled voice.

Ohls sighed and looked at me. I said: 'He doesn't have to admit that. I have his gun.'

Ohls said: 'I wish to Christ I had a dollar for every time I've had that said to me. What's funny about it?'

'It's not meant to be funny,' I said.

'Well, that's something,' Ohls said. He turned away. 'I've called Wilde. We'll go over and see him and take this punk. He can ride with me and you can follow on behind in case he tries to kick me in the face.'

'How do you like what's in the bedroom?'

'I like it fine,' Ohls said. 'I'm kind of glad that Taylor kid went off the pier. I'd hate to have to help send him to the death-house for rubbing that skunk.'

I went back into the small bedroom and blew out the black candles and let them smoke. When I got back to the living-room Ohls had the boy up on his feet. The boy stood glaring at him with sharp black eyes in a face as hard and white as cold mutton fat.

'Let's go,' Ohls said, and took him by the arms as if he didn't like touching him. I put the lamps out and followed them out of the house. We got into our cars and I followed Ohls's twin tail-lights down the long curving hill. I hoped this would be my last trip to Laverne Terrace.

Taggart Wilde, the District Attorney, lived at the corner of Fourth and Lafayette Park, in a white frame house the size of a carbarn, with red sandstone *porte-cochère* built on to one side and a couple of acres of soft rolling lawn in front. It was one of those solid old-fashioned houses which it used to be the thing to move bodily to new locations as the city grew westward. Wilde came of an old Los Angeles family and had probably been born in the house when it was on West Adams or Figueroa or St James's Park.

There were two cars in the driveway already, a big private sedan and a police car with a uniformed chauffeur who leaned smoking against his rear fender and admiring the moon. Ohls went over and spoke to him and the chauffeur looked in at the boy in Ohls's car.

We went up to the house and rang the bell. A slick-haired blond man opened the door and led us down the hall and through a huge sunken living-room crowded with heavy dark furniture and along another hall on the far side of it. He knocked at a door and stepped inside, then held the door wide and we went into a panelled study with an open French door at the end and a view of dark garden and mysterious trees. A smell of wet earth and flowers came in at the window. There were large dim oils on the walls, easy chairs, books, a smell of good cigar smoke which blended with the smell of wet earth and flowers.

Taggart Wilde sat behind a desk, a middle-aged plump man with clear blue eyes that managed to have a friendly expression without really having any expression at all. He had a cup of black coffee in front of him and he held a dappled thin cigar between the neat careful fingers of his left hand. Another man sat at the corner of the desk in a blue leather chair, a cold-eyed hatchet-faced man, as lean as a rake and as hard as the manager of a loan office. His neat well-kept face looked as if it had been shaved within the hour. He wore a well-pressed brown suit and there was a black pearl in his tie. He had the long nervous fingers of a man with a quick brain. He looked ready for a fight.

Ohls pulled a chair up and sat down and said: 'Evening, Cronjager. Meet Phil Marlowe, a private eye who's in a jam.' Ohls grinned.

Cronjager looked at me without nodding. He looked me over as if he was looking at a photograph. Then he nodded his chin about an inch. Wilde said: 'Sit down, Marlowe. I'll try to handle Captain Cronjager, but you know how it is. This is a big city now.'

I sat down and lit a cigarette. Ohls looked at Cronjager and asked: 'What did you get on the Randall Place killing?'

The hatchet-faced man pulled one of his fingers until the knuckle cracked. He spoke without looking up. 'A stiff, two slugs in him. Two guns that hadn't been fired. Down on the street we got a blonde trying to start a car that didn't belong to her. Hers was right next to it, the same model. She acted rattled so the boys brought her in and she spilled. She was in there when this guy Brody got it. Claims she didn't see the killer.'

'That all?' Ohls asked.

Cronjager raised his eyebrows a little. 'Only happened about an hour ago. What did you expect – moving pictures of the killing?'

'Maybe a description of the killer,' Ohls said.

'A tall guy in a leather jerkin – if you call that a description.'

'He's outside in my heap,' Ohls said. 'Handcuffed. Marlowe put the arm on him for you. Here's his gun.' Ohls took the boy's automatic out of his pocket and laid it on a corner of Wilde's desk. Cronjager looked at the gun but didn't reach for it.

Wilde chuckled. He was leaning back and puffing his dappled cigar without letting go of it. He bent forward to sip from his coffee cup. He took a silk handkerchief from the breast pocket of the dinner-jacket he was wearing and touched his lips with it and tucked it away again.

'There's a couple more deaths involved,' Ohls said, pinching the soft flesh at the end of his chin.

Cronjager stiffened visibly. His surly eyes became points of steely light.

Ohls said: 'You heard about a car being lifted out of the Pacific Ocean off Lido pier this morning with a dead guy in it?'

Cronjager said: 'No,' and kept on looking nasty.

'The dead guy in the car was chauffeur to a rich family,' Ohls said. 'The family was being blackmailed on account of one of the daughters. Mr Wilde recommended Marlowe to the family, through me. Marlowe played it kind of close to the waistcoat.'

'I love private dicks that play murders close to the waistcoat,' Cronjager said. 'You don't have to be so goddamned coy about it.'

'Yeah,' Ohls said. 'I don't have to be so goddamned coy about it. It's not so goddamned often I get a chance to be coy with a city copper. I spend most of my time telling them where to put their feet so they won't break an ankle.'

Cronjager whitened around the corners of his sharp nose. His breath made a soft hissing sound in the quiet room. He said very quietly: 'You haven't had to tell any of *my* men where to put their feet, smart guy.'

'We'll see about that,' Ohls said. 'This chauffeur I spoke of that's drowned off Lido shot a guy last night in your territory. A guy named

Geiger who ran a dirty book racket in a store on Hollywood Boulevard. Geiger was living with the punk I got outside in my car. I mean living with him, if you get the idea.'

Cronjager was staring at him levelly now. 'That sounds like it might grow up to be a dirty story,' he said.

'It's my experience most police stories are,' Ohls growled and turned to me, his eyebrows bristling. 'You're on the air, Marlowe. Give it to him.'

I gave it to him.

I left out two things, not knowing just why, at the moment, I left out one of them. I left out Carmen's visit to Brody's apartment and Eddie Mars's visit to Geiger's in the afternoon. I told the rest of it just as it happened.

Cronjager never took his eyes off my face and no expression of any kind crossed his as I talked. At the end of it he was perfectly silent for a long minute. Wilde was silent, sipping his coffee, puffing gently at his dappled cigar, Ohls stared at one of his thumbs.

Cronjager leaned slowly back in his chair and crossed one ankle over his knee and rubbed the ankle-bone with his thin nervous hand. His lean face wore a harsh frown. He said with deadly politeness:

'So all you did was not report a murder that happened last night and then spend today foxing around so that this kid of Geiger's could commit a second murder this evening.'

'That's all,' I said. 'I was in a pretty tough spot. I guess I did wrong, but I wanted to protect my client and I hadn't any reason to think the boy would go gunning for Brody.'

'That kind of thinking is police business, Marlowe. If Geiger's death had been reported last night, the books could never have been moved from the store to Brody's apartment. The kid wouldn't have been led to Brody and wouldn't have killed him. Say Brody was living on borrowed time. His kind usually are. But a life is a life.'

'Right,' I said. 'Tell that to your coppers next time they shoot down some scared petty larceny crook running away up an alley with a stolen spare.'

Wilde put both his hands down on his desk with a solid smack. 'That's enough of that,' he snapped. 'What makes you so sure, Marlowe, that this Taylor boy shot Geiger? Even if the gun that killed Geiger was found on Taylor's body or in the car, it doesn't absolutely follow that he was the killer. The gun might have been planted – say by Brody, the actual killer.'

'It's physically possible,' I said, 'but morally impossible. It assumes too much coincidence and too much that's out of character for Brody and his girl, and out of character for what he was trying to do. I talked to Brody for a long time. He was a crook, but not a killer type. He had two guns, but he wasn't wearing either of them. He was trying to find a way to cut in on

Geiger's racket, which naturally he knew all about from the girl. He says he was watching Geiger off and on to see if he had any tough backers. I believe him. To suppose he killed Geiger in order to get his books, then scrammed with the nude photo Geiger had just taken of Carmen Sternwood, then planted the gun on Owen Taylor and pushed Taylor into the ocean off Lido, is to suppose a hell of a lot too much. Taylor had the motive, jealous rage, and the opportunity to kill Geiger. He was out in one of the family cars without permission. He killed Geiger right in front of the girl, which Brody would never have done, even if he had been a killer. I can't see anybody with a purely commercial interest in Geiger doing that. But Taylor would have done it. The nude photo business was just what would have made him do it.'

Wilde chuckled and looked along his eyes at Cronjager. Cronjager cleared his throat with a snort. Wilde asked: 'What's this business about hiding the body? I don't see the point of that.'

I said: 'The kid hasn't told us, but he must have done it. Brody wouldn't have gone into the house after Geiger was shot. The boy must have got home when I was away taking Carmen to her house. He was afraid of the police, of course, being what he is, and he probably thought it a good idea to have the body hidden until he had removed his effects from the house. He dragged it out of the front door, judging by the marks on the rug, and very likely put it in the garage. Then he packed up whatever belongings he had there and took them away. And later on, sometime in the night and before the body stiffened, he had a revulsion of feeling and thought he hadn't treated his dead friend very nicely. So he went back and laid him out on the bed. That's all guessing of course.'

Wilde nodded. 'Then this morning he goes down to the store as if nothing had happened and keeps his eyes open. And when Brody moved the books out he found out where they were going and assumed that whoever got them had killed Geiger just for that purpose. He may even have known more about Brody and the girl than they suspected. What do you think, Ohls?'

Ohls said: 'We'll find out – but that doesn't help Cronjager's troubles. What's eating him is all this happened last night and he's only just been rung in on it.'

Cronjager said sourly: 'I think I can find some way to deal with that angle too.' He looked at me sharply and immediately looked away again.

Wilde waved his cigar and said: 'Let's see the exhibits, Marlowe.'

I emptied my pockets and put the catch on his desk: the three notes and Geiger's card to General Sternwood, Carmen's photos, and the blue notebook with the code list of names and addresses. I had already given Geiger's keys to Ohls.

Wilde looked at what I gave him, puffing gently at his cigar. Ohls lit one of his own toy cigars and blew smoke peacefully at the ceiling. Cronjager leaned on the desk and looked at what I had given Wilde.

Wilde tapped the three notes signed by Carmen and said: 'I guess these were just a come-on. If General Sternwood paid them, it would be through fear of something worse. Then Geiger would have tightened the screws. Do you know what he was afraid of?' He was looking at me.

I shook my head.

'Have you told your story complete in all relevant details?'

'I left out a couple of personal matters. I intend to keep on leaving them out, Mr Wilde.'

Cronjager said: 'Hah!' and snorted with deep feeling.

'Why?' Wilde asked quietly.

'Because my client is entitled to that protection, short of anything but a Grand Jury. I have a licence to operate as a private detective. I suppose that word "private" has some meaning. The Hollywood Division has two murders on its hands, both solved. They have both killers. They have the motive, the instrument in each case. The blackmail angle has got to be suppressed, as far as the names of the parties are concerned.'

'Why?' Wilde asked again.

'That's okey,' Cronjager said dryly. 'We're glad to stooge for a shamus of his standing.'

I said: 'I'll show you.' I got up and went back out of the house to my car and got the book from Geiger's store out of it. The uniformed police driver was standing beside Ohls's car. The boy was inside it, leaning back sideways in the corner.

'Has he said anything?' I asked.

'He made a suggestion,' the copper said and spat. 'I'm letting it ride.'

I went back into the house, put the book on Wilde's desk and opened up the wrappings. Cronjager was using a telephone on the end of the desk. He hung up and sat down as I came in.

Wilde looked through the book, wooden-faced, closed it and pushed it towards Cronjager. Cronjager opened it, looked at a page or two, shut it quickly. A couple of red spots the size of half-dollars showed on his cheekbones.

I said: 'Look at the stamped dates on the front end-paper.'

Cronjager opened the book again and looked at them. 'Well?'

'If necessary,' I said, 'I'll testify under oath that that book came from Geiger's store. The blonde, Agnes, will admit what kind of business the store did. It's obvious to anybody with eyes that that store is just a front for something. But the Hollywood police allowed it to operate, for their own reasons. I dare say the Grand Jury would like to know what those reasons are.'

Wilde grinned. He said: 'Grand Juries do ask those embarrassing questions sometimes – in a rather vain effort to find out just why cities are run as they are run.'

Cronjager stood up suddenly and put his hat on. 'I'm one against three here,' he snapped. 'I'm a homicide man. If this Geiger was running indecent literature, that's no skin off my nose. But I'm ready to admit it won't help my division any to have it washed over in the papers. What do you birds want?'

Wilde looked at Ohls. Ohls said calmly: 'I want to turn a prisoner over to you. Let's go.'

He stood up. Cronjager looked at him fiercely and stalked out of the room. Ohls went after him. The door closed again. Wilde tapped on his desk and stared at me with his clear blue eyes.

'You ought to understand how any copper would feel about a cover-up like this,' he said. 'You'll have to make statements of all of it – at least for the files. I think it may be possible to keep the two killings separate and to keep General Sternwood's name out of both of them. Do you know why I'm not tearing your ear off?'

'No. I expected to get both ears torn off.'

'What are you getting for it all?'

'Twenty-five dollars a day and expenses.'

'That would make fifty dollars and a little gasolene so far.'

'About that.'

He put his head on one side and rubbed the back of his left little finger along the lower edge of his chin.

'And for that amount of money you're willing to get yourself in Dutch with half the law enforcement of this county?'

'I don't like it,' I said. 'But what the hell am I to do? I'm on a case. I'm selling what I have to sell to make a living. What little guts and intelligence the Lord gave me and a willingness to get pushed around in order to protect a client. It's against my principles to tell as much as I've told tonight, without consulting the General. As for the cover-up, I've been in police business myself, as you know. They come a dime a dozen in any big city. Cops get very large and emphatic when an outsider tries to hide anything, but they do the same thing themselves every other day, to oblige their friends or anybody with a little pull. And I'm not through. I'm still on the case. I'd do the same thing again, if I had to.'

'Providing Cronjager doesn't get your licence,' Wilde grinned. 'You said you held back a couple of personal matters. Of what import?'

'I'm still on the case,' I said, and stared straight into his eyes.

Wilde smiled at me. He had the frank daring smile of an Irishman. 'Let me tell you something, son. My father was a close friend of old Sternwood.

I've done all my office permits – and maybe a good deal more – to save the old man from grief. But in the long run it can't be done. Those girls of his are bound certain to hook up with something that can't be hushed, especially the little blonde brat. They ought not to be running around loose. I blame the old man for that. I guess he doesn't realize what the world is today. And there's another thing I might mention while we're talking man to man and I don't have to growl at you. I'll bet a dollar to a Canadian dime that the General's afraid his son-in-law, the ex-bootlegger, is mixed up in this somewhere, and what he really hoped you would find out is that he isn't. What do you think of that?'

'Regan didn't sound like a blackmailer, what I heard of him. He had a soft spot where he was and he walked out on it.'

Wilde snorted. 'The softness of that spot neither you nor I could judge. If he was a certain sort of man, it would not have been so very soft. Did the General tell you he was looking for Regan?'

'He told me he wished he knew where he was and that he was all right. He liked Regan and was hurt the way he bounced off without telling the old man good-bye.'

Wilde leaned back and frowned. 'I see,' he said in a changed voice. His hand moved the stuff on his desk around, laid Geiger's blue notebook to one side and pushed the other exhibits towards me. 'You may as well take these,' he said. 'I've no further use for them.'

CHAPTER 19

It was close to eleven when I put my car away and walked around to the front of the Hobart Arms. The plate-glass door was put on the lock at ten, so I had to get my keys out. Inside, in the square barren lobby, a man put a green evening paper down beside a potted palm and flicked a cigarette butt into the tub the palm grew in. He stood up and waved his hat at me and said: 'The boss wants to talk to you. You sure keep your friends waiting, pal.'

I stood still and looked at his flattened nose and club steak ear.

'What about?'

'What do you care? Just keep your nose clean and everything will be jake.' His hand hovered near the upper buttonhole of his open coat.

'I smell of policemen,' I said. 'I'm too tired to talk, too tired to eat, too tired to think. But if you think I'm not too tired to take orders from Eddie Mars – try getting your gat out before I shoot your good ear off.'

'Nuts. You ain't got no gun.' He stared at me levelly. His dark wiry brows closed in together and his mouth made a downward curve.

'That was then,' I told him. 'I'm not always naked.'

He waved his left hand. 'Okey. You win. I wasn't told to blast anybody. You'll hear from him.'

'Too late will be too soon,' I said, and turned slowly as he passed me on his way to the door. He opened it and went out without looking back. I grinned at my own foolishness, went along to the elevator and upstairs to the apartment. I took Carmen's little gun out of my pocket and laughed at it. Then I cleaned it thoroughly, oiled it, wrapped it in a piece of canton flannel and locked it up. I made myself a drink and was drinking it when the phone rang. I sat down beside the table on which it stood.

'So you're tough tonight,' Eddie Mars's voice said.

'Big, fast, tough and full of prickles. What can I do for you?'

'Cops over there – you know where. You keep me out of it?'

'Why should I?'

'I'm nice to be nice to, soldier. I'm not nice not to be nice to.'

'Listen hard and you'll hear my teeth chattering.'

He laughed dryly. 'Did you – or did you?'

'I did. I'm damned if I know why. I guess it was just complicated enough without you.'

'Thanks, soldier. Who gunned him?'

'Read it in the paper tomorrow – maybe.'

'I want to know now.'

'Do you get everything you want?'

'No. Is that an answer, soldier?'

'Somebody you never heard of gunned him. Let it go at that.'

'If that's on the level, some day I may be able to do you a favour.'

'Hang up and let me go to bed.'

He laughed again. 'You're looking for Rusty Regan, aren't you?'

'A lot of people seem to think I am, but I'm not.'

'If you were, I could give you an idea. Drop in and see me down at the beach. Any time. Glad to see you.'

'Maybe.'

'Be seeing you then.' The phone clicked and I sat holding it with a savage patience. Then I dialled the Sternwoods' number and heard it ring four or five times and then the butler's suave voice saying: 'General Sternwood's residence.'

'This is Marlowe. Remember me? I met you about a hundred years ago – or was it yesterday?'

'Yes, Mr Marlowe. I remember, of course.'

'Is Mrs Regan home?'

'Yes, I believe so. Would you—'

I cut in on him with a sudden change of mind. 'No. You give her the message. Tell her I have the pictures, all of them, and that everything is all right.'

'Yes . . . yes. . . .' The voice seemed to shake a little. 'You have the pictures – all of them – and everything is all right. . . . Yes, sir. I may say – thank you very much, sir.'

The phone rang back in five minutes. I had finished my drink and it made me feel as if I could eat the dinner I had forgotten all about; I went out leaving the telephone ringing. It was ringing when I came back. It rang at intervals until half past twelve. At that time I put my light out and opened the windows up and muffled the phone bell with a piece of paper and went to bed. I had a bellyful of the Sternwood family.

I read all three of the morning papers over my eggs and bacon the next morning. Their accounts of the affair came as close to the truth as newspaper stories usually come – as close as Mars is to Saturn. None of the three connected Owen Taylor, driver of the Lido Pier Suicide Car, with the Laurel Canyon Exotic Bungalow Slaying. None of them mentioned the Sternwoods, Bernie Ohls or me. Owen Taylor was 'chauffeur to a wealthy family'. Captain Cronjager of the Hollywood Division got all the credit for solving the two slayings in his district, which were supposed to arise out of a dispute over the proceeds from a wire service maintained by one Geiger in the back of the bookstore on Hollywood Boulevard. Brody had shot Geiger and Carol Lundgren had shot Brody in revenge. Police were holding Carol Lundgren in custody. He had confessed. He had a bad record – probably in high school. Police were also holding one Agnes Lozelle, Geiger's secretary, as a material witness.

It was a nice write-up. It gave the impression that Geiger had been killed the night before, that Brody had been killed about an hour later, and that Captain Cronjager had solved both murders while lighting a cigarette. The suicide of Taylor made Page One of Section II. There was a photo of the sedan on the deck of the power lighter, with the licence plate blacked out, and something covered with a cloth lying on the deck beside the running board. Owen Taylor had been despondent and in poor health. His family lived in Dubuque, and his body would be shipped there. There would be no inquest.

CHAPTER 20

Captain Gregory of the Missing Persons Bureau laid my card down on his wide flat desk and arranged it so that its edges exactly paralleled the edges of the desk. He studied it with his head on one side, grunted, swung around in his swivel chair and looked out of his window at the barred top floor of the Hall of Justice half a block away. He was a burly man with tired eyes and the slow deliberate movement of a night watchman. His voice was toneless, flat and uninterested.

'Private dick, eh?' he said, not looking at me at all, but looking out of his window. Smoke wisped from the blackened bowl of a briar that hung on his eye tooth. 'What can I do for you?'

'I'm working for General Guy Sternwood, 3765 Alta Brea Crescent, West Hollywood.'

Captain Gregory blew a little smoke from the corner of his mouth without removing the pipe. 'On what?'

'Not exactly on what you're working on, but I'm interested. I thought you could help me.'

'Help you on what?'

'General Sternwood's a rich man,' I said. 'He's an old friend of the DA's father. If he wants to hire a full-time boy to run errands for him, that's no reflection on the police. It's just a luxury he is able to afford himself.'

'What makes you think I'm doing anything for him?'

I didn't answer that. He swung round slowly and heavily in his swivel chair and put his large feet flat on the bare linoleum that covered his floor. His office had the musty smell of years of routine. He stared at me bleakly.

'I don't want to waste your time, Captain,' I said and pushed my chair back – about four inches.

He didn't move. He kept on staring at me out of his washed-out tired eyes. 'You know the DA?'

'I've met him. I worked for him once. I know Bernie Ohls, his chief investigator, pretty well.'

Captain Gregory reached for a phone and mumbled into it: 'Get me Ohls at the DA's office.'

He sat holding the phone down on its cradle. Moments passed. Smoke drifted from his pipe. His eyes were heavy and motionless like his hand. The bell tinkled and he reached for my card with his left hand. 'Ohls? . . . Al Gregory at headquarters. A guy named Philip Marlowe is in my office. His card says he's a private investigator. He wants information from me. . . . Yeah? What does he look like? . . . Okey, thanks.'

He dropped the phone and took his pipe out of his mouth and tamped the tobacco with the brass cap of a heavy pencil. He did it carefully and solemnly, as if that was as important as anything he would have to do that day. He leaned back and stared at me some more.

'What you want?'

'An idea of what progress you're making, if any.'

He thought that over. 'Regan?' he asked finally.

'Sure.'

'Know him?'

'I never saw him. I hear he's a good-looking Irishman in his late thirties, that he was once in the liquor racket, that he married General Sternwood's older daughter and that they didn't click. I'm told he disappeared about a month back.'

'Sternwood oughta think himself lucky instead of hiring private talent to beat around in the tall grass.'

'The General took a big fancy to him. Such things happen. The old man is crippled and lonely. Regan used to sit around with him and keep him company.'

'What you think you can do that we can't do?'

'Nothing at all, in so far as finding Regan goes. But there's a rather mysterious blackmail angle. I want to make sure Regan isn't involved. Knowing where he is or isn't might help.'

'Brother, I'd like to help you, but I don't know where he is. He pulled down the curtain and that's that.'

'Pretty hard to do against your organization, isn't it, Captain?'

'Yeah – but it can be done – for a while.' He touched a bell button on the side of his desk. A middle-aged woman put her head in at a side door. 'Get me the file on Terence Regan, Abba.'

The door closed. Captain Gregory and I looked at each other in some more heavy silence. The door opened again and the woman put a tabbed green file on his desk. Captain Gregory nodded her out, put a pair of heavy horn-rimmed glasses on his veined nose and turned the papers in the file over slowly. I rolled a cigarette around in my fingers.

'He blew on the 16th of September,' he said. 'The only thing important about that is it was the chauffeur's day off and nobody saw Regan take his car out. It was late afternoon, though. We found the car four days later in a garage belonging to a ritzy bungalow court place near the Sunset Towers. A garage man reported it to the stolen car detail, said it didn't belong there. The place is called the Casa de Oro. There's an angle to that I'll tell you about in a minute. We couldn't find out anything about who put the car in there. We print the car but don't find any prints that are on the file anywhere. The car in that garage don't jibe with foul play, although there's a reason to suspect foul play. It jibes with something else

I'll tell you about in a minute.'

I said: 'That jibes with Eddie Mars's wife being on the missing list.'

He looked annoyed. 'Yeah. We investigate the tenants and find she's living there. Left about the time Regan did, within two days anyway. A guy who sounds a bit like Regan had been seen with her, but we don't get a positive identification. It's goddamned funny in this police racket how an old woman can look out of a window and see a guy running and pick him out of a line-up six months later, but we can show hotel help a clear photo and they just can't be sure.'

'That's one of the qualifications for good hotel help,' I said.

'Yeah. Eddie Mars and his wife didn't live together, but they were friendly, Eddie says. Here's some of the possibilities. First off Regan carried fifteen grand, packed it in his clothes all the time. Real money, they tell me. Not just a top card and a bunch of hay. That's a lot of jack but this Regan might be the boy to have it around so he could take it out and look at it when somebody was looking at him. Then again maybe he wouldn't give a damn. His wife says he never made a nickel off old man Sternwood except room and board and a Packard 120 his wife gave him. Tie that for an ex-legger in the rich gravy.'

'It beats me,' I said.

'Well, here we are with a guy who ducks out and has fifteen grand in his pants and folks know it. Well, that's money. I might duck myself, if I had fifteen grand, and me with two kids in high school. So the first thought is somebody rolls him for it and rolls him too hard, so they have to take him out in the desert and plant him among the cactuses. But I don't like that too well. Regan carried a gat and had plenty of experience using it, and not just in a greasy-faced liquor mob. I understand he commanded a whole brigade in the Irish troubles back in 1922 or whenever it was. A guy like that wouldn't be white meat to a heister. Then, his car being in that garage makes whoever rolled him know he was sweet on Eddie Mars's wife, which he was, I guess, but it ain't something every poolroom bum would know.'

'Got a photo?' I asked.

'Him, not her. That's funny too. There's a lot of funny angles to this case. Here.' He pushed a shiny print across the desk and I looked at an Irish face that was more sad than merry and more reserved than brash. Not the face of a tough guy and not the face of a man who could be pushed around much by anybody. Straight dark brows with strong bone under them. A forehead wide rather than high, a mat of dark clustering hair, a thin short nose, a wide mouth. A chin that had strong lines but was small for the mouth. A face that looked a little taut, the face of a man who would move fast and play for keeps. I passed the print back. I would know that face, if I saw it.

Captain Gregory knocked his pipe out and refilled it and tamped the tobacco down with his thumb. He lit it, blew smoke and began to talk again.

'Well, there could be people who would know he was sweet on Eddie Mars's frau. Besides Eddie himself. For a wonder *he* knew it. But he don't seem to give a damn. We check him pretty thoroughly around that time. Of course Eddie wouldn't have knocked him off out of jealousy. The set-up would point to him too obvious.'

'It depends how smart he is,' I said. 'He might try the double bluff.'

Captain Gregory shook his head. 'If he's smart enough to get by in his racket, he's too smart for that. I get your idea. He pulls the dumb act because he thinks we wouldn't expect him to pull the dumb play. From a police angle that's wrong. Because he'd have us in his hair so much it would interfere with his business. *You* might think a dumb play would be smart. I might think so. The rank and file wouldn't. They'd make his life miserable. I've ruled it out. If I'm wrong, you can prove it on me and I'll eat my chair cushion. Till then I'm leaving Eddie in the clear. Jealousy is a bad motive for his type. Top-flight racketeers have business brains. They learn to do things that are good policy and let their personal feelings take care of themselves. I'm leaving that out.'

'What are you leaving in?'

'The dame and Regan himself. Nobody else. She was a blonde then, but she won't be now. We don't find her car, so they probably left in it. They had a long start on us – fourteen days. Except for that car of Regan's I don't figure we'd have got the case at all. Of course I'm used to them that way, especially in good-class families. And of course everything I've done has had to be under the hat.'

He leaned back and thumped the arms of his chair with the heels of his large heavy hands.

'I don't see nothing to do but wait,' he said. 'We've got readers out, but it's too soon to look for results. Regan had fifteen grand we know of. The girl had some, maybe a lot in rocks. But they'll run out of dough some day. Regan will cash a cheque, drop a marker, write a letter. They're in a strange town and they've got new names, but they've got the same old appetites. They got to get back in the fiscal system.'

'What did the girl do before she married Eddie Mars?'

'Torcher.'

'Can't you get any old professional photos?'

'No. Eddie must have had some, but he won't loosen up. He wants her let alone. I can't make him. He's got friends in town, or he wouldn't be what he is.' He grunted. 'Any of this do you any good?'

I said: 'You'll never find either of them. The Pacific Ocean is too close.'

'What I said about my chair cushion still goes. We'll find him. It may take time. It could take a year or two.'

'General Sternwood may not live that long,' I said.

'We've done all we could, brother. If he wants to put out a reward and spend some money, we might get results. The city don't give me the kind of money it takes.' His large eyes peered at me and his scratchy eyebrows moved. 'You serious about thinking Eddie put them both down?'

I laughed. 'No. I was just kidding. I think what you think, Captain. That Regan ran away with a woman who meant more to him than a rich wife he didn't get along with. Besides, she isn't rich yet.'

'You met her, I suppose?'

'Yes. She'd make a jazzy week-end, but she'd be wearing for a steady diet.'

He grunted and I thanked him for his time and information and left. A grey Plymouth sedan tailed me away from the City Hall. I gave it a chance to catch up with me on a quiet street. It refused the offer, so I shook it off and went about my business.

CHAPTER 21

I didn't go near the Sternwood family. I went back to the office and sat in my swivel chair and tried to catch up on my foot-dangling. There was a gusty wind blowing in at the windows and the soot from the oil burners of the hotel next door was down-draughted into the room and rolling across the top of the desk like tumbleweed drifting across a vacant lot. I was thinking about going out to lunch and that life was pretty flat and that it would probably be just as flat if I took a drink and that taking a drink all alone at that time of day wouldn't be any fun anyway. I was thinking this when Norris called up. In his carefully polite manner he said that General Sternwood was not feeling very well and that certain items in the newspaper had been read to him and he assumed that my investigation was now completed.

'Yes, as regards Geiger,' I said. 'I didn't shoot him, you know.'

'The General didn't suppose you did, Mr Marlowe.'

'Does the General know anything about those photographs Mrs Regan was worrying about?'

'No, sir. Decidedly not.'

'Did you know what the General gave me?'

'Yes, sir. Three notes and a card, I believe.'

'Right. I'll return them. As to the photos I think I'd better just destroy them.'

'Very good, sir. Mrs Regan tried to reach you a number of times last night—'

'I was out getting drunk,' I said.

'Yes. Very necessary, sir, I'm sure. The General has instructed me to send you a cheque for five hundred dollars. Will that be satisfactory?'

'More than generous,' I said.

'And I presume we may now consider the incident closed?'

'Oh, sure. Tight as a vault with a busted time lock.'

'Thank you, sir. I am sure we all appreciate it. When the General is feeling a little better – possibly tomorrow – he would like to thank you in person.'

'Fine,' I said. 'I'll come out and drink some more of his brandy, maybe with champagne.'

'I shall see that some is properly iced,' the old boy said, almost with a smirk in his voice.

That was that. We said good-bye and hung up. The coffee shop smell from next door came in at the windows with the soot but failed to make me hungry. So I got out my office bottle and took the drink and let my self-respect ride its own race.

I counted it up on my fingers. Rusty Regan had run away from a lot of money and a handsome wife to go wandering with a vague blonde who was more or less married to a racketeer named Eddie Mars. He had gone suddenly without good-byes and there might be any number of reasons for that. The General had been too proud, or, at the first interview he gave me, too careful, to tell me the Missing Persons Bureau had the matter in hand. The Missing Persons people were dead on their feet on it and evidently didn't think it worth bothering over. Regan had done what he had done and that was his business. I agreed with Captain Gregory that Eddie Mars would have been very unlikely to involve himself in a double murder just because another man had gone to town with the blonde he was not even living with. It might have annoyed him, but business is business, and you have to hold your teeth clamped around Hollywood to keep from chewing on stray blondes. If there had been a lot of money involved, that would be different. But fifteen grand wouldn't be a lot of money to Eddie Mars. He was no two-bit chiseller like Brody.

Geiger was dead and Carmen would have to find some other shady character to drink exotic blends of hooch with. I didn't suppose she would have any trouble. All she would have to do would be to stand on the corner for five minutes and look coy. I hoped that the next grifter who dropped the hook on her would play her a little more smoothly, a little more for the long haul rather than the quick touch.

Mrs Regan knew Eddie Mars well enough to borrow money from him. That was natural, if she played roulette and was a good loser. Any gambling house owner would lend a good client money in a pinch. Apart from this they had an added bond of interest in Regan. He was her husband and he had gone off with Eddie Mars's wife.

Carol Lundgren, the boy killer with the limited vocabulary, was out of circulation for a long, long time, even if they didn't strap him in a chair over a bucket of acid. They wouldn't, because he would take a plea and save the county money. They all do when they don't have the price of a big lawyer. Agnes Lozelle was in custody as a material witness. They wouldn't need her for that, if Carol took a plea, and if he pleaded guilty on arraignment, they would turn her loose. They wouldn't want to open up any angles on Geiger's business, apart from which they had nothing on her.

That left me. I had concealed a murder and suppressed evidence for twenty-four hours, but I was still at large and had a five-hundred-dollar cheque coming. The smart thing for me to do was to take another drink and forget the whole mess.

That being the obviously smart thing to do, I called Eddie Mars and told him I was coming down to Las Olindas that evening to talk to him. That was how smart I was.

I got down there about nine, under a hard high October moon that lost itself in the top layers of a beach fog. The Cypress Club was at the far end of the town, a rambling frame mansion that had once been the summer residence of a rich man named De Cazens, and later had been a hotel. It was now a big dark outwardly shabby place in a thick grove of wind-twisted Monterey cypresses, which gave it its name. It had enormous scrolled porches, turrets all over the place, stained-glass trims around the big windows, big empty stables at the back, a general air of nostalgic decay. Eddie Mars had left the outside much as he found it, instead of making it over to look like an MGM set. I left my car on a street with sputtering arc lights and walked into the grounds along a damp gravel path to the main entrance. A doorman in a double-breasted guards coat let me into a huge dim silent lobby from which a white oak staircase curved majestically up to the darkness of an upper floor. I checked my hat and coat and waited, listening to music and confused voices behind heavy double doors. They seemed a long way off, and not quite of the same world as the building itself. Then the slim pasty-faced blond man who had been with Eddie Mars and the pug at Geiger's place came through a door under the staircase, smiled at me bleakly and took me back with him along a carpeted hall to the boss's office.

This was a square room with a deep old bay window and a stone fireplace in which a fire of juniper logs burned lazily. It was wainscoted in walnut and had a frieze of faded damask above the panelling. The ceiling was high and remote. There was a smell of cold sea.

Eddie Mars's dark sheenless desk didn't belong in the room, but neither did anything made after 1900. His carpet had a Florida suntan. There was a bartop radio in the corner and a Sèvres china tea set on a copper tray beside a samovar. I wondered who that was for. There was a door in the corner that had a time lock on it.

Eddie Mars grinned at me sociably and shook hands and moved his chin at the vault. 'I'm a pushover for a heist mob here except for that thing,' he said cheerfully. 'The local johns drop in every morning and watch me open it. I have an arrangement with them.'

'You hinted you had something for me,' I said. 'What is it?'

'What's your hurry? Have a drink and sit down.'

'No hurry at all. You and I haven't anything to talk about but business.'

'You'll have the drink and like it,' he said. He mixed a couple and put mine down beside a red leather chair and stood crosslegged against the desk himself, one hand in the side pocket of his midnight-blue dinner jacket, the thumb outside and the nail glistening. In dinner clothes he looked a little harder than in grey flannel, but he still looked like a horseman. We drank and nodded at each other.

'Ever been here before?' he asked.

'During prohibition. I don't get any kick out of gambling.'

'Not with money,' he smiled. 'You ought to look in tonight. One of your friends is outside betting the wheels. I hear she's doing pretty well. Vivian Regan.'

I sipped my drink and took one of his monogrammed cigarettes.

'I kind of liked the way you handled that yesterday,' he said. 'You made me sore at the time but I could see afterwards how right you were. You and I ought to get along. How much do I owe you?'

'For doing what?'

'Still careful, eh? I have my pipe-line into headquarters, or I wouldn't be here. I get them the way they happen, not the way you read them in the papers.' He showed me his large white teeth.

'How much have you got?' I asked.

'You're not talking money?'

'Information was the way I understood it.'

'Information about what?'

'You have a short memory. Regan.'

'Oh, that.' He waved his glistening nails in the quiet light from one of those bronze lamps that shoot a beam at the ceiling. 'I hear you got the information already. I felt I owed you a fee. I'm used to paying for nice treatment.'

'I didn't drive down here to make a touch. I get paid for what I do. Not much by your standards, but I make out. One customer at a time is a good rule. You didn't bump Regan off, did you?'

'No. Did you think I did?'

'I wouldn't put it past you.'

He laughed. 'You're kidding.'

I laughed. 'Sure, I'm kidding. I never saw Regan, but I saw his photo. You haven't got men for the work. And while we're on that subject don't send me any more gun punks with orders. I might get hysterical and blow one down.'

He looked through his glass at the fire, set it down on the end of the desk and wiped his lips with a sheer lawn handkerchief.

'You talk a good game,' he said. 'But I dare say you can break a hundred and ten. You're not really interested in Regan are you?'

'No, not professionally. I haven't been asked to be. But I know somebody who would like to know where he is.'

'She doesn't give a damn,' he said.

'I mean her father.'

He wiped his lips again and looked at the handkerchief almost as if he expected to find blood on it. He drew his thick grey eyebrows close together and fingered the side of his weatherbeaten nose.

'Geiger was trying to blackmail the General,' I said. 'The General wouldn't say so, but I figure he was at least half scared Regan might be behind it.'

Eddie Mars laughed. 'Uh-uh. Geiger worked that one on everybody. It was strictly his own idea. He'd get notes from people that looked legal – were legal, I dare say, except that he wouldn't have dared sue on them. He'd present notes, with a nice flourish, leaving himself empty-handed. If he drew an ace, he had a prospect that scared and he went to work. If he didn't draw an ace, he just dropped the whole thing.'

'Clever guy,' I said. 'He dropped it all right. Dropped it and fell on it. How come *you* know all this?'

He shrugged impatiently. 'I wish to Christ I didn't know half the stuff that's brought to me. Knowing other people's business is the worst investment a man can make in my circle. Then if it was just Geiger you were after, you're washed up on that angle.'

'Washed up and paid off.'

'I'm sorry about that. I wish old Sternwood would hire himself a soldier like you on a straight salary, to keep those girls of his home at least a few nights a week.'

'Why?'

His mouth looked sulky. 'They're plain trouble. Take the dark one. She's a pain in the neck around here. If she loses, she plunges and I end up with a fistful of paper which nobody will discount at any price. She has no money of her own except an allowance and what's in the old man's will is a secret. If she wins, she takes my money home with her.'

'You get it back the next night,' I said.

'I get some of it back. But over a period of time I'm loser.'

He looked earnestly at me, as if that was important to me. I wondered why he thought it necessary to tell me at all. I yawned and finished my drink.

'I'm going out and look the joint over,' I said.

'Yes, do.' He pointed to a door near the vault door. 'That leads to a door behind the tables.'

'I'd rather go in the way the suckers enter.'

'Okey. As you please. We're friends, aren't we, soldier?'

'Sure.' I stood up and we shook hands.

'Maybe I can do you a real favour some day,' he said. 'You got it all from Gregory this time.'

'So you own a piece of him too.'

'Oh not that bad. We're just friends.'

I stared at him for a moment, then went over to the door I had come in at. I looked back at him when I had it open.

'You don't have anybody tailing me around in a grey Plymouth sedan, do you?'

His eyes widened sharply. He looked jarred. 'Hell, no. Why should I?'

'I couldn't imagine,' I said, and went on out. I thought his surprise looked genuine enough to be believed. I thought he even looked a little worried. I couldn't think of any reason for that.

CHAPTER 22

It was about ten-thirty when the little yellow-sashed Mexican orchestra got tired of playing a low-voiced prettied-up rhumba that nobody was dancing to. The gourd player rubbed his finger tips together as if they were sore and got a cigarette into his mouth almost with the same movement. The other four, with a timed simultaneous stoop, reached under their chairs for glasses from which they sipped, smacking their lips and flashing their eyes. Tequila, their manner said. It was probably mineral water. The pretence was as wasted as the music. Nobody was looking at them.

The room had been a ballroom once and Eddie Mars had changed it only as much as his business compelled him. No chromium glitter, no indirect lighting from behind angular cornices, no fused glass pictures, or chairs in violent leather and polished metal tubing, none of the pseudo-modernistic circus of the typical Hollywood night trap. The light was from heavy crystal chandeliers and the rose-damask panels of the wall were still the same rose damask, a little faded by time and darkened by dust, that had been matched long ago against the parquetry floor, of which only a small glass-smooth space in front of the little Mexican orchestra showed bare. The rest was covered by a heavy old-rose carpeting that must have cost plenty. The parquetry was made of a dozen kinds of hardwood, from Burma teak through half a dozen shades of oak and ruddy wood that looked like mahogany, and fading out to the hard pale wild lilac of the California hills, all laid in elaborate patterns, with the accuracy of a transit.

It was still a beautiful room and now there was roulette in it instead of measured, old-fashioned dancing. There were three tables close to the far wall. A low bronze railing joined them and made a fence around the croupiers. All three tables were working, but the crowd was at the middle one. I could see Vivian Regan's black head close to it, from across the room where I was leaning against the bar and turning a small glass of bacardi around on the mahogany.

The bartender leaned beside me watching the cluster of well-dressed people at the middle table. 'She's pickin' 'em tonight, right on the nose,' he said. 'That tall back-headed frail.'

'Who is she?'

'I wouldn't know her name. She comes here a lot though.'

'The hell you wouldn't know her name.'

'I just work here, mister,' he said without any animosity. 'She's all alone too. The guy was with her passed out. They took him out to his car.'

'I'll take her home,' I said.

'The hell you will. Well, I wish you luck anyways. Should I gentle up that bacardi or do you like it the way it is?'

'I like it the way it is as well as I like it at all,' I said.

'Me, I'd just as leave drink croup medicine,' he said.

The crowd parted and two men in evening clothes pushed their way out and I saw the back of her neck and her bare shoulders in the opening. She wore a low-cut dress of dull green velvet. It looked too dressy for the occasion. The crowd closed and hid all but her black head. The two men came across the room and leaned against the bar and asked for Scotch and soda. One of them was flushed and excited. He was mopping his face with a black-bordered handkerchief. The double satin stripes down the side of his trousers were wide enough for tyre tracks.

'Boy, I never saw such a run,' he said in a jittery voice. 'Eight wins and two stand-offs in a row on that red. That's roulette, boy, that's roulette.'

'It gives me the itch,' the other one said. 'She's betting a grand at a crack. She can't lose.' They put their beaks in their drinks, gurgled swiftly and went back.

'So wise the little men are,' the barkeeper said. 'A grand a crack, huh. I saw an old horseface in Havana once—'

The noise swelled over at the middle table and a chiselled foreign voice rose above it saying: 'If you will just be patient a moment, madam. The table cannot cover your bet. Mr Mars will be here in a moment.'

I left my bacardi and padded across the carpet. The little orchestra started to play a tango, rather loud. No one was dancing or intending to dance. I moved through a scattering of people in dinner clothes and full evening dress and sports clothes and business suits to the end table at the left. It had gone dead. Two croupiers stood behind it with their heads together and their eyes sideways. One moved a rake back and forth aimlessly over the empty layout. They were both staring at Vivian Regan.

Her long lashes twitched and her face looked unnaturally white. She was at the middle table, exactly opposite the wheel. There was a disordered pile of money and chips in front of her. It looked like a lot of money. She spoke to the croupier with a cool, insolent, ill-tempered drawl.

'What kind of a cheap outfit is this, I'd like to know. Get busy and spin that wheel, highpockets. I want one more play and I'm playing table stakes. You take it away fast enough I've noticed, but when it comes to dishing it out you start to whine.'

The croupier smiled a cold polite smile that had looked at thousands of boors and millions of fools. His tall dark disinterested manner was flawless. He said gravely: 'The table cannot cover your bet, madam. You have over sixteen thousand dollars there.'

'It's your money,' the girl jeered. 'Don't you want it back?'

A man beside her tried to tell her something. She turned swiftly and spat something at him and he faded back into the crowd red-faced. A door opened in the panelling at the far end of the enclosed place made by the bronze railing. Eddie Mars came through the door with a set indifferent smile on his face, his hands thrust into the pockets of his dinner jacket, both thumb-nails glistening outside. He seemed to like that pose. He strolled behind the croupiers and stopped at the corner of the middle table. He spoke with lazy calm, less politely than the croupier.

'Something the matter, Mrs Regan?'

She turned her face to him with a sort of lunge. I saw the curve of her cheek stiffen, as if with an almost unbearable inner tautness. She didn't answer him.

Eddie Mars said gravely: 'If you're not playing any more, you must let me send someone home with you.'

The girl flushed. Her cheekbones stood out white in her face. Then she laughed off-key. She said bitterly:

'One more play, Eddie. Everything I have on the red. I like red. It's the colour of blood.'

Eddie Mars smiled faintly, then nodded and reached into his inner breast pocket. He drew out a large pinseal wallet with gold corners and tossed it carelessly along the table to the croupier. 'Cover her bet in even thousands,' he said, 'if no one objects to this turn of the wheel being just for the lady.'

No one objected. Vivian Regan leaned down and pushed all her winnings savagely with both hands on to the large red diamond on the layout.

The croupier leaned over the table without haste. He counted and stacked her money and chips, placed all but a few chips and bills in a neat pile and pushed the rest back off the layout with his rake. He opened Eddie Mars's wallet and drew out two flat packets of thousand-dollar bills. He broke one, counted six bills out, added them to the unbroken packet, put the four loose bills in the wallet and laid it aside as carelessly as if it had been a packet of matches. Eddie Mars didn't touch the wallet. Nobody moved except the croupier. He spun the wheel lefthanded and sent the ivory ball skittering along the upper edge with a casual flirt of his wrist. Then he drew his hands back and folded his arms.

Vivian's lips parted slowly until her teeth caught the light and glittered like knives. The ball drifted lazily down the slope of the wheel and bounced on the chromium ridges above the numbers. After a long time and then very suddenly motion left it with a dry click. The wheel slowed, carrying the ball around with it. The croupier didn't unfold his arms until the wheel had entirely ceased to revolve.

'The red wins,' he said formally, without interest. The little ivory ball lay in Red 25, the third number from the Double Zero. Vivian Regan put her head back and laughed triumphantly.

The croupier lifted his rake and slowly pushed the stack of thousand-dollar bills across the layout, added them to the stake, pushed everything slowly out of the field of play.

Eddie Mars smiled, put his wallet back in his pocket, turned on his heel and left the room through the door in the panelling.

A dozen people let their breath out at the same time and broke for the bar. I broke with them and got to the far end of the room before Vivian had gathered up her winnings and turned away from the table. I went out into the large quiet lobby, got my hat and coat from the check girl, dropped a quarter in her tray and went out on the porch. The doorman loomed up beside me and said: 'Can I get your car for you, sir?'

I said: 'I'm just going for a walk.'

The scrollwork along the edge of the porch roof was wet with the fog. The fog dripped from the Monterey cypresses that shadowed off into nothing towards the cliff above the ocean. You could see a scant dozen feet in any direction. I went down the porch steps and drifted off through the trees, following an indistinct path until I could hear the wash of the surf licking at the fog, low down at the bottom of the cliff. There wasn't a gleam of light anywhere. I could see a dozen trees clearly at one time, another dozen dimly, then nothing at all but the fog. I circled to the left and drifted back towards the gravel path that went around to the stables where they parked the cars. When I could make out the outlines of the house I stopped. A little in front of me I had heard a man cough.

My steps hadn't made any sound on the soft moist turf. The man coughed again, then stifled the cough with a handkerchief or a sleeve. While he was still doing that I moved forward closer to him. I made him out, a vague shadow close to the path. Something made me step behind a tree and crouch down. The man turned his head. His face should have been a white blur when he did that. It wasn't. It remained dark. There was a mask over it.

I waited, behind the tree.

CHAPTER 23

Light steps, the steps of a woman, came along the invisible pathway and the man in front of me moved forward and seemed to lean against the fog. I couldn't see the woman, then I could see her indistinctly. The arrogant carriage of her head seemed familiar. The man stepped out very quickly. The two figures blended in the fog, seemed to be part of the fog. There was dead silence for a moment. The man said:

'This is a gun, lady. Gentle now. Sound carries in the fog. Just hand me the bag.'

The girl didn't make a sound. I moved forward a step. Quite suddenly I could see the foggy fuzz on the man's hat brim. The girl stood motionless. Then her breathing began to make a rasping sound, like a small file on soft wood.

'Yell,' the man said, 'and I'll cut you in half.'

She didn't yell. She didn't move. There was a movement from him, and a dry chuckle. 'It better be in here,' he said. A catch clicked and a fumbling sound came to me. The man turned and came towards my tree. When he had taken three or four steps he chuckled again. The chuckle was something out of my own memories. I reached a pipe out of my pocket and held it like a gun.

I called out softly: 'Hi, Lanny.'

The man stopped dead and started to bring his hand up. I said: 'No. I told you never to do that, Lanny. You're covered.'

Nothing moved. The girl back on the path didn't move. I didn't move. Lanny didn't move.

'Put the bag down between your feet, kid,' I told him. 'Slow and easy.'

He bent down. I jumped out and reached him still bent over. He straightened up against me breathing hard. His hands were empty.

'Tell me I can't get away with it,' I said. I leaned against him and took the gun out of his overcoat pocket. 'Somebody's always giving me guns,' I told him. 'I'm weighted down with them till I walk all crooked. Beat it.'

Our breaths met and mingled, our eyes were like the eyes of two tomcats on a wall. I stepped back.

'On your way, Lanny. No hard feelings. You keep it quiet and I keep it quiet. Okey?'

'Okey,' he said thickly.

The fog swallowed him. The faint sound of his steps and then nothing. I picked the bag up and felt in it and went towards the path. She still stood there motionless, a grey fur coat held tight around her throat with an ungloved hand on which a ring made a faint glitter. She wore no hat. Her dark parted hair was part of the darkness of the night. Her eyes too.

'Nice work, Marlowe. Are you my bodyguard now?' Her voice had a harsh note.

'Looks that way. Here's the bag.'

She took it. I said: 'Have you a car with you?'

She laughed. 'I came with a man. What are you doing here?'

'Eddie Mars wanted to see me.'

'I didn't know you knew him. Why?'

'I don't mind telling you. He thought I was looking for somebody he thought had run away with his wife.'

'Were you?'

'No.'

'Then what did you come for?'

'To find out why he thought I was looking for somebody he thought had run away with his wife.'

'Did you find out?'

'No.'

'You leak information like a radio announcer,' she said. 'I suppose it's none of my business – even if the man was my husband. I thought you weren't interested in that.'

'People keep throwing it at me.'

She clicked her teeth in annoyance. The incident of the masked man with the gun seemed to have made no impression on her at all. 'Well, take me to the garage,' she said. 'I have to look in at my escort.'

We walked along the path and around a corner of the building and there was light ahead, then around another corner and came to a bright enclosed stable yard lit with two floodlights. It was still paved with brick and still sloped down to a grating in the middle. Cars glistened and a man in a brown smock got up off a stool and came forward.

'Is my boy friend still blotto?' Vivian asked him carelessly.

'I'm afraid he is, miss. I put a rug over him and run the windows up. He's okey, I guess. Just kind of resting.'

We went over to a big Cadillac and the man in the smock pulled the rear door open. On the wide back seat, loosely arranged, covered to the chin with a plaid robe, a man lay snoring with his mouth open. He seemed to be a big blond man who would hold a lot of liquor.

'Meet Mr Larry Cobb,' Vivian said. 'Mister Cobb – Mister Marlowe.'

I grunted.

'Mr Cobb was my escort,' she said. 'Such a nice escort, Mr Cobb. So attentive. You should see him sober. *I* should see him sober. Somebody should see him sober. I mean, just for the record. So it could become a part of history, that brief flashing moment, soon buried in time, but never forgotten – when Larry Cobb was sober.'

'Yeah,' I said.

'I've even thought of marrying him,' she went on in a high strained voice, as if the shock of the stick-up was just beginning to get to her. 'At odd times when nothing pleasant would come into my mind. We all have those spells. Lots of money, you know. A yacht, a place on Long Island, a place at Newport, a place at Bermuda, places dotted here and there all over the world probably – just a good Scotch bottle apart. And to Mr Cobb a bottle of Scotch is not very far.'

'Yeah,' I said. 'Does he have a driver to take him home?'

'Don't say "yeah". It's common.' She looked at me with arched eyebrows. The man in the smock was chewing his lower lip hard. 'Oh, undoubtedly a whole platoon of drivers. They probably do squads right in front of the garage every morning, buttons shining, harness gleaming, white gloves immaculate – a sort of West Point elegance about them.'

'Well, where the hell is this driver?' I asked.

'He drove hisself tonight,' the man in the smock said, almost apologetically. 'I could call his home and have somebody come down for him.'

Vivian turned around and smiled at him as if he had just presented her with a diamond tiara. 'That would be lovely,' she said. 'Would you do that? I really wouldn't want Mr Cobb to die like that – with his mouth open. Someone might think he had died of thirst.'

The man in the smock said: 'Not if they sniffed him, miss.'

She opened her bag and grabbed a handful of paper money and pushed it at him. 'You'll take care of him, I'm sure.'

'Jeeze,' the man said, pop-eyed. 'I sure will, miss.'

'Regan is the name,' she said sweetly. 'Mrs Regan. You'll probably see me again. Haven't been here long, have you?'

'No'm.' His hands were doing frantic things with the fistful of money he was holding.

'You'll get to love it here,' she said. She took hold of my arm. 'Let's ride in your car, Marlowe.'

'It's outside on the street.'

'Quite all right with me, Marlowe. I love a nice walk in the fog. You meet such interesting people.'

'Oh, nuts,' I said.

She held on to my arm and began to shake. She held me hard all the way to the car. She had stopped shaking by the time we reached it. I drove down a curving lane of trees on the blind side of the house. The lane opened on De Cazens Boulevard, the main drag of Las Olindas. We passed under the ancient sputtering arc lights and after a while there was a town, buildings, dead-looking stores, a service station with a light over a night bell, and at last a drugstore that was still open.

'You better have a drink,' I said.

She moved her chin, a point of paleness in the corner of the seat. I turned diagonally into the kerb and parked. 'A little black coffee and a smattering of rye would go well,' I said.

'I could get as drunk as two sailors and love it.'

I held the door for her and she got out close to me, brushing my cheek with her hair. We went into the drugstore. I bought a pint of rye at the liquor counter and carried it over to the stools and set it down on the cracked marble counter.

'Two coffees,' I said. 'Black, strong and made this year.'

'You can't drink liquor in here,' the clerk said. He had a washed-out blue smock, was thin on top as to hair, had fairly honest eyes and his chin would never hit a wall before he saw it.

Vivian Regan reached into her bag for a packet of cigarettes and shook a couple loose just like a man. She held them towards me.

'It's against the law to drink liquor in here,' the clerk said.

I lit the cigarettes and didn't pay any attention to him. He drew two cups of coffee from a tarnished nickel urn and set them in front of us. He looked at the bottle of rye, muttered under his breath and said wearily: 'Okey, I'll watch the street while you pour it.'

He went and stood at the display window with his back to us and his ears hanging out.

'My heart's in my mouth doing this,' I said, and unscrewed the top of the whisky bottle and loaded the coffee. 'The law enforcement in this town is terrific. All through prohibition Eddie Mars's place was a night club and they had two uniformed men in the lobby every night – to see that the guests didn't bring their own liquor instead of buying it from the house.'

The clerk turned suddenly and walked back behind the counter and went in behind the little glass window of the prescription room.

We sipped our loaded coffee. I looked at Vivian's face in the mirror back of the coffee urn. It was taut, pale, beautiful and wild. Her lips were red and harsh.

'You have wicked eyes,' I said. 'What's Eddie Mars got on you?'

She looked at me in the mirror. 'I took plenty away from him tonight at roulette – starting with five grand I borrowed from him yesterday and didn't have to use.'

'That might make him sore. You think he sent that loogan after you?'

'What's a loogan?'

'A guy with a gun.'

'Are you a loogan?'

'Sure,' I laughed. 'But strictly speaking a loogan is on the wrong side of the fence.'

'I often wonder if there is a wrong side.'

'We're losing the subject. What has Eddie Mars got on you?'

'You mean a hold on me of some sort?'

'Yes.'

Her lip curled. 'Wittier, please, Marlowe. Much wittier.'

'How's the General? I don't pretend to be witty.'

'Not too well. He didn't get up today. You could at least stop questioning me.'

'I remember a time when I thought the same about you. How much does the General know?'

'He probably knows everything.'

'Norris would tell him?'

'No. Wilde, the District Attorney, was out to see him. Did you burn those pictures?'

'Sure. You worry about your little sister, don't you – from time to time.'

'I think she's all I do worry about. I worry about Dad in a way, to keep things from him.'

'He hasn't many illusions,' I said, 'but I suppose he still has pride.'

'We're his blood. That's the hell of it.' She stared at me in the mirror with deep, distant eyes. 'I don't want him to die despising his own blood. It was always wild blood, but it wasn't always rotten blood.'

'Is it now?'

'I guess you think so.'

'Not yours. You're just playing the part.'

She looked down. I sipped some more coffee and lit another cigarette for us. 'So you shoot people,' she said quietly. 'You're a killer.'

'Me? How?'

'The papers and the police fixed it up nicely. But I don't believe everything I read.'

'Oh, you think I accounted for Geiger – or Brody – or both of them.'

She didn't say anything. 'I didn't have to,' I said. 'I might have, I suppose, and got away with it. Neither of them would have hesitated to throw lead at me.'

'That makes you just a killer at heart, like all cops.'

'Oh, nuts.'

'One of those dark deadly quiet men who have no more feelings than a butcher has for slaughtered meat. I knew it the first time I saw you.'

'You've got enough shady friends to know different.'

'They're all soft compared to you.'

'Thanks, lady. You're no English muffin yourself.'

'Let's get out of this rotten little town.'

I paid the check, put the bottle of rye in my pocket, and we left. The clerk still didn't like me.

We drove away from Las Olindas through a series of little dank beach towns with shack-like houses built down on the sand close to the rumble of the surf and larger houses built back on the slopes behind. A yellow window shone here and there, but most of the houses were dark. A smell of kelp came in off the water and lay on the fog. The tyres sang on the moist concrete of the boulevard. The world was a wet emptiness.

We were close to Del Rey before she spoke to me for the first time since we left the drugstore. Her voice had a muffled sound, as if something was throbbing deep under it.

'Drive down by the Del Ray beach club. I want to look at the water. It's the next street on the left.'

There was a winking yellow light at the intersection. I turned the car and slid down a slope with a high bluff on one side, interurban tracks to the right, a low straggle of lights far off beyond the tracks, and then very far off a glitter of pier lights and a haze in the sky over a city. That way the fog was almost gone. The road crossed the tracks where they turned to run under the bluff, then reached a paved strip of waterfront highway that bordered an open and uncluttered beach. Cars were parked along the pavement, facing out to sea, dark. The lights of the beach club were a few hundred yards away.

I braked the car against the kerb and switched the headlights off and sat with my hands on the wheel. Under the thinning fog the surf curled and creamed, almost without sound, like a thought trying to form itself on the edge of consciousness.

'Move closer,' she said almost thickly.

I moved out from under the wheel into the middle of the seat. She turned her body a little away from me as if to peer out of the window. Then she let herself fall backwards, without a sound, into my arms. Her head almost struck the wheel. Her eyes were closed, her face was dim. Then I saw that her eyes opened and flickered, the shine of them visible even in the darkness.

'Hold me close, you beast,' she said.

I put my arms around her loosely at first. Her hair had a harsh feeling against my face. I tightened my arms and lifted her up. I brought her face slowly up to my face. Her eyelids were flickering rapidly, like moth wings.

I kissed her tightly and quickly. Then a long slow clinging kiss. Her lips opened under mine. Her body began to shake in my arms.

'Killer,' she said softly, her breath going into my mouth.

I strained her against me until the shivering of her body was almost shaking mine. I kept on kissing her. After a long time she pulled her head away enough to say: 'Where do you live?'

'Hobart Arms. Franklin near Kenmore.'

'I've never seen it.'

'Want to?'

'Yes.'

'What has Eddie Mars got on you?'

Her body stiffened in my arms and her breath made a harsh sound. Her head pulled back until her eyes, wide open, ringed with white, were staring at me.

'So that's the way it is,' she said in a soft dull voice.

'That's the way it is. Kissing is nice, but your father didn't hire me to sleep with you.'

'You son of a bitch,' she said calmly, without moving.

I laughed in her face. 'Don't think I'm an icicle,' I said. 'I'm not blind or without senses. I have warm blood like the next guy. You're easy to take – too damned easy. What has Eddie Mars got on you?'

'If you say that again, I'll scream.'

'Go ahead and scream.'

She jerked away and pulled herself upright, far back in the corner of the car.

'Men have been shot for little things like that, Marlowe.'

'Men have been shot for practically nothing. The first time we met I told you I was a detective. Get it through your lovely head. I work at it, lady. I don't play at it.'

She fumbled in her bag and got a handkerchief out and bit on it, her head turned away from me. The tearing sound of the handkerchief came to me. She tore it with her teeth, slowly, time after time.

'What makes you think he has anything on me?' she whispered, her voice muffled by the handkerchief.

'He lets you win a lot of money and sends a gunpoke around to take it back for him. You're not more than mildly surprised. You didn't even thank me for saving it for you. I think the whole thing was just some kind of an act. If I wanted to flatter myself, I'd say it was at least partly for my benefit.'

'You think he can win or lose as he pleases.'

'Sure. On even money bets, four times out of five.'

'Do I have to tell you I loathe your guts, Mister Detective?'

'You don't owe me anything. I'm paid off.'

She tossed the shredded handkerchief out of the car window. 'You have a lovely way with women.'

'I like kissing you.'

'You kept your head beautifully. That's so flattering. Should I congratulate you, or my father?'

'I liked kissing you.'

Her voice became an icy drawl. 'Take me away from here, if you will be so kind. I'm quite sure I'd like to go home.'

'You won't be a sister to me?'

'If I had a razor, I'd cut your throat – just to see what ran out of it.'

'Caterpillar blood,' I said.

I started the car and turned it and drove back across the interurban tracks to the highway and so on into town and up to West Hollywood. She didn't speak to me. She hardly moved all the way back. I drove through the gates and up the sunken driveway to the *porte-cochère* of the big house. She jerked the car door open and was out of it before it had quite stopped. She didn't speak even then. I watched her back as she stood against the door after ringing the bell. The door opened and Norris looked out. She pushed past him quickly and was gone. The door banged shut and I was sitting there looking at it.

I turned back down the driveway and home.

CHAPTER 24

The apartment house lobby was empty this time. No gunman waiting under the potted palm to give me orders. I took the automatic elevator up to my floor and walked along the hallway to the tune of a muted radio behind a door. I needed a drink and was in a hurry to get one. I didn't switch the light on inside the door. I made straight for the kitchenette and brought up short in three or four feet. Something was wrong. Something on the air, a scent. The shades were down at the windows and the street light leaking in at the sides made a dim light in the room. I stood still and listened. The scent on the air was a perfume, a heavy, cloying perfume.

There was no sound, no sound at all. Then my eyes adjusted themselves more to the darkness and I saw there was something across the floor in front of me that shouldn't have been there. I backed, reached the wall switch with my thumb and flicked the light on.

The bed was down. Something in it giggled. A blonde head was pressed into my pillow. Two bare arms curved up and the hands belonging to them were clasped on top of the blonde head. Carmen Sternwood lay on her back, in my bed, giggling at me. The tawny wave of her hair was spread out on the pillow as if by a careful and artificial hand. Her slaty eyes peered at me and had the effect, as usual, of peering from behind a barrel. She smiled. Her small sharp teeth glinted.

'Cute, aren't I?' she said.

I said harshly: 'Cute as a Filipino on Saturday night.'

I went over to a floor lamp and pulled the switch, went back to put off the ceiling light, and went across the room again to the chessboard on a card table under the lamp. There was a problem laid out on the board, a six-mover. I couldn't solve it, like a lot of my problems. I reached down and moved a knight, then pulled my hat and coat off and threw them somewhere. All this time the soft giggling went on from the bed, that sound that made me think of rats behind a wainscoting in an old house.

'I bet you can't even guess how I got in.'

I dug a cigarette out and looked at her with bleak eyes. 'I bet I can. You came through the keyhole, just like Peter Pan.'

'Who's he?'

'Oh, a fellow I used to know around the poolroom.'

She giggled. 'You're cute, aren't you?' she said.

I began to say: 'About that thumb—' but she was ahead of me. I didn't have to remind her. She took her right hand from behind her head and started sucking the thumb and eyeing me with very round and naughty eyes.

'I'm all undressed,' she said, after I smoked and stared at her for a minute.

'By God,' I said, 'it was right at the back of my mind. I was groping for it. I almost had it, when you spoke. In another minute I'd have said "I bet you're all undressed." I always wear my rubbers in bed myself, in case I wake up with a bad conscience and have to sneak away from it.'

'You're cute.' She rolled her head a little, kittenishly. Then she took her left hand from under her head, and took hold of the covers, paused dramatically, and swept them aside. She was undressed all right. She lay there on the bed in the lamp-light, as naked and glistening as a pearl. The Sternwood girls were giving me both barrels that night.

I pulled a shred of tobacco off the edge of my lower lip.

'That's nice,' I said. 'But I've already seen it all. Remember? I'm the guy that keeps finding you without any clothes on.'

She giggled some more and covered herself up again. 'Well, how *did* you get in?' I asked her.

'The manager let me in. I showed him your card. I'd stolen it from Vivian. I told him you told me to come here and wait for you. I was – I was mysterious.' She glowed with delight.

'Neat,' I said. 'Managers are like that. Now I know how you got in tell me how you're going to go out.'

She giggled. 'Not going – not for a long time . . . I like it here. You're cute.'

'Listen,' I pointed my cigarette at her. 'Don't make me dress you again. I'm tired. I appreciate all you're offering me. It's just more than I could possibly take. Doghouse Reilly never let a pal down that way. I'm your friend. I won't let you down – in spite of yourself. You and I have to keep on being friends, and this isn't the way to do it. Now will you dress like a nice little girl?'

She shook her head from side to side.

'Listen,' I ploughed on, 'you don't really care anything about me. You're just showing how naughty you can be. But you don't have to show me. I knew it already. I'm the guy that found—'

'Put the light out,' she giggled.

I threw my cigarette on the floor and stamped on it. I took a handkerchief out and wiped the palms of my hands. I tried it once more.

'It isn't on account of the neighbours,' I told her. 'They don't really care a lot. There's a lot of stray broads in any apartment house and one more won't make the building rock. It's a question of professional pride. You know – professional pride. I'm working for your father. He's a sick man, very frail, very helpless. He sort of trusts me not to pull any stunts. Won't you please get dressed, Carmen?'

'Your name isn't Doghouse Reilly,' she said. 'It's Philip Marlowe. You can't fool me.'

'I looked down at the chessboard. The move with the knight was wrong. I put it back where I had moved it from. Knights had no meaning in this game. It wasn't a game for knights.

I looked at her again. She lay still now, her face pale against the pillow, her eyes large and dark and empty as rain barrels in a drought. One of her small five-fingered thumbless hands picked at the cover restlessly. There was a vague glimmer of doubt starting to get born in her somewhere. She didn't know about it yet. It's so hard for women – even nice women – to realize that their bodies are not irresistible.

I said: 'I'm going out in the kitchen and mix a drink. Want one?'

'Uh-huh.' Dark silent mystified eyes stared at me solemnly, the doubt growing larger in them, creeping into them noiselessly, like a cat in long grass stalking a young blackbird.

'If you're dressed when I get back, you'll get the drink. Okey?'

Her teeth parted and a faint hissing noise came out of her mouth. She didn't answer me. I went out of the kitchenette and got out some Scotch and fizzwater and mixed a couple of highballs. I didn't have anything really exciting to drink, like nitro-glycerine or distilled tiger's breath. She hadn't moved when I got back with the glasses. The hissing had stopped. Her eyes were dead again. Her lips started to smile at me. Then she sat up suddenly and threw all the covers off her body and reached.

'Gimme.'

'When you're dressed. Not *until* you're dressed.'

I put the two glasses down on the card table and sat down myself and lit another cigarette. 'Go ahead. I won't watch you.'

I looked away. Then I was aware of the hissing noise very sudden and sharp. It startled me into looking at her again. She sat there naked, propped on her hands, her mouth open a little, her face like scraped bone. The hissing noise came tearing out of her mouth as if she had nothing to do with it. There was something behind her eyes, blank as they were, that I had never seen in a woman's eyes.

Then her lips moved very slowly and carefully, as if they were artificial lips and had to be manipulated with springs.

She called me a filthy name.

I didn't mind that. I didn't mind what she called me, what anybody called me. But this was the room I had to live in. It was all I had in the way of a home. In it was everything that was mine, that had any association for me, any past, anything that took the place of a family. Not much; a few books, pictures, radio, chessmen, old letters, stuff like that. Nothing. Such as they were they had all my memories.

I couldn't stand her in that room any longer. What she called me only reminded me of that.

I said carefully: 'I'll give you three minutes to get dressed and out of here. If you're not out by then, I'll throw you out – by force. Just the way you are, naked. And I'll throw your clothes after you into the hall. Now – get started.'

Her teeth chattered and the hissing noise was sharp and animal. She swung her feet to the floor and reached for her clothes on a chair beside the bed. She dressed. I watched her. She dressed with stiff awkward fingers – for a woman – but quickly at that. She was dressed in a little over two minutes. I timed it.

She stood there beside the bed, holding a green bag tight against a fur-trimmed coat. She wore a rakish green hat crooked on her head. She stood there for a moment and hissed at me, her face still like scraped bone, her eyes still empty and yet full of some jungle emotion. Then she walked quickly to the door and opened it and went out, without speaking, without looking back. I heard the elevator lurch into motion and move in the shaft.

I walked to the windows and pulled the shades up and opened the windows wide. The night air came drifting in with a kind of stale sweetness that still remembered automobile exhausts and the streets of the city. I reached for my drink and drank it slowly. The apartment house door closed itself down below me. Steps tinkled on the quiet pavement. A car started up not far away. It rushed off into the night with a rough clashing of gears. I went back to the bed and looked down at it. The imprint of her head was still in the pillow, of her small corrupt body still on the sheets.

I put my empty glass down and tore the bed to pieces savagely.

CHAPTER 25

It was raining again the next morning, a slanting grey rain like a swung curtain of crystal beads. I got up feeling sluggish and tired and stood looking out of the windows, with a dark harsh taste of Sternwoods still in my mouth. I was as empty of life as a scarecrow's pockets. I went out to the kitchenette and drank two cups of black coffee. You can have a hangover from other things than alcohol. I had one from women. Women made me sick.

I shaved and showered and dressed and got my raincoat out and went downstairs and looked out of the front door. Across the street, a hundred feet up, a grey Plymouth sedan was parked. It was the same one that had tried to trail me around the day before, the same one that I had asked Eddie Mars about. There might be a cop in it, if a cop had that much time on his hands and wanted to waste it following me around. Or it might be a smoothie in the detective business trying to get a noseful of somebody else's case in order to chisel a way into it. Or it might be the Bishop of Bermuda disapproving of my night life.

I went out back and got my convertible from the garage and drove it around front past the grey Plymouth. There was a small man in it, alone. He started up after me. He worked better in the rain. He stayed close enough so that I couldn't make a short block and leave that before he entered it, and he stayed back far enough so that other cars were between us most of the time. I drove down to the boulevard and parked in the lot next to my building and came out of there with my raincoat collar up and my hat brim low and the raindrops tapping icily at my face in between. The Plymouth was across the way at a fireplug. I walked down to the intersection and crossed with the green light and walked back, close to the edge of the pavement and the parked cars. The Plymouth hadn't moved. Nobody got out of it. I reached it and jerked open the door on the kerb side.

A small bright-eyed man was pressed back into the corner behind the wheel. I stood and looked in at him, the rain thumping my back. His eyes blinked behind the swirling smoke of a cigarette. His hands tapped restlessly on the thin wheel.

I said: 'Can't you make your mind up?'

He swallowed and the cigarette bobbed between his lips. 'I don't think

I know you,' he said, in a tight little voice.

'Marlowe's the name. The guy you've been trying to follow around for a couple of days.'

'I ain't following anybody, doc.'

'This jaloppy is. Maybe you can't control it. Have it your own way. I'm now going to eat breakfast in the coffee shop across the street, orange juice, bacon and eggs, toast, honey, three or four cups of coffee, and a toothpick. I am then going up to my office, which is on the seventh floor of the building right opposite you. If you have anything that's worrying you beyond endurance, drop up and chew it over. I'll only be oiling my machine-gun.'

I left him blinking and walked away. Twenty minutes later I was airing the scrubwoman's Soirée d'Amour out of my office and opening up a thick rough envelope addressed in a fine old-fashioned pointed handwriting. The envelope contained a brief formal note and a large mauve cheque for five hundred dollars, payable to Philip Marlowe and signed, Guy de Brisay Sternwood, by Vincent Norris. That made it a nice morning. I was making out a blank slip when the buzzer told me somebody had enterd my two by four reception-room. It was the little man from the Plymouth.

'Fine,' I said. 'Come in and shed your coat.'

He slid past me carefully as I held the door, as carefully as though he feared I might plant a kick in his minute buttocks. We sat down and faced each other across the desk. He was a very small man, not more than five feet three and would hardly weigh as much as a butcher's thumb. He had tight brilliant eyes that wanted to look hard, and looked as hard as oysters on the half-shell. He wore a double-breasted grey suit that was too wide in the shoulders and had too much lapel. Over this, open, an Irish tweed coat with some badly worn spots. A lot of foulard tie bulged out and was rain-spotted above his crossed lapels.

'Maybe you know me,' he said. 'I'm Harry Jones.'

I said I didn't know him. I pushed a flat tin of cigarettes at him. His small neat fingers speared one like a trout taking the fly. He lit it with the desk lighter and waved his hand.

'I been around,' he said. 'Know the boys and such. Used to do a little liquor-running down from Hueneme Point. A tough racket, brother. Riding the scout car with a gun in your lap and a wad on your hip that would choke a coal chute. Plenty of times we paid off four sets of law before we hit Beverly Hills. A tough racket.'

'Terrible,' I said.

He leaned back and blew smoke at the ceiling from the small tight corner of his small tight mouth.

'Maybe you don't believe me,' he said.

'Maybe I don't,' I said. 'And maybe I do. And then again maybe I haven't bothered to make my mind up. Just what is the build-up supposed to do to me?'

'Nothing,' he said tartly.

'You've been following me around for a couple of days,' I said. 'Like a fellow trying to pick up a girl and lacking the last inch of nerve. Maybe you're selling insurance. Maybe you knew a fellow called Joe Brody. That's a lot of maybes, but I have a lot on hand in my business.'

His eyes bulged and his lower lip almost fell in his lap. 'Christ, how'd you know that?' he said.

'I'm psychic. Shake your business up and pour it. I haven't got all day.'

The brightness of his eyes almost disappeared between the suddenly narrowed lids. There was silence. The rain pounded down on the flat tarred roof over the Mansion House lobby below my windows. His eyes opened a little, shined again, and his voice was full of thought.

'I was trying to get a line of you, sure,' he said. 'I've got something to sell – cheap, for a couple of C notes. How'd you tie me to Joe?'

I opened a letter and read it. It offered me a six months' correspondence course in fingerprinting at a special professional discount. I dropped it into the waste basket and looked at the little man again. 'Don't mind me. I was just guessing. You're not a cop. You don't belong to Eddie Mars's outfit. I asked him last night. I couldn't think of anybody else but Joe Brody's friends who would be that much interested in me.'

'Jesus,' he said and licked his lower lip. His face had turned white as paper when I mentioned Eddie Mars. His mouth drooped open and his cigarette hung to the corner of it by some magic, as if it had grown there. 'Aw, you're kidding me,' he said at last, with the sort of smile the operating-room sees.

'All right. I'm kidding you.' I opened another letter. This one wanted to send me a daily news-letter from Washington, all inside stuff, straight from the cook-house. 'I suppose Agnes is loose,' I added.

'Yeah. She sent me. You interested?'

'Well – she's a blonde.'

'Nuts. You made a crack when you were up there that night – the night Joe got squibbed off. Something about Brody must have known something good about the Sternwoods or he wouldn't have taken the chance on that picture he sent them.'

'Uh-huh. So he had? What was it?'

'That's what the two hundred bucks pays for.'

I dropped some more fan mail into the basket and lit myself a fresh cigarette.

'We gotta get out of town,' he said. 'Agnes is a nice girl. You can't hold that stuff on her. It's not so easy for a dame to get by these days.'

'She's too big for you,' I said.'She'll roll on you and smother you.'

'That's kind of a dirty crack, brother,' he said with something that was near enough to dignity to make me stare at him.

I said: 'You're right. I've been meeting the wrong kind of people lately. Let's cut out the gabble and get down to cases. What have you got for the money?'

'Would you pay it?'

'If it does what?'

'If it helps you find Rusty Regan.'

'I'm not looking for Rusty Regan.'

'Says you. Want to hear it or not?'

'Go ahead and chirp. I'll pay for anything I use. Two C notes buys a lot of information in my circle.'

'Eddie Mars had Regan bumped off,' he said calmly, and leaned back as if he had just been made a vice-president.

I waved a hand in the direction of the door. 'I wouldn't even argue with you,' I said. 'I wouldn't waste the oxygen. On your way, small size.'

He leaned across the desk, white lines at the corners of his mouth. He snubbed his cigarette out carefully, over and over again, without looking at it. From behind a communicating door came the sound of a typewriter clacking monotonously to the bell, to the shift, line after line.

'I'm not kidding,' he said.

'Beat it. Don't bother me. I have work to do.'

'No you don't,' he said sharply. 'I ain't that easy. I came here to speak my piece and I'm speaking it. I knew Rusty myself. Not well, well enough to say "How's a boy?" and he'd answer me or he wouldn't, according to how he felt. A nice guy though. I always liked him. He was sweet on a singer named Mona Grant. Then she changed her name to Mars. Rusty got sore and married a rich dame that hung around the joints like she couldn't sleep well at home. You know all about her, tall, dark, enough looks for a Derby winner, but the type would put a lot of pressure on a guy. High-strung. Rusty wouldn't get along with her. But Jesus, he'd get along with her old man's dough, wouldn't he? That's what you think. This Regan was a cockeyed sort of buzzard. He had long-range eyes. He was looking over into the next valley all the time. He wasn't scarcely around where he was. I don't think he gave a damn about dough. And coming from me, brother, that's a compliment.'

The little man wasn't so dumb after all. A three for a quarter grifter wouldn't even think such thoughts, much less know how to express them.

I said: 'So he ran away.'

'He started to run away, maybe. With this girl Mona. She wasn't living with Eddie Mars, didn't like his rackets. Especially the side lines, like blackmail, bent cars, hideouts for hot boys from the east, and so on. The talk was Regan told Eddie one night, right out in the open, that if he ever messed Mona up in any criminal rap, he'd be around to see him.'

'Most of this is on the record, Harry,' I said. 'You can't expect money for that.'

'I'm coming to what isn't. So Regan blew. I used to see him every afternoon in Vardi's drinking Irish whisky and staring at the wall. He don't talk much any more. He'd give me a bet now and then, which was what I was there for, to pick up bets for Puss Walgreen.'

'I thought he was in the insurance business.'

'That's what it says on the door. I guess he'd sell you insurance at that, if you tramped on him. Well, about the middle of September I don't see Regan any more. I don't notice it right away. You know how it is. A guy's there and you see him and then he ain't there and you don't see him until something makes you think of it. What makes me think about it is I hear a guy say laughing that Eddie Mars's woman lammed out with Rusty Regan and Mars is acting like he was best man, instead of being sore. So I tell Joe Brody and Joe was smart.'

'Like hell he was,' I said.

'Not copper smart, but still smart. He's out for the dough. He gets to figuring could he get a line somehow on the two lovebirds he could maybe collect twice – once from Eddie Mars and once from Regan's wife. Joe knew the family a little.'

'Five grand worth,' I said. 'He nicked them for that a while back.'

'Yeah?' Harry Jones looked mildly surprised. 'Agnes ought to have told me that. There's a frail for you. Always holding out. Well, Joe and me watch the papers and we don't see anything, so we know old Sternwood has a blanket on it. Then one day I see Lash Canino in Vardi's. Know him?'

I shook my head.

'There's a boy that is tough like some guys think they are tough. He does a job for Eddie Mars when Mars needs him – trouble-shooting. He'd bump a guy off between drinks. When Mars don't need him he don't go near him. And he don't stay in LA. Well it might be something and it might not. Maybe they got a line on Regan and Mars has just been sitting back with a smile on his puss, waiting for the chance. Then again it might be something else entirely. Anyway I tell Joe and Joe gets on Canino's tail. He can tail. Me, I'm no good at it. I'm giving that one away. No charge. And Joe tails Canino out to the Sternwood place and Canino parks outside the estate and a car comes up beside him with a girl in it. They talk for a while and Joe thinks the girl passes something over, like maybe dough. The girl beats it. It's Regan's wife. Okey, she knows Canino and Canino knows Mars. So Joe figures Canino knows something about Regan and is trying to squeeze a little on the side for himself. Canino blows and Joe loses him. End of Act One.'

'What does this Canino look like?'

'Short, heavy set, brown hair, brown eyes, and always wears brown clothes and a brown hat. Even wears a brown suéde raincoat. Drives a brown coupé. Everything brown for Mr Canino.'

'Lets have Act Two,' I said.

'Without some dough that's all.'

'I don't see two hundred bucks in it. Mrs Regan married an ex-bootlegger out of the joints. She'd know other people of his sort. She knows Eddie Mars well. If she thought anything had happened to Regan, Eddie would be the very man she'd go to, and Canino might be the man Eddie would pick to handle the assignment. Is that all you have?'

'Would you give the two hundred to know where Eddie's wife is?' the little man asked calmly.

He had all my attention now. I almost cracked the arms of my chair leaning on them.

'Even if she was alone?' Harry Jones added in a soft, rather sinister tone. 'Even if she never run away with Regan at all, and was being kept now about forty miles from LA in a hideout – so that law would keep on thinking she had dusted with him? Would you pay two hundred bucks for that, shamus?'

I licked my lips. They tasted dry and salty. 'I think I would,' I said. 'Where?'

'Agnes found her,' he said grimly. 'Just by a lucky break. Saw her out riding and managed to tail her home. Agnes will tell you where that is – when she's holding the money in her hand.'

I made a hard face at him. 'You could tell the coppers for nothing, Harry. They have some good wreckers, down at Central these days. If they killed you trying, they still have Agnes.'

'Let 'em try,' he said. 'I ain't so brittle.'

'Agnes must have something I didn't notice.'

'She's a grifter, shamus. I'm a grifter. We're all grifters. So we sell each other out for a nickel. Okey. See can you make me.' He reached for another of my cigarettes, placed it neatly between his lips and lit it with a match the way I do myself, missing twice on his thumb-nail and then using his foot. He puffed evenly and stared at me level-eyes, a funny little hard guy I could have thrown from home plate to second base. A small man in a big man's world. There was something I liked about him.

'I haven't pulled anything in here,' he said steadily. 'I came in talking two C's. That's still the price. I come because I thought I'd get a take it or leave it, one right gee to another. Now you're waving cops at me. You oughta be ashamed of yourself.'

I said: 'You'll get the two hundred – for that information. I have to get the money myself first.'

He stood up and nodded and pulled his worn little Irish tweed coat tight around his chest. 'That's okey. After dark is better anyway. It's a leery job – buckin' guys like Eddie Mars. But a guy has to eat. The book's been pretty dull lately. I think the big boys have told Puss Walgreen to move on. Suppose you come over there to the office, Fulwider Building, Western and Santa Monica, four-twenty-eight at the back. You bring the money, I'll take you to Agnes.'

'Can't you tell me yourself? I've seen Agnes.'

'I promised her,' he said simply. He buttoned his overcoat, cocked his hat jauntily, nodded again and strolled to the door. He went out. His steps died along the hall.

I went down to the bank and deposited my five-hundred-dollar cheque and drew out two hundred in currency. I went upstairs again and sat in my chair thinking about Harry Jones and his story. It seemed a little too pat. It had the austere simplicity of fiction rather than the tangled woof of fact. Captain Gregory ought to have been able to find Mona Mars, if she was that close to his beat. Supposing, that is, he had tried.

I thought about it most of the day. Nobody came into the office. Nobody called me on the phone. It kept on raining.

CHAPTER 26

At seven the rain had stopped for a breathing spell, but the gutters were still flooded. On Santa Monica the water was level with the pavement and a thin film of it washed over the top of the kerbing. A traffic cop in shining black rubber from boots to cap sloshed through the flood on his way from the shelter of a sodden awning. My rubber heels slithered on the pavement as I turned into the narrow lobby of the Fulwider Building. A single drop light burned far back, beyond an open, once-gilt elevator. There was a tarnished and well-missed spittoon on a gnawed rubber mat. A case of false teeth hung on the mustard-coloured wall like a fuse box in a screen porch. I shook the rain off my hat and looked at the building directory beside the case of teeth. Numbers with names and numbers without names. Plenty of vacancies or plenty of tenants who wished to remain anonymous. Painless dentists, shyster detective agencies, small sick businesses that had crawled there to die, mail order schools that would teach you how to become a railway clerk or a radio technician or a screen writer – if the postal inspectors didn't catch up with them first. A nasty building. A building in which the smell of stale cigar buts would be the cleanest odour.

An old man dozed in the elevator, on a ramshackle stool, with a burst-out cushion under him. His mouth was open, his veined temples glistened in the weak light. He wore a blue uniform coat that fitted him the way a stall fits a horse. Under that grey trousers with frayed cuffs, white cotton socks and black kid shoes, one of which was slit across a bunion. On the stool he slept miserably, waiting for a customer. I went past him softly, the clandestine air of the building prompting me, found the fire door and pulled it open. The fire stairs hadn't been swept in a month. Bums had slept on them, eaten on them, left crusts and fragments of greasy newspaper, matches, a gutted imitation-leather pocket-book. In a shadowy angle against the scribbled wall a pouched ring of pale rubber had fallen and had not been disturbed. A very nice building.

I came out at the fourth floor sniffing for air. The hallway had the same dirty spittoon and frayed mat, the same mustard walls, the same memories of low tide. I went down the line and turned a corner. The name: 'L.D. Walgreen – Insurance', showed on a dark pebbled glass door, on a second dark door, on a third behind which there was a light. One of the dark doors said: 'Entrance.'

A glass transom was open above the lighted door. Through it the sharp birdlike voice of Harry Jones spoke, saying:

'Canino? . . . Yeah, I've seen you around somewhere. Sure.'

I froze. The other voice spoke. It had a heavy purr, like a small dynamo behind a brick wall. It said: 'I thought you would.' There was a vaguely sinister note in that voice.

A chair scraped on linoleum, steps sounded, the transom above me squeaked shut. A shadow melted from behind the pebbled glass.

I went back to the first of the three doors marked with the name Walgreen. I tried it cautiously. It was locked. It moved in a loose frame, an old door fitted many years past, made of half-seasoned wood and shrunken now. I reached my wallet out and slipped the thick hard window of celluloid from over my driver's licence. A burglar's tool the law had forgotten to proscribe. I put my gloves on, leaned softly and lovingly against the door and pushed the knob hard away from the frame. I pushed the celluloid plate into the wide crack and felt for the slope of the spring lock. There was a dry click, like a small icicle breaking. I hung there motionless, like a lazy fish in the water. Nothing happened inside. I turned the knob and pushed the door back into darkness. I shut it behind me as carefully as I had opened it.

The lighted oblong of an uncurtained window faced me, cut by the angle of a desk. On the desk a hooded typewriter took form, then the metal knob of a communicating door. This was unlocked. I passed into the second of the three offices. Rain rattled suddenly against the closed window. Under its noise I crossed the room. A tight fan of light spread from an inch opening of the door into the lighted office. Everything very convenient. I walked like a cat on a mantel and reached the hinged side of the door, put an eye to the crack and saw nothing but light against the angle of the wood.

The purring voice was now saying quite pleasantly: 'Sure, a guy could sit on his fanny and crab what another guy done if he knows what it's all about. So you go to see this peeper. Well, that was your mistake. Eddie don't like it. The peeper told Eddie some guy in a grey Plymouth was tailing him. Eddie naturally wants to know who and why, see.'

Harry Jones laughed lightly. 'What makes it his business?'

'That don't get you no place.'

'You know why I went to the peeper. I already told you. Account of Joe Brody's girl. She has to blow and she's shatting on her uppers. She figures the peeper can get her some dough. I don't have any.'

The purring voice said gently: 'Dough for what? Peepers don't give that stuff out to punks.'

'He could raise it. He knows rich people.' Harry Jones laughed, a brave little laugh.

'Don't fuss with me, little man.' The purring voice had an edge, like sand in the bearings.

'Okey, okey. You know the dope on Brody's bump-off. That screwy kid done it all right, but the night it happened this Marlowe was right there in the room.'

'That's known, little man. He told it to the law.'

'Yeah – here's what isn't. Brody was trying to peddle a nudist photo of the young Sternwood girl. Marlowe got wise to him. While they were arguing about it the young Sternwood girl dropped around herself – with a gat. She took a shot at Brody. She lets one fly and breaks a window. Only the peeper didn't tell the coppers about that. And Agnes didn't neither. She figures it's railway fare for her not to.'

'This ain't got anything to do with Eddie?'

'Show me how.'

'Where's this Agnes at?'

'Nothing doing.'

'You'll tell me, little man. Here, or in the back room where the boys pitch dimes against the wall.'

'She's my girl now, Canino. I don't put my girl in the middle for anybody.'

A silence followed. I listened to the rain lashing the windows. The smell of cigarette smoke came through the crack of the door. I wanted to cough. I bit hard on a handkerchief.

The purring voice said, still gentle: 'From what I hear this blonde broad was just a shill for Geiger. I'll talk it over with Eddie. How much you tap the peeper for?'

'Two centuries.'

'Get it?'

Harry Jones laughed again. 'I'm seeing him tomorrow. I have hopes.'

'Where's Agnes?'

'Listen—'

'Where's Agnes?'

Silence.

'Look at it, little man.'

I didn't move. I wasn't wearing a gun. I didn't have to see through the crack of the door to know that a gun was what the purring voice was inviting Harry Jones to look at. But I didn't think Mr Canino would do anything with his gun beyond showing it. I waited.

'I'm looking at it,' Harry Jones said, his voice squeezed tight as if it could hardly get past his teeth. 'And I don't see anything I didn't see before. Go ahead and blast and see what it gets you.'

'A Chicago overcoat is what it would get *you*, little man.'

Silence.

'Where's Agnes?'

Harry Jones sighed. 'Okey,' he said wearily. 'She's in an apartment house at 28 Court Street, up on Bunker Hill. Apartment 301. I guess I'm yellow all right. Why should I front for that twist?'

'No reason. You got good sense. You and me'll go out and talk to her. All I want is to find out is she dummying up on you, kid. If it's the way you say it is, everything is jakeloo. You can put the bite on the peeper and be on your way. No hard feelings?'

'No,' Harry Jones said. 'No hard feelings, Canino.'

'Fine. Let's dip the bill. Got a glass?' The purring voice was now as false as an usherette's eyelashes and as slippery as a watermelon seed. A drawer was pulled open. Something jarred on wood. A chair squeaked. A scuffing sound on the floor. 'This is bond stuff,' the purring voice said.

There was a gurgling sound. 'Moths in your ermine, as the ladies say.'

Harry Jones said softly: 'Success.'

I heard a short sharp cough. Then a violent retching. There was a small thud on the floor, as if a thick glass had fallen. My fingers curled against my raincoat.

The purring voice said gently: 'You ain't sick from just one drink, are you, pal?'

Harry Jones didn't answer. There was laboured breathing for a short moment. Then thick silence folded down. Then a chair scraped.

'So long, little man,' said Mr Canino.

Steps, a click, the wedge of light died at my feet, a door opened and closed quietly. The steps faded, leisurely and assured.

I stirred around the edge of the door and pulled it wide and looked into blackness relieved by the dim shine of a window. The corner of a desk glittered faintly. A hunched shape took form in a chair behind it. In the close air there was a heavy clogged smell, almost a perfume. I went across to the corridor and listened. I heard the distant clang of the elevator.

I found the light switch and light glowed in a dusty glass bowl hanging from the ceiling by three brass chains. Harry Jones looked at me across the desk, his eyes wide open, his face frozen in a tight spasm, the skin bluish. His small dark head was tilted to one side. He sat upright against the back of the chair.

A tramcar bell clanged at an almost infinite distance and the sound came buffeted by innumerable walls. A brown half-pint of whisky stood on the desk with the cap off. Harry Jones's glass glinted against a castor of the desk. The second glass was gone.

I breathed shallowly, from the top of my lungs, and bent above the bottle. Behind the charred smell of the bourbon another odour lurked, faintly, the odour of bitter almonds. Harry Jones dying had vomited on his coat. That made it cyanide.

I walked around him carefully and lifted a phone book from a hook on the wooden frame of the window. I let it fall again, reached the telephone as far as it would go from the little dead man. I dialled information. The voice answered.

'Can you give me the phone number of Apartment 301, 28 Court Street?'

'One moment, please.' The voice came to me borne on the smell of bitter almonds. A silence. 'The number is Wentworth 2528. It is listed under Glendower Apartments.'

I thanked the voice and dialled the number. The bell rang three times, then the line opened. A radio blared along the wire and was muted. A burly male voice said: 'Hello.'

'Is Agnes there?'

'No Agnes here, buddy. What number you want?'

'Wentworth two-five-two-eight.'

'Right number, wrong gal. Ain't that a shame?' The voice cackled.

I hung up and reached for the phone book again and looked up the

Wentworth Apartments. I dialled the manager's number. I had a blurred vision of Mr Canino driving fast through rain to another appointment with death.

'Glendower Apartments. Mr Schiff speaking.'

'This is Wallis, Police Identification Bureau. Is there a girl named Agnes Lozelle registered in your place?'

'Who did you say you were?'

I told him again.

'If you'll give me your number I'll—'

'Cut the comedy,' I said sharply, 'I'm in a hurry. Is there or isn't there?'

'No. There isn't.' The voice was as stiff as a breadstick.

'Is there a tall blonde with green eyes registered in the flop?'

'Say, this isn't any flop—'

'Oh, can it, *can it*!' I rapped at him in a police voice. 'You want me to send the vice squad over there and shake the joint down? I know all about Bunker Hill apartment houses, mister. Especially the ones that have phone numbers listed for each apartment.'

'Hey, take it easy, officer. I'll co-operate. There's a couple of blondes here, sure. Where isn't there? I hadn't noticed their eyes much. Would yours be alone?'

'Alone, or with a little chap about five feet three, a hundred and ten, sharp black eyes, wears double-breasted dark grey suit and Irish tweed overcoat, grey hat. My information is Apartment 301, but all I get there is the big razzoo.'

'Oh, she ain't there. There's a couple of car salesmen living in three-o-one.'

'Thanks, I'll drop around.'

'Make it quiet, won't you? Come to my place, direct?'

'Much obliged. Mr Schiff.' I hung up.

I wiped sweat off my face. I walked to the far corner of the office and stood with my face to the wall, patted it with a hand. I turned around slowly and looked across at little Harry Jones grimacing in his chair.

'Well, you fooled him, Harry,' I said out loud, in a voice that sounded queer to me. 'You lied to him and you drank your cyanide like a little gentleman. You died like a poisoned rat, Harry, but you're no rat to me.'

I had to search him. It was a nasty job. His pockets yielded nothing about Agnes, nothing that I wanted at all. I didn't think they would, but I had to be sure. Mr Canino might be back. Mr Canino would be the kind of self-confident gentleman who would not mind returning to the scene of his crime.

I put the light out and started to open the door. The phone bell rang jarringly down on the baseboard. I listened to it, my jaw muscles drawn into a knot, aching. Then I shut the door and put the light on again and went across to it.

'Yeah?'

A woman's voice. Her voice. 'Is Harry around?'

'Not for a minute, Agnes.'

She waited a while on that. Then she said slowly: 'Who's talking?'

'Marlowe, the guy that's trouble to you.'

'Where is he?' sharply.

'I came over to give him two hundred bucks in return for certain information. The offer holds. I have the money. Where are you?'

'Didn't he tell you?'

'No.'

'Perhaps you'd better ask him. Where is he?'

'I can't ask him. Do you know a man named Canino?'

Her gasp came as clearly as though she had been beside me.

'Do you want the two C's or not?' I asked.

'I–I want it pretty bad, mister.'

'All right then. Tell me where to bring it.'

'I–I—' Her voice trailed off and came back with a panic rush. 'Where's Harry?'

'Got scared and blew. Meet me somewhere – anywhere at all – I have the money.'

'I don't believe you – about Harry. It's a trap.'

'Oh stuff. I could have had Harry hauled in long ago. There isn't anything to make a trap for. Canino got a line on Harry somehow and he blew. I want quiet, you want quiet, Harry wants quiet.' Harry already had it. Nobody could take it away from him. 'You don't think I'd stooge for Eddie Mars, do you, angel?'

'No–o, I guess not. Not that. I'll meet you in half an hour. Beside Bullocks Wilshire, the east entrance to the parking lot.'

'Right,' I said.

I dropped the phone in its cradle. The wave of almond odour flooded me again, and the sour smell of vomit. The little dead man sat silent in his chair, beyond fear, beyond change.

I left the office. Nothing moved in the dingy corridor. No pebbled glass door had light behind it. I went down the fire stairs to the second floor and from there looked down at the lighted roof of the elevator cage. I pressed the button. Slowly the car lurched into motion. I ran down the stairs again. The car was above me when I walked out of the building.

It was raining hard again. I walked into it with the heavy drops slapping my face. When one of them touched my tongue I knew that my mouth was open and the ache at the side of my jaws told me it was open wide and strained back, mimicking the rictus of death carved upon the face of Harry Jones.

CHAPTER 27

'Give me the money.'

The motor of the grey Plymouth throbbed under her voice and the rain pounded above it. The violet light at the top of Bullocks green-tinged tower was far above us, serene and withdrawn from the dark, dripping city. Her black-gloved hand reached out and I put the bills in it. She bent over to count them under the dim light of the dash. A bag clicked open, clicked shut. She let a spent breath die on her lips. She leaned towards me.

'I'm leaving, copper. I'm on my way. This is a get-away stake and God how I need it. What happened to Harry?'

'I told you he ran away. Canino got wise to him somehow. Forget Harry. I've paid and I want my information.'

'You'll get it. Joe and I were out riding Foothill Boulevard Sunday before last. It was late and the lights coming up and the usual mess of cars. We passed a brown coupé and I saw the girl who was driving it. There was a man beside her, a dark short man. The girl was a blonde. I'd seen her before. She was Eddie Mars's wife. The guy was Canino. You wouldn't forget either of them, if you ever saw them. Joe tailed the coupé from in front. He was good at that. Canino, the watch-dog, was taking her out for air. A mile or so east of Realito a road turns towards the foothills. That's orange country to the south but to the north it's as bare as hell's back yard and smack up against the hills there's a cyanide plant where they make the stuff for fumigation. Just off the highway there's a small garage and paintshop run by a gee named Art Huck. Hot car drop, likely. There's a frame house beyond this, and beyond the house nothing but the foothills and the bare stone outcrop and the cyanide plant a couple of miles on. That's the place where she's holed up. They turned off on this road and Joe swung around and went back and we saw the car turn off the road where the frame house was. We sat there half an hour looking through the cars going by. Nobody came back out. When it was quite dark Joe sneaked up there and took a look. He said there were lights in the house and a radio was going and just the one car out in front, the coupé. So we beat it.'

She stopped talking and I listened to the swish of tyres on Wilshire. I said: 'They might have shifted quarters since then but if that's what you have to sell – that's what you have to sell. Sure you knew her?'

'If you ever see her, you won't make a mistake the second time.

Goodbye, copper, and wish me luck. I got a raw deal.'

'Like hell you did,' I said, and walked away across the street to my own car.

The grey Plymouth moved forward, gathered speed, and darted around the corner on to Sunset Place. The sound of its motor died, and with it blonde Agnes wiped herself off the slate for good, so far as I was concerned. Three men dead, Geiger, Brody, and Harry Jones, and the woman went riding off in the rain with my two hundred in her bag and not a mark on her. I kicked my starter and drove on down-town to eat. I ate a good dinner. Forty miles in the rain is a hike, and I hoped to make it a round trip.

I drove north across the river, on into Pasadena, through Pasadena and almost at once I was in orange groves. The tumbling rain was solid white spray in the headlights. The windshield wiper could hardly keep the glass clear enough to see through. But not even the drenched darkness could hide the flawless lines of the orange trees wheeling away like endless spokes into the night.

Cars passed with a tearing hiss and a wave of dirty spray. The highway jerked through a little town that was all packing houses and sheds, and railway sidings nuzzling them. The groves thinned out and dropped away to the south and the road climbed and it was cold and to the north the black foothills crouched closer and sent a bitter wind whipping down their flanks. Then faintly out of the dark two yellow vapour lights glowed high up in the air and a neon sign between them said: 'Welcome to Realito.'

Frame houses were spaced far back from a wide main street, then a sudden knot of stores, the lights of a drugstore behind fogged glass, the fly-cluster of cars in front of a movie theatre, a dark bank on a corner with a clock sticking out over the pavement and a group of people standing in the rain looking at its windows, as if they were some kind of a show. I went on. Empty fields closed in again.

Fate stage-managed the whole thing. Beyond Realito, just about a mile beyond, the highway took a curve and the rain fooled me and I went too close to the shoulder. My right front tyre let go with an angry hiss. Before I could stop the right rear went with it. I jammed the car to a stop, half on the pavement, half on the shoulder, got out and flashed a spotlight around. I had two flats and one spare. The flat butt of a heavy galvanized tack stared at me from the front tyre. The edge of the pavement was littered with them. They had been swept off, but not far enough off.

I snapped the flash off and stood there breathing rain and looking up a side road at a yellow light. It seemed to come from a skylight. The skylight could belong to a garage, the garage could be run by a man named Art Huck, and there could be a frame house next door to it. I tucked my chin down in my collar and started towards it, then went back to unstrap the licence-holder from the steering post and put it in my pocket. I leaned lower under the wheel. Behind a weighted flap, directly under my right leg as I sat in the car, there was a hidden compartment. There were two guns in it. One belonged to Eddie Mars's boy Lanny and one belonged to me. I took Lanny's. It would have had more practice than mine. I stuck it nose down in an inside pocket and started up the side road.

The garage was a hundred yards from the highway. It showed the highway a blank side wall. I played the flash on it quickly. 'Art Huck – Motor Repairs and Painting.' I chuckled, then Harry Jones's face rose up in front of me, and I stopped chuckling. The garage doors were shut, but there was an edge of light under them and a thread of light where the halves met. I went on past. The frame house was there, light in two front windows, shades down. It was set well back from the road, behind a thin clump of trees. A car stood on the gravel drive in front. It was dark, indistinct, but it would be a brown coupé and it would belong to Mr Canino. It squatted there peacefully in front of the narrow wooden porch.

He would let her take it out for a spin once in a while, and sit beside her, probably with a gun handy. The girl Rusty Regan ought to have married, that Eddie Mars couldn't keep, the girl that hadn't run away with Regan. Nice Mr Canino.

I trudged back to the garage and banged on the wooden door with the butt of my flash. There was a hung instant of silence, as heavy as thunder. The light inside went out. I stood there grinning and licking the rain off my lip. I clicked the spot on the middle of the doors. I grinned at the circle of white. I was where I wanted to be.

A voice spoke through the door, a surly voice: 'What you want?'

'Open up. I've got two flats back on the highway and only one spare. I need help.'

'Sorry, mister. We're closed up. Realito's a mile west. Better try there.'

I didn't like that. I kicked the door hard. I kept on kicking it. Another voice made itself heard, a purring voice, like a small dynamo behind a wall. I liked this voice. It said: 'A wise guy, huh? Open up, Art.'

A bolt squealed and half of the door bent inward. My flash burned briefly on a gaunt face. Then something that glittered swept down and knocked the flash out of my hand. A gun had peaked at me. I dropped low where the flash burned on the wet ground and picked it up.

The surly voice said: 'Kill that spot, bo. Folks get hurt that way.'

I snapped the flash off and straightened. Light went on inside the garage, outlined a tall man in overalls. He backed away from the open door and kept a gun levelled at me.

'Step inside and shut the door, stranger. We'll see what we can do.'

I stepped inside, and shut the door behind my back. I looked at the gaunt man, but not at the other man who was shadowy over by a workbench, silent. The breath of the garage was sweet and sinister with the smell of hot pyroxylin paint.

'Ain't you got no sense?' the gaunt man chided me. 'A bank job was pulled at Realito this noon.'

'Pardon,'I said, remembering the people staring at the bank in the rain. 'I didn't pull it. I'm a stranger here.'

'Well, there was,' he said morosely. 'Some say it was a couple of punk kids and they got 'em cornered back here in the hills.'

'It's a nice night for hiding,' I said. 'I suppose they threw tacks out. I got some of them. I thought you just needed the business.'

'You didn't ever get socked in the kisser, did you?' the gaunt man asked me briefly.

'Not by anybody your weight.'

The purring voice from over in the shadows said: 'Cut out the heavy menace, Art. This guy's in a jam. You run a garage, don't you?'

'Thanks,' I said, and didn't look at him even then.

'Okey, okey,' the man in the overalls grumbled. He tucked his gun through a flap in his clothes and bit a knuckle, staring at me moodily over it. The smell of the pyroxylin paint was as sickening as ether. Over in the corner, under a drop light, there was a big new-looking sedan with a paint gun lying on its fender.

I looked at the man by the workbench now. He was short and thick-bodied with strong shoulders. He had a cool face dark eyes. He wore a belted brown suède raincoat that was heavily spotted with rain. His brown hat was tilted rakishly. He leaned his back against the workbench and looked me over without haste, without interest, as if he was looking at a slab of cold meat. Perhaps he thought of people that way.

He moved his dark eyes up and down slowly and then glanced at his finger-nails one by one, holding them up against the light and studying them with care, as Hollywood has taught it should be done. He spoke around a cigarette.

'Got two flats, huh? That's tough. They swept them tacks, I thought.'

'I skidded a little on the curve.'

'Stranger in town you said?'

'Travelling through. On the way to LA. How far is it?'

'Forty miles. Seems longer this weather. Where from, stranger?'

'Santa Rosa.'

'Come the long way, eh? Tahoe and Lone Pine?'

'Not Tahoe. Reno and Carson City.'

'Still the long way.' A fleeting smile curved his lips.

'Any law against it?' I asked him.

'Huh? No, sure not. Guess you think we're nosy. Just on account of that heist back there. Take a jack and get his flats, Art.'

'I'm busy,' the gaunt man growled. 'I've got work to do. I got this spray job. And it's raining, you might have noticed.'

The man in brown said pleasantly: 'Too damp for a good spray job, Art. Get moving.'

I said: 'They're front and rear, on the right side. You could use the spare for one spot, if you're busy.'

'Take two jacks, Art,' the brown man said.

'Now, listen—' Art began to bluster.

The brown man moved his eyes, looked at Art with a soft quiet-eyed stare, lowered them again almost shyly. He didn't speak. Art rocked as if a gust of wind had hit him. He stamped over to the corner and put a rubber coat over his overalls, a sou'wester on his head. He grabbed a socket wrench and a hand jack and wheeled a dolly jack over to the doors.

He went out silently, leaving the door yawning. The rain blustered in. The man in brown strolled over and shut it and strolled back to the workbench and put his hips exactly where they had been before. I could have taken him then. We were alone. He didn't know who I was. He looked at me lightly and threw his cigarette on the cement floor and stamped on it without looking down.

'I bet you could use a drink,' he said. 'Wet the inside and even up.' He reached a bottle from the workbench behind him and set it on the edge and set two glasses beside it. He poured a stiff jolt into each and held one out.

Walking like a dummy I went over and took it. The memory of the rain was still cold on my face. The smell of hot paint drugged the close air of the garage.

'That Art,' the brown man said. 'He's like all mechanics. Always got his face in a job he ought to have done last week. Business trip?'

I sniffed my drink delicately. It had the right smell. I watched him drink some of his before I swallowed mine. I rolled it around on my tongue. There was no cyanide in it. I emptied the little glass and put it down beside him and moved away.

'Partly,' I said. I walked over to the half-painted sedan with the big metal paint gun lying along its fender. The rain hit the roof hard. Art was out in it, cursing.

The brown man looked at the big car. 'Just a panel job, to start with,' he said casually, his purring voice still softer from the drink. 'But the guy had dough and his driver needed a few bucks. You know the racket.'

I said: 'There's only one that's older.' My lips felt dry. I didn't want to talk. I lit a cigarette. I wanted my tyres fixed. The minutes passed on tiptoe. The brown man and I were two strangers chance-met, looking at each other across a little dead man named Harry Jones. Only the brown man didn't know that yet.

Feet crunched outside and the door was pushed open. The light hit pencils of rain and made silver wires of them. Art trundled two muddy flats in sullenly, kicked the door shut, let one of the flats fall over on its side. He looked at me savagely.

'You sure pick spots for a jack to stand on,' he snarled.

The brown man laughed and took a rolled cylinder of nickels out of his pocket and tossed it up and down on the palm of his hand.

'Don't crab so much,' he said dryly. 'Fix those flats.'

'I'm fixin' them, ain't I?'

'Well, don't make a song about it.'

'Yah!' Art peeled his rubber coat and sou'wester off and threw them away from him. He heaved one tyre up on a spreader and tore the rim loose viciously. He had the tube out and cold-patched in nothing flat. Still scowling, he strode over to the wall beside me and grabbed an air hose, put enough air into the tube to give it body and let the nozzle of the air hose smack against the whitewashed wall.

I stood watching the roll of wrapped coins dance in Canino's hand. The moment of crouched intensity had left me. I turned my head and watched the gaunt mechanic beside me toss the air-stiffened tube up and catch it with his hands wide, one on each side of the tube. He looked it over sourly, glanced at a big galvanized tub of dirty water in the corner and grunted.

The teamwork must have been very nice. I saw no signal, no glance of meaning, no gesture that might have a special import. The gaunt man had the stiffened tube high in the air, staring at it. He half turned his body, took one long quick step, and slammed it down over my head and shoulders, a perfect ringer.

He jumped behind me and leaned hard on the rubber. His weight dragged on my chest, pinned my upper arms tight to my sides. I could move my hands, but I couldn't reach the gun in my pocket.

The brown man came almost dancing towards me across the floor. His hand tightened over the roll of nickels. He came up to me without sound, without expression. I bent forward and tried to heave Art off his feet.

The fist with the weighted tube inside it went through my spread hands like a stone through a cloud of dust. I had the stunned moment of shock when the lights danced and the visible world went out of focus but was still there. He hit me again. There was no sensation in my head. The bright glare got brighter. There was nothing but hard aching white light. Then there was darkness in which something red wriggled like a germ under a microscope. Then there was nothing bright or wriggling, just darkness and emptiness and a rushing wind and a falling as of great trees.

CHAPTER 28

It seemed there was a woman and she was sitting near a lamp, which was where she belonged, in a good light. Another light shone hard on my face, so I closed my eyes again and tried to look at her through the lashes. She was so platinumed that her hair shone like a silver fruit bowl. She wore a green knitted dress with a broad white collar turned over it. There was a sharp-angled glossy bag at her feet. She was smoking and a glass of amber fluid was tall and pale at her elbow.

I moved my head a little, carefully. It hurt, but not more than I expected. I was trussed like a turkey ready for the oven. Handcuffs held my wrists behind me and a rope went from them to my ankles and then over the end of the brown davenport on which I was sprawled. The rope dropped out of sight over the davenport. I moved enough to make sure it was tied down.

I stopped these furtive movements and opened my eyes again and said: 'Hello.'

The woman withdrew her gaze from some distant mountain peak. Her small firm chin turned slowly. Her eyes were the blue of mountain lakes. Overhead the rain still pounded, with a remote sound, as if it was somebody else's rain.

'How do you feel?' It was a smooth silvery voice that matched her hair. It had a tiny tinkle in it, like bells in a doll's house. I thought that was silly as soon as I thought of it.

'Great,' I said. 'Somebody built a filling station on my jaw.'

'What did you expect, Mr Marlowe – orchids?'

'Just a plain pine box,' I said. 'Don't bother with bronze or silver handles. And don't scatter my ashes over the blue Pacific. I like the worms better. Did you know that worms are of both sexes and that any worm can love any other worm?'

'You're a little light-headed,' she said, with a grave stare.

'Would you mind moving this light?'

She got up and went behind the davenport. The light went off. The dimness was a benison.

'I don't think you're so dangerous,' she said. She was tall rather than short, but no bean-pole. She was slim, but not a dried crust. She went back to her chair.

'So you know my name.'

'You slept well. They had plenty of time to go through your pockets. They did everything but embalm you. So you're a detective.'

'Is that all they have on me?'

She was silent. Smoke floated dimly from the cigarette. She moved it in the air. Her hand was small and had shape, not the usual bony garden tool you see on women nowadays.

'What time is it?' I asked.

She looked sideways at her wrist, beyond the spiral of smoke, at the edge of the grave lustre of the lamplight. 'Ten-seventeen. You have a date?'

'I wouldn't be surprised. Is this the house next to Art Huck's garage?'

'Yes.'

'What are the boys doing – digging a grave?'

'They had to go somewhere.'

'You mean they left you here alone?'

Her head turned slowly again. She smiled. 'You don't look dangerous.'

'I thought they were keeping you a prisoner.'

It didn't seem to startle her. It even slightly amused her. 'What made you think that?'

'I know who you are.'

Her very blue eyes flashed so sharply that I could almost see the sweep of their glance, like the sweep of a sword. Her mouth tightened. But her voice didn't change.

'Then I'm afraid you're in a bad spot. And I hate killing.'

'And you Eddie Mars's wife? Shame on you.'

She didn't like that. She glared at me. I grinned. 'Unless you can unlock these bracelets, which I'd advise you not to do, you might spare me a little of that drink you're neglecting.'

She brought the glass over. Bubbles rose in it like false hopes. She bent over me. Her breath was as delicate as the eyes of a fawn. I gulped from the glass. She took it away from my mouth and watched some of the liquid run down my neck.

She bent over me again. Blood began to move around in me, like a prospective tenant looking over a house.

'Your face looks like a collision mat,' she said.

'Make the most of it. It won't last long even this good.'

She swung her head sharply and listened. For an instant her face was pale. The sounds were only the rain drifting against the walls. She went back across the room and stood with her side to me, bent forward a little, looking down at the floor.

'Why did you come here and stick your neck out?' she asked quietly.

'Eddie wasn't doing you any harm. You know perfectly well that if I hadn't hid out here, the police would have been certain Eddie murdered Rusty Regan.'

'He did,' I said.

She didn't move, didn't change position an inch. Her breath made a harsh quick sound. I looked around the room. Two doors, both in the same wall, one half open. A carpet of red and tan squares, blue curtains at the windows, a wallpaper with bright green pine trees on it. The furniture looked as if it had come from one of those places that advertise on bus benches. Gay, but full of resistance.

She said softly: 'Eddie didn't do anything to him. I haven't seen Rusty in months. Eddie's not that sort of man.'

'You left his bed and board. You were living alone. People at the place where you lived identified Regan's photo.'

'That's a lie,' she said coldly.

I tried to remember whether Captain Gregory had said that or not. My head was too fuzzy. I couldn't be sure.

'And it's none of your business,' she added.

'The whole thing is my business. I'm hired to find out.'

'Eddie's not that sort of man.'

'Oh, you like racketeers.'

'As long as people will gamble there will be places for them to gamble.'

'That's just protective thinking. Once outside the law you're all the way outside. You think he's just a gambler. I think he's a pornographer, a blackmailer, a hot car broker, a killer by remote control, and a suborner of crooked cops. He's whatever looks good to him, whatever has the cabbage pinned to it. Don't try to sell me on any high-souled racketeers. They don't come in that pattern.'

'He's not a killer.' She frowned.

'Not personally. He has Canino. Canino killed a man tonight, a harmless little guy who was trying to help somebody out. I almost saw him killed.'

She laughed wearily.

'All right,' I growled. 'Don't believe it. If Eddie is such a nice guy, I'd like to get to talk to him with Canino around. You know what Canino will do – beat my teeth out and then kick me in the stomach for mumbling.'

She put her head back and stood there thoughtful and withdrawn, thinking something out.

'I thought platinum hair was out of style,' I went on, just to keep sound alive in the room, just to keep from listening.

'It's a wig, silly. While mine grows out.' She reached up and yanked it off. Her own hair clipped short all over, like a boy's. She put the wig back on.

'Who did that to you?'

She looked surprised. 'I had it done. Why?'

'Yes. Why?'

'Why, to show Eddie I was willing to do what he wanted me to do – hide out. That he didn't need to have me guarded. I wouldn't let him down. I love him.'

'Good grief,' I groaned, 'and you have me right here in the room with you.'

She turned a hand over and stared at it. Then abruptly she walked out of the room. She came back with a kitchen knife. She bent and sawed at my rope.

'Canino has the key to the handcuffs,' she said. 'I can't do anything about those.'

She stepped back, breathing rapidly. She had cut the rope at every knot.

'You're a kick,' she said. 'Kidding with every breath – the spot you're in.'

'I thought Eddie wasn't a killer.'

She turned away quickly and went back to her chair by the lamp and sat down and put her face in her hands. I swung my feet to the floor and stood up. I tottered around, stiff-legged. The nerve on the left side of my face was jumping in all its branches. I took a step. I could still walk. I could run, if I had to.

'I guess you mean me to go,' I said.

She nodded without lifting her head.

'You'd better go with me – if you want to keep on living.'

'Don't waste time. He'll be back any minute.'

'Light a cigarette for me.'

I stood beside her, touching her knees. She came to her feet with a sudden lurch. Our eyes were only inches apart.

'Hello, Silver-Wig,' I said softly.

She stepped back, around the chair, and swept a package of cigarettes up off the table. She jabbed one loose and pushed it roughly into my mouth. Her hand was shaking. She snapped a small green leather lighter and held it to the cigarette. I drew in the smoke, staring into her lake-blue eyes. While she was still close to me I said:

'A little bird named Harry Jones led me to you. A little bird that used to hop in and out of cocktail bars picking up horse bets for crumbs. Picking up information too. This little bird picked up an idea about Canino. One way and another he and his friends found out where you were. He came to me to sell the information because he knew – how he knew is a long story – that I was working for General Sternwood. I got his information, but

Canino got the little bird. He's a dead little bird now, with his feathers ruffled and his neck limp and a pearl of blood on his beak. Canino killed him. But Eddie Mars wouldn't do that, would he, Silver-Wig? He never killed anybody. He just hires it done.'

'Get out,' she said harshly. 'Get out of here quickly.'

Her hand clutched in midair on the green lighter. The fingers strained. The knuckles were as white as snow.

'But Canino doesn't know I know that,' I said. 'About the little bird. All he knows is I'm nosing around.'

Then she laughed. It was almost a racking laugh. It shook her as the wind shakes a tree. I thought there was puzzlement in it, not exactly surprise, but as if a new idea had been added to something already known and it didn't fit. Then I thought that was too much to get out of a laugh.

'It's very funny,' she said breathlessly. 'Very funny, because, you see – I still love him. Women—' She began to laugh again.

I listened hard, my head throbbing. 'Let's go,' I said. 'Fast.'

She took two steps back and her face set hard. 'Get out, you! Get out! You can walk to Realito. You can make it – and you can keep your mouth shut – for an hour or two at least. You owe me that much.'

'Let's go,' I said. 'Got a gun, Silver-Wig?'

'You know I'm not going. You know that. Please, please get out of here quickly.'

I stepped up close to her, almost pressing against her. 'You're going to stay here after turning me loose? Wait for that killer to come back so you can say so sorry? A man who kills like swatting a fly. Not much. You're going with me, Silver-Wig.'

'No.'

'Suppose,' I said, 'your handsome husband *did* kill Regan? Or suppose Canino did, without Eddie's knowing it. Just suppose. How long will *you* last, after turning me loose?'

'I'm not afraid of Canino. I'm still his boss's wife.'

'Eddie's a handful of mush,' I snarled. 'Canino would take him with a teaspoon. He'll take him the way the cat took the canary. A handful of mush. The only time a girl like you goes for a wrong gee is when he's a handful of mush.'

'Get out!' she almost spat at me.

'Okey.' I turned away from her and moved out through the half-open door into a dark hallway. Then she rushed after me and pushed past to the front door and opened it. She peered out the wet blackness and listened. She motioned me forward.

'Good-bye,' she said under her breath. 'Good luck in everything but one thing. Eddie didn't kill Rusty Regan. You'll find him alive and well somewhere, when he wants to be found.'

I leaned against her and pressed her against the wall with my body. I pushed my mouth against her face. I talked to her that way.

'There's no hurry. All this was arranged in advance, rehearsed to the last detail, timed to the split second. Just like a radio programme. No hurry at all. Kiss me, Silver-Wig.'

Her face under my mouth was like ice. She put her hands up and took hold of my head and kissed me hard on the lips. Her lips were like ice, too.

I went out through the door and it closed behind me, without sound, and the rain blew in under the porch, not as cold as her lips.

CHAPTER 29

The garage next door was dark. I crossed the gravel drive and a patch of sodden lawn. The road ran with small rivulets of water. It gurgled down a ditch on the far side. I had no hat. That must have fallen in the garage. Canino hadn't bothered to give it back to me. He hadn't thought I would need it any more. I imagined him driving back jauntily through the rain, alone, having left the gaunt and sulky Art and the probably stolen sedan in a safe place. She loved Eddie Mars and she was hiding to protect him. So he would find her there when he came back, calm beside the light and the untasted drink, and me tied up on the davenport. He would carry her stuff out to the car and go through the house carefully to make sure nothing incriminating was left. He would tell her to go out and wait. She wouldn't hear a shot. A blackjack is just as effective at short range. He would tell her he had left me tied up and I would get loose after a while. He would think she was that dumb. Nice Mr Canino.

The raincoat was open in front and I couldn't button it, being handcuffed. The skirts flapped against my legs like the wings of a large and tired bird. I came to the highway. Cars went by in a wide swirl of water illuminated by headlights. The tearing noise of their tyres died swiftly. I found my convertible where I had left it, both tyres fixed and mounted, so it could be driven away, if necessary. They thought of everything. I got into it and leaned down sideways under the wheel and fumbled aside the flap of leather that covered the pocket. I got the other gun, stuffed it up under my coat and started back. The world was small, shut in, black. A private world for Canino and me.

Half-way there the headlights nearly caught me. They turned swiftly off the highway and I slid down the bank into the wet ditch and flopped there breathing water. The car hummed by without slowing. I lifted my head, heard the rasp of its tyres as it left the road and took the gravel of the driveway. The motor died, the lights died, a door slammed. I didn't hear the house door shut, but a fringe of light trickled through the clump of trees, as though a shade had been moved aside from a window, or the light had been put on in the hall.

I came back to the soggy grass plot and sloshed across it. The car was between me and the house, the gun was down at my side, pulled as far around as I could get it, without pulling my left arm out by the roots. The car was dark, empty, warm. Water gurgled pleasantly in the radiator. I peered in at the door. The keys hung on the dash. Canino was very sure of himself. I went around the car and walked carefully across the gravel to the window and listened. I couldn't hear any voices, any sound but the swift bong-bong of the raindrops hitting the metal elbows at the bottom of the rain gutters.

I kept on listening. No loud voices, everything quiet and refined. He would be purring at her and she would be telling him she had let me go and I had promised to let them get away. He wouldn't believe me, as I wouldn't believe him. So he wouldn't be in there long. He would be on his way and take her with him. All I had to do was wait for him to come out.

I couldn't do it. I shifted the gun to my left hand and leaned down to scoop up a handful of gravel. I tossed it against the screen of the window. It was a feeble effort. Very little of it reached the glass above the screen, but the loose rattle of that little was like a dam bursting.

I ran back to the car and got on the running board behind it. The house had already gone dark. That was all. I dropped quietly on the running board and waited. No soap. Canino was too cagey.

I straightened up and got into the car backwards, fumbled around for the ignition key and turned it. I reached with my foot, but the starter button had to be on the dash. I found it at last, pulled it and the starter ground. The warm motor caught at once. It purred softly, contentedly. I got out of the car again and crouched down by the rear wheels.

I was shivering now but I knew Canino wouldn't like that last effect. He needed that car badly. A darkened window slid down inch by inch, only some shifting of light on the glass showing it moved. Flame spouted from it abruptly, the blended roar of three swift shots. Glass starred in the coupé. I yelled with agony. The yell went off into a wailing groan. The groan became a wet gurgle, choked with blood. I let the gurgle die sickeningly, on a choked gasp. It was nice work. I liked it. Canino liked it very much. I heard him laugh. It was a large booming laugh, not at all like the purr of his speaking voice.

The silence for a little while, except for the rain and the quietly throbbing motor of the car. Then the house door crawled open, a deeper blackness in the black night. A figure showed in it cautiously, something white around the neck. It was her collar. She came out on the porch stiffly, a wooden woman. I caught the pale shine of her silver wig. Canino came crouched methodically behind her. It was so deadly it was almost funny.

She came down the steps. Now I could see the white stiffness of her face. She started towards the car. A bulwark of defence for Canino, in case I could still spit in his eye. Her voice spoke through the lisp of the rain, saying slowly, without any tone: 'I can't see a thing, Lash. The windows are misted.'

He grunted something and the girl's body jerked hard, as though he had jammed a gun into her back. She came on again and drew near the lightless car. I could see him behind her now, his hat, a side of his face, the bulk of his shoulder. The girl stopped rigid and screamed. A beautiful thin tearing scream that rocked me like a left hook.

'I can see him!' she screamed. 'Through the window. Behind the wheel, Lash!'

He fell for it like a bucket of lead. He knocked her roughly to one side and jumped forward, throwing his hand up. Three more spurts of flame cut the darkness. More glass scarred. One bullet went on through and smacked into a tree on my side. A ricochet whined off into the distance. But the motor went quietly on.

He was low down, crouched against the gloom, his face a greyness without form that seemed to come back slowly after the glare of the shots. If it was a revolver he had, it might be empty. It might not. He had fired six times, but he might have reloaded inside the house. I hoped he had. I didn't want him with an empty gun. But it might be an automatic.

I said: 'Finished?'

He whirled at me. Perhaps it would have been nice to allow him another shot or two, just like a gentleman of the old school. But his gun was still up and I couldn't wait any longer. Not long enough to be a gentleman of the old school. I shot him four times, the Colt straining against my ribs. The gun jumped out of his hand as if it had been kicked. He reached both his hands for his stomach. I could hear them smack hard against his body. He fell like that, straight forward, holding himself together with his broad hands. He fell face down in the wet gravel. And after that there wasn't a sound from him.

Silver-Wig didn't make a sound either. She stood rigid, with the rain swirling at her. I walked around Canino and kicked his gun, without any purpose. Then I walked after it and bent over sideways and picked it up. That put me close beside her. She spoke moodily, as if she was talking to herself.

'I–I was afraid you'd come back.'

I said: 'We had a date. I told you it was all arranged.' I began to laugh like a loon.

Then she was bending down over him, touching him. And after a little while she stood up with a small key on a thin chain.

She said bitterly: 'Did you have to kill him?'

I stopped laughing as suddenly as I had started. She went behind me and unlocked the handcuffs.

'Yes,' she said softly. 'I suppose you did.'

CHAPTER 30

This was another day and the sun was shining again.

Captain Gregory of the Missing Persons Bureau looked heavily out of his office window at the barred upper floor of the Hall of Justice, white and clean after the rain. Then he turned ponderously in his swivel chair and tamped his pipe with a heat-scarred thumb and stared at me bleakly.

'So you got yourself in another jam.'

'Oh, you heard about it.'

'Brother, I sit here all day on my fanny and I don't look as if I had a brain in my head. But you'd be surprised what I hear. Shooting this Canino was all right I guess, but I don't figure the homicide boys pinned any medals on you.'

'There's been a lot of killings going on around me,' I said. 'I haven't been getting my share of it.'

He smiled patiently. 'Who told you this girl out there was Eddie Mars's wife?'

I told him. He listened carefully and yawned. He tapped his gold studded mouth with a palm like a tray. 'I guess you figure I ought to have found her.'

'That's a fair deduction.'

'Maybe I knew,' he said. 'Maybe I thought if Eddie and his woman wanted to play a little game like that, it would be smart – or as smart as I ever get – to let them think they were getting away with it. And then again maybe you think I was letting Eddie get away with it for more personal reasons.' He held his big hand out and revolved the thumb against the index and second fingers.

'No,' I said. 'I didn't really think that. Not even when Eddie seemed to know all about our talk here the other day.'

He raised his eyebrows as if raising them was an effort, a trick he was out of practice on. It furrowed his whole forehead and when it smoothed out it was full of white lines that turned reddish as I watched them.

'I'm a copper,' he said. 'Just a plain ordinary copper. Reasonably honest. As honest as you could expect a man to be in a world where it's out of style. That's mainly why I asked you to come in this morning. I'd like you to believe that. Being a copper I like to see the law win. I'd like to see the flashy well-dressed mugs like Eddie Mars spoiling their manicures in the rock quarry at Folsom, alongside of the poor little slum-bred hard guys that got knocked over on their first caper and never had a break since. That's what I'd like. You and me both lived too long to think I'm likely to see it happen. Not in this town, not in any town half this size, in any part of this wide, green and beautiful USA. We just don't run our country that way.'

I didn't say anything. He blew smoke with a backward jerk of his head, looked at the mouthpiece of his pipe and went on:

'But that don't mean I think Eddie Mars bumped off Regan or had any reason to or would have done it if he had. I just figured maybe he knows something about it, and maybe sooner or later something will sneak out into the open. Hiding his wife out at Realito was childish, but it's the kind of childishness a smart monkey thinks is smart. I had him in here last night, after the DA got through with him. He admitted the whole thing. He said he knew Canino as a reliable protection guy and that's what he had him for. He didn't know anything about his hobbies or want to. He didn't know Harry Jones. He didn't know Joe Brody. He did know Geiger, of course, but claims he didn't know about his racket. I guess you heard all that.'

'Yes.'

'You played it smart down there at Realito, brother. Not trying to cover up. We keep a file on unidentified bullets nowadays. Some day you might use that gun again. Then you'd be over a barrel.'

'I played it smart,' I said, and leered at him.

He knocked his pipe out and stared down at it broodingly. 'What happened to the girl?' he asked, not looking up.

'I don't know. They didn't hold her. We made statements, three sets of them, for Wilde, for the Sheriff's office, for the Homicide Bureau. They turned her loose. I haven't seen her since. I don't expect to.'

'Kind of a nice girl, they say. Wouldn't be one to play dirty games.'

'Kind of a nice girl,' I said.

Captain Gregory sighed and rumpled his mousy hair. 'There's just one more thing,' he said almost gently. 'You look like a nice guy, but you play too rough. If you really want to help the Sternwood family – leave 'em alone.'

'I think you're right, Captain.'

'How you feel?'

'Swell.' I said. 'I was standing on various pieces of carpet most of the night, being bawled out. Before that I got soaked to the skin and beaten up. I'm in perfect condition.'

'What the hell did you expect, brother?'

'Nothing else.' I stood up and grinned at him and started for the door. When I had almost reached it he cleared his throat suddenly and said in a harsh voice: 'I'm wasting my breath, huh? You still think you can find Regan.'

I turned round and looked him straight in the eyes. 'No, I don't think I can find Regan. I'm not even going to try. Does that suit you?'

He nodded slowly. Then he shrugged. 'I don't know what the hell I even said that for. Good luck, Marlowe. Drop around any time.'

'Thanks, Captain.'

I went down out of the City Hall and got my car from the parking lot and drove home to the Hobart Arms. I lay down on the bed with my coat off and stared at the ceiling and listened to the traffic sounds on the street outside and watched the sun move slowly across a corner of the ceiling. I tried to go to sleep, but sleep didn't come. I got up and took a drink, although it was the wrong time of day, and lay down again. I still couldn't go to sleep. My brain ticked like a clock. I sat up on the side of the bed and stuffed a pipe and said out loud:

'That old buzzard knows something.'

The pipe tasted as bitter as lye. I put it aside and lay down again. My mind drifted through waves of false memory, in which I seemed to do the same thing over and over again, go to the same places, meet the same people, say the same words to them, over and over again, and yet each time it seemed real, like something actually happening, and for the first time. I was driving hard along the highway through the rain, with Silver-Wig in the corner of the car, saying nothing, so that by the time we reached Los Angeles we seemed to be utter strangers again. I was getting out at an all-night drugstore and phoning Bernie Ohls that I had killed a man at Realito and was on my way over to Wilde's house with Eddie Mars's wife, who had seen me do it. I was pushing the car along the silent, rain-polished streets of Lafayette Park and up under the *porte-cochère* of Wilde's big frame house and the porch light was already on, Ohls having telephoned ahead that I was coming. I was in Wilde's study and he was behind his desk in a flowered dressing-gown and a tight hard face and a dappled cigar moved in his fingers and up to the bitter smile on his lips. Ohls was there and a slim grey scholarly man from the Sheriff's office who looked and talked more like a professor of economics than a cop. I was telling the story and they were listening quietly and Silver-Wig sat in a shadow with her hands folded in her lap, looking at nobody. There was a lot of telephoning. There were two men from the Homicide Bureau who looked at me as if I was some kind of strange beast escaped from a travelling circus. I was driving again, with one of them beside me, to the Fulwider Building. We were there in the room where Harry Jones was still in the chair behind the desk, the twisted stiffness of his dead face and the sour-sweet smell in the room. There was a medical examiner, very young and husky, with red bristles on his neck. There was a fingerprint man fussing around and I was telling him not to forget the latch of the transom. (He found Canino's thumbprint on it, the only print the brown man had left to back up my story.)

I was back again at Wilde's house, signing a typewritten statement his secretary had run off in another room. Then the door opened and Eddie Mars came in and an abrupt smile flashed to his face when he saw Silver-Wig, and he said: 'Hello, sugar', and she didn't look at him or answer him. Eddie Mars fresh and cheerful, in a dark business suit, with a fringed white scarf hanging outside his tweed overcoat. Then they were gone, everybody was gone out of the room but myself and Wilde, and Wilde was saying in a cold, angry voice: 'This is the last time, Marlowe. The next fast one you pull I'll throw you to the lions, no matter whose heart it breaks.'

It was like that, over and over again, lying on the bed and watching the patch of sunlight slide down the corner of the wall. Then the phone rang, and it was Norris, the Sternwood butler, with his usual untouchable voice.

'Mr Marlowe? I telephoned your office without success, so I took the liberty of trying to reach you at home.'

'I was out most of the night,' I said. 'I haven't been down.'

'Yes, sir. The General would like to see you this morning, Mr Marlowe, if it's convenient.'

'Half an hour or so,' I said. 'How is he?'

'He's in bed, sir, but not doing badly.'

'Wait till he sees me,' I said, and hung up.

I shaved, changed clothes and started for the door. Then I went back and got Carmen's little pearl-handled revolver and dropped it into my pocket. The sunlight was so bright that it danced. I got to the Sternwood place in twenty minutes and drove up under the arch at the side door. It was eleven-fifteen. The birds in the ornamental trees were crazy with song after the rain, the terraced lawns were as green as the Irish flag, and the whole estate looked as though it had been made about ten minutes before. I rang the bell. It was five days since I had rung it for the first time. It felt like a year.

A maid opened the door and led me along a side hall to the main hallway and left me there, saying Mr Norris would be down in a moment. The main hallway looked just the same. The portrait over the mantel had the same hot black eyes and the knight in the stained-glass window still wasn't getting anywhere untying the naked damsel from the tree.

In a few minutes Norris appeared, and he hadn't changed either. His acid-blue eyes were as remote as ever, his greyish-pink skin looked healthy and rested, and he moved as if he was twenty years younger than he really was. I was the one who felt the weight of the years.

We went up the tiled staircase and turned the opposite way from Vivian's room. With each step the house seemed to grow larger and more silent. We reached a massive old door that looked as if it had come out of a church. Norris opened it softly and looked in. Then he stood aside and I went in past him across what seemed to be about a quarter of a mile of carpet to a huge canopied bed like the one Henry the Eighth died in.

General Sternwood was propped up on pillows. His bloodless hands were clasped on top of the sheet. They looked grey against it. His black eyes were still full of fight and the rest of his face still looked like the face of a corpse.

'Sit down, Mr Marlowe.' His voice sounded weary and a little stiff.

I pulled a chair close to him and sat down. All the windows were shut tight. The room was sunless at that hour. Awnings cut off what glare there might be from the sky. The air had the faint sweetish smell of old age.

He stared at me silently for a long minute. He moved a hand as if to prove to himself that he could still move it, then folded it back over the other. He said lifelessly:

'I didn't ask you to look for my son-in-law, Mr Marlowe.'

'You wanted me to, though.'

'I didn't ask you to. You assume a great deal. I usually ask for what I want.'

I didn't say anything.

'You have been paid,' he went on coldly. 'The money is of no consequence one way or the other. I merely feel that you have, no doubt unintentionally, betrayed a trust.'

He closed his eyes on that. I said: 'Is that all you wanted to see me about?'

He opened his eyes again, very slowly, as though the lids were made of lead. 'I suppose you are angry at that remark,' he said.

I shook my head. 'You have an advantage over me, General. It's an advantage I wouldn't want to take away from you, not a hair of it. It's not much, considering what you have to put up with. You can say anything you like to me and I wouldn't think of getting angry. I'd like to offer you your money back. It may mean nothing to you. It might mean something to me.'

'What does it mean to you?'

'It means I have refused payment for an unsatisfactory job. That's all.'

'Do you do many unsatisfactory jobs?'

'A few. Everyone does.'

'Why did you go to see Captain Gregory?'

I leaned back and hung an arm over the back of the chair. I studied his face. It told me nothing. I didn't know the answer to his question – no satisfactory answer.

I said: 'I was convinced you put those Geiger notes up to me chiefly as a test, and that you were a little afraid Regan might somehow be involved in an attempt to blackmail you. I didn't know anything about Regan then. It wasn't until I talked to Captain Gregory that I realized Regan wasn't that sort of guy in all probability.'

'That is scarcely answering my question.'

I nodded. 'No. That is scarcely answering your question. I guess I just don't like to admit that I played a hunch. The morning I was here, after I left you out in the orchid house, Mrs Regan sent for me. She seemed to assume I was hired to look for her husband and she didn't seem to like it. She let drop however that "they" had found his car in a certain garage. The "they" could only be the police. Consequently the police must know something about it. If they did, the Missing Persons Bureau would be the department that would have the case. I didn't know whether you had reported it, of course, or somebody else, or whether they had found the car through somebody reporting it abandoned in a garage. But I know cops, and I knew that if they got that much, they would get a little more – especially as your driver happened to have a police record. I didn't know how much more they would get. That started me thinking about the Missing Persons Bureau. What convinced me was something in Mr Wilde's manner the night we had the conference over at his house about Geiger and so on. We were alone for a minute and he asked me whether you had told me you were looking for Regan. I said you had told me you wished you knew where he was and that he was all right. Wilde pulled his lip in and looked funny. I knew just as plainly as though he had said it that by "looking for Regan" he meant using the machinery of the law to look for him. Even then I tried to go up against Captain Gregory in such a way that I wouldn't tell him anything he didn't know already.'

'And you allowed Captain Gregory to think I had employed you to find Rusty?'

'Yeah. I guess I did – when I was sure he had the case.'

He closed his eyes. They twitched a little. He spoke with them closed.

'And do you consider that ethical?'

'Yes,' I said. 'I do.'

The eyes opened again. The piercing blackness of them was startling coming suddenly out of that dead face. 'Perhaps I don't understand,' he said.

'Maybe you don't. The head of a Missing Persons Bureau isn't a talker. He wouldn't be in that office if he was. This one is a very smart cagey guy who tries, with a lot of success at first, to give the impression he's a middle-aged hack fed up with his job. The game I play is not spillikins. There's always a large element of bluff connected with it. Whatever I might say to a cop, he would be apt to discount it. And to *that* cop it wouldn't make much difference what I said. When you hire a boy in my line of work it isn't like hiring a window-washer and showing him eight windows and saying: "Wash those and you're through." *You* don't know what I have to go through or over or under to do your job for you. I do it my way. I do my best to protect you and I may break a few rules, but I break them in your favour. The client comes first, unless he's crooked. Even then all I do is hand the job back to him and keep my mouth shut. After all you didn't tell me *not* to go to Captain Gregory.'

'That would have been rather difficult,' he said with a faint smile.

'Well, what have I done wrong? Your man Norris seemed to think when Geiger was eliminated the case was over. I don't see it that way. Geiger's method of approach puzzled me and still does. I'm not Sherlock Holmes or Philo Vance. I don't expect to go over ground the police have covered and pick up a broken pen point and build a case from it. If you think there is anybody in the detective business making a living doing that sort of thing, you don't know much about cops. It's not things like that they overlook if they overlook anything. I'm not saying they often overlook anything when they're really allowed to work. But if they do, it's apt to be something looser and vaguer, like a man of Geiger's type sending you his evidence of debt and asking you to pay like a gentleman – Geiger, a man in a shady racket, in a vulnerable position, protected by a racketeer and having at least some negative protection from some of the police. Why did he do that? Because he wanted to find out if there was anything putting pressure on you. If there was, you would pay him. If not, you would ignore him and wait for his next move. But there was something putting a pressure on you. Regan. You were afraid he was not what he had appeared to be, that he had stayed around and had been nice to you just long enough to find out how to play games with your bank account.'

He started to say something but I interrupted him. 'Even at that it wasn't your money you cared about. It wasn't even your daughters. You've more or less written them off. It's that you're still too proud to be played for a sucker – and you really liked Regan.'

There was a silence. Then the General said quietly: 'You talk too damn much, Marlowe. Am I to understand you are still trying to solve that puzzle?'

'No. I've quit. I've been warned off. The boys think I play too rough. That's why I thought I should give you back your money – because it isn't a completed job by my standards.'

He smiled. 'Quit nothing,' he said. 'I'll pay you another thousand dollars to find Rusty. He doesn't have to come back. I don't even have to know where he is. A man has a right to live his own life. I don't blame him for walking out on my daughter, nor even for going so abruptly. It was probably a sudden impulse. I want to know that he is all right wherever he is. I want to know it from him directly, and if he should happen to need money, I should want him to have that also. Am I clear?'

I said: 'Yes, General.'

He rested a little while, lax on the bed, his eyes closed and dark-lidded, his mouth tight and bloodless. He was used up. He was pretty nearly licked. He opened his eyes again and tried to grin at me.

'I guess I'm a sentimental old goat,' he said. 'And no soldier at all. I took a fancy to that boy. He seemed pretty clean to me. I must be a little too vain about my judgment of character. Find him for me, Marlowe. Just find him.'

'I'll try,' I said. 'You'd better rest now. I've talked your arm off.'

I got up quickly and walked across the wide floor and out. He had his eyes shut again before I opened the door. His hands lay limp on the sheet. He looked a lot more like a dead man than most dead men look. I shut the door quietly and went back along the upper hall and down the stairs.

CHAPTER 31

The butler appeared with my hat. I put it on and said: 'What do you think of him?'

'He's not as weak as he looks, sir.'

'If he was, he'd be ready for burial. What did this Regan fellow have that bored into him so?'

The butler looked at me levelly and yet with a queer lack of expression. 'Youth, sir,' he said. 'And the soldier's eye.'

'Like yours,' I said.

'If I may say so, sir, not unlike yours.'

'Thanks. How are the ladies this morning?'

He shrugged politely.

'Just what I thought,' I said, and he opened the door for me.

I stood outside on the step and looked down the vistas of grassed terraces and trimmed trees and flowerbeds to the tall metal railing at the bottom of the gardens. I saw Carmen about half-way down, sitting on a stone bench, with her head between her hands, looking forlorn and alone.

I went down the red brick steps that led from terrace to terrace. I was quite close before she heard me. She jumped up and whirled like a cat. She wore the light blue slacks she had worn the first time I saw her. Her blonde hair was the same loose tawny wave. Her face was white. Red spots flared in her cheeks as she looked at me. Her eyes were slaty.

'Bored?' I said.

She smiled slowly, rather shyly, then nodded quickly. Then she whispered: 'You're not mad at me?'

'I thought you were mad at me.'

She put her thumb up and giggled. 'I'm not.' When she giggled I didn't like her any more. I looked around. A target hung on a tree about thirty feet away, with some darts sticking to it. There were three or four more on the stone bench where she had been sitting.

'For people with money you and your sister don't seem to have much fun,' I said.

She looked at me under her long lashes. This was the look that was supposed to make me roll over on my back. I said: 'You like throwing those darts?'

'Uh-huh.'

'That reminds me of something.' I looked back towards the house. By moving about three feet I made a tree hide me from it. I took her little pearl-handled gun out of my pocket. 'I brought you back your artillery. I cleaned it and loaded it up. Take my tip – don't shoot it at people, unless you get to be a better shot. Remember?'

Her face went paler and her thin thumb dropped. She looked at me, then at the gun I was holding. There was a fascination in her eyes. 'Yes,' she said, and nodded. Then suddenly: 'Teach me to shoot.'

'Huh?'

'Teach me how to shoot. I'd like that.'

'Here? It's against the law.'

She came close to me and took the gun out of my hand, cuddled her hand around the butt. Then she tucked it quickly inside her slacks, almost with a furtive movement, and looked around.

'I know where,' she said in a secret voice. 'Down by some of the old wells.' She pointed off down the hill. 'Teach me?'

I looked into her slaty blue eyes. I might as well have looked at a couple of bottle-tops. 'All right. Give me back the gun until I see if the place looks all right.'

She smiled and made a mouth, then handed it back with a secret naughty air, as if she was giving me a key to her room. We walked up the steps and around to my car. The gardens seemed deserted. The sunshine was as empty as a head waiter's smile. We got into the car and I drove down the sunken driveway and out through the gates.

'Where's Vivian?' I asked.

'Not up yet.' She giggled.

I drove on down the hill through the quiet, opulent streets with their faces washed by the rain, bore east to La Brea, then south. We reached the place she meant in about ten minutes.

'In there.' She leaned out of the window and pointed.

It was a narrow dirt road, not much more than a track, like the entrance to some foothill ranch. A wide five-barred gate was folded back against a stump and looked as if it hadn't been shut in years. The road was fringed with tall eucalyptus trees and deeply rutted. Trucks had used it. It was empty and sunny now, but not yet dusty. The rain had been too hard and too recent. I followed the ruts along and the noise of city traffic grew curiously and quickly faint, as if this were not in the city at all, but far away in a daydream land. Then the oil-stained, motionless walking-beam of a squat wooden derrick stuck up over a branch. I could see the rusty old steel cable that connected this walking-beam with half a dozen others. The beams didn't move, probably hadn't moved for a year. The wells were no longer pumping. There was a pile of rusted pipe, a loading platform that sagged at one end, half a dozen empty oil drums lying in a ragged pile. There was the stagnant, oil-scummed water of an old sump iridescent in the sunlight.

'Are they going to make a park of all this?' I asked.

She dipped her chin down and gleamed at me.

'It's about time. The smell of that sump would poison a herd of goats. This the place you had in mind?'

'Uh-huh. Like it?'

'It's beautiful.' I pulled up beside the loading platform. We got out. I listened. The hum of the traffic was a distant web of sound, like the buzzing of bees. The place was as lonely as a churchyard. Even after the rain the tall eucalyptus trees still looked dusty. They always look dusty. A branch broken off by the wind had fallen over the edge of the sump and the flat leathery leaves dangled in the water.

I walked around the sump and looked into the pumphouse. There was some junk in it, nothing that looked like recent activity. Outside a big wooden bull wheel was tilted against the wall. It looked like a good place all right.

I went back to the car. The girl stood beside it preening her hair and holding it out in the sun. 'Gimme,' she said, and held her hand out.

I took the gun out and put it in her palm. I bent down and picked up a rusty can.

'Take it easy now,' I said. 'It's loaded in all five. I'll go over and set this can in that square opening in the middle of that big wooden wheel. See?' I pointed. She ducked her head, delighted. 'That's about thirty feet. Don't start shooting until I get back beside you. Okey?'

'Okey,' she giggled.

I went back around the sump and set the can up in the middle of the bull wheel. It made a swell target. If she missed the can, which she was certain to do, she would probably hit the wheel. That would stop a small slug completely. However, she wasn't going to hit even that.

I went back towards her around the sump. When I was about ten feet from her, at the edge of the sump, she showed me all her sharp little teeth and brought the gun up and started to hiss.

I stopped dead, the sump water stagnant and stinking at my back.

'Stand there, you son of a bitch,' she said.

The gun pointed at my chest. Her hand seemed to be quite steady. The hissing sound grew louder and her face had the scraped bone look. Aged, deteriorated, become animal, and not a nice animal.

I laughed at her. I started to walk towards her. I saw her small finger tighten on the trigger and grow white at the tip. I was about six feet away from her when she started to shoot.

The sound of the gun made a sharp slap, without body, a brittle crack in the sunlight. I didn't see any smoke. I stopped again and grinned at her.

She fired twice more, very quickly. I don't think any of the shots would have missed. There were five in the little gun. She had fired four. I rushed her.

I didn't want the last one in my face, so I swerved to one side. She gave it to me quite carefully, not worried at all. I think I felt the hot breath of the powder blast a little.

I straightened up. 'My, but you're cute,' I said.

Her hand holding the empty gun began to shake violently. The gun fell out of it. Her mouth began to shake. Her whole face went to pieces. Then her head screwed up towards her left ear and froth showed on her lips. Her breath made a whining sound. She swayed.

I caught her as she fell. She was already unconscious. I prised her teeth open with both hands and stuffed a wadded handkerchief in between them. It took all my strength to do it. I lifted her up and got her into the car, then went back for the gun and dropped it into my pocket. I climbed in under the wheel, backed the car and drove back the way we had come along the rutted road, out of the gateway, back up the hill and so home.

Carmen lay crumpled in the corner of the car, without motion. I was halfway up the drive to the house before she stirred. Then her eyes suddenly opened wide and wild. She sat up.

'What happened?' she gasped.

'Nothing. Why?'

'Oh, yes it did,' she giggled. 'I wet myself.'

'They always do,' I said.

She looked at me with a sudden sick speculation and began to moan.

CHAPTER 32

The gentle-eyes, horse-faced maid let me into the long grey and white upstairs sitting-room with the ivory drapes tumbled extravagantly on the floor and the white carpet from wall to wall. A screen star's boudoir, a place of charm and seduction, artificial as a wooden leg. It was empty at the moment. The door closed behind me with the unnatural softness of a hospital door. A breakfast table on wheels stood by the chaise-longue. Its silver glittered. There were cigarette ashes in the coffee cup. I sat down and waited.

It seemed a long time before the door opened again and Vivian came in. She was in oyster-white lounging pyjamas trimmed with white fur, cut as flowingly as a summer sea frothing on the beach of some small and exclusive island.

She went past me in long smooth strides and sat down on the edge of the chaise-longue. There was a cigarette in her lips, at the corner of her mouth. Her nails today were copper-red from quick to tip, without half-moons.

'So you're just a brute after all,' she said quietly, staring at me. 'An utter callous brute. You killed a man last night. Never mind how I heard it. I heard it. And now you have to come out here and frighten my kid sister into a fit.'

I didn't say a word. She began to fidget. She moved over to a slipper chair and put her head back against a white cushion that lay along the back of the chair against the wall. She blew pale grey smoke upwards and watched it float towards the ceiling and come apart in wisps that were for a little while distinguishable from the air and then melted and were nothing. Then very slowly she lowered her eyes and gave me a cool hard glance.

'I don't understand you,' she said. 'I'm thankful as hell one of us kept his head the night before last. It's bad enough to have a bootlegger in my past. Why don't you for Christ's sake say something?'

'How is she?'

'Oh, she's all right, I suppose. Fast asleep. She always goes to sleep. What did you do to her?'

'Not a thing. I came out of the house after seeing your father and she was out in front. She had been throwing darts at a target on a tree. I went down to speak to her because I had something that belonged to her. A little revolver Owen Taylor gave her once. She took it over to Brody's place the other evening, the evening he was killed. I had to take it away from her there. I didn't mention it, so perhaps you didn't know it.'

The black Sternwood eyes got large and empty. It was her turn not to say anything.

'She was pleased to get her little gun back and she wanted me to teach her how to shoot and she wanted to show me the old oil wells down the hill where your family made some of its money. So we went down there and the place was pretty creepy, all rusted metal and old wood and silent wells and greasy scummy sumps. Maybe that upset her. I guess you've been there yourself. It was kind of eerie.'

'Yes – it is.' It was a small breathless voice now.

'So we went in there and I stuck a can up in a bull wheel for her to pop at. She threw a wingding. Looked like a mild epileptic fit to me.'

'Yes.' The same minute voice. 'She has them once in a while. Is that all you wanted to see me about?'

'I guess you still wouldn't tell me what Eddie Mars has on you.'

'Nothing at all. And I'm getting a little tired of that question,' she said coldly.

'Do you know a man named Canino?'

She drew her fine black brows together in thought. 'Vaguely. I seem to remember the name.'

'Eddie Mars's trigger man. A tough hombre, they said. I guess he was. Without a little help from a lady I'd be where he is – in the morgue.'

'The ladies seem to—' She stopped dead and whitened. 'I can't joke about it,' she said simply.

'I'm not joking, and if I seem to talk in circles, it just seems that way. It all ties together – everything. Geiger and his cute little blackmail tricks, Brody and his pictures, Eddie Mars and his roulette tables, Canino and the girl Rusty Regan didn't run away with. It all ties together.'

'I'm afraid I don't even know what you're talking about.'

'Suppose you did – it would be something like this. Geiger got his hooks into your sister, which isn't very difficult, and got some notes from her and tried to blackmail your father with them, in a nice way. Eddie Mars was behind Geiger, protecting him and using him for a cat's-paw. Your father sent for me instead of paying up, which showed he wasn't scared about anything. Eddie Mars wanted to know that. He had something on you and he wanted to know if he had it on the General too. If he had, he could collect a lot of money in a hurry. If not, he would have to wait until you got your share of the family fortune, and in the meantime be satisfied with whatever spare cash he could take away from you across the roulette table. Geiger was killed by Owen Taylor, who was in love with your silly little sister and didn't like the kind of games Geiger played with her. That didn't mean anything to Eddie. He was playing a deeper game than Geiger knew anything about, or than Brody knew anything about, or anybody except you and Eddie and a tough guy named Canino. Your husband disappeared and Eddie, knowing everybody knew there had been bad blood between him and Regan, hid his wife out at Realito and put Canino to guard her, so that it would look as if she had run away with Regan. He even got Regan's car into the garage of the place where Mona Mars had been living. But that sounds a little silly taken merely as an attempt to divert suspicion that Eddie had killed your husband or had him killed. It isn't so silly, really. He had another motive. He was playing for a million or so. He knew where Regan had gone and why and he didn't want the police to have to find out. He wanted them to have an explanation of the disappearance that would keep them satisfied. Am I boring you?'

'You tire me,' she said in a dead, exhausted voice. 'God, how you tire me!'

'I'm sorry. I'm not just fooling around trying to be clever. Your father offered me a thousand dollars this morning to find Regan. That's a lot of money to me, but I can't do it.'

Her mouth jumped open. Her breath was suddenly strained and harsh. 'Give me a cigarette,' she said thickly. 'Why?' The pulse in her throat had begun to throb.

I gave her a cigarette and lit a match and held it for her. She drew in a lungful of smoke and let it out raggedly and then the cigarette seemed to be forgotten between her fingers. She never drew on it again.

'Well, the Missing Persons Bureau can't find him,' I said. 'It's not so easy. What they can't do it's not likely that I can do.'

'Oh.' There was a shade of relief in her voice.

'That's one reason. The Missing Persons people think he just disappeared on purpose, pulled down the curtain, as they call it. They don't think Eddie Mars did away with him.'

'Who said anybody did away with him?'

'We're coming to it,' I said.

For a brief instant her face seemed to come to pieces, to become merely a set of features without form or control. Her mouth looked like the prelude to a scream. But only for an instant. The Sternwood blood had to be good for something more than her black eyes and her recklessness.

I stood up and took the smoking cigarette from between her fingers and killed it in an ashtray. Then I took Carmen's little gun out of my pocket and laid it carefully, with exaggerated care, on her white satin knee. I balanced it there, and stepped back with my head on one side like a window-dresser getting the effect of a new twist of a scarf around a dummy's neck.

I sat down again. She didn't move. Her eyes came down millimetre by millimetre and looked at the gun.

'It's harmless,' I said. 'All five chambers empty. She fired them all. She fired them all at me.'

The pulse jumped wildly in her throat. Her voice tried to say something and couldn't. She swallowed.

'From a distance of five or six feet,' I said. 'Cute little thing, isn't she? Too bad I had loaded the gun with blanks.' I grinned nastily. 'I had a hunch about what she would do – if she got the chance.'

She brought her voice back from a long way off. 'You're a horrible man,' she said. 'Horrible.'

'Yeah. You're her big sister. What are you going to do about it?'

'You can't prove a word of it.'

'Can't prove what?'

'That she fired at you. You said you were down there around the wells with her, alone. You can't prove a word of what you say.'

'Oh that,' I said. 'I wasn't thinking of trying. I was thinking of another time – when the shells in the little gun had bullets in them.'

Her eyes were pools of darkness, much emptier than darkness.

'I was thinking of the day Regan disappeared,' I said. 'Late in the afternoon. When he took her down to those old wells to teach her to shoot and put up a can somewhere and told her to pop at it and stood near her while she shot. And she didn't shoot at the can. She turned the gun and shot him, just the way she tried to shoot me today, and for the same reason.'

She moved a little and the gun slid off her knee and fell to the floor. It was one of the loudest sounds I ever heard. Her eyes were riveted on my face. Her voice was a stretched whisper of agony. 'Carmen . . . Merciful God, Carmen! . . . Why?'

'Do I really have to tell you why she shot at me?'

'Yes.' Her eyes were still terrible. 'I'm – I'm afraid you do.'

'Night before last when I got home she was in my apartment. She'd kidded the manager into letting her in to wait for me. She was in my bed – naked. I threw her out on her ear. I guess maybe Regan did the same thing to her some time. But you can't do that to Carmen.'

She drew her lips back and made a half-hearted attempt to lick them. It made her, for a brief instant, look like a frightened child. The lines of her cheeks sharpened and her hand went up slowly like an artificial hand worked by wires and its fingers closed slowly and stiffly around the white fur at her collar. They drew the fur tight against her throat. After that she just sat staring.

'Money,' she croaked. 'I suppose you want money.'

'How much money?' I tried not to sneer.

'Fifteen thousand dollars?'

I nodded. 'That would be about right. That would be the established fee. That was what he had in his pockets when she shot him. That would be what Mr Canino got for disposing of the body when you went to Eddie Mars for help. But that would be small change to what Eddie expects to collect one of these days, wouldn't it?'

'You son of a bitch!' she said.

'Uh-huh. I'm a very smart guy. I haven't a feeling or a scruple in the world. All I have the itch for is money. I am so money greedy that for twenty-five bucks a day and expenses, mostly gasolene and whisky, I do my thinking myself, what there is of it; I risk my whole future, the hatred of the cops and of Eddie Mars and his pals, I dodge bullets and ear saps, and say thank you very much, if you have any more trouble, I hope you'll think of me, I'll just leave one of my cards in case anything comes up. I do all this for twenty-five bucks a day – and maybe just a little to protect what little pride a broken and sick old man has left in his blood, in the thought that his blood is not poison, and that although his two little girls are a trifle wild, as many nice girls are these days, they are not perverts or killers. And that makes me a son of a bitch. All right. I don't care anything about that. I've been called that by people of all sizes and shapes, including your little sister. She called me worse than that for not getting into bed with her. I got five hundred dollars from your father, which I didn't ask for, but he can afford to give it to me. I can get another thousand for finding Mr Rusty Regan, if I could find him. Now you offer me fifteen grand. That makes me a big shot. With fifteen grand I could own a home and a new car and four suits of clothes. I might even take a vacation without worrying about losing a case. That's fine. What are you offering it to me for? Can I go on being a son of a bitch, or do I have to become a gentleman, like that lush that passed out in his car the other night?'

She was as silent as a stone woman.

'All right,' I went on heavily. 'Will you take her away? Somewhere far off from here where they can handle her type, where they will keep guns and knives and fancy drinks away from her? Hell, she might even get herself cured, you know. It's been done.'

She got up and walked slowly to the windows. The drapes lay in heavy ivory folds beside her feet. She stood among the folds and looked out, towards the quiet darkish foothills. She stood motionless, almost blending into the drapes. Her hands hung loose at her sides. Utterly motionless hands. She turned and came back along the room and walked past me blindly. When she was behind me she caught her breath sharply.

'He's in the sump,' she said. 'A horrible decayed thing. I did it. I did just what you said. I went to Eddie Mars. She came home and told me about it, just like a child. She's not normal. I knew the police would get it all out of her. In a little while she would even brag about it. And if dad knew, he would call them instantly and tell them the whole story. And some time in that night he would die. It's not his dying – it's what he would be thinking just before he died. Rusty wasn't a bad fellow. I didn't love him. He was all right, I guess. He just didn't mean anything to me, one way or another, alive or dead, compared with keeping it from dad.'

'So you let her run around loose,' I said, 'getting into other jams.'

'I was playing for time. Just for time. I played the wrong way, of course. I thought she might even forget it herself. I've heard they do forget what happens in those fits. Maybe she has forgotten it. I knew Eddie Mars would bleed me white, but I didn't care. I had to have help and I could only get it from somebody like him. . . . There have been times when I hardly believed it all myself. And other times when I had to get drunk quickly – whatever time of day it was. Awfully damn quickly.'

'You'll take her away,' I said. 'And do that awfully damn quickly.'

She still had her back to me. She said softly now: 'What about you?'

'Nothing about me. I'm leaving. I'll give you three days. If you're gone by then – okey. If you're not, out it comes. And don't think I don't mean that.'

She turned suddenly. 'I don't know what to say to you. I don't know how to begin.'

'Yeah. Get her out of here and see that she's watched every minute. Promise?'

'I promise. Eddie—'

'Forget Eddie. I'll go see him after I get some rest. I'll handle Eddie.'

'He'll try to kill you.'

'Yeah,' I said. 'His best boy couldn't. I'll take a chance on the others. Does Norris know?'

'He'll never tell.'

'I thought he knew.'

I went quickly away from her down the room and out and down the tiled staircase to the front hall. I didn't see anybody when I left. I found my hat alone this time. Outside the bright gardens had a haunted look, as though small wild eyes were watching me from behind the bushes, as though the sunshine itself had a mysterious something in its light. I got into my car and drove off down the hill.

What did it matter where you lay once you were dead? In a dirty sump or in a marble tower on top of a high hill? You were dead, you were sleeping the big sleep, you were not bothered by things like that. Oil and water were the same as wind and air to you. You just slept the big sleep, not caring about the nastiness of how you died or where you fell. Me, I was part of the nastiness now. Far more a part of it than Rusty Regan was. But the old man didn't have to be. He could lie quiet in his canopied bed, with his bloodless hands folded on the sheet, waiting. His heart was a brief, uncertain murmur. His thoughts were as grey as ashes. And in a little while he too, like Rusty Regan, would be sleeping the big sleep.

On the way downtown I stopped at a bar and had a couple of double Scotches. They didn't do me any good. All they did was make me think of Silver-Wig, and I never saw her again.